Little Bird

Jennifer R C

Copyright © 2022 by Jennifer Reynolds-Cook

All rights reserved.

No portion of this book may be reproduced in any form without written permission from the publisher or author, except as permitted by Canadian copyright law.

Contents

1. 1 Dum Spiro Spero — 1
2. 2 Schwellenangst — 9
3. 3 Hiraeth — 19
4. 4 Wabi-Sabi — 31
5. 5 Limerence — 41
6. 6 Metamorphosis — 51
7. 7 Haphephobia — 63
8. 8 Plucking Feathers — 75
9. 9 Verschlimmbessern — 87
10. 10 Cacoethes — 97
11. 11 Taphophobia — 107
12. 12 Sehnsucht — 119
13. 13 Stealing Light, Stealing Breath — 129
14. 14 Stuck — 141
15. 15 Edwardian Dreams — 153
16. 16 Deja-Visite — 169

17.	17 Tu Me Manques	183
18.	18 The Untea Party	197
19.	19 Éperdument Amoureux	209
20.	20 Ghosts	223
21.	21 Twisted	233
22.	22 La Douleur Exquise	245
23.	23 Girl with many faces	263
24.	24 Trouble	279
25.	25 Deviation	291
26.	26 Two peas in a pod	307
27.	27 Down the rabbit hole	323
28.	28 Shit, trash	339
29.	29 Lilith	349
30.	30 Smudge	361
31.	31 Seven devils and a boy	379
32.	32 Stain	391
33.	33 Nefelibata	407
34.	34 A pretty mess	425
35.	35 Saudade	437
36.	36 Walls & Boundaries	447
37.	37 Rub till it's numb	461
38.	38 Forelsket	471
39.	39 Torn	489
40.	40 Hikikomori	503
41.	41 Enfant Épouvantable	511

42.	42 Mutterseelenallein	525
43.	43 Once upon a time..	535
44.	44 Thirteen knots	551
45.	45 Lebensmüde	563
46.	46 Blue	581
47.	47 Commuovere	583
48.	Epilogue	603
49.	Acknowledgments	611

1 Dum Spiro Spero

Brendon Cook gathered the sparks, imagined them dropping like spiky raindrops, slashing through the cottony layer of clouds, and disintegrating before they reached the earth. His father sat beside him; listing the names of senior judges recommended for the Supreme Court of the United Kingdom. Angry disappointment furrowed his father's brow. Brendon hoped it meant David Cook was having a hard time choosing who to advocate for. Brendon would title the flight home from Germany, 'Die kacke ist am dampfen, the shit is hitting the fan.'

Sunshine illuminated the meticulously groomed grass. Once nothing more than a weed infested field, two sets of dilapidated bleachers and standard goal nets, a hefty donation transformed Taunton Park into the envy of any visiting Southern League team. Steel bleachers rose from the ground, housing black and blue molded stadium seating, Taunton First in block lettering on a royal blue awning. Five First players chased after the ball, hollering 'get after it' and 'push up.' Brendon braced himself, grass squelched beneath his cleats. He grinned confidently, snatched the ball, and rolled it back on the pitch.

"I've let three in. Is anyone going to get one past Mr. Football?" William McGregor said.

"Nothing gets past my mate. He's the top keeper in the Southern League," Troy Spence said, beaming.

Brendon tugged at the hem of his Borussia Dortmund jersey and swiped it over his brow. A girl with waves of red hair bent her fingers in the shape of a heart and held them up. Heat slithered over Brendon's cheeks. He jerked down his jersey and scowled.

"Don't they have better things to do?"

"Tilly and Rachel think we like the giggling and cheering," Troy said.

Brendon rubbed the back of his neck and pulled his gaze from the ogling girl.

"I wish they wouldn't. I come here to practice."

William placed his hand against his heart and swooned. "What I would give to spend one night snogging Matilda Morimoto."

Brendon picked up the ball and passed it to Troy. Matilda gave the illusion she was aloof and mysterious. A lustrous onyx fringe hid her ebony eyes. The constant gum chewing, and giggling put an end to the bougee façade.

"Did you forget about your girlfriend, Gemma?" Troy said, bouncing the ball from knee to knee.

"There is no harm in looking," William said, throwing a confident wink in her direction. "Who would you choose?"

"None. I'm taken."

"What about you, Mr. Football? Who would you snog?"

Brendon grabbed a pylon and stacked it on top of another. He tossed the tower towards the dressing room door, sparks lit.

"Can we finish the drills? I've had an awful morning."

"Your girlfriend isn't around, Cook, pick."

Brendon plucked a water bottle stuffed into the net and chugged.

"Rachel Jones."

William snickered. "I've shagged her."

"Who hasn't," Troy said.

Brendon crinkled the bottle in his hand and glared. "I didn't say I fancied her. I like her hair."

"Temper, temper."

"Shut it Will. We're supposed to be practicing, not talking about girls."

A flutter floated in Brendon's belly. Talk of Rachel Jones had flooded the dressing room for years. She was as bold as the untamed locks that tumbled over her shoulders.

"I think we're done."

"Who made you, coach?"

"My mate's in charge when Liam isn't here. He earned the role of team leader."

"Taunton's bleeding hero," William said, batting the ball between his feet. "You're bollocks at corner kicks."

Brendon tossed the ball up in the air and smirked. "Says the second-choice keeper."

William flipped up two fingers and ambled over to the girls.

"I survived a two-hour flight with my dad. I'm not in the mood for Will's shit."

"He's pissed off your back."

"He wears the bloody jersey to pull a girl."

"He needs all the help he can get."

"How did the Man U trial go?"

"I was bleeding nervous mate. I got into my head, couldn't concentrate."

"There will be scouts out all season. I could ask Walt to have Lukas fly in."

Troy chuckled. "And play for the Bundesliga? The Premier League is the only place for me. Manchester United all the way."

"Germany is football. Superb coaches, inexperienced players get a chance, consistency. Should I go on?"

"Your daft mate. Premier players are ace, Old Trafford, Emirates Stadium."

"The Bundesliga have the highest average attendance."

"Cause the ticket prices are so low."

They stepped into a dressing room that could rival any professional team. Each player had their own wood cubby, their jerseys hung, game ready. Offside the dressing room was a training area equipped with a variety of high-tech machines. Winning began in the dressing room and this one had winning all over it.

"Disappointed to be back?"

Brendon grabbed his body wash and towel. "A promise is a promise."

"At least you have a contract, mate. I'll be stuck on the farm forever if someone doesn't notice me."

"You're more than a defender. Liam can put you at midfield, right wing with that brilliant footwork. Someone will notice."

"I'll keep trying and wishing."

"You got manure on your boots," William said. "No professional team will want a player stinking of cow shit."

"Do you have to be a wanker?"

"Not everyone can pay one of the Bundesliga's top scouts to watch them play. Look at the money your mum dumped into this place. You're a shoe in for any pro team."

Tiny sparks flickered. Brendon inhaled, counted to four, and exhaled.

"I'm a good keeper."

"You've got money, that pretty face."

"My face has nothing to do with it."

Brendon crammed his practice jersey into his backpack, his body tense. "A punch will wipe the bloody smirk off your face."

Troy wound a towel around his neck and rubbed Brendon's shoulder. "Keep breathing, mate. Wait until the second half of the season to punch him."

"Always bloody Switzerland."

"Someone must be."

"You should have stayed in Dortmund," William said, tearing his backpack from the hook.

"And let you fuck up the season."

William stomped from the dressing room. Brendon grinned and plunked onto the bench.

"Will has blabbed around school. Walt's getting married."

"That's the rumour."

"Who is she?"

"He met her in a park in Paris. That's all I know."

Troy's blue eyes twinkled mischievously. "Is she anything like that Russian girl he was dating?"

"Anastasia Morozova. She has over 100,000 Instagram followers."

"How come Walt didn't propose to her? They dated for a year."

"She wanted to move to LA to model. A billionaire was sending her DMs and enticed her to fly to California. She never came back."

"Blimey! Was Walt upset?"

"Walt doesn't get upset over women. There's always another one waiting in the queue."

"There won't be now if he gets married. I looked forward to meeting Walter's newest girlfriend."

"She hasn't said yes yet."

***

Walter Pratt stepped out of the taxi; grabbed the picnic basket and smiled. The sky was clear blue, the air perfumed with the scent of dahlias. Parc Floral was luminescent under the sun's brilliance. Just as she promised, Angelene Hummel lazed on the park bench. The slip of yellow cotton barely covered her thighs and looked as if picked off the rack at a charity shop. Charcoal pencils and papers surrounded her bare feet. The concentration on her face as she sketched was captivating.

"You didn't run from me today."

"You've been hassling me since April, Mr. Fancy Suit."

Walter set the picnic basket on the ground and slid beside her.

"I would call it dating. Few wives run from their husband."

"We aren't married yet."

"You'll marry me," Walter said, tucking a strand of hair behind her ear. "Your sketch is fascinating."

Angelene shuffled her sketches into a pile and crammed them into a book. "It's Lucifer's side of the story. Is it fascinating now?"

"I guess everyone's story must be told."

Walter opened the picnic basket and grabbed a bottle of wine. The game had been fun, chasing and wooing. He liked a challenge. Angelene Hummel had been his biggest yet.

"Your words are black, Monsieur Pratt. Not lovely night sky black, but dynamic black."

Walter handed her a glass. "Call me Walter or darling, something other than Monsieur Pratt."

"Why did you choose me? Out of all the women in Paris, you picked a girl in cheap clothes."

"I see something in you," Walter said, his eyes crinkled as he smiled.

He wanted to be the talk of Taunton. Not because his wife was almost half his age, because she was stunning. He would do a better job than Henry Higgins. Angelene Hummel would outshine all the other women in Taunton. He would see to it.

"You don't know what you're getting yourself into." Angelene guzzled a mouthful of wine, ran her finger over a dribble on her lip. "Maybe my drawing is my story."

"Maybe, and maybe it's poor Lucifer," Walter said. "Take it easy, that's a Chateau Mouton Rothchild. This wine is for sipping."

"Wine is wine, non?"

"No, it isn't." He opened the basket and set a baguette, brie, and grapes between them. "What made you stop running?"

"Strong hands," Angelene said, popping a grape in her mouth, "You have a strong exterior and a stronger interior. You're the epitome of normal. Goodbye kisses, dinner on the table. Normal has never fit. It will now."

There wasn't anything normal about the waif sitting beside him.

A concrete beast rose into the clouds. Newspaper and food wrappers drifted in a river of rainwater collected in the gutter. Limp laundry clung to the rusting steel slates. The occasional pot of flowers added a pop of orange or red to the dismal beige complex. Walter gazed from graffiti tagged walls to a man plodding back and forth in the foyer, push broom in hand.

"I'll walk you to the door."

Angelene bristled and flapped her hand. "See you next Saturday."

"I'm a gentleman. A gentleman walks a lady to the door."

"I am no lady Monsieur Pratt."

"You haven't invited me into your flat yet."

1 DUM SPIRO SPERO

"I promised God, I would not bring you to my apartment."

"I won't be staying long. I'm having dinner with a friend, a scout for the Bundesliga."

A beefy hand slapped against the glass door and shoved it open. The gold chandelier and porcelain tiles would give the impression the building was posh and impressive. Years of neglect caused the ceiling to buckle. An out-of-order sign swung from the elevator door.

"Where have you been, little bird?"

The man grunted and marched across the fleur-de-lis tiles. Little whirlwinds of dust flew around the broom as he wheezed back and forth.

"None of your business."

Walter curled his fingers around her shoulder.

"You promised to wash my sheets."

"Tomorrow."

The man grumbled, slapped the broom on the floor, and puffed around the corner.

"Who was that man?"

"My landlord, Emile Douchette."

"Why did he call you little bird?"

Angelene opened the door to the stairwell. Walter glanced up the dirty steps; the air was dank.

"I'm not his little bird."

"It's fitting. You're so tiny and delicate, like a baby bird finding her wings."

"Don't call me little bird, I'm Angelene. Although I don't like to be called that most days."

Walter accompanied her up the stairs. Each floor held a distinct scent. Cumin, boiled potatoes, floor four smelled sweet and earthy. Walter cleared his throat, took hold of Angelene's elbow, and nodded towards the door to floor five.

"Yasmine, what are you doing? It isn't safe."

"I forgot my key," she said, collecting her crayons, "are you the man mama told Mademoiselle Hummel to stay away from?"

Walter grinned, reached into his pocket, and handed her a handful of Walkers toffee.

"Mama says you're too fancy."

"Come wait in my apartment. You've been practicing drawing."

"I added lots of detail, like you said."

"I like the knot in the tree and the owl hiding inside."

Walter collected a glittered backpack, following them down a peppery scented hall. Years of abuse dulled the beige walls and tiles.

"You can leave now."

The slap of the broom and heavy, asthmatic breaths reverberated off the walls. Walter took the key from Angelene and unlocked the door. The sun set the scratched parquet floors on fire. A sticky breeze lifted a cornflower print tea towel, moving the scent of sandalwood and stale cigarette smoke through the stagnant air.

"I'll stay until the girl's mother arrives."

"May I sit on the windowsill? I love the view from your flat. All mama and I can see is the garbage bins."

"It's my favourite spot to sit. Go ahead."

Yasmine smiled and scrambled onto the sill. "Your bed is in the living room."

Walter's stomach quivered. There was something unsettling about the flat, like it housed unpleasant memories and sorrow.

"The view of the stars is nicer here."

Walter gazed at a tattered green velvet chair and spindle-legged table muddled with jars of paintbrushes and pencils. Her breakfast of boiled egg and cheese sat next to a stuffed ashtray.

"Where's your telly?"

"Why do I need a television? I have my books."

"Where do you sit? That chair has seen better days."

"On the window ledge, Monsieur," Yasmine said, twirling the end of her pigtail. "What is your name?"

"Walter."

"You aren't French."

"Monsieur Pratt is from England,"

A knock rattled the puny apartment. Angelene's cheeks paled. She drew Yasmine into her side.

"You forgot your key again, silly girl," Lisette Gagnon said.

Walter stuck out his hand. "I should introduce myself. I'm…"

"Mr. Secretary of Defence. Come Yasmine, you have bothered Angelene enough."

"I couldn't leave her alone. Douchette is wheezing around the halls. He would have pestered her."

Walter snaked an arm around Angelene's shoulders. She shrunk away and scrambled to the kitchen table.

"Take these. You'll be a proper artist now."

"Look mama, charcoal pencils."

"Neither you nor I have the money for art supplies."

"Angelene will have the world. I'll see to that."

"We'll see Monsieur."

"Tough woman."

"She's protective of me." Angelene rambled to the window ledge and nestled into the corner.

"Next Saturday, Parc Floral with Father Charbonneau and the peacocks."

"I haven't said yes yet."

Walter grinned and settled beside her. "I have something for you."

He pulled a velvet box from a silk lined pocket. Walter examined her face, waiting for a smile, a gasp. She stared blankly at the diamond pendant, fumbling around her books for a cigarette.

"I won't accept it."

Walter lifted the chain from its velvet cushion and laced it around her neck. He leaned towards her and puckered his lips. Angelene ducked, slipped past him, and dropped into the armchair.

"Is Taunton peaceful?"

"I live in the countryside, in a pretty home. Right next door to my friend."

"Is this the friend you live in London with?"

"David Cook. Rosewood manor has been in his family for decades."

"His wife?"

"Sofia is a wonderful woman. She can be feisty. She balances out David's dull side."

"Do they have children?"

"One. He's a decent kid. Not the trouble maker I was," Walter said, lifting his cuff, "I must meet my friend, Lukas. He was ecstatic when Brendon signed."

Angelene peeked over the chair. "Is there something special about him?"

"He's an extraordinary footy player."

Walter rose, laid a hand on Angelene's cheek, and studied her grey-green eyes. "I'm glad you finally stopped running."

"I promised God I wouldn't speak to men. You kept pestering me."

"I'm not any man. I'm Walter Pratt."

"I asked God if I made a mistake."

Walter grinned and smoothed her hair. "What has God said?"

"He hasn't answered yet."

"I suppose I shouldn't ask for a kiss goodbye."

"Go away Mr. Fancy Suit."

Walter touched her cheek and blew a kiss. He didn't need to wait for God. He had done the right thing.

***

Angelene slid onto a wooden chair and clutched her rosary. The sun radiated through the stain glass windows, washing her face in a glow of red, yellow, and blue. Praying from her apartment window was getting her nowhere. She needed to try God's house. Saint Etienne-du-Mont was her favourite of all the churches in Paris. The asymmetrical wonder had taken one hundred years to build. The white spiral staircases that flanked each side of the pulpit and the cherubs brought her peace. God had to give her a sign. She appreciated His forgiveness and love. God's love was the best kind of love.

'Please God, I've been waiting for you. I sat with Victor Hugo and told him I would miss him. I visited the Dean and told her to wish Professor Piedmont well. Her office smelled of moldy potpourri and her books, squished together. The covers torn. I wanted to save them all.'

Angelene pushed her shoulders back and stared at the cross.

'If you flutter my hair, I'll know you're happy with me. If you poke my belly, I'll run.'

The air was still and heavily scented with frankincense. Angelene clutched her rosary, sweat dribbled down her back. The memory was vivid.

Monsieur Krieger, you're back.

What makes you so sad, little bird? Who has made you feel so tiny you feel all life's storm are faced alone?

2 Schwellenangst

Brendon stared at the clock. The constant tick of the antiquity drummed in his ears. The only phrase he understood was 'sapre Aude, dare to know.' It had been Taunton College's motto since the school opened in 1880. The only thing Brendon dared to know was the Bundesliga team stats. A trickle of sunlight glinted across the layers of wood stain and bounced onto the paper. He didn't know why his father thought Latin was an important subject. It made no sense, and after surviving all his classes, he couldn't care less about carpe diem. All he wanted to seize, a football before it went into the net. Outside the classroom, the end of the day was sweeping down the hall, feet shuffled, students chatted. He shifted in the cramped desk, loosened his tie and jot down another attempt at an answer.

"Destitutus ventis, remos adhibe." Theodore Campbell stood by his desk in a navy blazer, fingering his bowtie, expressionless. "If the wind fails, use the oars."

Brendon rolled his eyes, dropped his unfinished quiz on the desk, and followed the flow of students. A museum curator could have decorated the hallway. It was as stodgy and archaic as the classrooms.

"You looked brilliant on the pitch."

Rachel Jones reached for his tie, moving her fingers up and down the plaid silk. "Are we still on for German lessons? I wouldn't want you wandering around Dortmund not knowing how to ask for the loo."

Brendon tugged his tie from her fingers and tore his gaze from her ample chest. "That's the plan."

"Did you know your name means prince?"

"Get your jubblies off my mate."

Troy nudged through the crowd, stepping between them. "Did you know your name means tart?"

"Rachel means beautiful in form," she said, wiggling her hips. "It's in the Bible."

"Since when do you read the Bible?"

Rachel flicked Troy's chin and beamed. "The prince of the pitch. It suits you. Auf wiedersehen."

A group of girls giggled, turned, shaped their fingers into hearts and called out a 'hiya Brendon' in unison. His flush deepened to maroon.

"Never a problem with the girls."

Troy inspected his hair in a classroom door and grinned. "Must be nice."

"Rachel gave my tie a wank in front of Mr. Campbell. It's embarrassing."

"Girls have been chatting you up since reception. First day of school Ellie Harker shared her biscuit and kissed your cheek."

"I don't pay any attention. I have a girlfriend."

Girls had always made him nervous. He would get tongue tied and agitated at his blazing cheeks; embarrassment layered on embarrassment.

"Troy Spence, you were supposed to meet me."

Charlotte Donovan swung her hobo bag back and forth like a cricket bat. She tucked a wisp of chestnut brown hair into her fishtail ponytail and pouted. Charlotte was a spoiled fashionista. A slender, shapely, cooing dove with a blue eyed, 'please little crumpet' stare. Her makeup, perfection, nails manicured to match the Manchester United kit. Brendon laughed inwardly; the practiced pout was working on Troy.

"Where have you been, babes?"

"Can't I meet up with my mate?"

"Not when you're supposed to meet me. Give me your keys and I'll wait at your car." She grasped his square jaw and nibbled his chin. "I love my little crumpet."

Charlotte bumped the door open with her hip and skipped across the grass in her navy Doc Marten boots.

"You want to go to the pitch? I've been practicing my volley kicks."

"Can't. I promised dad I would catch up on the school work I missed."

Waiting patiently by his car was Margaret Thornton. Kilt knee length, white cotton blouse, buttoned to her chin, fresh faced with blue blossom eyes. The type of girl who found peace in the library.

"Part of my punishment."

Troy's face burst into a smile. "When you get bored with studying, sneak off to the Beemer for a snog."

"There will be no time for snogging. Not when the library is involved."

"Hurry my delectable little crumpet,"

Brendon glanced from Maggie to Charlotte's fluttering kilt. His eyebrows raised; her panties were lace.

"I'm down here," Maggie said.

"Do you wear lacy knickers?"

"Don't be daft. Mum would give me an ear bashing if I wore anything like that."

He kissed the top of her head and lifted the hem of her kilt.

"Nice one, mate," Troy yelled.

Maggie giggled and brushed his hand away.

"Ms. McGregor was at the salon and told mum, Walter got married."

"Mum's been bloody cranky. I assumed it was me. She's been grumbling over lists and whispering to dad about being disappointed."

"Who is this girl?" Maggie said, gnawing on her thumbnail, "Walter's ex, the Russian tart, fancied you."

"Mum mentioned Walt should bring her to Taunton in a Pram."

"I'm glad you're back. These last four weeks have been awful."

2 SCHWELLENANGST

Sunlight illuminated the assemblage of Victorian buildings. Lush lawns enveloped Taunton College, with fields and trees on all sides. They strolled past the chapel and ivy-covered administration office. Brendon kept his eyes on the ground. The headmaster, Julian Dawson, popped up in the window.

"Three strikes Mr. Cook."

Maggie silenced a laugh and tugged open the library door. "Mr. Dawson, not happy you're back?"

"He was happy to see mum."

Brendon hooked his foot around the chair leg and fell onto it. He scrubbed his cheeks and sighed. An irritated 'shh' blew from between the rows of books.

"Look what I did for you."

Maggie pointed to a chart and grinned. "I did it in Dortmund's team colours."

Brendon looked at the mapped-out assignments, each class printed in bold black and highlighted in yellow. English, French, History and Latin.

"You went to a lot of trouble. Thanks."

Brendon kissed her cheek and slipped his fingers between her thighs.

"Stop before someone sees."

"I missed you. Let's snog."

"I told your dad I would help you get organized. You've missed two weeks."

"Those were the happiest days of my life."

"You're starting with The Sorrows of Young Werther in English, Henry the VIII..."

"Can we talk about something else?" Brendon tapped the diamond solitaire on her finger, "like how bloody brilliant I played for Dortmund's U19 squad." He nuzzled her neck and raised his middle finger at the tsk-tsking coming from within the aisles.

"I was gutted when you were away."

"I called you every night at ten." Brendon dropped his voice to a whisper. "I dreamt about you."

Her eyes fluttered shut. The kiss was tender and sweet.

"Not in the library, Mr. Cook. Three strikes," the librarian said sternly.

"Does the whole bloody school know?"

Maggie clicked her pen and listed the due date of a French assignment. "People have been placing bets for weeks. Someone bet five quid you'd only last a day in Dortmund."

"I don't want to talk about it." Brendon loosened his tie, tilting the chair back. "I talked to Rachel. I thought you should know; in case the wagers start."

Maggie scrunched her nose and flipped through her notebook. "What did Taunton's tart want?"

"She's going to teach me German. Madame Lafavre recommended her."

"I promised after the Franca incident I wouldn't get jealous."

"I need help. I couldn't understand the goal coach."

Brendon pushed her glasses up her nose. "I promise I'll follow dad's daft Gentlemen's code."

Maggie rested her cheek against his arm. "I'm glad you're back. I missed you horribly."

Brendon kissed her and peered at the growing list of assignments and quizzes. "All that in one year?"

"It's Sixth Form. What did you expect, worksheets and colouring pages?"

The walls of books shrank around Brendon. The smell of dust and aging paper tickled his nose. He wanted to tell Maggie about the mistake he made, the regrets he had. There was something about the way her glasses sat precariously on her nose, how her eyes reminded him of the bluebells in springtime, made him change his mind. He had seen enough disappointed people since arriving home.

"You want to get out of here?"

"Your dad will be mad if you don't start an assignment."

"I'll take you for pizza."

Maggie shoved her notebook in her bag and folded her glasses. "Can we go for a walk in Vivary Park after?"

Brendon grabbed her overstuffed book bag. "We'll find a bench and start the history homework. I should have brought you to Dortmund with me. I might have done better."

"Next time," Maggie said.

***

Angelene stared at the building across the street. His spirit wavered in the window; she laid her hand against the glass. A ghostly touch, the smell of rose and pomegranate, haunted her. She followed the sun's glow to the faded peony wallpaper. Roman Krieger brought the hand painted paper back from London. It was one of the few occasions she saw her mother smile. Angelene sniffed and wiped her nose on her sleeve. She had cried among the tired walls, screamed, hid, and cuddled in the faded green chair with Roman.

"Will you look at this place? I can't see an inch of the floor."

Jars of wilted flowers camouflaged the kitchenette and spilled from the bedrooms. Price tags hung from clothes slathered over the kitchen table. Angelene touched the emerald-cut diamond that extended the length of her slim finger and forced a smile.

"You could open a boutique." Yasmine bounced on the armchair and draped a shawl around her.

"Monsieur Pratt has been very generous."

"Your husband," Lisette said. She picked up a bottle of perfume and sniffed. "Pretty."

"Keep it," Angelene said, sliding off the window ledge. "He doesn't like patchouli oil. Roman used to bring it home from India for mother. I liked how it smelled on her skin. It was the only thing I liked about her."

Lisette picked up the box. Her eyebrows lifted. "190 euros, I couldn't."

"I don't want to smell like flowers."

Yasmine smoothed the shawl across her cheek. "This feels soft, like a bunny."

"It's angora sweet pea," Lisette said, removing the wrap from Yasmine's fingers, "and expensive. What do you know about this man?"

Angelene twisted her fingers through her hair. "We've discussed this."

"Did God give you a sign?"

"There were too many. Walter's a politician, you know this."

"Him, not how he makes his money."

Yasmine whirled a pashmina scarf around her shoulders. "He wears fancy suits, mama."

"Is it the money?"

Angelene lit a cigarette, took a hearty drag and slung her arm out the window. "This is my chance to get out of Clichy-Sous-Bois."

"Do you love Walter?"

Angelene tossed the cigarette and paced. "I'm not sure. I like his tattoo."

"Is that it, an anchor tattoo?"

"Walter's been extremely kind to me."

"Clothes and jewellery are just things," Lisette said, fingering the price tag of a Christian Dior blazer, "your soul mate could be out there. He could be in Taunton. What will you do? You're married to a man you don't love."

"Love will come."

"You make awful decisions."

Lisette held up a black silk dress and shook it. "This is not you. Where is the colour? The patterns?"

"I still have my patterns. My whole life has been nothing but patterns."

"Your perfume, your clothes, shouldn't he love you for you?"

"I suppose. I've never had a normal relationship."

"You've made poor choices."

"It's too late for a lecture. Walter will be here soon."

Yasmine peered over the chair and dug her fingers into the faded velvet. "Douchette. Where will I go when I forget my key?"

Angelene stopped pacing and sank to her knees. "Where's your key?"

Yasmine searched in her sundress pocket and dangled the key. Angelene unclasped the diamond necklace and laced the chain through the hole. "Now you'll never forget."

"Monsieur Pratt gave that to you."

"He can afford another."

"Give her a piece of ribbon, some string," Lisette said.

"Promise to never take it off. You must protect your light."

"I insist you take it back."

"It will keep her safe."

Lisette seized Angelene's shoulders and shook her. "You frustrate me."

"I have something else." Angelene held out a book and an assortment of coloured pencils.

"You love A Bell for Ursli. Monsieur Krieger gave you this book," Yasmine said.

"I have my memories. It is your turn to help Ursli chase winter away."

Angelene turned from Yasmine, gathered an armful of clothes, and tossed them into a bag. The perfume was next, the angora shawl and navy blazer.

"Take them."

"Walter bought these for you."

"Wear them, sell them, I don't care. Please keep Yasmine's light safe."

"In my pocket, in case you get hungry on the plane."

Angelene shoved her hand in Lisette's cardigan and pulled out a rectangular box. "Lemon macaron."

"Only the French can make a macaron. Be safe."

Angelene blew a flurry of kisses and collapsed onto the armrest. Patterns, poor decisions. She had been exceptionally good at both.

The elevator doors whirred and jerked open. Angelene pushed her bottom against the door and dragged a duffle bag inside. She stared at the numbers as the elevator lurched and clunked between floors. She would have new stairs to count, a proper kitchen to mess. The elevator hissed open, Angelene heaved the bag through the lobby. Slivers of sunlight shimmered between the buildings; the concrete scenery was her home.

"Little bird."

Angelene crossed her arms over her chest and tapped her foot against the cracked pavement.

"What do you want?"

"You forgot something," Douchette said. "I was going to throw it down the garbage chute."

Angelene ripped a jewellery box from his hand, unzipped the duffle bag and shoved it among the clothes. Douchette placed his lips on her neck. His plump fingers snaked through her hair.

"Walter will be here soon. If he sees you touching me."

"Your lover will not want to muss his fancy suit."

"He's not my lover. He is my hus... husband."

"You still have trouble saying that."

Douchette's breath hissed in her ear. An empty Orangina can clanged across the asphalt. In the distance, a horn beeped. Angelene wiggled free as the black Rolls Royce she had spent the summer travelling in pulled alongside the curb.

"Always the big shot. Sac de merde."

"Be quiet Emile."

She tugged at her blouse and teetered in her shoes. A glass of wine, a cigarette would be the medicine she needed to settle the tremors shredding through her stomach.

"It's a magnificent afternoon," Walter said.

"If you say so."

Angelene gave the building another look. She had always hated the concrete monstrosity, today she was in love.

"Hand me your bag. We have an airplane to catch."

"I've never been on a plane. I'm afraid."

"We have our own suite. It will help you relax."

Douchette huffed. "Don't listen to him. You sit in a seat and pray it doesn't fall from the sky."

Angelene clutched Walter's suit jacket, her eyes frantic. "I'm not getting on that plane."

"He's a fool. We'll be in the air for an hour. You can have a glass of champagne. It will be fine."

Angelene shook out her hands and wiggled her fingers. The voices in her head squabbled. Stay, run.

"You shouldn't be leaving. You're French."

"She'll still be French, just in Taunton."

Douchette shook his head, his chins wiggled. "This is her home. She's my little bird."

"Stop," Angelene said, holding her hands over her ears, "I can't listen to the two of you bickering. My own thoughts are enough."

"You think there is heaven in her, Pratt? She's all devil."

"I'll take my chances."

"Angelene," Yasmine called.

Angelene stumbled and glared at Walter. "Why did you buy me these ridiculous shoes?"

"They're Louboutin."

Angelene bent and clutched Yasmine's shoulders. "You drew me a picture. Is that my home in England?"

"It will be spring every day."

Angelene dragged Yasmine into her arms, pressed her nose in her apple scented hair. "Your light is so bright. I'll miss you." She glanced up at Douchette, her eyes damp. "Run to your mother. Go now."

Angelene licked her lips and rubbed at an ache in her chest. The building warped, Lisette's 'see you soon' swept down from their balcony. Memories flooded over her in scents and colours.

"I'm homesick and we haven't left."

"You have a new home now."

Angelene waved to Lisette and Yasmine. "How will Lisette protect Yasmine?"

"Don't worry about the Gagnon's. I have a plan for them, too."

Angelene pressed her thumb on her pulse. Thirteen listless beats. The farmhouse was modest, with black framed dormer windows, its walls and walkway covered in wisteria. The trees surrounding the drive sheltered it, casting shadows across the lawn. Grass crept up around the door in scraggly patches, weeds choked the marigold. Angelene shivered. It was like the sun never reached its walls or warmed its rooms.

"It looks haunted."

"If you want ghosts, head to the manor. There's one in every room."

"Is the forest part of the property?"

"All the way to the manor. There's a path that leads from here to Rosewood."

Angelene stepped out of the car and swallowed mouthfuls of air. This was her home now. A farmhouse in the middle of a moor, in the middle of nowhere with no one. She dug her fingernails into her wrist, 'what have I done' stuck in her throat.

Shadows waltzed across the foyer and over the dull, white walls; the sharp sting of bleach bit her nose.

"Amelia was here. I must send her flowers."

"Who's Amelia?"

"The Cook's housekeeper. She's more family than employee."

"Do you have a housekeeper?"

"I prefer to do my own cleaning. I'm very particular."

She cocked her head and glanced into the front room. Nothing but a leather recliner. Angelene rubbed the goosebumps erupting over her skin.

"Wh... where's the kitchen?"

"Right this way. I keep thinking I should remodel it. I have fond memories here. The island is new."

The space was rough hewn and charming, whitewashed cupboards, a sea foam green, white, and beige backsplash. Angelene licked her lips and ran her hand over the weathered wood island. "I can't cook."

"You'll learn. That's the sitting room."

Angelene spun on her heels and gazed at a sofa and gargantuan television sitting atop an antique bread hutch.

"It's not what I expected."

"What more does a man need? A telly, a sofa. Were you expecting something posher?"

"You're so particular about your clothes, your fancy watches."
"Between London and travelling for work, I'm not here much."
Angelene shrunk into the island, overwhelmed and out of place.
"Let me show you the upstairs."
Angelene followed, surrounded by more white walls and empty rooms.
"You said there would be a room where I can paint."
"There's one at the end of the hall," Walter said. "This is our room. I'll grab the luggage."
A mammoth bed dominated the room. It was an unsightly focal point, making the knotted pine dresser and nightstand insignificant. Angelene drooped onto the bed and clutched the duvet.
'The closet is bigger than my flat. A bathroom, right here in my bedroom.'
A thud shook the thoughts from her head. She gathered her hair around her face and twisted the sun-bleached strands around her fingers. "I can't breathe."
"What's the matter?"
"This room is ugly."
Walter smiled his crinkly smile and brushed his lips over her hair. "I suppose the entire house needs a makeover."
"I want to go home."
"This is your home now."
"Do you have to work in London?"
"I thought you enjoyed being alone."
"I'm overwhelmed. I must go to this party, remember all the rules. No gulping the champagne, no fidgeting."
"Please stop picking. I spent forty euros on your manicure."
She shook out her hands, lifted her bottom, and shoved her fingers underneath.
"Where will I go? What will I do? Back home I could go to the Parc Floral or sit with Hugo."
"We have parks here."
Angelene stood, tugged on the pull of the duffle bag. The jewellery box rose on a wave of clothes. It tipped; Edelweiss tinkled in the air.
"What's that?"
"Just an old box."
She closed the lid and cradled it against her chest.
"There will be no secrets in my home."
"It's a few old memories, nothing more."
Walter unzipped a Chanel garment bag; it housed a saffron dress with beaded straps.
"Where is the dress I bought you?"
"I gave it to Lisette."
"You want to wear this? My friends will be there, my colleagues."
"I love that dress. It's my favourite colour. It will make me yellow, less frightened."
"Do you know what that dress cost?" Walter touched her trembling lips and grinned. "Of course, you don't. This dress will have to do."
"I'm sorry."
"No need for apologies. I'll make you a cuppa. Did you see the window bench in the kitchen? It has a wonderful view of the moors."
Angelene scraped up and down her arm. She had lived her life blending into the background, trying to fit in, trying to do normal and be normal.

"My stomach hurts. Roman used to say it was my nerves. Mother said it was God's punishment. Is God trying to tell me something?"

"You hardly ate today. Just pecked at your breakfast, pecked at your lunch. Just like a little bird pecking away."

"I feel dizzy."

"A cup of tea will help. You can sit in the window," Walter said, reaching into the depths of the duffel bag, "you have your book, The Hunchback. Everything will be fine."

"Please don't leave me alone tomorrow."

"I promise."

3 Hiraeth

Brendon drove along Taunton Road, following a charm of goldfinch. They dipped above the treeline, over the farmhouse, settling into an arch of ancient trees enclosing the laneway. Brendon zoomed through the tunnel of contorted trees. The branches unravelled and presented Rosewood Manor. The stately Georgian home sat elegantly atop the hill. Ivy clung to the ivory stucco walls and framed the windows that overlooked the gardens. Generations of Cooks had lived in the 18th century masterpiece. It was his mother's pride and joy, his father's burden and, one day, his. The house had always been a silent sentinel, overlooking the moors, it was humming with activity. Caterers carried in crates of vegetables and bulging paper sacks. Decorators came and went, arms full of twinkle lights and urns. Brendon parked beside his mother's Maserati, grabbed his backpack, and stepped over boxes of pressed linens. He pushed open the servant's door, his eyes widened at the buzz of activity. A team of people had hijacked the spacious kitchen. Silver tiered trays crowded the black walnut island. Opened boxes of petit four and pastries sat between piles of vegetables and fruit. Brendon leaned into the counter and smiled. Amelia Potter flew from the pantry and slammed jars of spices into a mess of flour. A cloud of white mushroomed into the air. Amelia coughed and sputtered, scampering between the chefs like a determined mouse dodging a trap.

"Ame, you're not humming."

Amelia crumpled onto the stool and tucked a strand of grey hair into her bun. "I'll be humming the death march soon. Look at my kitchen."

The chefs had ransacked the cupboards, bottles of olive oil and vinegars covered the countertops. Crumbs and vegetable peels dusted the travertine tiles. The ordinarily spotless and obsessively organized room was in disarray.

"I'll have to alphabetize my spices again."

Amelia jumped from the stool and lifted a dome, exposing artfully arranged slices of Battenberg cake, Victoria sponge, and cannoli.

"Help yourself," Amelia said, scowling at the head chef, "he barged into my kitchen, ordering me about. Go on, mess up his fancy display."

Brendon hitched his backpack over his shoulder and snatched a piece of cake. "Where's mum?"

"I have no idea. I told Sofia a posh meal with a few close friends would be fine." Brendon chuckled. "Mum doesn't do simple."

"Miss Amelia, I need basil, fresh, not dried."

"I would leave before he puts you to work."

"It's almost over," Brendon called.

He dodged men carrying urns of red roses and stopped in the middle of the foyer. Peter, their groundskeeper, leaned into a ladder, polishing the crystals dangling from the chandelier. Brendon ducked around a parade of decorators carting displays of fruit and buckets of champagne and bounded up the split staircase. Chandeliers created a sparkly pathway leading to the nine bedrooms. Each decorated in a specific theme, one remained locked.

Brendon flipped on the light and tossed his knapsack. There were signs a teenager lived amongst the built-in bookcases and antique furniture. Clothes dangled over a chair, bundles of football magazines, a collection of scrunched Red Bull cans cluttered the dresser. Nestled among his favourite childhood stories sat Paddington Bear. The bear was well-loved and had played every imaginary football match in the garden. Brendon thrummed with energy. His parents had said little about the mysterious woman who stole Walter's bachelorhood. Over the years, Walter had introduced him to a collection of brunettes and raven-haired models. Anastasia had been the last of Walt's beauties. The flirty brunette would comment on his dimpled grin and dark eyes. He would blush, Sofia would curse. His looks had earned him the title of the Southern league's dishiest player. The scruff on his face and tousled locks had not deterred the girls. It only irritated his mother. Brendon flopped on his bed, opened his Latin text, and stuck a pen in his mouth. From deep within the house, an ear-splitting crash and stream of Italian reverberated off the walls. Brendon laughed; he pitied the poor soul who had to deal with a furious Sofia Cook.

"Why didn't you say hello?"

His mother's entrance was grand, like a commander going to war. She marched to the bookshelf, adjusted the trophies and Paddington, and marched to the bed, her silver bangles jangling. Sofia Cook was strength, sophistication, passion, silk, and red lips. She had a face that turned men's heads and a body his friends ogled.

"I just got home."

Sofia brushed her lips over his cheek and planted herself on the bed. She moved a pillow, angled another, adjusted, and readjusted.

"What are you working on?"

"Latin. I don't understand."

"Ask your father for help."

"He'll get frustrated and tell me I'm not applying myself. I'll ask Rachel tomorrow."

"Who's Rachel."

"A girl."

Brendon jotted out an answer, reworked the sentence and scribbled it out.

"Are you still upset we wouldn't let you stay in Dortmund?"

"I don't want to talk about it."

"If Walter hadn't brought Lukas around, the Bundeswhatever wouldn't know who Brendon Cook is. You'd be here in Taunton with me."

"I don't want to be in bloody Taunton." Brendon tossed his pen and rubbed his brow. "I tried. It was a lot, studying and football."

"Education is important to your father. He doesn't put value in sports like you do."

"Lukas had his eye on me when I was seven. Dortmund wanted me at sixteen. You two said no."

Sofia tapped a ruby red fingernail against his textbook. "None of them care about you. You're a commodity."

Brendon had heard this for years. He'd be in his twilight years at thirty with a broken body and nothing to fall back on. David Cook's son would be well rounded, respectful, and wise.

"I'm trying. Doesn't that count for something?"

"I'm not the only one looking for a hiding place. It's a circus down there."

If there was a picture beside the word respect in the dictionary, Brendon would place his father beside it. David Cook, in his tailored suit, silk braces and stylish taper cut, exemplified respect.

"You two talk," Sofia said, adjusting David's braces. "I want you both with me when Walter arrives. Twenty-five years old. Unbelievable."

"Everything good in parliament, Lord Chancellor?"

"The usual. Argue and debate, debate and argue."

"Is she really twenty-five?"

"I told Walter to think about marrying someone so young. He did it anyway. I have my fingers crossed."

"William told everyone she modelled nude."

"Word travels fast around Taunton, doesn't it?"

"Everyone knew about my mishap in Dortmund before the plane arrived at Heathrow."

"She posed for art students, not in those magazines you and your friends look at."

Heat crept over Brendon's neck. There was Mr. Respectable again. He slid his notebook in his backpack and dragged his fingers through his messy fade.

"Done your homework?"

"I'll do it later."

"You promised you'd try harder."

"Dortmund wanted me to stay."

"You didn't learn your lesson last spring. You've gone and messed things up again."

"Aren't we supposed to be getting along? Mum expects a perfect family."

"My apologies. You're trying, again. Has mammina laid out our suits?"

Brendon pointed to a garment bag hanging from the closet door. "Did you expect them not to be? I'll have my homework done before school."

Brendon wiped his sweaty hands and wiggled his tie. Sofia paced and fidgeted with her bracelets.

"Will you sit? You're making me dizzy," David said.

"Maybe it's the scotch."

Brendon grinned at his mother's remark. "You'd think Prince William and Kate were coming over."

"I wish you two would stop. Five months and married."

"I knew at sixteen I would marry you."

"Troy fell in love with Charlie the first time he saw her."

"We were together for two years. Isn't anyone worried?"

Headlights lit up the den, Brendon shifted on the edge of the desk. The moment had arrived. Blonde, brunette, youthful, sophisticated?

"Get over here. I want to hold your hands."

"Bloody hell, mum, you'd think we were marching to the gallows."

"Ten quid, she's Swedish, and moved to Paris to chase her dreams of becoming an artist," David said.

Sofia arched an eyebrow and smirked. "She's Spanish, a runway model."

"She's an exotic dancer with legs a mile long and fiery red hair."

"Walter would not date an exotic dancer."

"There was that girl from Liverpool."

Sofia frowned and snapped David's suspender. "We don't talk about that girl."

Brendon smothered his laugh. The doorbell rang. They looked at one another; the answer was on the other side of the door.

"Bloody hell. Is no one going to answer it?"

Brendon let go of his mother's hand and yanked open the door. His smile dropped. The world slowed and softened. She was neither Swedish nor Spanish. No mile long legs, red hair or over plumped anything. She was the most beautiful woman Brendon had ever seen.

"Angelene, meet my friends." Walter nudged her and jerked her strap over her shoulder.

The yellow dress skimmed over her body, highlighting her delicate curves and breasts. Brendon swallowed; she wasn't wearing a bra.

"Bonjour."

"It's nice to meet you," David said. "Let's head to the ballroom. I opened the Lagavulin for you."

Walter tugged his sleeve from Angelene's fingers and clapped a hand on David's shoulder.

"Your home is lovely." Angelene's eyes darted around the foyer as fast as her chest rose and fell.

"David wants to sell it. He's sick of the ghosts."

Angelene hooked a finger beneath the gilded strap and tugged it over her shoulder.

"I've never seen so many exquisite things. Only in books or at the Musée des Arts Décoratifs."

"Did Walter pick out that dress?"

"He bought me another. I gave it to my friend Lisette," Angelene said, drawing the strap over her shoulder, "he's not happy."

"You gave it away?"

"Lisette deserves a pretty dress."

A waiter strolled past. Brendon snatched two flutes of champagne and handed one to Sofia, the other to Angelene. She murmured, thank you, gripped the glass so tight, the strap slipped and hung down her arm. His mind emptied of football. He couldn't think of anything besides the yellow dress.

"You could play football in here," Angelene said.

"I have."

Brendon scanned the ballroom. Candles flickered from ornate candelabras, illuminating the food stations. The scents of roses and a melange of hors d'oeuvres perfumed the air. A jungle of red roses covered every inch of the room. The baby grand was in danger of collapsing under the weight of roses arranged on its lid. It was everything Angelene wasn't, elegant and posh.

"Where abouts in Paris did you live?" Sofia asked.
"Clichy-Sous-Bois."
"Those riots happened there. Two boys died."
"They were hiding from the police in a substation. The electrocution knocked the power out, cars were on fire, it was chaos. I didn't leave my apartment for weeks. The neighbourhood has never been the same."
"Dad said the boys didn't have police records. They were just two kids playing footy."
"Is your mother still there?"
"I don't know where she is. She's good at running from things. I have a serious lacuna in my family tree, quite the desolate gap. It says a lot about me and my values, or lack of."

Brendon touched Sofia's fingers as she clicked her bangles.
"The seafood station is unacceptable. Excuse me," Sofia said.
Angelene picked at her manicure. Tiny specks of raspberry polish landed on the gleaming parquet. She scowled at the fallen strap.
"Merde!"
Brendon moved the strap over her shoulder and tightened the clasp.
"What are you doing?"
"It shouldn't fall down now."
Waiters strolled past, offering trays of mini beef wellington and Scottish salmon. Couples Brendon didn't recognize floated into the ballroom, blurted out hellos and exchanged curious glances at the girl in the yellow dress.
"You're sweating."
Brendon handed her a handkerchief. She blotted her collarbone and clutched it. Tiny sparks burned inside Brendon. Walter was greeting guests. His mother was arguing with the chef. Women hid their looks of disapproval behind flutes of champagne. There were no hellos. Everyone was pretending not to stare.
"Can I get you something to eat?"
Angelene shook her head and scraped at her nails.
"Ang, come meet my friends."
Walter's voice carried over the music. All eyes were on her. Instinctively, Angelene shrunk into Brendon's arm.
"I'm going to trip in these ridiculous shoes."
"Do you want to hold my arm?"
Angelene pressed the handkerchief in his hand. Brendon held it to his nose. The odour was curious, smoky, earthy, sultry.
"You're brooding, sweetheart," Sofia said. "I can't make sense of Ms. Pratt."
Angelene hid beneath Walter's arm. No smile, cheeks pale.
"It must be overwhelming."
"The others were so vocal. They never had enough to say."
This girl was not like the others. What was it about Angelene that tugged at his heart and made his belly flop? She was awkward, unconventionally pretty. He cleared his throat and reached for a glass of champagne.
"She can barely stand in those shoes. Why isn't Walt holding her hand?" Brendon guzzled the champagne and set the glass between trays of antipasti. "Ms. Batra is staring down her new nose at her."
"She's gawking at you, sweetheart. I had to remind her she has a daughter your age."
"None of your friends have spoken to Ms. Pratt."

"She hasn't mingled."

Brendon jabbed a bocconcini with a toothpick, nibbling it. "Why would you when everyone is giving you the evils?"

"Speaking of my friends. I'm going to save your father from Victoria McGregor. He doesn't do well with gossip."

Sofia presented her cheek, Brendon kissed her and glanced at the ceiling as a whisper of 'he's such a good boy' reached his ears. He stepped away from the table. Walter was centre stage, the crowd mesmerized. Just like the fans who cheered Cook, Walter had his own audience. The person who needed his attention stood offside, hidden among the urns of roses.

"This is like a proper do."

Brendon gazed at Angelene. A little voice in his head reminded him of the Gentlemen's Code, rule number eleven, don't covet another man's girl.

"I texted you to say I was here. A bloke wearing white gloves escorted me."

"I had to leave my phone in my room. Dad didn't want me watching the highlights."

"How do I look?"

"Brilliant."

"You haven't looked at me. Charlie said my dress looked posh. No one would know I got it off the sales rack at Debenhams."

Brendon tried to think of something dazzling to say. Thoughts of Angelene held the words hostage.

"Are you going to introduce me to Walter's wife?"

Collywobbles stormed Brendon's stomach. It wasn't the house prickling his skin; it was the odd attraction to Angelene and the words 'Walter's wife.'

"Is she dead gorgey? The kids in drama were placing bets," Maggie said, snatching a blini topped with caviar. "Farrah Swindon heard she was on the cover of French Vogue."

"She's just a girl."

Brendon blotted his forehead with his tie. The code bumped around his head, take Maggie's hand, don't curse, be polite.

"Here's Taunton's hero."

"I wish you wouldn't say that. I'm just a keeper."

"Don't be so modest. Number one in the Southern League."

"Maggie, this is... Ms. Pratt."

Walter withdrew his arm, pressed his fingers into the small of Angelene's back. She wobbled forward.

"Angelene. Bonjour."

"It's nice to meet you," Maggie said. "That's some ring."

"I wanted something that said she was Walter Pratt's wife."

Brendon glanced at the glimmering diamond. It roared she belonged to Walter Pratt.

"Sorry Davy boy, wouldn't let you stay in Dortmund."

"Dad wants a kid with an education. Now he'll get it."

Walter snorted and clapped Brendon's shoulder. "I told you he was a good kid; always does as he's told."

"I don't want to fight anymore. What's eleven months?"

"An entire season," Walter said, scanning the crowd, "I'll be damned. Patrick Carrington is here. You must meet Paddy. We were in the Royal Navy together. Chin up, Brendon, we'll get you back to Dortmund."

Angelene's eyes pierced his. He could have sworn he saw 'help me' flickering in her eyes.

"Ahem," Maggie said, jabbing her elbow, "you can stop staring at Ms. Pratt."

Brendon rubbed his side. "Bloody hell, I wasn't staring at her."

"You were gawking at someone. I doubt it was Ms. McGregor."

Brendon's thoughts were a mess of 'why? Who is she? How come I fancy her? She isn't pretty. She's beautiful.' He grabbed Maggie's hand and scanned the ballroom. Angelene had disappeared.

"Are you going to admit you fancy her?"

"No, I'm not."

"I'm not a dolt. You had that same daft look on your face when that French exchange student called you her Petit chou."

Sparks twitched and sizzled. "I thought you were working on your jealousy."

Brendon eyed a tray of champagne; heat crawled over his skin; sparks fluttered.

"Did you see her dress? She isn't wearing a bra."

"I hadn't noticed."

"Every man here has noticed."

She stared at him in a way that said, 'I adore you,' guilt took hold of him and shoved the Gentlemen's Code in his face. Rule number four, 'treat a girl the same way you'd treat your mother.'

"Do you want something to drink?"

"Something fizzy, not champagne. It gives me the hiccups."

Brendon shook the sparks away and left the ballroom. He stepped into the kitchen, opened the fridge, and grabbed two cans of soda. A glowing orange orb caught his eye. He rubbed his eyes, the glowing dot disappeared then appeared. Brendon stared at the doorway, then back to the glow. Rule number seven, help a woman in distress.

"What are you doing out here?"

"Hiraeth." Angelene dragged on the cigarette. Smoke curled around the words. "I'm homesick. I can't go back. I can't breathe."

Brendon peeled off his suit jacket and held it towards her. "Put this on."

"I shouldn't."

"I'll feel bad if you catch a cold. Besides, it's the gentlemanly thing to do, rule number six."

Angelene wrapped the jacket around her shoulders. It was as long as her dress. "That's my problem."

"Do you catch colds easily? I usually get the lurgy around this time of year."

Angelene tilted her head and hid her smile behind her fingers. "I don't think I dive right in."

Her accent was raspy and syrupy. Angelene dropped the cigarette and slammed her heel into it.

"I'm not good enough or pretty or sophisticated. Your mother is so elegant, so fucking confident."

"You're the most beautiful woman I've ever seen." Mortified, Brendon looked away and cursed.

"Your words are brown, you're brown." She shrugged off his jacket and handed it to him. "Call me Angelene. I'm having trouble with Ms. Pratt."

Brendon fanned his tie over his heated cheeks. He said she was beautiful, her response he was brown. He didn't know what that meant. His hair is brown, his eyes the same deep shade. It was an odd thing to say. She was an odd girl.

'*It was just a dream.*' The conversation, the compliment, handing her his jacket, all a dream. With every step to the ballroom, he repeated, '*it was just a dream,*' guilt hurt less.

"What took you so long?" Maggie said.

Rule number five, honesty.

"I was talking to Ms. Pratt."

"You've been chatting up Ms. Pratt."

A groan rumbled deep in Brendon's throat. He chugged the soda and crinkled the can.

"You think I was pulling Walt's wife?" Sparks smoldered; guilt pecked away at him.

"I bet she's a tart."

The words were harsh. Brendon was sure the women at the party thought that.

"You don't know her. Nobody does."

"Is that what you were talking about? Poor Ms. Pratt, nobody likes me," Maggie said, chewing her thumbnail, "if she wore something that didn't show off her bits, people wouldn't stare."

"Stop whingeing over Ms. Pratt. Did you bloody hear that? MS. Pratt."

Sparks whirred, setting his limbs on fire. He inhaled slowly and imagined the sparks as ash.

"Are you going to accuse me of pulling Rachel? I'll tell her to forget about German lessons if that's the case."

"Nice boys don't pull girls like Rachel Jones."

'*Breathe Brendon, you know Maggie is the jealous type.*'

"I'm curious about Ms. Pratt, just like everyone else."

Maggie pulled her thumbnail from her mouth and grinned. "I forgive you, only because I want to try the dumplings. I have ten stations to sample before I go home."

Brendon kissed her cheek and scanned the crowd. Simone Batra smiled and winked. Victoria McGregor stood next to the dessert station; her plate piled high. His parents sat by the fire. He spotted Walter by the bar, no Angelene. Brendon glanced around the food stations, the loggia. A tiny tug pulled at his heart. Angelene was alone. He wasn't doing anything wrong; no one was talking to her.

"Would you like anything? Champagne? Something to eat?"

Angelene fiddled with her bracelets and slowly shook her head. "I can't have anymore champagne. It is for sipping. I gulp when I'm nervous."

"Did Walter say that?"

"He's so happy his friends came to celebrate. I don't want to make a terrible impression." She hid her smile behind her fingers and laughed softly. "I've already made the wrong impression."

"There's a lot of people here. I'm overwhelmed."

"Were you given instructions? Were you told how to act?"

"Give a firm handshake, say hello, be polite, use a napkin, don't ramble on about football."

"Je veux aller à la maison."

"I'm bollocks at French."

Angelene weaved her fingers. "I want to go home."

"I'll get Walter and tell him you feel iffy."

"My home. My flat in Paris with the faded peony wallpaper and the stars out my window."

"We have lots of stars in Taunton,"

"I don't understand how to be a wife."

"You just have to be you."

"Your light is powerful."

"Liam, my coach, talks about firing up the dragons before a match. Is that the same thing?"

"It's within you, sometimes dull, sometimes intense and blinding. Mine is barely a flicker."

"It's not so bad here. Mum grew up in Milan. She didn't like Taunton at first."

Vanilla scented the air. Maggie jerked on his suit jacket.

"I was just talking to Ms... she was alone."

"Taunton is cleaner than Paris. No offence," Maggie said.

"I hear that a lot. To me, Paris is beautiful."

"Ms. Pratt was just telling me about the light people have."

"Everyone has it. It's what drives you. Have a dumpling,"

Brendon's lips flattened as he chewed. He caught another smile hidden behind Angelene's fingers.

"Walter is finally alone. Thanks for keeping me company." She teetered to her feet, held out her hands to steady herself, and walked away.

"Do you think she's Einstein? Everyone knows about a person's light." Maggie gobbled the last dumpling and patted her mouth. "I've eaten about a hundred of those."

"Why would you tell her Paris is dirty?"

"When Charlie and I visited, I nearly stepped in dog poo about a hundred times. There was trash in the streets."

Brendon spotted Angelene. She hid beside Walter, her head bowed. Prior to the party, he had given little thought to who she was or what she may look like. He couldn't get her out of his mind.

***

"Why her? You spend all week with Walter. What's so special about her?"

Sofia peered at her reflection in the mirror, touching the fine lines around her eyes.

"She makes him smile."

David pressed his lips against her gardenia scented shoulder, running a hand under her hair.

"He said that about Anastasia."

"She shared quotes from her favourite books. She paints."

"She could barely stand in those shoes. She picked at her nail polish. It was all over the floor."

"Walter likes a challenge."

Sofia dissolved into David's chest. "There's something about Angelene, something I can't put my finger on."

"Have you been talking to your mother? She'd make anyone suspicious."

"As soon as we met, the hair on the back of my neck stood up."

"It could be my father; you know he haunts the den."

"Her eyes are so sad."

"Give her a chance to settle in."

"Did you not see the fidgeting?"

He covered her mouth with his, slipping his fingers under the silky strap. "She was nervous."

"Are you seducing me?"

"Yes."

People said if there were a couple meant to find each other, it was David and Sofia. Sofia couldn't say the same about Walter and Angelene.

***

Angelene perched on the nightstand, smoke streamed from her mouth. The party had flown by in a dizzying array of colours and sounds. The only colour that stood out was brown. She inhaled sharply and tossed the cigarette out the window.

"I hung up your dress."

"You can throw it out."

"You shouldn't have given the Chanel to Lisette."

"I was the talk of that ridiculous party."

"People want to get to know you."

"You left me alone."

Angelene jerked at the blankets and squirmed underneath. She wrestled the sheets to her chin, made a cocoon, and squeezed her eyes shut.

"You should have introduced yourself to Victoria or Simone. They just got back from Provence."

"Sofia doesn't like me."

Walter tugged at the blankets and curled his body around her. "She doesn't know you. If you continue to hide away, she never will."

"Let me sleep."

"I'll ask Sofia and Brendon to stop by. You liked his company."

Angelene reached for her cigarettes. "He was the only person who spoke to me."

"No more. They're stinking up the house."

"It calms me."

Walter traced his thumb around her nipple. "I know another way."

Angelene pushed his hand away and shrunk under the blankets.

"I've given you a new life. No beast of a landlord. No more scraping by."

"Become a servant of God. You have proof of heroic virtue. I'll be a miracle, the improved Angelene. The Vatican will canonize you, Saint Walter."

"You say the most amusing things." He slipped his hand under the blankets and cupped her breast. "Every woman envied you tonight."

Angelene flicked his hand. "You're full of yourself."

Walter laughed, kissed her neck, running his fingers along her stomach. "Guess who I bumped into before we left Paris?"

Angelene clamped her thighs together, imprisoning his hand. "Brigitte Bardot."

"Your friend, Pierre Piedmont."

"How do you know Pierre?"

"I donated to the Sorbonne. You love the Hugo statue," Walter said, prying her legs open. "He was coming out of the Dean's office. I heard her mention they had let you go."

"Why did you speak to him?"

"I was curious how he knew you."

"You should have left him alone."

Walter pressed his mouth against her ear. "I told him I married you. Do you know what he said?"

His fingers slid into her panties. She squirmed; a cold tremor slithered down her back.

"If you want to fuck me, just do it and stop talking."

"He said, good luck."

4 WABI-SABI

Brendon stared at the English assignment, list the character traits of Lotte. He had thought of two, flawless and angelic. The list had transformed into what he liked about Angelene. The scent of her skin, earthy, spicy, musky, the yellow dress.

"Brendon Cook. You're behind two weeks. I suggest you get your head out of the clouds," Harriot Hudson said. She had been part of the faculty for over twenty-five years, bled Taunton plaid and could recite random quotes from Dickens, Bronte, and Shelley. She was squat, stodgy, and bland. Brendon had never seen her in anything but beige. Even her squared off bob was boring brown.

"Psst, mate." Troy laid a chewed pencil on the edge of the desk, pinging it. Brendon shot out his hand and snagged it.

"You heard Ms. Hudson; I need to concentrate."

"You haven't told me about Walt's wife? All Maggie told Charlie was the dumplings were brilliant."

Brendon leaned across the desk and concealed his mouth with the novel. "Promise you'll keep your gob shut? That means no telling Charlie."

Troy rolled the novel into a tube and nodded.

"Walt pulled a tidy one. She had on this yellow dress. You could see everything."

"Was she better than that Polish girl or Anastasia?"

"I hope you are discussing Werther and not football," Ms. Hudson said.

Brendon lowered the book and flashed a dimpled smile. "I was telling Troy, Werther's love interest is named Charlotte."

"Perhaps he'll read the novel then."

Brendon sunk into the chair and lowered his voice. "She wasn't wearing a bra. I'm not sure she had knickers on."

"What were her jubblies like?"

Brendon peeked over the novel. Ms. Hudson flipped through papers, cheerfully slashing red pen across them. Warmth crept over his cheeks. "Small, but not too small. They were perky."

"I've got to meet her."

"I shouldn't be talking about her that way. She's Walt's wife."

"No harm in looking, mate."

Brendon shoved his notebook in his bag. Troy's philosophy, a peek doesn't hurt, was simple. Make it quick. Brendon had peeked and stared. She had haunted him since the party.

"Good luck in French."

"I'm meeting Maggie first," Brendon said, pushing open the door. "She's doing a fantastic job pretending not to be nervous about German lessons."

"Keep away from Rachel, mate. That list is infamous."

"What list?"

Troy smiled and sprinted across the lawn. Streams of yellow light filtered through the treetops, sparkles of amber twinkled along the branches and bark. Angelene was all around him. The girl he should be thinking about was walking towards him. Brendon took Maggie by the arm, dragged her behind a cedar and pressed his lips against hers. She tasted like a fairy cake.

"Someone might see."

"We have five minutes. Kiss me."

Her breath danced over his lips. "We shouldn't."

I'm not good enough or pretty... you're the most beautiful woman I've ever seen

"No more. Mr. Dawson patrols the grounds between classes."

"Just a little longer."

"I can't be late for class."

"Can we meet in the car park after German lessons? I parked under the willow tree."

Maggie fixed her kilt and hiked her overstuffed book bags over her shoulders.

"Everyone knows what happens under the willow tree. Behave yourself with the ginger tart."

"I'll follow every daft rule in the Gentlemen's Code."

"You better. No thinking about any other girls. That goes for..." she stopped herself and stood on tiptoes.

"What were you going to say?"

"One more kiss."

Brendon pecked her lips and flicked her kilt. "Lace knickers today."

"You've been incredibly randy since coming home from Dortmund. See you at lunch."

'*No thinking about Ms. Pratt, bloody dolt.*'

The German flag drooped over the chalkboard, framed posters of Karl Marx, Bach, and Goethe hung in various corners of the room. A dish of roasted almonds, an Oktoberfest must, sat beside a bruised apple. Brendon's leg bounced; his cheeks were hot. The Gentlemen's Code flicked through his brain like pages of a book.

"Guten Tag, mein gutaussehender Prinz."

Rachel strolled into the classroom and tossed her hair over her shoulder. She dragged a chair across the floor and straddled it. His eyes darted from her freckled inner thighs to her globe sized breasts squeezed into her blouse. The Gentlemen's Code flew out the window.

"I'm surprised Thornton allowed you to meet me."

"I need to learn German."

"Won't Dawson let you take it again?"

Brendon pressed open his notebook and dug into his pocket for a pen. "I called Mr. Lochmann a poofter, told him he could shove his roasted almonds up his arse. He won't have me in his class."

"Now you're stuck in French."

"My dad thinks everyone should know two languages."

"Why didn't you take Spanish? I liked it better."

"Mr. Klaussen didn't want me either."

Rachel scooted the chair closer and scrunched herself next to him. She had him pinned to the wall. Brendon's nose filled with the scent of cigarette smoke and tuberose perfume.

"Wurst du man Freund sein," Rachel said. She brushed her pinky over his. "Will you?"

Brendon wiped his palms on his thighs. He didn't know where to look, the chart of German expressions, the sky.

"I don't know what you said."

"I asked, will you be my friend?"

"Why do I need to know that? What if I need to ask for a bloody taxi or directions?"

"You want to be my friend, don't you?"

Brendon ran his tie over his forehead and swallowed nervously. Her smile was intense, eyes amber, red hair, breasts, freckled thighs. He was speechless, flustered.

"You're fit as fuck." Rachel didn't blush or look away. "You have the perfect footballer's physique. What are you, six-foot two?"

Compliments were nothing new to Brendon, never so bluntly and never without followed by giggles.

"Am I making you nervous?"

"Bloody hell yes. Can we get to the German?"

"You're even dishier when you blush."

"I'm going to leave if you don't stop."

Rachel flashed him an 'you're no fun' pout and plucked the pen from his hand. "Ich brauche Ein taxi."

Brendon repeated the phrase and relaxed against the wall.

"You can ask for a taxi now. Try this one, ich wurde gerne der Gründe für deine schlaflose Nacht sein."

"Bloody hell, you're going to have to say that slower." Heat bloomed over his neck and cheeks. "What did you bloody say?"

"I would like to be the reason for your sleepless night. I'll write it in your book."

Brendon flicked her hand away. "Don't bloody do that. Maggie will want to know what it says. There go German lessons."

"You're no fun."

"What if I get lost and need to find Signal Iduna Park?"

"Wo ist Signal Iduna Park?"

"What if I need to use the loo?"

"Wo ist die toilette. I'll write them down for you."

Brendon twirled a strand of coppery red hair around his finger. It hit him. He fancied the girl no boy fancied. Brendon pushed the feeling deep inside. Rachel was not the type of girl he fancied; gentlemen chose a lady.

"Why did you ask me for help? I could ruin your reputation."

"I need someone who can speak German brilliantly."

"You think I'm a slag."

Brendon had heard the rumours, listened to Maggie and Charlotte go on about the tarts of Taunton. He never gave it any thought. She was just a girl with fantastic red hair.

"I asked Madame Lafavre who was the best student in Mr. Lochmann's class, she said you."

She glanced at him and grinned coquettishly. "Twice a week at dinner break?"

"Are we done? It's only been thirty minutes."

"I've got to eat and have a ciggie before classes start. See you in Latin, mein Lieblings fursball spieler."

"You didn't ask for a kiss, did you?"

"Next time."

Brendon had spent most of Latin ignoring Rachel's advances. It had been hard to concentrate when she wiggled her tie at him or fluttered her thickly mascaraed lashes. He was glad the school day was over and happier to be home. Brendon opened the front door. Sofia angled a Derby vase, moved a framed photo, and repositioned the vase again. She wore a black pencil skirt and a blouse the colour of red wine. The afternoon sun glowed through the transom window, casting a spotlight on her raven hair and curves.

"Blimey," Troy said.

"That's my bloody mum."

Sofia turned; her ruby red lips quirked. She exhaled.

"Your home."

She swooped in; her arms outstretched like silk wings. Brendon shot up his middle finger at Troy and shrunk away from her embrace.

"Every day around this time."

"Don't be cheeky. How was your day?"

"I pissed Mr. Campbell off. That's the fourth time this week."

"What did you do?"

"He was staring at Rachel's jubblies."

"It was a quick peek. Mr. Campbell sent her to the back of the classroom."

"Did her jubblies distract him too?" Troy said.

"She asked if there was a scroll in my trousers or if I was happy to see her."

"What a thing to say," Sofia said. "You've missed two weeks. Can't you pay attention?"

"It's Latin."

Troy laughed. "English, French, history."

"You're not helping, bloody prat."

"Your father rang this morning. Walter would like your help."

Brendon stared at his feet; he had made it through the rest of the day not thinking about Angelene. The mention of Walter's name shot her back into his head; her trembling fingers, the way her mouth moved when she spoke, the yellow dress.

"He's planned his own party and wants you to mow the lawn and hack away at those overgrown hedges. I told your father; you're not a gardener."

"Add it to my list of punishments."

"That's what your father said." Sofia clicked through her silver bangles and arched an eyebrow. "He wants us to check in on her. If she's so lonely, buy her a cat. Don't those creative types like cats?"

"I've got nothing better to do. You in?"

"I said I'd like a look at..." Troy hung his head, rubbing the back of his neck. "I've got more experience mowing."

"The idea of you pruning and mowing that mess."

"Walt's done lots of stuff to help me out."

"Your dressed for it," Sofia said, tugging on his hoodie. "Ever since that ridiculous poll was on social media, you've completely given up on your looks. So, what if people find you attractive?"

"I've told you a million times, I'm a keeper, not a face."

Amelia scurried across the foyer, humming an upbeat rendition of Memory from Cats. "That's how footy players make extra money. Look at Beckham toting those swanky underpants."

"Don't be too long. I'm making spezzatino di manza."

"Bloody hell, if you don't stop, we'll be there until midnight."

Brendon grasped Troy's shoulders and twisted him out the door.

"Your mum cooks?"

"Don't be a dolt."

"Every time I'm at yours, Amelia is toiling away. You have a perfectly good mum to make you dinner."

"Mum's busy."

"Doing what? Looking fit. My mum has fed the cattle, prepared supper, got things ready for the stall, all before nine."

They rambled down the hill. The grass gleamed, the air sweet, the farmhouse, a few steps away.

"Why doesn't Walter have a gardener?"

"He likes to do this stuff. He says it keeps him grounded."

"Your dad and Walt are like us."

"What are you talking about?"

"You're a nancy and I have to muck stalls, feed the chickens."

"Stop talking bollocks."

"What was that? I couldn't hear you; your silver spoon is in the way."

Brendon paused at the edge of the farmhouse drive. He grabbed the hem of his hoodie and twisted it between his sweating hands. He was steps away from the girl who had changed his world and shouldn't have.

"This is ace mate. I can't wait to get a look at her." Troy smoothed his bangs, straightened his Manchester United t-shirt, and smiled boyishly. "I'm all set."

"Don't be acting like a dolt. She's shy."

"Hurry mate, before my hair gets mussed."

Brendon lifted the door knocker and rapped. His body buzzed; every nerve zapped with electricity. The door opened. He felt like he was standing under a heat lamp. She wore holey jeans, a flimsy shirt, her hair was as gold as the day, her eyes bright green. Troy fixed his gaze on her, blinked, glanced at Brendon, then back. He scratched his hair, smoothed his bangs, and blinked.

"Got something in your eye?"

"No, mate. I'm... blimey, I don't get it."

They stumbled into a clutter of paint cans and rollers. The scent of turpentine and fresh paint hung in the air. The front room was bare. All that remained were three shades of blue swiped across the wall and a tarp covered in wood trim and nails. Brendon glanced from Troy's puzzled face back to her. She was imperfect, hesitant to smile and as she dug in a bowl for a skeleton key, Brendon imagined the graceful movements of her fingers on his skin.

"Thanks for helping Walter."

Her syrupy voice snapped him from his revery. He floated behind her; his eyebrows lifted; her bottom was the shape of a heart.

"You've got drool on your chin, mate."

"I'm not drooling."

He didn't think he was. He had never seen a bottom that shape before. A flush stung his cheeks. He wasn't doing anything wrong. A quick peek was harmless. Brendon cursed under his breath; he was staring.

They stepped into the mudroom, over broken trim, and cardboard boxes filled with yellowed curtains. When Brendon was younger, the green door led to an imaginary pitch and thousands of squealing fans. Walter would take him to extraordinary places where mermaids seduced, and pirates were ready to loot and pillage. The little room took on a new meaning.

"Qui est votre ami?"

Troy hurled out his hand. "Troy Spence."

"Il est mignon."

Troy's eyebrows raised, he swatted Brendon's arm. "Did you hear what she said, mate?"

"I'm bollocks in French."

"She said I was cute."

Angelene laid her hand over her mouth, clinging to her smile, like it didn't belong.

"Will you visit me sometime? This house frightens me."

Brendon wiped his palms on his jeans. "Sure, I mean, I guess until you get used to the house."

"Come on, Casanova, I have chores to do."

"You live on a farm?"

"Unfortunately."

"Do you have animals?"

"Cows and chickens."

"You don't like the farm?"

"Getting up at dawn, manure wafting in my bedroom window." Troy lifted his shirt and sniffed. "The constant noise."

"What's the matter?"

"Sometimes you can't get the smell out."

Angelene stepped closer, placing her nose in his neck, Troy's cheeks flushed.

"You smell nice. What is it?"

"Eau du chicken feed."

"Thanks mate."

Brendon laughed and shielded his chest from Troy's fist.

"Do you play football?"

"I'm part of the defence team. I protect his pretty arse."

"I'll have to get Walter to take me to a match."

Tiny flutters split through Brendon's belly. He envisioned Angelene in the bleachers, cheering and shouting 'Cook.' The flutters disappeared; she would be with Walter.

"Everything you need is in there." Angelene pointed to a shed surrounded by woolly willow and butcher's broom. "I'll let you get to work. You'll be okay, oui?"

"Sure Ms. Pratt."

"Please Brendon, call me Angelene. I'm struggling with being a Ms."

She held his gaze and walked away.

"I didn't see it at first, mate."

They trudged through the overgrown grass. The sun was beginning its descent, lighting the moors on fire.

"I was expecting Miss. Poland, I got Miss. Awkward instead. Has Walter lost the plot?"

"I think she's beautiful."

"I wouldn't say beautiful," Troy said, glancing back at the farmhouse. "Something about her sticks in your head."

Brendon understood. She had been in and out of his thoughts, confusing him, enticing him, and giving him a harsh case of the guilts.

"You sure Walt didn't meet her in a creche?"

"What the bloody hell is that?"

Brendon shoved the key in the padlock. The door screeched open, releasing a dank odour into the air.

"Daycare mate."

"Age doesn't matter. You love who you love."

Brendon combed through the garden tools and held up shears. "Prune or mow?"

Troy grabbed the shears, pointing them towards a hawthorn bush. "I'll prune and start right over there."

Angelene had burrowed in the corner of the window bench, book in hand. A cigarette dangled from her mouth.

"I thought she wasn't pretty."

"It's strange mate. I didn't think she was. It's like she crawled inside me, and I need a second look."

Brendon sparked the mower to life. "It's a quiet beauty. It creeps up on you."

He pushed the mower past the window. She glanced over the book. A knot tightened in his belly. Something haunted her eyes and he looked away. Who was Angelene Pratt? Shy, awkward, a mystery. Brendon mowed the length of the garden, met her gaze. She was sunshine hidden behind a wall of clouds, wintry and pale. His body filled with anxious tremors.

***

The town library was one of Maggie's favourite places. Books made excellent company when Brendon had practice. It wasn't cool, hanging out at the library. Maggie had never been cool, not until she started dating Brendon. The kids at school still questioned how she had scored Taunton's hero. Her friends thought the pairing of athlete and scholar peculiar. Weird or not, Maggie thought she was the luckiest girl alive. A studious thespian, the girl rated six out of ten, had the most popular boy in school.

"I love history. I could study it all day."

"You're daft," Charlotte said, dumping her purse onto the table, "I cut my shopping trip short. This better be good."

'Shh,' hissed from behind a colossal bookshelf.

"Maybe if you spent more time in the library, you'd get better grades."

"I'm only finishing sixth form for daddy." Charlotte thumbed through a book and scrunched her nose. "I have one plan and one plan only."

"You should go to school for fashion. You have a brilliant sense of style."

"I'm going to be Ms. Troy Spence, live in a posh house, run all over Manchester with the other footballer's wives."

"Those are some ambitious dreams."

"How was the do? You haven't talked about anything but those dumplings."

Maggie set her glasses on the table. "Brendon and I got into a spat."

Charlotte smeared lip gloss over her lips, smacked and applied another layer. "Was Ms. Batra chatting Brendon up again? That gobby cow told babes he had a nice bum."

Maggie glanced around the library and jammed her thumbnail in her mouth. "We fought about Ms. Pratt."

Charlotte's blue eyes brightened. "Rumours are she looked poorly, pale faced, skinny."

"She's different."

"Does she have an arse face?"

"You remember Mr. Pratt's last girlfriend?"

Charlotte tapped her finger against her cheek. "There's been so many."

"The Russian. He brought her to a football match, the entire team was gawking at her."

"Miss photoshopped face, I gave babes the biggest pinch for staring at her."

Maggie tore at her fingernail and sucked at the blood bubbling around her cuticle. "Ms. Pratt is tiny, barely came up to Mr. Pratt's waist and plain. She's quiet."

"That's rubbish. Mr. Pratt wouldn't marry someone like that," Charlotte said. "Was she wearing a banging outfit? Something from Chanel or St. Laurent?"

"Her dress looked like it came from a charity shop, what there was of it. Her arms were more covered up, bracelets to her elbows." Maggie rubbed her finger under her nose; the colour faded from her face. "Brendon couldn't take his eyes off her."

"Shouldn't you be worried about the ginger tart?"

"It was the way Brendon looked at her, like he fancied her, but didn't fancy her or was confused about fancying her."

"Have you considered humping him?"

"It always comes back to sex."

"Don't you get a flutter in your fanny when you're snogging Brendon?"

Maggie tore at the tip of her fingernail, picking the glittery bit off her tongue. "Do you?"

"As soon as babes' lips touch mine." Charlotte snatched Maggie's hand from her mouth and grimaced at the mauled manicure. "His spunk won't kill you."

"Mum says the stuff is as bad as the plague," Maggie said, tapping her highlighter against her notebook. "I don't want people to think I'm like Tilly and Rachel."

"No one will think you're a slag," Charlotte huffed. "You can't expect Brendon to bang one out every time you get scared."

"That's disgusting. You don't think he does that, do you?"

"Every boy wanks."

A smile replaced the disgust on Maggie's face. "Do you think he does it in the shower?"

Charlotte clutched her stomach and laughed. "They'll touch their knobs any chance they get. Dawson caught Philip Morris in the custodian's cupboard last term."

Maggie stopped giggling and bit into her lip. "I bet Brendon did that after the do, thinking about Ms. Pratt."

Charlotte wrapped her arm around Maggie and squeezed. "He might have, or he might have fallen asleep. Worry about Rachel and her list, not homely Ms. Pratt."

"I can't get her out of my head."

"You've had a rough go. Brendon left, came back, moodier than ever. Rachel has her tart hands all over him."

"You want to go to the pub? I know you hate this place."

"We can be sophisticated and drink g&t's."

Maggie gathered her books and shoved them into a tote. A feeling like something dark was going to happen prickled her skin.

***

Smoke curled around Angelene's head; ash dripped to the floor. Images of Brendon haunted her: broad shoulders, slender waist, lean muscles. He had an incredible glow. His light was bright. She called him her boy in brown.

"Forgive me, God, for thinking such things. It's my pattern."

Angelene squished the cigarette, dropped it on an ash filled plate and tugged at her hair.

I got here as fast as I could. I had to wait for father to fall asleep.
The quiet is killing me. My scars are on fire, ready to burst.
I'll fill them with gold. Kintsugi, you'll be even lovelier.
You're ridiculous. My scars are ugly.
Wabi-sabi, embrace your imperfections. There is beauty in your scars.

Angelene fell onto the bed and cradled the pillow.

You don't go looking for trouble; it falls at your feet.

The words strangled her. It had been her pattern, greeting trouble and asking God for forgiveness.

5 Limerence

Brendon bound down the steps of the modern languages building. The sky had clouded over. Vast stretches of grey engulfed the Victorian buildings. Maggie was waiting by the dining hall, prettily composed. The crimson glow on her cheeks told him differently. There was a storm brewing inside her. He'd use Troy's tactic, compliment, then a kiss. If that didn't work, beg for forgiveness.

"You look nice."

She crossed her arms and scowled. "I look the same every day."

He bent to kiss her; she swatted at his arm.

"Bloody hell, did you not get the part of what's her name?"

A glimmer of frustration shot through him. His scoop saves had been brilliant. He hadn't stumbled over the agility ladder. All the exhilaration he felt at training puddled at his feet. He smothered the sparks and shoved his hands in his pocket.

"Her name is Ophelia. Michael is going to be my Hamlet."

Brendon chuckled. "You and that swot again."

"Michael is a brilliant actor."

"What the bloody hell is the matter? I've had a brilliant morning."

"My mother forgot to wash my favourite tights; these are horribly itchy. Jack sucked on his finger and stuck it in my toast."

"How is your brother spitting in your brekky my fault?"

A gang of students dawdled around the dining hall doors. A couple Brendon recognized from Latin loitered around the privet hedges and placed their bets. Two-pounds Maggie Thornton was ready to have a tantrum.

"For two years, at exactly ten, the theme from Zeffirelli's Romeo and Juliet plays."

"Is something wrong with your ringtone?"

"No, wanker. I waited over an hour for you to give me a ring, half an hour the other night."

Brendon scraped his fingers through his hair and glared at the crowd of bystanders.

"I've been busy."

"You never forget. Even when you were in Dortmund, you gave me a bell."

"Troy and I were at Walter's. The Bayern, Dortmund highlights were on. Bloody homework."

"You saw Ms. Pratt?"

"You're seriously asking if I was with Ange, Ms. Pratt?"

Maggie's mouth tipped into a pout. Wagers whispered in the wind, 2p Maggie was about to cry. 1p Brendon would explode.

"Walt asked me to mow the fucking grass. Was I not supposed to talk to her? She bloody lives there."

Maggie's chin trembled, she sniffed and ran her blazer over her nose. Hot sparks filled his hands and fingers. He curled and uncurled his fists.

"Will you lot fuck off."

The crowd scattered; peals of laughter followed Brendon into the dining hall. Conversations about who was pulling who, and the Christmas formal, created a joyful hum.

"I got you the veg lasagna, mate. It's a far cry from your Nonna's."

Brendon mumbled thanks and slumped onto a chair.

"You're dark and broody, Mr. Football. Didn't make a save this morning?" Charlotte said. She smothered Troy's cheek with kisses and ran her finger over his ear. "I wish I were an octopus. I could touch all the parts I love."

Maggie flumped onto the chair; her breasts pressed against him; her perfume was cloyingly sweet.

"Ask your friend why I'm pissed off."

"Don't blame Magpie," Charlotte said. "Shall we go to the pub tonight? We'll celebrate me getting the part of Queen Gertrude. I'm not sure why Ms. Baxter gave it to me. She didn't like the dress I chose for auditions."

Maggie giggled. "They didn't wear mini dresses in the eleventh century."

Brendon flipped over a layer of lasagna and ran his fork through the roasted vegetables. A debate started in his head, '*go to Angelene, leave her alone.*'

"I have to help mum after football."

"Can't Amelia or Peter help?" Troy said.

"It's part of my punishment."

"We haven't been to the pub in a while."

The chatter clogged Brendon's ears, Maggie's perfume assaulted his nose and, in his head, Angelene.

"We went to the pub before I went to Dortmund. I got bladdered and barfed at training. Liam fined me twenty quid."

"Cut the apron strings, mate."

"Come over Saturday after the match."

"Ooh, babes, I can show you my new bikini."

"That isn't a bikini. It's a pile of strings," Maggie said. Her breath tickled his ear. Brendon wrenched his arm free and loosened his tie. The dining hall was as hot as a desert.

"You going to barf, mate?"

Brendon tugged at his collar. He needed to escape from Maggie, from the thoughts reeling around in his head. Brendon yanked at his cuff and dabbed his forehead.

"I need some air."

"I'll come."

"Talk girlie stuff with Charlie. We'll be five minutes."

Brendon dodged around the tables; conversations halted. He barged through the double doors, scanned the hallway for the exit, and barreled down the hall, tearing off his blazer.

"Blimey mate, what's up?"

"Maggie was hanging all over me. My mind is racing about... the match. I couldn't breathe."

"Maggie can be clingy."

Brendon was confused. How could a thought about Angelene leave him feeling suffocated?

"Don't tell Liam about this. If he thinks I'm not in top form, he'll put Will in."

"I just got you back in net. It's our secret."

I'm not good enough, pretty...

Angelene's voice whispered through his ears. She slithered inside his mind and through his thoughts. A little shiver trickled down his spine. He loosened his tie and unbuttoned the top buttons.

"If Dawson sees, you'll get a uniform infraction."

"I'll fix it before class."

"Tidy yourself up, mate. Your mum will have you benched if you fool around."

"She only said that to make dad happy."

The dining hall doors burst open. Students milled about the lawn, their eyes on Brendon. He had a reputation for angry outbursts. They had never seen him shaken.

"Walk me to class, babes."

"You going to be okay, mate?"

Brendon nodded and stuffed his hands in his pockets.

"Guten tag Mr. Football."

Brendon wrapped an arm around Maggie and jerked her into his side.

"You looked brilliant at training. That tip over the bar, ace."

"Maggie and I are on our way to history."

He inventoried Rachel, nice hair, amazing breasts, freckles on her collarbone. His skin tingled. She was an eight out of ten.

"Go away," Maggie said.

Rachel ran her tongue over her glossy lips. "Can we watch the highlights again?"

Maggie swung her bags into his hip. Guilt slapped him hard in the face. He had fantasized about Angelene, sized up Rachel like a piece of meat.

"That was a one off. I had to see if Gladbach moved up the standings."

"What's the tart going on about?"

"We better get to history. I'll see you in Latin."

Rachel lifted his cuff and glanced at his watch. "You have a tattoo. You're even dishier now."

"Get your hand off my boyfriend."

"I'll save you a seat, knuddlebär."

Heat stormed his cheeks. Students moved around them, sneaking glances, fingers pointed, muffling their laughter. Brendon held up his middle finger and scowled.

"She just asked you to cuddle or called you cuddle bear. Cheeky cow."

"She wants to piss you off."

"Are you going to tell me what was the matter? And don't say the veg lasagna, it was delish."

"This place."

Drizzle cooled Brendon's face. *'Visit, don't visit. Respect Uncle Walt. I'll decide after classes.'*

"Why did you watch football with her? That's our thing."

"What match did we watch Sunday?"

"One team had blue shirts, the other red."

Brendon held open the door. "See, you don't watch, and I didn't ask her. She moved her chair next to mine."

"Ignore her next time."

"She's harmless."

Maggie's mouth dropped open. "Everyone knows you're at the top of her list."

"What list?"

"Don't play innocent. You know what kind of list the tart keeps."

Brendon wrapped his hands around Maggie's waist and lifted her into his arms. "Hold my kilt down. I don't want people staring at my bum."

"I'd have to touch it then."

"Put me down."

He dropped her to her feet and stole a kiss as a gravelly 'ahem' bellowed down the hall.

"Into class," Mr. Clark said.

Brendon glanced at the man who believed his ancestors belonged to the House of Tudor. He was short, stout, and spherical. His blonde beard was tidy, hairline receding and if he had worn a fur trimmed crown, Brendon may have been convinced.

"You may enter my classroom once you straightened your tie. Three strikes Mr. Cook."

Brendon wiggled the knot in place and prepared himself for an overenthusiastic lecture on Mr. Clark's family tree.

Brendon cast a brief glance at the farmhouse. Rain dribbled from the sills and dripped from the wisteria. Sorrow and drab clouds swathed the house.

'Go home. This is daft.'

He put the car in reverse and hit the brake. She had asked him to visit. A ten-minute check-in wouldn't hurt. Brendon jiggled his keys and stepped into the rain. He jumped over puddles and thumped the door knocker. Rain melted his hoodie to his chest. Brendon pressed his ear to the door. It slowly opened, he stumbled over the threshold.

"Look at you."

Brendon ran his hand through his wet hair and grinned. She wore patched jeans, a stretched t-shirt, and a sloppy ponytail. Teeny blobs of black paint covered her forearms. She didn't seem to care that she looked dishevelled.

"I was just driving by, I thought. I'm not sure what I was thinking."

"Do you like it?"

White paint replaced the dismal ivory walls. She had stained the cove moulding deep amber and hung Linolscnitt prints of rabbits and birds. Teal, orange and white, added a touch of whimsy to the puny foyer. Sandalwood incense snaked into the entry in long, twisting swirls.

"Go sit by the fire. I'll get you a towel. I haven't put the laundry away yet. Walter would be so upset."

Brendon rubbed the back of his neck. This was Uncle Walt's house, his wife. If he stayed, all the strange, confusing emotions that had made him irritable and dizzy might return. Brendon sighed and stepped into the front room. It took a second for the changes to sink in. A hulking olive-green settee leaned into an indigo blue wall. Turquoise, vermillion, and floral print pillows smothered the couch. She had piled enormous plum and teal pillows by the fireplace. Brendon ran his fingers over a peacock feather. A cluster of black ink illustrations, faceless creatures, and dancing fairies lined the mantle.

"Do you like it? The wall colour is the same shade as a friend's eyes."

"It isn't Walt's taste."

Angelene handed him a towel. "Walter has no taste. Will you stay for tea?"

Brendon clenched the towel. He should be grumbling over his homework or at the pub. He stumbled through a quick mental list of why he should stay: she was sad, lonely.

Brendon collapsed onto the worn brick ledge. He yanked off his soggy hoodie and laid it on the warmed bricks. "One cup."

"Your mother came to visit me today." Angelene poured tea and passed it to him. He quivered as her fingers skimmed over his.

"How was mammina?"

Angelene held up a pitcher and sugar bowl. "Votre mère est intimidant."

"Just milk."

"She told me in the politest manner, if I hurt her family, she would send me back to Paris." Her fingers weaved in and out, press and push.

"I'm sorry."

"Don't be sorry. She adores you." Angelene thrust her hands under her thighs. "You're wearing a cross."

"I'm Catholic."

Angelene withdrew her hands, wiggled her fingers, and picked up her teacup. "Me too. Do you go to church?"

"When I was younger. Mum had a question for God. He didn't answer. She lost her faith."

"I'm glad you stopped by."

"The first time I went to the football camp in Dortmund. I was bloody afraid. You must feel the same way."

"I'm feeling many things, fear, elation, loneliness. I'm also grateful, hopeful." She laid a plum pillow at his feet and nestled onto it.

'I fancy you, I don't. I think you're beautiful, I don't. I want to be with you. I shouldn't. You're in my head and out of my head. I'm losing my bloody mind.'

"Bloody hell, it's hot in here."

Brendon plucked at his t-shirt. She had done it again, slithered into his head and lit a fire in places she shouldn't.

"What do you do all day, other than redecorating?"

"I read and paint. Would you like to see my artwork?"

Curiosity spurred inside him, another layer to the mysterious girl.

Brendon set down his cup and followed her up the stairs. Paint cans, rollers, and splattered tarps cluttered the hallway. She had smeared a stripe of chocolate brown, sienna, and burnt umber on the wall. An assortment of throw pillows, swatches of fabric and a can of paint sat in the centre of each room he passed.

"This is where I spend most of my day."

The room smelled of turpentine, walnut oil, and sandalwood. Brendon didn't recognize Walter's boyhood room. The walls were white. She had clipped yellow saris to the brass curtain rods and angled a saffron lounge between the two windows. Brendon approached a spindle-legged table. Illustrations of contorted trees, distorted figures, dancing horned creatures laid between a palette and tubes of acrylic paint. The collection of drawings was haunting and morose, another layer to peel away.

Angelene laid her hand on his arm. A flutter rippled through his belly; her hair smelled like lavender. "Yellow is my favourite colour. I thought if I decorated this room yellow, I would be yellow too. What is your favourite colour?"

"You can guess."

He picked up a sketch of a woman with the head of a goat reaching for her horns; her body stretched like elastic.

"You drew all these?"

"Do they frighten you?"

"They make me sad."

She buried into his side; his heart surged. She fit perfectly against him. "Tell me why."

"The woman in the painting doesn't like what she's become. She's trying to break free." Brendon thumbed through the drawings. "Something has happened to all these women. They're running, hiding, or trying to beat a creature off. There's no one protecting them."

Angelene scraped along a faint scar. Brendon wrapped his fingers around hers and inspected her forearm, faded crisscrossed lines, little crosses.

"Please don't do that." He traced along a faded cross, beautiful, bruised, Uncle Walt's. "Do something else, scream, punch a wall like I do. Well, used to do. I'm working on my temper."

"My screams are as lost as I am."

Brendon pushed his thumb under a watch band. Angelene tugged her arm free, hid her smile as he yawned.

"You're sleepy."

"I get up early to train, rush home, rush to school."

"Is that how you spend your day? Rushing around Taunton?"

"Mum and dad are making me finish my A-levels. Liam, my coach, keeps us on an intense schedule. I'm busy."

He followed her out of the bedroom. The stairs creaked under his feet. They stood silently in the foyer. A strange sense of comfortability wrapped around him. The silence was as loud as the rain pelting against the door. After a few minutes, Angelene spoke. Her voice was far away.

"I love football."

"What's your favourite team?"

"Paris St. Germain."

"I thought you'd be the art gallery type."

"I am. I love a good match. Walter said you play professionally."

"Semi-pro in Taunton. I'm on loan with Dortmund's U19 squad."

"Your words are black, disappointed blue."

"Education is important to dad." Sparks flared and dissolved. "I didn't do well last year. I've had a few mishaps with my tutors."

"Football is your passion, non?"

"It's a long story."

"Will you share it with me sometime?"

"It's a tale of a boy whose dreams got shattered by expectations and ghosts."

"I would like to hear it and watch you play."

Brendon opened the door. The wind whirled wisteria petals into a dizzying waltz, depositing them at her bare feet.

"You're in luck. We have a match Saturday."

Her hand covered her smile. The urge to pull her hand away tingled in Brendon's fingers.

"I'll beg Walter. Cry if I must."

Rain battered against his back and pooled under his feet. Brendon looked into her eyes; he was curious about her story. He titled the night, 'Silent screams, scars and the tugging thread that ties us.'

"I'm happy you came."

Angelene rose on tiptoes, brushing her lips over his chin. He touched the spot. It radiated like the happiness, confusion, and guilt raging inside him.

"Will you be, okay? You haven't had dinner. Bloody hell, there's a mess on the floor."

The words spilled from his mouth. The spot her lips touched was warm.

"Don't worry about me. Go home."

"The highlights will be on. You'll have to sit through the Premier league first. They'll eventually get to Ligue 1."

"The puddle will soon be an ocean."

"Goodnight, Ms... Angelene."

"See you soon."

Brendon flew to his car, branches swayed, chilly rain pierced his skin. There would be a next time and another after that. There was nothing wrong with checking in and chatting. They could talk about football, and he could persuade her the Bundesliga was better than Ligue 1. He pulled into the carport, the thread that tied him to her tightened. He touched his chin; the spot tingled. If he found himself lost, the thread, the odd, wrong, and unbelievable connection would lead him to her. He dashed to the door; water splashed around his feet.

"Mammina."

Brendon ran his t-shirt over his face and walked to the dining room. Candle wax and cedar lingered in the air. Rain and the midnight blue walls made the room darker, ominous. The ornamental header above the window added charm to the outside. Shadows cast across the table looked like prison bars. The theme for this room, 'obliterate any trace of Richard Cook.' Brendon swore his grandfather joined them at meals. Pissed off, Sofia had replaced the heirloom Chippendale table for a mid-century Gangso Mobler masterpiece.

"You didn't answer my text. I was worried something happened to you."

Brendon clenched the back of the chair. "Bloody hell, don't do that."

"You could have been dead in the ditch. Two texts ignored."

Brendon sunk onto a chair and stared at the rain snaking through the ivy. The narrow ribbons crisscrossed through the leaves, like Angelene's scars. Brendon rubbed the chill from his arms. He had carried her scars home.

Sofia handed him a plate and slowly arched an eyebrow. "Where have you been?"

Brendon ran his fork through the sweet potatoes. He could lie, say he was at the pitch, lying went against the code.

"I was at Walter's."

"What were you doing?"

Brendon crumbled under her stare, poking at the rosemary scented chicken breast. "Making sure she was okay."

Sofia tightened the tie on her silk robe. "I want you to stay away."

"Did you see the front room? I thought you were obsessed with pillows. Heaps of them and in the nicest colours. It doesn't look like Walt's place at all."

"The style is Bohemian."

"Did you look at her drawings?"

"I thought the crayon drawing was terrific."

"Not that one, bloody hell, it had the name Yasmine in the corner. The ink sketches."

Sofia gripped the back of the chair. "They're dreadful, like nightmares."

"Where do you think the ideas come from?" Brendon scooped up a forkful of potato and chicken and shoveled it into his mouth.

"Manner's sweetheart," Sofia said, tossing at a napkin at him, "her imagination."

"Do you think the paintings could be about her life?"

"I hope not. I need you to stay away from her. Those sketches frightened me."

"I saw worse paintings in my art history class. There was one titled Severed Heads. Ms. Pratt is harmless."

A frown wrinkled Sofia's forehead. Brendon laid his fork across his plate and reached for her hand.

"I won't visit Ms. Pratt anymore."

"You didn't get a strange feeling when you were with her, that, be aware feeling?"

"I see a girl with twitchy fingers." His cell phone buzzed in his pocket. "That's Mags, she'll be whingey if I don't answer."

He rambled into the kitchen, set the phone on the counter, and hit speaker.

"It's not ten yet."

"Where were you?"

He could tell by her sour tone she was sulking. Brendon tugged open the fridge, grabbed the milk, and spun off the cap. He glanced towards the doorway and gulped.

"First mum, now you."

He chugged another mouthful, whirled the cap on, and shoved it back in the fridge. If he wanted to end his night peacefully, he needed to choose his words carefully. If he gave her a compliment, it would be insincere. He knew she would be in either unicorn or mermaid print pyjamas. Before he left for Dortmund, he snuck her in to sleep over. He hoped for a frilly baby doll but got mermaid jimjams, an old bear crammed between them, and a horrible case of the guilts.

"You looked nice today."

A groan bellowed through the speaker. Stupid, he had used that one already.

"Don't charm me. Where were you? I called Troy, Charlie answered the phone, giggling. I don't know what Troy was doing. She could barely speak."

"He was probably visiting Australia, down under, you know."

"That's disgusting."

"It sounds bloody smashing."

"I'm waiting."

"I was at Walter's." He closed his eyes and waited for the backlash. All he got was a breathy, agitated sigh. "She's redecorating and needed help to move furniture."

"You must be tired. You helped your mum, Ms. Pratt."

Brendon leaned his head in his hand. He forgot about the lie he told at school.

"Can you drop it? I'm bloody knackered."

"Limerence."

"Bloody hell, you're as bad as my dad, always dropping words I don't understand."

"Charlie learned about it in psych. It's infatuation, deep longing, like how I felt about you after our first date. You better not be obsessed with Ms. Pratt."

"Good night, Mags. I love you. I'll see you in the morning, sweet dreams."

The whiny sigh turned into a giggle. Danger of a miserable Maggie, averted.

"You're a wanker, but you're my wanker and I love you."

Brendon looked at the tattoo on his wrist, 'Dum Spiro Spero.' The Latin phrase, 'While I breathe, I hope' had ruled his life. He had hoped to be in net for Dortmund, it had come true. He clung to the hope he could finish sixth form with no trips to the headmaster's office. Despite his mother's warning, he would see Angelene again.

***

Angelene filled a glass with wine, picked up her book and shuffled to the front room. Wind rattled the windows and blasted rain against the panes. Had she not been frightened of her new surroundings, she would have gone for a walk, let the wind lash through her hair and the rain soak the Ecole Nationale Supérieure d'Architecture t-shirt. Angelene lounged on the sofa. Something black caught her eye. She crawled across the couch and peeked over the armrest. Her heart slowed; her breath returned. Angelene held Brendon's hoodie to her nose and breathed in the scent of lemons and bergamot. The smell was invigorating. If she were to put a colour to it, it would be dazzling amber. Angelene tugged it over her shoulders and lounged into the cushions.

"God, please don't see this as bad. He smells so clean, pure white. I promise to return it."

Her gaze drifted to Yasmine's drawing. She held her cuff covered hand to her mouth and smiled. It was not springtime in Taunton. It was the season of unknowing and unwanted transformation.

"I painted the wall the colour of your eyes. Now I have you with me."

Angelene tucked her nose into the collar, his scent was all around her.

'The devil lives within him. His devil wants to break free.'

6 Metamorphosis

Sofia blotted her nose and examined the sky. It had been a fickle morning. The sun would shine, then clouds would flood the sky, threatening rain. The weather matched her mood. She had spent most of the morning swinging between calling off the lunch date and hoping someone else would. David had reassured her, a quiet meal with proper introductions; would be good for Angelene. Sofia watched Angelene teeter down the walkway. She wasn't so sure.

"I phoned Walter and said I had a stomachache. He said I needed to meet people." Angelene dropped her cigarette and burrowed into the seat.

Sofia grinned at the confession. "You'll love my friend Kate. She has a bit more couth than the other two."

"I don't do well in social settings."

"Brendon told me he stopped by." Sofia glanced at Angelene and argued with herself. What was she looking for? Blushing, a twinkle in the eye?

Angelene's voice was brittle and faint. "He's a nice boy."

"All those years David drilled the Gentlemen's code into Brendon's head. He did the respectable thing."

"Gentlemen's Code?"

"David and Walter wrote it when they were fourteen. They vowed to live their lives by it."

Sofia pulled into the car park of a rustic cottage turned Italian eatery. Cucina Povera was upscale, yet cozy, the perfect spot for a 'get to know you' lunch.

"You ready?"

"I've been rehearsing what to say. I'm afraid I'll forget something or disappoint Walter."

"Just be yourself."

"It's hard to be me."

"Then act. Everyone at the table will put on their best performance."

They stepped out of the car; Angelene wobbled. Sofia took her elbow, camouflaging her impatience with a smile.

"How do I look? Walter said to wear a dress. Trousers were more comfortable. I hoped my yellow blouse would make me calm."

"Is it working?"

Angelene smoothed the ends of her hair. "I'm afraid not. You look beautiful."

"I've had years of practice. Now, do as I do, shoulders back, chin up. People will think you own the place."

Angelene's shoulders sagged, her lips trembled around the words. "I can't."

"Yes, you can. Take a breath."

"When have you ever felt like this?"

"I've had moments. What's something that calms you, besides the colour yellow?"

Angelene buried her fingers between Sofia's bangles and clutched her wrist. "His eyes. They're as dark as the Makonde figurines I saw on display at the Louvre."

The hairs prickled under the sophisticated knot tied at the nape of Sofia's neck. It was like looking into a cracked mirror.

'I'm not scared of you, little bird. You have no control over me or my son.'

"You'll be fine Angelene. I'm right here."

Sofia opened the door. The aromas of focaccia and roasted garlic floated from the dining room. She gave Angelene a slight nudge and took her elbow as she teetered.

"Merde, merde. These silly shoes."

"I've tripped over my gown before. Those two have stumbled."

Victoria McGregor and Simone Batra whispered at each other from behind their wine glasses. Victoria was an all about impressions woman. From her frosty blonde hair to the Botox ironing out her face, she was over-processed, brassy, and squeezed into her blazer and skirt. Simone Batra's enthusiastic nasally voice was enough to get her noticed. Her philosophy, stay forever youthful, at whatever price.

"Have a seat before you fall over," Sofia said, dragging out a chair. "Walter should have purchased you pumps instead of stilettos."

Sofia slid onto a chair, hooking her purse strap over the back. "You remember Victoria and Simone."

Angelene nodded and clasped her hands in her lap.

"This is my friend, Kate."

"It's nice to meet you," Kate said.

"And you," Angelene chirped.

Friends for twenty-three years, Sofia could rely on Kate to calm her when things got crazy. Kate was not a worrier. She focused on the present, looked for reasons, reeling Sofia in before things spun out of control. Kate was the type of woman who could knock back a few cocktails in a designer dress and look good while doing it. She took care of herself and stood up for others, while keeping her hands clean. Sofia thought Kate was a catch. She had yet to be caught.

"We missed you at the do. Was it too difficult?" Victoria said.

"I was in London, wedding dress shopping with my niece. I hear it was a lovely evening."

"Nothing but the best for Walter," Sofia said. The server set down two glasses of wine. She thanked him and passed one to Angelene.

"Weren't you and Walter in Paris? Still harbouring feelings for him?" Simone said.

"I loathe Walter. He's chauvinistic, cocky," Kate said, her tone softened, "and the most charismatic man I've ever met. However, I respect him and his decision."

Victoria leaned into Simone's shoulder and smirked stiffly. "Does that bother you, Angelene, knowing Walter and Kate dated?"

Sofia arched an eyebrow at Victoria and lowered her gaze to Angelene's weaving fingers.

"Walter mentioned you're a barrister?"

"I am. What did you do in Paris?"

Sofia's ears perked up. She had heard bits and pieces from David, the gossip that vomited from Victoria's mouth. There had to be more to Angelene Hummel than frightening paintings and twitchy fingers.

"I worked at the Sorbonne." Angelene's flushed cheeks deepened to crimson, the twitching stopped, she froze.

"Ooh," Simone said, leaning into her arms, "tell us more."

Sofia held up her glass and shook it at the waiter.

"It's okay Angelene, no one here will judge you."

"How's Brendon? I haven't stopped thinking about him since the party. I told Eshana he's the one to go after," Simone said.

Sofia's jaw tensed; she forced a grin. "My son is fine. Breathe Angelene, it will help."

"Every time my heart beats this fast, a friend, Monsieur Krieger, would say, breathe little bird." Angelene exhaled a slow, ragged breath. The words, 'I did some modelling' hung off the end of it.

"You're a little short. My niece walks the runway. She's five-foot ten. What are you, five feet?" Victoria said.

"You don't need height to be an artist model," Sofia said.

"Don't artist models pose nude?" Simone said. She turned to Victoria and struggled to raise an eyebrow.

"Not necessarily. David mentioned you did some other work for the university."

Sofia took a small sip of wine; Brendon would be proud of her. She was being a friend, steering the conversation away from Victoria and Simone's nosy questions.

"I set up the art rooms."

"Angelene paints and draws. She has an incredible imagination."

Angelene knitted her fingers. Her gaze flitted from one exit to the other.

"I love Kandinsky. The notes of a song became a colour and an image. I found that interesting," Kate said.

Sofia grinned; Kate was playing the game of 'keep Ms. Pratt comfortable,' too.

"Kandinsky had a theory that geometrical elements make up every painting. There was the point, line, and basic plane. A friend drew a castle using Kandinsky's Point theory."

Victoria nudged her elbows on the table and clasped her hands. "Were you born in Paris?"

"Did you surround yourself with artistic men? Voulez-vous coucher avec moi ce soir. Right, girls?" Simone said.

"That's a silly phrase," Angelene said, twisting the napkin, "no one in France says that."

"Just ignore her. She's worse than a teenager," Sofia said.

"I was born in Marseilles."

Victoria clapped her ring clad hands together, her face cracked into a smile. "We took a trip to Marseilles. Sofia begged us to drive to Italy."

"I suggested it, Simone pushed. You wanted to discover the men of Turin."

The server set a platter of antipasti in the middle of the table. Sofia picked up her fork and rolled two olives on her plate, lifting her eyebrows at Kate.

"How did you end up in Paris?" Kate said, smoothing her auburn hair.

"Who cares about that? I want the juicy details," Victoria said, stuffing salami in her mouth. "How did you meet Walter? I can't imagine a man who was in the Special Forces taking an art class."

Laughter dominated the breezy sound of Vivaldi's Stabat Mater. Diners turned their heads and stared. Angelene gripped her glass, sipped, then gulped. "We met in Parc Floral."

"One of Walter's favourite places," Kate stated.

Sofia patted her heated cheeks. The tiny slurps and hearty guzzles grated on her nerves.

"Didn't you think it was odd, a man of Walter's age interested in you?"

"I've been with someone older."

Victoria leaned into Simone's ear. "Probably married."

The attempt at a whisper did not go unheard. Diners peered over menus, raising eyebrows at the accusation. Sofia looked at Kate with wide 'you've got to be kidding' eyes. Angelene hobbled to her feet. The dishes clattered; wine spilled. Sofia steadied the table.

"What's the matter with you?'

"It must be true. Look at her, trying so hard to fit in," Victoria said.

Sofia glared at Victoria; her smile was as fake as her hair colour. "You would know. She's gone and hid in the bathroom."

"We've all done things we aren't proud of," Kate said, pointing her fork at Simone. "You invited that young man back to your room in Ibiza."

Simone patted her mouth, flipping her golden-brown hair over her shoulder. "He played for Real Madrid."

"We all have baggage, that's all I'm saying," Kate said.

Victoria stabbed at a rigatoni and pointed her fork. Sauce flicked across the table. "Angelene has steamer trunks."

Sofia shifted her gaze to the hallway. The escape to the loo had done nothing to ease Angelene's trembling. She hobbled towards them, her hands clenched and unclenched.

Sofia touched Angelene's shoulder as she crumpled onto the chair.

"You'll love the orecchiette. It's comfort in a bowl."

Angelene murmured a thank you and dragged her napkin over her lap. Sofia had seen Brendon anxious before a match. She had seen no one dissolve the way Angelene had.

"Is it Burnham on Sea or Milan?" Kate said.

The sour expressions on Victoria and Simone's faces screamed they had no desire to hear about vacation plans. Sofia didn't care. She had lunch to rescue.

"I'm hoping for Milan. You know how much David loves Burnham."

"There wouldn't be a choice. If I said we were going to Milan, that would be the end," Victoria said.

"I'm with you. All those Italian men," Simone said, between bites.

"I'm the single one, yet you keep going on about men," Kate said.

Angelene kept her eyes on the bowl, poking at the pasta. "You have a home in Italy?"

"It belonged to my uncle. He left it to me and my brother, Gianni."

"You're lucky to have visited so many places," Angelene said.

"Have you not travelled?" Kate said.

Angelene set down her fork and fiddled with the ropes of sea pearls around her wrist. Sofia gazed curiously. The night of the party, strands and strands of bracelets, today the same. The day she visited the farmhouse, she wore a collection of copper and silver bangles.

"My friend Monsieur Krieger travelled for business. He would tell me about the places he visited. I vacationed through him."

"Those bracelets are lovely. Did Walter buy them?"

"Walter thinks my jewellery looks cheap."

Sofia exchanged a look with Kate. "He means well."

"My friend Lisette said Walter was trying to change me."

Sofia tapped her fork against her lip, searching for the words. "Walter sees the beauty in you. He's trying to bring it out."

"I guess."

"You guess?" Kate said, buttering bread, "you have gorgeous bone structure. Women would die for a complexion like yours. We'll plan a spa day, the works."

"That will be wonderful," Victoria said.

"No one is inviting you," Sofia said.

Silence fell over the table. Relief washed over Sofia; pasta had taken precedence over the interrogation. The feeling that gripped her at the wedding reception zipped around her belly.

"You're still good for tonight?" Kate said.

Simone laid a napkin over her empty bowl. "What are we doing?"

"We're doing nothing," Sofia said.

"Cheeky mare," Victoria said. "What made you decide to marry Walter? Was it his looks? I never go for the rugged type."

Simone chortled at Victoria's serious expression. "We know your type, Sofia's David."

"Did you enjoy your meal, Angelene?"

"Stop twisting the conversation. I want to know what drew her to Walter," Victoria said.

"Walter was a fool marrying me."

Sofia glanced at Kate, who glanced at Simone, who struggled to raise an eyebrow at Victoria. Sofia was curious now. She didn't know where to take the conversation or if she wanted to continue it. The annoying feeling swarmed her stomach.

"I'm a mess. I have been for a while."

The silence that hung over the table thundered louder than Sofia's beating heart. Sofia grappled with the comment. What did mess mean? Her appearance? Her story?

***

Dusk had painted the sky purply grey. Brendon could hear his mother telling him to stay away. Another voice told him it was okay. A tug of war battered his brain, '*visit, go home.*' Brendon raised the door knocker. It was heavy in his hand. Stay, go, follow the rules. Stay won.

"You should keep the door locked."

Angelene strolled from the front room, wearing Walter's pyjama bottoms, fingertips smudged; hair piled into a chaotic mess. She was beautiful chaos, melancholic and dishevelled.

"You're wearing my hoodie."

Angelene tugged at the waistband and lifted it over her chest.

"You can wear it."

He knew he should take it back. She wore a look that said she needed comfort. Brendon told guilt to 'fuck off' and flopped onto the sofa.

"I tried. I was drowning," she said, in a raspy slur.

"Would you like a cuppa?"

Angelene held up a glass of amber liquid. "I have this."

"Scotch?"

"C'est dégoûtant."

The coffee table was a muddle of illustrations, smudged paper towel and pencils. Brendon picked up a sketch. Two women cackled into their wineglasses; their faces stretched taut across their skulls.

"I hope that isn't mum."

"It's Victoria and Simone."

She guzzled the scotch, cringed, and dropped the glass to the floor. "Your mother and Kate were kind. I call that drawing tweedle dee and tweedle dum."

Angelene yawned, crept across the couch, and curled against him. Guilt, or someone with exceptional marksmanship, shot an arrow and pierced his heart. She held him like he used to cuddle Paddington when the ghosts visited. Her breathing was drawn-out and steeped in scotch.

"I'm a monster."

"Don't be daft. You're just a little rumpled."

Angelene flapped her hand over her mussed appearance. "Someone so beautiful and pure. Here you sit, with this."

"I wanted to make sure you survived lunch."

She squeezed him, squished into the cushions, and swiped her cigarettes from the table. "Tell me about your day. What's your school like?"

"Bloody pretentious. Your somebody if you go to Taunton College."

Angelene dragged on the cigarette. "What are you studying?"

"You really want to hear about this?"

Angelene nodded. The cigarette smoldered between her fingers.

"I have English. We're reading a book called The Sorrows of Young Werther. The ending is going to be sad. I know it."

"Good books have tragic endings."

"Then I have French, history. I had a match today, so I had permission to bunk off Latin."

Brendon fanned the smoke from his face. "You shouldn't smoke."

Angelene tossed the cigarette onto an ashy plate and wiped her fingers. "Did you win?"

"I stood around most of the match." He glanced at his watch and hesitated. "I need to go."

"Do you have to?"

His mother's warning assaulted his brain. He didn't want to leave her with her friends, scotch and ciggie. It was best he went home. He was still walking a fine line after the Dortmund fiasco.

"I have a ton of homework to complete. If I don't start applying myself, dad will never forgive me."

Brendon screwed the cap on the scotch and hid it behind a mountain of pillows. He shoved his hands in his pocket; the room fell quiet. He had never been a 'fall head over heels' type of guy. This mess of a girl had changed his mind. He had fallen into the 'can't breathe, can't concentrate, can't think about anything but her' trap. He had fallen for Uncle Walt's wife.

"I'll stop by again." Brendon tripped over his feet and his words. "Sometime, after practice or when Walt's home."

"Let me see your hands."

He held out his hands. Shivers skittered up his spine as she traced over the lines.

"Your lifeline is deep. You're in good health."

"You see that?"

"I see two loves."

"Only two?"

"Only two, mon ami."

The urge to squeeze all the sadness out of her filled him. Brendon spotted a cell phone entombed in a glass bowl filled with keys and trinkets. "Is that yours?"

"Walter said I needed one. I'm trying to figure it out."

"You've never owned a phone? How did people ring you?"

"They called Lisette. Yasmine used to love running to my flat to tell me I had a call."

"I'm going to put my number in it. If you need me, I'll come."

The voices in his head screeched at him. He shooed them away and swiped open her phone.

"Do you want a picture on your lock screen?"

"I don't understand."

Brendon dug out his cell and tapped it. The Dortmund logo lit the screen. "That didn't impress Maggie. Bloody Troy has a picture of Charlie, made me look like a dolt. What's a painting you love?"

"The Witches Sabbath by Goya."

Brendon typed; the painting appeared. "You sure do like some interesting paintings."

"I'll see you Saturday."

"You're coming to the match?"

"Walter says I must watch you play."

Angelene looped her arms around his waist and pressed herself against him. He held his arms at his side. A voice warned him, *'she'll steal your light, run home.'* Another cackled, *'hold her.'* She fit in his arms like she was meant to be there.

"I can stay, make you something to eat. I'm not the best cook."

"We have something in common."

"Text if you need anything."

He jingled his car keys and took one last look.

The doorbell rang. Brendon sprinted down the hall, slid across the marble and jerked open the door.

"What are you doing here?"

Maggie smoothed her pink hoodie and dug into her lip. "I dropped Jack off at karate. I thought I'd say hello. You didn't text after the match."

Angelene jumped into his head. He pulled at his collar.

"You don't care about my matches."

He led her into a room his mother called 'la mia magnifica stanza,' magnificent it was. The panelled walls were cream. Leather sofas gleamed in the fire's glow. Handmade rugs in navy, ivory, and brown pulled the richness of the furniture together. Sofia had filled the room with luxurious fabrics and antiques, transforming it from depressingly drab and haughty to vibrant and cozy.

Brendon snatched the remote from within a hulking Baroque armoire. The sportscasters' lively banter filled the cypress and cedar scented air. Brendon stared at the television and winced as the ball soared past the Dortmund defenders and blew into the net.

"Bloody hell, he should have tipped that one over the crossbar."

"Can't you skip the highlights? It's just football."

Brendon bit down on the curse words. Football was the greatest game on earth and Angelene was coming to his match. The hug resurfaced. She had squished herself so tightly against him, there had been no space between them. What was he doing thinking about Angelene? His Nonna had once said, 'In God's eyes, the slate is clean if you make amends.' It was time to make amends. He clicked off the television and plunked beside her.

"Mum will be home soon. We might as well make the most of it."

"Why didn't you tell me she was out? You know the rule."

Brendon slid across the sofa and parted his lips. A wave of heat washed over him. He eased her into the mound of throw pillows. Her body was stiff under his. Maggie's face swirled, coming apart like a jigsaw puzzle, reassembling into a green-eyed blonde. He slipped his fingers under her shirt. The warmth of her skin sent pleasant shivers over his body.

"I don't want to wait until July."

Maggie gripped the cushion and dragged herself from beneath him. "We've talked about this a million times."

"Eleven months is a long time to wait."

"I don't want to be up the duff like Camille Dunlop. Her parents made her go to school with that massive belly."

"I have condoms."

He slipped his hand in her sweater and cupped her tiny breast.

"Why do you have condoms? We aren't... Did you meet a girl in Dortmund?"

Brendon slapped his hands against the cushion and walked to the French doors, never ending black wrapped around the loggia and roses.

"Troy gave me some. It was supposed to be my birthday present."

Maggie shoved a mauled fingernail in her mouth. "I'm scared."

Sparks crackled. "Scared of bloody what? People have sex all the time."

"Sweetheart, I'm home."

Brendon switched on the television, imagining the sparks as snowflakes, melting away.

"Hello, my love," Sofia said, cupping his cheeks. "You're flushed."

Brendon pulled his face away and forced a smile. "How was lunch?"

Sofia unraveled a cashmere wrap and raised an eyebrow. "Exhausting. You know the rules."

"It's my fault, Ms. Cook. I took Jack to karate; I didn't hear from Brendon."

"I forgot to text; blame me, mammina."

"You're a saint, listening to those annoying commentators."

"I don't mind. Come July, the only way I'll see Brendon is on the telly."

"No talk of July. The thought of losing my baby again kills me."

"I'm not a bloody baby."

Sofia bent down and kissed his mussed locks. "You'll always be my baby. I'm going to call your father. I miss him."

Brendon inhaled, counted to four and exhaled in one long breath. Liam taught him the yoga breathing, pranayama, after a red card incident. It was to relieve the sparks before he reacted with bitter words or his fists. He counted his breaths, blew the ashy sparks away and took her hand.

"Mum's home now, you're safe."

"Every time we kiss, you turn into a wanker."

"Is it bloody wrong to want to hump my girlfriend?"

Maggie screwed up her face and tore at her fingernail. "You've never pushed."

Brendon stretched his arms overhead and clamped his hands together. "You keep promising. Bloody hell, we kiss, my knob gets excited?"

"It was never important before. It's all you think about lately."

"I'm a guy. We think about humping."

Maggie whipped her purse over her shoulder and nibbled her fingernail. "Be patient."

"Patient, got it."

He battled with the sparks and followed her to the foyer.

"Are you going to pick me up before the match?"

"Have Charlie drive you."

She hesitated at the door and gnawed her fingernail.

"Everything is fine." Brendon kissed her and patted her bottom. "I'll see you at the pitch." He watched her leave, confused. He hadn't summoned Angelene into his mind, she appeared. Brendon was torn between what was right and what was wrong. Maggie was right, springtime pretty and his. He had to get Angelene out of his head.

"Your father is leaving London early. He's excited about your match."

"He goes because it's what a dad is supposed to do."

"That's not true. He enjoys watching you play. It gives him something to brag about."

"The only thing he spews around the House of Commons is when I fuck up."

"You're in a fine mood."

The evening thrashed around his head, the hug, reading his palm, squirming, pleading.

"I'm bloody fine."

"Swearing and brooding in my foyer is fine?"

"You wouldn't understand."

"I know what was going on."

"You mean what wasn't."

Warmth rolled over his body. He tugged at his hoodie and whipped it at the stairs.

"Why do you want to be like Troy and William sticking their pisello into every gnocca that walks by?"

"Troy sticks his pisello in Charlie. I don't give a shit who Will, Jesus Christ mum."

He moved in long strides and flicked on the kitchen light. Brendon swung open the fridge and gazed around the immense box.

"Don't involve Jesus." Sofia said, flicking the charms dangling from her bracelet.

"Since when do you care about JC? You're angry with him and God. You have been for years."

He grabbed a container of roasted chicken and slid it across the counter. A tub of mixed greens ricocheted off the backsplash and into the sink.

"Can we talk about this tomorrow?"

"We'll talk about it now. I don't want you grumbling around the house."

Angelene floated into his mind. He could feel her arms around him. He cursed, shook her from his head, and forked mixed greens into the container. Brendon sliced through a tomato and placed the wedges on the salad.

"I think Kate still has a thing for Walter."

"She called him an arrogant donkey."

Brendon chopped a red pepper, dumped it on the chicken and sliced into a cucumber.

"I know she still loves him."

"Did she tell you that, or are you making an assumption?"

He swept the cucumber into the container, poured on the dressing, and leaned against the counter.

"She beams when she talks about him. Sit sweetheart, it's better for your digestion."

"Kate made it seem like she didn't care what Walt did."

He crammed a bite into his mouth and wiped a splotch of dressing from his chin.

"Use a kitchen towel," Sofia said, tearing a section from the roll. "Simone called you dishy."

"I can't get past her nose. I would have asked for my money back." He ran a forkful of greens through a puddle of dressing and munched. "What did Kate think about Angelene?"

He studied his mother's reaction; worry wrinkled her brow.

"She expected a glamazonian and got... Angelene."

"She's not that bad."

"You didn't see her at lunch. She picked at her meal, kneaded her knuckles, barely said two words."

"I'd be nervous around Ms. McGregor."

"Kate doesn't know what to make of her, and neither do I?"

Brendon smeared lettuce around the container and stuck it in his mouth. He was having his own trouble trying to figure her out.

"I'm afraid if Walter pushes her too hard, she'll push back. There's a feisty side to her. I saw a hint of it today."

"You worry too much," Brendon said, rinsing the container. "Uncle Walt wouldn't have married her if he didn't see something."

"What about this feeling I keep getting?"

"It's the same feeling you get when I fly to Dortmund, when Walter first brought Anastasia around, when Kate dated that guy from Wales."

"I spent most of lunch trying to calm Angelene."

"I'm proud of you for trying to make her feel comfortable."

"What will I do when you're gone?"

"Fly to Dortmund every weekend."

He watched Sofia walk away, a little quiver rolled in his belly. Angelene was harmless, consumed by her own fears and insecurities. She was just a girl trying to play a role she knew nothing about. The only thing Brendon questioned was how she got stuck in his head.

***

Angelene loved nighttime. The rest of the world slept. Everything was peaceful and dreamy. Her love for all things washed in black escaped her. The forest was dark and distorted. The quiet was violent and terrifying.

'It was an exhausting day, God. I rehearsed what to say and forgot. I pleaded with myself to remember the rules, sit up straight, sip my wine. I was my bumbling self.'

Angelene lit a cigarette and gulped back streams of smoke. Lunch had been a crazy pattern of colours. Victoria had been pickle green and just as sour. Simone had been turquoise and not the turquoise she dreamed of dipping her toes in but, boastful turquoise. Sofia had been her usual elegant black and Kate, in her navy sheath and sensible pumps, was encouraging, and confident, teal. It surprised Angelene Walter had never dived into Kate's teal. She had found it quite attractive. The phenomena, seeing words in colour, started when Angelene was a child. Her teacher had asked her to spell the word apple. Every letter had been a different colour: red, green, green, yellow, blue. She remembered the children laughing and her teacher yelling spiky red words. Veronique Hummel declared her daughter a witch. Her teacher had called it synesthesia. It was another thing that made her odd.

'God, forgive me for hugging Brendon. I cannot believe how brilliant his light is. It's not mine to have.'

She dropped the cigarette into the glass and drew the blankets to her chin.
"Sleep. I beg you to come."

Her mind filled with the boy who looked like a man, the football hero, her boy in brown. A strange feeling fluttered in her belly; she dug at her wrist.

'I'm supposed to be playing normal, being a wife, learning to love Walter. God, take Brendon from my mind. Forgive me for wanting his light. Forgive me for asking for forgiveness.'

7 Haphephobia

It had been an intense first half. The play bounced between both ends, with a heavy attack coming from Taunton and Dorchester. There had been chances to score. Nothing had gotten past Brendon or Dorchester's keeper. It was the type of match Brendon lived for.

After years of being stuck in the middle of the standings, Taunton First began the hunt for a new coach. Word around Taunton, an ex-striker from the Shamrock Rovers, was teaching physical education at a community school. Liam McMahon had a reputation of driving the school team to success, making him a solid choice for the fledging football club. Liam worked the team hard. He treated them like pro footballers and had a list of infractions in place to keep them focused. The team admired his winning spirit and for the hero he once was.

The fans burst into rowdy cheers. Handmade posters and flags waved as they made their way onto the pitch. Brendon tightened his gloves. The dragons soared. He was ready for battle.

"I didn't think I'd see you back here," Liam said.

Brendon stared down a Dorchester attacker. "Things didn't go as planned."

"Bets at the bookies have us taking the win."

Brendon took a sip of water and dropped the bottle at the side of the net. "There are holes in their defence. We just need the opportunity to get the ball through."

"The keeper's good. Word is Tottenham is interested."

"He's quick but gets out of position."

"They're putting up a good fight."

"Their plays are weak. They're too focused on winning."

"I'm glad you're back."

"I'm not."

Liam chuckled and patted Brendon's shoulder.

Brendon scanned the crowded stands. He spied Angelene squeezed between Walter and his father. There was no smile on her face. A rosy glow brightened her cheeks. A burning sensation stabbed Brendon in the chest. Walter laid his arm around Angelene and brushed his lips over her hair. Every visit to the farmhouse, Angelene had been his. She was Walter's wife again.

"Nice to see Ms. Pratt out," Troy said.
"She's a minger," William said.
"She's no arseface, pretty, in a plain way," Troy said.
Brendon breathed through the flickering sparks. There were forty-five minutes left to play. He had to forget about the jealousy brewing inside him and concentrate on the match.
"Mum said she hid in the restaurant loo." William's tone was easy and arrogant. "She also said Ms. Pratt was involved with a married man."
Sparks glowed, Brendon flexed his fingers and glared. "How does your mum know that?"
"She just does."
"Your mum's a bloody gossip."
The whistle blew, stirring the fans into a frenzy.
"Walt's got himself a slapper." William's laugh was so controlled it sounded artificial.
"Your mum should be concerned about your dad. I've heard stories."
William twisted Brendon's jersey and scowled. "What are you going on about?"
"Ask your bloody mother. She knows everything." Brendon jerked his jersey free. "Get your fucking hands off me and take your seat on the bench."
Brendon took his position in net. He caught sight of Maggie nibbling on her thumbnail. Resentment fuelled the dragons. A hand job would be nice, a quickie. He tore his eyes from Maggie, snagged the ball, and slammed it to midfield. Rachel was two rows up, waving a Cook #1 poster. An attacker approached. Brendon kept his eye on the ball and snatched it. The crowd cheered and stamped their feet. Brendon kicked it to midfield and glanced into the crowd. Angelene smiled behind her fingers. Joy brightened her face. Brendon followed the ball, it bounced off Troy's head. Dorchester picked up the rebound, Brendon sank to his knees, skidded across the pitch, and cradled the ball. He rolled it back onto the pitch. Troy barreled in, kicked, and cleared it. Brendon wiped blood from his grass-stained knees, held his breath. First put the ball in the net.
"Keep it in their end. Push up," Brendon yelled.
The team listened; it was a victory for Taunton First.

The mood in the dressing room was euphoric. The season had started with a draw and a loss. Taunton First was back to their winning ways. Brendon ran a towel over the water gliding down his back. He had been sharp and Angelene had been there to see it. He never believed in love at first sight. The only thing he had fallen head over heels for was Signal Iduna Park. He believed in moments. There had been moments with Angelene, her finger on his palm, the kiss, the hug. Beautiful, wrong moments.
"You know that saying, undressing you with your eyes, Rachel had you starkers all match," Troy said.
Brendon rubbed his hair with a towel. "I didn't notice. My eyes were on the pitch."
"I saw you looking." Troy dug in his shaving kit for pomade. "I'll meet you at the manor. Charlie and I have to celebrate."
"How do you know she'll be up for it?"
"We always hump after a win." Troy laughed. "Or a loss."
"You wouldn't know about that; would you Cook?" William said.

A ripple of 'oohs,' 'No Brendon, stop,' 'I'm a good girl,' floated on the menthol scented steam. Brendon flung his jersey in the laundry bin and shrugged the tension away.

"She's built like a girl too," William said.

"I'd shut my mouth if I was you."

Brendon jabbed a finger into William's chest, knocking him onto the bench. His temper had always been unpredictable. It had put him in the headmaster's office, parked him on the bench, and took his father back to a place he wanted to forget.

Do you know why you are here?

I pushed Freddy. He said I was a daft keeper. He said my house has ghosts and people died there.

Do you believe you're a bad keeper?

My Uncle Walt's friend, Lukas, watched me play. He called me a word that started with a p.

A prodigy.

Yes, sir.

A plaster will not cover that gash over Freddy's eye.

Mr. Oakes, I'm sorry. I get these sparks in my belly. I can't help it.

Walk away next time. One day, you're going to do more than cut someone's face.

"Knock, knock," Troy said, tapping his knuckles on Brendon's head, "you in there?"

Brendon breathed through the ashy aftermath.

"Analyzing the match."

He grabbed his keys and left the dressing room. His father's Jaguar was gone. Maggie waited by his car; an umbrella embossed with mermaids over her head.

"My parents didn't stick around?"

"They had to go to Tesco for groceries. Walter is making a French dish called hachis parmentier."

"Dad needs to take notes. His bolognese was dodgy."

"It was burnt," Maggie said, closing her umbrella. "We ate it anyway."

Brendon pulled out of the car park; his mind tangled with memories, the scent of lavender in Angelene's hair, the little tears in her chapped lips. Brendon glanced at Maggie and took her hand. He turned onto the laneway and threw out an intention to anyone listening, shoo Angelene from his head.

"You didn't get your hump in."

"My brothers put me in a headlock."

"There's plenty of time for snogging, babes. Daddy said I could stay over."

"Your parents are letting you sleep at Troy's?" Maggie said.

Brendon led the pack to the door. It would be a chilly day in hell before his parents allowed a girl to sleep over, even the virtuous Maggie.

"I promised daddy I would help Ms. Spence with chores. He never says no."

"Not even your mum?" Maggie said.

"Mum likes to have romantic evenings with daddy. I can just imagine what they get up to when I'm not around."

"Charlie is the best egg collector in Taunton. The chickens love her, except for Lucy."

"Any time babes is near me, that mangey bird pecks at my ankles."

Brendon chuckled. "Pick a room. You can use the loo in the hallway."

"Can't I change with Charlie?"

"If dad comes home and catches the two of you snogging, you'll be out on your arse."

"I won't hump her with your parents around."

The girls giggled up the stairs. The Mediterranean inspired room would be perfect for a pool side afternoon.

"You have no control when you see Charlie naked."

"She has a lovely body. There's a little freckle on her hip. It's the most brilliant thing I've ever seen."

"Better than her arse and jubblies?"

"I kiss it every time we get naked."

Brendon shook envy away and climbed the stairs. He flicked on his bedroom light, stripped out of his clothes, and dropped them in the laundry basket. Patchouli clung to the puff of air. An ache ballooned and pressed into his ribs. He couldn't have Angelene. He shouldn't want her either. She was Walter's girl. Springtime Maggie, with her blue blossom eyes and head full of knowledge, was his.

Brendon wrenched towels from the vanity. With every step down the hall, he repeated, *'Maggie is my girl.'* The front door burst open; Brendon smiled at Sofia's exasperated look.

"That store is just dreadful."

"It's not that bad, mum."

"Potatoes are potatoes no matter where you buy them," David said.

"I got you some fig bars. I know you like them at halftime. It used to be Smarties when you were little."

"I still like Smarties, just the blue ones."

"I hope you don't make Maggie pick out the blue Smarties," David said.

"Why would I do that? She saves them for me." Brendon reached for the bags. "I'll help."

"Go see your friends."

"You sure?"

Brendon studied David's face. It could be a test, see if he ran from the code. David's grin was genuine.

"Your mother can help, if it's not beneath her."

Sofia took a bag of vegetables. "Stai attento a come parli."

"You played brilliantly, son."

David had never been an athlete. Academics was how he exercised. David tolerated football and would tune in to random Bundesliga matches to appease Sofia. It was not who David Cook was, but it was a compliment, Brendon would take it.

"Think we can get a snog in before the Pratt's arrive?" David said.

"That's bloody gross," Brendon called.

He made his way down the hall, past portraits of his ancestors, their eyes following him, and into a room with walls of glass, soaring to a vaulted ceiling of exposed beams. Modelled after a Tuscan farmhouse, the pavilion stretched into the forest. A fireplace encased in mosaic tiles was built into a stone wall. Copper urns of ferns, teak lounges, and chairs cushioned in yellow and royal blue decorated the pool deck.

"Come in, mate."

Charlotte climbed out of the pool, adjusting the triangles barely covering her breasts. "Stop pouting, Magpie. The water is brilliant."

Brendon turned away. Maggie laid on the lounge in a magenta one-piece, no cut-outs, no plunging neckline, no strings holding anything in place.

"Let's go in."

"Soon."

Brendon tossed the towels onto the floor. "Why won't you come in?"

"I don't feel like it right now."

Brendon flashed her a knowing pearly white smile and perched on the lounge. "Is it Charlie?"

"There isn't anything to that bathing suit."

"You could wear a bikini. A little pink number with ruffles on your bum."

"Where did you see a bathing suit like that, in the children's section at Debenhams?"

"Last years Sports Illustrated."

"I wouldn't look like those models."

Brendon leaned across the lounge and caged her in his toned arms. "You'd look like you."

Brendon brushed his lips over Maggie's. The curtains covering the French doors fluttered.

"I could live in here," Angelene said.

"By the pool?" Walter said.

"I could paint, sit by the fire, float all day. How do you not spend every day in here?"

Brendon muttered. "I'm a busy guy."

"You should come in Ms. Pratt," Troy said, shielding his nipples, "Meet my girlfriend, Charlotte."

"Bonjour. Another time."

Guilt ate away at Brendon. Two voices duelled inside his subconscious, *'do the right thing, stare at the pretty Ms. Pratt.'*

"You both played brilliantly today," Walter said.

Brendon's cheeks warmed; he lowered his gaze to the bruise forming around the abrasions on his knees.

"How do those scouts not see your talent?"

Troy swam to the edge of the pool. "I keep attending the football trials. No luck yet."

Brendon kept his gaze on his knees. The voices raged, *'You want her; she belongs to someone else.'*

"I'll talk to Lukas. He knows a few scouts in London. I'll put in a good word."

Walter placed his hand on Angelene's hip. Reality stabbed Brendon as they walked away. She was Walter's wife.

"Come in the pool with me."

"Not yet."

Brendon swept Maggie into his arms. She kicked wildly, her arms flailing as he tossed her into the pool. Brendon dove in, swam to her, and wiped her hair from her eyes. "I'm sorry."

"For staring at Ms. Pratt again."

"I've never seen anyone react like that. It's a bloody pool."

He drew her into his arms. She felt good and right. The tangled ball of 'what if's' and 'follow the code' tightened. Guilt was heavy.

A gasp tickled Brendon's ear. Maggie's arms squeezed his neck.

"What's the matter?"

"She's watching you."

There was nothing in the hall but a fading shadow.

"It was Richard the prick. He floats around the pool, pissed off mum had the extension built."

"Your grandfather doesn't have blonde hair?"

"Then it was one of the other ghosts that lurks around here."

The shadow was gone.

Brendon waved goodbye to Troy and Charlotte and shut the door. He wanted to believe Angelene had been staring at him. Maybe he crept inside her brain and hung out like she did his. Maggie's insecurity over Charlotte's itty-bitty bikini had to be the culprit of the mysterious shadow.

"Take this bottle to your mum. I'm going to start the washing up. Walter's an excellent cook. He sure makes a mess."

"Have they gone through a bottle of wine already?"

"Angelene can drink. Nervous habit, I think."

Brendon took the bottle and walked to the great room. He promised himself not to stare, not even a peek. The sound of sparks popping, and the fire crackling, filled the silence. Brendon clutched the wine bottle and cursed softly. Angelene gripped the wineglass, her knuckles white. It had taken exactly five seconds to break his promise.

"Put that here, sweetheart," Sofia said, pushing aside an empty bottle. "Would you like a glass?"

Brendon shook his head and sunk onto the couch beside Maggie. "Can I put the telly on?"

"That would be rude, sweetheart. We have guests."

"No one is talking."

"We'll talk. Let's talk," Sofia said. "I was thinking about your drawings. They look like the illustrations from that old Grimm's fairy tale book Richard owned."

Angelene stared at the bottle like it was a decadent dessert. A line of desperation materialized between her eyebrows.

"I hated that book." It was time to swoop in for the rescue before she downed another bottle.

"He used to shove that picture of the witch stuffing children into the oven in Brendon's face. You remember, sweetheart?"

"How could I forget? I still have nightmares."

"My pops read me Beatrix Potter. I loved Peter Rabbit," Maggie said.

"Do you get your inspiration from books?" Sofia said.

Angelene blew out a hefty sigh, poured wine into her glass, and gulped. "They come from my dreams."

Brendon raised his eyebrows. "Those are some dreams."

"I rarely bid on art at the auctions. Most of the paintings in the house belonged to David's father."

"Don't get too excited. They're bloody boring. Landscapes, and creepy looking people."

Angelene hid her smile behind her wineglass. He stared into his lap.

"I didn't know you were such a connoisseur, sweetheart. Would you prefer paintings of football pitches and Bundesliga logos?"

"I took art history."

Sofia sipped her wine and grinned. "You attempted art history."

"I wrote your final essay," Maggie said.

"I did the research." His fingers tingled to steal the glass from Angelene. She could grip his hand instead. "It was on the artist I liked; the poster was in the classroom. It was colourful, had all sorts of squares and circles. The couple was kissing."

Angelene sat up. "Klimt?"

"That's it. I thought his name was funny. It reminded me of a girl's fanny."

"Oh, mio dio, you say the most inappropriate things," Sofia said.

Brendon grinned at his mother's displeasure and pointed to the darkened corner. "We have one here."

"You have a Klimt?"

"It's hanging over my Nonna's credenza. Water Serpents."

Angelene set her glass down and scrambled from the sofa. Brendon turned, dragging Maggie with him. Angelene touched her full lips, studying the painting.

"She looks like she's going to cry," Maggie said.

"Ms. Dolman said art should move you. She's been bloody moved."

The look on Angelene's face was dreamy, like she was floating with the women in the painting. Was it love, infatuation, limerence? Brendon didn't know. The feeling marched through his insides, up his spine, making a home in his heart. Maggie leaned her cheek on his shoulder. Brendon blinked, refocused, told himself to pay attention to Maggie.

"What's everyone looking at?" David said.

"Mum told Ms. Pratt about the Klimt painting."

"We should have sold it."

"And not see Angelene's reaction?" Sofia kissed David's cheek and leaned into his ear. "Two and a half bottles."

"I hate that painting."

"It's better than those creepy portraits."

"Some of those creepy people are your ancestors."

Angelene grabbed her glass from the coffee table. "Why don't you like it?"

"It reminds me of my father. He paid more attention to that painting than he did mum and I."

"Do you like it?"

Brendon fiddled with the clasp on his watch. Maggie's ragged fingernails dug into his arm. His mother raised an eyebrow. David looked impressed he had paid attention in class.

"The women are beautiful. They look like they're floating in the water."

"Klimt loved women. Many of his paintings are erotic. Klimt was a rebel," Angelene said.

"That's why Richard loved it. He re-titled it those glorious lesbians," David said.

Brendon rubbed at the red indents puckering his forearm.

"Bloody hell, you nearly tore into my skin."

"Do you believe me now? She couldn't take her eyes off you."

"She asked me a question. Was I supposed to ignore her?"

The glow of the fire brightened the midnight blue walls. Brendon pulled out Maggie's chair. The scent of warmed brioche, onions, and garlic filled the air. Brendon did his best to keep his attention on Maggie, passed her a plate of Walter's French creation, filled her water glass. He was finding it difficult.

"It tastes like shepherd's pie, Uncle Walt."

Brendon scooped up a forkful of potatoes, waiting for someone to reply. His mother and father nodded in agreement; Walter grimaced and covered Angelene's wine glass with his hand.

"It's brilliant Mr. Pratt. Just moreish."

"What is shepherd's pie?" Angelene said.

Brendon flipped his fork around his fingers with the dexterity of a drummer. The question floated around the dining room for anyone to answer. Her eyes were on him.

"It's, uh, like this."

The fork flung from Brendon's hand and clattered across the table. Sofia arched her eyebrow at the potato and gravy Jackson Pollock created on the damask tablecloth.

"I'll make it for you sometime. It's similar." The veins in Walter's neck pulsed. "Put some food in your belly, peck, peck, peck."

Angelene's hand shot out. She hooked her finger in her wineglass and finished it. Brendon grinned. Klimt's rebel spirit had rubbed off on her.

Walter grabbed her glass, shoved his napkin in it, and tapped his knife against Angelene's plate. "Are you still going to university for teaching?"

"I'm hoping to be accepted at the University of Cambridge," Maggie said.

Brendon kept his glances subtle, hidden behind bites of food and sips of milk. The wine bottle had disappeared.

"Your parents will celebrate when I'm gone."

"My parents like you."

"Since when?"

"How could they not like my baby? Look at that face," Sofia said.

His mother's cooing didn't erase the line creased across Walter's forehead.

"Cambridge's education department is one of England's best," David said.

"Can you manage a long-distance relationship?" Walter said.

The ring Brendon had placed on Maggie's finger gave the impression he could. It had been impulsive and came with a lecture from his father about his habit of breaking promises. It had seemed the right thing to do before heading to Dortmund. There was a part of him that wanted Maggie to join him in Dortmund. Another was unsure. As he stared at Angelene's wistful eyes, doubt resurfaced.

"We did." Sofia touched David's hand and looked at him with eyes of a love-struck teenager.

"Richard was happy to get rid of mother and I."

"Relationships are hard no matter where you live," Brendon said.

"If you play like you did today, they'll be no time for a relationship."

"Walter." Sofia shifted her eyes towards Maggie.

"We'll figure something out. That's what you do, right? Adapt, learn, and accept."

Brendon aimed the words at Walter. As far as Brendon was concerned, Walter needed to do all three.

"Vous serez une grande star du football."

Held in her fervent, grey-green gaze, red heat stormed Brendon's cheeks. The flush rolled down his neck in slow waves.

"Finish your meal, sweetheart," Sofia said, her eyes and words were steely.

"What did you say, Ms. Pratt?"

Maggie dug her tooth into her lip and chewed. "She said you'll be a big football star."

7 HAPHEPHOBIA

"Don't tell me you're failing French," David said.

"He needs to learn German." Walter jammed his fork into a pile of potatoes and presented it to Angelene.

"He already tried German. The teacher won't have him back," David said.

Walter snort. "Got a temper like Richard. A little fire in the belly doesn't hurt."

"Someone from school is helping me learn German."

Brendon inventoried Walter. He smiled his crinkly smile, his cheeks blazed crimson, knuckles white. If anyone knew about fire in the belly, it was Walter.

"Who? None of the teachers will have you. Your mother had to beg Madame Lafavre."

"I didn't beg dear."

"Rachel Jones," Maggie said.

"Miranda Jones's daughter? If she's anything like her mother, I'd watch out," Walter said.

"She's the tart..."

"You're making the distance between Cambridge and Dortmund very inviting, Mags."

Sparks lit in fierce pops. Walter's knife tapped against Angelene's plate. Chewy mouth sounds came from Maggie. Sofia clicked through her silver bangles.

"Brendon David, what a thing to say. What type of girl is Rachel Jones?"

Brendon scrubbed at his ears. Tap, smack, click. He closed his eyes, counted his breaths, and imagined the sparks as powdery soot.

"Dad thinks knowing a second language is important. I'm only doing what I'm told."

"If you were doing as I asked, you would have kept your mouth shut last term and not ended up in the headmaster's office. Every teacher in the modern languages department is afraid of you."

"I warned Mr. Lochmann the sparks were flying."

Brendon locked eyes with David. Silence swept through the dining room. He rocked the chair on its back legs, counting his breaths with each tilt.

"We're working on his temper. Brendon knows the consequences if his grades slip," Sofia said.

David stacked his plate on Sofia's and kissed her cheek. "My apologies. We don't need to broadcast our problems. We have Victoria McGregor for that."

Walter dropped a forkful of mince on Angelene's plate and stood. "I'll help finish the washing up."

"Maggie, come tell Angelene and I about your trip to Paris."

"No more wine, little bird. I'll bring you in a cuppa and a slice of roly-poly. You might eat that."

Brendon yanked the napkin from his lap and tossed it on the table. The sound of Angelene scratching her jeans filled the silence.

"You going to join mum?"

"I want to go home."

"Do you have a headache? I do. The bloody conversation was daft. The constant tapping on your plate."

Angelene staggered to her feet, held a hand to her forehead, and wobbled.

"You're bladdered."

"If that means drunk, then I'm afraid I am."

She let go of the chair and swayed. Brendon hesitated and unglued his feet. It was the gentlemanly thing to do, help a damsel in distress.

"Take my arm."

"Get me another glass. Mother always said one more to straighten you out."

"Your mother was wrong." He flexed his arm as she took hold and leaned into him. "Walt's angry."

"He's smiling and laughing."

"Last season, this punter waited for me in the car park. I let in two goals. He blamed me for the loss. Walter stepped in, lifted him off the ground. He was smiling the whole time."

"Did he hurt the man?"

"Dad stepped in and stopped him. You never see Walt coming."

"Like you?"

"Everyone knows when I'm mad, I snap. I'll slam my fist into anything or say bloody, awful things. Read Walt's face."

They stood in the foyer. Brendon surveyed the distance to the great room. There were ten steps to get her to the sofa. Then she was Walter's problem.

"What do I look for?"

"His eyes turn icy blue. He's smiling, his eyes are crinkly but there's no laughter in them."

"I mustn't make him mad."

"No more wine tonight."

She laid her cheek against his arm. "I'll have a cigarette."

"Some tea and roly-poly. That will make you feel better."

"What is rollee-pollee?"

"It's jam and sponge. We aren't fancy like the French, with your eclairs and those biscuits Maggie likes, macaroons."

"It's macaron. They're my favourite," Angelene said, swaying. "Vous êtes merveilleux."

Her breath, scented with wine, was warm against his skin. The expression in her eyes sent his heart racing.

"Merveilleux means wonderful. I only know that because Madame Lafavre said it when she learned I was in her class. I'm far from wonderful."

"You're my only friend."

He had been, when he wasn't supposed to be, when he went against his promise.

"Brendon"

He jerked his head up and stared into Sofia's blazing eyes.

"Maggie and I have been waiting."

Brendon untangled her arm and placed a hand on her shoulder.

"It's my fault. I've had too much to drink. I'll go for a cigarette; the fresh air will help."

He took a step as she staggered. Sofia stood in front of him. "She's not your concern."

"Was I supposed to leave her at the table? Walter knows she's soused. He left her sitting there."

"I told you to stay away from her. The feeling is back."

"Dad and I got into it. Your perfect family didn't look so perfect."

Sparks zipped as he brushed past Sofia. She snagged him by the wrist.

"This feeling has nothing to do with you and your father bickering. She couldn't take her eyes off you. Stay away from her."

Brendon wrenched his wrist free. "For fuck's sake."

"Stop swearing," Sofia said, her face softened. "I'm sorry, sweetheart. My stomach is in knots, and I don't know why."

"She's drunk. That makes you nervous."

"Be a good boy, go to Maggie. I'm going to see if your father needs any help and tell Walter he needs to take Angelene home."

Brendon rambled into the great room. Maggie stared at him with wide blue eyes and her best 'I'm not jealous' smile.

"Sorry I took so long."

"I understand."

"I didn't even tell you where I was."

He collapsed beside her and drew her into the crook of his arm.

"You were with Ms. Pratt."

"She's bloody pissed."

"You did what you're supposed to do, be a gentleman. You held back Gemma's hair at William's birthday bash when she barfed."

Brendon's heart was warm and tingly. He wanted to be with Maggie and Angelene. He liked the smell of Maggie's perfume, but not the scent of wine permeating from Angelene. Maggie was his, smiling in that way that said, 'I adore you.' Angelene was drunk and married.

"You want to go to my room and snog?"

"No, I don't."

"I'm sorry about the dinner conversation. You knew about Dortmund before we started dating."

"It's been in the Taunton Times since you were eight, Taunton's hero."

"Just because I'm in Germany, doesn't mean we have to break-up."

"My cousin went to school in Canada and her relationship ended. The distance was too hard."

Brendon hadn't thought about the relationship's survival. All he wanted was to get to Dortmund.

"We'll try. Let's go to my room and snog."

He kissed her softly. His gaze shifted to the arched doorway. Angelene walked in precise steps to the painting, fell to her bottom and hugged her knees. He was falling for her again. The voices in his head argued, *do the right thing. Sit, and stare.*

"You want to go play FIFA 18? I promise no snogging."

"Can we play something else? I never win that football game."

"Sure, you can pick."

"Should we tell Ms. Pratt we're leaving?"

"I'm not sure she knows we're here."

***

Angelene dragged on a cigarette, blowing smoke towards the ceiling. She pictured herself, chin deep in Brendon's glow. A brief pang struck her belly. God spoke; she was doing a lousy job being a wife.

"I made you some tea."

Angelene dropped the cigarette, cranking the window closed.

"I told you I get anxious around people."

Walter grabbed a can of air freshener, aiming it in Angelene's direction.

"A group of strangers I can understand. Those are my friends, your friends."

Angelene wiped the spray from her cheeks, bowing her head. Explanations, expectations. The shot to the belly was stronger, fierce. God was angry.

"Why aren't you wearing one of those nightgowns I bought you?" Walter waved his arm and drenched the air with spray. "Do you suffer from haphephobia?"

"Why must you use big words? I don't understand."

Walter set the can down and passed her a cup of tea. "Do you fear me touching you? You squirm, roll away. An old pair of boxers will surely keep me away."

"They belonged to a friend. I have little to remember him by. I won't get rid of them."

She studied Walter's face, looking for icy eyes, a façade of a smile. The after effects of overindulging fogged her brain.

"Another lover?"

Angelene groaned and slid off the nightstand. She thumped to the bathroom and flung open the medicine cabinet. Walter's razor hummed at her. Act this way, wear this, sit up straight, eat, no more wine. A distinct emotion clung to every word; the beehive of electricity was dizzying. Angelene bit into her tongue, grinding until she tasted blood. She brushed her teeth and spit a crimson blob into the sink. The buzzing softened to a whisper.

"Next time we go to dinner, you'll watch the drink. You didn't even join us for tea and pudding, just stared at the painting."

"Have you looked at it? It's exquisite."

She tossed the toothbrush on the vanity, scrambled across the floor, and tucked herself under the blankets.

"Give me a kiss."

Angelene flicked his lips and curled into a ball. "Go away."

Walter finished her tea, walked to the bathroom, and grabbed his toothbrush. "Haphephobia, little bird."

"I don't kiss. You taste a person's breath, their teeth."

"Kissing is lovely; makes you feel like a teenager again."

She tugged the blankets around her neck, memories collided around her head. "Kissing is disgusting, spit dripping in your mouth."

Walter set his toothbrush in a cup; the mattress creaked as he laid on the bed. "Plenty of women would be thrilled to have sex with me."

"You've told me before."

"I suppose you have a headache."

"We have a party to prepare for. You'll want me on my best behaviour. Let me sleep."

Walter grumbled and thumped to his side.

Tomorrow was another day; she would try normal again. Be the perfect host, present a beautiful home, mingle, and shine.

'With what light?' Angelene tugged the blankets over her head. *'Mine has been lost for years.'*

8 Plucking Feathers

Beams of sunlight stabbed through the clouds, illuminating a black silk dress.

"Isn't it lovely?" Walter said. He took a cigarette from Angelene's fingers and slipped it into his pocket.

"I'll look like the nuns outside Sacre Coeur."

Angelene slumped on the edge of the nightstand, shook a cigarette from the pack, and lit it.

Walter rubbed his tense jaw. "Must you be so incorrigible?"

"I don't know what that means."

"You don't want to reform, improve."

"There's nothing wrong with me."

She inhaled deeply and blew out a mouthful of smoke. Walter grabbed the air freshener and squirt it at her.

"That dress isn't me. I should be able to pick out my own clothes."

"It's a Stella McCartney."

Angelene ran her arm over her face and raised her chin defiantly. "Who's that?"

"A popular fashion designer, Paul and Linda's daughter." Walter pulled the cigarette from her fingers, smashed it in the ashtray, and wiped his hands. He slid a tiffany blue box out of his pocket, snapping it open. "Would these make you feel better?"

Angelene stared at the Tahitian pearls. "Always wanting to hide my wrists."

"My friends aren't daft. I won't give them anymore to talk about."

"Why are you trying to change me?" Angelene said, sliding her foot into a black pump. "These shoes impressed Victoria. What is it about red soles?"

"I'm not trying to change you, just the way you dress."

Angelene kicked off the shoe. It shot like an expensive bullet, tumbling at Walter's feet.

"I'm going to read."

Walter marched behind her. He had convinced himself over a round of scotch with colleagues, he would make a good husband. He had sowed his wild oats, been the envy of the House of Commons. The defiant mood was making it difficult to enjoy matrimonial bliss.

"Two glasses of wine tonight."

"I'll be a good girl."

"I almost forgot. For you."

He handed her a black silk bag. The contents rattled and clicked.

"What's this?"

"Makeup. My secretary Juliette said it was all the essentials."

Angelene tossed the bag on the island and scrunched her eyebrows. "I don't like makeup. I don't know how to wear it."

"You're an artist. Paint your face like you would a canvas."

"It's not the same."

"You'll find some magazines in my briefcase. Study the models."

Angelene filled the kettle, set it on the stove and clicked on the burner. "I don't want to look like a clown."

Walter rubbed her back and brushed his lips over her hair.

"Poor little January girl, always so wintry."

Angelene touched her lips and smiled. "Hello friend."

Walter grabbed olives and cheese from the fridge, setting them on the counter. "Who are you speaking to?"

"A rabbit."

He grinned and grabbed two knives. "Will you help?"

"You're smiling. You're not angry anymore. I asked God to make you happy."

"I wasn't angry, more annoyed," Walter said, unscrewing the lid. "I'm trying to help you feel comfortable. Has someone said you don't deserve nice things?"

Angelene dumped the olives into a crystal bowl. "My mother."

"You look the part. People will stop talking," Walter said, slicing through a brick of cheddar. "Taunton will see an improved Angelene."

"Why are you going to so much trouble? Planning a party, buying me a fancy dress?"

"I want my friends to know I'm happy."

Angelene swiped a piece of cheddar, pecking at it.

"You want a perfect wife. I doubt it's in me. However, I'll try normal again. It's a little ill-fitting."

Walter chuckled and tossed a tea bag in the pot. "We'll be the power couple of Taunton."

"Not the Cooks'?"

"You'll have more influence than Sofia." Walter poured water into the pot and scrutinized his little bird. Tangled waves of blonde, delicate fingers, pale skin. Pluck a few more straggly feathers and she'd be perfect.

"I've never fit in at school, work, or as a daughter."

"Everything I touch turns to gold."

"Shall I call you King Midas?" A shadow of a smile haunted her mouth. "Golden fingertips."

Walter stretched a sheet of plastic wrap over the bowl. It was a fitting nickname. He poured tea into a cup and handed it to her.

"Just how you like it, black."

"No milk or sugar? You aren't trying to change that?"

Walter grabbed his mug and followed her to the garden. They sat on the stoop, warmed by the sun, 'anxious' Angelene prevented.

"What have we learned about one another?"

"You like the Rolling Stones, cheddar cheese, and you want an elegant wife. Now you."

"You love Dickens, Psalm 51. You made friends with a rabbit." Walter nodded towards the remains of beams and stone. "He's over there by the barn. Should I take it down?"

"It looks like it has grown from the soil. Leave it."

"I have some splendid memories in there."

Angelene propped her elbows on her knees and cradled the mug in her hands. "Share them with me."

Walter rested against the door frame and grinned nostalgically. "David and I smoked and drank in there, talked about girls."

"You smoked? And David?"

"We thought ciggies made us look cool. It lasted a week."

Angelene took a small sip, her eyes moved along the golden horizon and up the hill. "Why wouldn't you sit at the manor? All those rooms and gardens?"

"Richard. The expectations he put on David were ridiculous and the temper. The man was a brute."

"Where's David's mother?"

"Elizabeth passed after David got married. She hung on long enough to know he would be safe. That used to be her room," Walter said, pointing to Brendon's window. "She would sit and knit, waiting for David to come home. Elizabeth was a kind woman."

"Your light has dimmed. King Midas has a heart," Angelene said. "How did she pass?"

"Years of abuse and neglect took her before cancer did. That house, as beautiful as it is, has seen more sadness than happy times."

"What happened to Richard?"

"He got what was coming to him," Walter said, swallowing back the tea. "I lost my virginity in the barn."

Angelene hid her smile and snuggled into Walter's arm. "With the animals watching?"

"Her name was Prudence. Everyone called her Pru."

"What happened to Prudence?"

"She's about three times the size and has six nippers."

Angelene hooked her thumb through the mug handles. "That's not kind."

They walked into the house; Walter laughed. "It's the truth. I saw her at Tesco pushing two trolleys. One with groceries, the other full of kids."

"What are we doing now?"

"This," Walter said, pointing to a recipe in a worn cookbook, "a favourite of mine."

"Potted cheese? Do you serve it on the stove like fondue?"

Walter stared at the girl, who was nothing like the others.

You think there's heaven in her, she's all devil. Douchette's warning hijacked him, raising the hairs on the back of his neck.

Loving her would be like a slice to the throat. Quick and fast.

Angelene ran her hand over his. "I thought the ghosts lived at Rosewood manor. You're spooked."

"Haunted by memories, little bird, back to the potted cheese."

"Do you plant it like a seed and wait for something delicious to grow?"

"You blend the ingredients and spread it on baguette."

"Your words are green."
Walter would have coloured himself cowardly yellow.

***

Four on four, not a goal scored, not from a corner kick or a rebound. He had been on fire. Brendon was happy.
"Do you have your suit?" Sofia said.
David turned down the newspaper and grinned at the disdain on Brendon's face.
He slid onto a stool, poured a cup of coffee, and scratched at the stubble on his chin. "You've asked a hundred bloody times."
"Are you going to shave that stuff off your face?"
"I don't have time. Maggie's waiting."
Sofia dunked the toast into a poached egg. "You look scruffy like that riffraff we saw hanging around the docks in Clevedon,"
"Leave him alone. Isn't it enough he's giving up an evening to hang out with his parents?"
"You have such a lovely face. Why hide it?"
"It doesn't look that bad."
Brendon studied himself in the toaster. The dark stubble disguised his lovely face.
"You can't see the cleft in your chin."
"No one cares, mammina."
He grabbed a slice of toast, rose, and draped the garment bag over his arm.
"I do. Isn't there something in your code about appearance?"
"Don't get me involved," David said.
Brendon stuffed the toast in his mouth, crumbs dusted his hoodie.
"Where are your manners lately?"
Brendon gobbled the toast in three bites. "I'm saving them for tonight." He chuckled at Sofia's displeasure; his cell phone buzzed.
"Wipe your mouth. Then give me a stubbly kiss."
Brendon stared at the screen. Every contact had a Bundesliga team logo attached to it, except for Troy. He had the Premier league lion. He ripped a paper towel off the roll, swiped it across his lips, and shoved it in his pocket. His phone rang again.
"I'd give her a kiss, son, or you'll be stuck here all day."
He brushed his lips over Sofia's cheek, puzzled.
"If your mother asks. You want to go to Burnham," David called.
Brendon stuffed his feet into his trainers and swiped his finger across the phone. "I can't understand you... stop crying... I'll be right there."
He ran to his car, hung the garment bag, and slid behind the wheel. Puffs of sand blew up around the tires. Brendon turned onto the farmhouse lane, texted Maggie an apology and rambled up the walkway. He pushed open the front door. Lemony cleaners masked the fresh paint smell. The floors sparkled; banister glistened. The house was tidy and deathly quiet. Brendon walked towards the mudroom; the door was ajar. He stumbled, jamming his heels into a line of wellies. Angelene clutched a rabbit to her chest. Her face washed in tears.

"There was a goshawk. It's dead."

She trembled and fell into his chest. Brendon could feel the heat of the animal through his hoodie.

"I couldn't find anything to scare it away."

Brendon scanned the sky, followed the wisps of clouds. There was no bird, just endless blue.

"It's gone."

"Are you sure? Check the trees."

He gazed along the tree line; a thump hit his chest. Another whack knocked his stomach. Its black nose twitched.

"The rabbit is alive. There's no blood."

Angelene sniffed and nuzzled its tawny neck.

"Put it down. It'll hop to its den."

Angelene knelt, the rabbit stretched and bounced from her arms. They walked into the house. Angelene sagged onto a stool.

"Where's Walter?"

"He's gone for bits of bob."

"It's bits and bobs. Is Walter excited about the party?"

"It's all he's talked about."

"Why did you ring me?"

Her shoulders drooped, her mouth full and pretty, pouted. Brendon tucked the moment away.

"I'm not sure. You were busy."

"I was listening to mum complain about my stubble."

A dribble of snot filled the bow of her lip. He reached inside his pocket and dabbed her nose.

"Walter wouldn't have come home to help."

Brendon handed her the crumpled napkin. "Not for a rabbit. He hunts."

"He doesn't understand how precious God's creatures are. The peacocks, pigeons, even Victor Hugo was my friend."

A pang struck Brendon's heart. "Who's Victor?"

"The statue at the Sorbonne."

"You were friends with a statue?"

"It's Victor Hugo," Angelene said, in a tone that suggested everyone would make friends with a statue. "The Hunchback of Notre Dame is one of my favourite books. I would sit at his feet every day. He never judged."

"He isn't real."

"He was real to me."

Brendon stuffed his hands in his hoodie pocket. Friends with a rabbit, a statue. She gave a new meaning to the word lonely.

"I've had very few friends; most have gone away." Angelene flicked the magazine across the island. "Look at that girl. Do you think she's pretty?"

"Too much makeup."

"Walter wants me to look like that."

The model was pretty in a 'made up' kind of way. There was nothing special, nothing interesting or unique. Nothing captivated his attention quite like the wistful girl sitting in front of him.

"I think you're beautiful just the way you are."

"You don't think I need makeup?"

"I don't, but if Uncle Walt asked, then it's best you do."

"Your mother wants you to shave, and you don't."

"It feels good to go against mammina."

"Your light is incredibly bright today."

"I don't get this light you're talking about. Most people would say I'm a moody arse."

"I don't believe it."

"I get in my head, brood as mum says."

"I only see light and a handsome boy. Brooding or not, you're beautiful."

Brendon cursed. The attempt to downplay his looks kept failing.

"My agent got me an ad campaign for a protein powder. He said it helps get you noticed. It got me noticed in the wrong way. I want to be known for being ace on the pitch."

"You are and you will continue to be."

"Not if girls keep putting lists on Facebook. They never say the best keepers in the Southern league, just the dishiest."

"Beauty is more than a handsome face. You fought for ninety minutes yesterday, the determination and passion."

Angelene twisted her hair into a braid. "I wish I had a light like yours."

Brendon breathed in the moment. Her slight smile, her clear eyes.

"You sure see the world differently."

"There's beauty in everything. The leaves on the tree, a cloudy sky, the prickly thistles, you."

Her honesty swept over him. Guilt stepped in and knocked him back to reality.

"I should get going. I was supposed to be at Maggie's over an hour ago. It isn't right to keep her waiting."

It wasn't right to allow Angelene to sink into his head. It wasn't right to find her so beautiful.

Brendon leaned against the car, preparing himself for an afternoon of babysitting. He glanced into the bay window. Jack jumped on the sofa, still in his pyjamas, hair sticking up like he stuck his finger in a light socket. The first time Maggie introduced Jack; Brendon had asked if he liked football. The response was a spray of spit and a karate kick to the shin.

Brendon grabbed his garment bag and sauntered up the walkway. Yarrow and grass sprouted between the cobblestones. Brendon opened the smudged door. The scent of sweaty socks and fabric softener wafted around him.

'There's beauty in everything. Find the bloody beauty.'

He kicked his shoes into a mountain of overturned wellies and trainers.

"Jack, come eat or you can go to you room."

"Brendon the dolt is here."

A whoosh of black fabric blew past Brendon. Jack skidded to a stop, stuck out his tongue and sprayed a mist of spit across the hardwood.

"Listen to your sister, go eat."

"You can't tell me what to do." Jack slid into Maggie, ripped a box of cereal from her hand, laughing maniacally.

Maggie swiped her hand over her forehead. "I hate Sundays."

Crumbs crunched under Brendon's feet as he followed Maggie to the front room. Newspapers and hair magazines cluttered the coffee table. Overturned buckets of blocks covered the battered hardwood. Brendon wiped a half-eaten biscuit to the floor and sunk onto the threadbare sofa.

"Will Walter's party be as posh as your mum's?"

"Don't expect caviar and champagne. Think more lager and sausage rolls."

"I tried caviar at your mum's do. I didn't like how it burst in my mouth."

"You wouldn't."

"Gosh, Brendon." Maggie pushed an assortment of books to the floor and flopped beside him. "What's Walter celebrating?"

"Walt wants to do things married couples do, have dinner parties and stuff."

Maggie pulled at a pill on a throw pillow. "I hope she's covered up this time. You'll be gawking at her again."

Brendon shoved his hands under his arms and dropped his head against the tattered cushion. "I wish you would stop obsessing over Ms. Pratt."

The voice in his head spoke, *'so should you.'*

"Do you think she's pretty? Troy thinks she has lovely eyes. He got a pinch for saying that."

"Not really."

He leaned across the couch and silenced her with a kiss.

"Yuck. I'm telling mum you were snogging Brendon." Jack arched his arm, pressed his tongue against his upper lip and whipped Batman across the room. Brendon shot out his hand and caught it. Jack dashed from the room; wet, bubbly laughter exploded through the house.

"Sorry," Maggie said, smiling.

Brendon didn't know if she was smiling an apologetic 'I'm sorry my brother is a dolt' grin or an amused 'That's what you get for fancying Ms. Pratt' grin.

"Sunday wouldn't be Sunday without getting covered in spit or having toys chucked at my head."

He scooted across the couch and kissed her.

"No snogging."

Brendon closed his eyes and breathed away the frustration. He reached for the remote, flicked through the channels, and stopped at the football highlights.

"Do you want a brew?"

"I can think of something better than tea."

"You're such a wanker."

"I wouldn't be if you'd do it for me."

Brendon settled into the couch; a block jabbed his back. He whipped it into the explosion of coloured blocks and analyzed an Arsenal goal.

"Bloody hell. Why didn't he move left? He would've made the save."

"What are you going on about?"

"The keeper. He didn't read the play, no wonder Tottenham scored."

"Do you ever NOT think about football?"

"It's the greatest sport on earth." He sipped the tea, making a face. "You put sugar in it."

"Milk and sugar, right?"

"We've been together two years and you still can't get it right. Just milk."

A heavy bounce and thump stomped overhead; silence swept over the house.

"Is Jack getting some kip?"

A crash and thud kicked hope out of Brendon.

"He barely napped as a baby. Why would he start now?"

"To give me a bloody break. Bouncing out of bloody bed, bouncing around the house."

"Jack is a spirited child."

A block flew from the foyer. It spiralled in the air, plunked into Brendon's mug, splashing tea on his hoodie. Brendon set the mug down and dabbed at the stain. Jack fluttered his cape and flung himself into a karate stance.

"Hiya." He spun around, slicing his hand past Brendon's face. "Why can't Charlie come over?"

"I'll see if her and Troy can come next Sunday."

"I don't like Troy either. The last time he was here, he kept kissing Charlie and smiling that daft smile of his." Jack wiggled his tongue at Brendon, flapped his cape and charged from the room.

"Jack fancies Charlie. The only time he sits still is when she's here. He stares at her with this look on his face."

"You better tell Troy he has competition."

"Jack looks at Charlie like you do, Ms. Pratt."

"I'm trying to figure her out like everyone else."

"Do you think she has lovely eyes?"

Brendon clenched his hands, sparks lit. "I'm going home if you don't quit."

"Answer the question."

"I think... bloody hell, can you drop it? I've missed the Premier league highlights. Troy and I will have nothing to talk about in English."

"You could talk about the novel."

Brendon scrubbed his face and groaned. Rule seven, honesty.

"Sometimes I think she's pretty and sometimes she looks like a girl I'd pass on the street."

"I get a strange feeling when she is around."

'Me too,' Brendon thought. "Mum said the same thing."

"It's like something bad is going to happen and I won't be able to stop it, like someone is going to get hurt."

"Don't be daft. Ms. Pratt is awkward and shy, that makes people uncomfortable."

A thunder of footsteps boomed above their heads.

"Want to go for ice cream? The place on Sycamore Close has gelato."

"You sure you want to take Jack for ice cream?"

"I want to stop the running around the house."

It wasn't how Brendon wanted to spend his afternoon. If it meant he didn't have to listen to Jack's bouncing or Maggie's strange feeling, he'd do it.

Brendon fixed his tie, smoothing it against his chest. The voices in his head had awakened from their slumber, hissing, stretching through his mind and thoughts, entrancing him under a spell of anxiety. *Leave Ms. Pratt alone. Sneak a peek. Look at your girlfriend, pretty, springtime Margaret. Pure, virginal, good little girl.*

"How do I look? Mum did a great job with my hair. It's a knotted ponytail, so sophisticated."

"You look beautiful."

It wasn't a lie. She looked pretty, typical Maggie pretty.

"You behave yourself with my girl," Kevin Thornton said, slapping an overworked hand on Brendon's shoulder. "I worked on your mum's Maserati. The parts are as expensive as the car."

"Another bash?" Rosie Thornton said. "Is that all you toffs do?"

"Yup, Ms. Thornton, every bloody night."

8 PLUCKING FEATHERS

Outside, the air was fresh and wonderful. It snaked through Brendon's lungs, warm and clean. He opened the car door for Maggie, curious if Angelene could pull off being a host.

"You'd think it was our first date," Maggie said.

They coasted past the moors darkened by night's arrival. Thoughts of Angelene cluttered his mind. Had she slaved all day, prepping for the party, planned the perfect menu, a signature cocktail? It would take a level of comfortability to prep and plan, Brendon grinned. Comfortable, and Angelene went together like vinegar and bleach.

"Your mum's proud to be middle class. She works hard, which makes her better than my mum. She thinks footballers are egotistical womanizers."

"It doesn't matter what mum thinks, I like you."

Brendon parked beside the ditch. The house was alive and bright. He took her hand and led her up the walkway. Wisteria drooped overhead.

"What's that smell?" Maggie said, fanning her nose.

'It doesn't smell like bloody feet.'

"Incense."

"What did she do to Walter's front room?"

"Decorated it."

"It's... I don't know how to describe it."

"I like it. The blue wall is nice."

"You would."

The upbeat tempo of the Rolling Stones floated into the foyer. Aromas-buttery pastries and cider- drifted from the kitchen. The display of artisanal cheeses, crudité, and hors d'oeuvres was grand and decadent.

"At least the sitting room looks normal," Maggie said.

The walls were chalk white, splashes of shamrock green livened the curtains and throw pillows. A monstrous sofa had taken up residence in the once barren room. It was dull compared to the colour and patterns in the rest of the house.

"Sweetheart, over here."

Women smiled a 'what a good boy,' grin. He mumbled polite hellos and edged through the crowd.

"This is some turnout."

"Free food and drink, more opportunity to gossip. Why wouldn't they come." Sofia said.

Brendon searched the sea of faces. Victoria grinned at him from behind an overfilled plate. Simone winked and mouthed a sultry 'hello.'

"Where's Uncle Walt?"

"I haven't seen him since we got here," David said.

Brendon rubbed his finger under his nose. "No, Ms. Pratt?"

"She's getting ready," Sofia said.

David grinned and patted Sofia's hip. "If she's anything like you, we'll be waiting all night."

"It takes time to look this good."

The absence of host and hostess raised a prickle of uneasiness in Brendon. Everywhere he looked, guests smiled, ate, sang along with Mick Jagger. This was Walter's time to shine. 'Look at me, look at my beautiful home, my perfect wife.' Brendon tossed a sausage roll at Maggie; his stomach twisted.

"I'm going to the loo."

"Stay away from Ms. Batra. She's as bad as Rachel."

Brendon slipped from the room. The stairs creaked, muffled 'put the damn dress on' seeped from behind the closed door. Heavy footsteps approached; Brendon ducked into the bathroom. A groan floated down the hall, followed by thumps and Walter apologizing for Angelene's tardiness. Something about a stuck zipper. Brendon rubbed his hands on his trousers.

'Go back to Maggie, eat, talk football, get ogled by Ms. Batra.'

Something pulled him towards the bedroom. Angelene sat on the edge of the bed, little bits of torn tissue at her feet.

"We had a wonderful day. I was doing normal things. His eyes changed to icy blue so quickly."

Brendon wiggled his tie and peered over his shoulder. Conversation, Van Morrison, laughter. He stepped over the threshold and froze. He was in Walter's room, with Walter's wife.

Angelene walked to the full-length mirror, dabbing the mascara staining her cheeks. She gripped handfuls of chartreuse silk; her shoulders sagged.

"This dress is me."

"Walt means well. He used to pick out clothes for Anastasia. She bloody loved it."

"He throws names at me like I'm supposed to know who they are." Her face went slack. She slashed at her thighs. "I want to wear my clothes. It would be easier to do normal things if I were comfortable."

"If it makes you feel better. Mum picked out mine and dad's suits."

He had checked in, made sure she was okay, promise not broken. It was time to get back to his normal.

"I hate that dress. I hate Walter demands I wear it."

"You want those women to stop gossiping, don't you?"

Brendon glanced into the hall. The conversation had turned to Brexit, Tom Jones replaced Van Morrison. He lifted her chin and ran his thumb over a smudge of mascara. "Put the dress on. They'll have nothing to talk about."

"Those women won't stop talking whether I wear this or that hideous dress. What's wrong with my dress?"

The chartreuse shift skimmed over her body, highlighting her curves and pert breasts.

"I wish you could see what I do. You'd understand how bloody wrong this dress is."

"I thought Walter would want to show me off. He rambles on and on about his reputation and image."

"He wants you to look as posh as he does. That's how Walt makes an impression."

He yanked a tissue from the box and dabbed her cheeks.

"I don't look like that girl in the magazine anymore."

"Not quite."

Angelene jerked the dress from the hanger and tossed it on the bed. "I will wear the McCartney. She's the daughter of people I'm supposed to know." She held up the dress and scrunched her nose at the white satin lapels. "I have this persistent knot in my belly, reminding me how out of place I am. My zipper please."

Brendon's gaze drifted down her spine to the swoop of her bottom. Creaks and rattles came at him from every corner. Brendon tugged at the pull. The dress fell around her feet. He ran his fingers through his hair, black lace panties.

"Will you do me a favour?"

"Don't turn around, please."
"Will you keep your lamp on for me, so I know you're always there?"
"I promise."

***

Angelene stared at the glow in Brendon's window. Walter's soft breathing filled the room. The night had been long. She listened to Simone prattle on about her love of Paris and talked about antiques with Sofia. It had been a dizzying day of emotions. Mourning the rabbit that was not dead, feeling something for Walter, then despising him. Washing herself in Brendon's light.

'Is it wrong God to be Brendon's friend? I could break a pattern this time.'

She had been an okay wife for part of the day. Normal sort of fit. *'I promise to continue to do wife things, keep a clean house, practice cooking. If I can do that part of normal, I can be a normal friend too.'*

9 Verschlimmbessern

English had not been on Brendon's mind. He bumbled through French and fell asleep in the dining hall. The promise to leave his lamp on had him dragging his ass through training and school. Brendon stripped off his school kit and tossed it on a stack of clean clothes. He dug around the closet for his usual, t-shirt, hoodie, jeans and dressed.

"It looks like Burnham on Sea won. We're off to Bridgwater Bay," Sofia said.

"I thought you liked that house. You're always going on about old bones and Edward."

He picked up a notebook, flipped through the pages and tossed it on to the dresser.

"The house is Edwardian, and it's lovely. The Pratt's are joining us."

An ache bounced up Brendon's spine and coiled around his shoulders. He dug under a stack of football magazines, grabbed a notebook decorated in Dortmund logos and jammed it into his backpack.

"You haven't given her a chance. No one has."

"There are things in her past that are." Sofia paused and rattled her bangles. "Questionable."

"You sound like your friends."

"Do you know why she was late for the party?" She fluffed the throw pillows, rearranged, and rearranged again. "She refused to wear the dress. It was a McCartney."

"Who cares? She should be able to wear what she wants."

He yanked a textbook from a teetering tower. The stack toppled and banged on the floor. Sparks lit and sizzled.

"Walter has certain expectations; slinky dresses don't fit it."

Brendon snatched the book off the floor. He bit down on the words, sorting through what he wanted to say and what he should.

"She must have dressed like that in Paris."

"Why are you so concerned with how people treat her? It's about respect for her husband."

"People should respect her."

"Sexy isn't about letting everything hang out. Sexy is leaving things to the imagination."

"I doubt Angelene is trying to be sexy, end of conversation."

Sofia grabbed a hanger from beneath the mountain of clothes and hung his blazer.

"Why are you in a mood? School's over."

"I ignored Margaret at Walt's do. She's making me study."

He tore his backpack off the bed and marched to the hall.

"If Simone wasn't cornering you, you were staring at Angelene."

Brendon pounded down the stairs. "I wasn't staring at Ms. Pratt, bloody hell mammina."

Amelia scurried into the foyer, an apple and protein bar in hand. "Don't forget your snack." Brendon counted his breaths, one... two. The sparks crackled.

"Thank you, Ame."

She patted his arm and smiled warmly. "Breathe, breathe the entire way to Maggie's."

"No kiss?" Sofia said.

"You accused me of staring at Ms... No."

He left the foyer, breathed through the sparks, guilt twisted around his throat. Had it been that obvious? He had mingled, talked to Kate about football, entertained Simone's flirting. Brendon dropped onto the seat and started the car, cursing himself and Angelene's lace knickers.

Dense grey clouds dominated the sky. Taunton was brooding with him. Brendon drove along the crumbling tarmac. The world changed from fields of green to rows of brown. The aging terraced homes leaned into one another, joined by brick fenced gardens. Maggie's cat, Suki, laid across the bricks, her paws crossed, keeping a watchful eye on the street. Brendon parked alongside the curb and imagined fat raindrops, pummelling the sparks, one plunk, two plunks.

"I started my laptop."

"No hello." Suki purred around his ankles. He ran his hand over her fur and threw his backpack into the front room.

"Your mood hasn't changed."

Brendon brushed past Maggie, wiped crumbs from the cushion and dropped onto the sofa. He could come clean, tell her Angelene has a heart-shaped bottom, confess he had followed the hills and valleys of her spine. Brendon leaned across the sofa and kissed her.

"You taste sweet."

"I ate a bag of jelly cherries."

Brendon gently tugged her hand towards his crotch.

"Homework."

"In a bit."

"Will you quit it? What's got into you?"

Black lace knickers.

"Do you know what Troy and Charlie did today?"

Maggie unzipped his backpack, grabbed his notebook, tossing it in his lap. "They did it in the custodian's cupboard."

"Tilly thought it was funny. She almost peed her knickers. She was laughing so hard."

"Matilda sounds like a pig when she laughs, squealing and snorting. It's as annoying as her gum chewing."

Brendon folded open his notebook and stared at the question, 'find a quote that shows Werther's love for Lotte'.

"I heard something else today."

"I'll get expelled before first term ends."

"Rachel gave you an origami envelope filled with blue Smarties?"

Brendon groaned and pressed open the novel.

"Did she?" Maggie said, digging her tooth into her lip. "Your ears are red."

Brendon flipped through the novel. The stuffy sock smelling air was scorching and smothering.

'I have so much in me, and the feeling for her absorbs it all; I have so much, and without her it all comes to nothing. Bloody hell, Goethe, you hit the nail on the head.'

"I gotta go."

A war began in Brendon's head. A gentle voice whispered, *go back to Maggie, and apologize.* The other, he had named Padre Diavolo, pushed him to the farmhouse and willed his hand to knock on the door.

"Bonjour mon ami."

She looked as sad as her voice. Holey black leggings, his hoodie, hair in a messy ponytail. She rubbed the cuff over her bloodshot eyes and tugged his hand. Brendon followed her up the stairs. Paint cans and rollers littered the hall; she had painted the walls chocolate brown.

Brendon froze at the bedroom door. Clothes laid like dead bodies strewn over the floor and bed.

"Bloody hell, if Walt sees this."

He picked up a beaded camisole, folded it into a square, and set it on the dresser.

"Walter can fuck off." Her tone was sharp and piercing. "I've disappointed him, embarrassed him. Your mother will take me shopping for clothes."

"What can I do to help?"

"Stay and have tea. I need to sort through this mess. I'm afraid of what I may do to myself."

Brendon glanced at the faded scars on her forearm. "I'll stay."

"Tea first. Milk, oui?"

"You remembered, bloody hell, Maggie still can't get it right."

She touched his chin, his belly fluttered. "How do I take mine?"

"Black."

"Always remember how to make a girl's tea or coffee. It's as important as remembering a birthday."

Brendon dragged a box to his feet, picking up a piece of jade chiffon. He couldn't tell if it was a skirt or shirt. Tossing it into the box, Brendon held up a spaghetti strap dress. He heard the shuffle of feet and glanced up. "You can't keep this?"

Angelene set the cups on the nightstand. "I'm afraid not."

Brendon grabbed the mug and stared over the rim. How could Maggie accuse him of fancying Angelene? There was nothing special about her. She was plain, dishevelled, with bloodshot eyes and colourless cheeks.

"That's too bloody bad. Does it all have to go?"

Her presence took over the room, snatched his breath, disarming his defences. She had spilled her disaster at his feet. Her vulnerability was beautiful.

"I can only keep what he bought me in Paris and London."

"These are your things. He's asking you to throw yourself away."

Angelene held up a beaded slip. "Ms. Secretary of Defence wouldn't wear something like this."

"You could if you were my wife. I wouldn't care what anyone thought."

Angelene grinned behind her mug. "You wouldn't want me for a wife."

He unravelled a slinky raspberry chemise and grinned. "Are you bloody kidding? If you were in this."

"Once you get to know me, you'll change your mind."

"Walter says he wants to improve you. He's making things worse by wanting to change you."

Angelene scooped up an armful of clothes. "There's a German word for that, Verschlimmbessern."

Brendon tossed a shirt into the box. "I think you just smiled. If you'd move the clothes out of the way, I could see."

"Mother used to get angry when I smiled. If she wasn't full of joy, I had no right to be happy."

She leaned across the bed and brushed her lips over his cheek. "Thank you."

"I said I would be here for you. I meant it."

"You have a beautiful face. I could paint you."

Brendon stared into his teacup. A flush stained his cheeks. "I'm trying to get away from that, remember?"

"You shouldn't be upset about some silly list. At least you aren't ugly."

He looked at her tangled hair, wistful eyes, and wrapped an arm around her. "You don't think you're ugly, do you? There's beauty in everything. You said so."

"I struggle to see it in me. Sometimes I stare in the mirror and wish my face would change, my body."

"I wish I had spots and a receding hairline."

Brendon took her hands and walked her to the full-length mirror. "Don't you see it? You smell like cigarettes but, you're beautiful."

Angelene leaned into his stomach, drawing his arms around her. Brendon's gaze swept over the anchor alarm clock, a Royal Navy hoodie. Walter was everywhere.

"I'll help you finish." He bent down and picked up a low-cut cocktail dress. "This is brilliant."

"In the box."

He held a lacy blouse against his chest. "This too?"

"Throw it all in. It'll be less painful."

He grabbed an armful of denim and silk, dropping it in the box.

"How will I ever learn to be the wife he wants?"

"I'm sorry Walt was a dick."

"Your mother will help me. I'll be a better version of me."

"Where should I put this?"

"By the front door. Your mother and I are dropping the clothes... what did Walter call it?"

"A charity shop."

"That's it."

Brendon walked down the stairs and dropped the box by the door. Her thumbnail scratched and pulled the thin polyester leggings. Soft cracks and pops clattered from behind the walls, leaves rustled, and somewhere among the trees, an owl hoot.

"Don't do that."

"It's another bad habit."

He folded the cuff around her fingers like a mitten and held tight. "Is there anything else that makes you feel better?"

Angelene stared at the stucco ceiling and sighed. "Booze, cigarettes."

"Healthy things."

"A bath," she fell into his chest and inhaled, "your comforting brown."

"Bloody hell, I feel dizzy."

"If you visited Parc Floral, and you saw me, would you want to speak to me?"

She rubbed his back, meandered to the stairs, and dissolved onto the step.

"I have a feeling you would have run away."

"I might have. I do an excellent job at running."

"Healthy things tonight."

"I'll have a bath and eat."

"Don't let mammina pick out your clothes. She wears a lot of black. You're more of a colour kind of girl."

"You're a sweet boy."

"Black tea, yellow and Victor Hugo."

"Borussia Dortmund, tea with milk, and a dislike of school." She tugged on the sleeves and wound them around her like a scarf.

"Visit me again?"

Mammina's warning pulsed in his head. Padre Diavolo cackled.

***

Maggie studied the timeline in her agenda. She had mapped out all her assignments in pink and lime green ink. She placed her chin on her hand and cracked open the chemistry text. Maggie enjoyed doing homework at Charlotte's. The house was quiet, her bedroom was glam. There was no Jack to contend with.

"Thanks for letting me come over."

"I thought you were hanging out with Brendon?"

"He barely spoke," Maggie said, chomping on her thumbnail, "We didn't even get to his homework. He rushed out the door, said he had to go."

Charlotte rubbed a towel over her legs and pitched it into the laundry basket. "Do we have to do homework?"

"We can talk about Rachel giving Brendon Smarties. She picked out the blue ones, daft cow."

Charlotte wiggled into a t-shirt and relaxed onto the bed. "That feels better. I had a bit of babes' goo on my bum. It itched all day."

"You're disgusting. Mr. Dawson could have suspended you two."

"When the mood strikes."

Maggie wrote out an answer and grumbled as Charlotte copied it.

"You could open your textbook; the answers are on page 221."

"I can't concentrate when I wear one of babes' t-shirts. One smell and I miss my crumpet horribly."

"You've got a collage of pictures on the wall; you can't stare at it then look for the answer?"

"What's else has got your knickers in a twist?"

"I haven't slept in days. I get a chunk of sleep, then I'm awake."

"Did you dream about humping Brendon and now you feel guilty?"

"I dreamt he cheated on me."

"Mr., I do everything mummy and daddy say."

Maggie lounged into a pile of velvet and glittered pillows and crossed her arms over her chest.

"He was snogging Ms. Pratt, and he was ready to, you know, when my mum walked in and called him a wanker. Then I failed all my classes."

Charlotte grinned an 'you're a nutter, but I love you,' grin and snuggled next to her. "Brendon would never cheat, and you're the smartest person I know. There's no way you'll fail."

Maggie blew her bangs from her eyes and sniffed. "He's been distant. You should have seen him at Walter's do. He was making the Charlie face at Ms. Pratt."

"Is that like the O face? I asked babes if I made one."

Maggie poked Charlotte with her pen. "It has nothing to do with that. It's the face Jack makes when he sees you."

"Ooh, does he have a crush?"

"Don't let on you know. He's a handful as is."

"Brendon is a nice bloke. He signs autographs for the little footy players. He volunteered as a goal coach for the youth team."

"He's always around Ms. Pratt or sneaking a peek. He doesn't know I've caught him." Maggie shoved the pen in her mouth and chewed. "Didn't you find Ms. Pratt weird?"

"What do you mean by weird? Like a nutter weird or like the swots in physics? One of their paper airplanes got stuck in my hair."

"I've accepted girls stare at Brendon. I just bite my lip and hope the jealousy goes away. The day we swam at Brendon's, Ms. Pratt was hiding behind the curtain, staring at him."

"You need to worry about Rachel, not Ms. Pratt."

Maggie studied Charlotte's face. The weird feeling flitted around her stomach. It was a brush-off.

"I told Brendon she was staring at him; he didn't believe me. She was there, I swear."

"Have you forgotten she's married? Mr. Pratt's ace for an old bloke. His eyes crinkle when he smiles. He's like a young Sean Bean."

"Will you be serious? Ms. Pratt is the worst kind of pretty, dangerous, like she doesn't know she's beautiful."

"Give Brendon a pinch when he gawks. Babes will never look at her again."

"It's like she has a scream stuck in her throat."

"Ms. Pratt is one of those introverts I read about in psych. They make people uncomfortable because they're quiet."

"I'm not sure."

"Ah, Magpie, maybe you need to hump Brendon."

Maggie touched the diamond solitaire. "My mum would cut off Brendon's thing if he came near me."

"It's brilliant how two people fit together. Babes and I are a perfect match."

"I'm sure that's what Ms. Spence was thinking. Please God, give me a boy to fit perfectly with Charlotte Donovan."

"Humping might take your mind off Ms. Pratt."

A tickle crawled up Maggie's spine. She knew this feeling. It whispered, she's there, stealing breath, watching, waiting.

***

Angelene sifted her fingers through the dirt. The smells of damp earth enchanted her, she moved on. Upturned soil turned to velvety green. She stumbled onto gravel and Spence Farm. The coop door squeaked, she kneaded her knuckles, excuses danced around her head: *'I have trouble sleeping, I lose track of time when walking.'* Her anxious gaze met Troy's; the words tumbled from her mouth.
"I was walking and ended up here."
"Do you always walk around at night?"
"I don't sleep well. I've been meaning to explore the property. Now seemed like the right time."
Troy closed the gate and smiled. "It's late. I'll walk you home."
"I'll find my way back. I've troubled you."
"I was finishing my chores. It's not a big deal."
Angelene hesitated. Troy's presence was luminous, golden yellow. It filled the laneway and glowed against her. She touched her chest. Could he hear her heart pounding?
"Troy, I've perfected my Piledriver. I want to show you," Callum Spence yelled.
"Show Brian."
Feelings, colours, words electrified Angelene like an overloaded circuit board. *'Always stumbling into things, tripping over your feet, anything to drench yourself in their light.'*
Angelene pressed her fingers into her forehead, buzz, crackle, buzz.
"Bonne nuit."
"Mum said no more wrestling. Troy!"
"I'll be right back, Callum."
"Who's the girl?"
"Go inside. I'll run back; it'll take less than a minute."
"Sounds like you have a busy house."
"Four boys. My older brother Gavin is at uni. Brian and Callum want to be professional wrestlers. Busy doesn't describe it."
"I don't have any siblings." Angelene plucked a feather from a patch of clover and twirled it between her fingers. "Family might have meant something to me. We could have protected one another."
"Sometimes I wish I were an only child; I never get a moment's peace. Brian threw me over the ropes after dinner. The sofa in case you were wondering."
"It sounds wonderful to me."
"The only good thing, chores get divided up."
The buzzing hummed; the crackling stopped. Troy's glow calmed the noises. She liked his smile, every part of his face twinkled. When he spoke, the words shot from his mouth in vibrant, sunburst yellow. Angelene looped her arm through his, touched her throat, and asked God to forgive her.
"Blimey Ms. Pratt," Troy said, plucking at his collar, "it took three days to stop thinking about you."
"I like your sunshine. I can feel it through your skin."

"That's my heart racing. If Charlie finds out, I'll get a horrible pinch."

"I don't mean to make you uncomfortable. Your smile is contagious."

"You get into my head; it makes me feel like a wanker."

"Do I annoy you? I do that often, annoy people."

"That day, Brendon, and I worked in Walt's Garden. I couldn't stop thinking, what is it about you? It was hard to look at Charlie."

Angelene tightened her grip. She had heard it before. She wasn't entirely sure how it happened.

"You're in love?"

"Charlie was meant to be my girl."

"It must be an amazing feeling. My mother said love makes you crazy."

"It does, but it's the good kind of bonkers."

"Is Brendon in love with Maggie?"

She tried to stuff the words back in. It was the wrong question. She didn't know why she asked it.

"I thought he was. Before he left for Dortmund, they were all over each other. Since he came back, he's, I don't know, different."

They ducked under a gnarled hornbeam branch, Angelene glanced at Rosewood manor, touched her lips, and smiled. His lamp was on.

"I would say Brendon is in like."

"Charlotte is lucky to have you."

"It's the other way around. It's rare a girl like her wants to be with a guy like me."

"I don't understand what you mean, a guy like you. You're special."

"You're doing it again, giving me those eyes. I'll be thinking about you when I fall asleep."

"What is one thing you love about Charlotte?"

"That's a hard one. I love so many things about her."

"You make love seem easy. If love were a colour, you and Charlotte would be pink. If love had a look, you both wear it."

"You'll fall in love with Walter and see how simple love is."

"I'm trying my best to trust love and fall deeply into it. I need to get normal right first. Be comfortable playing, wife."

"Think about all the things you like about Walter. It'll be easy then."

"I'll start tonight," Angelene said, opening the door, "thank you for walking me home."

"Bonne nuit, Ms. P."

"Bonne nuit. Petit à petit, l'oiseau fait son nid, des grandes choses peuvent être réalisées."

Troy cocked his head and smiled.

"Little by little, the bird makes its nest, great things can be achieved. Never give up on your dreams, Au revoir."

Angelene slipped into the house and slid the deadbolt in place. She enjoyed walking arm in arm with Troy, the scent of hay on his clothes. She liked it and it wasn't right. With each step up the stairs, she recited a 'hail Mary.' She knelt by the bed and clasped her hands.

"God, please forgive me for taking Troy's arm and falling into his sunshine. It's my patterns. I fall into them before I realize I have, please forgive me. Amen."

Angelene stripped off her clothes and buried under the mussed blankets. She scrunched into a ball and imagined herself in a field of green filled with the bluest cornflower and prettiest buttercups. God shone his love down and every scar on her body disappeared. Her heart was whole, and all the lost pieces fit into place. Sleep came in a wave of golden yellow.

10 Cacoethes

Brendon gripped the steering wheel. Kakos, bad, ethos, disposition, cacoethes, the uncontrollable urge to do something unadvisable. It was a terrible decision, leaving school, and for what, a desperate text. Sand blew up around the tires. He left the engine running and sprinted to the door. Brendon peeked in the kitchen, frowning at a clutter of dishes, eggshells, and the smell of burnt toast. He followed the sound of soft whimpering to the bedroom. Clothes covered the unmade bed; price tags gleamed in the sunlight.

"What the bloody hell are you doing?"

Brendon stood in the closet doorway and held out his hand.

"I'm supposed to be hanging up my clothes. They've been laying on the bed for a few days now."

"Mum nags about the clothes on my floor. I don't cry."

"Walter and I got into a horrible fight. He let me decorate the house, I must wear the clothes. I told him I want to be me, and he said he didn't like me. He hates the brown walls."

Brendon brushed a damp strand of hair from her cheek. "What a dick."

"He changed his tune when I cried." Angelene wiped her eyes on her sleeve and poked at her belly. "He wants a miniature, Sofia. I need a church. I fell asleep after the argument and dreamt about mother. She was screaming at me, calling me ugly and stupid. I... it's a terrible habit."

Brendon held her arm and ran his thumb over the red scratches. "I told you not to do that."

"Please take me to a church. I need to feel God. I need Him to know I'm sorry for hurting myself."

Tears created lines through her makeup. Brendon grabbed a wrap from the bed and draped it around her shoulders.

"I told you healthy things."

"Please, no lecture. I've heard enough from Walter about my drinking and smoking."

"You should have called me before you cut yourself. What did you use?"

"A hanger."

Clouds swept in, swallowing the blue. Rain fell in steady plunks, turning the street slick black.

"What else is the matter? Walter's been a dick before. You didn't cut yourself."

"Nobody has ever liked me, not even my mother. No one, except Roman, Francois and the boy with liquid blue eyes."

"I like you."

Angelene twisted in the seat and pressed her nose against the window.

"What's this?"

"St. Theresa's."

"It looks like a school. Where are the statues and stained glass? What about the steeple?"

Sparks flit around his belly. "I bunked off school and you're upset there's no bloody stained glass?"

"I'm sorry. I'm acting like a brat. Will you come with me?"

"I'll wait here. I'm liable to burst into flames for all the bloody, terrible things I've done lately."

Brendon relaxed into the seat and tapped open the Champion's League app. He studied the match predictions; odds were in Dortmund's favour. He dropped his phone in the cup holder and watched wood pigeons peck at fallen beech nuts. Cutting, picking, scratching, little scars on her arms, hidden behind bracelets and long sleeves. There had been a girl in year six, caught in the art cupboard, digging a chisel into her arm. Brendon never understood what made Tabitha Harper cut herself. Rumour was, she felt dead inside and cutting made her feel alive. His heart hurt. Did Angelene feel the same way?

Voices carried along the wind; Angelene's face looked brighter.

"God forgave me. I felt it in my belly. I'm worthy of His love again." She laced her fingers through his and exhaled slowly.

"You're worthy of lots of things."

He backed out of the car park; her hand was warm on his.

"Is your mother angry with me? I tried on everything she passed over the fitting room door."

"She never mentioned anything."

"Her style scares me."

Brendon chuckled. "Her fashion sense or her?"

"She's so sophisticated. Those shop clerks ran right over to her when we walked in."

"They make bloody good commission, that's why."

"Everything was so expensive. The skirt she insisted I buy, a pencil skirt, cost more than a month of groceries."

"She has expensive tastes. Did she make you buy Italian? Mum swears Italian designers are superior."

"I think so. She got extremely excited about a jumpsuit by Miu Miu. I thought there was a cat in the store." Angelene flung her hand out the window and traced along the telephone wires. "My mother once said, if I were a cat, she would have drowned me."

"Bloody hell, your mum was a gobby cow."

She seemed happy enough. The tears had dried; the splotches had faded from her cheeks. He was okay to leave her and despite Madre Innocente, the other voice he had named, stabbing him with her staff of guilt, he was glad he bunked off school.

"I have an outfit for a cream tea, afternoon tea, high tea. I never knew there were so many ways to have a tea party."

Brendon pulled into the farmhouse laneway and parked beside the walkway. Rain misted the windscreen.

"No ciggies, no wine and no bloody hangers."

"I'll paint, read, soak in the tub, pretend I'm floating in the ocean."

He had never seen her eyes shine so brightly. Brendon blinked. It wasn't a hallucination. There was a twinkle of a smile.

"You've danced with the devil, mon ami; I can see him flickering in your eyes."

"I've got to know him well; his name is Padre Diavolo."

Angelene stared into her lap, pinching her knuckle. "Are you in love with Maggie?"

"I'm in like."

"She has a ring on her finger."

"I was leaving for Dortmund and thought it was the right thing to do. I jumped before thinking."

"I have a habit of doing that too."

"Have you always been quiet?"

Brendon laid his hand over hers. She stopped plucking and leaned her head against the window.

"The less I say, the less I get noticed."

"The quiet ones get noticed the most."

"You think."

"People don't know what you're thinking. It's scary."

Angelene traced along his finger. "I never know what to say. I practice for hours. The words stick in my throat."

"I'm the same." A little shiver travelled up his spine. Her touch was electric. "If I fail a test or screw up, I'll spend the entire day thinking of something to tell dad."

Brendon stared at her mouth. *'One kiss, a peck, just to say I hear you and I care.'*

"I wish it were the end of the day. We could watch the Dortmund, Barcelona match. I could tell you the difference between a cream tea and high tea."

"Go to school. I should have called a taxi," Angelene said. "Promise to give me a kiss on my brow when I'm dead. I shall feel it."

"Bloody hell, that's depressing."

"It isn't. It's Victor Hugo, Les Misérables. Au revoir."

Brendon waited until she was inside the house, then drove away. *'You're going to hell, Cook.'*

"Sorry I'm late. I had to go to Boots, headache, the queue was long."

Rachel glanced up from her phone. "Du bist der Mann meiner Träume."

"Bloody brilliant, what did you say?"

"You're the man of my dreams."

Brendon loosened his tie, releasing the heat tingling under his collar. He looked at the gallery of photos, amazed at the array of boys. "That's the attacker from Wellington."

"He was fun for a while. Movie dates and pints at the pub got boring."

"Edwin Bellingham, the swot?"

"He tried to dazzle me with his knowledge of subatomic particles, boring."

Brendon recognized the goalkeeper from Truro, the clerk from the sweet shop. The infamous list had to be true.

"That's me."

Rachel enlarged the photo and kissed it. "You look dishy in your black kit. The green one makes you look like a giant grasshopper."

"Have you been with all those boys?"

"Not all of them." Rachel glanced at him; tingles prickled his cheeks. "Dawson is going to have you by the goolies if he finds out you bunked off French."

"He isn't happy I'm back."

He eyed a water bottle decorated in a red rhinestone tiara and nodded towards it.

"Go ahead, knuddlebär. Du hast schone Augen. You have beautiful eyes."

"Why do I need to know that?"

"In case you meet a fit German girl," Rachel said, "say something about me."

Brendon took a sip, and sort through the German words floating around his head. He had heard different things from his teammates in Dortmund, Schön, hübsch, arsch, reizvolle. He didn't want to give Rachel the wrong idea. Brendon scraped his fingers through his hair and took another sip.

"Ich mag deine haare"

Rachel twirled a curl around her finger. "Boys never say they like my hair. Most tell me they like my tits or arse."

"Both are bloody brilliant. I was trying to be a gentleman."

"The rumours are true. You're a good boy."

"Depends on who you ask."

"Would you like to be a bad boy?" Rachel said, the buttonholes stretched as she slid towards him. "I think you secretly want to be bad."

Brendon tore his gaze from her freckled breasts. She had a way of lighting his insides on fire.

"I brought us something, Mittagessen."

"Should I know what that is?"

She leaned over the desk and dug in a monogrammed bag. Brendon tilted the chair back and peeked, lacy knickers.

"It's lunch. A German feast for German lessons."

She laid an embroidered tablecloth over the desks and handed him utensils wrapped in the same floral fabric.

"You didn't have to do that."

"I wanted to. Mum was out with her latest boyfriend. I was bored."

Brendon took the stack of containers and popped the lids. "Chef let you into the kitchen to heat it up?"

"I gave him a pack of Marlboro Gold," Rachel said, setting out plates, "Königsberger Klopse, Gruen Bohnen, Gurkensalat."

"It smells better than it sounds."

Rachel laughed and filled a plate. "Meatballs, green beans, and cucumber salad."

"You went to a lot of trouble."

"You're worth it."

He jabbed his fork into a meatball and popped it into his mouth. "Bloody hell, that's good."

"I'm glad you like it. I volunteer at the old age home on Trinity Road, delivering meals. The cook is German," Rachel said, nibbling a green bean, "you should come round to mine. I'll make you schnitzel."

"Can we start the lesson?" He stabbed a cucumber and smeared it through the sauce.

"Welches Bier wurdest du empfehlen."

Brendon munched on the cucumber and raised his shoulders.

"I said, which beer do you recommend? Give me your notebook and I'll write it down for you."

Madre Innocente stabbed his heart; he couldn't tear his eyes off Rachel. Her mouth looked pillowy and full of promise. She was pretty in a made-up kind of way.

"Is Thornton following you to Dortmund?"

"She's going to uni in Cambridge."

"Does that make you sad?"

She slid closer to him; a flurry of tingles rippled through his groin. He tried to squash them. She was the tart of Taunton; he was number one on her list. Pulling number one would give her bragging rights. Guilt tore through him; Rachel wasn't a slapper. She was a girl, a 9.25.

"I'll try to manage a long-distance relationship."

"I had a boyfriend in Lisbon, Miguel. He was a striker, ace at putting the ball in the net."

"What happened? By the look on your face, you really liked him."

"He moved to Torino," Rachel said, snapping on a lid.

"Does he play for Juve?"

"The youngest boy to play for the team."

"Bloody hell, you should have held on to that one."

"Italy is further away than Portugal. It wasn't meant to be," Rachel said. "I found a prettier boy."

"Who's the lucky guy?"

She moved closer, pressing her breasts against his arm. "Sitting here."

Brendon edged himself closer to the wall, running a finger under his collar.

"What do you plan on doing after school?"

"I'm planning on going to uni for nursing."

"Uni? Wow, I didn't..."

"Didn't think a girl like me would have ambition?"

"It's kind of hard to think when your jubblies are squished against me."

"You know who has no ambition, Charlotte. All she talks about is marrying Troy."

"It's all I've bloody heard for two years now. Charlotte will have no cares in the world when she's done school. People think I'm spoiled. Mr. Donovan will make sure she's taken care of even if that means he has to do it."

"Ahem."

Brendon fumbled with the utensils and passed them to Rachel.

"Hey Mags."

"I'll see you in Latin knuddlebär."

Brendon nodded and stared at his feet. "Thanks for everything."

Rachel smiled the flirtiest 'you're welcome' smile Brendon had ever seen; he tore his eyes off her wiggling hips and flashed his best dimpled smile. "You look ace today."

Maggie crossed her arms over her chest and shoved her thumbnail into her mouth. He stooped and kissed her mottled cheek.

"I've been texting you. Gemma said you weren't in French."

"I drove into town, headache."

"You could have gone on dinner break and missed German with the tart."

Brendon wiggled his tie; the pristine wood framed walls were shrinking around him. Kisses and compliments weren't going to work. It was time to pull on her heartstrings.

"Remember that time at the pitch when my head was pounding, and I barfed? It's that kind of headache."

He walked away, longing for fresh air. The pungent wood polish, vanilla and tuberose perfumes were stuck in his nose.

"Why can't she tutor you like a normal person? Not have her jubblies pushed up to her chin."

"She is tutoring me like a normal person. What she wears has nothing to do with it. Did you know she volunteers with old people?"

"She's a slag and a saint, brilliant. Why were you thanking her?"

Brendon slammed his hands against the door, welcoming a blast of cool, wet air. The lie was not a lie anymore. An ache crept through his skull. Padre Diavolo lit sparks, and Madre Innocente shamed him for being a liar.

"She made me lunch."

"Was it a German lesson or a date?"

"Bloody hell, will you quit it. I didn't ask her to do it."

"It's part of her tart plan, flatter you, do wonderful things. She'll be checking you off her list soon," Maggie said, grabbing the sleeve of his blazer, "slow down. My legs are shorter than yours."

Brendon tugged his arm free and wiped a film of drizzle off his face. "I'm trying to get away from you."

"You're a dolt. Can't you see she's flirting with you?"

"Rachel flirts with everyone. I don't think she knows how to act any other way."

"She tried to pull Mr. Torres last term. He left his position in the science department."

"That was a rumour. He had to go home to Valencia. His mother was sick."

"Rachel wants her number one. She wants to, you know."

"I like being her number one. It makes me feel good to know someone fancies me in that kind of way."

"That was a daft thing to say." Maggie jerked a tissue from her pocket and rubbed it under her nose. He had no idea where the comment came from. Frustration, guilt, Padre Diavolo? Brendon scraped his fingers through his hair, hug her, rub her back, call himself an arsehole. It wasn't in him to do any of those things. The day had been like a roller coaster, up, down, worry, frustration, joy. There had been more climbs and dips than he could manage.

"Don't bloody cry. People are staring."

"I fancy you," Maggie said, blowing her nose, "it shouldn't matter that some slapper who can't keep her hands off anything in a football kit likes you."

"Can you please stop crying? I need to take a few breaths. Who knows what I'll say to Mr. Clark."

"You don't care what you say to me, but god forbid you act like an arse to Mr. Clark."

Heat rippled over his body; Maestro Padre Diavolo orchestrated a symphony of sparks.

Maggie dabbed her eyes and scrunched the tissue. "Aren't you going to say sorry?"

"It's better if I keep my fucking mouth shut."

"Mr. Cook, language," Mr. Clark said, yanking open the door, "tuck in your shirt. Must I remind you of the dress code every day?"

"Will everyone give me a fucking minute."

The words flew from his mouth. Mr. Dawson snuck out from behind the privet hedges. Brendon cursed and stared into the blue-grey sky.

"Strike one."

"You've got to be bloody kidding. I asked for a minute so I can breathe. No one fucking listened."

"Is that strike two?"

"No sir."

"Go to the room outside my office."

"It smells like bloody barf in there."

"Plug your nose."

Brendon whipped his backpack over his shoulder and groaned. Damn Maggie for crying, Angelene for being needy and Padre Diavolo for stirring up the fire.

'Do as you're bloody told. Go to Latin and gawk at Rachel's boobs, payback for Maggie's whingeing.'

He jerked open the door. The secretary glared at him and pointed her pen at a room no bigger than a cupboard. There was nothing but a desk and a chair. No windows to look out, nothing but ivory walls and the overwhelming scent of vomit. Brendon dropped onto the chair; his backpack landed with a thud on the floor.

"Henry VIII's wives, where they were born, how the marriage ended and if they had children. I suggest you start."

Brendon dug in his backpack and threw the book on the desk.

"I heard that. Get that temper in check or I'll ring your mother."

'You'd love that. You get a bloody biggie every time you see her.' He flipped through the pages and folded open his notebook. "Who was your first victim, Henry?"

He scribbled Catherine of Aragon and listed the facts. A soft ping came from within his blazer pocket. Brendon stretched his neck and glanced around the office. His bad mood lifted. Angelene was sorry for acting like a brat. Brendon turned his attention back to the assignment. Bullet point after bullet point filled his notebook until he got to Catherine Parr. Fifty minutes was up.

"I'm sure Mr. Clark would have preferred paragraphs, but you've finished it," Mr. Dawson said dryly. "What have you used instead of dashes?"

"It's the Borussia Dortmund logo."

"You're an artist. How's your temper?"

"Concentrating on Henry's wives helped."

"What have you learned?"

"Henry was a prick like my grandfather, Richard. Is that strike two? Sometimes curse words just fly out of my mouth."

"Pay attention in Latin and you'll start back at three."

Brendon scrambled from behind the desk. "I promise."

"No football highlights and tuck in your shirt."

Brendon jammed his shirt in his trousers, burst through the door and gulped fresh air, clearing the smell of puke from his nose. Bolting across the lawn, he ripped open the door and raced down the hall, grinning at Mr. Campbell. He could be a model student for fifty minutes. Some of his dad's love of academia had to be in a gene or two.

"I heard you had to sit in that room." Rachel moved her chair closer; her hair tickled his forearm.

"News travels fast."

"They were making all kinds of bets in maths. Not me. I like when you get all fired up."

"It's got me a red card, suspended and back in Taunton. It's a pain."

"You've had quite the day, knuddlebär."

An assignment floated onto the desk. Brendon glanced up at Mr. Campbell. 'I have my eyes on you,' glinted in his steely grey gaze.

"Look at the list of nouns and decide which meaning is right, then divide the nouns into declensions. Why is the end of a noun crucial?"

Brendon shifted his gaze to Rachel's bouncing breasts as she flung her hand in the air.

"I hope you are going to give us the answer and not ask what's under Brendon's toga again."

Brendon stifled a laugh. He liked Rachel's wit. She was fearless and owned an abundance of lace bras. She was a 9.75.

"It tells us if the noun is singular or plural and what role it plays in the sentence."

German, Latin, Rachel was smart too. Despite his disdain for school, he found smart girls attractive. There was more to Rachel than a round bottom and full breasts. A little stir flickered in his belly; Rachel Jones was a ten.

"Look under the desk."

Brendon leaned back and peered into her lap. She had pulled up the Dortmund, Barcelona match on her phone.

"Dawson forgave the swearing. I need all three strikes to get me to July."

"Copy my answers. If Campbell comes around, just shove my phone up my kilt."

Brendon swallowed; Padre Diavolo snickered. Her legs were creamy white.

"You want me to put my hand up your kilt?"

"I dare you."

"Can I ask you something?"

"Will I go to dinner with you? I'd love to knuddlebär."

"Are you being nice to me because you're trying to conquer this list, I keep hearing about."

She reached for his tie and ran her fingers over the silk. "I don't need to act nice to knock you off my list."

"Really."

"I see you staring at my jubblies."

Brendon scratched down an answer and glanced at the screen. It was 0-0. He liked when Rachel touched him or played with his tie. He liked it too much. It was bad enough he struggled with the warm, buzzy feeling around Angelene. Now he had to contend with flutters in his groin. Padre Diavolo whispered, '*it's just harmless fun.*' Brendon put some space between him and Rachel. It went against the code and despite his annoyance with Maggie; she was his girl. Brendon pushed Padre Diavolo out of his mind. It was easier to concentrate without him snickering in his ear.

***

Walter pulled out a leather stool and settled on it. "Isn't this pub a little trendy for you?"

David pushed a pint of lager across the bar and unfolded his napkin. "Beatrice said the steak and mushroom pie is the best in London."

Walter cradled the glass, glancing at the young crowd. "Your sixty-year-old secretary dines here?"

He took a hearty slug and plunked the glass on the shiny bar. Walter studied the menu, deconstructed dishes, reinvented British classics. It intrigued him. How does one deconstruct fish and chips? It would be a sin not placing it in a paper lined basket.

"My bash was a complete disaster."

"Everyone had a wonderful time."

"I was hoping Ang would come out of her shell and mingle. Put on that frock and be damn normal."

David picked up his spoon and cracked open the pastry lid. Rosemary and peppery steam escaped the bubbling stew.

"You could have let her wear what she wanted. She might have been more comfortable."

Walter pointed to the fish and chips and laid the board on the bar.

"Go through the same humiliation as last time. It's a damn dress. I didn't ask her to cut off her arm."

"The day you saw her in broken sandals and a dress you said came from a charity shop, did it bother you?"

"I assumed once she got a taste of Chanel and Louboutin, she'd be a new and improved Angelene."

David blew on a spoonful of pie. "Did you make the right decision? Marrying a project?"

"I love a good project. Maybe I was meant to be a bachelor."

"You're navigating your way through marriage," David said, washing the mouthful down with a swig of beer. "You're adjusting."

The barkeep set a basket before Walter. Malt vinegar wafted into his nose. He was happy the fish and chips hadn't been deconstructed.

"Have I told you about her moods? One minute she's happy, as happy as Ang can be. The next, she's pouting. She's messy, incorrigible, shy."

"Sofia is headstrong and smothering. I wouldn't want her any other way," David said, dunking a wedge of pastry into the gravy.

Walter stared into his pint. Single had been a choice for him. Random dates, the occasional steady girlfriend. He had been okay with nights alone on the sofa. Marriage was the ultimate project. He couldn't fail. He wouldn't.

"Ang is an unusual girl, no moral compass, no fixed personality. I see so much potential in her. Have you looked at her face?"

"I have, but not in the way you mean."

"She's a mix of Claudia Schiffer and Brigitte Bardot. Under that mess of hair and charity shop clothes, she's stunning."

"Have you told her this?"

Walter shook his head and sliced through the crispy batter. "I've been focusing on the negatives."

"Give it time. You'll accept Angelene's quirks and fall madly in love."

"The shopping trip didn't go well."

David laid the napkin over the bowl. "Have you shopped with Sofia? It would make anyone miserable."

"Is it so bad wanting her to look classy and respectable, not like those slappers we see at our local?"

David chuckled. "It depends on your definition of classy and respectable."

"The other day she was trying to make me an omelette. A bird landed on the windowsill, there went brekky."

"Accept all the parts of Angelene, the weird, wonderful, and give her some time to settle in before you demand so much of her."

"You're a smart man, Lord Chancellor. Too damn smart."

Walter pointed to their empty mugs and relaxed onto the stool. Caterpillar to butterfly. This was a challenge he liked, the fight to see it blossom into something beautiful. It had only just begun.

***

She was angry, spiky red.

'You shouldn't have asked him to leave school. You shouldn't be holding his hand. You're a needy, desperate girl. Shame on you Angelene Greta Hummel.'

Angelene ran her fingers over her faded yellow t-shirt, praying the colour would bleed into her red and she'd be vibrant orange.

Angelene lit a cigarette, pressed dial, and paced.

"I'm red Lisette."

"I better sit then."

"I shopped with Sofia. It was a painful experience. I missed myself even more."

"Did she pick out your clothes?"

"She suggested things," Angelene said, smoke curled around the words. "Black, everything black. Walter said black was a powerful colour. I told him black was not a colour, it is absent of light, true black doesn't exist. He hung up."

"I told you to wait. You had to run off to England."

"I'm tired of following the rules. The only time life is peaceful is when I'm with Brendon and Troy. Troy's sunshine is intoxicating, and Brendon comes at me in electric sparks."

"Angelene, you promised God you would stay away from men. You married a stranger and now, two more."

"This time will be different. I'll remember things like boundaries and rules."

"You're not good at being friends with men. You've tried, it failed, horribly."

Angelene stared into the colourless night. The cigarette dangled between her fingers. "Sofia goes into protection mode when I'm around."

"I take it one of those boys is her son. Haven't you learned anything?"

"I'll prove to God I can break the pattern and be a friend."

"The price will be hefty, being this boy's friend."

"He's worth it."

11 Taphophobia

Brendon sprawled along the sofa, laying the newspaper in his lap. His plans for the day, analyze his match, watch a Dortmund game, enjoy an empty house.

"No one in the house," Sofia said.

Brendon clasped his hands, reached overhead, and stretched his muscles. "Yes, mammina."

A smile teased Sofia's ruby-red lips. "I spoke to Mr. Dawson. You were watching football highlights again."

"He'd find any excuse to give you a bell. He's got a biggie for you."

"Who's got a biggie for my wife?"

"Mr. Dawson. The prick told me mum has a lovely shape."

David glanced at his wife's curves and smiled. "You sure you don't want to come?"

Brendon tossed a section of the newspaper on the floor, spreading out the sports section. "Antiquing in Yeovil, I'll pass. Dortmund and Bayern play today." He scanned the headlines and grinned, 'Brendon Cook is back and at the top of his game.' "Here's another for your scrapbook."

"Put it on your father's desk," Sofia said, wiggling his chin, "you look older in the photo. Shave for mammina please."

"Leave him alone," David said, tugging her arm, "you want to join us for dinner? We're meeting Kate at that Italian place on Eastgate."

"There's a freezer full of food. Football and quiet, sounds like the best bloody day ever!"

"Kate's bringing a date. He's from Dublin. Aren't you curious to meet him?"

"You can tell me about him when you get home."

"Suit yourself," Sofia said, kissing his eucalyptus scented hair, "I'm going to miss this smell."

"I'll leave you the bottle."

"Stop teasing. I hate the sound of that, leaving. It makes it seem like I'll never see you again."

"You might not if you don't stop," David said.

"Maybe I'll start hunting for homes in Dortmund."

"Isn't it time you got on the road. The M5 is crazy on a Saturday."

David rubbed Sofia's arm. "We're not buying a home in Germany. Enjoy your quiet."

"See you later, arrivederci, ti amo."

Brendon relaxed into the sofa and studied the football standings. His phone vibrated, he shot up his finger and went back to the paper. It buzzed again, Brendon grabbed it and stared; Paris St. Germaine's logo filled the screen. If he kept the conversation short, Padre Diavolo couldn't rise and convince him to visit. He pressed speaker and tossed the phone on the sofa.

"Were you ignoring me?" Her voice was raspy, untroubled, almost joyful.

"I was reading the newspaper."

"Watch football with me."

The better choice, join the Thornton family outing to the Wookey Hole Caves, play the devoted boyfriend. If he went round to Walter's, the door would open again, Angelene would be stuck in his head and Maggie would be an after thought.

Brendon tossed the newspaper on the sofa. "I'm supposed to go to Maggie's for dinner."

"I don't want to be alone."

Brendon leaned into the cushions and stared at the ceiling. "One match."

He clutched his phone and tapped it against his forehead. He would talk football, give her his own play by play, nothing more than Brendon the commentator. It was just a match, like watching football with Troy.

Guilt swept through him as he swiped his keys off the umbrella stand. Angelene was a friend, nothing more. He locked the house and trudged through the grass, flicking the pull on his hoodie. All sorts of reasons as to why this was a bad idea raced through his head: Walter could come home; his parents might decide a walk around the roses would make for a better afternoon, Troy could show up looking to play one on one. Brendon wiped his hands on his jeans, it was one match.

"Why are you standing at the end of the laneway?"

He raised a reluctant hand, his heart knocked about, pink cheeks, cherry red lips, he couldn't tear his eyes away. Brendon pushed guilt aside and rambled up the drive.

"The Dortmund match is about to start," Angelene said.

He slid out of his shoes and followed her to the sitting room.

"It's bloody boring in here. White, green, and gray, a little plain for you."

Angelene bristled and yanked two bottles of beer from the fridge. "Walter does not like my colourful walls or the patterns I picked out."

"You're a better decorator than Walt."

"Tell him that," Angelene said, holding up a bottle, "join me."

"I'm not a big drinker. I barf when I've had too many."

Angelene passed him a bottle. "Don't make me drink alone."

"One and that's it."

Brendon was crazily uncomfortable. He wasn't sure where to sit, the ottoman, the barrel chair, beside her.

"Isn't the sofa wonderful, two people can lie on it," Angelene said, running her fingers over the plush pewter velvet, "we can stretch out."

An uproar of cheering fans and overjoyed commentators took Brendon's attention from the gigantic sofa, goal for Dortmund. Brendon swallowed a mouthful, he was supposed to be watching the match, not cuddling. Annoying flutters stormed his belly, the heat from the fire penetrated his hoodie. Angelene's eyes bore into him with that 'I need to be close to you' stare. He eased onto the oversized cushions and stretched out his legs, his gaze darted nervously to the doorway. Walter could come home and catch them cuddling on the sofa for two.

"Can you hold this?" He handed Angelene the bottle and swiped his cuff over his brow. A great furnace door opened inside him; his neglected sexual fire roared to life. His skin flushed, his hands and eyes were hot. "I can't relax."

"Are you worried about Walter?"

"I'm having a cuddle with his wife."

He turned his attention to the match and pushed his body deeper into the cushions. *'I'm worried I'll feel something I shouldn't.'*

"Walter won't be home until tomorrow. He is going to something called a stag for a Monsieur Huntington."

"Dad mentioned something about that. He's, our MP."

She looked at him puzzled; her expression was adorable.

"Taunton's member of parliament."

A little wrinkle formed between her brows.

"He's getting married. A stag is a do, a party."

"Your father isn't going?"

"He's hunting for treasures with mammina."

"He loves your mother," Angelene said, wistfully.

"They're like a couple of teenagers. It's awful."

The roar of the fans exploded into the room. Brendon smiled, another goal for Dortmund.

"The keeper should have saved that one," Angelene said.

"He had no chance. No defence out front."

"I'll be watching you on the television, remembering the day you kept me company."

'We're friends, nothing more, just mates watching football.'

"You'll be busy going to charity galas and discovering the world with Walt. You'll forget about me."

"I forget to take out the garbage or put the milk back. I don't forget moments."

He held her gaze, she looked at him like it was the last time they would see one another. Time slowed, sounds muffled, his heart raced like the wings of a hummingbird. He leaned closer, applause and cheers broke through the silence and brought him back to Uncle Walt's sitting room.

"Bloody hell what a save." Brendon pushed himself deeper into the sofa, his mind whirred, had he almost kissed her?

"His dive is as impressive as yours. Does Maggie watch with you?"

"She sits with me. Football isn't her thing."

"Oh, my goodness, football is the greatest sport."

"Can you be anymore perfect? You're pretty and you love football."

Brendon had no idea where the words came from, they spilled from his mouth carelessly. It was the truth and not right.

"Walter wants me to start going to auctions and lunch with those nasty ladies, I won't do it."

"You'll make him angry."

"You have beautiful eyes. A little Mephistopheles, a little Archangel Michael. You are the knees of bees."

"I have no idea what you mean but, it's the bees' knees."

She laid her head on his arm and dragged her fingers over his. Every nerve in his body stirred and tingled. The beer, courage, Padre Diavolo, pushed him closer to her.

"Mephistopheles serves Lucifer. Michael is a warrior angel who carries a beautiful sword of light. You have both in you."

"Are you saying I'm the bloody devil?"

"We all have the devil in us, it's how you choose to play with him."

The roar of the fans thundered off the walls, she gripped his hand, the flutters gently floated.

"Did you ever watch PSG play?"

"We didn't have money for tickets. Sometimes my friend and I would sit outside the Stade de France and pretend we were in the stadium."

Sadness flooded Brendon. He had been to Chelsea matches with Walter and Kate. Manchester United with Troy, Dortmund, Bayern, the list went on.

Angelene took his beer bottle and set it on the floor. "I'm glad you came. You're my sign."

"Charlie's into that stuff. She was chuffed to know scorpio and taurus are a brilliant match. I'm a leo, and Maggie is a pisces. According to mystic Charlotte, Mags and I aren't."

"No silly," Angelene said, tracing along the veins in his hand, "I asked God for a sign that I made the right decision moving to Taunton. I saw your face when I prayed and then your lamp turned on. God answered. As for astrology, I'm a cancer, to some, quite literally."

"Bloody hell, who would say that?"

"Just know that leo and cancer are a match."

The promise to stay away dissolved. He would never forget this afternoon, watching his favourite team with the most beautiful woman he had ever known, his perfect match.

"How come you never talk about your mum?"

"She was not like Sofia, any mother for that matter."

"Do you look like her?"

He pictured a taller, blonder version with hopeless green eyes.

"Mama had dark hair. She was obsessed with old Hollywood. She was a bitch like Joan Crawford and aloof like Greta Garbo. There was always someone adoring her."

Her voice was small and tight, she let go of his hand and dug her fingernails into her forearm.

"Please don't do that."

"I told you, it's a habit."

Brendon moved her hand away and ran his thumb over the indents. "Break it."

"There's another match on."

"Bayern and Leverkusen. It'll be brilliant. Lewandowski is one of the greatest players in the Bundesliga."

"Stay please."

Maggie's dinner invitation flashed in is mind. Madre Innocente rammed her staff of guilt into his ribcage. Padre Diavolo snickered delightfully.

"No more talk about Walter or your mum. We're going to watch the match and you can help me analyze the plays so I can persuade Troy the Bundesliga is better than the Premier league."

Angelene buried her nose in his neck, his heart sputtered. "I love how you smell."

"Have you eaten?"

It was a stupid thing to ask. The flutter of her eyelashes on his neck was heating up his furnace again.

"I've smoked and drank that beer."

"Bloody hell you take lousy care of yourself. What would you like? I can make a decent fry-up."

"I would like to try fish and chips."

"You haven't tried fish and chips, bloody hell, its a British classic!"

"Walter has promised, we have yet to go."

"Would you like fish and chips?"

"You'll have to drive into town."

Brendon grabbed his hoodie and wrestled his arms through the sleeves. "I'm not getting mushy peas, they're bloody disgusting."

"What is a mushy pea? Peas should not be mush-shee."

Brendon chuckled. "No, they shouldn't."

He watched her curl into the corner of the sofa, the urge to kiss her lingered. He liked kissing. Maggie liked slow, gentle kisses without roaming hands. His first kiss had been with a girl he met on the beach in Burnham. Brendon climbed the hill and sprinted to his car. Angelene's lips, chapped, still kissable. Stay, go, weaved through his thoughts, innocent or led by his devil? *'I'm falling for her.'*

The smell of upturned earth and apple trees heavy with fruit, swept over the moors and through the car windows. The clouds had blown away, the sky was pale blue, gold glowed over the town centre. Brendon parked and stepped onto the pavement. He swung the door open, brass bells jingled, releasing the scent of canola oil and beer batter into the breeze.

"I'll be damned, what's it been, a year, two?"

Diners looked up from feasting on chips to see who John Ball was making a fuss over. Brendon's cheeks burned, he pulled up his hood.

"Hey Mr. Ball. Can I get two orders."

"Salt and malt?"

"Is there any other way?"

Brendon dragged a chair away from a table and sunk onto it. He swiped open his phone and tapped the Dortmund app, scrolling through the team news. The bells clanked, a random straw wrapper blew across the black and white checkered floor.

"Look who it is."

Brendon glanced up from the screen and forced a smile. "Bugger off Will."

"What's the Prince of Taunton doing in a greasy takeaway?"

"I could ask you the same thing."

"I don't follow that daft diet Liam gave me."

Brendon slid his phone in his pocket. "Where's your girlfriend?"

"Working. Tilly and I are just friends."

"Is that what you call it?" Madre Innocente gave him a quick jab.

Tilly wound a string of gum around her finger and smirked. "Rachel's having a bash tonight, you should come."

"I'm busy."

"Margaret got you on a short leash?"

Mr. Ball grinned and plunked a brown paper bag on the counter.

"Two orders? Who's the lucky girl?"
"None of your business."
Brendon kicked the chair under the table and rambled to the counter.
"On the house. The way you've been playing, you deserve free fish and chips for a year."
Brendon tossed twenty pounds on the counter. "I haven't played better than anyone else."
"You're a good kid."
Brendon grinned. If Mr. Ball knew what he was up to, he might change his mind.
William stared at himself in the napkin dispenser, fixed his hair and grabbed a handful. "Rachel puts on a great party."
"Are you taking Gemma or this tart."
"You're sharing lunch with that girl from the pitch. She had to have your autograph."
"Nope, now fuck off."
William jabbed a straw through the plastic lid. "Poppy McKenzie? She's been trying to get into your knickers since primary."
"Ellen Barker from French?" Tilly said.
"Who said it was a girl."
"Bets at school, you've gone off Thornton," William said.
"Have a bloody brilliant time at Rachel's."
"You're right, Willie." Tilly blew a bubble and pierced it with a talon-shaped fingernail. "He is a poofter."
"Ciao."
Brendon waved to Mr. Ball; the door jingled behind him. The sparks flitting in his belly, fizzled. Brendon slid into the car; his mind filled with excuses in case one of them opened their mouth. He could deny being at Ball's. Maggie would believe him over William and Matilda. He could be honest and tell her Angelene was alone or say Walter begged him to check in on her. Brendon turned into the farmhouse laneway, *'please have Will and Tilly get soused so they'll forget.'* He'd watch the Bayern match, eat, and go home. He'd call Maggie, be attentive and listen about her adventure at the Wookey Hole Caves. He might even throw in an, I love you. Brendon grabbed the bag, who was he kidding, he was, in like.
"The commentators said this would be the match of the day."
Angelene was smiling her sometimes smile, no hand covering it, no trembling fingers.
"Fish and chips."
He rolled his eyes at his lame remark and dropped onto the sofa beside her.
"We'll eat out of the box. No utensils, no napkins."
Brendon ripped open the grease-stained bag, releasing the warm scent of malt vinegar
"You're being a rebel today."
She puffed out her chest, scrunched her brow and wagged a finger. "All I hear is no, no, no. You'll get fat, ladies don't do that. I go into town and its hello Ms. Pratt, no Angelene, just Ms. Pratt."
"You should have kept your maiden name."
"I don't like Hummel either."
Brendon chuckled and handed her a box. She held the carton to her nose and inhaled the malty steam.

"Who's in net for Bayern?"
"Neuer. He's one of the top keepers in the Bundesliga."
"Better than you?"
"Bloody hell, yes. I still have a lot to learn."
Angelene tore into the fish, crispy bits of batter scattered across her lap. "You'll be better than Monsieur Neuer."
"Thanks for the vote of confidence."
"Your passion for the game will take you far. People notice you."
He wanted to ask her if she noticed him but kept the comment to himself, why ruin a perfect day when he knew the answer.
"I'll come to Dortmund to watch you play."
"Walter will want to visit Lukas."
"Not with Walter, just me."
Brendon clutched the box. The idea of her sitting in the stands at Signal Iduna Park was incredible and silly.
"You think Walter will let you travel to Germany alone?"
"I'll tell him I'm visiting Lisette and Yasmin; I'll take the train. I might go to Switzerland and find Roman."
Brendon nibbled a chip, A burning sensation tingled in his chest. "Who's Roman?" One point for stupidity and one for jealousy.
"Roman was one of mother's lovers."
Brendon dropped his half-eaten dinner on the table. "You were close?"
"Roman was my hopeful poppa."
"Did you not know your father?"
Angelene wiped her fingers on her shirt and tossed the empty carton in the torn bag.
"When I visit Dortmund, you can take me on a date. Imagine me, Angelene Hummel out with a handsome keeper."
"Why are you changing the subject?"
"It would be my own fairy tale, like I've been asleep for years and finally woke up."
Warmth spread over his cheeks. He forgot the 'who's your father' question. It sounded wonderful, Angelene in Dortmund, the two of them discovering the city. It was a fairy tale, a story about a girl rebelling against her demanding husband.
"Did you forget you're married?"
"Who would know?"
"That rock on your finger might give it away. If I were taking you on a date, I wouldn't want it to be a secret."
"I've always been someone's secret. It would be normal for me." She laid her cheek in his palm, a surge of electricity swept through him. "It's a beautiful story, you, and me in Dortmund. I would be tripping into my old ways."
"I'd have the prettiest girl on my arm."
She smiled the tiniest smile; he ran his thumb over her lip.
"Mama and I used to clean for the Dupont's, it was my job to straighten their travel brochures. Once the Dupont's had planned their adventure, it was never a trip or vacation, always an adventure. They would give me the brochures." She reached under the newspaper for her cigarettes and lit one. "I covered an entire wall with pictures. When mama was entertaining one of her lovers, I would go to my room and stare at it."

Brendon waved at a plume of smoke; her eyes were far away like she transported herself to one of the countries she longed to visit.

"I dreamed of the Serengeti Plains, walking through the tulips in Tivoli gardens. Neuschwanstein Castle, picking wild cornflower."

He grabbed the cigarette pack and tossed it on the island, something told him this was a two cigarette story.

"Walter can take you to all those places. He loves to travel."

Brendon scrunched the bag, stood, and stuffed it into the garbage. He went to the stove and set the kettle on the burner.

"They're just dreams."

"Dreams come true. I've wanted to play for Dortmund. I've been on loan for a year. I'll be back in July."

Brendon dropped a tea bag in the pot and leaned into the counter. Smoke rings danced around her head like a vapoury wreath, she remained far away, Holland, the Alps.

"You want to see the world, tell Walt. All it takes is money and he has plenty."

The kettle whistled, Brendon tipped water into the pot and dug in the fridge for milk. He stared at the television, watching the ball move around the pitch.

"They're going to pick up the rebound if the defence don't get it out."

"You knew Bayern were going to score."

"I'm good at reading plays. It's like a sixth sense, I feel the players vibes, I can see where the ball is going to go. When I walk onto the pitch, I know if we'll win or lose. I feel it in my stomach."

She smashed out the cigarette and stared into the cup. "It's black."

"I remembered."

"Maybe I don't want to see the world with Walter."

"Are we back to that? He's your husband. Mum and dad travel somewhere every year. They went to Morocco last spring."

"It wouldn't be fun with Walter. He would tell me how to act, dress. If we went to Italy, it would be all your mother's favourite places."

"Then you'll have to go by yourself or with your friend Lisette."

He sipped his tea, studying Neuer as he moved around the net.

"I'll start my travels in Dortmund."

"Why not the Czech Republic? You can visit Prague Castle."

She set her cup down, crawled across the couch, and snuggled into his side. His mother said there was power in a hug, a person could communicate without saying anything. He had mastered the mum hug, the friend hug. He had a hug for everyone in his life but this hug, how she tucked herself close to him and clutched his shirt like she was afraid he might slip away, was the best.

"You would pick me cornflower. You would let me wear my shortest skirt. We would drink as much beer as we wanted."

"Now you are dreaming."

"It's a beautiful dream."

A sting of warmth tugged his thundering heart and even though Madre Innocente was scolding him, he wound his arm around her.

"It would be bloody brilliant if you were in Dortmund. I'm terrified to join the first team. What if I'm bollocks and forget everything I've learned, they'd toss my contract away."

"You won't fail," Angelene said, snaking her fingers through his, "you're a star, a bright, beautiful star. I see it and it's incredible."

11 TAPHOPHOBIA

"You make my heart feel like its going to explode. I like it. I like how you make me feel."

"You've been there for me; I'll be there for you. I'll take a train, run, swim. I'd even get on an airplane, it frightened me horribly, I would do it so I could hold your hand."

Padre Diavolo whispered, *'kiss her.'* She glanced up from his chest, he pushed guilt aside, parted his lips. A knock bounced off the walls. Brendon pulled away; his gaze darted nervously around the sitting room. The knock grew louder.

"Answer the bloody door before they break it down."

Brendon rubbed his hands on his jeans, trying to digest what happened. They had been talking, she would be there for him. He was her friend, he had told himself no more visiting, Brendon swallowed, this was more than a visit.

"Go see who it is?"

Angelene dragged herself from the sofa and tiptoed to the doorway.

"Bloody hell. Go look out the window."

He listened to her shuffle across the foyer. She gasped and rushed back. "I feel like I've been buried alive. I can't breathe."

"Taphophobia." was all he could say.

"It's a terrible fear," Angelene said, clawing at her knuckles, "it's why I avoid funerals."

"What's going on? Did you not hear us?" David said.

An excuse, he needed something sharp, believable, nothing came.

"I stopped him. I went for a walk and when I got back, I heard noises."

"The house is old," David said.

Brendon glanced at his mother; she was assessing the room. What little he had eaten churned in his stomach. The highlights lit up the sitting room, two cups of tea, mussed throw pillows on the sofa for two.

"What do you mean you stopped him?" Sofia said.

"I heard a car, and I ran outside. I was scared."

"Perfect timing sweetheart."

"I was keeping Troy company at the stall. I drove by, saw Ms. Pratt."

"Its time you went home," Sofia said.

"I should look around, maybe someone is in here."

"Go home son. I'm sure it's the pipes or mice."

"I can help. What if it's a machete wielding nutter?"

"Do as your told," Sofia said, tapping her lip, "Why are there two cups of tea?"

"Wasn't I supposed to go home?"

"I offered him a cup. It's my fault."

"I'd be more upset if it was candles and wine," David said.

Driving into the car port, Brendon switched the car off and shuffled to the front door. It had been a confusing day, a lovely day. Brendon walked across the dark foyer and climbed the stairs, longing for his bed. Angelene wouldn't come to Dortmund. He stripped out of his clothes, sprawled onto the bed, and jerked the blankets over his head. He heard the front door close and Sofia's footsteps, Brendon shut his eyes and laid as still as his raging heart would allow. Dim light flooded the bedroom, he held onto his laughter, Sofia tsked the clothes he had dropped on the floor. She pulled back the blankets and ran her fingers through his hair.

"I can't lose you. What would I do?"

'I'll always be there mammina. I love you, now go away so I can dream about everything Angelene said.'

Sofia switched off the lamp, Brendon shot out his hand and touched her wrist.

"Turn it on please."

"How do you sleep with the lamp on?"

"Richard the prick has been visiting again."

Brendon snuggled the pillow. He closed his eyes and imagined Westfalenpark, a park bench and the prettiest girl sitting upon it.

***

The 'something is going to happen' feeling fluttered in Sofia's stomach. From within the manor, the sound of tinkling piano keys danced on the draught. She recognized Fur Elise; it had been Elizabeth's favourite piece to play.

"We need the house blessed again. Brendon's been sleeping with his lamp on. Richard the prick has been visiting."

David played a haunting melody, his fingers gentle on the keys. "I made you coffee, I know you prefer it over tea."

"Thank you darling. Why did you stop?"

"Music hasn't sounded the same since mum died," David said. "I can feel her hands on mine when I play, smell her lily of the valley perfume. I wish you could have spent more time with her."

"I knew her long enough to know she was a good woman who deserved better than Richard."

"Do you remember the summer you stayed here?"

"How could I forget. My father pouted for days."

"It was the best summer of my life. Richard had flown to Copenhagen for business or a lover. Mum was her old self."

Sofia cozied into David's arm; her heart swelled with memories. "Mother promised papa, you'd be a perfect gentleman."

"And I was."

"We ate in the garden, Elizabeth talked about planting roses, she'd be happy."

"Mum played Fur Elise, we danced."

"You stepped on my toes."

David laughed. "The number of times I squashed your foot under mine, you still smiled, even with bruised toes."

"We've been through a lot, haven't we?"

"We've faced many storms."

"What do we do about hurricane Angelene?" Sofia said, sipping her coffee, "I looked in her eyes tonight. There was this desperate need to be forgiven."

"You haven't liked any of Walt's girlfriends."

"Only Anastasia. She couldn't keep her hands off Brendon."

"There's a childlike quality about Angelene like she doesn't feel safe in the adult world."

"You feel sorry for her, don't you?"

"Sometimes."

"What does Walter know about her family? What if her father was worse then Richard?"

David closed the cover, picked up his cup and sipped. "I don't think she knows who her father is?"

"Even better, daddy issues. Don't you see the incredible sadness?"

"All the more reason to welcome Angelene and ease her into that group of women you choose to be friends with." David finished his tea and wrapped his arm around her. "I'm tired. All this talk of Angelene and ghosts has exhausted me."

"Too tired for romance?"

"I'm not that tired," David said, glancing at the piano, "I wish things could have been different for mum."

"All Elizabeth wanted was for you to be safe and loved. She died knowing her wish came true."

They walked hand in hand, Sofia rubbed David's arm as he shivered against her.

"Has Richard moved from Brendon's room to the foyer?"

"Every room in this house holds a chapter of my life, not many are worth reading."

"There must be a happy memory somewhere. The ballroom where we danced. What about here, think."

David scanned the foyer. "All I can hear is Richard calling me a brat."

"Think harder."

"Signal Iduna Park, 80,000 fans sitting in the imaginary stands."

"Every night you came home from work, Brendon would be playing football here."

"He'd trip over that Dortmund jersey."

"You see, not every room holds a bad memory."

"Some are good, like the ones in our bedroom."

"Cheeky Lord Chancellor."

"Tu sei I amore della mia vita."

"You're the love of my life."

The feeling fluttered in Sofia's chest. If the walls could talk, Rosewood manor would have quite the story to tell. She was sure Angelene had one too.

***

Angelene paced.

"There are no ghosts, no creatures lurking in the attic. The ghosts are in me."

12 Sehnsucht

Morning came at Walter, hard and forceful like the thump in his head. He dropped a duffel bag of dirty clothes and followed the scent of brewed coffee. The kitchen sparkled; the floors shined. If there had been an intruder, he had been neat. Filling a mug, Walter sipped and made a face. The brew could burn a hole in one's chest. He sighed and glanced up the stairs at the brown walls. Angelene had called it chocolate, he called it mud. Plumes of sandalwood and cigarette smoke trickled down the hall. He gulped the coffee, erasing the pungent smells from his throat.

"Your cigarette has burned to the filter."

Angelene stood in front of the easel, paintbrush in hand, cigarette dangling precariously from her mouth. He turned his attention to the canvas. A cloaked figure with bony hands clawed at a girl in a yellow dress. Alarm bells rattled in his head.

"Can't you paint joyful things?"

He dragged a spindle-back chair across the weathered parquet and settled onto it.

"It's all I know."

Walter sipped and coughed. "Look around you. The view is lovely."

Angelene dabbed crimson paint across the child's fingers, the blobs ran onto the wilting flowers.

"Are you going to tell me about the intruder?"

"I went for a walk. When I came home, I heard scratching and rattling. You have ghosts."

"They live at Rosewood manor. Could be rats."

She dunked the brush in a jar of cloudy water and sort through a can of brushes. "It sounded like footsteps. I got myself all worked up."

"If you painted happier things, you might not have imagined a nutter roaming around our home."

"What I paint has nothing to do with the sounds I heard."

He followed the slow rise of her chest, locking his inquisitive gaze on her unimpressed stare

"Why are you staring at me?"

"I learned about kinesics interrogation from a friend."

"Was her name Dominique? Madeline?" Angelene said, chewing on the end of the paintbrush, "do you think I'm lying, Admiral Pratt?"

Walter pressed his lips to the mug and sucked down the syrupy, acrid brew. "I wasn't an Admiral. I was Lieutenant Commander with the Special Boat Service."

"Did you sail magical ships?"

"The Special Boat Service is an elite counter-terrorist unit. The operations I took part in were highly classified. We were the best of the best."

Angelene swept grey paint through the cloak. "Should I be impressed?"

"Most people are, then again, you aren't most people."

He cradled the mug against his chest and walked to the table cluttered with canvases and tubes of acrylics. Walter shuffled through drawings of smirking gnomes, wicked fairies, and stopped at an unfinished sketch of a man's back.

"Back to the intruder."

Angelene groaned, swishing the brush in the water. "Enough talking. You're giving me a headache."

"Why Brendon? Why not call David or me?"

"I ran outside, Brendon drove by." Angelene stepped back from the easel and studied the painting. "It could have killed me."

"Rats? Rusty pipes?"

"The stag was more important than me."

She threw up her hands and rushed from the room.

"I'm here now. Give me a kiss."

"I don't kiss when I'm angry."

"You don't kiss at all. Stop running and show me you're happy I'm home."

He met her halfway down the stairs, cupped her chin and kissed her.

"You need to be kissed; you'll like it."

"Should I call you Rhett Butler?"

"You're familiar with Gone with the Wind?"

"I didn't like the book. Scarlet O'Hara was a brat."

"Does she remind you of yourself? Paint something pretty while I'm at the pub," Walter said. "I'll check for rats when I get back. You can hold the ladder."

Angelene splashed coffee in a mug, stomped to the fridge and poured cream. "Aren't you afraid I might leave you in the attic to rot?"

Walter rinsed his mug and set it in the sink. "Pretty things, trees, the moors, the roses up at the manor."

"You can control what I wear, not what I paint. It helps me."

"Bloodied creatures, terrified little girls?"

"It's a release."

"What have you seen in your twenty-five years to make you paint such horrific things?"

"I don't want to talk about it."

"One more kiss and I'll leave you alone,"

She pursed her lips together and squished her eyes closed.

"I was Lieutenant Commander Ms. Pratt. Think about that when I'm gone."

***

Brendon wandered into the kitchen in rumpled shorts, a sleeveless t-shirt, his hair more mussed than usual. The air held the warm odours of coffee and toasted ciabatta. Sofia buttered toast and stared thoughtfully out the window. Muted gold flickered through the forest canopy, casting a glittering sheen across the bark. The forest looked pretty, not the formidable monster she had steered him clear of.

"Jeans and a pullover, how pedestrian mammina. It suits you."

"Flattery will get you everywhere."

Brendon grabbed yogurt and berries from the fridge. He popped the lid, dumped the berries over it, and flopped onto a stool.

"Why did you stop at Walter's? I don't believe the intruder story." Sofia poured coffee and shoved the mug towards him.

Brendon dropped his spoon. It clattered against the container, flinging a blueberry across the island and onto Sofia's plate.

"I just woke up. Maggie's been blowing up my phone. We'll talk later."

"Don't get angry," Sofia said, popping the blueberry in her mouth. "It was strange, don't you think?"

"Maggie ringing my phone and texting obsessively?"

Sofia tore the toast in two and pointed a triangle at him. "Who would wander around Taunton Road at night?"

"Walter's house is bloody creepy."

"Let your father and I worry about Angelene. She drinks too much, smokes too much. You don't need to be around a woman like that."

Brendon pushed the container away; a slow grumble rose from his throat.

"You should be concerned about the girls hanging around the pitch."

"Rosie Thornton calls them the tarts of Taunton."

"I don't know any tarts."

A series of chirps rose from the depth of his pocket. He fumbled for his phone and grumbled. "This is the fifth time Maggie's rang. There's about a hundred texts."

"My goodness, you're grumpy. What's the matter?"

"Your questions, bloody Maggie. I'm about to explode."

"Do that breathing thing. I can't have you exploding all over my kitchen."

He took a small breath, wrestling with the tie on the bread bag. "Jesus Christ."

"Give it here," Sofia said, tugging the bag from his hand. "Call Troy, kick the ball around until you simmer down. Eat your yogurt."

Brendon dragged the container with this spoon. He didn't know what was causing the sparks. Madre Innocente and her staff of guilt. Padre Diavolo and his pitchfork of temptation, the incessant beeping, his mother's questions.

"You don't like Ms. Pratt, do you?"

"I'm finding it hard to get to know her. She flits about trying not to draw attention to herself. All she's doing is drawing attention to herself."

"You didn't answer the question."

Sofia set down the plate, walked to the fridge, pouring him a glass of milk. "I can't get past this feeling you and your father dismiss."

A muffled ping filled the air. Brendon bit into the toast and grimaced.

"I can see why you're annoyed. Your phone has beeped five times in the last ten minutes."

"Maggie invited me for dinner."

"You hung around the Spence's stall instead? That wasn't nice."

Brendon chugged the milk and ripped a kitchen towel from the roll. "You've never had dinner at Mags. Jack pings food at me. Ms. Thornton glares and Mr. Thornton takes the mick out of me for being a toff."

"I've told you a hundred times, you accept the invitation and tolerate it."

His phone chirped; Brendon dropped his toast on the plate. "Jesus Christ."

"Stop saying that."

"Since when do you care about insulting Jesus?"

"It's God I have the problem with. He gave me you; I think it was God. It might have been Satan with that mouth of yours."

"I think dad might have had more to do with it. You can thank Richard the prick for my mouth."

"I wish you had inherited Richard's love of learning and not his temper," Sofia said, snuggling his neck. "A hug used to calm you. Your shoulders are tight."

"I do have a love for learning. Ask me about Dortmund, the Bundesliga, what it takes to be a great keeper." He reached out from beneath Sofia's embrace and took a bite. "You're making it very hard for me to finish my brekky."

"Promise me you'll leave Angelene alone."

"No more Ms. Pratt."

As he said the words, Madre Innocente jabbed his heart. Padre Diavolo patted his back. He would try.

"She scares me."

Brendon swirled his spoon through the yogurt. "Nothing scares you."

"That forest frightens me. I hate flying."

"I can understand the forest but flying, you've been all over the world."

"Your temper scares me. Those horrible things Angelene paints."

"She's just an odd girl you didn't get to meet before Walt married her."

"What's that supposed to mean? I have no control over Walter."

"You would have done everything in your power to stop him from putting a ring on her finger."

"You're a cheeky thing."

"And you're bloody squishing me."

"Every time you walk out that door, I can't breathe. Please, no more visiting Angelene."

"Bloody hell, mammina, I won't visit her or go into the forest. I'll practice my breathing, use a bloody condom."

Sofia smooched her lips against his cheek. "Do you know how happy you make me?"

"Even when I'm cheeky?"

"You came into my life and filled all my empty spots. Ti amo."

"Ich Liebe dich, mammina."

"You'll pay attention to some girl, not Madame Lafavre. Ruby danced in the Paris Opera Ballet."

"Rachel looks better."

"I suppose you told me you loved me."

"I did. Rachel is teaching me all sorts of important stuff."

Sofia arched an eyebrow and poured coffee into her mug. "I love you, is important?"

"Rachel's always telling me she loves me." He scraped up the last of the yogurt and tossed his spoon into the sink. "She taught me another word, Sehnsucht."

Sofia opened a moleskin journal and clicked her pen. "I'm afraid to ask what it means."

"It means an intense yearning for something."

Brendon rinsed the container, opened the cupboard, and dropped it in the recycling bin. The sofa for two, her eyelashes tickling his neck, her love of football. *'I wonder if she's thinking of me.'*

Madre Innocente struck his heart. She was probably enjoying breakfast with her husband, spinning a tale about the mysterious intruder.

"Make sure you apologize to Maggie. No wonder Rosie doesn't like you."

Brendon glanced at Sofia's agenda, aperitivo, antipasti, formaggi e frutta, and dolce.

"Planning an afternoon tea?"

"It's my turn to have the girls over," Sofia said, listing prosecco and olives. "Your phone beeped again. You best be on your way."

"See you later mammina."

Sofia looked up from her notebook and pointed at his rumpled shorts. "You haven't showered."

"I brushed my teeth. If I don't get over to Mags, she'll have either chewed through her lip or gnawed her bloody fingers off."

"Put a hoodie on."

"I set it on the banister."

His mother, the most intimidating woman he knew, feared Angelene. Brendon jerked on his hoodie, puzzled. The only feeling he got from Angelene was a pleasant simmering in his belly. Angelene was more afraid of herself.

Suki crouched on the bricks, her tail swishing. The cat took a cautious step, wiggled its bottom, and pounced on a bug.

'Be like the cat, tread bloody lightly.' He'd need a handful of compliments, kisses, and his dimpled grin to avoid an aggravated Maggie. He raised his hand to knock, the door swung open. Brendon dragged her into his arms. Her chewed fingers were damp against his back.

"I didn't think you were going to show. You never answered a text or rang me."

Brendon soaked in the silence. Sehnsucht, blossomed, glowed, expanded, suffocated.

"Where's everyone?"

"Mum and dad took nanna for fish and chips. I should be there. We should be there."

"We'll bloody go then."

Brendon sagged into the wall; his keys dug into his palm. The pain distracted him from the sparks.

"If you would have answered your phone or come round for dinner, you would have known."

"I'm sorry. I watched football and fell asleep."

Maggie scraped the thumbnail off her tongue and flicked it towards him. "Have I done something? William's acting dodgy. The largest bet at school, William fancies the gum chewing tart."

Brendon counted the shoes at the door, twelve pairs. The scent, guilt, was strangling him.

"You couldn't text to say you were having a kip?"

Brendon rubbed the indents on his palm.

"Have you gone off me?"

He searched for the words she wanted to hear, he loved her; he fancied her, she was pretty. The urge to run tingled through his limbs. He could tell her he had to meet his dad and Walter at the pub or Troy at the pitch. Aching heat crawled down his back. He tore off his hoodie, bunched it in his hands and wandered into the front room.

"Charlie says when boys act distant, they want to break up."

"I haven't gone off you."

"Of course, you haven't. I'm worrying about nothing."

He flung Batman to the floor, plunked onto the flattened cushions, and reached for the remote. Her pout returned.

"I can't watch football highlights."

"I want to talk."

Brendon dropped the remote on a crumb covered magazine and stretched his legs across the cluttered coffee table.

"The Dortmund match was bloody brilliant. I'd like to study the keeper's saves."

"They loop through the highlights all day. We need to plan what we'll wear to the Christmas formal."

"I'll wear my black Armani."

"Your navy suit is ace," Maggie said, nibbling a mauled fingernail. "Do you fancy a snog?"

"What if your parents come home?"

"Charlie says a snog is the best way to end a row."

He drew her into his arms, her lips tasted like cotton candy, her body, warm. There were no stirs in his belly, no heat in his groin.

You would pick me cornflower. Imagine me with a handsome football player.

The almost kiss with Angelene played in his mind. He peeled back Maggie's blouse and slid his hand over her cotton clad breast. Gripping the collar of his shirt, Brendon yanked it over his head and dropped it to the floor. Tingles took over the sparks and invaded all the ignored parts of his body. Troy had instructed, one afternoon in the dressing room, he needed to kiss Maggie gently, add a bit of tongue and slowly dry hump until she was panting and begging for it. Maggie was not panting or begging. There were no moans. She hadn't clawed at his back in the throes of ecstasy. He pulled his mouth away; her cheeks were bright pink, she blinked as if something was stuck in her eye. Brendon tugged at the button on her jeans, just like he expected, pink cotton.

"Do you have a condom?"

"Why would I bring one? I'll pull out."

"How will you know when you're...."

"A guy knows when it's going to happen. Stop bloody talking or I'll lose my biggie."

He wiggled at the waistband of his shorts and smothered her mouth with his.

"That's how mum got pregnant."

"Don't fucking do this again."

"My parents will be home soon. You know Jack can only sit for so long before he's bouncing all over the restaurant."

"Can we go to your room?"

Maggie wiggled from beneath him, hunkered into the arm of the sofa, and dragged her blouse over her chest.

"You're not allowed upstairs."

"Bloody hell, I'm about to explode. Can't you give me a wank?"

"Go to the loo and do it."

All the lovely warmth puddled at his feet. He was empty, unsatisfied. A different heat rushed through him, blazing with sparks.

"How can you be gagging for it, then say no. Charlie told me she gets tingly, don't you?"

"I wasn't gagging for it. You don't even have a condom."

"You can't keep saying no."

"You want it so bad. We'll go to Vivary Park and do it in the rear seat of your car."

"Whatever."

He jerked his shirt over his head and dragged his hoodie from between the cushions. Sparks whizzed through his body; it was hard to breathe.

I would fly home and take a train. We would walk hand in hand.

He could feel Angelene's hand in his, smell her perfume, he missed her, sehnsucht.

"Before you leave for Germany."

"Should I ask Kate to write up a contract?"

He ignored the sigh, raised his hands above his head and rapped his knuckles on the wall.

"We can try in Burnham. I'm more relaxed away from home."

"Family only. Mum's rules."

The lie slipped out, easily. He stared at his hands; his muscles tensed. What was he thinking? Angelene would be there with Walter. There would be no walks on the beach or time alone. Maggie might be an excellent distraction.

"Can't you stay home?"

"Walt and Angelene are coming. She's having a hard time settling in. Dad thought a weekend away would help her feel part of the family."

"Is it because I said no again?"

Brendon placed his hands behind his head and stared at the ceiling. The sparks settled, his breathing slowed, Angelene resurfaced, smiling her sometimes smile.

"I'm going to go."

Brendon shoved off the sofa, wincing as he stepped on Batman's arm. He crooked his toe under the toy and flung it across the room. "My nanna wants to see you."

"She doesn't like me anymore than your parents. She greets me with, hello numpty."

"You can watch the daft highlights."

"I'm not in the mood to get stuff thrown at me."

Maggie sniffed; her lips twitched in a smile.

"Will you give me a bell later?"

Brendon kissed her cheek and flashed her a 'please understand' smile.

"Everything is fine. I want to watch the highlights in peace before dad harps on me to do my homework."

He flung up his hand in a meager wave and grabbed his cell. She would make him feel better.

***

Angelene stood at the mouth of a path. The branches of the beech and poplar trees had bent into a natural arch, knotting, and twisting into a magnificent green canopy. Angelene stepped under the claustrophobic tangle of branches. The breeze brought the smell of wild mint and damp leaves.

"I came as fast as I could."

"I couldn't breathe."

"I'm feeling the same. Walter has been hovering over me, complaining about my paintings." Angelene ran her sweater over her face and clasped her hands. "Did you argue with Maggie?"

"I got frustrated, and she started sniffing, which means she's going to cry."

"Your eyes are so dark. I think I've found my pretty thing to paint."

"I'm sure Walter would appreciate that."

"What's troubling you? We're here for each other, non."

"I don't want you to think I'm a bloody pig."

Angelene dragged his arm across her lap and laid her hand over his. "It would take a lot for me to think of you as anything but beautiful."

"I need to respect the bloody code. I shouldn't be pushing Maggie into doing anything she isn't comfortable doing."

"Are you talking about sex? I'm the last person you should talk to."

"If we were a couple, would you, you know, want to…" Brendon shifted in the seat, "do that."

"Is Maggie a virgin?" Angelene touched his crimson cheek and smiled. "Are you?"

"Will was fourteen. Troy was sixteen."

"You think sex will make you a man?"

"It'll stop my friends from taking the piss."

"Your light is more beautiful now."

"My light isn't getting me humped."

"You must respect her. Don't force her."

"I'm going to bloody burst."

Rain fell through the webbed canopy, tapping a soothing rhythm on the car. Angelene traced along the vein in his arm, her heart wrenching as old wounds opened.

"Don't dim your light because you're horn-nee. Stay away from temptations, like that flirty girl at school."

"Be patient, right?"

"Wait for Maggie. It will mean the world to her."

"We both needed to run away from someone today."

"We're so different, yet so similar." Angelene traced along his vein. "Instead of a Tale of Two Cities, we're a tale of two people. Au revoir, mon ami."

"I'll drive you home."

"I enjoy walking in the rain. I would hate Walter to question why we're together."

"I was driving home from Mags and saw you. Mention the code, he'll understand."

"Do you feel better?"

"I'm bloody randy but, yes."

"Oh, my goodness, think about football."

"I'm just being honest, mon chou."

Angelene giggled softly and touched the nape of his neck. "Where did you learn that?"

"A French exchange student, Selena, she called me mon chou. The other, Raisa, used to yell mon petitou every time she saw Troy. He had bruised nipples for weeks."

Déjà vu overwhelmed her like they had met in a past existence. The fleeting moment of alignment was perfect, eerie.

"I wish we could watch the highlights together. You really watched the match, not pretended to."

"My friend, the boy with liquid blue eyes, told me a person knows they're in love when they can't experience anything without wishing that person was there to see it, too. He showed me all his favourite places in Paris."

"Are you saying I'm in love with you? Bloody hell, I don't love Maggie."

"I don't love Walter, so we have something else in common. Hold on to your light. Once it's dim, it doesn't take much for it to fade out. See you soon."

A prayer of forgiveness screamed in Angelene's head. She rambled down the road, looking for pretty things. Prickly brambles poked at her. All around her was misty grey. The wisteria wept as she hurried along the walkway.

"How was your walk?" Walter said, handing her a cup of tea.

"The air is lovely here. I can smell autumn coming."

"Would that be Spence farm?"

"No silly. I can smell the apples and the soil," Angelene said, sipping her tea.

"Goldfinger is on the telly. Would you like to watch it?"

Angelene rubbed the chill from her arms, smiling a practiced smile, "Is it a documentary about you?"

Walter brushed his lips over her temple, chuckling. "It's a James Bond film with Sean Connery. The only true James Bond."

"I know the books. I've never seen a movie."

It was getting easier to play normal and be a wife. She had twisted Brendon into a mixture of colours so she could be Walter's wife. She had a habit of twisting things, squeezing tight, until they strangled.

She flopped onto the sofa and buried herself into the cushions and pillows.

"David said Brendon's been having some trouble with Margaret."

She knew the answer but refrained from saying it, conversations she'd had with Brendon could slip.

"Do you not like Maggie?"

It was an odd question, Angelene studied Walter's face, he was neither puzzled nor surprised.

"It doesn't matter whether or not I like her. Margaret is a bit of a bore. Brendon would do better with a girl with fire in her belly, someone wild."

A strange numbness tingled down Angelene's spine and lashed out at her heart. The weird prickles marched through her body and settled in her fingers, yearning, and itching for his light.

"A femme fatale?"

Walter laughed and set down a plate of lemon macaron, "Pardon me?"

"A femme fatale, a seductress. You want a woman who uses her parts to entice and enchant?"

Walter settled onto the sofa, dragging her into his chest, "Why would you want pleasant and innocent when you could have a wild fire blazing at your fingertips?"

"Maggie is a nice girl, respectable." "Now that I think of it, nice girls can come in some incredibly sexy packages."

Angelene shook the tingles from her fingers and plucked a cookie from the plate, "So can the devil."

"You are the most devout person I know, and you mention the devil." Walter said with a snort, "I have yet to see a horned red monster impaling the sinners of Taunton. The devil does not exist."

"He's always present," Angelene said, touching her tongue to the lemony filling, "Sometimes he is incredibly attractive, the most beautiful thing you've ever seen. Other times, he wears a disguise of magnificent light. He is your enemy prowling around like a roaring lion looking for someone to devour, Peter 5:8. I have seen him. I have watched him fall."

Walter sipped his tea, running a hand over her leg, "This is why I don't put faith in religion, too much storytelling and condemnation. It's a about making choices, not the devil made me do it. It's an excuse to appease guilt."

"The devil lives in all of us. I believe that."

"You have lived through some terrible things little bird. Your memories are your devil. It's that voice in your head, not Satan."

The voices in her head were her saboteur and ruled by Lucifer. The devil was real and alive, burning to get out. She had seen him hovering over Brendon and in herself every time she looked in the mirror.

"You have to stop listening to those voices. Have you not looked in the mirror?"

'It's my disguise, my devil playing dress-up.' She snuggled into Walter's chest, all the talk about the devil, Brendon and Maggie had exhausted her spirit, tangled her thoughts, and drained her yellow to gray.

"All this talk of the devil has frightened you little bird?"

"Please don't call me that. It used to mean something, it doesn't anymore."

"It suits you. You sound like a little bird when you talk, you peck away at your food and flit about like you are just learning to fly. It's endearing."

Angelene breathed in the peppery scent of his cologne and pointed to her tea, "I don't want to talk about me anymore, it makes me anxious and uncomfortable." Walter handed her the cup and she sipped, "Tell me more about James Bond."

"He is highly intelligent and cunning. One may see him as arrogant, manipulative, or hot tempered. I see him as a man that pushes himself to the limit, sets goals and is very loyal to his institutions. I admire that."

"In other words, you are James Bond Monsieur Secretary of Defence, Lieutenant Commander."

Walter laughed, kissing her cheek, "We have some similar qualities. Bond is a lone wolf, I'm a people person."

"We are the extrovert and the introvert."

"What's wrong with that? I can bring the best out in you, and you can reign me in a little."

Angelene smiled softly, it was an interesting way to put it. He would have to dig very deep to find the best in her and she doubt anyone could reign him in. Taking Walter's hand, Angelene stared at his palm.

"What do you see?"

There were breaks in the main line slicing through his palm, islands, and chain structures. She ran her finger over her cross, masking the uneasy look with a grin, "What do you think I see? Fortune, success, golden fingertips." Mère de tous les diables said.

13 Stealing Light, Stealing Breath

Maggie handed Charlotte a basket of clothes and flopped onto Troy's bed.

"Troy has more pictures of you than Man U posters. It must be nice to rate higher than a football club."

Charlotte slid a stack of jeans on the dresser and flicked her hair over her shoulder. "Doesn't Brendon have pictures of you in his room?"

"He has one. It's usually knocked over."

The door creaked open; Maggie grinned at a younger version of Troy. While Brian had Evelyn Spence's sandy blonde hair and serious grey eyes, Callum, Troy, and Gavin inherited Harrison's chocolate brown hair and twinkly blue eyes.

"Shall I ring Mr. Dawson? Let him know you didn't barf," Callum said. He grinned mischievously and pointed to Maggie. "You don't have cramps."

"This match is important to crumpet. He expects me there," Charlotte said, picking a t-shirt off the floor and holding it to her nose, "I'll tell you bunked off too."

"I guess all three of us faked stuff today," Callum said, leaning towards her, "You want to stay here and be my ring girl?"

"Are you chatting Charlie up?"

Maggie grabbed her purse and grinned at Callum's red cheeks.

"Troy would have me by the goolies if I did that."

"I adore you," Charlotte said, ruffling his hair. "Take it easy on Brian when he gets home."

"You should have seen the Piledriver. Are you coming for dinner tonight?"

"Your mum is making pie and mash. I never miss that."

"Can I sit beside you? You be in the middle between Troy and I?"

"What would your girlfriend think?" Charlotte said.

"I broke it off. She smelled like cough medicine, tasted like it too."

"I thought my brother's crush was bad," Maggie said.

"Chloe Burton was talking about you."

"Are you telling me a porkie? She smells like blackcurrant jam."

"I heard her," Maggie said, giggling into Charlotte's shoulder, "she said you have a dishy smile."

"She likes that you're taller than the other boys, just like my little crumpet, tall, lean, and twinkly."

"Blooming brilliant," Callum said, dreamily.

They left Callum and his crimson cheeks, skipping to the car. Maggie flopped onto the seat, humming along to the radio.

"I need to put some lippy on. This acting ill does nothing for my looks."

Maggie tossed Charlotte a tube of lip-gloss, gasping. "Charlie, stop."

Charlotte jammed the car into park. They scrambled from the car.

"Ms. Pratt, are you okay?"

"I didn't hit you, did I?"

"It was my fault. I was daydreaming about the house on the sea that's really a bay."

"Are you hurt?"

"Daddy will kill me if I dent his car," Charlotte said, examining the bumper.

"I'm fine," Angelene said, glancing over Maggie's shoulder, "Were you visiting the cows?"

"I was doing some laundry..."

Maggie tugged at Charlotte's sleeve and shook her head. "Charlie felt ill, and I have cramps. Troy's house is the closest."

"Il est mon soleil."

A chill prickled Maggie's skin. She pulled her blazer tighter around herself. "Troy, is your sun?"

"His smile lights up the world, painting everything gold."

"Babes has a dishy smile."

"Your words are pink and you, Maggie, are cherry pink and white."

Maggie laughed nervously and took two steps back.

"It's the way I see people," Angelene said. "When Charlotte talks about Troy, the words are pink, that's love."

"I love my babes."

Maggie knocked her elbow against Charlotte's arm. "We've missed kick-off."

"What does love feel like?"

A strange flash struck Angelene's eyes, Maggie pawed her honey-blonde hair. Something felt wrong, but not wrong all at the same time.

"Don't you love Mr. Pratt?"

"I love Walter's hands. They're powerful and not in the sense they're big, more like they build beautiful things. He smells like cardamom and pepper, like a man who has travelled, like a man I once knew."

Maggie hooked her arm through Charlotte's. The chill rippled down her spine. Angelene was smiling a pleasant 'we're friends aren't we' smile, yet her presence was snowy and bracing.

"I may have felt something once. It was odd and made me extremely uncomfortable. I ran from it to Sacre-Coeur Basilica and asked God to help me understand. You both should know what love feels like."

Maggie tugged Charlotte's arm. "You tell her, Charlie, so we can go."

"It feels like home, safe and comfortable. You miss them when they aren't around, like right now. I miss crumpet."

13 STEALING LIGHT, STEALING BREATH

"I once knew someone who made every second of the day mean something. I lost him."

"I wish we could stay and talk, but we have to get to the pitch."

"Does Brendon feel like home?"

Maggie stumbled into the bumper. *'She wants something of mine.'*

"You take care of my sunshine. You hold the key to his light. If you hurt... a bientôt."

Maggie gripped Charlotte's hand. They scrambled back to the car, dove onto the seats, slamming their hands on the locks.

"Did she threaten you?"

"She's a bleeding nutter Magpie."

The drive to the pitch was quiet. The look in Angelene's eyes haunted Maggie, longing, desperation, sadness. She couldn't put a finger on it.

"Babes is going to be so upset I missed kick-off."

Maggie tugged her purse over her shoulder and grabbed a blanket from the rear seat.

"I doubt Brendon even noticed."

They slid their tickets under the glass, smiled shaky smiles, and edged their way to the seats.

"I'm freezing Magpie, share the blanket with me."

Maggie shook it out, winding it around them. "I feel the same way. It isn't even cold today."

The look in Angelene's eyes lingered, *'stealing light, stealing breath.'* One look from Angelene and she had come undone. It was scary to think someone so tiny could have so much power over her. Maggie snuggled closer and focused on a bigger problem.

"If my mum finds out, I told a lie to get out of classes, she'll murder me."

"Margaret Thornton would never tell a porkie. Poor little muffin with cramps."

"I saw the secretary's face. She didn't believe we were both ill?"

"I had a prop. Ms. Baxter would be chuffed at my performance."

"What did you do?"

"I dumped the fish pie in a Tesco bag and mixed in some milk. The smell was disgusting."

Maggie closed her eyes and breathed away the flutters upsetting her belly. "I'm done with this month's Cosmo." She pulled the magazine out of her purse and handed it to Charlotte. "I didn't read the whole thing. The last few pages were stuck together."

"It's babes' spunk. We read the article, 'Twenty positions to blow his mind.' I gave him a wank."

Maggie scrunched her nose and groaned. "I touched that disgusting stuff. You could have warned me."

Charlotte pressed open the pages and pointed to a pink silhouette on her hands and knees, a blue silhouette behind it. "Wouldn't you like to try that?"

"Not very romantic. Your bum stuck up in the air."

"It's not my favourite. This one is."

Maggie studied the pink silhouette straddling the blue one. "Do you just sit on it? Doesn't it hurt to have his thingy shoved all the way up there?"

"You're the sweetest muffin. It feels brilliant. I can look at my crumpet the whole time. He has the cutest 'O' face."

"I've seen 'O' faces in movies; they look daft."

"You don't know what you're missing."

"I forgot to do the quiz." Maggie hooked a ragged fingernail under the page and flicked the magazine open. 'Are you toxic?' jumped out in vibrant, red writing.

'Stealing light, stealing breath, stealing Charlie's sunshine,' seared through Maggie's brain.

"You're not toxic, Magpie. Toxic people have deep wounds. Nothing bad has happened to you unless you count Jack."

Maggie glanced at the first question, *'do you discover people's weaknesses and use them against them? You know Charlie loves Troy. You knew if you threatened her, she'd buckle. I saw Charlie's face. You scared her.'*

Maggie pulled out her glasses and pushed them over her nose. *'Do you regularly play the victim? Brendon's always running to you, falling for the pathetic, poor me pout.'*

"Stop with the quiz. You need to read the article on sexual positions. Start with missionary, you'll love it."

'Do you always have something sad to say? She's a spiritual vampire.'

"Maggie." Charlotte closed the magazine, tucked it in her purse, and pulled out her cell phone. "You're not a toxic person. You're the sweetest muffin. Which I'm sure Brendon would love to dive into."

"I thought I was ready on Sunday; I couldn't do it. He got mad, then I got mad at myself for thinking I should just do it to make him happy."

Charlotte scrolled through the gallery, tapping on a picture of Troy. "It shouldn't be that confusing. Do you want my advice?"

"If it involves me getting on all fours, then no."

"Wait until the Cook's have gone to bed and sneak into Brendon's room. You'll hear the bay outside his window, it'll be very romantic."

"I'm not going to Burnham on Sea."

Charlotte held up her phone, aimed it at Troy, snapping a series of photos. "You always go."

"Not this time."

"That attacker is going to run right into my crumpet." Charlotte dropped her cell in her lap, covered her eyes, and peeked through her fingers. "Not his hair!"

The whistle blew, the referee waved a yellow card at the Hayes player.

"Ms. Cook wants a family weekend."

"That shows him, nasty wanker, elbowing babes."

"Brendon told me the Pratt's are going," Maggie said, eyeing Charlotte's gallery. "How many photos do you have now? A thousand?"

"You're one to talk. You filled your bedroom with pictures of Brendon," Charlotte said, snapping a photo. "Here comes that attacker again!"

"Brendon will make the save," Maggie said soberly. "Don't you think it's weird, Ms. Cook making Brendon go?"

"Hayes has been in our end for twenty minutes now. Babes will be too exhausted for a snog."

"Are you listening to me?"

"Of course, luv. Babes is playing brilliantly; I'll be in Manchester yet."

"Ms. Cook likes when I come to Burnham. We go shopping and have lunch at a posh restaurant. You know the type where there's nothing on the plate but a leaf of lettuce and a blob of sauce."

Maggie gnawed at her nails, tugging, and pulling on the loose cuticles.

"You know what I think," Charlotte said, jerking Maggie's hand away.

"I'm not sure you're entitled to an opinion. You haven't taken your eyes off the pitch."

"The next eleven months are going to be hell for you. Ms. Cook has been clingier since he got back."

"I keep asking Brendon why she's like that. He won't talk about it."

"Some mums are just like that. Did you say you were up for a hump on Sunday?"

Charlotte held up her cell, tapped a fingernail on the camera and kissed the photo.

"I'm trying to have a serious conversation and you're back to taking pictures. I think he's gone off me."

"If you don't stop whingeing, Brendon will run as fast as he can. Put a smile on your face and let's go meet our men."

"I wish I was half as confident as you."

"I have bad days, too. Remember when I wanted to try blonde highlights, and they turned orange? I felt ugly for weeks."

"I couldn't tell."

"I'm a better actor than Ms. Baxter thinks. I cried on babes' shoulder for days. Act Magpie, you're the best actor in drama."

"You sound like Ms. Cook."

"You're always going on about how so and so looks, if their jubblies are bigger or their clothes are nicer. People only put the good stuff on social media. They don't put pictures of themselves with spots or in their jimjams."

Maggie loosened her tie and undid the top button. "Bets at school are we're on the outs."

"Brendon's been on his best behaviour. It's all they have to bet on."

"Should we mention almost running Ms. Pratt over?"

"I don't want to talk about it. It'll make me get the collywobbles again."

Maggie placed her thumb in her mouth and chewed. Monsters came in all shapes and sizes. This one was tiny and helpless.

***

Troy turned into the pub car park. Charlotte ran her hand over his thigh. He twisted his mouth, pecking at her lips.

"Do you think Maggie's pretty? She's feeling down."

"Will it get me a pinch? That attacker ran into me, bleeding hard. I have a bruise on my hip."

"It'll make her feel better."

"Michael Collins is always following her around. Ask him."

"I'm asking you." Charlotte slid her hand into his jeans, biting into her lip. "Tell me babes."

"She has bee stings."

"I didn't ask about her boobs."

"She's pretty in that scrubbed clean kind of way."

"Do you think she's a minger?"

"I think she's sweet like a fairy cake and smells like one too," Troy said, drawing in a breath as her lips teased his belly. "She's too smart for me."

Charlotte looked up from his lap. "Are you saying I'm dumb?"

"You're smart at the right stuff." Troy gasped and moved his fingers through her hair. "Like whom plays for Man U and how to pick out my outfits for posh do's. I'd take that over the Scientific Method any day."

"Turn up the radio." Charlotte's breath was hot on his thighs. "It's our favourite Nicki Minaj song."

A warm, tingly sensation flickered through Troy's body. "It's going to happen."

"Hold my hair back."

Troy's belly muscles contracted; he gripped the grab bar. "There's a napkin in my pocket." Charlotte wiped her mouth, reached into the console, and shook out a piece of gum.

"Did you like that? I tried something new."

"It was bleeding brilliant. Are you sure you want to go for a drink? Will asked Tilly and Rachel."

Troy glanced out the car window. Brendon and Maggie had arrived and were standing toe to toe, scowling and pouting.

"Those tarts don't bother me."

"We can finish watching that Netflix series."

"By the looks of things, Magpie needs me."

"My mate needs a hump!"

"Is that it?"

"Is that it?" Troy said, flipping down the visor and smoothing his bangs. "My mate hasn't really touched a set of jubblies yet."

"If he wasn't so obsessed with football. He might have humped sooner."

"Maggie does nothing."

"What if I never wanted a hump or was scared? Would you get all whingey?"

"You've always been up for it."

"Are you saying I'm a slag?"

"You can't be a tart if you've only been with one bloke. You let me touch your jubblies and put my hand down your knickers."

"You do that tickle from the inside thing."

Troy snapped the visor and kissed Charlotte's neck. "Tell Maggie how good it feels. Brendon can give her a tickle, too."

"Brendon's been spending time with Rachel. Does he fancy her?"

"I have a theory; you can't say anything."

"Hurry, it looks like the two if them are going to kill one another."

"He fancies Ms. Pratt. He gets this dreamy look on his face whenever she's around."

"Her eyes lit up when she spoke about him."

"What are you going on about?"

"Nothing," Charlotte said, gripping his nipple. "She's anorexic, needs a tan and has a crooked tooth. Plus, she's a nutter."

Troy batted her hand away. "Bleeding heck, she's not that bad. Get a good look at her."

"Have you been hanging around Mr. Pratt's Garden again?"

"No, uh, I saw her and Walt out walking."

Charlotte held her fingers over his nipple and glared. "You look like the two of you shared a moment."

Troy wrestled into his hoodie and planted a kiss on her cheek. "There's something about Ms. Pratt that creeps up on you."

"Like the flu."

"Ms. Pratt loves football. Of course, Brendon would have a crush."

"He sticks his knob in anyone else and I'll kill him," Charlotte said, dabbing shimmery gloss on her lips. "You stay away from Ms. Pratt."

"Why should I stay away?"

"She steps inside you and sticks like glue. She's creepy."

"Has something happened?"

Charlotte dropped the lip gloss in the console and tousled her chestnut waves. "It's a feeling I get when she's around, like she's preying off my spirit and energy."

"What is she? A bleeding vampire?"

"I've been craving your mum's pie and mash all afternoon. I promised Callum I'd sit between the two of you."

Troy had felt nothing but guilty the night he walked Angelene home. It had taken a while to knock her out of his head, but he hadn't felt drained. No one knew Angelene Pratt. She was a stranger with strange habits and strange things to say. It wasn't a fear of vampires or soul suckers; it was the unknown.

***

"Are you going to tell me what's bothering you?"

Sparks whizzed through Brendon's body. They had lingered over porridge and berries, through his school day and onto the pitch. The plus side of the nagging sparks, he played a feisty, no-fear game of football.

"I won't stand in the car park all night. Bloody talk."

The setting sun washed the horizon in sweeps of melancholy pastels. A battle waged inside him, run to little bird or console Margaret Grace.

"You looked bloody miserable throughout the entire match."

"I'm worried the school called mum," Maggie said, plucking at a decimated fingernail.

Brendon crossed his arms and leaned into the car. "If they gave out awards for attendance, you'd win."

"You've been acting dodgy since you were at mine. We've barely said two words to each other."

"I'm trying not to lose my temper."

William and Tilly strolled across the car park wearing 'we know something you don't' smirks.

"Lover's quarrel?"

"Fuck off Will."

"Why isn't he with Gemma? Are you hanging around cheaters now?"

"I don't hang around Will."

"Are you going to tell us who you were buying the fish and chips for?" William said. His 'try to get out of this one' grin accentuated his overbite, fuelling the sparks dipping in and out of Brendon's turbulent stomach.

"You told me you were knackered and fell asleep."

Brendon's hands tingled with sparks. Maggie was too smart for excuses.

"I grabbed one for dad."

Maggie jerked her lapels back and forth. "He was in Yeovil with your mum."

"He had a craving when he got home."

William laughed like he was hatching an evil plan. "Sounds like a lie to me, Mr. Football."

Brendon shook his hands, hoping the sparks would fly out of his fingers. Every inch of him was on fire. The lie was easy but wrong, wanting to kiss Ms. Pratt and run from Maggie. Wrong.

"Get in the car, Maggie."

"You look guilty, Mr. Football. Adios."

Light flooded the car park. Troy flung up his middle finger at William and jogged to Brendon. "You coming inside? Rachel keeps asking where you are. Charlie's going to slap her."

"I'm liable to punch Will in the nose."

"Maybe that's what the wanker needs."

"Dad and I have been getting along lately. I don't want any aggro, smooth sailing until July, that's my plan."

"What's up? We won, you played brilliantly."

The secret was eating a hole in Brendon. He had a crush on Angelene and a crazy voice by the name of Padre Diavolo pestering him to do things he shouldn't. Spilling everything would undo the knots but, it would get back to Charlotte, who would tell Maggie. There was only one person he trusted. She understood expectations and had rules. She would take a train and hold his hand. The girl that wasn't his.

"Maggie's my problem." Brendon picked up a stone and whipped it across the car park. "You're getting a bloody bj and I'm listening to her whine about bunking off school."

"Charlie and I were snogging mate."

"I may be a fucking virgin; I know what was going on."

"Don't tell Charlie you saw. It'll never happen again."

"Your secret is safe with me."

"You gone off Maggie?"

"Why do people keep asking me that?"

"You used to carry her book bags. You used to text her after a match."

Brendon imagined a violent wind battering the sparks, sweeping through him, silencing the raging fire.

"Do you fancy someone else, Rachel, Ms. Pratt?"

Brendon shoved his hands in his pocket and stared at his feet. *'The truth will set you free. The truth will get me a bloody blubbering Maggie.'*

"Don't be daft."

"I'm just asking, mate. I say her name and you get this look on your face."

"I feel sorry for Ms. Pratt. People treat her like shit."

"Rachel?"

"No one fancies Rachel. She's jubblies and an arse. Both of which I like but, never in my lifetime would I fancy her. She doesn't even rate."

"What would you give her out of ten?"

"Two, one for her arse and one for her tits."

"Be nice to Maggie. She loves you. See ya, mate."

Brendon strolled to the car and plunked onto the seat. "Don't ask about the fish and chips."

"I wasn't going to."

"I don't want to talk either."

"I took a quiz today about toxic people."

13 STEALING LIGHT, STEALING BREATH

"Not talking."

Brendon gripped the wheel, Madre Innocente scolded him. He hurt Maggie, lied, allowed William to get under his skin and all for a girl he couldn't have.

"Toxic people are emotionally manipulative. They get you under their control. You bend over backwards for them."

"No more talking."

"They take your time for granted," Maggie said, sliding her hands between her thighs.

What is this? Where are the sculptures and stained glass? It looks like a school.

Brendon flicked the indicator, Angelene had complained about the church. She didn't seem to care he had bunked off school. She needed forgiveness, and that took precedence.

"Toxic people need your help to get through things." Maggie bit into her lip. Her eyes were wide, vibrant blue. Brendon gripped the steering wheel, sweat gathered in his armpits. Maggie's brain was in overdrive.

"Do you know what Charlie did in the car park?"

Brendon parked along the brick fence. It seemed like an excellent strategy, avoid conflict by changing the subject, fling some dirt in her direction, make her feel guilty, *'toxic Brendon, manipulative prick.'*

"It's a nasty thing to do in front of everyone's local."

"I bet Troy didn't think so. I'm sure he enjoyed it."

Maggie hooked the plethora of straps over her arms and tore into a jagged fingernail. "I'm sure he did."

Brendon didn't understand how feelings could change from 'I'm in serious like, here's a ring' to; 'I'm falling for Uncle Walt's wife.' He had spent little time with Angelene. All he knew was the moments shared meant something. If anyone was toxic, it was him.

Shadowy darkness veiled the farmhouse, the dormer windows glowed sinister yellow. He told himself to follow the code, go home, call Maggie, and apologize for being a prick. Despite his best intention to follow the code, he needed to see her. Brendon parked under the willow tree, jerked on his hood, and rambled up the walkway.

"I was going to text and ask if you would stop by."

Her voice was raspy, sparkling with happiness. She peeked around the door, smiling a rosy, pink smile. This was not toxic. This was paradise.

"You should have seen the save I made today. The ball slammed into my chest and bounced right into the Hayes player's foot. He tried to put it in the right corner. The dive I made, bloody brilliant."

"I wish I had been there," Angelene said, grabbing two plates from the drying rack. "Take your hood off so I can see your face. Are you hungry?"

Brendon yanked at his hood. The island was a mess of lettuce, green beans, and boiled eggs. An opened tin of tuna and black olives sat on the cutting board.

"I thought you were a terrible cook."

"You can't mess up a salad. Will you join me?"

The voices in his head argued, *'go home, stay.'* The battle continued with Madre Innocente leading her army of guilt and Padre Diavolo charging through with his pitchfork of pleasure.

"I'll eat at home. I don't know why I came."

"For someone who played an amazing game, your light is dull. Stay and talk. We're here for each other, non?"

'If she were toxic, she wouldn't want to hear about my day or wonder why I was upset. She'd tell me about a fight with Walter or tell a sad story, deflect the attention back to her. Toxic, my ass.'

"What are we having?"

"Salad Niçoise. I had it at a café with Roman. I thought I was special dining with a handsome businessman. The server thought we were father and daughter. We played along."

"Can I help?"

"Grab the salad dressing from the fridge. Bring me the tuna and olives."

"You made the dressing?"

"Mother was so mad Roman took me to lunch. He had to make her one for dinner. Olive oil, lemon juice, Dijon and Roman's secret, honey."

He set the tuna and olives beside the plates and went to the fridge, grabbing the jar. "Your mum was a bloody cow."

"She didn't like when her men paid attention to me," Angelene said, slicing into a tomato, "I'm done talking about my mother. Tell me what's wrong, so your light brightens. Peel the eggs, please."

"William gives a whole new meaning to taking the piss. He never shuts his bloody gob, always digging at me."

"He's jealous. He'll cast a shadow over you because your light is so bright and his is dull. What else?"

He rolled an egg over the counter, cracking the shell. "Maggie was whingey all day."

She took the eggs and sliced them, arranging the halves on the lettuce. Brendon was both happy and sad. The simple pleasure of constructing a salad together made his insides tingle and his heart hurt.

"Why is Maggie upset?"

"She bunked off school."

"We'll sit on the sofa. I have a bottle of wine open."

"Have you been drinking all day?"

"I had one glass after my walk, honest."

Brendon plunked onto the sofa. Loose sheets of paper, stubs of charcoal and smudged tissues, covered the coffee table. The ash tray was empty, the bottle almost full. Her mood, the glorious, sunny yellow mood, was all her.

"Has Maggie never lied before?"

"Once. She told her mum she was sleeping at Charlie's so she could stay at mine. Worse night of my life. She slept in mermaid pyjamas, felt guilty. I had to drive her home."

Angelene set down her plate and shuffled through the drawings. "I drew these today."

"Bloody hell, those are me. What will Uncle Walt think?"

"I'm going to give one to Sofia. Maybe she'll like me then."

Brendon set down his fork and studied each illustration. Every detail was right, from his widow's peak to the cleft hidden beneath the stubble.

"Walter will not like this."

"Other than the one I'm giving your mother; he'll never know."

Brendon pushed a pile of lettuce through the dressing. He didn't know what to think, flattered, embarrassed, panicked.

"Why did you draw these?"

"I enjoy sinking into your light."

"What about your light?"

"I lost mine years ago and have struggled to find it."

Brendon shovelled in the last bites of salad, set his plate on the coffee table, and laced his fingers through hers. "Who hurt you?"

"I knew a boy who was a lot like you. His passion was architecture. He saw the world in lines and shapes. He knew the history of every famous structure in France."

"What happened to him?"

"He loved Casa Batlló, the House of Bones in Barcelona. I'm sure he is daydreaming on one of its balconies."

Brendon slumped into the cushions, wiggling his fingers within hers. For a tiny girl, her grip was unbelievably strong.

"You need to know math and physics to study architecture. Bloody hell."

"Be creative, a visionary, a dreamer. He put triangles, arches, and squares together to make incredibly beautiful things."

"I failed geometry."

"School does not make you smart. Life and God are your best teachers."

She unwrapped her fingers and dug under the illustrations for a book wrapped in Van Gogh's Starry Night. Angelene thumbed through the pages, stopped, and tapped a charcoal-stained fingertip on it. "This is The Nightmare by Fuseli."

"That's a perfect title."

"What do you see in the painting?"

Brendon nuzzled against her, studying the picture. "She must be having a bad dream with that thing sitting on her chest."

"Go on."

"She should be scared. She looks like she's enjoying the dream, like the girls in the video Will showed us in the dressing room."

"What kind of video was that?"

Brendon ran a finger around his collar and swallowed. "An inappropriate one. She looks like she's, bloody hell, being satisfied by that thing."

Angelene grinned and touched his warmed cheek. "The creature is an incubus, a demon. They have their way with women."

"Good thing she's asleep. If she saw what she was humping."

"Does the painting scare you?"

"She looks at peace, like she's enjoying it."

He slid his arm around her and buried his nose in her hair. The day's tension unravelled and burned away.

"I hear you're coming to Burnham."

"Walter is excited. Will you be there?"

"Mum wants me to go."

"You don't want to go to the house on the sea that's really a bay?"

"I'd rather have a break from my parents. Since I came home from Dortmund, things have been tense." Her touch was gentle, no one toxic could have fingers this soft. "Mammina is clingier. Dad's pretending to be over it."

"What did you do? Walter said you flew home twice."

Brendon laid his cheek on her head. Just as she didn't want to talk about her mother, he wanted to forget about the day his world blew up.

"It was the opportunity of a lifetime that came with a list of expectations and promises."

He buried his nose in her hair and closed his eyes. The scent of lavender and the slow beat of her heart lulled him.

"What are you thinking about mon ami?"

"You and me in Westfalenpark."

"We could go to Oktoberfest, eat potato dumplings and bratwurst, drink until we can't stand."

"You'll be cleaning up barf."

"I'll wipe your chin like you do my nose."

Brendon opened his eyes and grinned sleepily. "I better get home before mum sends out a search party."

He stared at her mouth, memorizing the shape of her lips.

"I'm glad you came. You make Taunton a little less frightening and normal, a little easier."

Brendon stretched and yawned. "I hope that bloody incubus doesn't pay me a visit."

"It would be a succubus."

"Are you telling me there is a female version of that thing?"

"There's a seductress in the Dead Sea Scrolls, with horns and wings full of sin. Someone said I carried my sins on my broken wings and stole light like a succubus."

"Who ever said that was a dick."

"Get home to Sofia before she worries herself sick and her elegant black turns to grey."

"Have you always seen people in colour?"

"All my life," Angelene said, taking his hand, "when someone speaks, their words come at me in colour and surrounds them. I know all about a person just by their colour."

"I'm boring brown."

"Brown is wise and grounding, like the mighty oak. Sweet like chocolate." Angelene opened the door and grinned. "What colour am I?"

"You've been a bit of a chameleon tonight. You were yellow when I got here, then sad grayish blue, then faraway purple and now I'd say you're pale yellow, kind of happy."

"You're right. I'm kind of happy, sweet dreams, my boy in brown."

He walked away immersed in her yellow.

***

Angelene stared at Fuseli's Nightmare.

"I'm a succubus, stealing light, stealing breath, stealing their wings."

14 Stuck

He followed a trail of feathers; twisted branches tore at his skin. He dropped to his knees and cradled her. Blood flowed from wounds in her palms and feet. Wake up, little bird.

"Wake up knuddlebär."

Brendon blinked and rolled his head across the panelled wall. Rachel grinned at him, her mouth the colour of raspberries, the buttons on her blouse, ready to pop.

"What are you doing at school so early?"

"Mum and I had a meeting with Dawson. If it isn't my blouse, it's my shoes. I need to tie my hair up, lower my kilt, wear tights or those itchy trousers."

"Wouldn't be much fun for me."

"You ready for your lesson today, knuddlebär?"

"I've been practicing all morning."

"Really?"

"With every box jump, eins, Zwei, drei. I got to twenty-nine and forgot how to say thirty."

"Dreißig."

"Right."

"Why didn't you come into the pub?" Rachel said, unwrapping a Double Lolly. "Was it Will? I don't know what Tilly sees in him." She placed the powdery lollipop in her mouth, licking the residue off her lips.

"I was knackered."

"That's not what I heard." She flicked her tongue around the lolly. His mind took him to a place it shouldn't. "I heard you and Thornton were having a row."

"We were debating stuff."

Rachel tugged at the top buttons; her breasts sprang from their cotton restraint. "That's better."

"You could have warned me." Brendon said. A bloom of heat stained his cheeks.

"Was it because Tilly and I were sitting at the table?"

"We were discussing toxic people."

"They're insecure." Rachel bit the lollipop. She slowly licked sugar from her lips and tossed the stick into the bin. "It makes them feel better to make people miserable."

"Like when you call me knuddlebär. You don't think that upsets Maggie?"

"I can't help it. I bet you give great cuddles."

Brendon liked how her eyes shined like polished amber and she wore Converse high tops instead of flats. She was different. He was curious. Did she own a battery-operated boyfriend like William said? How long was the famous list? "Did your private chef make your lunch today? I've seen you in the dining hall with a bagged lunch."

"She's our housekeeper and yes, Amelia did. I've got a sandwich, salad, nuts, fruit."

Rachel lowered her gaze, her voice softened. "You're brilliant, you know that."

"If you want me to share my lunch, just ask." Brendon patted the floor beside him. "It's the least I could do after you cooked for me."

Rachel looked at him quizzically. "You want me to sit? Boys never want to talk to me, like really talk to me."

"I enjoy talking to you."

The hallway filled with students. Brendon flicked the end of his tie between his fingers. He ignored the curious stares and raised eyebrows, patting the floor again. "How do you say red in German."

Rachel dropped to the floor; her kilt ballooned around her as she stretched out her legs. "Rot."

He flattened his tie against his chest, touching a curl. "Your hair is rot."

"Dein haar ist braun."

"How do you say beautiful again?"

The vent whirred, showering him in heat. He loosened his tie and undid a button. Her exposed cleavage and perfume doubled the temperature.

"Schön." Rachel pulled two lollies from her blazer pocket and dropped one into his lap. "Indulge knuddlebär."

"I haven't had a double lolly in years. My dad used to hide them in his briefcase. When he came home from work, I would carry it to the den. There was always one stuck between the pens." Brendon unwound the wrapper, tucking the crinkly plastic in his pocket. "He started buying buckets of them and hiding them from mum. I'd get one if I finished my homework."

"Why did he hide them?"

"Mum didn't want me eating candy. I overheard her telling dad I was hard to settle at bedtime. She had an excuse for everything."

"Has your mum always been protective of you? I'm lucky if I get a goodnight."

Brendon stuck the lolly in his mouth, the tart cherry flavour tingled on his tongue. "From what I ate, where I could play. Even the bloody sheets I slept on. Dad and I can't say goodbye. It's see you soon. How do you say delicious?"

"Lecker."

"And brilliant?"

"Brilliant or hervorragend." Rachel said, unzipping her purse.

Brendon's eyebrows raised at the collection of lollypops tucked amongst the lighters, packs of cigarettes, and her change purse.

"Take a couple."

"Don't tell Liam. He'll fine me for each one."

He took a handful of lollies and shoved them in the front pocket of his backpack.

"Even your coach is protective of you."

"As mammina says, I'm a commodity. Liam's protecting Dortmund's investment."

"I won't tell."

"You didn't buy all those sweets, did you?"

"You know the sweet shop across from Ball's?"

"It sells jelly unicorns. I bought Mags a bag for her birthday. I've never seen anyone so happy over bloody sweets."

"The owner, Mr. Lawson, calls me his strawberry muffin. He gives me handfuls."

"Bloody creepy, don't you think?"

"He doesn't stare at my tits or anything. He feels sorry for me."

"Why?"

"He knew my dad before he ran out on us," Rachel said, grabbing her phone.

"Bloody hell. Did he just up and leave?"

"Last I heard, he moved back to Liverpool, bleeding scouser."

Brendon glanced over her shoulder at a photo of her and Tilly. "Can you tell Tilly to stay away from Will? It isn't helping my situation with Maggie."

"William isn't even her number one. Mr. Walker is. Keep that to yourself."

"The physics teacher? He's bloody married."

"Tilly doesn't care about that stuff," Rachel said, tapping on the camera icon.

"Do you have any married blokes on your list?"

"I may be a tart, but married guys are off limits. My mum got involved with a banker. He had a perfect life back in London, a wife, daughters. I hated my mum the two months they were humping."

"I'm on your list. I have a girlfriend. Troy too."

"Girlfriends come and go. A wife is supposed to be forever. Once you take those vows, you respect them. My dad had some slappers on the side. I think that's why mum lost faith in commitment."

"My dad takes his vows bloody seriously. One time we were at the pub with his best friend, Walt, these women came in."

"You're talking about Walter Pratt? His crinkly smile and that 'I sailed the seven seas' vibe is brill. Mum thinks he's dishy."

"Walt told dad and I to look. All dad said was they looked like nice ladies."

"I've seen your mum; he'd have no reason to look. My mum says she's a stuck-up cow."

"People think she is. Nonna raised her to command a room, take no prisoners."

"I wish my mum were like that. Every time a relationship ends, she's a miserable cow. She fills the freezer with ice cream, doesn't leave her room until the next one comes along." Brendon had seen his mother rattled. The worry on her brow had Angelene attached to it.

"My mum stresses when things aren't perfect. She likes everything, including dad and I, to be just so."

"I'd like my mum to fuss over me," Rachel said, holding up the phone. "Let's take a pic together."

A cacophony of laughter and voices echoed through the hall. Maggie's drama cronies glared. Boys looked at him like 'what are you doing with the slag?'

Someone bet he'd have her in the back of his Beemer. It was just a photo between friends.

"Just one, and don't be bragging about it. Maggie will kill me."

He laid his cheek against hers. Her reflection was pretty, a softer Rachel.

"When I say Dortmund, smile."

She counted down from three. As she said Dortmund, Brendon crossed his eyes and stuck out his tongue.

"Oh, bollocks. I wanted to remember this moment. You ruined the photo."

"You want to remember these musty halls?"

"You're the first boy who hasn't tried to chat me up."

A feeling of 'I like you' bombarded Brendon. One simple thing like a photo meant the world to her. She wasn't a tart; Taunton had labelled her like Angelene.

Brendon leaned against her and flashed his best dimpled smile. Her hair smelled like the sweet peas Amelia grew on the kitchen windowsill.

"You look dead gorgey. When you're famous, I can brag I knew you. Can we take another?"

"I'm getting the evils from those drama swots."

"So, what," Rachel said, extending her arm. "Something silly this time, like duck lips."

Brendon pursed his lips. He heard someone say, 'they've been taking pictures together' and the clunk of bags and buckles. Maggie clomped towards them; Brendon mumbled a string of curse words.

"What are you doing?" Maggie said, kicking her foot into his shoe. "Is this why you didn't pick me up? You wanted to spend time with her."

Brendon pushed himself off the floor, extending a hand to Rachel. "Bloody hell, relax."

"I'll see you at dinner break."

"No, you won't, daft cow."

"What have you got in these bags, Magpie?" Charlotte said, hurling the totes at Maggie's feet.

"Stuff," Maggie said, sticking her tongue out at Rachel. "No German today, no German ever. Auf wiedersehen."

Rachel smirked a 'just try to stop me' grin and wiggled her hips. "See you, knuddlebär."

"He's not your cuddle bear."

Bets swamped the hallway. 50p Thornton was going to cry, 2pound Cook would end up in Dawson's office.

"You're a dolt." Maggie said, jabbing her fist in his belly.

Brendon winced and rubbed the sting. "Has Jack been teaching you karate strikes again?"

Students paused in doorways, teachers strolled past, tapping their watches. Sparks flared and shot like firecrackers.

"You can give him an ear bashing at lunch, Magpie."

"Why were you early for school?"

"I needed to get away from mum. She was going on about Dortmund and missing me."

The temperature in the hallway rose another ten degrees, sparks crackled and whirred like a Catherine Wheel. Brendon loosened his tie and counted a shallow breath.

"You didn't text or give me a bell."

"Let it go Magpie."

"Did your little crumpet ring you after training?"

"I promised to help with geoggers. I never got to tell him the importance of river hydrographs. Callum put babes in a headlock."

"Listen to Charlie and go to class before I lose my temper. I'll end up in the room that smells like barf and lose a strike." Crack, whir, inhale, exhale.

"You're not meeting the ginger tart."

"It's just a photo. Babes took one with a girl at the pitch a few weeks ago. The only photos that matter are the ones of you and him," Charlotte said, glaring at Brendon. "You're a wanker."

Brendon practiced his breaths with every enraged step to the classroom. *I am calm. I'm as bloody cool as a cucumber.'*

"What did you do this time, mate?"

"Where do I bloody start? I didn't call her. I was talking to Rachel. I didn't pick her up this morning."

Tilly skipped into the room, chirping an animated, 'bleeding tart, you did what?' into her phone.

"Matilda Morimoto, put your phone away and spit out that gum. It's a disgusting habit."

She leaned over the bin and spit a lump of magenta goo into it.

"You made Rachel so happy this morning," Tilly said, spinning in her chair. "She'll never delete the photos."

"Turn around Ms. Morimoto or it's off to see Mr. Dawson."

"You better do it. You'll end up in the room Camilla Barton was sick in. The scent sticks in your nose all day," Troy said.

"If Charlotte doesn't want to live on the farm with you. I'm more than willing. I love cows and chickens," Tilly said.

Quiet flooded the classroom. Brendon stretched his legs into the aisle and sank into the chair.

"So far, we have concentrated on Werther's love for Lotte. Today, we will look at his sorrow. Mr. Spence a quote."

Brendon hid behind his book and smiled at Troy's flushed cheeks.

"Have you read the book?"

"I've tried, it's depressing. Werther is always whingeing about Lotte. There had to be other girls. He walked around Walheim a lot."

A burst of air expelled between the gap in her teeth. "I'm sure there were, Mr. Spence, that wouldn't make a good story. Matilda, can you find a quote?"

"I haven't been focusing on the sad parts, just the love parts. I'm with Troy. It's horribly depressing."

Brendon glanced at the page and read a few sentences. Out of the ashes, a pathetic spark lit and stung his heart. He slowly raised his hand.

"Why, it's a miracle. Dazzle us Mr. Cook."

"I have so much in me, and the feeling in her absorbs it all, I have so much and without her it all comes to nothing."

Werther pined for Lotte and could only be a friend. He, too, was nothing more than Angelene's friend.

"She gets stuck."

"Pardon me Mr. Cook."

Heat flashed across his cheeks. Troy smothered a laugh and the rest of the class stared at him in disbelief. The kid who made it perfectly clear he hated Taunton College had become a model student.

"It's the book. Poor bloody guy."

"I'm curious what you're thinking. There's five minutes left. Why not continue to impress me," Ms. Hudson said, wedging her ample bottom on the corner of her desk.

"Sometimes you meet someone and even though you know it's not right, you fancy them anyway. When they aren't with you, they're stuck in your head. You go about your day, wanting to see them. You know it's wrong, but they're there, stuck."

Tilly held a hand to her heart and gushed. "I'm telling Rachel. You're the sweetest."

"Thank you, Mr. Cook, for making the girls swoon. Quotes, I want quotes."

"What was that?" Troy said, hiking his backpack over his shoulder.

"Don't you love Charlie like that? The first time you saw her, you couldn't get her out of your head."

His phone buzzed, Brendon pinched his lips together and edged through the mob of students.

"Slow down mate."

Brendon stomped to a stop; a misty breeze cooled his cheeks. "I'm going to throw my phone into the bushes if Maggie doesn't stop."

"Why don't you answer it?"

"And have another row. I've got to before I explode."

"You got the sparks in your belly?"

"It's a bloody fire."

"Not a good idea, mate. You bunk off and you'll be down a strike."

"There's Ms. Morrison from the Career Centre."

"She's looking fit today. What are you going to do, mate?"

Brendon strolled across the lawn, kneading his forehead. "Ms. Morrison, do you have a minute?"

"Of course, Brendon," the willowy blonde said. "What can I do for you? You already know where you're headed."

"My head is bloody pounding. I feel like I could honk, can I leave?"

He gave her the eyes he used when he needed mammina to forgive him.

"I can't give you permission to leave."

Brendon touched her arm. "I'll make an appointment to see you. You like Leverkusen, don't you? I'll tell you about the team. They're fifth in the standings."

"I'll get in trouble."

He held a hand to his stomach and wobbled. "Talk to Madame Lafavre. I've seen the two of you eating together."

She leaned into him, rubbing his back. "Do you promise to make an appointment? I'd love to talk football with you."

Brendon nodded, clutching his stomach.

"You best get home."

"Did you do something different with your hair?"

"I asked for beachy waves and caramel highlights. Do you like it?"

"It's very pretty."

"Come on mate, you don't want to honk all over Ms. Morrison's shoes," Troy said. "You only have three strikes."

"If I don't go, I'll lose all three and mum may follow through on that daft rule her and dad made."

"This isn't you."

Troy was right. It wasn't him. Sure, he hated school; he despised the long days, the jail sentence. He went out of duty, respect, it's what a good boy does.

"Go to French mate."

Brendon watched Troy walk away, rattled the keys in his hand. He needed to breathe. He needed her.

A frog hopped from within the bullrushes to a lily pad. Brendon counted the ripples that moved over the water. There was a list of things he had done wrong. He enjoyed his time with Rachel in a way he shouldn't have, ignoring Maggie. He had manipulated Ms. Morrison, gave her a desperate look, complimented her, promised a meeting he had no intention of keeping. Birds scattered through the tangled canopy, butterflies tripped out of their cocoons, churning his stomach, filling him with sweaty waves of nausea. He was getting good at making poor decisions.

"I found some feathers."

A smile tugged at Brendon's lips. Her hair was windblown, cheeks vibrant pink, and tucked into the pocket of her denim shirt were three white feathers. The list disappeared; Madre Innocente shrunk away. Padre Diavolo whispered, *'she's beautiful.'*

"Have you had a good morning?"

"Non. Walter called; he could not find his notes. He had me searching all over the house. It was my fault because I hadn't tidied," Angelene said, peeling his hand off the steering wheel, "Your light is dim."

"The day started good. I was ace a training. I got to school earlier than usual. I even dazzled Ms. Hudson."

"It sounds like everything is okay."

"Maggie and I got in a row. She's pissed off I was talking to Rachel."

"Stay away from Mademoiselle femme fatale. She's a troublemaker."

Brendon agreed. Rachel made him think lots of inappropriate things. Nice or not, Rachel would jump all over him if given the chance.

"The novel we're reading in English really got to me. That bloody guy is in love, like the world stands still and she's all you think about, love. He can't be with Lotte because she's married, and it made me think about you." He locked eyes with Angelene, butterflies stormed his stomach. "I can't stop thinking about the things you said."

The words came. The butterflies flinched and crawled into their cocoons, frightened by his honesty.

"Would you come to Dortmund?"

He searched her face. It was sombre.

"Maggie should be the only person on your mind."

"You just pop into my head. I could be at the pitch, watching telly, when I can't sleep. You're there."

"We're friends, my only friend. Please don't make me repeat the pattern." She let go of his hand and weaved strands of hair between her fingers.

"All those things you said meant nothing?"

He unravelled her hair and rubbed the red marks. She wore a look like she had run to a far-off place, from the pattern, from him.

"I dreamt we were in the Black Forest, running. Something was chasing us."

"Was it mum?"

Angelene trembled and inched closer to the vent. "I don't know. We just ran."

"You think about me?"

"I do. God is not happy."

"Those things you said, truth or one of your fairy tales?"

"I need you to think of me as your friend. I need to please God and show him I can break the pattern." The desperation in her voice tugged at his heart. Reality slapped him. He hated Walter for bringing her to Taunton. "Please help me keep my promise to God."

"I guess being your friend is better than nothing."

"I need your help to break the pattern. Go back to school, apologize to Maggie."

"Arselick, you mean."

"Apologize. She's a good girl."

"For you. I'll drive you home, its starting to piss down."

"I'll walk."

"If you come to Dortmund, would you go to the Football Museum with me?"

"Only if you come to the Museum am Ostwall."

He took her hand and ran his thumb over the dots of paint on her fingers. "I'd go anywhere with you."

"And I with you. Go tell Maggie you love her."

"Right. Maggie, Apologize."

"There's a quote from the book Paris Spleen by Charles Baudelaire. La plus belle des ruses du diable est de vous persuader qu'il n'existe pas. The devil's finest trick is to persuade you that he doesn't exist. He is here, He is in all of us. Protect your light."

"You're too pretty to have the devil in you."

"I have the worst kind. I hope you never have to meet them."

Brendon peered through the sweeps of rain; the devil was wandering down the road. He slowed the car, opened the window, and smiled at Rachel's soggy kilt and high tops."Get in."

She tossed a waterlogged cigarette in a puddle, climbed into the car, and rubbed her goose pimpled thighs.

"I am glad to see you."

"There's a hoodie on the rear seat."

She reached over the console. His gaze shifted to the rear-view mirror. Orange lace knickers.

"You had the same idea as me."

"Thornton and her swot brigade have been giving me the evils all morning. Michael even told me to stay away, cheeky bugger."

"Since when do you care?"

"It's frustrating. You'd think we had snogged or something. I guess Thornton has banned me from teaching you German."

"I should be able to talk to you without Mags getting pissed off."

"She needs to write to an agony aunt," Rachel said, squeezing her hair between the folds of her blazer.

"How about you teach me now? I'll share my lunch with you."

He reached to unzip his backpack; his fingers brushed over her thighs.

"You'll get more aggro from Thornton."

"I'm already in trouble."

He opened the brown paper sack and pulled out a sandwich. Brendon unfolded the waxed paper and passed half, biting into the tower of chicken and spinach.

"Is that Branston pickle?"

"Amelia says it makes a sandwich." He dumped a container of dressing over a salad, closed the lid and shook it. "I only have one fork."

"This is enough. Wir sollten morgen frühstücken"

"I'm supposed to understand that." Brendon said, jabbing his fork into a mound of kale and rocket.

"We should have breakfast tomorrow."

"You have the devil in you."

"I'm just a girl who knows what she wants. Satan isn't telling me what to do," Rachel said, licking pickle off her finger, "I'm going to quiz you knuddlebär, you up for it?"

Brendon nodded, cracking open a can of sparkling water.

"How do you say yes?"

"Bloody easy, ja."

"And no."

"Nein."

"How do you say please?"

"Bitte."

"Kann ich einen küss bekommen?"

Brendon stashed the container in the bag and tossed it into the rear seat.

"I thought you were quizzing me?"

"Do you know what I said?"

He shook his head, biting into the sandwich. "Nope."

"I asked for a kiss."

"You never give up, do you?"

"I bet you're a brilliant kisser."

Padre Diavolo snickered. *'Time to come out and play.'*

"We better head in. I should apologize to Maggie for being a prat."

"Sit beside me in Latin? I downloaded the Bundesliga app. I'll have the news feed ready for you."

They stepped out into the pounding rain, Brendon reached for her hand, they raced across the lawn. He opened the door, shaking the rain from his hair. His eyes shifted from Rachel's rain-soaked shirt to Maggie.

"Mr. Cook."

Rachel winked and ducked into the bathroom. Brendon's shoulders dropped. He stared at the ceiling and cursed. Mr. Dawson marched towards him, slinging his long, elastic arms.

"You missed French."

"I told Ms. Morrison; I was feeling iffy."

"You've made a miraculous recovery."

"I pulled over on the way home and honked. My head bloody hurts, but I'm here."

"Next time you feel like missing class, talk to me. Ms. Morrison believed that rubbish."

"I guess that's a strike?"

"I spoke to Ms. Hudson; your insight into the novel impressed her. Take that enthusiasm to history."

One bullet dodged, onto the next. He tossed the intention 'wish me luck or have the roof cave in' into the air and plastered on a grin.

"Headache again?"

"You know I get migraines like dad."

"Why were you with the ginger tart? An impromptu German lesson?"

"I was driving back to school and saw her walking. It's pissing out."

"I've been texting you, gave you a bell twice. You could have answered."

Sparks glided through his body. Entertained students walked by, whispering, and grinning at Maggie's sour expression.

"Can we talk later? I haven't finished the homework."

"Of all the people you choose to spend time with, it's a girl you would never talk to."

"We weren't spending time together. It's no different than you reciting lines with Michael, or what about that time you studied with Ciaran Cealleagh? I never said a thing."

"Neither one of those boys tried to chat me up. Everyone knows what Rachel wants, Mr. Number One."

"Have I ever given you reason to doubt me? I haven't snogged anyone else. I've kept my knob in my trousers. I haven't even touched you inappropriately. My father expects me to be respectful. Just like it's written in the bloody code."

"You're a wanker."

Brendon kneaded his knuckles across the ache in his forehead. The stares and giggles from passing students and Maggie's sweet perfume had turned his lie into truth.

"Take these," Maggie said, whipping a bottle of paracetamol. It bounced off his chest and rolled into the wall. "Nice save, Mr. Football."

Brendon snatched the bottle off the floor and skulked into class. The only available desk was in front of Mr. Clark. The day couldn't get any better.

***

Angelene poured a cup of tea and walked to the island. She studied the treasures she found on her walk, the feathers, a pebble, a bouquet of wildflowers tied with a stem of mint. She picked up an oak leaf, twirled it in her fingers, and grinned at a box she had discovered buried in the barn. The plan for the old box, clean it, paint it, add all the treasures she had found. She'd title the assemblage, 'the day the pattern fell apart.'

The oven timer pinged, Angelene placed the leaf in the box. She grabbed an oven mitt, opened the door, the warm scent of garlic and simmering chicken blew across her cheeks. It was picture perfect. She set the dish on the stove and swiped open her phone.

"You'd be so proud of me."

"No hello. What are you doing, little bird?"

"Hello husband. I'm plating my dinner. I found a recipe in that book of yours for cassoulet. I did it, I made dinner."

She scooped beans and chicken onto her plate. His laughter was gold and shimmery.

"That's wonderful. You'll be a chef yet."

"I can feel the pattern breaking. For the first time, things are falling into place, into a new pattern with normal things."

"I wish I were home with you."

"I wish you were here, too. You could try my cassoulet. You'd see the floors are spotless and the loo, as you call it, is sparkling clean."

"I'll book you an appointment at the salon to celebrate. A makeover before Burnham."

She dropped onto a stool; the smile fizzled from her lips. "What is wrong with me now?"

"Nothing. Women like going to the salon."

"I'll do it for you because wives are supposed to look pretty for their husband."

'Would you like Sofia to join you?"

"Non, I must do it on my own. I will take a taxi and discover Taunton."

She was yellow, bright, shining from the inside, yellow. The pattern would be different, solid, unbreakable yellow. Brendon would be a friend, like a brother

'I can do it. I can break the pattern. Brendon is nothing more than a brother.'

15 Edwardian Dreams

Troy sulked into his tea.

"Does Bronwyn still live in Burnham," Maggie said, squirting a blob of ketchup on her plate, "Brendon had the nerve to tell me her lips tasted like strawberry sponge."

"Can we talk about something else? The entire drive here, I miss Brendon, why hasn't he texted?"

"I bet he doesn't miss me. I'm gutted, just gutted."

"I'm sure he misses you muffin. Babes, text Brendon and remind him how important it is to keep Magpie happy."

"I'm not getting involved," Troy said, piling bacon on toast. "He doesn't need to know you're pouting."

"You're my mate too. Text him, for me," Maggie pleaded.

"He'll be gone for a weekend. He's been away longer."

"His dad laid down all those rules. I knew he wouldn't be in Dortmund long."

"You're a bleeding nutter."

"I'm in love."

"Love makes you do crazy things," Charlotte said, slurping her tea, "that boy shaved his head last term when he heard Ms. Morrison fancied Jason Statham."

"Do you know anything? We've had a row every day."

"What do you think babes knows? He tells me everything, then I tell you."

Troy smiled an 'of course I tell you everything' smile and shrugged. "It pissed him off for letting that goal in. Any nipper in the kiddie league could've made that save."

"It's more than that. I talked to Gemma last night. She's feeling the same way about William."

Troy dipped his toast into an egg, golden yolk spilled onto the plate. "He has said nothing to me."

"Do you think he fancies Rachel? Gemma thinks William fancies Matilda. I don't know why. Her gum chewing is incredibly annoying."

"So is your whingeing."

Troy dropped his fork and flung his arm over his chest as Charlotte's fingers dove in for the pinch.

"Troy Alexander, what a nasty thing to say."

"See what you did? I'm not her little crumpet now."

"Don't get angry, babes. After school, we'll have a cuddle. I'll tell you about this dishy footy player named Troy Spence, who becomes more famous than Beckham and Ronaldo. Tell Magpie Brendon doesn't fancy anyone but her."

"I swear to you. Brendon doesn't fancy anyone."

"Why is he being such a dolt?" Maggie said, latching on to her bottom lip.

Troy wiped his mouth, tossing the napkin on his plate. "You could always give him a wank."

"It always comes back to that."

"Now muffin, I could show you how to do it on a cucumber or have a peek at Brendon's face while you're doing it. You'll know if he's enjoying it."

"I don't want to look at his face. That's revolting."

"What about Ms. Pratt babes?"

Troy tapped his fork against the table. "Did you have to mention that?"

"Charlotte Elodie Donovan, you're supposed to be my bestie."

The server strolled over to the table, dropping the receipt. Troy sniffed; her perfume smelled familiar, woodsy, spicy. The hidden smile. Her arm looped through his.

"Oh my gosh, you're making the Charlie face."

Troy stuffed his hands in his pockets and slid down the booth. "I don't know what that is."

"It's the face Jack makes when he stares at me. Do you have a crush on Ms. Pratt, too?"

"Brendon has a crush on Ms. Pratt. I knew it!" Maggie said.

"I don't fancy Ms. Pratt, neither does Brendon."

"You said it after I gave you a special treat, which you'll never get again if you fancy her."

Troy didn't know what it was or how to describe it. Angelene popped into his head and swarmed his insides. He was sure Brendon got warm and gooey inside, too.

"Ms. Cook is fit. I don't make excuses to go round to the manor to have tea with her."

"Brendon has gone to the Pratt's to work in the garden, move furniture. Any opportunity to talk to her and he's there."

"You fancy Ms. Cook?" Charlotte said.

Troy groaned and laid thirty pounds on the receipt. "I'm her meatball."

"You're my little crumpet," Charlotte cooed.

"All I'm saying is Brendon had a crush. It's over. He only has eyes for you."

"Remember when we sat in the hayloft," Maggie said, chewing on her pinky, "remember that brilliant spider web."

"We get spiders in the barn all the time. What's your point?"

"We called her Penelope. She amazed us at how long and hard she must have worked on her web. Every day, she sat, sitting, looking beautiful, waiting for her prey. She devoured that poor fly."

Troy smiled at Maggie, guiltily amused. "Are you comparing Ms. Pratt to a spider?"

"The deadliest."

15 EDWARDIAN DREAMS

"I'll admit she's odd, but dangerous. You're losing the plot," Charlotte said, wrapping her fingers around Troy's.

Her face looked unnerved, like it did when they went on the ghost tour of the Wookey Hole caves.

"You okay luv?"

"I hate spiders, you know that."

"Are you sure it was a crush? I swear Brendon's gone off me."

"He fancied her for like a day."

"Do you think she's the devil? Regan, in the Exorcist, could speak different languages."

Troy laughed. "For a smart girl, you're awful stupid. Ms. Pratt is French."

"Babes, let's stop by the sweet shop and get some jelly unicorns, so Magpie stops worrying."

"Can I come over tonight? I don't want to be alone," Maggie said.

"No, you may not. I'm tired of talking about Brendon."

Troy could have sworn Charlotte had been uneasy. He was sure Brendon still had a crush on Ms. Pratt. She could be a devil, tempting boys with her pretty disguise, a black widow, quietly stalking her prey. Troy doubted it.

***

Brendon pressed the top down. The moors flashed by in shades of green; the sun bobbed behind the clouds, flickering through the trees. There were a million smells along Taunton Road, sweet clover, apple trees heavy with ripe fruit, curing hay. The world around him was fresh and beautiful, especially the girl waiting by her front door. Walter had texted, asking him to drive Angelene to Burnham. Poor little bird had paced all night.

Brendon backed the BMW in, left it idling while he rambled up the walkway, stopping. There was something different about her. She was more refined, made up.

"Have you been waiting long?"

"A minute or two. I had to finish packing. Walter said the weather could be fickle, like me."

"He told you that?"

"He says my affection bounces all over the place."

Brendon grabbed her luggage. "Your husband is bloody charming."

"He can be."

"You got your hair done. You look pretty."

Angelene tucked her purse at her feet and relaxed into the seat.

"Walter wanted me to look like Brigitte Bardot."

"Was she fit?"

"Bardot was a beautiful woman. I couldn't believe my reflection in the mirror. It didn't look like me. I paced."

"How come you didn't wake Walt?"

Golden light washed over her pale skin. Delicate, too perfect for the world. She had a grip on his heart; it wasn't right, harbouring a crush on Walter's wife.

"He'd be grumpy if I disturbed him. I need him happy. I'm feeling yellow and I don't want the feeling to leave."

The traffic bunched up; Brendon slowed the car. The moment was perfect. While drivers cursed and gripped their steering wheels, he savoured how peaceful Angelene looked and how calm his heart was.

"You want to talk about your mum?"

"I don't like to think about her."

"Don't you have any happy memories?"

"My memories, even the bad ones, are precious to me. I prefer to keep them hidden."

A precision of cars snaked down the motorway. Exhaust fumes perfumed the air. It was gridlock.

"You can trust me. You should know that."

"I promised Walter no more sad stories."

"I'm asking you to share. We'll be stuck in traffic for a while."

The pink faded from her cheeks. She became one of her paintings, colourless, pained, and haunted.

"My mother was a beautiful, empty shell," Angelene said, pulling the ends of her sleeves over her trembling fingers. "She loved looking glamorous. The makeup didn't hide her poor decisions. She wore them better than the old Hollywood looks she tried to mimic."

"Your dad?"

"It could be the man from Spain who spoiled her with gifts of Turron and Vermouth. It could be the traveller from Istanbul. It could be the man she left Germany with. I may be parts of all three."

Brendon dug under the wool cuff and held her hand.

"Mother wanted to leave me at the hospital. God convinced her to keep me. I was punishment for the madness she felt with those men." She continued between shaky breaths. "Mother wanted a life where she could flaunt her beauty and be free. I stole her freedom. I need a cigarette."

"Keep holding my hand."

"She never had to attract men. They circled her like wolves, hungry for their prey. It was mother who devoured them."

"Roman Krieger was one of those wolves. You made it seem like he was a nice man."

"He courted mother. He could have saved us."

The traffic thinned; Brendon put the pedal to the floor. He had seen the same stretch of trees and moors for fifteen years. It had always been a boring drive; stuck in the rear seat, flipping through football magazines with nothing but the M5 to look at. The sky was bluer, the air sweeter. The highway could go on forever.

"Mother didn't like when her men paid attention to me, especially Roman. She never said, but he was her favourite."

"Maggie's mum was up the duff at fifteen. She never regretted being a mum."

"Gustav, her Danish lover, asked mother if he could make love to me, like it was normal to seduce a child. I thought I stepped into a chapter of Lolita by Nabokov." Angelene paused and shrank into the seat. "Gustav's favourite quote from the book was I knew I had fallen in love with Lolita forever, but I also knew she would not be forever Lolita. It resonated with him. I never wanted to read that book."

"What did your mum do? Mammina would have killed him."

Angelene's smile was close-lipped. "She left."

"How bloody old were you?"

15 EDWARDIAN DREAMS

"Thirteen."

Brendon breathed in the briny air. He was dizzy with disbelief. How does a mother leave her child? Angelene dragged his arm across her breasts, bringing his hand to her mouth. Her lips danced over his knuckles as she spoke. "My only refuge was the Victor Hugo statue. He was my saviour. Please Brendon, one cigarette."

"Keep holding my hand. I'll tell you about my life, the Dortmund training camp, the U19 squad, bloody school."

"What were you like as a child?"

"Richard, the prick would have said a brat. Mum calls me her miracle and dad... he's never really said."

"Did you always want to play professional football?"

"I wanted to be a pirate."

Angelene twisted in the seat and smiled. All the colours that made her glow overtook her pale cheeks; she was pink, sparkling green, and brilliant yellow.

"Did you search for buried treasure?"

"Walt, Paddington, and I would sail the seven seas. Walt was a brilliant pirate. He planned the best adventures."

"You keep talking about this, Paddington. He must be special."

"He was my best friend, other than Troy. The greatest defender of all time. I'll introduce you sometime."

Heat danced on his cheeks; little flutters took flight in his belly. He wasn't supposed to be feeling this way. She was a friend. A beautiful, wounded friend.

"You must have had some happy times."

Angelene gazed at a gull, screeching, and soaring through the streaks of white clouds. She hung her arm out the window, catching handfuls of peaty, algae kissed wind.

"When Roman visited."

"What was one of your favourites?"

"He took me to Notre Dame. I wanted to meet Quasimodo. Did you know his name means half-made? I identified with Quasimodo. Like Paddington, he was a special friend."

Brendon tucked a strand of hair behind her ear. The warmth from her cheek seeped into his finger. He held onto the moment.

"Are you happy now?"

"The blue sky, salty air, wind in my hair. I'll remember every second of this drive and how you made me glow."

Brendon turned off South Esplanade onto a dirt road lined with oak and walnut trees. She had shared parts of her story and held his hand so tight; he couldn't feel his fingers. She had been his for forty-five minutes. It was time to tuck the flutters away. They were friends. No matter how lovely the time was; he had to respect her wishes.

"Is that the house?" Angelene unbuckled the seatbelt and bounced to her knees, gazing at the Edwardian home. He had never seen her so happy. Sunshiny liquid gold.

"It's lovely. A sign too, Cook and Pratt, extraordinary!"

A stacked fence framed the property, September wildflowers poked between layers of glimmering stone. As a child, Brendon would balance along the top of the wall, walking the entire length to the shoreline. He could picture Angelene, arms outstretched, doing the same.

"The porch is a work of art," Angelene said. "Look at the decorative windows and stained glass. I thought Rosewood manor was impressive. I prefer the house by the sea."

She leapt from the car, holding her hands to her mouth, gazing with childlike wonder.

Brendon stood, stretched his arms. He had happy memories of the house. This would be his happiest.

"Little bird, you're here."

Walter wore a pleased with himself smile, a towel around his neck, his sandy brown hair damp. "Sofia can finally breathe. You made it one piece."

"One of these days, she's going to faint. I'll pop the boot."

Brendon plunked the suitcases on the ground. Angelene jumped into Walter's arms. An ache filled Brendon's chest. The drive had been sweet. He had chipped away at her wall and digested her story. The sunshine left him; hers glowed.

"This is quite the welcome. You're positively radiant this morning," Walter said, lowering her to the ground.

"The drive was lovely. I've never driven in a convertible before."

"What did you talk about? Walter said, picking up her suitcases.

Brendon grinned nervously. "Football, what else?"

"You're a saint. An hour listening to this one prattle on about football."

"I know all about the Bundesliga now."

"You're impressed with the outside. Wait until you see the inside."

Brendon heaved his backpack over his shoulder, grabbed his Dortmund duffel bag, and shuffled to the door. The sun shone through the stained-glass fanlight, casting a rainbow of colours across the tessellated floor.

"You made it," Sofia said, swooping towards him. "How was the drive?"

"The usual, heavy traffic."

Moments of the drive circulated around Brendon's head. He tried to stop his heart from shrivelling. It was stupid to think he meant anything to her. He was a friend like the Victor Hugo statue.

"Did she fill your head with sad stories?"

"We talked about football. I'm going to take my stuff upstairs."

Brendon climbed the stairs, shutting out Angelene's 'ooh's' and syrupy, 'c'est beau'. The walnut floor glimmered like a golden pathway leading Brendon to a narrow door. When he was little, the doorknob was an enormous diamond and the claustrophobic, creaky staircase led him to the belly of a pirate ship or the dressing room at Signal Iduna Park. It had always brought him joy to hide away in the attic turned bedroom. He dropped his bags on the floor. Nothing about the room spoke to his tastes other than the framed photo of him in his Borussia Dortmund kit. The furniture was ostentatious, the walls painted subdued blue. Brendon leaned into the dresser; his fingers wrapped around a fuzzy pink cardigan. Guilt crept in and knocked around his head. He had done it again, dived into hope, dismissed Maggie, and struggled with being Angelene's friend.

"We're going into town to have lunch on the pier."

Sofia's voice brought him back to his bedroom. He pulled off his ball cap, tossed it on the bed, and scratched out his flattened hair. "I'll stay here."

"It's that restaurant you like. We can share a bowl of Eton mess."

"I fell asleep before I finished my homework. I'll sit in the conservatory and work on it."

15 EDWARDIAN DREAMS

"Is everything all right, sweetheart? You're smiling, but there's no twinkle in your eye." She held up her palm. Brendon took hold of her hand, stopping the dreaded 'Oh my goodness, he's ill' swipe to the forehead.

"I swear to God I'm fine. I worked myself too hard at training."

"Don't swear to Him. He's an awful listener. I'll make you some tea," Sofia said, rubbing his arm. "I brought some fruit. There are crisps in the pantry. Here." A box rattled towards him. Brendon snagged it, shaking the Smartie container. "You can pick out the blue ones."

Brendon moved to the circular window, heartsick. The water moved as peacefully as the memories floating through his mind. Elaborate sandcastles housing pretty princesses, driftwood pirate ships, his first kiss. They were together in his mind, walking hand in hand along the beach. She was glowing bright yellow and all his.

If Brendon had a paintbrush, he would have created a masterpiece, titled 'Edwardian Dreams.' Sofia had researched the era to ensure the sitting room stayed true to its charm. The fireplace was white. A sequence of photos telling the story of David and Walter's friendship lined the ornate mantle. The walls were pistachio with white crown moulding. White shears framed the windows, the furniture, pebble grey. It was clean and functional, Sofia but not Sofia. The memories Brendon had in the room were long and happy.

Brendon gazed from Walter to his parents and decided a more fitting title would be 'Bedtime.' The only person who didn't look like they had taken a dose of sleeping pills was Angelene. She sat on the edge of the sofa; her legs bounced as if she were powering up to fly. The nervous energy spilled across the floor, taking hold of him. New title, 'the caged bird.'

"That was a pretty heated game of Scrabble," Walter said, laying a hand on Angelene's bouncing knee.

Brendon scratched his head at words like fozy, zaxes, and zek. He had a feeling he knew who ruled the Scrabble board. 'Who won?'

"Your father. He's the only person I know who can make words with X's and Z's."

"Did you play?" Brendon said.

Angelene pried Walter's hand from her knee and gently rocked. "Non, je me sentais stupide."

Walter draped his arm over her lap, clinking the ice around in his glass. "You could have used French words."

Brendon rubbed his upper lip, hiding his smile. Angelene pushed Walter's arm off her legs, bouncing to the edge of the sofa.

"Did you enjoy the bubble and squeak? It's a favourite of mine and Walter's," David said.

"I liked the potatoes," Angelene said, gripping the cushion. She rocked and bounced, lifting herself up and down. Brendon's smile faded. Walter wound his arm around Angelene, gripping her shoulder.

"Ang eats more potatoes than that Irish bird I dated. What was her name?"

"Branagh," Sofia said.

Walter's eyes were piercing blue. Sparks lit, hot and fiery. Bounce, grip, bounce, grip.

"Are you coming to my match on Sunday?"

Steer the conversation to football before he dove across the sitting room and snagged Walter by the throat.

"Beatrice told me I needed to get out to more matches, show my support," David said.

"We'll go sweetheart. I can see the new extension."

Brendon rolled his neck, trying to ease the tension that bound him like a noose. *'Walter should hold her hand or take her for a walk, bloody hell.'*

"I spoke to Lukas the other day."

"How's my friend?" Walter said.

"He was in Stuttgart, got his eye on a sixteen-year-old midfielder."

Walter braced Angelene's shoulder. Curse words slapped against Brendon's mouth, *'let her go, you stupid fuck.'*

"Lukas has an eye for talent. He saw it in you and here you sit."

David knocked back his scotch and set down his glass. "Twice, dear friend. He's blown it twice."

"He could do a lot for the Bundesliga. Every damn team was begging for him." Walter said. He loosened his grip on Angelene's shoulder and rubbed his brow. "Sit still. You're making me uncomfortable."

An awkward silence fell over the room. David stared out the window, disappointment darkening his face. Sofia ran a hand over his neck, her gaze transfixed on the relentless bouncing.

"Can we go out?"

Angelene's voice was small and taut.

Brendon grinned at the sleepy 'are you serious look' on Walter's face.

"Does anyone look like they could go into town?"

"New places make me nervous. I need to get out."

"Tomorrow."

Brendon glanced from her bouncing to the harried look in her eye. He had to do something before she had a tantrum or jetted herself through the roof.

"I could take her into town."

"I don't think that's a good idea, sweetheart."

"I'm not tired."

"The pubs close at eleven," David said.

"There's that dance club. I'll take you tomorrow."

The conversation was over. Silence swept back into the room.

"I'm going to call Maggie and finish my homework."

A chorus of 'good nights' followed Brendon. He shuffled from the room and climbed the stairs. He trudged up the hidden staircase, stripped out of his clothes, and buried under the blankets. Brendon heaved his Latin text onto the bed. A sheet of paper decorated in hearts and 'fancy a snog' fell onto his lap.

'Break the pattern, friends helping friends.' He repeated the mantra. Sleep kidnapped him and took him to a place he didn't recognize.

Run, run fast. He slammed into a golden birdcage and gripped the icy bars. A little bird swung back and forth, her wings clipped and frayed. Feathers floated around him, tickling his nose and neck.

"Are you awake?"

Brendon rubbed his eyes and grinned. "Someone fixed your wings."

"Get up, sleepy boy."

He shot up, frantically clutching the sheets, "Bloody hell, what are you doing?"

Angelene tossed jeans and a black thermal shirt on the bed, her eyes wild. "Quick, get dressed."

"Is everyone asleep? What bloody time is it?"

"11:30, your jeans, hurry."

"Uncle Walt said no."

"To hell with Walter. I'll smother him if I don't leave."

Brendon tugged on his jeans and socks, rushed to the bathroom. He splashed water on his face and scrubbed his teeth, his mind whirling.

"This isn't a good idea."

"I need to get out. I can't breathe."

"Mum has insomnia, dad usually gets up for a snack."

"Do you want to play with your devil tonight?"

A fire raged in her eyes, intoxicating green, scorching his heart. The adventure was dangerous, not him.

"Padre Diavolo is a dickhead."

"Père Satan meet Mère de tous les Diables."

Shadows followed them down the hall. Every creak and rattle bellowed and boomed in Brendon's ears. His heart thrummed louder and louder. He glanced at Angelene, jeans, V-neck Henley, the famous, red-soled shoes. He didn't see a pitchfork or horns hidden beneath the waves of blonde.

"Can we walk?"

Brendon covered the deadbolt with his hand and slowly turned the latch. "It would take about an hour."

A blanket of grey clouds hid the moon. There were no nighttime sounds, no crickets, no owls hooting, no sounds from the water, just quiet. Cold sweat prickled Brendon's skin. The world was much too quiet.

"If dad finds out I took you into town after Walt said no, he'll have me by the goolies."

He took a few breaths to steady his heart and shaky limbs.

"Let's play with the devil. Lucifer has a lot of suppressed anger; we don't want to upset him."

"If I keep saying yes to him, I'll like it too much."

Brendon gently twisted the key in the lock and nodded towards the BMW.

"Have you ever driven a car?"

"Pierre tried to teach me. He gave up when I kept stalling it."

"Just shift it into neutral."

He tossed her the keys; she snagged them from the air.

"There's a keeper in you. I'll get you out on the pitch."

"I would love that."

Brendon put his hands on the hood. They slid across the gleaming black paint. He wiped his palms on his thighs, cursed Padre Diavolo, and pushed. The car rolled onto the road. He knocked on the roof and scrambled into the car.

"Aren't you afraid?"

"Non." She ran her hand over his, eyes chaotic green. "This is what friends do. They help one another, and I need you."

Brendon tapped his fingers against the steering wheel. The rhythm was as relentless as his thundering heart.

"We could sit in the garden and talk."

"You must stop smoking little bird," she said, flapping her hands, "Watch the bread, but he devours a loaf. All his fucking rules, you understand, don't you?"

The town unfolded in front of them, a jumble of century old shops and modern boutiques. Street lamps lit the pavement in an amber glow, illuminating the alley. Brendon maneuvered around crates and flattened cardboard boxes; thumping bass bounced through the white brick walls.

"You ready mon ami?"

"I should be in my bed. I was having a dream. I'd like to know what happened."

"You can go back to your dream later. I can finally breathe."

Every part of him was alive. Electric music thumped and chugged. Late night smells of coriander and cumin laced the brackish air.

"It's your turn to hold my hand."

Angelene wound her fingers through his. He rested his palm against a red-painted door. The music pulsed through the wood. A blast of hot, stuffy air scented with hops, perfume, and desperation hit his face. White, blue, and pink strobe lights ignited the dance floor, the chugging rhythm bounced in his chest. Brendon tore his gaze from a couple entwined like snakes to a scarred and sticky bar. Dim globe lights barely illuminated the empty cocktail glasses scattered among bowls of lemons and limes. The bartender chewed on a toothpick, flexing his muscles, flirting with two scantily clad women.

"Two pints of whatever and a bottle of wine," Angelene said, sliding two fingers into her pocket, "make it two."

Brendon pulled out his wallet. Angelene wagged her finger, tossing fifty pounds on the grungy bar.

'Where did you get the money?"

Brendon grabbed the mugs, following her through a maze of white melamine tables and silver pedestal stools.

"Walter's wallet."

"Won't he know it's missing?"

They found a white lacquered booth and slid onto the zebra print bench.

"Walter shoves wads of euros and pounds in his wallet. He thinks it makes him look important."

"There's a lot of alcohol on the table. I don't really drink."

A steady stream of fog puffed from hidden smoke machines; Brendon coughed. Laser lights blasted the crowd with rays of vivid red.

"Did you forget who we are playing with?"

"Padre Diavolo wants to get me into trouble."

"How do you feel right now?"

An image of Sofia running through the house searching for him battered his brain. "Nervous, scared, alive."He chugged back the pint in a series of throat quenching gulps. Rebellion flickered in Angelene's eyes. Lucifer had disobeyed and revolted against God, so had the woman sitting across from him. Her God was six feet tall with rock-like hands.

"You're yellow right now mon ami, not pretty yellow but scared yellow."

"Shouldn't I be red like the devil?"

"The devil isn't red. He's white, cold, and empty." Angelene ran her finger around the rim of the mug and took a slug. "Lucifer doesn't like when people ignore him. He does things to get their attention. No one listened to his side."

"For someone who loves God so much, won't He be upset you're sympathizing with the devil?"

"I have empathy, that's a good thing. I understand how Lucifer felt, never having a voice."

15 EDWARDIAN DREAMS

Brendon held up his mug, shook it, grabbing the bartender's attention. He fixed his eyes on Angelene. The glass was cumbersome in her hand. The rebellious look had morphed into something he had never seen before; like she was searching for something, missing pieces, freedom, a scream that had been stuck. He thanked the bartender, handed him ten pounds, and took a long sip.

"You look beautiful."

He supped his beer and relaxed into a mess of feathery pink pillows.

"Is that Father Satan talking? He's a liar."

"He's also a thief and a tempter. It's me, not the devil or the beer."

She finished the lager and poured wine into the lingering froth. "Do this, don't do that. Wear this, speak this way."

Brendon emptied the mug, filled it with wine, and sipped. It tasted of vinegared berries.

"Get good grades, be respectful, lead by example."

"You do the last naturally. The boys on the team gravitate towards you."

"Did you see the look on dad's face when Walt told him I should be in Dortmund?"

Angelene laughed. "David puts a lot of faith in education. I can just imagine what he thinks about me."

"With knowledge comes power, dad lives by that motto."

"Genuine power comes from evolving, using the knowledge you have and challenging yourself. It comes from the heart, not filling your head with information."

"Richard used to lock dad in his room and force him to study. Richard didn't want a dolt for a son, neither does dad. I'm not the son he wanted."

Angelene set down the mug and ran her thumb over his hand.

"How could he not want someone as gifted as you?"

"I'm not supposed to talk about it."

The glow of black lights shined on the packed dance floor. Gigantic warehouse fans showered Brendon in sweaty, perfumed air. He had held tight to the rules and the code, yes mammina, no dad, I'll be a good boy and do good things. *'They're not made of stone. Break the rules, it's one night. Break one, say fuck you to the code and it's so long, good boy.'* Brendon licked his lips, chugged, his throat remained dry. Stay, go, apologize, face the consequences.

"I'll take you home. The music is giving me a bloody headache."

"Can we go to the beach? I'm not ready to end the night yet."

'Break free, slip through the bars that have penned you in for so long'.

"I'll grab us another bottle."

"Padre Diavolo is back."

"He's a fucking prick."

Brendon slid out of the booth, found his feet, rambling to the bar.

"Am I still scared yellow?"

He grabbed the bottle and her hand.

"You're maroon, fiery red, slashed with white."

A sliver of moon cut through the clouds, silver streaks lit a path through the alley, leading them to the street. No one would believe the adventure he was having. He titled this chapter, 'The night I played with Satan.'

"If we walk far enough down the beach, we won't have to hear that bloody music. You'll see the Low lighthouse."

"I know the way."

She led him through the alley, past a whitewashed pub with bright green shutters and a convenience store. The beach was a few steps away.

"How did you... how..."

"I don't know. Everything seems so familiar, like your hand in mine."

They trudged through the sand, littered with pebbles, ropes of marram grass and bony driftwood limbs, until the techy boom-boom was a whisper. A breeze swept in from the shimmery black water. Angelene unscrewed the cap, took a long sip, and passed it. Brendon drank, took another, and flopped onto the sand.

"Tell me more about Paris, and you."

"Why? do you like sad stories?"

Brendon picked up a pebble, the pink and ivory stripes glimmered in the moonlight. It would look nice in his bowl of treasures. A reminder of the night he met the mother of all devils.

She passed the bottle and draped her arm around his waist. He nuzzled her hair, breathed in lavender, and shoved the bottle into the sand.

"I want to understand where your light went."

"You make it very hard to break the pattern."

"I know all about Charlie. She loves every shade of purple. She lives off sweets and if you asked her to choose her favourite, she'd tell you five different things. Nicki Minaj is her favourite singer. She loves Troy and that farm. I could go on."

"No one has really cared to ask."

"What about Lisette?"

He unscrewed the cap, held the bottle to his nose. It smelled like the chocolate-covered cherries Nonna loved.

"Lisette thought I made poor choices."

"What about Piedmont?"

"The men I've known wanted to fuck me."

She took a gulp, handed him the bottle, resting her cheek against his arm.

"Not me." Brendon hiccupped and grinned a tipsy grin. "I wouldn't know what to do. Troy tells me things, but honestly, I'm bloody scared."

"It isn't all it's cracked up to be."

"Troy said it's as brilliant as stopping someone from scoring."

"It's not that exhilarating."

She dug in her purse, tossed a pack of cigarettes and a silver monogrammed lighter on the sand.

"He doesn't want you to smoke, but he buys you a lighter?"

"At least I'll look classy."

It was as if he had stepped onto the pitch at Signal Iduna Park. His heart climbed to his throat, butterflies tiptoed out of their cocoons and began a nauseating dance. The feeling was back. He drank another mouthful. The wine had to drown the butterflies.

"When you were dreaming of playing football in Dortmund, I dreamt about surviving."

Brendon pressed his lips against Angelene's temple. She leaned into his ribs and melted against him.

"Imagine if mum and dad were touring Paris, and they found you, thirteen years old, sitting at Hugo's feet. They could have brought you to Rosewood manor."

"You would have been six years old."

Brendon took a long sip, passing her the bottle. "You could have played football with me and Paddington. Mum might have let me play in the forest."

She would have been a sister if his parents had rescued her. He told himself to think of her as a sister. It would be easier to follow the code and be her friend.

"Imagine me growing up at Rosewood manor. I would hold my tea cup properly, say the right things. My scars would disappear. I wouldn't be afraid of mirrors."

"You'd have to study and get good grades."

"I wouldn't mind sitting behind that desk, learning about the world from David. I would have been someone."

Tears swarmed her eyes; Brendon rested his chin on top of her head. "I wish you saw what I did."

"What you see is not what you get."

"I don't want you to cry. I want to finish the wine, talk about daft things, things that make you beautiful yellow."

"Sometimes the tears just sit there and blur my eyes. Sometimes it's harder to breathe."

"Which is it now?"

"Breathe."

She took a deep drag, her eyes focused on the water. Smoke slipped from between her lips, spiralling through the air like a ghost. Her mouth was full and pretty, the smoke was magical; the smell mingled with her perfume, captivating him.

"Fuck, these damn butterflies."

"I don't see any butterflies. There is nothing but water and sand."

"The butterflies are in my belly. It could be the wine; it tastes bloody awful."

"Sofia has spoiled you with luxurious food and wine. It tastes fine to me."

Brendon shimmied his phone out of his pocket and swiped his finger across it. "Can we take a picture? We'll always have this moment."

"Have evidence we snuck away? It must be Father Satan speaking to me right now."

He tapped the camera, adjusted it to selfie and held the phone in front of them.

"I don't like it. Turn it off."

"Move your hands."

"You see my crooked tooth when I smile."

He held the camera at arm's length and pressed his cheek against hers. "Grin then."

A whisper of a smile brightened her face. The photo was perfect.

"What time do you think it is?"

Brendon squinted at the lock screen. "Three."

"The devil's hour."

"Bloody hell, you really put a scary spin on things."

"Satan is powerful at this time."

"Let's hope Satan uses his power to get us home."

Brendon staggered towards a cement embankment, bracing himself against a damp pillar. He unzipped his fly, showering the stone. She fell against his back, snaking her arm around his waist. Her fingers pressed into his belly, sending a flurry of flutters through his body.

"Did the devil tell you to hug me while I was going wee?"

"I'll ask God to forgive me."

They climbed the concrete steps. There was no life on the streets. Sludgy light glowed from the streetlights.

"Our Lord Chancellor will be pissed off if I get caught driving drunk."

The pavement bent and bobbed under his feet.

"We can't leave your car here."

"I don't know what's worse, driving drunk or confessing."

"Drive slow."

Brendon gripped her hand, swaying left and right.

"Watch the barf."

He guided her around a technicolour puddle and opened the car door. His insides twitched. He'd drive slowly, keep his focus on the road and hope Padre Diavolo and Uncle Gianni the reckless would help guide him home. Brendon eased his foot on the gas and somehow found the end of the alley.

"I needed this," Angelene said.

She traced along his neck; each tiny hair stood on end. Her touch was intense, like she had reached inside, wrenched his heart, scooped the breath from his lungs.

"Stop touching me. The butterflies are fucking out of control. I'm going to barf."

He wasn't going to vomit. Uncle Reckless and Padre Diavolo were going to coax him to pull over and kiss her.

"I thought it might relax you."

"It feels too good."

Brendon switched off the headlights, racking his brain. Had he parked beside the Aston Martin or the Jaguar? He was sure he had parked beside Walter's car. He remembered staring at the number plate. It had always amazed him that the random set of letters assigned to Walter's plate were his initials, WAP. Brendon parked, relieved. He did not know how he did it, but they were home.

Brendon held a finger to his lips; the staircase looked a mile away.

Her body weaved and bobbed. She clasped the heel of her shoe, collapsing into the wall.

"You need to get to bed."

"I don't want to disturb Walter. He might think it's an invitation for sex."

The floor shifted; the walls tilted like he was back in the funhouse in Blackpool. He led her to the sofa. They tripped onto the cushions. Every creak and rattle rising from the vents stirred his insides.

"I'll remember this night."

"Me too."

He moved toward her, resting his hand on her cheek. His body tensed. It was dangerous and stupid. It was just a kiss. Angelene pushed on his chest, her eyes wide.

"Please, I can't breathe." She buried into the cushions, dragging a throw over her shoulders.

Brendon staggered to his feet, bumping his shin on the coffee table. He cursed, clutched the armrest, and placed his lips on hers. Angelene squirmed into the cushions, touching her lips. His brain stuttered. He had kissed her.

***

15 EDWARDIAN DREAMS

Angelene stared at the hulk of a man tangled among the sheets. She tiptoed into the room and dropped her shoes on her suitcase.

"You're awake, little bird."

She froze, a cold prickle crept over her cheeks and neck. "I couldn't sleep. I was going for a walk."

Walter scratched out his hair and yawned. "It looks like it's going to rain."

Angelene stared at the steely grey clouds, touching her lips. "Mother said God was crying when it rained. I need to feel God."

"I'll come with you," Walter said, tearing back the blankets.

Angelene dug through the mound of clothes, cringing at the pain in her temples. She grabbed a wrap and wound it around her trembling shoulders.

"The promise is broken."

"Did you promise God you'd go for a walk?"

"I need him to help break the pattern."

"You're talking nonsense this morning," Walter said, pulling on his jeans. "We best be on our way before God sheds his tears."

'He's already crying'

16 Deja-Visite

Wind blustered the walnut trees, rain tumbled from the clouds, tapping a cacophony of plunks and clacks against the window. Sofia envied people who slept well. When she first moved to Rosewood Manor, the ghosts had kept her awake. Over the years, party plans, the transformation of Taunton Park, stories to keep Brendon out of the forest took precedence over sleep. Last night had been no different. Walter's prattling on about potatoes and Brendon staying in Dortmund had rattled around her brain. She could have sworn she had heard footsteps around four o'clock.

"It doesn't look like the rain is going to stop," David said.

"I was hoping for tea in the garden."

"Scones and posh sarnies. Angelene will love that," David said, pouring himself a coffee.

"She might."

David grinned and kissed her cheek. "Do you think Angelene ever settled down?"

"I thought I heard footsteps this morning. I was going to see if it was her but, the house was cold, you were warm."

"Angelene paces when she can't sleep."

"I can't imagine being that anxious."

"You do other things, play with your bracelets, wear my old jumper. People do things to ease the nerves."

"Even you Lord Chancellor."

"I fly through my speeches. Beatrice writes slow down on my notes to remind me."

"You're incredibly charming when you give a speech, you look so confident."

"I hide it very well."

Sofia rested her hand on his, mulling over Walter's remark.

"Do you think we should have let Brendon stay in Dortmund?"

"Walter has made you doubt we did the right thing?"

"It was a dream come true. We took it away."

"We've been through this. We let him go, we brought him home. He punished us by calling the entire modern languages department pricks," David said, pouring cream in his coffee. "Brendon promised again at the start of this term."

"Some professional football players start at sixteen."

"And some at eighteen," David said, sipping his coffee. "You weren't ready to let him go. You smiled when we picked him up at Heathrow."

"I was happy to see him."

"You were over the moon he was coming home."

"I contacted the Professional Football Scouts Association after Lukas set his sights on him. I hoped to keep Brendon in England."

"Clubs in France, Italy, wanted him. Dortmund won. He broke his promise and now he'll do his time at Taunton College."

Sofia ran her finger over her bracelets, *'Shift your worry Sofia, there are bigger issues.'*

"Do you think Walter and Angelene will make it?"

"I don't know. He needs someone like Kate to put him in his place."

"I know Walter likes a challenge... I worry about him."

David pressed his lips against the wrinkle on her brow. "Worry about Brendon finishing school."

The door burst open. A spray of cool, wet wind followed Walter and Angelene. Walter pulled off his hood, shaking his damp hair. He unwound Angelene's soggy wrap, puddles of water pooled under their feet.

"Hand me a kitchen towel Davy boy, these floors cost a fortune."

David tossed the roll and grinned. "Where have you two been?"

Walter dropped a strip of paper towel on the floor, running his foot over the puddle. "The farmer's market. We got all sorts of goodies: blood sausage, fresh goat cheese. We'll have a proper fry-up."

Sofia rubbed David's arm. "You did enough last night. Why don't you let us make it?"

Walter chuckled. "Burnt toast and frittata? We're celebrating this soggy, beautiful country we live in."

Sofia flicked through her bracelets. Angelene hadn't shared in Walter's joy or laughed at their drenched clothes and hair. Her breath was shallow and raspy. She scrubbed at her wrist as if trying to remove a stain.

"Did you enjoy the walk?"

Angelene bowed her head and wiggled out of her wet sneakers. "It was nice until God cried."

"My mother used to tell me God was playing a game of bocci when it stormed."

"God is crying. Excuse me."

Sofia edged herself closer to David and snuggled under his arm.

"Why would God do that? He doesn't weep. He gets pleasure watching someone suffer."

"Ang didn't sleep well," Walter said in a disconcerted tone. "This weekend is exactly what she needs. I'll change and start brekky."

Sofia pulled a stack of plates from the cupboard, setting them on the island. "She couldn't look at me."

David gathered the cutlery and laid them next to the plates. "You intimidate her. Even Liam shudders when you're at the pitch."

Sofia positioned a place mat, aligning it precisely with the stool, moving to the next. "She better get used to me if you and Walter expect us to be friends."

16 DEJA-VISITE

Sofia floated around the island, centering each placemat, then the plates. The utensils were next, lined up perfectly on either side. Sofia studied the soapstone countertop and grinned. Everything looked perfect, everything except Angelene.

"I'm not sure she'll ever be comfortable with you," David said, grabbing a bowl of oranges. "I'm going to start squeezing. Why don't you see if sleeping beauty is awake?"

Sofia stepped into the foyer, gasped, flinging her hand to her chest.

"Oh, mio dio."

Angelene pushed and pulled on her knuckles. An uneasiness stole Sofia's breath.

"I'm on sausage and bacon duty. Roman used to say blood sausage was the heart and soul of the United Kingdom. It sounds disgusting to me."

"I agree. It's as bad as black pudding," Sofia said, wrinkling her nose. "We'll stick to bacon."

"I'll put extra slices in the pan."

Sofia released an exasperated breath and climbed the stairs. Walter's rendition of Brown Sugar mingled with the rain pummelling the roof. She opened the door to the secret staircase. Laughter from five-year-old Brendon haunted the tiny space. She couldn't count the number of times she had chased him up the stairs, Paddington dangling at his side, the Dortmund jersey hiked up around his ankles. Memories ran in slow motion. She wanted to be there, climbing into the belly of Queen Anne's Revenge, or heading to the dressing room at Signal Iduna Park. Sofia reached the top of the stairs; a distinct memory invaded her mind, her brother, Gianni the reckless. Her smile dropped. The room smelled of stale wine and vomit. Sofia's gaze moved from the clothes tossed on the floor to the lump hidden under the blankets. Angelene could barely look at her. She had been twitchy, lost in thought. God was crying for her.

'You're being silly, Sofia.' She backed out of the room, sweat tickled her back. She followed the sound of laughter and stood in the kitchen doorway. Angelene was touching David's arm, staring up at him. *'Looking for what? Approval? Love? Flirting?'*

"Angelene and I are shopping after breakfast. You can get your son up."

Sofia tied a Pucci scarf around her neck, applied her signature red lipstick and tossed the tube on the vanity. She grabbed her Prada bag and walked down the hall. Angelene stood in the middle of the bedroom in her underwear, beads strung around her wrists, clothes strewn across the bed.

"Is something the matter?"

Angelene threw up her hands, jerking her arms through a grey jersey pullover. "I can't seem to put an outfit together. I don't understand the rules."

Sofia sighed softly and marched into the room. "Stop fretting over something as silly as an outfit."

"Sometimes normal fits and other days, it's too loose, too tight."

"Today, it's going to fit right," Sofia said, handing her a pair of jeans. "Can you look at me?"

Their eyes met, and a shiver trickled down Sofia's spine. Guilt, longing, sadness, a mixture of all three. *'Forgiveness, she wants me to forgive her.'*

"Now what?" Angelene said, tugging at the hem of her shirt. "This doesn't look fabulous."

Sofia hid her worry behind a grin. "Accessories. Hand me the indigo and white wrap."

She snapped it open and tied it, pulling waves of blonde from beneath the layers.

"Bracelets, check. Your Vuitton bag, lipstick."

Angelene pointed to the dresser. Sofia paraded across the room and dug through the bulging makeup bag. Classic red, tawny pink, and nude.

"Not the red. I haven't worked up to that colour yet. I'm feeling pink today and not in the way Troy looks at Charlotte."

"What are you talking about?" Sofia said, choosing the pink.

"I'm feeling emotional and timid."

Sofia applied the lipstick and took a step back. "You look lovely. Riding boots or booties?"

"What are you wearing?"

"My ankle boots. You ready?"

"I don't want to disappoint Walter. I have disappointed God, which is enough for today."

"I wouldn't worry about disappointing God. He has a terrible habit of disappointing people."

"God is always beside me. Today he's weeping for me."

They walked down the stairs. Sofia slid on her boots and grabbed the keys from an antique wash basin. Sofia opened the door, popped an umbrella, and studied the dismal sky.

"Looks like God will cry all day."

She took hold of Angelene's hand, and led her down the soggy walkway, unlocking the car.

"May I?" Angelene said, fumbling for her cigarettes. "You look worried. Is something troubling you?"

Sofia put down the window. Her fingers struck the steering wheel in a series of staccato taps.

"Brendon's room stunk of wine; he doesn't drink. He might have a glass of wine with dinner."

Angelene took a long drag, tossing the cigarette into the rain-soaked wind. "He's been arguing with Maggie lately."

Sofia angled the Jaguar into a spot out front of a line of shops. "Why talk to you? Why not Troy or me?"

"Je suis désole. I'm upsetting you."

Sofia walked around the car, taking Angelene's hand.

"You think Brendon drank because he had an argument with Maggie?"

Rain pummelled the pavement, Sofia tugged open the door, the tiny shop shone as if built from gem stones and glass, ammonia lingered in the air. Sofia set the umbrella by the door and adjusted Angelene's scarf.

"Sometimes people turn to unhealthy things to cope."

"Beautiful things can make a person reckless."

Sofia reached for a silver and gold cuff; the lacy pattern shimmered under the track lighting. She slid it on her wrist, rotating it left and right. "Do you agree Angelene?"

"Beautiful things always get me into trouble."

The look on Angelene's face shifted like a kaleidoscope, endlessly changing from one emotion to the next.

"Brendon doesn't drink his troubles away."

"You know your son better than me," Angelene said, clenching her hands, "or are you asking because you've watched me drink the nerves away?"

Sofia wiggled the bracelet off and handed it to the salesclerk with her charge card. "It's an opinion."

"People do all sorts of things when they can't control their emotions. Brendon has a temper."

"He broke a boy's nose. David had to work some incredible magic so the family wouldn't press charges. He pushed a boy on the playground, split Freddy Chaney's forehead open."

"Isn't it better he drank."

"You seemed upset Walter wasn't in the mood to go into town," Sofia said, sliding her charge card in her wallet. "It's silly of me to think of you and..."

"Do you think Brendon and I went into town?"

Sofia tried to distinguish the look in her eyes. Shame, disappointment?

"It's hard for me to settle in unfamiliar places. I've hardly slept since coming to Taunton."

Sofia held up a gold charm bracelet, wiping the thought from her mind. Brendon was a good boy. The charms tinkled in her fingers. A good boy who would help his friend.

"This would look lovely on you."

Angelene shrank away, wrapping her hand around her wrist. "No bracelets."

"You should buy something. The rings are exquisite."

A tray of baubles locked beneath the glass, winked, and glittered under the bright lights.

"Can you bring out the display to give her a better look?"

The salesclerk unlocked the cabinet and set the tray on the glass counter. Angelene picked up an oblong ring set with jade and diamonds.

"It reminds me of my mother."

"Really?" Sofia said, perplexed. She hadn't answered the question. It was a simple yes or no. She avoided her eyes, twisted the subject.

"My mother loved Greta Garbo." Angelene's finger shook as she slid the ring on. "She loved the scene from Grand Hotel where Garbo says, I want to be alone. She said it often to me and in such a way, it made my insides scream. Garbo wore a ring like this in a picture mother had framed."

"Buy it, in honour of your mother."

Angelene handed the clerk the ring and fumbled within her purse for her wallet.

"I'll buy it in honour of Roman. He thought Garbo was beautiful."

"Shoes are next. We'll get you some sensible pumps. You can work your way up to the stilettos Walter wants you to wear."

Sofia popped open the umbrella, guiding Angelene onto the drenched pavement. They walked side by side, a steady stream of rain pinged against the black monstrosity. Angelene pushed the door open with her hip. Sofia patted her upper lip with her scarf, stunned. *'How did she know this was the store?'*

"Did Walter tell you... how..."

"I don't know, deja visite. It's happened before."

"Is it like deja vu?"

"Similar yes, I knew we had to walk precisely ten steps from the jewellery store."

The sales clerk, in a pinstriped suit and shined Zanotti shoes, swirled his lacquered pompadour, grinning handsomely at Sofia. "It's twenty-five and sunny in Milan."

"Where is the nightclub?"

"Looking to go dancing, Ms. Cook?"

"Is it close by?" Sofia said, click, click, clicking her bracelets.

"It's a two-minute drive, Pier Street, then Esplanade. Who's this? You must have snatched her off the runway."

Angelene glanced over her shoulder, the store was empty.

"He's talking about you. Stephano, meet Angelene Pratt."

"As in Walter Pratt? I never thought he'd marry. That cheeky bugger."

"It happened rather quickly."

"It's nice to meet you. We just got the Prada winter collection in, you two sit."

He pointed to a burgundy chaise that looked like a giant pair of lips and snapped his fingers. "Eloise, champagne for Ms. Cook and Ms. Pratt."

Sofia settled onto the curved sofa; her eyes fixed on Angelene's knitting fingers. "Walter never told you about this store?"

She passed Angelene a flute of bubbly, her chest grew tight.

"He talked about River Parret, the Bristol Channel. I know Burnham. I feel like I've been here before."

"Get that into you. You need to relax."

Sofia could feel the emotions roiling through Angelene, with every fidget and slurpy, panicked sip. '*It could be me. My thoughts are racing, so many questions.*'

"This store isn't me." Angelene's voice was tiny, shaky, drawing Sofia out of her thoughts.

"The last pair of shoes I bought was from the Marche aux Puces de la Vanes for ten euros."

Sofia took a small sip; a wall of boxes formed in front of them. Deja visite, the stink of stale wine and vomit. It had to be memories of Gianni that had her rattled. After a brief silence, Sofia spoke.

"Walter expects you to play the part. You need props. A fabulous pair of shoes is the best."

"I don't belong in these stores. I can't breathe."

"You have every right to shop here." Sofia held up a strappy red stiletto. She slid her foot in, angling it from side to side. "Brendon uses a breathing technique when the sparks light. That's how he describes his anger, fiery sparks. Try it, breathe in, and slowly exhale."

Angelene laid her hand on her chest, breathed in, quickly releasing it. Angelene didn't have the gumption to stand up to Walter. Sofia doubted she'd have the courage to persuade Brendon to sneak out and get drunk. Sofia set the red stiletto back in the box and reached for a peep toe slingback.

"Try this on. It looks like something Garbo would have worn."

"Teal is an introverted colour. It suits me. People who like the colour appreciate things that are different and don't want to fit in. I've belonged nowhere."

"Where do you get these ideas?" Sofia said, examining the wooden heel of an espresso pump.

"I see letters and numbers in colour. I read palms. Mother hated it. She said I needed an exorcism to rid the devil."

Sofia tilted her head, set the shoe down, and held out her hand. "What does mine say?"

16 DEJA-VISITE

"You have breaks in your life line, trauma, and loss. Three, no I see four."

Sofia steadied her hand; her heart raced. "Go on."

"Your heart line curves upwards, you're passionate. You have a sun line. No wonder you're so confident."

"Are you sure you see four breaks?"

Angelene ran her finger along Sofia's palm. "I'm positive about three. The fourth, I'm not sure it's happened yet."

Sofia tugged her hand away and smiled nervously. "Who knew you could see so much in a person's hand."

"People think eyes are the window of the soul, it's a person's hands. Touch is a language all its own."

"What do you see in Walter's hands?"

"Power, hard work. He has golden fingertips."

"Are you happy?"

"Sometimes I feel yellow and sometimes I'm a jumble of colours waiting to come together, like a kaleidoscope."

"How are we making out here? More champagne," Stephano said.

"No, thank you. I'm ready." Sofia said, handing him two boxes. "Angelene?"

"I'll take these. Teal suits me."

"Nothing beats a good pair of shoes. I'll set them by the register," Stephano said.

"Does Walter make you happy?"

"I'm learning to be a wife. My friend Lisette made it look easy. You make it look easy."

Sofia handed her charge card to Stephano. She had never considered herself a wife, she was a partner. Marriage took work, Sofia wasn't sure Angelene had it in her.

"It hasn't been easy. You saw it in my lifeline."

"You're in love. That's all you need."

Sofia thanked Stephano, grabbing the umbrella. She studied the pewter sky; rain fell in fat plunks. God hadn't finished weeping.

"You need more than love. You need to see each other as equals."

"Walter will never see me as his equal. That's why he married me."

"He's learning to be a husband. King Midas will surely turn you into gold."

Sofia unlocked the car, sagged behind the steering wheel, drained.

"Do you believe that?"

"It isn't about changing who you are, just the props, like choosing accessories."

"A boy told me I didn't need to change. He likes my messy hair and holey jeans. I'm patched, stitched together. My clothes are a representation of that."

"Was that boy Brendon?" Sofia clung to the silence; her heart dropped to her stomach.

"It was just a boy, a boy surrounded by beautiful brown."

Sofia parked beside the Aston Martin; she was home. She needed a fix of David and Brendon, joy to overtake the heaviness.

"What are you wearing to dinner? I must start thinking about it, so I don't keep everyone waiting."

"A black wrap dress and my new red shoes."

"I'll wear black too with my teal shoes. I'll channel my inner Sofia and dazzle King Midas."

"Have you read Walter's palm?" Sofia said, grabbing her purse and shopping bag.

"He thinks it's nonsense. I studied his palm one night while we were watching television. He has one break in his lifeline, only one true love."

A chill swept over Sofia. She hurried up the walkway and stepped into the house.

"I'm home."

"You didn't buy the store out?" David said.

"I was tempted. Italians make the best shoes."

"The best shoes, clothes, purses. Shall I go on?"   "Where's Walter?"

"Upstairs. We stopped at a football shop before coming home. He bought a Chelsea shirt and wanted to try it on. He bought one for you too, Angelene."

Angelene fumbled through a shaky smile and left the foyer. Sofia collapsed into the door.

"Tired?"

"Exhausted. Where's Brendon?"

"Did you know Miranda Jones's daughter does his Latin for him?"

"It wouldn't surprise me."

"He's in his room finishing his homework. I made some tea. Join me in the conservatory?"

The bags clattered to the floor. She set the umbrella by the door and followed David. Her movements were sluggish, like she was wading through quicksand. Sofia sagged onto an ivory and azure floral club chair with heavy eyelids.

"She mentioned nothing about love. She skirted around all my questions."

"Were you prying again?"

"She isn't in love with Walter. Her eyes lit up when she mentioned a boy with brown light."

"I'm not sure if Walter loves her."

"What the hell are they doing together?"

"Walter has a way of dazzling women."

"He has golden fingertips. Did you know that?"

"Angelene certainly has an interesting way of seeing things."

"She reads palms," Sofia said, sliding her fingers over her bracelets. "She saw four breaks in my lifeline. Has Walter told her anything?"

"I told him not to. Not yet."

"Four. Doesn't that concern you?"

"There's no truth behind that stuff. You've had a long day, you're tired."

"It's a strange tired. I feel empty, drained, dry."

"Angelene's melancholy wears on people."

"How was Brendon?"

"He stared into his ginger ale. Walter went on again about the fuss their making in Dortmund. Brendon couldn't look at Walter or me."

'The boy in brown, the boy who likes her as she is, messy, stitched together. Who did she mean?'

"Let's go cuddle. I need to rest."

"Can we snog?" David said.

"Can we kiss, yes."

Sofia looped her arm through David's, tucking herself close to his side. The feeling overwhelmed her, no love, golden fingertips, a boy in brown. Questions flitted around Sofia's head. She would lie down, concentrate on her husband. Hopefully see things a little clear over dinner.

***

What are we going to do today, Uncle Walt?
Do you see that piece of driftwood? What does it look like?
A ship. It has a mermaid on the bow.
Then we're pirates in search of treasure.
I love you. Mummy says you should always tell someone you love them just in case something happens.
Before you were born, I loved you very much. I held my hand against your mother's belly and introduced myself as your Uncle Walt; you kicked. I said, Sofie, you've got yourself a footy player.

Brendon jerked and blinked his eyes. The Latin text clunked onto the floor. There was no beach, no driftwood pirate ship, no Uncle Walt. Shoving his notebook off his lap, Brendon swallowed, moistening his parched throat. He groaned at the pain throbbing in his temples. He couldn't remember if he had kissed Angelene or if she had kissed him. What he remembered; she had pushed him away.

Brendon closed the door to his room and made his way downstairs. He glanced into the sitting room and braced himself against the door frame. Angelene dipped a paintbrush in a jar of water, then swirled it in a beige paint pod, gently stippling small dots on the paper. Brendon took a deep, pained breath and stuffed his hands in his pockets. Madre Innocente shouted instructions, *'leave, call Maggie, Troy, go back to your room.'.*

"I see you standing there."

Brendon blew out a heavy breath and perched himself on the edge of the sofa. He glanced at the painting, admiring the waves and tiny pearl shells.

"That's nice."

Angelene dropped the paintbrush in the water. Her eyes were as grey as the day.

"I was remembering last night and how special it was. You ruined it. I need God to forgive me."

"He needs to forgive me, not you."

"Sofia asked if we went into town."

He had no memory of getting into bed. All he remembered was waking, covered in sweat, and stumbling to the bathroom to vomit. He was sure Sofia tried to wake him for breakfast.

"What did you say?" Brendon's voice was thick and unsteady.

"Our secret's safe. That's why God won't stop crying."

"You bloody begged me to go. I'm sure that's why God is pissed off. You and your fucking devil. I told you, Padre Diavolo is a prick."

Angelene smeared brown paint over the painting and groaned.

"What about..." Brendon lowered his voice, picking at his fingernail. "The kiss."

"We were drunk. You ruined everything."

"Did you enjoy kissing me?"

She crumpled the painting, tossing it on the coffee table. "It made me uncomfortable. I can't trust you."

Brendon picked up the painting and smoothed it across his lap. Memories of the beach flooded over him. She was a tease, worse than Rachel. At least he knew the intention behind Rachel's tickling fingers. Angelene had sucked him in, made him have the feels, then spat him out.

"I didn't try to hump you. You touched me in a way that said you wanted to kiss me."

"You should have fucked me. It was what you wanted," Angelene said, gruffly.

"Not everyone has bad intentions. You looked at me like Charlie does Troy."

"That wasn't me."

"What if I told you I loved you."

"You're stupid. Things happen to people who fall in love with me."

Sparks whirred. He tossed the painting at her, jamming his hands in his pockets. "Walter would have liked that painting."

Brendon stormed from the room; his thoughts as crumpled as the painting. Slumping onto a stool, Brendon tapped his phone open. He stared at Maggie's number and drummed his fingers against the counter. Brendon pushed his phone away, mumbling a string of spark infused curse words.

"Having a row with Margaret?"

Madre Innocente pointed a benevolent finger at him. *'Look at the man who loves you like a son. Make your amends and leave his wife alone.'*

"Have you ever tried to be friends with a girl?"

Walter reached inside the fridge, grabbing two bottles of water.

"I'm friends with Kate."

Brendon ran the bottle over his warmed cheeks and forced himself to look at Walter.

"You've kissed Kate. That makes you more than friends?"

"Kate and I tried; it didn't work out."

"You stayed friends. It doesn't make things awkward?"

"Have you kissed Miranda Jones's daughter? I won't tell your dad. Just because I helped write that code doesn't mean I've always followed it."

This was his way out. Confess he had snuck out, got drunk and kissed Angelene. Brendon practiced the speech, his head flooded with memories. Walter had been there for him, supported him, defended him.

"I kissed her."

"That Jones girl is fit, eighteen going on thirty."

Brendon swallowed, chugged the water, and swallowed again. This was his chance to do the right thing. Release the guilt and brace himself for the beating of a lifetime.

"I didn't mean for it to happen."

"Do you feel sorry for what you did?"

"It felt like the right thing to do. Now I feel like a bloody dolt."

"Monogamy is a tricky thing."

"Mum and dad love Maggie."

"If there ever was a girl, you took home to your parents, it's Margaret Thornton. Do you love her?"

Angelene stormed into Brendon's brain. He clamped his fingers around the bottle and squeezed. "I thought I did. I can't stand her."

Walter laughed. "I understand. Ang can drive me completely mad some days."

"What if I want to kiss her again?"

"Then ask yourself if you want to be in a relationship with Margaret."

"I know one thing I want. Maggie has made it perfectly clear she doesn't want that."

"I feel your pain. Ang is reluctant to do anything intimate, even kiss. Who doesn't like to kiss?"

The words hovered around Brendon; her resistance made sense. A simple kiss was no different from sex. He had forced himself on her.

"I broke her bloody trust."

"Don't beat yourself up. Just don't do it again."

"I hear footsteps. I better start getting ready. Mum will expect me in my bloody suit."

"We can't have a simple getaway without Sofia wanting us to get all dolled up."

"I'm sorry."

Walter smiled his crinkly grin. "For what"

"I was a dick when I came home from Dortmund. I was an arse to you."

"I would've been pissed off, too. You're a good kid."

She didn't kiss Walter. When he could get her alone, he would apologize and promise not to kiss her again. He would keep his lamp on, so she felt safe and be her friend.

"Brendon, our reservation is in thirty minutes," Sofia said. "I came to wake you this morning and your room, it smelled…"

"I argued with Maggie and drank some wine. Daft."

"Bottles?"

"Enough for me to barf mammina."

"Five minutes and do something with your hair."

The bottle crinkled in his hand. He had a two-hour meal to get through, with no Charlie face or guilt etched on his brow. He would become the dutiful son, consume himself in the character, the sweet prince of Rosewood manor.

Dinner had gone as Brendon expected. Angelene had downed an old-fashioned, five to be exact. Walter talked about past conquests, how Sofia was the perfect politician's wife and Angelene's consumption of alcohol. He didn't have to use any of his acting skills. Walter and his drunk wife had taken centre stage.

Brendon loosened his tie and strolled into the sitting room. He swiped the remote off the nest of books and clicked on the television. Walter's hushed and displeased voice travelled into the sitting room. Brendon tiptoed to the doorframe, pinning his back to the wall.

"Can you make it up the stairs, little bird?"

"You and your women."

An explosion of sparks lit.

"Kate, Branagh, the Russian princess, even Sofia. Does David know you lusted after her?"

"Bed now, before the whole damn house hears you."

"Enculer."

"Fuck you too. What about you and your married men."

Brendon stepped away from the wall, his hands clamped in tight fists. He could use the Gentlemen's Code as an excuse and step in front of Angelene, save the damsel in distress.

"I need a cigarette."

"Go on, little bird. Your words become very sharp when you drink. It's no wonder people leave you."

Brendon exhaled the sparks and flopped onto the sofa. His first instinct was to protect her. Something, a flutter, Madre Innocente, warned him to protect himself. He heard the door close. Angelene hobbled across the floor and plopped beside him. Patchouli permeated from her skin, spicy and musky. There was a snag in her stockings. She was drunk, pouting, and beautiful.

"Pour me a glass."

"I thought you didn't like scotch?"

"Just fucking pour it."

Brendon held up his hands. "Bloody hell don't be a bitch to me. I was a good boy tonight, no elbows on the table, chewed with my mouth closed, napkin on my lap."

"Did you hear that ridiculous conversation?"

"Unfortunately."

"Walter was a playboy, oui?"

Brendon held onto his laugh. "He loves women."

"He has made love to all his ex's, bought them expensive gifts."

"Not all of them. Kate wouldn't until he promised her a commitment."

"She's more wonderful now, smart and classy, not some gutter girl from Paris."

She downed the scotch and slid the glass across the table. It ricocheted off the books and fell at his feet. Brendon picked it up and ran his foot over the spill.

"Why do you call yourself that?"

"You have no idea what I've done. All the poor decisions and stupid patterns I trip in to."

"Speaking of poor decisions. I'm sorry for kissing you. I made you uncomfortable."

Angelene poked her finger through the run, digging into her thigh.

"It was a strange uncomfortable. I can't describe it."

"I'd love to find those pricks that hurt you and punch them in their fucking mouths."

Angelene glanced up and grinned wistfully. "My hero."

"You doubt your worth. I see your light."

Brendon held his hand over hers and hesitated. She was calm, a hurricane raged in her eyes. Deciding it was worth the risk, he grasp her hand. "Who made you hate yourself so much, you can't see how brilliant you are?"

"You sound like Roman."

"You can't listen to that voice in your head. I never should have listened to Padre Diavolo."

"He's a prick, oui?"

"As bad as the mother of all devils." Her fingers wrapped around his.

"Sometimes I blame myself when we lose. I'll analyze every move I made and criticize myself. Self-doubt is a bloody confidence shaker."

"I've felt nothing but shame and guilt. God must be annoyed with me, asking for forgiveness all the time."

"That's his job, right?"

"I must exhaust Him."

"Probably."

"Can you pour me another?"

"No bloody way. I'll make you a coffee."

Brendon pulled her from the sofa. They walked silently to the kitchen. He pulled out a stool and patted the cushion.

"Sit."

Brendon filled the kettle and clunked it on the stove. He opened the cupboard, pushed aside tins of soup and tea, grabbing coffee.

"I'm sorry for kissing you. You need to know that." He spooned a heap of coffee into the mug and leaned into the counter. "I'm sorry for telling you I love you. I don't love you that is, I fancy you but love, no way."

"I don't like the word."

"I said fancy, a strong like."

The kettle boiled, Brendon tipped water in the mug and went to the fridge, adding cream. He set the mug before her and drooped onto a stool.

"How come you frown every time Walt calls you little bird?"

"I was Roman's little bird. It meant something different when Douchette called me his little bird. It took everything sweet away from it. I've asked Walter not to call me that."

"What colour are you right now?"

"Weepy blue, staticky red and grey."

"Then we need to make you yellow. A happy memory."

"A Bell for Ursli."

"What the bloody hell is that?"

"It was a book Roman used to read to me. We used to chase winter away like Ursli."

"Some of my best memories is mum reading me the Paddington stories."

"I bet you looked sweet curled up beside her."

"I'd have on my Dortmund shirt, Paddington in my arms. I'd squeeze myself so tight against her. She was the best storyteller. Yellow yet?"

"Grey."

"You better tell me something else, then."

"I loved when Roman spoke about Switzerland. He used to tell me about the edelweiss and alpine aster. I used to dream about running through the fields listening to the cowbells. Roman said I would surely find my wings. Switzerland is magical." She gulped back the coffee, rose, and rinsed the mug in the sink. "Please be my friend."

"Whenever you need me, I'll be there."

"I'm a hint of yellow."

"Keep thinking about running through the fields in Switzerland with Roman. You'll be yellow by the morning." He brushed her hair from her face and held her cheek in hand.

"When I turn my lamp on tomorrow night, I want you to turn yours on, too. I'll know you're yellow. Deal?"

"Deal."

They walked hand in hand to the foyer. Angelene glanced from her heels to the stairs. "I'm not meant to wear high heels."

"You're pissed."

"I need you to be my friend and help me."

"We'll destroy the pattern together."

"I wanted to tell you how handsome you looked tonight."

He leaned into her ear. "Don't. I'll want to kiss you again."

"My mother liked a man in a suit. It was one of the few things we agreed upon. You were meant to wear suits."
"Mammina says the same thing."
"Will you help me?"
"I'll always be there."

***

Angelene slipped on a lacy nightgown. It was scratchy and uncomfortable. The weekend had turned into an alcohol-soaked tangle of memories, some to remember and others she couldn't wait to forget. Normal had been difficult. God was angry with her. She was willing to play wife again, see if it fit. This was her fourth attempt.

"You're wearing a nightgown. You look lovely." Walter said, flicking off the bedroom light.

Angelene inhaled deeply. Sex was part of normal. She gazed out the window. Brendon's lamp was on and just as she promised, she switched hers on too.

"I thought you liked the lights off?"

"I'm not sleepy. Will it bother you if I leave it on to read?"

"Not at all, little bird. All that fresh air made me tired."

"Are you too tired for that?"

Walter eased her onto the bed, kissing her jaw. "That, as you call it, will make me sleep like a baby."

He raised her nightgown. She turned her head, staring at the glow coming from Brendon's window. Angelene gripped the sheets and squeezed her eyes shut. She painted herself yellow and shut out Walter's moans.

"I'm trying Walter."

"I know Little bird."

She leaned towards him; swallowed through her rattled nerves and pecked his cheek.

"It'll be the lips next time. Fais de beaux rêves."

Angelene reached for Tale of Two Cities and flipped to a dog-eared page.

'I wish you to know that you have been the last dream of my soul. Did you write that about Brendon, Mr. Dickens? If there ever was a sweeter dream. Fais de beaux rêves, mon ami. Deja visite, I've been here before.'

17 Tu Me Manques

Chickens clucked and pecked at the feed surrounding Troy's feet. He dug under a feathery belly, smiled, and tossed an egg at Charlotte.

"What if I missed? Ms. Nutter is making a special trip for these eggs."

"Be nice." Troy pressed his tongue against his lip, pilfering under a plume of tawny feathers. "That should be twelve."

"How come you have to do this, not Brian or Callum?"

"I bunked off chores yesterday to meet Brendon for pre-pre-match warm-up."

Troy peered down the laneway, flicking the pull on his Manchester United sweatshirt. Angelene approached, daydreamy and golden. She was a different Ms. Pratt than the one that stumbled into the coop, polished but not entirely comfortable. Angelene smiled a tiny, 'I won't say a thing' smile. It was as if she had slipped into his mind and read his guilt.

"Your eggs," Charlotte said, shoving the carton at her.

"Did you gather these yourself?"

Charlotte flung out her hand and grasped his nipple. "Babes did. He's gentler than me, babes."

Troy sucked in his breath, unclasping her fingers. "What did you think of the match, Ms. P?"

He draped an arm over his chest and tugged Charlotte into his side.

"I thought the corner kick would've gone in. You were right there."

Troy pressed his mouth against Charlotte's hair. Heat swept over his cheeks. "Babes is a brilliant defender."

"Walter mentioned scouts were at the match."

"I've got my fingers and toes crossed. I need to leave the farm."

"I'll put you in my prayers," Angelene said.

Troy was crushing on a woman who was nothing like he had ever fancied. There was an aura surrounding Angelene, it struck him like a viper.

"Still two pounds ninety-five?"

"She isn't a spider. She's a witch."

Charlotte's elbow sunk into his ribs. "She asked if the eggs were still…"

"I heard her."

Troy shook his head. Angelene had done it again, worked her magic, cursing him with a love spell.

"Mum said to give them to you."

"Are you feeling ill? You're pale."

"He's suffering from the Charlie face," Charlotte said.

"Is that some kind of disease?"

"It's inflicting the boys around Taunton. Nothing a snog can't cure."

Troy rubbed the back of his neck and forced a grin. "I was thinking about how I can prove myself to those scouts."

"I see the spark; God sees it and He will make your light shine."

Troy licked his lips. Only a witch could turn the pleasant tingles into excruciating knots.

"You have it, it's in your hands and those miraculous feet." Angelene waved, gave a slight smile, and walked away.

"She sees a spark. That gobby cow, no one sees a spark in my little crumpet but me."

"I didn't have the Charlie face."

"You did babes, she was looking at you like you were a bag of Jelly Babies."

"She wasn't."

"I heard Mr. Pratt call her little bird at the match. He should call her little cat."

"Why's that?"

"What's that saying, the cat that got the cream? She looked smug, proud of herself for something."

"Can we change the subject, please?" Troy said, scraping his boots on a cinder block. "I want to start the day on a pleasant note."

"If you give Ms. Nutter the Charlie face again, I'll give you a pinch you'll never forget."

They walked towards the house, which was once a regal manor. The relic of sombre stone and weathered wood was as tired and ancient as the moors. Troy opened the door to a room smelling of oats and mown hay, cluttered with muddied boots and dusty jackets.

"I love you."

"I know babes. I don't blame you for looking. A new hairstyle can make the ugliest girls look good."

"That's all it was. I still think you're the prettiest girl in England."

The house was brighter than a big top and just as noisy. Brian stood on the sofa while Callum held out his scrawny arms, ready for the clinch. Brian jumped from the sofa, clutched Callum's blazer, grunting as he took him to the floor.

"Nice one, Bri," Troy said.

They walked into the kitchen, flour dusted the counters, scraps of pastry were stuck to a well-loved rolling pin.

"Mum made pasties."

"I'm coming for dinner. Your mum's pastry is scrummy," Charlotte said, peeking into a bowl of beef filling.

Troy poured tea, passed one to Charlotte, and took her hand. The feeling of never wanting to let go made his heart swell. It was just the gentle push needed to knock Angelene out of his head.

"Mum! Charlie's coming for dinner tonight."

Evelyn Spence's voice came from somewhere within the house. "You have an hour before school. Don't be late."

17 TU ME MANQUES

"Brendon didn't send Magpie a text, nothing all weekend."

They walked deeper into the house to a puny box that had once been the tack room. The window framed a picture-perfect view of the barn and coop. A constant reminder of where he had been born and where he might stay.

"He was getting game ready."

"All weekend?"

Troy flicked on the light; the wall of Manchester United posters cast a red glow over the mess of clothes creeping from the drawers.

"He didn't meet up with that girl, did he?"

"Don't be daft. He didn't talk about Burnham," Troy said, yanking off his t-shirt, "he seemed distracted, like his mind was elsewhere."

"On the match, training?"

Troy stared down at his hands. "Like happy moments."

"He met up with that tart."

"No, he didn't. I'm going to shower."

"Come sit babes. You know your brothers are going to burst in here. I haven't perfected my piledriver yet."

A crash and bang exploded from the sitting room; laughter rippled down the hallway. Troy stripped out of his grass-stained jeans, twisted the lock, and squirmed into the mess of blankets.

"That'll be you on the cover one day." Charlotte slid a Match magazine off the nightstand and pecked Troy's nose. "Troy Spence, brilliant defender."

She dropped the magazine to the floor, scrunching her nose at a buxom blonde wrapped in a pink satin bow. Charlotte picked up the magazine. The centre page fell open in three swishes.

"Look at the size of her jubblies," she said, glancing at her own doctored breasts. "What are you doing looking at this?"

"Will passed it around the dressing room and stuck it in my rucky. He said I could compare your jubblies to hers."

Charlotte bat him with the magazine and dropped it in the bin.

"You're a million times prettier than that girl."

"You're just saying that, so I don't give you a pinch."

Troy groaned, resting his head on her shoulder. "I like the highlights in your hair. Your nail polish is ace."

"Are your parents going to the caravan soon?"

Troy ran his hand over hers. A purple rhinestone decorated her ring finger. "No, why?"

"We need to have a proper do. Magpie may be up for it if she has a few alcopops."

"Should you be plotting this stuff?"

"I think she wants to hump. She asks a lot of questions, turns a brilliant shade of pink."

"I'll get Brendon to ask his mum. She never says no to him," Troy said, sliding his hand over her stomach. "Fancy a snog?"

"Your brothers will barge in here to put you in a chokehold."

He pecked her cheek, shuffling through the mess on the floor.

"Mum! Charlie and I are doing homework. Tell Brian and Callum not to bother us. I need to finish English."

"You mean biology," Evelyn Spence hollered.

Troy shut the door, turned the lock, and sprung onto the bed.

"Your mum knows we're having a hump?"
"She has four randy boys. She isn't daft."
He unbuttoned Charlotte's shirt, pressing his lips against her stomach. "You still coming to Manchester with me or London or where ever?"
"Liverpool, Germany, France. Wherever babes."
Troy ran his hands over her bottom and tugged at her kilt, grinning at her cherry print knickers. The old walls rattled; feet stomped down the hall, followed by peals of laughter.
"I need to leave here."
"You will."
He kissed a trail up her stomach, gazing into her ocean blue eyes. "All I think about is playing football. There isn't anything else I see myself doing."
"We're going to Manchester. Don't give up hope."
"I don't know why you chose me."
"The chickens make me laugh and you look dead gorgey holding a pitchfork," Charlotte said, winding her legs around his waist, "even dishier in your football kit."
"Brendon looks like a proper footy player. He doesn't even have to try, posh car, posh clothes."
"You don't need those things to be a talented football player. Now be quiet and concentrate. You need to hit that spot that makes me tingle."
Fists hammered against the door, rattling it on its hinges. "Troy! I knocked Brian out."
"Go away Callum. We're busy."
"Slow down, babes."
"I want to finish before they break the bleeding door down," Troy said, gripping her hands. "Go away."
A fit of laughter erupted outside the door. "When you're finished having some rumpy-pumpy, come to the sitting room."
Troy dropped his forehead on Charlotte's shoulder. "If I'm not up to my knees in manure, it's those two bothering me."
"I know what will help."
She clamped her thighs around his waist, tossed him to his back, and rose above him.
"You should wrestle the Inquisitor with a leg lock like that."
"Just close your eyes, let me do all the work. Poor crumpet has had quite the morning."
You have it; I see the spark. God sees it and He will make sure your light shines.
"How do you do it?" Troy whispered.
"Quiet babes, you're making me lose my rhythm."
He blinked and stared; Charlotte was no longer Charlotte. She was blonde with piercing green eyes.
"Babes, your heart is going to beat out your chest."
Troy had never been frightened by things like clowns and heights. He didn't fear much in life. He didn't know what it was about Angelene, but he was afraid.

***

17 TU ME MANQUES

Overexuberant chatter buzzed in the dining hall. Huddles of students exchanged the latest gossip over their designer lunches. The once executive chef had convinced himself a stint at Taunton College would be less stressful than the restaurant he captained. He had spruced up the menu with French classics and gourmet twists. Over salted chips and burgers sans the gastrique was the only item that dazzled the finicky teenagers.

Brendon followed Troy to the lineup and studied the selections, fettucine al a poulet et béarnaise or Cumberland sausage.

"How was Burnham? You have mentioned nothing?" Troy said.

"Boring."

"No walks on the beach, no kisses."

Brendon kept his hands clenched to avoid wiping them on his trousers. He could feel the weight of Troy's stare.

"Who would I be kissing, my dad?"

"You've been awful twitchy, mate. When Ms. Hudson asked you to describe how Werther's emotions govern his life, your voice cracked, like when we were twelve."

"Mum made me spend time with dad. Happy now."

The memory of Angelene standing beside his bed unfolded in his brain like the pages of 'A Bear Called Paddington.' The details were vivid, every touch, the desperate plea in her eyes.

They walked to the quietest corner and slid their trays across the table.

"Still being punished?" Troy said, slurping a forkful of noodles.

Brendon dug around the pasta. He was positive there was chicken buried under the pool of sauce and even more positive, Troy didn't believe him.

"Mum thinks I need to repair my relationship with dad. I had to play chess, and uh, scrabble."

Brendon knew he was in the wrong, lying to Troy. Their friendship had been effortless. They could watch football, not say a word, be completely comfortable in the silence. They didn't need a pact to be there for each other. It had been an unspoken rule since day one. He was lying to his best friend.

"Bollocks, mate, when dad and I spend time together, there's a Man U match on," Troy said, taking a slug of water. "What did the Pratt's do? Play chess and scrabble too?"

Brendon shifted in the chair; heat rolled over his cheeks; the secret was eating a hole in him.

"Married people's stuff."

'Argue, make up, argue.'

"Spend anytime with Ms. Pratt?"

"Don't be a wanker."

The dining hall doors squeaked open, every boy in the room gawked at Rachel, hips wiggling, a coquettish smile. Brendon met her gaze; she was the distraction he needed.

"Hiya number one and number three."

Rachel dragged a chair across the parquet and plonked onto it.

"We have names," Troy said.

"Can't a girl have any fun. Hello Troy, hello knuddlebär."

She slithered to the edge of the chair, lifted his cuff, and glanced at his watch.

"There's a bloody clock on the wall."

"I'd rather look at your posh watch. Fuck, you smell dishy," Rachel said, running her fingers over his knuckles, "do you?"

"Do I what?" Troy said.

"Smell as dishy as knuddlebär." She leaned across the table and sniffed. "William's a dolt. You don't smell like manure, you smell delicious."

"Can you sit down, please?"

"Like what you see?" Rachel said, wiggling her bottom.

"The entire dining hall can see up your bloody kilt."

"You're no fun. Neither are you number three." Rachel pulled an apple out of her purse and crunched. "You want a bite, knuddlebär?"

Troy rolled his eyes, twirling pasta around his fork. "What do you want? You're going to get me a pinch if you don't bugger off."

Rachel ran a sticky finger over Brendon's ear. Her breath was warm and sweet against his cheek. "I saw knuddlebär and thought I'd say hello. Margaret is making things difficult for me."

Brendon shrank away, rubbing his sleeve over his earlobe. "Do you mind? Michael and the drama swots are two tables over. They're probably texting Maggie right now."

Rachel whipped the apple core into the bin. "You're blushing, knuddlebär."

"You're as red as that apple she just ate, mate."

Rachel pulled a tube of lip gloss from her pocket, pumped the applicator up and down and layered it on her lips. "Thornton called me a schlampe."

"I don't know what that is."

"A trollop."

She leaned her breasts into his arm; the fork fell from his fingers. Her breasts looked like the cantaloupes Amelia had brought home from Tesco.

Troy pinched his lips and flung his bottle of water. "Cool off mate."

"Sorry, Maggie called you a trollop. Can you leave now?"

"Anything for you, knuddlebär, kisses."

"Your phone beeped. It's probably Maggie giving you shit."

Brendon tapped open his phone, read the text, and deleted it.

"You sure nothing else happened in Burnham? No Bronwyn? You didn't stumble upon any other girls on the beach?"

Brendon grabbed his water bottle, spun the cap off, and chugged. "Just chess and scrabble."

'I kissed her. I told her I loved her.'

"You're looking awful innocent, mate, which scares me."

***

Sofia flumped onto the sofa, her mind jumbled and blurred. Questions came home with her from Burnham and rode in the passenger seat to Kate's. She couldn't make sense of it. Had she imagined the smell? Had Angelene answered the question about love and the boy in brown?

"Every detail. The dimple on his left is deeper than his right, the cheeky twinkle in his eye. All from memory."

Kate set a plate of lemon madeleines on a Chinoiserie coffee table and snuggled into the corner of the sofa.

17 TU ME MANQUES

"What are you going on about?"

"Didn't I tell you? Angelene drew a portrait of Brendon."

"Angelene drew that? It's a little out of character for her. Shouldn't Brendon have glowing eyes or horns?"

"Have you heard of Tartini?"

"He's a composer."

"He had a terrible inferiority complex, suffered from depression. The devil appeared in his dream. He wrote his most famous piece, The Devil's Trill."

Kate smiled, shaking her head in disbelief. "What are you saying? Angelene's mastery of art is because she made a deal with the devil."

"Don't people usually sit for portraits? I don't want him around her."

"What's she going to do? Put a hex on him? Perform black magic?"

Sofia smoothed and re-smoothed her blouse, struggling to breathe through the flutters. "She looks at him in this way that makes me uncomfortable. Angelene frightens me. It's like she's constantly in a state of dying, like she gave up struggling to live and now floats, chin deep in the memories. There's a desperate look in her eyes, help me but, let me die."

"Tough weekend?"

"It was a damn roller coaster ride. David and I took Brendon to Alton Towers when he was little. It was my turn to ride the roller coaster. I ended up in the lady's room."

"I certainly hope you didn't spend the weekend in the loo."

"One minute Walter and Angelene were laughing, I think she was laughing, you never can tell with her, then she's pouting, he's angry."

"It's bound to take some time. They're still getting to know one another."

Sofia stuck a fingernail between her bracelets, flick, clack. "You put the Bible box on the mantle."

Kate rested her hand on Sofia's. "What's the matter?"

"I think Brendon snuck out with her."

"Really?"

"Angelene begged Walter to go into town. I thought she was going to bounce through the ceiling. She was that anxious. He said no, she pouted."

"What does that prove?"

Sofia stroked her eyebrow. Her throat was tight, clogged with questions. Brendon wasn't a liar. He wasn't a drinker, yet he smelled and looked like he had pickled himself in cheap wine. Angelene had worn the same look.

"I went to wake Brendon for breakfast, his room stunk of wine."

"Did you ask him about it?"

"I think she seduced him."

Kate bit into a cookie, smiling an 'you're so dramatic, but I love you,' smile. "If he sneaked out, and that's a big if, he did it on his own accord. I wouldn't blame him; it must be hard doing as he's told all the time."

"She had her hands all over David."

"Since when are you a jealous woman?"

Sofia met Kate's gaze; a small frown creased her brow. "I'm not jealous. She needs to understand boundaries, always touching and flirting."

"I don't think she means any harm."

"I wish I were as observant as my mother. I might understand her."

"Did you ask Angelene?"

"I hinted. She danced around it." Sofia picked up a madeleine, stared at it and dropped it back on the plate. "She's obsessed with my family."

"Your life is like a fairy tale, Rosewood Manor, the king and queen of Taunton, the prince. Who wouldn't want to be part of that story? What does she know about family?"

Sofia drudged up conversations with Angelene. Neglectful mother, absent father. While Sofia was trying to figure out the girl from Paris, Angelene was trying to figure out what family meant.

"I told Brendon you still love Walter."

Kate glanced at a photo of her and Walter on the beach in Burnham.

"I never loved Walter."

'Neither does Angelene.'

Sofia followed Kate's gaze, grinning softly. "Admit you love Walter."

"I'll always love him. Underneath all that bravado, he's a wonderful man."

"Angelene says he has golden fingertips."

"There's truth to it. Everything he touches turns to gold."

The unsettling feeling welled inside Sofia. It was too coincidental, Angelene begging to go out, Brendon hungover.

"Don't turn your back on, Walter."

"Are you worried about him, too?" "Their marriage seems strained, forced."

"She's more work than Walter expected."

Sofia ran her thumb over the breaks in her lifeline. "Angelene reads palms."

"A good Catholic girl."

"She saw things, things we don't talk about. She saw a fourth." Sofia pulled her cardigan tighter around her chest. Goosebumps prickled her skin.

"Give me your hand."

Sofia laid her hand on Kate's lap, her heart knocked wildly.

"I see a woman with a beautiful manicure, who loves antiques and worries."

"Something doesn't feel right."

"You're worrying for nothing. This is Walter's Mountain to climb, not yours. Did you ask Brendon if he snuck out?"

"He got into a fight with Maggie and drank his anger away. Brendon doesn't do that, Angelene does."

"This weekend has opened old wounds. It's only natural, you'd worry."

"Stay by Walter's side. Be there for him."

Kate wrapped her hand around Sofia's. "I'll always be there. No more worrying."

Sofia had no idea why the feeling lingered or what it meant. The look in Angelene's eyes haunted her like an omen. Something bad was going to happen.

***

"Do you think God heard my apology?"

"You've confessed your sins and thanked Him."

"Why hasn't He given me a sign?"

"Sometimes they're subtle, and you're too busy or troubled to notice. Be patient."

17 TU ME MANQUES

Angelene scrambled from the confessional, crossed herself, and pushed open the door. The September sun hit her face; it took a moment for her eyes to adjust. She rambled across the car park, no twinge in her belly, no flutter of her hair. Angelene tugged on the taxi door and dropped into the seat. The scent of brandy tobacco carried her back to the flat in Paris and Roman Krieger.

"Can you take me to the bookstore, please?"

"Which one? There's one on High Street and East Street."

"I'm not sure. It's beside a patisserie and a clothing store."

"Is that the one that sells witchy stuff?"

"I was looking for a special book. It was the only shop that could find it."

"You're new to Taunton?"

Angelene twisted her engagement ring around her finger. "I married a man from here. Perhaps you know him, Walter Pratt."

"I've driven him home from the pub a few times. You live in the farmhouse next to Rosewood manor."

Angelene slid her ring over her knuckle and turned to face the driver. "Do you know the Cook's?"

"From one generation to the next."

"You must know their son."

"Now there's a kid going places. Nice boy. Helped me change a tire once. I was stuck out on Taunton Road."

Angelene studied the driver's face, chubby cheeks, sky-blue eyes, bushy white moustache, head full of white hair. His words came out vibrant green.

"What's your name?"

"Malcolm."

"How long have you lived in Taunton?"

"Sixty-two years. Been driving a taxi since I was twenty."

"May I call you when I need a ride? The taxi I took earlier smelled like spoiled milk."

Malcolm pulled alongside the curb; he grinned; his moustache fluffed over his lip. "I'd be honoured."

"Can you wait? I'll only be a minute."

"I have to pick up Ms. Mulholland from the salon."

Angelene slid her purse strap over her arm. The attempt at a smile pained her. "I'll drop her off at home and come back."

"I'm still trying to find my wings. You've made me feel safe."

"Shouldn't that be your feet?"

"No, my wings. My feet lead me to all sorts of stupid places."

Malcolm chuckled. "You say some funny things, Ms. Pratt."

"Please call me Angelene. Ms. sounds strange to me."

She walked to the door, the breeze cool on her back. The boy with liquid blue eyes would have admired the Tudor façade. The sign, written in Old English lettering, creaked back and forth on its wrought iron frame, 'Where the Raven Flies.' Angelene stepped inside the dimly lit shop, yet it was as bright as the Tibetan singing bowls vibrating in the air. Plumes of incense snaked around the shelves of books and tables of spell infused candles. Angelene tapped a bell. A blood red sphere with lacy white veins weaving through it caught her attention. She touched the stone; a tiny shock zapped her fingertip; she drew her hand back.

The salesclerk, draped in a jade kaftan, appeared from behind a curtain of clacking beads.

"It's pretty, isn't it?"

"It made the hair on my arm stand up. What is it?"

"Crazy lace agate."

Angelene touched her lips, overjoyed. God had given her a sign. She picked up the crystal and rolled it between her fingers. The electricity tickled her hand.

"Agate has incredible healing powers. It makes you feel whole, less vulnerable."

"Do you think God has touched it?"

"If you're drawn to it, then God has touched it."

"It might help put me back together," Angelene said, laying the stone on the counter. "You found the book?"

The sales clerk slid out a book from beneath the cash register, presenting it like a sacred gift. Angelene's gaze darted over the illustration of Ursli and his cow bell. She drew in a breathless sigh.

"I've never seen anyone so happy about a book."

"A book takes you to places; makes you feel things. A story is magic."

"It makes me feel good knowing you'll love this book."

"This is more than a book. It's an old friend."

She pressed the book to her lips, breathed in the memories, breathed in Roman Krieger.

Angelene pushed open the door. A thin strip of sunlight severed the grey clouds, washing the street in pale gold. Angelene smiled, it was sign number two. She approached the black cab. Malcolm fiddled with his moustache; the newspaper spread over the steering wheel.

"Can you take me to Taunton Park?"

"There isn't a match today. The boys might be training."

"I like the energy there."

One by one, the street lamps turned on. Angelene memorized which shops she would like to visit, a charity shop, another bookstore.

"You'll be my driver from now on."

Malcolm laughed. The sound sprang from deep within his chest, lifting his cheeks and jiggling his belly. "You're a sweet girl."

The scent of brandy tobacco seeped from the heat vents, invading her nose and mind.

Roman, why do you pay so much attention to Angelene?

Angelene needs love and attention from you, her mother.

You're like Gustav, always staring at her.

I'm nothing like Mr. Jenssen. my heart breaks for her. She's going to end up like you, searching for love, receiving it, and running as fast as she can. Someone needs to love little bird.

"I thought you'd fallen asleep."

"I was daydreaming. It gets me into trouble," Angelene said, clutching her purse. "Drop me off here. I'll walk the rest of the way."

"Do you need me to wait? I'm expected home for tea. I can come back and get you."

"I have a ride home. Thank you, you'll make finding my wings much easier. See you soon."

Angelene walked along the pavement fringed with pennyroyal and knapweed. '*This is a test, see if I can be his friend. Please be with me.*' She crossed herself and grinned. Brendon paced, stopped to fumble with the pylons, then paced again.

"Are you nervous?"

"Where did you come from?"
"I had Malcolm drop me off at the corner."
"Who's Malcolm?"
"My taxi driver. He's the nicest man. I liked how his taxi smelled."
"They usually smell like armpit and kebobs."

Angelene laid her purse and the paper bag on the bench and grabbed a grass-stained ball. She looked at Brendon in rapt fascination. She thought God was beautiful and that beauty itself was an expression of God. God had done his best work creating Brendon Cook.

"You need gloves," Brendon said, digging in his duffel bag for a pair of Puma Evodisk gloves.

His voice pulled her from her rapture.

"They're big. They have your name on them." She held out her hands. He slid the gloves on, adjusting the Velcro. "My hands look like flippers. Why are they sticky?"

"It's latex. It gives the gloves a good grip."

"Now what?"

"Get in net. It's coming straight down the middle, centre shot."

Angelene walked across the field and stood behind the white line, her insides squishy. A strange feeling captured her. It was as if the pitch, trees, and the ball were magic, and she stepped into a dream.

"That was much too easy. Try again."

Brendon laughed at the serious look on her face. "You barely cover the net. What if I miss and I give you a black eye? I'd feel terrible."

"I'm waiting."

"Try to figure out where I'm going to put the ball."

She watched him pass the ball between his feet. He kicked it. She rushed to the right side.

"Easy again."

"I'm coming in for the rebound."

The ball soared above her head; she lost her balance and landed on her bottom.

"You, okay?"

Angelene burst into unrestrained laughter. "That was quite the shot."

"Are you having fun?"

A hitch tickled her throat. She couldn't remember the last time she laughed.

"Shoot again."

"You sure?"

She dusted the back of her jeans and took position. "This time don't stop. Keep trying to score on me."

"You're asking for it."

"Dortmund against PSG."

"No bloody competition."

Angelene walked backwards into the net, a car idled by the curb. Icy tingles snaked over her skin. She had learned over the years to trust her gut. It had always been right about Douchette, Gustav Jenssen. The car sat. The prickling moved down her spine and into her stomach.

"We have to go."

"What's the matter? You're white as a ghost."

The car idled at the stop sign, then drove off.

"It's dark. Sofia will wonder where you are."

"You afraid I'll get another past you?"

"There was a car. Someone was watching us."

"Was it a Fiesta?"

She shook her head and followed him to the BMW. Angelene looked up and down the street. She yanked at the sleeve of her shirt, dabbed at the sweat above her lip, and imagined herself washed in yellow.

"This is a test."

"Did I fail?"

"We promised to try again. I wanted to see if I could be with you without adoring your light."

"Do you fancy me?"

"Be serious. I had a feeling. It took my breath away and made God angry. I need to learn to live with your light and not want it."

"I had a feeling, too. Maybe we can't be friends."

"We're going to do this. I'm going to prove to God I can be friends with a boy, tell my devils to fuck off."

Angelene carefully slid the book from the bag. Many nights, the story had brought her comfort. Roman Krieger had grown up listening to the story of the brave little boy. The first time he shared it with her, the darkness of night lifted. She, too, could be brave like Ursli.

"You found your book."

"I gave my copy to Yasmine so she could chase winter away and welcome spring. I feel like I've put back a missing piece."

She reached into the bag and wrapped her hand around the crystal; it vibrated. God was pleased. She could do this, be Brendon's friend and not want his light. Warmth washed over her insides; the feeling was so powerful it stole her breath.

"Did I tell you Rachel made me lunch a while back? A German feast for German lessons."

"Mother would spend days planning a meal for a lover. It's the way to a man's heart, not that she cared. She stole their hearts and ran."

"Maggie said it was one of Rachel's tart tactics."

"My mother was an expert at luring men, their favourite foods, favourite positions. Mother thought her vagina was gold."

Angelene squeezed the crystal, resting her cheek against the seat, committing Brendon's profile to memory. She would never forget the day she had found her laugh.

"Mademoiselle femme fatale will tempt you. Padre Diavolo is strong in you."

"You sound like the priest Nonna made me sit with when I was ten."

"Why did she do that?"

"I was obsessed with jubblies."

Angelene shoved her fingers between her thighs. The blush on his cheeks was charming and tempting.

"Sofia's sweet boy, obsessed with breasts?"

"It started when we were in Italy and accidentally stumbled onto a topless beach, boobs everywhere," Brendon said, turning into the driveway. "In year five, Matilda Morimoto told the headmaster I was staring at my teacher's baps. Mum was so embarrassed."

"I can't imagine how David reacted."

"He lectured me about objectifying a woman."

A strange warmth fluttered through her belly; she squeezed her thighs tighter.

17 TU ME MANQUES

"Padre Diavolo has been with you a long time."

"It wasn't my fault. Ms. O'Malley wore low-cut dresses and whenever she bent over, it's all I saw."

"Are you still obsessed with breasts?"

"Bloody hell, I love them. I've never really touched one, just ran my hand over Maggie's."

"Padre Diavolo has filled your head with lusty thoughts."

Brendon flicked the BVB key chain. "Can I tell you something?"

"Don't tell me you want to kiss me. You'll ruin my day."

"I missed you today, in a friend sort of way."

"Never say I miss you; say tu me manques, you are missing from me."

18 The Untea Party

Brendon dropped an unfinished assignment on Mr. Clark's desk. Henry VIII hadn't been on his mind; memories of Angelene's laughter had bogged him down. He could still see the look on her face when it exploded from her mouth. It surprised her that a laugh still lived inside her. The 'I'm in love' feeling was relentless.

"Are you coming to my rehearsal tonight?" Maggie said.

Brendon launched himself through the door. The sun warmed his cheeks. He marched ahead of her. The leaves were turning, wavering in the breeze, holding on stubbornly, like Maggie.

"I said I would."

"You used to enjoy coming to my rehearsals. We'd go out after. It's been our thing."

It had been a thing for two years, celebrate her getting the lead role and force himself to sit in the musty theatre. He went out of duty and loyalty to the code.

"Bloody hell, I'll meet you after class and we'll drive over."

"Don't sit beside the tart," Maggie warned. "I have spies everywhere."

"Enjoy theatre studies."

Brendon walked away. The 'in love feeling' returned, transporting him to the pitch and the joy that overwhelmed Angelene.

"Knuddlebär, wait up."

Rachel snaked her arm around his waist. Maggie's warning flashed through his head. He spun out of her grasp.

"Dancing, are we?"

"Maggie has spies. They're probably watching me right now."

"I missed you today."

"It's tu me manques, you're missing from me."

Rachel lifted his blazer and smacked his bottom. "You have a brilliant bum, knuddlebär, it doesn't jiggle."

Brendon tugged at his blazer, nodding towards the laurel bushes. "There's some of Maggie's friends. I bet they're texting her right now."

"I was enjoying German lessons. Thornton has ruined everything," Rachel said, hooking her pinky in his belt loop. "Why don't you come round to mine? Thornton will never know."

"Bloody terrible idea," Brendon said, unhooking her finger.

"Don't trust me?"

The oak doors to the science building groaned open. Troy threw his hand up in a wave.

"Are you bothering my mate again?"

"It isn't bugging if he likes it."

"You need to keep those covered," Troy said, folding Rachel's lapels over her cleavage. "It's time for a party, mate."

"You're suggesting I have one."

"You have the biggest house."

"I could finally see inside Rosewood manor. I bet your bedroom is ace."

"You won't go anywhere near my mate's bedroom," Troy said, lifting his cuff. "Call mammina."

"It would be brilliant, knuddlebär."

Brendon grabbed his phone, tapped, and hit speaker.

"Shouldn't you be in class?" Sofia's voice was cool and curt.

"I have ten minutes. Did I tell you how brilliant you looked this morning?"

"What did you do?"

Troy laughed. Brendon held a hand over his mouth. "You won't get a call from Dawson."

"You're interrupting my party."

"Can I have a few people over this weekend?"

"Absolutely not. I'm flying to Brussels to see your father. I won't have my home turned upside down again."

"I'll keep everyone in the great room."

"You promised a few people the last time. Five turned into fifty. Amelia found condom wrappers in my Nonna's majolica vase."

Troy and Rachel burst into laughter. Brendon shot up his middle finger. "I won't let anyone hump in the house."

"Can't you say make love?"

"We're teenagers, we hump. Please, I need this."

"You needed the last party. The answer is no. Let me get back to my friends. You get to class."

Brendon raised his shoulders and slid his phone into his pocket.

"You heard her."

"Be a rebel, have it. Cheers, mate."

Brendon scratched at his tousled hair; he would need a foolproof plan. The list of rules would have to be extensive.

"Would you come?"

He opened the door; dust motes floated in the musty air.

"I missed the last one."

Should I or shouldn't I rolled through his mind. Padre Diavolo thought it was a smashing idea. Madre Innocente scolded him. He'd give himself until the end of Latin to decide.

"Both of you to the blackboard."

Mr. Campbell's snively voice snapped Brendon out of his reverie.

"I didn't have time to finish the assignment."

"You certainly find time to dazzle us on the pitch. Why not amaze us with your knowledge of Latin."

Brendon sent his backpack flying down the aisle, begging the sparks to go away.

"I will not tolerate your temper in my classroom," Mr. Campbell said. An arthritic finger poked Brendon's spine, pushing him into the ledge. His cheeks tingled and burned. Rachel grabbed a magnet and stuck her assignment on the blackboard. She nudged Brendon, nodding towards the paper. Chalk fell in white flakes onto the pink and blue smudged tray.

"Very good Mr. Cook. You can thank Rachel after class for providing you the answers."

Rachel shaped her fingers into a heart and winked. "Ich Liebe dich"

"I'm happy you love Brendon. Please go to your desks and start today's assignment."

Brendon dusted his hands and sauntered to his desk. A little paper crane dropped into his lap. "What's this?"

"Cranes stand for success and good fortune. All your dreams will come true, knuddlebär."

He examined the folded paper and sat it on the corner of his desk.

"Will you keep it?"

"I'll put it in my bedroom."

Rachel dug in her blazer pocket and placed a handful of Love Hearts on his notebook. He pushed a candy towards her. She smiled and popped it in her mouth.

"Kiss you, I would love to, knuddlebär."

He picked up a candy, the message, 'I love you.' Angelene was married. He had to respect that, even if it hurt worse than the time, he got a football boot in the stomach. He'd let her be Ms. Pratt.

"Knuddlebär."

Brendon shook Angelene from his head. A pink candy rolled across his desk, 'In love' written in white.

"Aren't you a love them and leave them kind of girl?"

Rachel held her notebook in front of her mouth. "Have a party. Show me around the manor."

"Get myself into trouble?"

"It isn't trouble if you want it to happen."

Brendon's cell phone vibrated against his thigh. He glanced at Mr. Campbell, hid his phone under his desk, and cursed at the angry emoji. Brendon scrubbed at his heated cheeks.

"Can I go to the loo?"

Theodore Campbell aimed his pen at the door, his face twisted. "I expect a completed assignment."

Brendon strolled out of the classroom. He walked down the hall to the toilets, surveying the stalls.

"What the bloody hell are you doing?"

"I should ask you the same thing. Charlie said you may have a party."

Brendon pressed his lips into a tight line and stared at the ceiling. "You got me out of Latin for this?"

"I know you've been eating sweets with the tart."

"Mammina said no."

"Your last party was a disaster. There were cigarette butts smashed in her carpets, you barfed in her roses."

Brendon scowled into his phone. To hell with Maggie, the Code, and the good boy. It was time to play with Padre Diavolo.

"Mum is going to Brussels. She'll never know."

"We can spend the weekend together. Go for a walk in the forest."

"You know I'm not allowed in there."

"You'll have a party but won't go into the forest."

Brendon knocked his phone against his forehead and sighed heavily. "It's bloody different. There are ghosts in the forest."

"There are no proof ghosts exist except the ones people create in their heads. Defying your mother is defying your mother."

"Mum has her reasons. It would bloody kill her if she found out I was in there."

"Don't have the party."

Brendon shook the tingles from his fingers, switched the phone and wiggled the sparks from the other. The plan would have to be rock solid to protect the illustrious manor from hordes of rowdy teenagers.

"I'm having it. If mammina finds out, I'll smile my best dimpled smile. She'll forgive me."

"What's the matter with you? Your dad is still upset about Dortmund. Don't you want to make things right?"

"Dad will lecture me, and I'll tune him out. I'm getting good at that lately."

"You're getting good at lots of daft things."

Brendon stared at the blank screen. The party was on.

***

Angelene's eyes drifted to the window. The sun hung low between the trees, casting a pale stream of grey, gold across the gleaming parquet floor. She did not know how long she had been at the manor. The only things she had noticed were a wall of books, the extravagant display of food, and Victoria McGregor's ritual. Pick up a sandwich, sniff and place it on her plate, pluck, sniff, stack.

"Angelene, you haven't eaten a thing."

She tore her gaze from the window, a twitchy grin on her lips. "I ate before I came. I keep forgetting afternoon tea means there is food."

"I thought holding the party in the library would make you comfortable. You love books like a mother would a child."

"You've been very considerate. Books make better friends then people."

Sofia glanced at Victoria, sniffing a radish and butter sandwich. "I imagine they could be."

"These sandwiches look like roses."

"That's herbed mascarpone with smoked salmon. There's Branston pickle and cheese, egg, watercress and, just for you, jambon-beurre. Walter said you liked ham and butter."

Simone stabbed an olive with a toothpick, jabbing the air. "You should get into event planning. It'll give you something to do when Brendon leaves."

Angelene took a plate off the stack, examined each tier, deciding on the ham and butter, a triangle of egg, and the Branston pickle. She grinned politely at Sofia and walked in light, precise steps to the sofa. *'How to sit like a lady. You read it this morning. Knees together, ease down gently, smooth my skirt, angle my feet. How do I do that and balance my plate? These ridiculous rules.'* Angelene flumped onto the cushion and cursed quietly.

"How's Brendon?" Simone said, pawing at her hair.

"He's fine."

"Eshana and I went to the last match. He was just brilliant, so dishy in his black kit. Why hasn't he asked Eshana out?"

Sofia sipped her tea and narrowed her eyes. "You or Eshana."

Angelene couldn't wait to get home and put the afternoon in her sketchbook. Sofia's annoyed face, Victoria's sniffing, the look of lust in Simone's eyes. She would title it, the Untea Party.

"Didn't you notice our William? He's just as handsome in his kit."

"He sits on the bench, Vic. What's to see?" Simone said.

Brown goo seeped from the corner of the sandwich. Angelene glanced around the room. Sofia and Simone had locked eyes. Victoria was studying the desserts. Angelene stuck her finger in the pickle and licked it. It was sweet and sour.

"Eshana would be a better match than Margaret Thornton. Similar backgrounds, similar lifestyles."

"You'd be able to gawk at him all the time," Victoria said, shoving her nose in a Bakewell tart. "Thank goodness Brendon is attractive. My William is smart. Smart gets you somewhere."

Something stirred within Angelene. Brendon had been there for her, now it was her turn. She swallowed; little flutters stirred in her belly.

"Brendon sees things in a unique way."

Victoria's crumb-filled mouth dropped open; Simone chuckled an 'oh dear. Angelene met Sofia's cool gaze. Mere de tous les diables had found her voice.

"Thank you Angelene, I don't pay attention to Victoria's opinion about Brendon. It's always a competition," Sofia said, jerking her silk cuffs, "She barged in, attached a price tag to the new chairs I bought David, inventoried the china, the fabrics, even the damn food."

"Well," Victoria poopooed. "It doesn't take brains to kick a football around."

"C'est des conneries. It takes concentration, foresight."

She needed a cigarette, a glass of wine, something to keep up the confident charade. Sofia's questioning gaze was chasing the mother of all devils away.

"You seem to know a lot about football," Simone said.

Victoria lifted herself off the sofa and marched to the credenza, helping herself to tea. "I could have sworn I saw you at Taunton Park. I finished handing out flyers for the gala. You asked me to do that and I'm still annoyed.

"Do you fancy Brendon too?" Simone said.

Angelene cleared her throat and picked at the black paint embedded under her fingernail.

"I fancy, as you call it, my husband."

"You must have a doppelgänger," Victoria said. The seams on her paisley dress stretched as she dropped onto the chair.

"Have you looked at the catalogue for the auction?" Sofia said.

"You weren't in net?"

Angelene twisted her bracelets around her wrist. Veronique had been a firm believer in St. Augustine's view. Lying was morally wrong. Over the years, Angelene realized, some lies were necessary and morally just, like the Christians that hid Jews from the Nazi's. There was nothing malicious about this lie, it was to protect Brendon.

"Was it Posy Partridge, the keeper from the girl's team? She's always hanging around the pitch asking for advice," Simone said.

Sofia plucked at the bow on her blouse. "You're still upset they chose me to plan the gala, aren't you?"

"No offence Vic but, Sofia has a knack for putting on a bash," Simone said.

Victoria bit into a tart. "You weren't in town?"

"I was, but not at the pitch. I went to St. George Church and a bookstore." Angelene set down her plate and kept her gaze on Victoria.

"Excuse me."

She wobbled to her feet and rambled from the library; Sofia's sigh followed her. Little earthquakes erupted inside her. Angelene climbed the stairs, glanced over her shoulder, and tiptoed down the hall. She snuck into the eucalyptus and citrus scented room, floating to the dresser. Tucked within the pages of a football magazine was a stack of photos. She slid them out, flipping through photos of Charlotte and Maggie, Troy with his sunshine smile. She stopped at a picture of Brendon, running her finger over his tousled hair and grin. Opening her clutch, she slid the photo in the pocket and tucked the rest into the magazine. Angelene turned from the dresser, spying a Borussia Dortmund shirt hanging from the side of the laundry basket. She picked it up and brought it to her nose.

"Please forgive me."

Angelene folded the jersey into a square and placed it deep within the giant rectangular purse. Walter had brought it home from London, raving it was the latest fashion. She had found it cumbersome and awkward; it was perfect now. She took one more glance around Brendon's bedroom, meeting the black bead eyes of a bear.

"You must be Monsieur Paddington. It's nice to meet you."

She squeezed her purse under her arm and hurried down the hall. Guilt sawed relentlessly at her gut, lies, stealing. *'Forgive me, I'll punish myself. Thirty-nine lashes.'*

"You weren't hiding in the bathroom again, were you?" Sofia said.

Angelene gripped the banister, her cheeks burned.

"I walked right past the bathroom to that green and white room. The view of the forest is beautiful."

"I can't say I like the view," Sofia said, straightening the bow on her blouse. "Ignore Victoria."

Sweat gathered in Angelene's armpit; she squeezed her purse tighter.

"I have no reason to be with Brendon."

"I know. Come have dessert."

Angelene summoned confidence. It ignored her. She dissolved onto the sofa.

Sofia ladled trifle into a bowl and passed it to Angelene. "David said Walter has business in Paris. Will you be joining him?"

"Not this time."

"Aren't you homesick?" Victoria said.

"Not really."

"You don't want to shop, Chanel, St. Laurent?" Simone said.

Angelene shifted among the cushions, picking through the berries and custard. Home, she still had no idea where she belonged or what it meant.

"Going home will open old wounds."

18 THE UNTEA PARTY

Victoria sucked the jam from her finger and wiped it on a napkin. "You're going to set Walter free in the City of Love?"

"He's working."

Sofia dunked a sugar cube in her tea and raised an eyebrow. "Walter is not a womanizer."

Angelene glanced up from her bowl. There was something unnerving about the way Victoria was staring at her. It could be guilt, paranoia. She was sure Victoria was taking inventory of her.

"I'm going to Brussels with David. He has a lovely weekend planned for us."

"David needs to give Taj a few pointers," Simone said.

"That Partridge girl is tall, built like an athlete. You never see her out of her Taunton Blues kit," Victoria said, stuffing a cookie in her mouth. "You ready Simone."

"I was hoping to say hello to Brendon."

"Thank you both for coming. I'll see you out."

Angelene set the bowl down and flopped against the sofa. Her breath rushed from her lungs to her mouth. She would have to stop the private meetings. It was part of a pattern, secret trysts, hiding, lying.

"Victoria is ridiculous. She never quits."

It was hard to tell if Sofia believed Victoria.

"I should head home, too."

"Don't let Victoria scare you off."

"My head is full."

"I understand. I need a long soak," Sofia said, peering out the window. "Shall I drive you? It looks like rain."

'It would be appropriate for God to cry.'

"I'll walk. It will help clear my head."

She grabbed her purse, clamping it against herself like a shield. Angelene teetered across the foyer, stopped at the door, and shivered.

"Something cold went through me."

"It's the ghosts," Sofia said. "David's mother sits at the piano. Richard roams from room to room. I still can't get rid of him."

"Are there any others?"

"One," Sofia said. "It's raining. Are you sure I can't drive you?"

"If I don't see you, have a wonderful time with David."

The wind nipped at her legs, pushing her along the drive. Angelene removed her shoes. Rain seeped through the canopy of branches, soaking her clothes.

'You're disappointed in me.' Mud oozed between her toes. *'Who will I have when Brendon leaves?'*

Headlights shone through the blinding rain. She recognized the glistening black paint. *'You're always here when I need you.'*

The car did a U-turn and idled beside her.

"What the bloody hell are you doing? Get in."

Angelene rushed around the car and slid across the leather seat, wiping her arm over her face.

"Walking home."

"Put this over you," Brendon said. He passed her his blazer and draped it over her lap.

"I survived the Untea party. I had a cheese and pickle sandwich."

"Did mum call it that?" Brendon said, cutting the engine, "sometimes she themes her tea parties."

"Tweedle dee and tweedle dum were there."

"I'm going to grab my backpack; I want to change out of my school kit."

Angelene ran up the walkway, unlocking the front door. She dropped her shoes and tossed his blazer onto the bricks in the front room. Angelene tore away her muddied stockings and rambled up the stairs. She hurried down the hall, peeled away her blouse, dropped her skirt to the floor, and kicked it into the bedroom. She lay her purse on the bed and wiggled into a pair of lounge pants and a sweatshirt. It had been a trying afternoon. A cup of tea might help the lingering jitters, a glass of wine would be better.

"Are you decent?"

"I'm putting my jeans on."

"I'll bring you tea. May I have a glass of wine?"

"No, you may not. The house is a bloody mess."

"I was in a hurry."

An apple core had browned beside a wedge of brie, dishes sat in the sink, stale cigarette smoke hung in the air. Angelene set the kettle on the stove and grabbed the cannister of tea bags. "I'd rather have a glass of wine."

"You spent the afternoon with Ms. McGregor. You'll drink the whole bloody bottle."

"She's a horrible woman."

"I made a fire," Brendon said, splashing milk into his mug. "Did you smoke an entire pack? The house stinks."

"Walter made me spiky red."

"What is it this time?"

They walked to the front room, the scent of cedar masked the cigarette smoke and incense. Angelene stretched along the sofa and tucked her feet under his thighs.

"I didn't want to go for tea. He said I must. I said I was wearing a navy dress, he said to wear a black skirt. I said I would wear a white blouse, he said wear black."

"You should have told him to fuck off."

The conversation with Walter littered her brain. Guilt strangled her, and a new feeling appeared. It was murky green.

"Victoria told Sofia she saw me at the pitch." Angelene blinked at the red spots flashing in her eyes. "Simone said it was Posy Partridge. Who's she?"

"The keeper for Taunton Blues," Brendon said. He pulled her feet from beneath his legs and laid them across his lap. "What did mum say?"

"She dismissed Victoria," Angelene said, rubbing her arms, "I practiced what to say, read a book on etiquette, I got to your house, and nothing came out. I couldn't speak until Victoria said you weren't smart."

Brendon grinned and sipped his tea. "Gobby cow. What did you say?"

"I defended you, like you do me."

"What did mum think of that?"

"I couldn't tell. She was upset about Posy Partridge. She wanted to have a pleasant party."

Angelene dug under a mess of illustrations, found a half-smoked butt, and placed it in her mouth. "Simone wanted to say hello to you. She wants you to date her daughter."

The spots flashed and flickered; her chest burned.

18 THE UNTEA PARTY

"Eshana? She jumps from one footy player to the next. A striker from Chelsea, a midfielder from Liverpool, and a defender from Tottenham. She's working her way through the Premier league."

"It'll be the Bundesliga next, a goalkeeper."

"She isn't my type. She's more bloody fake than Ms. Batra."

The spots flashed and spread, painting the room red. Her insides were on fire. God was angry with her. She stole, she lied. Normal had been suffocating.

"I scrub Walter's floors, do his laundry, hang his clothes in straight fucking lines and blocks of colour." Her hand shot out. The tea cup flew across the room and shattered against the wall. "I should have taken him as a lover. I could have been his slut in Paris."

She grabbed a mug from the coffee table, firing it at the fireplace, bits of blue porcelain sprinkled over the bricks.

"Are you done? Would you like to take a swing at me?"

"You should have seen the smug look on Victoria's face. She was happy you might have done something wrong."

"She thinks Will and I should share time in net."

"I want to tear everything up, including myself."

"We really would have a mess, wouldn't we?" Brendon said, winding his arm around her. She shot him a warning look.

"I'm not going to kiss you. The house is messy enough without you throwing more bloody stuff around."

Angelene snuggled into his chest and clutched his hoodie. "I thought if I put on the right clothes, it would be okay. I don't belong here."

"I wouldn't be able to give you this," Brendon said, handing her an ink drawing of cornflower, the words 'ihre Kornblum,' above the bouquet. "I drew it in Latin and asked Rachel the German way to spell it."

"That's so sweet." Angelene placed the drawing against her breast and yawned. "I'm so tired."

She gave him a little squeeze and curled into the corner of the sofa.

"Have I met one of your devils?"

"Roman used to sit with me until I fell asleep. I had terrible nightmares as a child. One night, I dreamt a man snuck into my room and stole my most precious thing. Roman held me and hummed Edelweiss."

"I'll stay, but I'm not singing."

"Je t'aime parce que tout l'univers a conspiré à me faire arriver jusqu'à toi."

"I need to pay attention in French."

"It's a quote from The Alchemist by Paulo Coelho. I love you because the whole universe conspired to make me get to you. The universe had a plan to bring Walter to Parc Floral and me to Taunton."

"Walter is a persistent guy. He wouldn't have left Paris without you."

"I think there's a bigger plan."

Sleep swept her down a rabbit hole.

Down, down she fell, tumbling into a field of cornflower. She jumped to her feet and brushed off her knees, greeted by a rabbit, limestone Hugo and a boy with incredible light.

Where am I? This is such a curious place.

She walked through the cornflower and stopped at the edge of a forest.

Will you come with me?

Mammina doesn't let me play in the woods.

I need your light.

The path snaked through gnarled limbs and tangled roots. She stumbled into the clearing, alone. Tweedle dee, in her too-tight dress, sat across from Tweedle dum who sipped tea from a gargantuan cup. The rabbit sat in the middle of the table, munching on cookies shaped like carrots. At the other end was the queen in robes of black and a crown of thorns. Dark, sullen music seeped from the burls.

Who invited her?

She doesn't belong here.

I'll have tea and leave. I must follow his light.

Would you say hello from me? He's a pretty thing; I could devour him.

Please don't, you'll steal his light.

What do you say, queen? You're the guardian of his light.

Off with her head!

Angelene jerked, clutched her neck, and gazed wide eyed around the room. She was safe at home, but things were different. The floor was clean. Pencils were in the jar, illustrations tucked in her sketchbook. The drawing of cornflower leaned against a candleholder. Angelene stood, held out her arms, steadying herself. She walked to the kitchen; the sink gleamed; the scraps of food had disappeared. Angelene carried herself up the stairs. The macabre music from her dream played in her ears. She lumbered to the bedroom, walked into the bathroom, lighting candles lining the window ledge. She put the plug in the drain, turned on the taps, and tipped in patchouli scented bubble bath. The hot water scorched her skin. Her mother swore a soak was as good as a baptism. It was a chance to wash oneself clean. She could hear her mother's voice, 'scrub Angelene, scrub.'

I missed you Roman. You were gone a long time.

I was in London; I brought you a copy of Through the Looking Glass. Alice reminds me of you.

Because of my blonde hair?

Something you said before I left, 'when I woke, I was Angelene Hummel but as the day went on, I lost myself a few times.' The same thing happened to Alice.

Angelene plunged under the water, twisted her hair around her hands and pulled. A scream forced its way out. Electricity surged through her veins, stay, run, hide, fight. She burst through the bubbles and panted for air.

"Changing, always changing. From mademoiselle Hummel to the lady of healthy things, to Ms. Secretary of Defence. All in a matter of a day."

Angelene dragged herself from the tub and scrubbed her body dry. She walked to the bed and nestled under the blankets. Her eyelids grew heavy. She tried to blink and banish sleep. She didn't want to go back to the queen and her thorny crown. The strange dream world was just as odd as the real world. She didn't fit. Happy thoughts and cheerful things, sunshine, and songbirds. She needed spring.

Your eyes are the deepest blue, like spilled ink.

I thought you were sleeping.

I had a nightmare.

I'll tell you a story, snuggle next to me. Once upon a time, there was a girl named Petite Oiseau. She lived in a nest of yellow ribbons high in an oak tree. One day, a boy looked up and saw the girl. She was the prettiest girl he had ever seen. He called to her to come down and walk through the fields of lavender with him. Her voice sang out, she had no wings to fly. Each day, the boy wandered through the streets collecting feathers and each day before he went home; he visited the nest and placed a feather in the nub until she had the most beautiful wings any bird had ever seen. They soared together through the sky. You will fly, Angelene.

19 Éperdument Amoureux

THE DECISION TO HOLD the world's greatest party stood.

Brendon wrapped his hand around a list tucked in his pocket. The plan was failproof.

"I'll miss you this weekend," Sofia said.

"You're going to walk around Bruges and Ghent, eat chocolate, waffles. You won't have a minute to miss me."

"You remember what I said."

"No friends over."

"Amelia will pop in Sunday morning to check on you."

"She doesn't need to do that. I'm not doing anything but watching the Dortmund match."

The part lie slipped from between his teeth. It was his plan on Saturday.

"You can stop worrying. All I'm doing tonight is watching my last match. I recorded it on my phone."

"That's it? Football?"

"You're going to miss your flight if you don't get on the road."

It was getting harder to look her in the eye. Her gaze had turned from suspicious to the worried, 'I may never see you again.' It kicked him square in the stomach. He grabbed the train case and followed her out to the Maserati.

"Don't you think you over packed?"

"I picked out all your father's favourite outfits."

Brendon raced back to the foyer, wheeling out the remaining suitcases. "Your entire cupboard."

Sofia held his cheeks in her hands and gave him her best 'do as you're told' look.

"Stay away from Angelene."

"Shouldn't I check in, make sure she's, okay?"

"Watch your football. Ti amo sweetheart."

He wrapped his arms around her, completing the performance with the world's greatest hug. He had done it, survived her 'I hate goodbyes, I love you too much to leave' look. Padre Diavolo flipped the excitement switch; it was time to get to work. Brendon raced into the house and up the stairs to change. He read the list: empty the great room, lock the liquor cabinet, roll up the handwoven rugs, lock the door to the laundry room so no one could discover the wine cellar, lock the pool, set out tin cans in the garden for cigarette butts. Guilt invaded the 'yes, mammina, I promise mammina, I would never do that dad' space in his brain, Padre Diavolo could wrestle with that. Brendon changed and bound down the stairs. He grabbed his great-Nonna's Cantagalli plate and a Limoges vase, strolling into the den. The Marti et Cie clock had to go, and the apple shaped tea caddy his mother said was a rare find. He carried them into the den and placed them on the desk. The doorbell snapped him out of his daze. Brendon laid an armful of frames on the desk and walked to the door. He glanced at the silhouette in the window, tiny, fidgety fingers. He opened the door; vivid gold spread across the moors.

"I wanted to thank you for cleaning my mess. I'm good at making all sorts of messes."

Brendon glanced at his feet and shrugged. "You were tired and upset. I didn't think you would want to deal with that when you woke up."

"It was sweet and, as usual, other people deal with my chaos." Angelene craned her neck, gazing around the foyer. "Did I interrupt you?"

"I was putting mum's antiques away."

"Is she redecorating?"

"I'm having a party."

A look of disapproval passed across her face. He was suddenly five years old, standing in front of his father.

"You mustn't."

"I've told all my friends."

She reached for his wrists and held them. "Don't answer the door, Sofia's beautiful things."

"I've been smart this time. There is a list of things I need to put away. I'll make sure everyone stays in the great room. You can help me."

Angelene let go of his wrists and held up her hands. "If Sofia knows I was a co-conspirator, she'll never forgive me."

Brendon laughed. "Do you remember sneaking out and getting pissed? I'll grab the keys; you can lock the door to the laundry room and pool."

He ducked into the den, opened the desk drawer, fumbling around scrapbooks for the key ring.

"I suppose Père diable has been whispering to you."

"The prick's been pestering me all week." Brendon rattled the keys, grinning. "The skeleton key is for the laundry room; the pool key has a P on it. Once you've done that, meet me in the great room."

"I won't be blamed if you get caught."

"You were never here."

Brendon sauntered into the great room and took an inventory of all the knick-knacks and antiques. There wasn't one thing in the room that didn't mean something to his mother. Pushing back the coffee table, Brendon rolled up the rug and shoved it towards the doorway. He walked to the mantle and swept his arm across it; the photos fell like oversized dominoes.

"I locked both doors."

"Can you lock the liquor cabinet? Dad's got an expensive bottle of scotch in there. It's the little key."

He laid the armful of frames on the sofa, his heart clunked. Brendon chased the feeling away. She was his friend, nothing more.

19 ÉPERDUMENT AMOUREUX

"What about the Klimt painting?"
Her voice pulled him back to the list. He had forgotten the Klimt masterpiece.
"I better take it down."
"I'll carry it to the den. Be careful not to touch the canvas, the oil and perspiration from your fingers will leave residue and ruin it."
They strolled to the corner of the room, stood side by side, and stared at the painting.
"My hands are bloody sweaty."
"You've listened to Padre Diavolo."
Brendon reached above the credenza and carefully grabbed the frame. "I don't know why dad doesn't like this painting. The blonde looks randy."
"Stop staring at the girl and focus on the painting."
"Are you sure you can carry it? It's as big as you?"
"Give it here," Angelene said, pinching her lips. "Is there a key to the den? No one should go in there."
"There's a key for every room in the house."
He gathered an armful of collectables and followed, impressed at how careful she was with the painting.
"Sofia has a Faberge egg?"
"It belonged to my great-grandmother Ruth. Dad found it hidden in the wall safe."
"It's beautiful."
"I'm going to grab my pictures."
"You didn't keep them on the mantle?"
"Have my friends take the piss."
They walked back to the great room, scanning for more treasures. "I'll grab the clock. It's one of the few German things mammina loves. Can you grab the lamp?"
Angelene unplugged it and wound the cord around her hand. "What does she have against Germany?"
"It stole me."
"The chairs by the fireplace were a present for David."
"I'll move them to the wall, drape a sheet over them and pray no one uses them for a trampoline."
"I'll pray too."
Brendon teetered the chair on its legs and hobbled it across the floor. He sat on the armrest, watching Angelene pick up an item and examine it. She took a moment with each, lightly touching the curve of a bowl or studying the details before she moved to the next.
'She does something to me every bloody time.'
"One last thing to do," Brendon said, pulling a remote from his pocket, "you can't have a party without music." A vibrant tempo travelled around the room. "Still got the keys?"
Angelene held up her wrist and jingled it. He slid the remote into the armoire and closed the doors. He had done it, followed through on a promise and protected the illustrious Rosewood Manor.
"Have you eaten?"
"I was working on a painting and lost track of time."
Brendon touched her elbow, guiding her into the kitchen. Beer, alcopops, and crisps covered the counter. He reminded himself to put the alcohol in the garden

and crisps on the coffee table. If Amelia's alphabetized pantry was out of order, he'd never hear the end of it.

"How many cigarettes have you had?"

Angelene dropped onto a stool and held up two fingers.

A note card addressed to her little man leaned against the pepper mill. A smiling face ended the instructions. He slipped his hand in a strawberry print oven mitt, warm air scented with lemon and dill filled the kitchen.

"Do you want butter for the veg? I use olive oil spread. Ame says she could polish the floors with it."

"You don't need to feed me. I can go home and make something."

"Do you want milk or water?"

"Water please, you eat."

"You'll go home, start painting and forget or smoke instead."

He turned on the tap and filled a glass. Digging in the fridge, Brendon grabbed the jug of milk and plunked it on the island. He set out a plate and arranged half the fish, rice, and broccoli.

"I planned to make harira. It's a Moroccan soup. Roman loved it, he'd make it for mama and me." "Just planned?"

"For three days now. I had Malcolm take me to Tesco for the ingredients."

Brendon piled fish and rice on his fork and frowned. "Don't tell me you haven't eaten for three days?"

"I've had some yogurt, some brie, an apple or two. Not a meal but, I've eaten."

"Bloody hell, eat up then and take a bag of crisps with you."

"Are you talking about sheeps?"

"A sheep like baa? Crisps, they're crunchy, made from potatoes."

Angelene smiled. "In France, we don't snack on them. We eat them with a meal."

"Mum would die. I put them on a sandwich once and she nearly had a heart attack. Take the salt and malt, they're my favourite."

They ate in silence. She took tiny bites, savouring each mouthful before the next. The moment sank deep into Brendon's bones. She looked beautiful, tiny, fragile like crystal. Drop her, she'd break.

"What colour are you right now?"

"Pink, green, red, murky, muddied. Éperdument amoureux, madly in love."

"With me?"

Angelene glanced up from her plate, her grin was slight. "The idea."

Brendon touched her fingers. A little spark drew him to her like they had been friends in an earlier existence, like a kindred spirit, like he had been madly in love with her before. Angelene pulled her hand away and flicked her fingers as if ridding herself of the connection.

"What can I help with now?"

Brendon took their plates, rinsed them, and set them in the sink. "You can help with the beer and sheeps." He stacked a pack of Fosters on top of a box of Becks and nodded towards the snacks. "Throw some on top, take the salt and malt."

"I'll eat them with my soup."

Angelene tossed bags onto the boxes and filled her arms with the rest. They walked to the great room. She dropped the armful of snacks and fetched the salt and malt from the pile. The music changed to a slower beat; an instrumental version of a movie theme song Brendon couldn't put his finger on. All he could remember was being stuck in the cinema, listening to Maggie cry for three hours.

"Dance with me."

Angelene shrunk away, twisting the cuffs of her sweater. "Non, I haven't danced with Walter. It isn't right."

"I won't kiss you; I promise."

"God won't be happy."

"If we were at a party, dad would expect me to dance with you. I'll be a perfect gentleman." He held out his hand. "I won't step on your toes. I was mum's date for the gala three years ago. She taught me the proper way to dance."

They swayed in silence; her palm was moist within his. Brendon clung to the moment, knowing it would be just that — a moment. He wished he could stretch it out and lay in the serenity. It was three and a half minutes of utter bliss.

"I can hear your heart," Angelene said.

"It's beating so hard, it hurts."

The CDs shuffled; a poppy dance beat boomed from the hidden speakers.

"Was that so bad?"

"I'll ask God to forgive me."

"God doesn't have to forgive anything. I've danced with Charlie, Kate, even Ms. Batra. She giggled worse than Maggie. Just enjoy it for what it was, a dance with a friend."

"I should go."

"I didn't mean to make you uncomfortable."

He followed her to the foyer. She cradled the bag of crisps in her arms.

"I enjoyed listening to your heartbeat. It was prettier than that song."

Angelene opened the door and wagged her finger. "Don't listen to Padre Diavolo. He'll convince you to do dreadful things."

"Like sneak off in the night and get pissed. Tu me manques."

"Faire de beaux rêves mon ami."

Brendon closed the door, the 'in love' feeling swarmed him. He wanted to hold her, chill on the sofa, watch football and eat 'sheeps'. Padre Diavolo had to flip on the excitement switch fast. The idea of a party with friends, friends of friends and strangers, had lost its appeal.

The door burst open. Troy smiled and pat Brendon on the back.

"This is going to be brilliant."

"There's more beer and cider in the kitchen. Help me carry it to the garden."

"I saw Ms. Pratt."

"Did you say hi to her?"

"She was halfway down the hill. I didn't want to make eye contact."

"What are you going on about?"

Troy tore open a box, grabbed a lager, and chugged. "Her eyes are magical, green, grey, sparkly, stormy." He scrunched the can and tossed it in the sink. "I had a dream I was humping her. That isn't right."

Dreams of making love to Angelene had haunted Brendon since the day he adjusted her strap and touched her skin. He wouldn't call it magical powers, just attraction.

"I was humping Charlie when it happened."

"I was snogging Maggie and imagined it was Angelene. Does that make you feel better?"

Troy grabbed a bag of crisps and slammed his hands against it. A spray of crisps flew into the air and scattered across the floor. "Not really. A snog is one thing, but shagging, that's bleeding bad."

Brendon placed the opened beer case on another and lifted the stack. "Promise to hump in one room. You did it in three last time. It pissed Amelia off she had to wash all that bedding."

Troy grappled with three cases of cider; his face brightened.

"I love waking up with Charlie. Morning humps are brilliant. You're both sleepy, like a beautiful dream."

"What about morning breath?"

"You really know how to ruin things," Troy said, walking into the great room, "spoon, wanker."

"Humping in the morning is ace. I'll remember that."

Brendon pulled open the door to the loggia. Troy's eyes lit up at the wall of alcohol. "Where did all this come from?"

"I picked up a few cases after school and the rest, Todd Watson."

They set down the cases and walked back into the great room.

"That swot?"

"He was bloody desperate for an invitation. I met him at Tesco. He filled the boot of my car."

"I guess when your best friend is a Bunsen burner, you'll do anything," Troy said, gazing around the room. "You cleared the room by yourself?"

"I had a plan and stuck to it."

The doorbell chimed; relief washed over Brendon. The longer he had to talk about his plan, the harder it would be to keep his accomplice a secret.

"That'll be Charlie."

"How do you know it isn't some guys from the team?"

"Charlotte doesn't like to be late."

Brendon opened the door and stumbled over his feet. Charlotte bound into the foyer and into Troy's arms.

"I brought those frilly knickers you like."

Brendon's eyebrows raised. "You brought frilly knickers?"

Maggie swung her overnight bag at him and poked her finger in his stomach. "Which room do babes and I get?"

"The one at the end of the hall past mum and dad's."

"Oh, babes, that's the blue and white room. I've always wanted to sleep in that bed, posh pillars, and a canopy. It's fit for a queen."

"It's perfect for you, luv."

"Don't be jumping all over it, it's from the tutor period."

"It's pronounced Tudor, with a d, wanker. We are studying Henry VIII," Maggie said. "I still can't believe you're doing this."

"Please don't ruin my night by being mum-like."

"I'm putting my stuff in your room."

"You're staying the night?"

"I overheard the queen slag and her troupe of tarts talking about coming. There's no way I'm leaving you alone with her."

Brendon didn't know what to say. For the first time in his life, he was happy to see William.

"Looks like the party can start now. I've arrived."

"The beer is in the garden. Go to the great room."

"Is that what you toffs call a sitting room?"

"Just go, bloody wanker."

"Did I walk into something? You're looking a little tense for someone having a party," William said.

"I'm staying the night. Tell your tarts to stay away from him."

"Maybe tonight will be the night, Cook."

"Please go. You're giving me a bloody headache."

William snickered and slapped Brendon's chest. "Rachel's always up for it."

"Gosh, I hate that dolt."

"Just ignore him. Since when does your mum let you stay over?"

"She doesn't. I said I was staying at Charlie's. I feel awful about lying, so don't be a wanker and make me feel worse."

A group of First players barged through the door followed by some girls Brendon recognized from Latin. A succession of Taunton College students and the Taunton Blues, led by Posy Partridge, greeted him with enthusiastic hellos. Brendon followed the mob, scanning the room. No one was jumping on the sofas, the smokers were in the garden, small groups had congregated in corners. Maggie's friends from drama stood in a circle by the fireplace, full of animation and gestures.

"Get this into you, mate. You got that gloomy look on your face all the girls find dishy."

Brendon cracked open the beer. "One, Mags. You're worse than me with alcohol."

Maggie twisted off the top of an alcopop and squished under his arm.

"People like that slag think I'm boring. I'm going to prove them all wrong."

Rachel waved and called over the music. "Du bist die Liebe meines Lebens."

"Cheeky cow! I think she said you are the love of her life."

"I wouldn't know. She can't tutor me anymore. Tutor with a T."

"Who's being cheeky now," Maggie said, gulping back the drink. She reached into her sweater pocket for a cider and cracked it open. "Why is she coming over here?"

Rachel's jeans looked as if she had poured them on. An oversized V-neck hung off one shoulder, exposing a galaxy of freckles. Her hair was wild and untamed. Femme fatale was on the pull.

"Your home is fucking brill. Will said you have an indoor pool and a ballroom. Who has a ballroom?"

"The house is old."

His teammates snickered at his red cheeks; Maggie scowled into her drink. Padre Diavolo wanted to introduce himself to Rachel.

"Can you give me a tour?"

"Go back to your slag friends," Maggie said, jerking him closer.

"I'm going for a ciggie. You want to come, knuddlebär? We can talk about the lineup for tomorrow's Dortmund match."

"He isn't going anywhere with you."

"Relax Thornton, I'm not chatting up your man. Auf Wiedersehen knuddlebär."

"Why do you have to be like that?"

"She's a slapper, trying to tell me she wasn't chatting you up, rubbish!"

Maggie gulped the fizzy drink and pulled another from her pocket. She hiccupped and swayed, nodding towards the loggia. "It looks like she's giving the cigarette a bj."

"What do you know about giving bj's?"

"The party is banging, mate."
Brendon forced a grin, keeping watch on the crowd. So far, so good.
"Let's get you some crisps. You need to soak up that alcohol," Charlotte said.
"That's a bloody smashing idea."
"I'm not leaving your side. You'll be staring at the tart's fat arse. Troy another," Maggie said, snapping her fingers, "strawberry this time."
Brendon balled his hands, sparks fluttered. The crowd had grown, conversations merged, laughter spilled over the music. Everyone was enjoying themselves, everyone but him.
"I need air."
"You got the sparks, mate?"
"I need to take a few breaths before I say something I'll regret."
"Don't be too long. You need to take care of your girl."
Brendon pushed open the door and walked onto the loggia. A tepid, earth and pine scented wind rushed by. Overhead, the sky was inky blue, sprinkled with stars. Padre diavolo had turned off the excitement switch.
'*I'm as blue as the sky.*' He smiled to himself, swiping the empty cans off the concrete bench. Angelene was rubbing off on him.
"Hiya knuddlebär."
"You've got thirteen freckles on your shoulder." Brendon traced from freckle to freckle. They came together to create a star.
"Does Thornton practice giving evils in the mirror?"
"It's the alcohol. Maggie doesn't get mad, she cries."
"You look fucking fit tonight, knuddlebär, a little sad, still dishy."
"You've had too many fizzy pops."
"I've had one, and it's the truth," Rachel said, running a finger over his tattoo. "What's the matter?"
Brendon stared at the farmhouse and shrugged. "I thought I was up for a party. I guess I'm not."
"Babysitting Maggie mustn't be fun."
"All it takes is two, and she's pissed. I think she's up to four now."
"I'll stay after everyone leaves and help you clean up."
"Maggie's staying the night. She'll throw a fit if you hang around."
Rachel got to the end of his tattoo; tiny shivers travelled up his spine, she continued along his vein. It was Angelene's thing to do, follow the veins in his hands and arms. She said it carried his light. Brendon glanced into the great room; Gemma Fowler wore the same irked expression as Maggie.
"Pull Tilly off Will; Gemma doesn't look impressed."
He laid her hand on her lap, tapping a German flag painted on her thumb.
"You worried about Maggie?"
"I told her to stop drinking. She's on her own." Brendon turned and grinned. Her eyes were wistful amber. "Do you want to stay and help?"
"Anything for you, knuddlebär." She stood and touched his cheek. "You make me tingly. Ich Liebe dich."
Brendon walked back into the great room. Crisp bags sprouted from the sofa cushions, battered tins cluttered the floor. He swiped up a handful and walked to the fireplace, where he had stashed a pile of bin bags. Brendon snapped one open, dropped the cans in, and slumped onto the chair. Small crowds of people stood around the room. There were no holes in the wall or scratches along the floor.

Everything was okay, everything except Maggie. He stared up at the ceiling and stretched his arms. It was time to be a wonderful boyfriend.

"How many bloody alcopops did you drink?"

Maggie clamped her hand over her mouth, her eyes widened. "I'm going to barf."

Brendon's gaze left the creature stirring in Maggie's belly to the loggia. Rachel was picking up cigarette butts. She had kept her word.

"You better get to the loo before you chunder all over mum's floor."

Maggie burped and pressed on her stomach. "Why is the ginger tart still here?"

"Lots of people are still here."

Brendon wound an arm around her and guided her up the stairs. Her stomach pitched and heaved against his palm.

"Hurry Mags."

"I'm trying, but my legs feel like they're filled with jelly."

"Don't honk on mum's runner. It came from her Nonna's home in San Siro."

"Will you shut it. I'm trying to concentrate on walking."

Brendon pushed open his bedroom door and released his grip. She staggered to the bathroom. A rainbow of colours and undigested crisps spilled into the sink. Brendon jerked his collar over his nose and sunk onto the toilet seat. The smell of fruity vodka and what he thought was cheddar and onion crisps seeped through the fabric.

"Oh, my gosh." Maggie bounced off the rim of the sink, stumbled over the threshold plate, and knocked her head on the edge of the door. "Why is your floor slanted?"

"It's you, not the bloody floor. Get into bed."

She tugged at her vomit splotched hoodie and fell onto the mattress.

"Can you help, please?"

"Unzip it."

He tugged at the pull, found a vomit free spot, and yanked her limp arms from the sleeves. "I finally get you out of your clothes and you're pissed."

"Your bed smells like barf."

Brendon switched on the lamp, walked to his laundry basket, and dug out a t-shirt. "Wear this."

"It's dirty."

"Sleep in your clothes then."

He tossed the t-shirt at her. She swayed back and forth; her eyelids blinked slowly.

"I can't find the armholes."

Brendon sighed, left his spot, and dragged her shirt over her rocking body. Maggie tumbled back and knocked her head on the headboard.

"My jeans please."

Brendon stared at her zipper, Padre Diavolo came out of hiding and snickered. *'Look at your girl, pathetic, can't handle other birds, can't handle her liquor.'*

He undid her jeans and shimmied them over her hips.

"Sit up so I can get my shirt over your head."

She flung herself up, hiccuped, and held up her arms. "Turn off your lamp and lay with me."

"You might need the loo again."

Maggie shoved the blankets back and crawled under. "Lay beside me."

Brendon flopped onto the bed; the mattress bounced. She groaned and clutched her stomach. The scent of vomit and vanilla wafted from her skin.

"Do you want to, you know."

"You're bloody pissed."

"I'm up for it."

"Go to sleep."

She smooshed her nose in his ribs. Soft murmurs warmed his skin. He could hear the door open and close; Troy was doing an excellent job saying good night to his guests. Brendon shimmied off the bed, draped the blankets over her, and headed downstairs to the great room. Troy smiled from behind a sandwich piled high with an assortment of meat and cheese.

"How's Maggie?" he said between chews.

"She's passed out."

"Are you leaving?" Charlotte said, stealing a corner of cheese. "We've tidied everything up."

"I want my tour," Rachel said.

"We're going to bed, right, mate?"

"You should be with Magpie. She's never been bladdered before."

"I promised Rachel, I'd show her the pool and ballroom, then she's leaving, right? You're leaving."

"If you want me to, then I will, knuddlebär. I wouldn't want to get you in trouble with your friends."

Troy squished the last bite into his mouth and pointed an accusatory finger. "No dancing in the ballroom and no swimming."

Brendon held up his hands and gave his best, 'I promise' grin.

"I was talking to Rachel."

"Behave." Charlotte tugged Brendon's arm. He bent down; she planted a kiss on his cheek. "Especially you. Don't work your tart charm on my friend. He's taken."

Guilt sizzled his lungs and burned his stomach. Rachel was beside him, ready to pounce. Maggie was upstairs, passed out. The song he and Angelene had danced to filled the room.

"Show me the ballroom, knuddlebär."

He shook the memory from his head, tried to make sense of his emotions and thoughts, do the right thing, follow his heart, keep loving the girl he shouldn't love or listen to his ignored body part.

"I've only seen a ballroom in movies."

"Don't get too excited. It's an empty room with a piano in it."

Rachel hooked her arm through his.

"Really?"

"A gentleman would escort a lady to the ballroom."

They walked arm in arm. He ran over the list of what went where, which photo adorned what table until they reached the darkened room. He pushed a switch; the chandeliers lit the expansive room. The smile on her face was dreamy and filled with wonder.

"Mum had Walt's wedding do here."

Rachel walked over to the piano and ran her fingers across the keys. "Do you play?"

"Dad does, well did. He hasn't played in years. I'll show you the pool."

"He never taught you?"

"He tried. I would sit for a minute, then kick the football around. The ballroom makes an impressive pitch."

They wandered down the hall to the French doors. Rachel pushed herself against the glass and squealed dramatically. "Is that a fireplace? By a pool, bleeding brilliant. You're so lucky."

"I guess."

"Have you looked around you?"

"They're just things, things don't make you lucky. Mammina loves me. That's all that matters."

"How could she not, knuddlebär, you're adorable. And your daddy, does he love you too?"

They strolled back to the great room. Heat crept over Brendon's cheeks. "I think he'd love me more if I was going to uni."

Rachel sunk onto the sofa, tugging him with her. "You've never liked school, have you?"

"I'm a bloody terrible student."

"That must upset our Lord Chancellor."

"He's proud I made the pros, only because it's part of the code, pursue and conquer. I know he wishes I were more like..."

Brendon could feel eyes burning into him from somewhere in the great room. He could hear scampering feet and the rustle of the curtains. His pulse quickened as a draught passed over him.

"Like whom?"

Brendon rubbed the chill from his arms and grinned. "My dad, who else."

"You know everything there is to know about football and you're learning German."

"Danke."

Rachel edged closer. He squeezed himself deeper into the cushions.

"Where did Tilly run off to? Didn't you come together?"

"She left with William."

"Poor Gemma."

"William fancies Tilly. Gemma is like Magg..." She stopped herself, licking her lips. "Matilda needs somebody. Everyone needs someone."

"Even, I don't give a fuck, Rachel?"

"Even me, knuddlebär."

She pressed her breasts into him. Padre Diavolo was back, begging him to touch her.

"I might smell like barf. Maggie passed out on me. She bloody reeks of it."

"I'll tell you." She brushed her lips over his neck; his belly flopped. "You smell as dishy as ever."

She stretched her legs over his and straddled his lap.

"What are you doing? Maggie is upstairs." He pushed himself deeper into the sofa, cushions separated, the frame stuck in his back. "Troy or Charlie could come down."

Rachel licked and sucked along his collarbone. "Do you think Troy is going to stop humping Charlotte to check on you?"

Padre Diavolo stirred up the tingles. Her fluttery kisses reached his ear. "Fancy a snog, knuddlebär?"

"Not a good idea."

"I'll give you a kiss and if you don't like it, I'll stop."

She traced the outline of his lips. The kiss was hard, then soft.

"Kiss me back knuddlebär."

Warmth diffused from her lips and slowly spread through his body, with it came insecurity. He didn't know what to do. Push her off, run his fingers over her back? He could use her, get his first time over with. It was obvious she wanted it and once he had given her his virginity, she'd cross him off the list and move on to number two. Should I or shouldn't I, danced in his head, Padre Diavolo gave his approval. Brendon shoved his hand up her shirt and cupped her breast. Troy had said more than a handful was too much. Brendon disagreed. Rachel wound her legs around his waist. He fell on top of her.

"I have a condom in my purse."

She fumbled with his belt, tugged at his jeans and boxers. Padre Diavolo instructed him to undo her zipper. It took some tugging to pull her jeans over her hips. Her knickers were lace, she was a natural redhead.

"Brendon? Where are you?"

Brendon dropped his forehead against Rachel's and cursed.

Rachel nudged his jeans further over his hips. "Ignore her."

"I'm going to barf again."

Madre Innocente jabbed her staff of guilt into his gut, her army of remorse charged through him. Brendon mumbled a string of curse words and pulled up his jeans and boxers.

"Doesn't your devil want to play? What did you call him, Father Satan?"

"I played with him once before and it got me into trouble."

"Brendon, hurry!"

Rachel grabbed her jeans and wiggled into them. "Just my luck, knuddlebär. I'll see myself out."

"I'm sorry."

"No, you're not, you're relieved. You're a good boy, cuddle bear. See you soon."

He rushed to the foyer. Maggie clung to the wooden railing, teetering precariously on the top step. He hurried up the stairs and unclamped her hand from the banister.

"Is that Rachel? Why is she still here?"

"She forgot her purse."

Maggie coughed and gagged. "Gosh, I didn't think there was anything left to throw up."

He lugged her down the hall and steered her into the bathroom. The sweet smell of artificial fruit hung in the air. He shoved her towards the toilet. She tumbled into the bowl and fell to her knees. A splash of pink and orange vomit filled the bowl. Madre Innocente scolded him for not holding her hair back. Maggie moaned and rested her head on the toilet seat. He took her hand and yanked her drooping body from the floor.

"Are you going to sleep with me?"

"I'll be right next door. It reeks in here."

"I want to wake up with you."

"I'll see you in the morning."

"I love you."

"Get some sleep."

"From the moment Charlie introduced us, maybe before that."

He stifled a yawn and glanced out the window. All the lights in the farmhouse were out. He wished Angelene sweet dreams and started to leave the bedroom.

"You never said it back."

"I, uh, love you."

He waited until her eyes closed, asked Madre Innocente to look after her, and shuffled next door. He dove onto his stomach. Exhaustion bulldozed over him, his mind on fire. He had to put the day to bed and forget about the almost hump, the copious amounts of vomit splashed in his toilet and the silly feeling of love.

**

Angelene puffed on a cigarette. His lamp light was on, but he was not in his bed. She felt it. Goldilocks had tripped into it.

"I had my first dance tonight. Please don't be angry with me God, I used to dance on Roman's feet until mother forbid it."

She took a long drag and crushed the cigarette on a plate. "Brendon started to dance and then I was too. I was dancing God. I felt his heart and the music. For the first time, I felt bliss."

Angelene pushed on her heated cheeks. Her breath hitched, and she crawled under the blankets.

"I know God, it should be shame I'm feeling."

20 Ghosts

Goldfinch chirped outside the window; the sun played peek-a-boo behind the clouds. Brendon rolled his head across the pillow and scratched out his rumpled hair. He yawned, walked to his bedroom, peeking around the door frame; Maggie stared over the blankets. The heady stench of vomit and sweaty vanilla hung like a toxic cloud over his bed. Brendon opened the window, a leaf pirouetted in the breeze, danced, and floated until it landed on the bench where he had sat with Rachel. A wave of nausea engulfed him; he had almost had sex.

Maggie inched her way up the headboard and flinched.

"My head hurts, my knees. My throat feels like sandpaper, all I can taste is barf."

He slipped into the bathroom; his stomach lurched. Reminders of Maggie's evening floated in the toilet bowl. Brendon jerked his shirt over his nose, swung open the cabinet, and grabbed a bottle of pills. He filled a glass with water and marched back to Maggie.

"Take some pills. I need to clean my bathroom and have a shower."

Maggie groaned and folded her arms over her chest. "Can't you sit for a minute? I feel awful."

"Give me ten minutes. I slept in my clothes; I can't get the smell of barf out of my nose."

Madre Innocente was up early. He had fallen asleep with the guilts and woke with them.

"Can I have a kiss?"

"Are you bloody mad?"

"Did we, gosh, we didn't. Remember when Davina got bladdered and did it with William."

"I may be a wanker but, I wouldn't take advantage of you when you're pissed. Bloody hell."

"There's my sweet little muffin. Have you got a poorly tumkins?" Charlotte said, fanning the air. "You ready? Daddy needs his car."

"I'm afraid to get out of bed. The room is spinning."

"Bend down," Charlotte said.

He stooped in front of her, Charlotte flung her arms around his neck and squeezed. "Thanks for letting babes and I stay over. It was a brilliant evening."

"I'm glad you had an enjoyable time."
"You'll let Charlie give you a hug but, you won't come near me."
"She smells like Swizzel Fizzers."
"Go shower, luv, I'll get Magpie up."

Brendon shut out Charlotte's mothering and flushed the fruity remnants away. He yanked off his t-shirt, a purply red mark shaped like Australia adorned his collar bone. He had been so busy concentrating on not prematurely exploding, he couldn't remember when it might have happened. Brendon stripped out of his clothes and stepped into the shower. Memories flipped through his head like a stack of photographs. He had to clear his head and focus. There was an entire house to put back together. He scrubbed his hair, ran a washcloth over his body, rinsed and turned off the taps. Brendon dried himself, wound the towel around his waist and reached for a bottle of cleaner. He aimed it at the sink, squirted the lemony bleach into the basin. The toilet was next. He gave it a good dousing, snapped a rag, and scrubbed the scent of vomit away. He washed his hands, brushed his teeth, and slowly opened the door. Charlotte was fluffing Maggie's hair. He ducked into the walk-in and shrugged on a t-shirt; the evidence hidden.

"She looks better, doesn't she?" Charlotte said.
"You're the colour of mushy peas."
"You're a wanker. Don't let me get drunk again."
"Here muffin, have some gum."
"I told you to stop."

He strolled to the dresser and pulled open a drawer. "Close your eyes. I'm putting on my boxers."
"Brendon, my bestie is right here."
"It's not like she hasn't seen a bare arse before."

Charlotte scanned his body, tilting her head from side to side. "You're fit, not as dishy as babes."
"I'm going to drop my towel."
"Go to the loo. Charlie will sneak a peek."
"You cheeky cow. I had my look."
"Just close your eyes."
"Just do it Magpie. I need to stop by the bakery. Netflix, my sweet little crumpet, and donuts. What a beautiful Saturday it's going to be."

Maggie peered through her fingers. "Haven't you seen enough of him?"
"Never."

Brendon slid on his boxers and tossed the towel in the basket. He finished dressing then walked to the walk-in to grab a hoodie, another layer to hide the evidence.

"Thanks again luv. I didn't make the bed; the sheets are a little mussed."
"I was planning to change them. I can't have one of mum's guests rolling around in crumpet's spunk."
"Can I have a kiss now? I chewed some gum."

Brendon pecked her forehead. "That's the best you're going to get. I'll walk you to the door."

They left the bedroom, pale light stretched across the foyer, bounced off the chandelier and cast little prisms on the stairs. Charlotte yelled an enthusiastic 'see you babes.' Brendon mouthed, 'I'll call you' and waved. He strolled to the kitchen and dug in the pantry for coffee. His thoughts pulled him in all directions, from setting up the house, to breaking the Gentlemen's Code. Brendon spooned coffee into the basket and clicked on the machine. It hissed and gurgled. Part of him wanted to ring Angelene and see if she would help. The other part, the rational part, said to put some space between them. The feeling of love was getting out of control, and it didn't feel warm and fuzzy like Troy said.

"Morning, mate." Troy plopped on a stool and sniffed the air. "What's that smell?"

"Bleach. Maggie honked all over the loo."

"I was having a brilliant hump while you were cleaning up barf."

"Do you have to rub it in? I finally get Maggie in my bed, and she's pissed."

Troy chuckled and reached for an apple. "Did Rachel stay long?"

Brendon turned to the coffeemaker, grabbed two mugs, and poured. He wanted to tell Troy about Rachel's lacy knickers and that her more than a handful of breasts were lovely, but he kept the tingly secrets to himself. Troy was just like David Cook, a poster boy for monogamy.

"I showed her the ballroom and pool, then she left."

Troy bit into the apple, screwing up his face. "You sure mate? Your cheeks are a pretty shade of pink."

"Tilly left with Will."

Change the subject to something scandalous, give him the gossip before it was the hot topic at school.

"Rubbish, mate. Will's a daft keeper, not a cheat."

He handed Troy a mug, yanked open the fridge, and grabbed the jug of milk. "William cheats on Gemma all the time. You're too in love to notice."

Troy crunched around the apple and tossed the core into the sink. "Rachel stayed longer, didn't she? We've been friends for thirteen years, I know you."

"I kept my hands to myself."

"What did you do, snog? Your first bj?"

A hot flush stained Brendon's cheeks. He yanked open the fridge door and hid. "Do you want brekky? I can fry you up all that greasy stuff you like."

"Close the bleeding door and sit your arse down."

Brendon hip-checked the door closed and dropped onto a stool. "It was her; I swear."

Troy tore a banana from a stalk, snapped the stem, and peeled it. "You didn't hump her, did you?"

"Maggie woke up before anything bloody bad happened."

Troy gobbled the banana in three bites. "I knew it. Did you touch her jubblies?"

Brendon rubbed the back of his neck. He'd give Troy the watered-down version, save himself a lecture.

"She climbed on my lap and kissed me."

"She kissed you?"

"She's bloody relentless. I asked her to stop, but she was grinding her fanny against me and did this thing with her tongue. It was one hell of a snog."

Troy flung the peel into the sink and tore into an orange. "Dry humping gets you every time."

"Are you going to tell Charlie? I feel bad enough I ignored Maggie all night. Can you imagine what she would be like knowing Rachel and I snogged?"

"Did she taste like cigarettes?"

"She must have chewed some gum; her mouth was minty."

"You need to stay away from Rachel," Troy said, popping an orange segment into his mouth. "She'll get you into heaps of trouble."

"I've been told."

Troy rose, swiped the orange peels into his hand, and walked to the sink. He hooked his foot under the cupboard door, jerked it open, depositing the fruit into the compost bin.

"I won't tell Charlie if you promise to avoid Rachel."

"I'll avoid her like the plague," Brendon said. "Have you got chores to do?"

"I promised Callum I would wrestle with him if he collected the eggs. What do you need?"

The tension drained from Brendon's body; the PG-13 version, accepted.

"I've got to put the house back together before the Dortmund match."

"I'll help. It was an ace party, mate."

They left the kitchen and headed towards the den. Brendon pulled the keys from his pocket and unlocked the door. "I organized everything by room. The stuff on the desk goes into the great room. The junk on the coffee table belongs in the foyer."

"I'm afraid to touch this stuff."

"Just be gentle."

"Doesn't everything have to be lined up at specific angles?"

"All I need you to do is carry the stuff to the great room and lay them on the sofa or coffee table. I'll do the arranging."

Troy exhaled slowly. "Your lucky I like you."

"I'll give us ninety minutes to get it done, the length of a match. After that, I'll make you something to eat."

"Is there any pizza dough in the freezer?"

"Amelia made some the other day. I'll take it out. You ready?"

"The first half just started. You best get that dough out of the freezer."

Brendon grabbed a few frames; it would be a miracle if they cleared everything from the den in ninety minutes. He imagined himself on the pitch. The referee blew the whistle. The first half had begun.

Brendon waved goodbye to Troy and walked across the lawn. He wandered to the forest's edge, contemplating the trees that stretched and spiked through the grey-blue sky. From within the shadows, the brambles rustled, and birds chirped. The gnarled hornbeam branches didn't look frightening in the afternoon sun. Sofia had been adamant about him venturing into the forest. He'd be defying her again. Deciding he had done enough rule-breaking, Brendon turned and flinched.

"Jesus Christ."

"Jesus isn't here. He's having tea with friends," Angelene said. "I was going to explore the forest for some inspiration. Will you come with me?"

Brendon gazed nervously at the dense canopy.

"I can't. I've got to be a good boy for the rest of the weekend."

"I don't know the property."

"Mum and dad made up all sorts of stories to keep me out. I'd lose you in there."

The forest hummed with life. Leaves shushed, branches clacked, the trunks moaned. A whisper of light broke through the wavering tree tops, lighting the path. It was a forest, not a raging beast.

"I did sneak in when I was ten."

"Now the truth comes out."

"It was Uncle Walt. We started to build a fort. Mum was pissed off when she found out. I promised I would never step foot in the forest again."

"Walter's a troublemaker. Shall we?"

"Who's the trouble maker now?"

They stepped onto an uneven path dotted with mossy rocks, patches of foxglove, and mushrooms. The green and brown canopy grew thicker, the air was damp, scented with the tang of pine needles, earth, and bark, light disappeared.

"You see that over there," Brendon said, pointing to a burl in an oak tree, "below the bump and behind the mushrooms."

"I see it."

'It's a faery door."

"Who told you that?"

"Walt did."

"Faeries are naughty."

"Now who's telling stories."

"Roman told me you must be kind to the faeries, or they'll play tricks on you. What did Walter say?"

"They're beautiful and randy."

The air became cooler, twigs snapped and crunched under their feet. Brendon stopped at the tangled roots of an oak. A tingly sensation prickled up his legs and back. The trees whispered, *go back*, a shadow floated over the roots, something watched him, waited. Brendon suppressed a shiver. The shadow disappeared into the knotted roots; the air cleared.

"Doesn't look like much, does it?"

Rot had warped the boards nailed between four alder trees. The makeshift plywood roof had bowed under the weight of broken branches and damp leaves.

"You never tried to finish it?"

"I've never seen mum so mad."

"Spiky red?"

Brendon ducked under the crumbling shell, brushing twigs, and curled leaves to the ground.

"Spiky red doesn't describe it."

"It would have been a fun place to play." Angelene picked up a stem of pine needles and swept it across her palm.

"Walt and I had so many adventures planned. It was the dressing room at Signal Iduna, our pirate ship."

"Would you like to pretend we're in the dressing room now?"

Padre Diavolo screamed, *'kiss her.'*

"I'll be in the real one soon enough."

"How was your party?"

"Maggie got pissed. She spent most of the night barfing." He hesitated and rubbed the back of his neck. "Rachel was there."

A brisk wind stirred up the leaves, Angelene snuggled into his arm. "I told you to stay away from her."

"Who said I went near her?"

"Your words are sludgy green."

"I kissed Rachel."

"We've kissed."

"If Maggie hadn't woken up, I would have humped Rachel on mum's bloody posh sofa."

"You protected your light."

"There's evidence."

He tugged his arm out of his hoodie and hiked up his t-shirt. Angelene poked at the purple splotch.

"Mon Dieu. Did she put her mouth there?"

"She would have put her mouth anywhere if I let her."

"Put your shirt down. Zut alors! You've kissed me, femme fatale."

He wiggled into his hoodie and swiped a pinecone from the ground. Brendon peeled back the sections and flicked them into the air.

"I think about kissing you all the time."

"Please don't start talking about kissing and all that nonsense. I don't like it."

"I've fallen for you."

"You mustn't. The boy with liquid blue eyes... non, I won't let it happen again."

Brendon whipped the pinecone. "It's hard shutting off my feelings." He held her hand and kissed the top of her head. "I've kissed Charlie like that, so don't get pissed off. It's just a friendly kiss, mon amie."

Brendon snapped a plant growing among a patch of ferns and handed it to her. "It isn't a cornflower but, it's something."

"It's nightshade, the devil's berries."

"Someone must have slipped me some last night. I feel like shit for snogging Rachel."

"That's a silly word, snogging. It sounds as bad as kissing."

"Kissing is the greatest thing on earth, other than football."

"It'll take a lot of convincing for me to believe a kiss is anything but exchanging spit."

"You won't let me kiss you, so you'll never know."

Kissing her will lead you to a place you should not go. Wanting it is just as dangerous.

The whispering words passed along the branches and rustled the leaves. Brendon shivered and drew her into his chest. She trembled against him.

"I wish I had been like you and Maggie." "Maggie might be okay with it; my goolies are aching."

"What you have is precious," Angelene said, her voice weak. "Mine was stolen. Don't take it from Maggie and don't fall victim to femme fatale."

"I'm sorry that happened to you."

"Roman told mother to protect me."

Brendon rested his chin on her head and held her tighter. "Roman sounds like a good man."

"He used to send me postcards from all the places he travelled. Mother got jealous and threw them away. She told Roman the postcards never came. He knew she was lying; he would sneak them into the flat."

"How could she be jealous? You were just a little girl."

"She loved Roman, she would deny it, but I knew. She was afraid of the love she felt for him and chased him away."

Her soul was his again. Another few bricks dismantled from her wall.

"What happened? Did he stop showing up?"

"Roman came to visit after a business trip. He brought me the prettiest yellow dress for Easter Mass. Mother was angry with him, worse than spiky red. She was a mixture of green, crimson, and electric black sparks."

Brendon's heart knocked about. He remembered a painting, a little girl in a yellow dress, a horrible monster clawing after her.

"He brought mother peonies and put them beside her bed. The flowers were cheap compared to my dress. She screamed." Angelene leaned her cheek against his arm and snuggled deeper into his chest. "I never heard mother scream like that. She must have bottled it up for years. I was so frightened, I ran to my room and sat on the windowsill with my fingers in my ears. That's when I saw Roman walk away. It was my turn to scream."

Brendon pressed his lips in her hair. He'd never turn his lamp off, always say see you soon and help find all her missing pieces.

"Mother, cut up my dress. There were shreds of yellow fabric and peony petals everywhere. We saw more of Paulo and Gustav."

"That was a long time ago. You're in Taunton now. No one can hurt you anymore."

"It doesn't matter where I am. The scars live in my heart and mind. I have years of evidence on my body."

He turned over her hand, pressed his thumb between the bracelets, and ran his thumb over the scar. "Why did you do that?"

Angelene jerked her hand free, fixing and adjusting the beads. "I don't talk about it. God wept and forgave me."

"What if I want to hear?"

"I haven't talked about it with Walter. He's embarrassed, that's why he keeps buying me bracelets."

She tucked herself deeper in the shelter of his armpit.

"You can trust me. I won't judge you." He brought her trembling hand to his lips. "I haven't yet."

"I was sixteen. Douchette asked me to make him raclette. All I could think about was the time Roman made it for me and we sat in the window eating it. The pot of potatoes boiled over; the cheese burnt." Her chest rose in shallow breaths. "Douchette hit me for spoiling his supper. He split my lip open, then bent me over his bed, shoved my face in the sheets. I can still smell the repulsive, sweaty smell. The noise, the terrible grunting."

"Bloody hell, he fucking raped... I would have killed him."

"I ran home, straight to the bath. I tried to scrub him away, but I couldn't. The smell lingered; the sounds stayed in my ears. I asked God to help. All he did was cry." Her hand was clammy in his, her heart thumped against his ribs. "It rained all night and into the next day. I stayed in the tub, scrubbing, and scrubbing until I was raw. I hoped slicing into my skin would release the scream bottled inside me."

"Somebody must have been looking out for you."

"I thought it was Roman wrapping my wrists and crying, little bird, what have you done?"

"Who found you?"

"Douchette," she whimpered. "Brendon, I feel like I'm drowning. I can't breathe."

"What can I do? Do you need a hug? Do you need to walk?"

"My sweet boy, always trying to help."

Brendon yanked on his cuff and blotted the tears on her cheeks.

"My scars don't disgust you?"

"We all have scars."

"You'd say anything to make me smile."

"Look." Brendon pulled down the waistband of his jeans and pointed. "There's my scar."

Her finger traced along the jagged line on his hipbone. His belly quivered.

"How did it happen?"

"An attacker was trying to catch the rebound and slammed his foot into what he thought was the ball." He let go of his waistband and grinned. "I made the save."

"Who knew football could be so dangerous."

"A scar is a reminder we've healed. You should be proud you survived."

Angelene stretched her arms, yawning. "I'm tired. I need sleep."

She shone differently now. The burden of horrible memories sunk her shoulders. Her light pulsed behind her scars, begging to break free.

"Try to think about happy things, like your friend the rabbit and football."

"I'll read the Hunchback."

"Give me a bell if you want to talk. I've got to change my sheets; they reek like bloody barf."

Brendon released a long, pent-up breath. Exhaustion wrapped around him, squeezing tight.

The crowd cheered and released ribbons of yellow onto the pitch at Signal Iduna Park. The roar of the fans had his heart knocking violently, knock, knock.

Brendon gazed sleepily around the room. The furious knock rose from the foyer. His eyes jerked open. It wasn't a dream or his heart. Every horror movie he had watched flashed through his mind. It was after midnight, windy. He was alone. The knock grew louder and more frantic. Hesitantly, he climbed out of bed. This was what every character did in the movies, searched the house and ended up butchered. He gripped the banister; the knocking persisted. He made it to the foyer and stared at the door. There was no peephole to see who was on the other side, no identifying rhythm. He was positive a six-foot seven machete wielding madman was on the other side. He walked to the den and ripped the letter opener from the penholder.

"Who is it?" he said, masking the quiver in his voice.

"Please open the door."

A whoosh expelled from his lungs. He tossed the letter opener into the den, struggling with the locks.

"Bloody hell, you scared me." He grabbed Angelene's wrist and dragged her inside.

"Have the ghosts followed me?"

Brendon scratched his hair, dazed.

"I thought about happy things. I thought about you then you faded away, no goodbye, no see you soon, you just vanished." She paced across the runner and rubbed her arms. "I thought about Roman, then I saw him walk away. I have a horrible ache in my belly. All the ghosts were in my room tonight."

"Did you call Walter?"

"He accused me of being drunk." She swayed; her accent was thicker.

Brendon crossed his arms. "You have been drinking."

"What do you want me to do? I hoped one would help me sleep and when it didn't, I had another."

His eyes shifted to a series of red welts on her arm. "Do you want to stay here?"

"I can't be alone. It isn't safe."

He took hold of her hand and led her up the stairs. "Which room do you want? Springtime in Ireland? The art déco masterpiece?"

"I want to stay with you."

His brain stuttered, he tried to decipher her words. Stay with him, in his bed, or have him nearby?

"You can hold Paddington, he's good at keeping ghosts away."

"I need you. I feel God in your fingertips."

"I'll stay until you fall asleep."

He went to the walk-in, tore a Nike t-shirt from a stack and handed it to her.

"I've got to wee."

This was one of the worst ideas he had ever had. It wasn't like he was going to make love to her, just sit beside her until she fell asleep. He wouldn't lie under the blankets or hold her. He flushed the toilet, washed his hands, and froze in the doorway. She didn't look like a woman. She looked like a terrified little girl. He slid onto the bed, pulled the blankets around her, and pushed Padre Diavolo from his mind.

"Tell me something wonderful, a favourite thing."

"My Nonna's meatballs."

"Was Borussia Dortmund always your favourite team?"

"The black and yellows forever."

A breathy laugh tickled his side. "Do you like Emma the bee?"

"You know Dortmund's mascot. What's Bayern's?"

"Berni the bear."

"And Man U? Troy will be disappointed if you don't know."

"Fred the Red after the club's nickname, the Red Devils. PSG is a lynx."

"Bloody hell, that's impressive."

"I've had a lot of time to read about things." She yawned and curled into a tight ball.

Brendon leaned his head against the pillow, losing himself in the rhythm of her breathing. Happiness engulfed him. His breathing slowed, and his eyelids grew heavy.

***

Angelene danced in a field of cornflower and buttercups.

21 Twisted

Brendon jerked himself onto his elbows. He had drifted off to visions of being in net surrounded by 80,000 Dortmund fans. Angelene had been one of them, in a yellow dress and now she was here, in his bed. Brendon rolled to his side, stared at a photo of him and Maggie, reached and flipped the frame over.

"Are you awake mon ami?"

She threaded her arm around his waist, her breasts squished into his back, his belly tightened. He turned his attention to the gentle splats of rain dribbling down the window and concentrated on what he was going to work on at the pitch. Her body was warm, inviting. Troy's bragging about morning sex infiltrated his thoughts.

"You smell even better in the morning."

"I shouldn't be here. You shouldn't be here."

She withdrew her arm, pushed the pillows against the headboard, and rested against them.

"It's been a long time since I slept that peacefully. You have a gift, like Roman."

Brendon rolled his head to the side and grinned. It was a stupid thing to do, fall asleep with her. If it meant she had a night of peace, then the stupid decision was worth it.

"I wish things could have been better for you."

"It's only a few chapters. I haven't finished writing my story yet."

She slid across the bed and shivered as her feet hit the floor.

"Would you like a coffee?"

Angelene lifted the t-shirt and dragged it over her head. "I don't know when Walter will be home. I've left a mess again."

Brendon picked up the pillow she had slept on. Lavender and patchouli stained the fabric.

"Can you invest in a bloody bra?"

"I don't like them. All I do is pull at it."

"No wine today and one cigarette."

She came round the bed, held his cheeks in her hands, little flutters floated in his belly. "You stay away from femme fatale, no more of that nasty kissing."

"I don't need another love bite."

"It's ugly. She bruised you," she said, scratching at his stubble. "Thank you for keeping the ghosts away."

"We're there for each other."

"See you soon."

He'd help her write the next chapter in her story and title it, 'The night we chased the ghosts away.'

Brendon gazed out the kitchen window. The rain had stopped, a slice of candescent light broke through the trees making them shine like glass, the bark crystalline. Brendon scraped his fingers through his hair. A melodic hum of Arthur's theme seeped into the kitchen. Amelia was as particular as his mother. She knew every inch of the house, what went where, and the angles Sofia preferred. He spooned up the last bite of yogurt and granola and crossed his fingers. It would meet her approval.

"Good morning," Amelia crooned. She set down grocery bags and dug through the drawer for an apron.

"Checking in on me?"

Brendon stood, rinsed his bowl, and placed it in the dishwasher. He chugged back a glass of milk and shoved a half-eaten piece of toast in his mouth.

"I'm freshening up the house and making one of your great Nonna's recipes."

"You drove all the way out here to make sauce and open windows?"

"It's Janina's bolognese. It must simmer. You'll be responsible after I leave."

"I'm going to the pitch then Maggie's."

"When you get back."

"You can look through the entire house. You won't find a thing."

"Who says I'm looking for anything?"

Brendon pecked her cheek and left the kitchen. He bound up the stairs. Despite the broken sleep, he had a surprising amount of energy. Brendon side-shuffled down the hall, preparing himself for a morning at the pitch. He stepped into the walk-in and ran his fingers over a row of Bundesliga shirts.

"Ame!"

"What are you hollering about?"

She stomped into the room, cradling a stack of clean towels.

"My practice jersey. I can't find it."

"Your First shirt is right there."

"Not that one."

He moved from the closet to a mountain of clothes piled on the chair and tossed handfuls to the floor.

"Which one? You have half the Bundesliga in your cupboard."

"The only one that matters, Dortmund."

"It wasn't in the basket when I did laundry."

He bent down and peered under the bed. No dust bunnies, no magazines, or lost socks.

"If you would put your clothes away."

Brendon pushed himself off the floor, marched to the laundry basket, dumped it, and kicked through the pile. He yanked open a dresser drawer, rooted through socks and boxers. Nothing. He moved to the second, nothing but never worn pyjamas.

"You have a cupboard full of jerseys to choose from."

Brendon grabbed his ball cap and yanked it over his mussed hair. "It's signed by the keeper. Every time I wear it, we win."

"Don't be superstitious. You've only lost one match so far and you said it was because no one's head was in the game, including yours."

"You don't understand."

"I hope you don't expect me to clean up this mess."

"Why would I?"

"Don't be cheeky," Amelia said, stacking towels on the vanity. She came out of the bathroom and stopped. Brendon swiped his keys off the dresser and glanced nervously from the scatter of clothes to his bed.

"I should be putting the blue sheets on, not taking them off. I have a system."

"Who has a system for changing sheets?"

"I do. It makes things easier."

"Maybe you put the blue sheets on by mistake."

"I never deviate from my system."

Brendon cursed, pounded down the stairs, and slammed out the door. Sparks darted around his body. What could he say? His room was hot, he felt feverish. That would send Sofia into a tailspin, worrying he was sick. Brendon blew through a red light, grumbled under his breath, and screeched into the car park.

"We've been waiting almost an hour," Troy said, bopping the ball with his head. "I could have had an extra snog with Charlie."

"I couldn't find my Dortmund shirt."

"We win when you practice in it."

"Let's hope Nike can bring us luck."

Brendon tromped to the net; grass squelched under his feet.

"We don't need a shirt for luck, Mr. Wonderful."

"Fuck off Will."

"I came here to have some fun, not listen to you two," Troy said. He dashed out front of William, stole the ball and fired it towards the net. Brendon reached and snagged it.

"Did you have fun Friday night?" William said. He aimed, Brendon jumped, caught it, and tossed it back on the pitch. It came soaring back at him. He dropped to his knees and snatched it.

"I heard Rachel stayed after everyone left."

"He gave Rachel a tour. That's it, right, mate?"

Brendon tipped the ball over the crossbar; sparks whirred and inflamed his limbs. He picked up the ball and whipped it at William.

"I hear she does this thing on the bell end."

"I wouldn't know."

"You didn't think Rachel would keep her gob shut, did you? She told Tilly, who told me."

"Can we just play? It was a daft mistake; my mate regrets it."

William thrust out his bottom lip and puckered his brow. "Poor Brendon, did Maggie ruin it for you?"

"You need to keep your bloody gob shut. We snogged, that was it."

Brendon lifted his ball cap and ran his t-shirt over his forehead. The entire weekend had been an onslaught of poor decisions.

"The poofter almost got down to it."

"You're any better? Running off with Tilly."

Brendon whipped his gloves to the ground. Sparks fluttered and burned.

"How did it feel to touch some jubblies?" William said.
"Put your gloves back on, mate. Will, you try to get the ball past me."
William smirked. "What was her fanny like?"
"You should bloody know you fucked her."
"I tried to shag her. I couldn't get hard. She's had a lot of knobs in her beaver."
"I left my brekky and Charlie to listen to this," Troy said, bouncing the ball from knee to knee. "Keep breathing, mate. I can see the sparks."
"Is that a love bite? You dirty wanker."
Brendon charged across the pitch and seized William. "You need to keep your fucking mouth shut. If Maggie finds out about this."
"Let him go, mate. He isn't worth it."
"Always bloody Switzerland."
"Someone has to be. Let go of his shirt. We need to practice."
"You wouldn't know where to put your knob."
Brendon twisted William's collar, dragging him to the ground. William kicked, the studs on his cleats pierced Brendon's knees. Everything went fuzzy and black. Brendon tightened his grip. William coughed and sputtered.
"If anything gets around school, or Taunton. I'll see you're never in net."
William jerked his shirt free and tossed a clump of grass. "Get off me."
Brendon rose, the trees, grass and bleachers came back into focus, sparks whizzed through his body like a firestorm.
"Have a drink, mate." Troy said, knocking a bottle of water against his chest.
"Do that again and my fist will be in that dishy face of yours," William said.
Brendon tossed the bottle to the ground and glared. "Try me."
"You two poofters enjoy the rest of the morning."
Brendon swiped the bottle from his feet and chugged the water. "I didn't get a chance to defend because of you two dolts," Troy said.
"Get out front. I'll try to get one past you."
"I hope Will keeps his mouth shut. Maggie will be gutted if she finds out."
Brendon dribbled the ball between his feet and ran towards the net. "He will."
"You think?"
"He was shaking in his football boots."
Troy poked his foot between Brendon's feet and grinned. "Too easy mate. I can see why you're a keeper."
Troy raced down the pitch. Brendon ran, fuelled by the sparks, and dove just in time to stop the ball from going into the net.
Brendon finished his sandwich and tossed the wrapper into the bag. He summoned his best dimpled grin, strolled up the weed infused walkway, meeting Maggie at the door.
"You look better than the last time I saw you. Not so green."
He hastily brushed his lips over Maggie's hair and kicked off his shoes into the jumble.
"You look awful."
Brendon glanced at the smears of dirt on his elbows and abrasions on his knees. "I came from the pitch. What did your mum say when you got home?"
Sweaters hung over the railing, books and toys trailed down the stairs, and spilled into the foyer.
"I got in so much trouble."
He followed her to the front room, flopped on the sofa and stretched his legs across the coffee table. Jack's footsteps thundered overhead.

"I told mum Charlie, and I drank champagne," Maggie said, nibbling her thumbnail, "I said nothing about being at yours."

Brendon dug between the cushions, grabbed the remote and flicked through the stations until he found the football scores.

"You smell sweaty."

He sniffed his armpit. "I smell fine. Bloody hell, I can go if it's bothering you."

"You used to go home and shower."

Footsteps pounded down the stairs. Jack raced into the front room, fired a block, and thumped away.

"Bloody hell, how do you stand him?"

"Do you want a cuppa?"

Brendon dropped his head against the cushion, thump, thump, thump, echoed through the house. He couldn't focus on the highlights or Maggie. His brain was shuffling through, kissing Rachel, Angelene and her knowledge of football mascots, waking beside her. Sparks were simmering in his belly. With every crash and bang, another lit.

"How do you stand the noise?"

"I'm used to it," Maggie said, winding the cord of her sweater around her finger.

"What do you want to do?"

"Watch the bloody highlights in peace."

"Can't we talk? Tell me about practice."

Rain tapped a melodic rhythm against the smudged window. Brendon clicked off the television. The house was unbelievably silent.

"It was the usual."

"Did anything happen?"

Brendon reached between the cushions, pulling out a bright blue block. He examined the ridges, the little nubs, plasticine wedged into the holes. This could be a set-up, bribe him with tea, stare at him with eyes that said she honestly cared about football.

"You sent out your spies, didn't you?"

"Are we in a Game of Thrones episode? I'm trying to make conversation."

Jack thumped into the room and shoved his finger up his nose. "Make me lunch."

"Looks like you're about to bloody have it."

Maggie gave him a 'you're being a baby' look and turned to Jack. "I told you an hour ago to get out of your jimjams and I would make you something."

"Batman and I had important stuff to do," Jack said, wiping his finger on his pyjamas. He licked at chocolate something staining his upper lip, dug into the other crusted nostril, and pulled out a green glob.

"What are you looking at?"

"A bloody disgusting brat."

"I'm looking at a big dolt."

Brendon held up the pillow as a series of colourful blocks flew towards him.

"Will the two of you stop," Maggie said. "I'll slap some peanut butter on bread, then belt up."

Jack grabbed a handful of blocks and aimed. "I'm going to tell mum you wouldn't make me anything to eat cause you were too busy snogging,"

"Will you make him a sarnie before he takes my eye out."

Maggie groaned and stomped from the room. "I feel like I'm babysitting two."

"I hate you." Jack dropped the blocks, tugged the cushions from the sofa and stacked them into a tower. "You smell gross. Give me the remote."

"You do my fucking head in."

"I'm going to tell my mum you swore. She'll never let you come over again."

"Good, I won't have to listen to you bang around the bloody house."

Bubbly laughter gurgled in Jack's throat. "Maggie barfed yesterday. It was her favourite colours, pink and green. Mum said she better not have gotten soused with you."

"Fuck off."

"Brendon." Maggie said, dropping the plate on the coffee table. "Leave Jack alone. Come with me."

Brendon kicked through the pile of blocks and followed her into the foyer. "Where are we going?"

"To my bedroom."

He booted a pathway through the toys and stopped at the bottom of the stairs. He didn't know how much longer he could keep up with the charade. His lunch was about to come up, his muscles ached. All the memories of the weekend swelled around him; he was drowning in his poor decisions.

"You're breaking your mum's number one rule, no Brendon in your bedroom."

He made his way upstairs and stood in the doorway. Everything was pink, frilly, and smelled cloyingly sweet. Stacks of things were everywhere, piled on the vanity, in corners, on the floor. Stuffed animals and textbooks cluttered the bed. It was as chaotic as the rest of the house.

"Jack could use this against me."

"Horrible Henry is on. He'll be glued to the telly for an hour."

Brendon stared at the scrapes on his knees. "No wonder he's such a brat."

"I have three tubes of Sherbert Dips to bribe him with," Maggie said, twiddling a stuffed bear's ear, "he broke mum's Hummel figurine last week. We glued it back together as best we could. I can threaten him with that."

Brendon lifted his ball cap and swiped his hand over his sweating brow. If he sat beside her, she could accidentally tug his t-shirt and expose the continent sized love bite. He had no excuse for snogging Rachel or falling victim to the 'in love' feeling. Brendon backed away and bumped into the pouf. He wasn't proud of his behaviour. Maggie's blue blossom eyes made him feel worse.

"Are you going to shave that stuff off your face?"

"Don't start nagging about the stubble. I get enough aggro from mum."

Stunned by the tone of his voice, Brendon forced himself to remember all the things that made his heart flutter two years ago. All he felt was empty. A chorus of clapping and 'Brendon smells gross,' exploded through the house, followed by a chair scraping across the floor. Maggie jumped from the bed and ripped open the vanity drawer. Brendon's eyebrows raised; the entire drawer was full of sweets. Jack chanted faster, thump, clang, bang.

"Will you do something about him."

Maggie swiped a handful of sweets and kicked the drawer shut. "Gosh, you're miserable."

Brendon's breath was heavy in his chest. He stepped over a tower of books, stared out the window, dismal grey swaddled the weatherworn bricks and gardens. Swallows had perched along the wet telephone wires. Every memory of Rachel and Angelene resurfaced, painful and sharp. The girl he wanted was

21 TWISTED

married. The other, he used to satisfy all his unsatisfied parts. His bad decisions hit him hard.

"Jack should be quiet now. He's eating ice cream; I gave him the sweets."

"I'm going to go."

"You just got here."

Brendon frowned at the display of photos lined up on the vanity. It was hard to look at himself.

"Is it Jack? He'll settle down now. I put on a Batman movie."

"It isn't your brother."

Sparks, heat, longing, rattled his insides.

"Is it because I got so bladdered?"

"I don't care you got pissed," he shifted from foot to foot and sighed, "I want to go home."

"Did Rachel really forget her purse?"

"Bloody hell. Why are you always going on about Rachel and Ms. Pratt?"

Maggie crossed her arms and dug her teeth into her bottom lip. "I haven't said a word about Ms. Pratt."

Brendon punted the pouf into the vanity. He couldn't count his breaths; the sparks were furious.

"I can't fucking breathe."

Maggie's lips quivered. He grabbed her arm and pulled her into his chest. She was springtime, Angelene was winter, Rachel was blazing like the summer heat.

"I'll call you later."

"Do you promise? You said you would call yesterday, you didn't."

"I'll bloody call." Madre Innocente skewered him with her staff. Every part of him hurt. "I need help with the history assignment."

Maggie ripped a tissue from a squished box and dabbed her nose. "At least I'm good for something."

"Don't be like that," Brendon said, fishing his keys out of his pocket. "Why do you have so many pictures of me?"

"I like looking at you."

Brendon kissed her and waited for the flutter. He kissed her again, gentler, slower, nothing. He took hold of her hand and led her from the bedroom, waiting for the tingles or swell of his heart.

"Bye, wanker."

Jack charged past; a handful of blocks fell like colourful bullets at Brendon's feet.

"Unfuckingbelievable."

A 'you deserve to be tortured by my brother,' smirk quirked Maggie's lips.

"History. Don't forget. I promised your father I would help you."

Brendon clacked his heels and shot his arm out in a salute. "Heil Thornton."

"Don't joke about that," Maggie said, opening the door. "I expect you to do your part of the assignment."

He kissed her. Nothing. Was he falling out of like, had two years been long enough? Had too much happened over the weekend, and he wasn't thinking clearly?

Brendon collected the clothes scattered on the floor. He shoved handfuls of boxers into the drawer, threw his dirty laundry back in the basket, and froze. Amelia had changed his sheets. Angelene's perfume lingered, crept off her skin, seeped onto flesh or fabric, clinging, screaming, *'remember me,' I'm always here.'*

Brendon rubbed his forehead. Amelia was known to break into a full-blown performance if she felt moved by a song. A show tune might have distracted her. The mess may have annoyed her, and she pulled the sheets away without bringing them close to her face. Brendon held his cross and raised his eyes to heaven. "Please God, bloody hell, who am I fooling."

Brendon grabbed his history text and notebook and walked down the stairs. There was nothing he could do, except hope his tantrum annoyed Amelia and she didn't notice. It was time for act two, appeasing Maggie. Brendon slid onto the sofa, flipped open his text and tapped his phone on. He set it to speaker and clicked on the television.

"You're watching the highlights?"

"No hello?"

"Do you have your book open?"

"Page 235."

"Turn off the telly. The assignment is on page 325. Tell me one of the key events of Henry VIII's life."

"He was fat and humped a lot of women. Bloody brilliant save, that's another clean sheet for Dortmund."

"Brendon."

"In 1531, he declared himself head of the English church."

"Sweetheart."

"My parents are home. I'll call you back."

Sofia and David waltzed into the great room like they had just stepped off the set of a steamy romance. Sofia's lips were set in a dreamy, love-struck grin. Cupid had pummelled David with his arrows.

Sofia floated to the sofa and wound her arms around his neck. "I missed you."

"You're bloody strangling me."

"Doing your homework?" David said. He gazed from the open textbook to the television. "With the telly on and talking on the phone." Disapproval overtook the love-struck look.

Sofia rubbed David's shoulder and grinned. "I have wonderful news. Your Nonna is coming to visit."

"Don't you mean coming to give her approval. You better warn Walt."

Sofia's gaze swept over the great room. He had set the mantle up correctly, cuckoo clock in the middle, his smiling mug on either side. The armchairs, placed at the perfect angle in front of the fireplace to keep his father warm when he read. Faberge egg under glass, the Klimt hung.

"Everything good, mammina?"

"I can't look at you when you're grumpy. You get this look in your eye, and it frightens me."

Brendon leaned across the sofa and planted a kiss on her cheek. "I can't wait to see Nonna. Instead of one woman nagging, I'll have two."

"No more football until you finish your studies," David said, clicking off the television. "I hope you talked to your mother. Angelene is shy. Nicola is bold."

"Mum says it like it is. Women could learn from her."

"Tell her to be gentle," David said, glancing at the doodles on the paper. "Was Maggie helping you with your homework?"

"Someone has to."

"This is just like the last time and the time before that. You say you're going to apply yourself and all you focus on is football."

"We had a lovely weekend. I can smell the Mastrioni Magico bolognese simmering. I'll see he does it in the morning."

"He can do it now." David's brow creased as he flipped through the notebook. There were more drawings than notes. "What have you been doing all weekend? Wasting time at the pitch? Laying in front of the television?"

"Who cares how many wives Henry VIII had."

"You don't like French, Latin. You hated your maths class. Need I go on?"

"Do you know how embarrassing it was, daddy yanking me from the U19 squad? All my friends got to hang out after training. I had to study."

Sparks sizzled like little sticks of dynamite, crackling, and exploding.

"Imagine an educated football player. When you're too old to play and not everyone's hero, you'll have something to fall back on."

"I'm not bloody smart like you."

"Why don't I go make tea," Sofia said.

"You best get it done or…"

"Or what? You going to keep me from going to Dortmund? Make me redo A-levels until I get the grades, you'll be happy with."

"I'll be happy to see you go."

"David, you don't mean that."

"Aren't you tired of fighting with him? It's been a struggle since year one."

Brendon gripped his textbook. Every ounce of him thrummed with fire, curse words danced on his tongue, ready to spit like bullets.

"I'll be in the den. I'll finish the bloody assignment."

Brendon stormed from the great room, followed by Sofia's sigh and David's annoyed growl. He slammed his elbow onto the light switch and tossed his books on the desk. Brendon flopped onto the chair and imagined the sparks flying out of his fingers and toes. He took himself back to Friday and the soft curve of Rachel's belly, the swell of her round breasts. He remembered Angelene curled into a tight ball, her breath warm on his ribs, her heartbeat in sync with his. Brendon jerked open the drawer and dug under file folders. He clasped a frame in his hand and stared at the picture.

"You fucking prick. Why'd you have to be so smart."

He whipped the photo back in the drawer and slammed it shut. A quote from the Tempest popped into his head. It was the only Shakespeare play he liked, 'Hell is empty, and all the devils are here.'

***

A hefty ache lingered in Angelene's chest. She had slipped into her old pattern, seduced by the light. It could have been Brendon's devil playing tricks on her. She knew Padre Diavolo well, and he was dangerous to Brendon's light.

Mademoiselle Hummel, what are you doing in here?

I'm looking for Professor Piedmont. I need to speak to him.

Pierre won't be in for a while.

Has something happened?

Pierre mentioned you had stolen the light. He kept repeating it. Please stay away.

Angelene shuddered, the walls creaked, a howl swept over the blackened moors.

Where have you been, little bird?

I was washing Monsieur Douchette's feet. Mother wanted quiet.

My coat is on the chair, little bird. There is a gift in every pocket. I need to speak to your mother. Veronique, what are you doing sending that precious girl to him? You must protect her light.

I'm late with rent. He said he would wait if Angelene anointed his feet like Mary Magdalene did Jesus. It's an act of kindness.

That man is not Jesus. You can't trust him around, little bird; I will pay your rent if it means Angelene's light is safe.

She stared at the glow in Brendon's window and dug her fingers into her forearm.

I have a gift for you, petite oiseau. Mother and I visited the lavender fields in Valensole. You should have seen it, purple as far as the eye could see. Your hair will smell as beautiful as the fields.

What did your mother say?

I told her it was for a girl at school.

That was a lie.

Not entirely. You're a girl, my girl. This will help you find your light.

"Still awake?"

"I'm thinking happy thoughts to keep the ghosts away."

She rubbed at the indents and jumped from the nightstand. Walter smiled his crinkly smile and sat on the bed. He took hold of her wrist and gently tugged her beside him.

"There are no ghosts in the house, just memories."

"There was knocking on the walls, taps coming from the attic."

"Old homes make noises."

"You thought I was drunk."

"Weren't you?"

"I was tipsy. I couldn't sleep. The sounds were coming from every corner."

Walter wound his arm around her and kissed her forehead. "I should have listened. I should have consoled you."

"I'm trying not to run to alcohol. It's a terrible habit. I have so many to get rid of. Please be patient."

"I have something for you."

An image of her curled beside Brendon slashed through her mind, striking her, electrifying the ache in her chest. "I don't deserve presents."

Walter reached into his jeans pocket and held up a gold chain. At the end, a simple cross. There were no diamonds, no flash, just a simple thread of gold. Angelene touched her mouth, tears blurred her eyes.

"I know how important the church is to you."

She gazed from the cross to his soft blue eyes and flung her arms around his neck. "I had to pawn mine. It was my favourite gift from Roman."

"Louboutin and Chanel don't seem to impress you. I thought this might make you happy," Walter said. "You're always touching your neck, searching for the necklace."

Angelene lifted her hair, Walter clasped the chain. She glanced down at the shimmering cross.

"I feel like a piece of me has returned."

"I'll keep trying until we find all the pieces, little bird. I'm going to brush my teeth."

Angelene clasped her hand around the cross. A sting, icy and sharp, pierced her heart. *'Please God, keep me away from his light. Something strange happens when I'm around Brendon. I don't understand it. It frightens me.'*

22 La Douleur Exquise

According to Edward Weiss, Taunton's most trusted doctor, there were four stages to anger, annoyed, frustrated, infuriated and hostile. By age seven, Brendon had learned at what stage he needed to put out the fire. At various times over the weekend, he had been at one stage or the other. The conversation between Sofia and Amelia had him intrigued, sweating, and on the verge of blowing.

"Does Maggie still wear that sweet perfume?"

"She smells like a bakery. Every time she visits, I get a craving for a faery cake."

Brendon stiffened and pressed his back against the wall.

"Margaret hasn't started smoking, has she?"

"She's a saint. What's with all the questions?"

"I was gathering the sheets on Sunday to get a head start on my Monday list. I have a system, a certain colour each week."

"And."

"They were the wrong colour."

Brendon cursed. Amelia Potter was the only person he knew who found joy in being excessively regimented.

"All this fidgeting because of the wrong colour sheets."

Brendon loosened his tie, skipped frustration, and slid into infuriated.

"I know that smell. My sister thought it masked the pot she smoked, patchouli oil."

Sparks flashed in Brendon's eyes. He balled his hands and stormed into the kitchen. Sofia stared at him with curious eyes.

"Did Maggie spend the night?"

"I said patchouli, not vanilla."

"What the bloody hell are you accusing me of, Ame?"

He shoved bread into the toaster, undid a button and jerked his collar open.

"I asked you a question. Turn around and look at me."

'Get a fucking grip.'

"It was Charlie."

"Go on."

"There was a party in the forest, close to the rugby club. I'm not allowed in the forest, any forest, so I stayed home. I wouldn't want to break the rules."

Heat crawled up his chest and stained his cheeks. He breathed, released the breath, surprised he wasn't spewing fire.

"Charlotte doesn't smoke," Amelia said, flapping her apron ties.

Brendon slammed his fists against the island. "Stay out of this. You've already said enough."

"Brendon David, control that temper."

"This is fucking daft. Charlie got drunk. Troy had a few and didn't think he should be driving. We carried Charlie to my bed and let her sleep while we watched the telly."

The toaster popped, Brendon ripped it from the slots and whacked a layer of jam across it.

"It's an odd perfume choice, don't you think?"

He wrapped the toast in a paper towel and stared at Sofia. "Charlie is always changing her perfume. I can't fucking believe you're asking me these bloody questions."

"Stop swearing."

"I fucking won't. I'm mad."

"Why didn't you tell dad and I Sunday night?"

"Dad wouldn't shut up about my homework. Since then, I've been angry. I'm almost at the hostile stage. I might lose all my fucking strikes today."

"You know the rule, no one in the house."

"Next time I'll let your little meatball drive bladdered. Sound good?"

"You're impossible this morning."

"You better hope the sparks go out before I get to school or my match this afternoon. Bloody unbelievable."

"I didn't mean to make you mad. I just thought Sofia should know."

"Your loyalty is bloody commendable. I need to go before I'm late, and Ms. Hudson makes me sit in the hallway."

"I suppose I shouldn't ask for a kiss."

"You've got to be bloody kidding."

Brendon stormed from the kitchen, snatched his backpack off the floor and prayed the sparks fizzled out before he got to school.

The sparks stuck with Brendon all morning and continued to simmer in his belly. He had sent Angelene two texts and no reply. The buzz in the garam masala scented dining hall dove into his ears. He checked his phone. Still no reply.

"If my mum asks, Charlie got pissed and slept it off in my bed."

"Why would Charlie sleep at yours when I live ten minutes away?"

"You were bladdered too."

Troy laughed into his bottle of water. "Did she find out about the party?"

Brendon swallowed a mouthful of salad and shook his head. "Ame changed my sheets. They smelled like perfume."

"So why did you say it was Charlie? Do you fancy my girl?"

"I couldn't say it was Maggie. Ms. Thornton would never let her stay over and if mum visited the salon and said something, it would create a bigger mess."

"Where did this party happen?"

"In the forest, beside the rugby pitch."

Troy gobbled a mouthful of Tikka Masala, his eyes twinkled playfully. "The forest? That's a daft place for a party, mate."

22 LA DOULEUR EXQUISE

"If I said it was at yours or someone from the team, she'd find out. Mum knows bloody everybody."

Brendon pressed on the ache in his belly.

"You got the collywobbles?"

Brendon dropped his fork into the salad. A splatter of thyme scented dressing dotted the tablecloth. He stared at his cell. Still no text. "My stomach is in bloody knots."

"It's pre-match jitters."

"Can you watch my stuff? I've got to go to the loo."

"You going to honk?"

"I'm going for a wee, bloody hell."

Brendon clutched his phone, lumbered around the tables, and burst through the dining hall doors, tucking himself beside a trophy case. He needed her voice. He had one class to get through before the match. Dragons in the belly were one thing, sparks could get him a yellow card or worse, a red. Brendon tapped his foot, cursing every ring.

"Are you ignoring me..., I don't care about bloody Walter or the beautiful gift he gave you, Amelia told mum my sheets smelled like patchouli... you're fucking right it's bad... I can't, I have to go to history, I was late everyday last week... Calm bloody down, I told mum it was Charlie... I can't come right now, I've been a prick all morning, Dawson's waiting for me to fuck up... I said no, I'll come after the match... I don't care if you need me now, where the fuck have you been? I've been texting all morning."

Brendon barged through the door, his heart beating in time with the sparks. Whispers of bets buzzed around him. 50p he would toss a chair, two pounds he would scream the F-Word. Brendon dodged around the tables, kicked a chair out of his way, and plunked down at the table. He choked back a bite of chicken and swallowed it with a gulp of water. Anger stirred inside him. He had been there for her, kept the monsters away, listened when she told him Walter had given her a cross. He had been there when Walter hadn't.

"What's the matter, mate?"

His voice was cold and sharp. "Nothing."

"Don't be an arse. I'm just asking."

Brendon impaled a pile of lettuce and shoved it into his mouth.

"Mum called when I was in the loo and started in about Charlie sleeping in my bed."

"You shouldn't feel guilty about something that didn't happen."

"You think someone will tell Maggie about Rachel?"

Troy pushed his plate away and grinned. "Feeling guilty? Just tell Maggie, she'll cry, you arse-lick. She'll forgive you; she loves you."

Brendon poked his fork in a piece of chicken and pushed it through a puddle of dressing. Angelene made him believe he was important by inviting him into her world. He was stuck in her messy life, drowning.

"You have two choices mate, come clean or break up with Maggie and hump the tart."

"She promised to come to Dortmund. She promised we'd walk in Westfalenpark."

"Are you talking about Rachel? She'd say anything to knock you off her list. Now finish that veg, you need fuel for the match."

"She's never had a boyfriend. She's never danced with a boy before."

The weekend and all its tender moments swarmed Brendon's brain. Angelene wanted him, not Walter.

"What do you care about Rachel? You fancy her?"

"I thought I did."

Brendon tapped an apology, sent the text, and stared at the screen. No reply.

"Let's walk, mate, before you explode."

Students snickered and whispered, someone rejoiced in their winnings, the bet, Troy would save the day. Brendon wiggled his tie and unbuttoned the top button. He needed her, and she was too busy. She needed him and the time wasn't right. His thoughts were messy, like her.

"Are you practicing your breaths?"

"I've been trying to breathe since the weekend."

"Let the explosion happen. We could go to the car park; you can let it all out."

"Have people think I'm a nutter?"

"It isn't good to keep it in either. It'll fester, mate and you'll bring it to the pitch."

A string of curse words spewed from his mouth. Brendon jerked his shirt tails loose, rubbing them over his sweating chest.

"That was impressive, mate, a dick fuck prick, bloody doing as your told c-word. I promised Charlie I would never say that word. You feel better?"

Brendon glanced at his phone, still no reply.

"You want to do sprints? A few quick ones to burn it away."

"I'm sweaty enough."

"I'm trying, mate. Breathe down the hall and think about being between the sticks."

"Breathe, got it."

"Promise me and think happy thoughts."

The girl who hated the title of wife and now suddenly loved it, had stolen all his happy thoughts.

"I'll think about a brilliant save the Dortmund keeper made."

"No jubblies?"

"That only reminds me of the daft thing I did."

"What's more than a handful feel like, mate?"

"I thought they would be squishy like a marshmallow. They were firmer than I thought."

"You're becoming a man," Troy said, slapping his shoulder, "tuck your shirt in."

Brendon burst through the door. The musty smell emanating from the heat vents choked him. He glanced at his phone. One message. Brendon hastily tucked in his shirt, looked around, and growled. Maggie wanted to know where he was.

"Just in time, take your seat." Mr. Clark said in a tone that was both surprised and irritated.

Brendon rambled down the aisle. His cell beeped. He clutched it, dropped onto a chair, and cursed.

'Happy thoughts mate.'

Sparks buzzed through his limbs. He had kept his lamp on, so she'd know she was safe. He had done everything for her and now she ignored him.

"Your final assignment is on what you feel was Henry's greatest accomplishment. No papers on how he could pull a woman. It's been done, that student failed."

22 LA DOULEUR EXQUISE

Brendon tapped his pen on the desk. The sparks were out of control. He had held Angelene's hand, listened to her sad stories, stuck up for her when Walter hadn't.

"Asleep Mr. Cook?"

Whispers of 'here we go' and 'ten quid Cook's going to blow' filled Brendon's ears.

"Do you know what we're discussing?"

"Bloody Henry VIII."

"You have no hero status in my class. Answer the question on the board."

"Have you heard about the stages of anger? I'm about to reach the fourth one. Please let me bloody breathe."

"Answer the question." He poked a stubby finger against Brendon's text and barked. "You aren't on the correct page."

The stench of stale coffee breath assaulted Brendon's nose; salad tossed about his stomach. He begged Madre Innocente to come out of hiding, shower him with calm and good judgement. Padre Diavolo cackled. *'Stick your pen in his eye.'*

"Every teacher at Taunton College knows what your punishment will be if your grades slip. One call is all it would take."

Brendon dropped his pen, clutched the corners of the desk. The room clouded. "Are you threatening me?"

The veins in Mr. Clark's neck bulged and throbbed. Silence swept through the classroom. "Answer question one. We spent Friday discussing it."

"If you weren't so bloody boring, I might have paid attention."

"Pardon me?"

Brendon lifted the desk and clunked it on the floor. "If you weren't so fucking boring, I might have listened."

"Get out!"

"Turn to page 355, Brendon, the answer is there," Maggie pleaded.

"Out!" Spit showered Brendon's sleeve. "All my years of teaching, I have never met an idiot quite like you."

Brendon rose, knocking the chair to the floor.

"Pick that up."

"Fuck off."

"Mr. Dawson will be notified about your behaviour."

"Tell him, I don't care."

Brendon stormed past Mr. Clark and swung the door open. It banged against the wall, rattling the map above the blackboard. He marched to his car, whipped his backpack in the rear seat and crumpled behind the wheel. The game of being there for one another weighed heavily on him.

"Guten tag."

Brendon rubbed his face and leaned back in the seat. "Shouldn't you be in class?"

"I told my teacher I had unbearable cramps and needed to go home."

"I have some paracetamol in my rucky."

Rachel laughed. "I told a porkie, knuddlebär. It's an easy excuse when I want to skive off school."

"You want to sit? The wind is chilly."

Rachel skipped around the BMW, jerked open the door, and slid onto the seat. "Why are you sitting in the car park?"

"I got kicked out of history."

"Oh, knuddlebär, that's so dishy."

"I've never seen Mr. Clark that mad."

Brendon stared at his palm and traced along his lifeline. Angelene saw strength. He didn't feel strong. Padre Diavolo and his orchestra of sparks had beaten him down.

"I need to relax so I can play my best today."

"You want to come round to mine?"

"I've got to find Dawson and apologize. You have no idea what could happen if I don't make this right."

Rachel leaned across the console and wrapped her hands around his arm. "I'll make you a cuppa. You can watch some highlights."

"The bus leaves at 3:30. I have to change into my suit or Liam will fine me 5 quid."

"You can change at mine."

Padre Diavolo stopped lighting the sparks and snickered. '*To hell with school. Fuck your father and his expectations. Fuck little bird, let her break her own patterns.*'

Brendon started the engine. The collage of Victorian buildings faded in the distance.

"Have a ciggie, knuddlebär."

"No, thanks."

"You're such a good boy."

Cursing, lying to his mother, kissing Uncle Walt's wife, fantasizing about Rachel's ginger landing strip. If anyone should pray for forgiveness, it was him.

Rachel flicked the cigarette out the window. She shook out a piece of gum and tossed it in her mouth.

"Would you rather have a proper drink? Mum's friend was visiting from Berlin. There's lager in the fridge," Rachel said, pointing, "turn left, second house."

Brendon turned onto a cul-de-sac lined with brown, rectangular boxes. Each house faced the tree-lined street with the same white framed windows and brick lined gardens. The only difference between Rachel's home and the others were the pots of cyclamen and pansies blooming outside the front door.

"Tea or beer?"

Brendon parked the car and wrestled with the jitters in his belly. One drink before the match wouldn't hurt. He'd add it to the list of stupid things he had done today.

"Beer."

'*Will power Brendon. Ignore Padre Diavolo.*' He rubbed his brow, sighed, and stepped into the floral scented foyer. The white-tiled floors shined; the wood gleamed. Brendon's gaze followed the various shades of white from the entry to the sitting room. The only speck of colour was the rattan settee, the walnut coffee table, and the blue floral pillows. Everything from the armoire to the fireplace looked as if covered in snow.

"Shall we go to my room, knuddlebär?"

"Can't we sit in there, watch telly?"

"I have a telly in my room."

His nerves were tattered, jumping in every direction. Sparks zipped and fizzled.

"You're not doing anything wrong."

"Everything about this is wrong."

22 LA DOULEUR EXQUISE

He followed her up the stairs, matte white continued down the hall, into the bedrooms and bathroom.

"My bedroom, knuddlebär."

Brendon poked his head into the white, golden brown and smoky blue room. He had expected a temptress' lair with red walls, black satin sheets, and handcuffs dangling from the bedpost. He got a neatly made bed in virginal white.

"It's warm in here."

He took off his blazer and laid it on an aquamarine fan back chair.

"Sit. I'll grab the drinks."

Brendon smiled stiffly and plunked on the edge of the bed. He glanced at a photo of Rachel and Tilly, all smiles, dressed to impress. A piece of paper stuck out from beneath the frame. She had listed the prices of tickets to a Dortmund match and decorated the words in hearts. It would cost sixty-five pounds to fly to Dortmund.

I would fly home and take a train. We would walk hand in hand in Westfalenpark.

Brendon rubbed his knuckles over his forehead, forcing her voice from his mind. She wouldn't sneak away from Walter to hold his hand. Walter was a prince now.

"One Helles for my knuddlebär."

Brendon took the glass and ran it over his inflamed cheeks.

"Here's to a win," Rachel said, raising her glass, "Prost."

Rachel took a long sip and set her mug down. She climbed onto the bed, sat behind him, kneading his shoulders.

"Does it feel good?"

The glass slipped in his sweating palm. She pressed her breasts into his neck and undid his tie. He could picture Angelene pacing, praying, clutching her cross, pleading for forgiveness. He should be with her, having tea, discussing the patchouli scented sheets.

"I should go. I'm in enough trouble."

He cursed Padre Diavolo for changing the angry sparks to tingly ones and sending a wave of heat to his groin. Rachel had managed to undo his tie and the buttons on his shirt. Brendon chugged the beer and set the glass next to hers. His shirt floated to the floor.

"Your turn now."

Rachel climbed off the bed, stood before him, jerking her tie loose.

"I shouldn't be here."

Angelene's pretty words cluttered his brain. He could see Maggie chewing away at her fingernails. Sparks of both kinds fluttered.

"Go on, knuddlebär, take my shirt off."

She guided his hand, her breasts sprung from their cage of cotton. Brendon touched the heart charm dangling from her belly button. He peeled away her shirt, his fingers tickled down her spine, and stopped at the zipper.

"Undo it."

Yes, no, bombarded his head. Padre Diavolo switched on the pleasure sensors. He unhitched the clasp and tugged at the tiny pull. Rachel stood before him in a turquoise lace bra and panties.

"Your turn now."

You must protect your light. That girl is no good. She's dangerous.

"Hurry, I'm cold," Rachel said, climbing into bed.

"Cold? It's about a hundred degrees in here."

He slid his trousers off, her bra landed at his feet; Brendon counted twelve freckles between her collarbone and sternum. He crawled under the blankets, his face and body heated. Rachel's minty ale tasting mouth clamped on his. She had him trapped with her arms, legs, and lips.

"You can touch me," Rachel said.

Brendon glanced from her breasts to the turquoise triangle. Both places looked inviting.

"Have you never touched a fanny before?"

He placed his lips on hers and tucked his fingers under the elastic band. To hell with Angelene and Maggie. His devil wanted to play.

"Go slower, knuddlebär, like this."

She laid her hand over his and guided his fingers in slow circles. She gasped against his mouth and reached into his boxers. All the gossip that had floated around the dressing room was true. She knew how to please a boy, and she was pleasing him. Pleasant twitches surged through his body; he fought the sensation, struggling to hold on.

"Bloody hell, I'm sorry."

She grinned and kissed his nose. "Don't apologize, knuddlebär, it was bound to happen."

She reached over him; his lips parted as her nipple grazed his mouth. She wiped his belly; it flexed and tingled. Rachel dropped the bundle in the bin and nibbled his chin.

"I love the stubble."

"Mum hates it. Maggie complains it scratches."

"Don't use that name in my bedroom."

"Who is she, Voldemort?"

Her fingers skated over his ribs and abdomen. He laughed. "Will you bloody stop."

"You're smiling now. Your eyes were dark before, they're twinkling now," Rachel said, kissing his shoulder. "I have a brilliant idea. Let's get starkers."

She lifted her bottom and wiggled out of her panties. Brendon fumbled with his boxers. He didn't want to be a gentleman or the 'I always do as I'm told' boy. He wanted nothing but this moment. Brendon opened his mouth, danced his tongue over hers, and slid his fingers between her thighs. A tip, Troy had shared crept into his mind, start with one finger, then two and crook them like he was tickling the inside of her belly. Rachel moaned. He sunk his fingers deeper. She gripped his forearm.

"Am I hurting you?"

"Keep doing what you're doing, knuddlebär."

Brendon had no idea what he had done, but by the look on Rachel's face, Troy's trick had worked.

"Do you have a condom?"

"In the nightstand," Rachel said, through delighted sighs.

Brendon yanked open a drawer, pushed aside papers and books until he found a strip of foil packets. He stared at the square, his body quivered and not in an 'I'm about to lose my virginity' way.

"Are you going to put it on?"

"I'm working up the nerve."

"You're so cute, knuddlebär, allow me."

22 LA DOULEUR EXQUISE

He laid on top of her, his breath rapid. He couldn't remember if Troy had said to go slow or fast. All he knew was the feeling was incredible. Her breath was warm on his neck. It surprised him at how tightly she held him.

"I'm afraid you'll think this is a mistake, knuddlebär."

He silenced her with a kiss. It was a mistake, a horrible, fantastic mistake. Brendon savoured the incredible warmth between them, sighing heavily in her ear. Padre Diavolo applauded, and Madre Innocente struck his belly with her staff. He stared at his clothes heaped on the floor. A cold realization slapped him back to reality.

"That was brilliant."

"Can I use the loo? I need to change into my suit. The bus leaves soon."

"Ignore mum's beauty products. She's worried about getting old," Rachel said, gathering the blankets around her. "Can you pass me my ciggies?"

Brendon tossed the package on the bed.

"You feel like an arse, don't you?"

Brendon gathered his school kit. His heart dropped to the pit of his stomach, crushing the sweet memories.

"You can keep this a secret, right?"

"I'll take it to my grave."

"I mean it, Rachel. No one can know about this. Maybe put a star beside my name instead of crossing it off."

He clutched his clothes, his mind wandered. Did he kiss her? Should he thank her for an enjoyable time?

"I can't be late for the bus. Liam fines us for that, too."

"I get it. You're taken," Rachel said, blowing out a mouthful of smoke. "Can I ask you something?"

He was getting impatient. The room felt hotter. He needed to run and fast before he fell back into her bed.

"Where did you learn to do that? For a boy who's never touched a fanny, bleeding heck, knuddlebär, that was a brilliant tingle."

"Troy. If I could ever get my hand down Maggie's knickers, I needed to know what to do."

"Know any other tricks?"

"I'm going to miss the bus. Fuck, my bloody suit is in the car."

Rachel set her cigarette on the edge of the vanity and pointed to a kimono. "Pass me my dressing gown."

Brendon lowered his gaze and handed her a cherry blossom print robe.

"Go to the loo. She who shall not be named will never find out."

Her body disappeared under the silky fabric; she ran her hand over his bottom.

"Bloody hell, don't you ever quit."

"You have a brilliant bum, knuddlebär."

Brendon touched his cross. *'Thanks for fighting off Padre Diavolo. You're never here when people need you.'*

He walked down the hall and snapped on the bathroom light. A floral scent clung to the seashell print shower curtain and roman blinds. Different sized wicker baskets stuffed full of serums and lotions sat on the countertop. Brendon dropped his school uniform to the floor, turned on the tap, pumped some fruity smelling soap on his hands and washed Rachel's scent away.

"You decent?"

"You've already seen me naked."

Rachel opened the door and held up the garment bag. She wore a smile Brendon didn't expect. She was supposed to be a 'I got what I want, now leave' girl, not grinning at him like she was love struck.

"Is that an Armani suit?"

"Mum thinks Italians make the best clothes."

"Impressive. I'm going to make a cuppa; you want one?"

"I've got to get a move on... should we kiss goodbye?"

"It's never goodbye, knuddlebär and no, you don't have to."

Brendon hung the garment bag from the towel rack and slumped into the counter. Madre Innocente wrapped him in an itchy cloak of regret, a heavy breath emptied from his lungs. He couldn't change what he had done, just shove it aside with all the other stupid decisions and try to forget it happened. Brendon unzipped the bag, trousers, shirt, tie. He looked the part of a respectable footy player. Brendon took one last look in the mirror, grinned an 'you're a bloody dolt' grin, and shoved his school kit in the bag. He walked down the stairs; the kettle whistled.

"I'm leaving."

"Bist bald knuddlebär. Viel gluck, mein Freund."

Brendon sprinted to his car. He had ten minutes to get to the pitch. His head was full of regret, his stomach in knots. He needed someone. He needed Angelene. Brendon kept his eyes on the road and tapped his phone.

"Pick up, please pick up."

The phone rang and rang. He jammed his finger on the screen and batted it to the floor mat. Brendon parked the car and tried again. Sparks flickered; it went unanswered. He inhaled slowly, plastered a grin on his face and tried to stir up the dragons. Brendon stared from one teammate to another, their faces sullen.

"Why does everyone look so bloody miserable?"

Troy kicked a stone and looked at him with an 'as if you don't know' smirk. The bus shook, Liam slammed down the stairs; a clipboard flew towards his head.

"You spoiled eejit."   "What the bloody hell have I done?"

Liam charged towards him, finger pointed, nostrils flared. Brendon batted Liam's finger away and took a step back. He had seen Liam angry, not where his face was crimson and the veins in his neck were ready to burst.

"Why are you acting like a bloody nutter?"

"You're benched. The headmaster called your mamm. What were you thinking bunking off school?"

"Let me call mum."

"You think your charm will work on her? There's no reasoning with that woman."

"We'll lose."

"You should have thought about that before you made a holy show of yourself."

Brendon rolled his head from side to side, sparks exploded like grenades.

"Mr. I'm so tough, I should have been a rugby player," Brendon said, stepping closer. "You're going to listen to my mother?"

"Do you know how much influence she has? Do you have any bleeding idea how much money she's dumped into the team?"

Brendon edged closer. "You knew about mum and dad's daft rule, didn't you?"

"Your father and I had a pint, and he mentioned it. He said you made a right bag of things in Dortmund. I will not argue with our Lord Chancellor."

"My parents have you by the goolies."

22 LA DOULEUR EXQUISE

Liam grabbed his lapels and shoved him into the bus. "You show up here in your posh suit, stinking of ale and perfume, expecting to play when your mamm warned you. I want fifty quid."

Brendon wrangled himself free. "For what?"

"For missing the team meeting. Drinking a pint before the match. Disrespecting your coach and breaking your parents' rule. Do you want me to go on?"

"My day has been bollocks, sparks all day."

"You should have practiced your breaths. Now get your bleeding arse on the bus and keep your gob shut. You better be in top form McGregor."

Brendon brushed off his suit jacket and ripped his backpack from the ground. He stomped onto the bus, jammed his knapsack on the overhead rack, and dropped on the seat. Sparks burned and swirled.

"Talk to me, mate?"

"Liam said to keep my mouth shut."

Brendon scrolled through the music on his phone, the sparks dimmed, he could finally breathe.

"Your mum could have you benched for the entire season. You should have found Dawson and begged for mercy."

"She's teaching me a lesson, avoiding aggro from dad. She'll feel bad, she always does."

"Where did you go?"

"For a drive."

Troy leaned in and sniffed his neck. "With whom?"

Brendon flicked at Troy's nose and stared at his phone. She hadn't returned his call or sent a text.

"Myself, that's who."

Troy's face twisted. "You smell like Rachel's perfume and spunk."

"Is that so?"

"You also have a daft look on your face, like you did something bad."

Brendon turned away from Troy. How does someone smell like sex? He had washed his hands, rinsed his mouth with mouthwash he found stuffed in a basket of potions and lotions. He leaned his head against the seat and stared at the steel rack.

"Charlie said Rachel complained about girly cramps and left psych. You better not have spent the afternoon humping."

"I wasn't humping Rachel."

"I swear mate, if you hurt Maggie. Charlie will have me by the nipples and the goolies."

"I haven't done anything. You always have sex on the brain."

"Why would you pick this day to tell Mr. Clark where to go? Weston is two points behind, now Will's in net. Bollocks."

Brendon couldn't agree more. The entire day had been bollocks.

***

Sofia walked into Johnstone, Harrnsworth, and Miller law offices. She smiled warmly and nodded towards Kate's office. The secretary pulled down her glasses and returned the smile.

"Go in Ms. Cook."

The corner office was bright and welcoming. An arched window overlooked the garden, filling the office with natural light. Kate's desk, an ornate gargantuan structure, sat squarely in the middle of an area rug. A notebook, Toby mug filled with her pens and pencils, three framed photos, one of her and Kate sipping espresso on a piazza, Brendon signing the contract with Dortmund and in his too-big Dortmund jersey, decorated the expansive desk. The built-in bookcases housed a variety of law books and journals. Two floral barrel chairs sat in front of the desk. It was more home than office.

"Sorry I didn't call," Sofia said, setting a cup of cappuccino on the desk. "I hope you aren't busy."

Kate glanced up from her notebook. "I'm trying to figure out how I can help a client keep her home and children. You're just the break I needed."

"She's a mother. Wouldn't it make sense she gets the home to raise her children?"

"Not when you're having an affair."

"I need your help."

Kate removed the plastic lid and blew on the milky foam. "It's just like you to get right to it."

"Do you still have that friend? The private investigator?"

Kate's brow wrinkled. "Hugh? I wouldn't call him a friend, more of a colleague."

"If I ask you to do something, promise not to tell David."

Kate took a small sip and shook her head. "I know what this is about, and the answer is no."

"Money isn't an issue."

"I thought you were done with Angelene?"

"How do you know it isn't about Lukas or a new groundskeeper?"

"No one knows roses like Peter, and you already asked about Lukas," Kate said. Her smile wavered. "There's only one person causing you to worry. She's five feet tall and blonde."

"I need to know about her family, the professor she worked with."

"Why? Angelene doesn't like to talk about her past. Respect that."

"Do it for Walter."

Kate wheeled the studded Edwardian chair back. She walked around the desk, perched on the corner, and folded her silk clad arms over her chest. "What else is troubling you? You're fiddling with your bracelets."

When Sofia became a mother, she took on the challenge like she did everything: headstrong and confident. Over the years, she found motherhood changed her, she worried, she got scared. She loved fiercely, found it hard to let go.

"It's Brendon."

"Angelene is not out to get Brendon."

"The picture she drew from memory, at the restaurant in Burnham she kept glancing at him over her cocktail."

"He's an attractive kid and not just his looks. He's worth a fortune."

"Angelene looks at him differently."

Kate rose, unclenched Sofia's fingers from the cup, and tossed it in the garbage bin. "We need to leave Angelene alone."

22 LA DOULEUR EXQUISE

"Amelia thought she smelled Angelene's perfume on Brendon's sheets. He said it was Charlotte. When Amelia gets a hunch, it's usually right. Her stomach was in knots the day I had to run into the forest."

"Why would Brendon have Angelene in his bed? Is Amelia suggesting they're having an affair?"

Fear settled into Sofia's chest. As far back as she could remember, women had always flirted with Brendon. This was more than flirting. There was a longing in Angelene's eyes, like she wanted to crawl inside him, cling to his heart and breath.

"Simone made that ridiculous comment. She'd love to get Brendon between the sheets."

"She was on her fifth margarita," Kate said, pulling down her cuff. "Have you spoken to Dr. Weiss, walked in the forest like he suggested? It might put an end to all the fear you carry around."

"David and I are dealing with it. We have been for years."

"When Brendon went to Dortmund in August, you redecorated a bedroom. When he was there last spring, you dug out all his baby pictures and started scrapbooking," Kate said. "What do you do when he leaves the house?"

"Hold my breath."

"Once he's home, you release it."

"You're not a mother. You don't know what it's like to have a child."

"You're right, I don't, but I know how it feels to love someone so much, you feel your heart break every time they walk away."

A Royal Dalton vase caught Sofia's eye; a hollow, achy feeling stuck between her ribs. "I still have the pieces of the Royal Dalton figurine Brendon broke. I remember the look on his face when he handed me the five pounds he got for his birthday. He made me a pasta necklace, painted each noodle red to match my lipstick. The string tore, but I kept every damn macaroni."

"This bedsheet nonsense has got you worried."

Sofia shivered and clutched Kate's hand. "Have you ever looked into Angelene's eyes?"

"They're sad and green."

"Some background information, please."

The wind rustled the leaves and pushed the clouds through a sooty sky. Goldfinch chirped and fluffed their yellow feathers in the concrete birdbath.

'Maybe Angelene envies Brendon's wings. She's looking to repair hers and only wants to steal a feather or two.'

"Why do I have a feeling there's more."

"I feel terrible. I promised David."

"What did you do?"

"Mr. Dawson called. Brendon told his teacher to fuck off."

"Is that all?"

"Isn't that enough?" Sofia said, clutching her handbag. "He was supposed to see Mr. Dawson. He left. This is not the first time either. He's been buying Boots out of paracetamol."

"I'm surprised he goes at all."

"David is so upset."

Sofia tapped her fingernails against her purse. She had never been a punisher. She reacted, then softened.

"I called Liam and had him benched."

"Way to hit below the belt."

"David and I told him if he didn't take his studies seriously, no football," Sofia said, flicking her bracelets, "I'm sure it's to see her. They always find one another."

"Who, Sofia?"

"Angelene. The mysterious intruder, Walter's party. The damn sheets."

"Brendon was probably at the pitch or driving around trying to cool off."

"The whole time I was talking to David, I could hear Walter laughing."

"Walter thinks you're overprotective."

"Walter can go to hell. If he hadn't called Lukas, I wouldn't be losing my son."

"Someone would have discovered Brendon."

Sofia had never forgotten the championship game. A group of scouts had swarmed Brendon. He knew all the moves. He could read the play as if stepping into the minds of the other players. His confidence was outstanding and all at seven. She had protected him from their sales pitch. They were there to steal her son. Angelene was no different from those men.

"I wouldn't ask if I didn't think it was important."

"I'll take you for curry, that place on High Street is getting brilliant reviews," Kate said. "We'll have a G&T, sort through your worries, then you can decide if you want me to ring Hugh."

Sofia pulled her wrap tighter around her shoulders. "Did I make the right decision? The only thing Brendon looks forward to is football."

"If it saves you arguing with David, then yes. Brendon will get over it like he always does with a few curse words and some brooding."

Sofia wasn't so sure.

***

Night came with chaotic splats of rain, charcoal smudged skies and frantic winds. Angelene enjoyed a night when God was furiously screaming at the world, not tonight. He was angry with her; she was tired. Tired of pacing, tired of waiting for God's forgiveness. She started the day yellow, said goodbye to the chocolate brown walls and hello to a hallway the colour of a chick's feathers. When Brendon called about the scented sheets, the yellow drained away and she was sickly grey. Cigarettes had not helped the tearing of her insides. Wine helped for a minute, then the tornado of emotions would reappear. She needed Brendon; he did not come.

A knock echoed through the house. Angelene plucked a bent cigarette from within a mound of ashes and squeezed her eyes closed.

I knew you would come. I don't need you now.'

She broke the cigarette in two and tugged at her braid. "Go away."

The knock grew louder, spirited, forceful. She brought her cross to her lips and kissed it.

"I want you to go away."

"Open the door. I need to talk to you."

"God is furious with me. Can't you tell by the rain and wind?"

"You promised to be there for me. Open the fucking door."

Brendon pushed into the foyer; she pinched the cross between her fingers.

"Go sit by the fire. I'll bring you a towel." She crushed her cross into her palm and marched to the laundry room. "You weren't there for me either."

22 LA DOULEUR EXQUISE

She whipped the towel at him and plunked onto the ottoman. "All day I paced trying to think of something I could tell Sofia. You should have come."

"I had one class and then I had to catch the bus for the match. I couldn't drop everything and run to you, not today." Brendon stripped off his suit jacket and glared. "It looks like you've been dealing with the problem."

She followed his gaze to a bottle of wine and ashtray full of butts. "What was I to do?"

"Call Walter. He bought you the necklace. He's bloody wonderful now. You could have made up a daft story and made him feel sorry for you. You're good at that."

"Padre Diavolo is extraordinarily powerful right now. Your eyes are so dark."

"The little fucker has been pestering me all day."

Brendon's black mood seeped into Angelene's skin. It tasted like soot. His dark thoughts jumped from his mind and stabbed into hers.

"Did you win?"

"Lost. 4-0"

"You let in four goals?"

"I couldn't play."

"Are you hurt?"

Brendon ran the towel over his neck and balled it in his hands. "I told my history teacher to fuck off. The headmaster called mum, and he told her about the other classes I bunked off."

"You shouldn't have listened to Padre Diavolo." "It wasn't bloody Satan, it was me. I've skived off school to help you. I've needed you all bloody day."

Staticky black surrounded him. Slashes of red like fiery lightning bolts lit up his abdomen and groin. "You're black, I see red. What have you done to your light?"

Brendon shifted on the bricks, clenched, and unclenched the towel. "I met up with Rachel and went back to her house."

Angelene shook out a cigarette and inhaled sharply. The tornado of emotions raged. This was not her boy in magnificent brown. It was his clothes, his citrusy smell and beautiful face but, it was not him.

"I had sex with Rachel."

Angelene choked on the mouthful of smoke. "You broke up with Maggie?"

"I cheated on her."

"I told you to stay away from that girl. I told you to protect your light."

"If you would have picked up the phone. You would have understood I needed to go to class."

Angelene smashed the cigarette into an ashy plate. Swampy green and hot red invaded her sickly grey.

"Don't blame me. I needed you, and you fucked that disgusting girl. You're dirty."

"I was pissed off, and she was there. Rachel was fucking there, not you," Brendon said, whipping the towel, "all that shit you said. Bloody hell, we kissed."

Angelene pressed her hands over her ears and squeezed her eyes shut.

"You can say we were drunk, and it meant nothing, but it meant something. It meant something to me."

"Stop, please stop."

"You slept in my bed. You hold my hand; not Walter's." His voice was brittle and cold, like a winter wind, sweeping over her skin.

"No more, please. I can't listen to you."

"You used me."

"Ask God for forgiveness. Stay away from that girl and your light will be bright again."

"I have nothing to say to God. Mum has been asking him the same question for nineteen years and he still hasn't answered her. What makes me special?"

Angelene pushed herself off the ottoman and paced. Her gut twisted. All the pieces of the pattern that had fallen away came together.

"I thought we could be friends; I've tried before, it ended horribly. It can't happen again."

"Stop fucking pacing. We're here for each other now." He rose and stepped in her path. "We can forget about the day and start over."

"I don't like you."

"Because I had sex? Everybody fucking humps. I'm still the same person."

His words were sludgy brown with shades of weepy blue.

"It's for the best we end this. I promised God I would be a better wife. Walter has been very patient."

"Give Walter time, and he'll be that cocky prick ordering you around. He'll complain about the yellow walls, and you'll paint them blue or white to appease him. Who'll be there to say it's okay? Not me."

He barged past and slammed the door. She dashed to the foyer, flung the locks in place, and ran up the stairs, falling to the bedroom floor. Angelene yanked out the jewellery box, spilling the contents. She picked up a news article, running a finger over Brendon's face. She lay the article in the box and held up the Dortmund jersey.

"I can't be your friend. La douleur exquise, you want my affection, I can't give it."

She lay the jersey over her lap and held up a sketch of the Pont des Arts. Her heart split.

"We held hands along the footbridge. You were going to build me a castle on the Ile de la Cite so I could have cake with Marie Antoinette's ghost."

She set the drawing in the box and picked up a postcard from Germany. Flipping it over, she read the words, longed for them, breathed them into her wrenched lungs, 'tu me manques, little bird.' Angelene pressed her lips against it and placed it in the box. The tornado inside her grew into a hurricane, blowing and smashing into her lungs and heart. She clamped her hands against her temples, voices screamed at her, bit into her flesh. She was no good, a cancer, infected by the devil. Angelene scrambled to the bathroom and whipped open the medicine chest. She shoved aside bottles of aspirin, aftershave, and vitamins. Whacking the door closed, she bolted from the bedroom, raced down the stairs. The voices mocked violently. She thumped to a stop; the paring knife she had used to slice an apple sang to her from the cutting board. Angelene clutched it and sank to the floor. She folded down the waistband of her jeans and gazed at the blue vein pulsing through her tissue paper skin. She was slow, steady, her breath blew out as hard as the wind.

Roman hurry, it's coming.

What is it, little bird?

A monster.

There are no monsters. I checked before you went to bed.

Mother said Satan takes little girls away when they're bad. She said she saw the devil in me.

You're wearing the cross I gave you. You said your prayers before you went to sleep. God is protecting you.

What if I dream about the wicked man and you aren't here?

I'll always be with you, little bird.

Angelene stretched her shirt and dabbed at the bubbles of blood. "What do I do when I need someone? Who will help me when life gets tangled, and I trip?"

Angelene grabbed the edge of the island and dragged herself off the floor. An ache settled into her forehead. Exhaustion dripped like honey, slow and oozy, following her like a sticky puddle to her bedroom. She stopped at the foot of the bed, holding her fingers to her mouth.

"Your lamp is on."

The pattern of run, hide, clutch, smother, wound around her. She pressed her palm against the tickle in her belly. Brendon had succumbed to fevered red. The loss swelled and choked her. La douleur exquise.

23 GIRL WITH MANY FACES

BRENDON'S EYES SWEPT OVER Nicola Mastrioni. He tried to decipher his Nonna's mood. All he saw was a slender woman with dazzling white hair and penetrating espresso eyes. While Brendon had a knack for reading a football play, making keen observations was in Nicola's DNA. Nicola could study a person, look in their eyes, watch for subtle twitches of the mouth or fidgeting fingers, gather the information she needed, and use it to her advantage. There was one look Brendon could read on his Nonna's face: how proud she was. Proud that the textile mill was still one of Milan's best, proud of her home, her happy marriage, and her children. She would go to the ends of the earth to protect her family, which included Walter Pratt and Kate Miller. The person she loved the most was staring at her.

"Amore mio, you're quiet tonight."

She rose from what Brendon would consider her throne, adjusted the upturned collar on her signature white blouse and lounged beside him.

"Let me look at that brooding face of yours. Sei Cosi bello." She held his chin and turned his face from side to side. "You look different, older."

"I look the same as I did when I saw you in August."

"You look like you've aged five years since then."

Brendon felt like he had. The week's events had left him empty, with a severe case of the guilts and pissed off.

"It's that stuff on his face," Sofia said.

"Dad, don't let her start."

The doorbell gonged, David stood and squeezed Sofia's shoulder. "Leave him alone. There are more important things to worry about than stubble."

Brendon hung his head and shooed away the sparks. This was not the night to let his temper get the best of him.

"What can I expect from Ms. Pratt," Nicola said, fingering her pearl necklace, "another leggy bimbo?"

"Quite the opposite," Sofia said.

"Am I going to get any substance? Intelligence?"

"She's interesting."

"Mum don't. She's just a girl."

A spark lit and whizzed around his stomach, followed by another. He didn't know why he cared about his mother's opinion. Angelene had dismissed him and broke their pact.

Voices carried from the foyer, Brendon straightened his tie and yanked on his cuffs, the sparks whirled in a frenzied tingle. He had to be cool, nonchalant. Nicola was all eyes and ears. She was sensing something was troubling him.

"Forced, uncomfortable sophistication in that designer dress and Louboutin shoes."

Brendon glanced from Nicola to Angelene, rubbing his palms on his thighs. She looked beautiful in her dress-up clothes.

"She looks no older than you."

"She's twenty-five."

"Exactly topolino, not much older than you."

"Angelene, meet my mother-in-law, Nicola Mastrioni."

Walter unglued her from his side, thrusting her forward. She stumbled. Brendon grinned. She still hadn't mastered the red-soled shoes.

"It's nice to meet you," Nicola said, extending a hand. "I would have been here sooner, but I had to attend the spring summer Settimana Della moda. Two designers used fabric from the mill."

"You're so lovely," Angelene said, in a raspy whisper, "You remind me of Audrey Hepburn."

"People would say I'm more Joan Crawford. I appreciate the compliment. Walter, how are you?"

'Irritated,' Brendon thought.

Walter kissed Nicola's cheeks. "Busy, but good."

"How's married life? It must be quite a change," Nicola said.

Walter accepted a glass of scotch from David and waved Angelene onto the sofa. Brendon curled his fingers, flexed, and shook out the itch to wipe the annoyed look from Walter's face.

"I'm adjusting. I'm not sure there's such a thing as domestic bliss."

"I'm sure Angelene is adjusting too," David said, relaxing onto the armrest. "New town, new friends, new lifestyle."

Brendon gave his father a point for sticking up for Angelene. It took the onus off him. He was having more fun trying to read Nonna's face. Angelene was fidgeting with the bracelets cluttering her wrists. As far as he could tell, the incessant clacking annoyed Nicola.

"Did you get my wedding gift?"

"It was very generous," Walter said.

"You're like a son to mother."

Brendon could have sworn there was a tone to his mother's voice, like she hoped Angelene realized she married into a tight-knit clan, blood or not.

"Sofia said the two of you met in Parc Floral. Anthony and I visited once. The flowers were lovely but those peacocks, strutting about."

"That's Ang's favourite thing about the park."

Walter laid his hand over Angelene's twitching fingers. Brendon smirked. The evening would be fun. He would title it 'Masquerade at Rosewood Manor.'

"I can see why Walter introduced himself. You're beautiful."

"I keep telling her that. She doesn't listen," Sofia said.

23 GIRL WITH MANY FACES

Sofia tapped a slow rhythm against her wineglass. David clinked the ice around in his scotch. Walter took small, annoyed sips, Angelene clicked through her bracelets. It was hard for Brendon to think above the noise.

"Are you ready to join the Italian league yet?"

"The Dortmund keeper's contract is up in summer. Rumour has it, I'll be playing on the first squad and not as second choice keeper."

"Why wouldn't they choose you, topolino? I'd prefer you played for Serie A, however, I'm proud of you."

Walter sipped and clinked the ice. "Brendon has done wonders for Taunton First. He didn't get to play the last match. Davy boy thought he needed to learn a lesson."

David wound his arm around Sofia and shot Walter a disapproving look. "Angelene is a football fan. You two have something to talk about."

"You enjoy football?"

Angelene burrowed deeper into the cushions. 'Oui' was all she said.

"Italy put France out in the World Cup."

"You'll have to excuse my mother. She's passionate about the game. You should have seen her the first time Brendon was on the pitch. You wouldn't have seen anyone prouder than her."

"Topolino will be the greatest keeper the Bundesliga has ever seen."

"I don't know about that. There's Neuer, Sommer."

"Lukas knows you'll be one of the Bundesliga's top five. I hope you'll be proud of him then, Davy boy."

The doorbell gonged; it came at just the right time before his father could lecture about the importance of education.

David handed his glass to Sofia. "I'll ignore that."

"It must be Maggie," Sofia said.

"You don't look happy, topolino."

"We've been arguing lately." He glanced at Angelene, then back to Nicola. "It's hard for her to accept I'm leaving in July."

"You had to give her that damn ring," Walter said.

"It's just a promise ring. Promises can be broken," Nicola said.

Brendon caught the subtle glance Nicola flashed at Angelene. Maggie and his father came back into the room, with Amelia scurrying behind them.

"Supper is ready."

"Thank you for coming back to help with dinner," Sofia said.

"It was no problem. I had supper with my family, listened to Tim whine about work. It's been nice to have some peace."

"We appreciate it," David said. "Brendon, take Maggie's arm."

Brendon glanced at his feet. It was hard to look into Maggie's eyes. Every time he did, all he saw was Rachel's curves. He stumbled around the coffee table and dutifully wound his arm through hers.

"I'll finish the trifle and go. I'm glad you're here Nicola. Night," Amelia said.

"How come you didn't answer the door?" Maggie said.

"I was talking to Nonna."

"About what?"

"Football, what else?"

The display of food was superb. Glistening roast beef, buttery carrots, parsnips, herbed potatoes, perfectly puffed yorkies, red wine gravy perfumed the air. Brendon plopped onto a chair; Nicola snapped open her napkin, shielded her mouth, and leaned into Brendon's shoulder.

"What do you see, topolino?"

Brendon grinned and whispered. "Dad's eyeing up that platter of beef like Troy does Charlie, and mum's proud everything looks perfect."

"Do you know what I see?" Nicola's voice almost disappeared. "Walter's adam's apple is bobbing up and down. He's agitated. Ms. Pratt is ready to crawl out of her skin and Maggie is more nervous than usual."

"You see all that?"

"Mother, we have guests. You're being rude."

"I'm sharing a moment with topolino. I have gifts in my suitcase for him."

"You could have told your little mouse earlier."

It surprised him Nicola hadn't read him and spoke of the nauseating guilt churning his stomach.

"Salad," Maggie said.

'Look at bloody Maggie, smile, arsehole.'

Nicola was on a roll. She was bound to put two and two together. Brendon brushed his lips across Maggie's cheek and filled his plate with salad.

"Sofia mentioned you worked at the Sorbonne," Nicola said.

The conversation was about to turn and this time, he wouldn't save Angelene, her husband could.

Walter spooned carrots on her plate and shifted uncomfortably. "Don't be shy."

"I helped in the art department."

"I've told you this mother," Sofia said, arranging the utensils around her plate, "I want a pleasant dinner party."

"Everything is lovely, gattina. I'm trying to get to know Ms. Pratt."

Brendon relaxed, stabbed his fork into a roasted potato, and smiled. The game was about to begin.

"Did you teach? Sofia says you paint." Walter sliced through a gravy-soaked slab of beef; his eyes never left his plate. "Wait until you see it — depressing stuff."

"Non, j'ai nettoyé la salle de class."

"Étiez-vous concierge?"

"I was not a janitor," Angelene said, choking out the words, "Bon sang."

Walter tapped his knife on Angelene's plate and cleared his throat. "Ang helped set up the classrooms. She did a bit of modelling."

"Your family?" Nicola said.

The splotches on Angelene's cheeks spread across her cheeks and crept over her neck. Curse words slammed around Brendon's head. *'I bloody hate her. Normal isn't fitting. She's struggling.'*

"Did you see the last AC Milan match? The keeper was bloody brilliant. You think I could replace him?"

Nicola met his gaze and mouthed, *'Nice save.'*

"Your family."

Angelene twisted the napkin in her hand, her voice strained. "I don't know where my mother is. I never knew my father."

"How does one not know who their father is? Last thing I knew, it took two people to make a baby."

"How's the mill doing?" David said.

"I was at AC's last match. I prefer Gianluigi Donnarumma, unfortunately he left for PSG. The mill is doing wonderful. We just signed a contract with a design house in Spain," Nicola said, slapping a spoonful of horseradish on her plate. "Walter, are you annoyed by my questions?"

"We're family. Speak up, little bird."

"My father could be any of mother's lovers."

"Your mother wasn't married?"

"My mother was a whore."

Brendon laughed, Sofia gasped, utensils clattered. Angelene hobbled away. Madre Innocente stuck him hard with her staff.

"She's probably gone for a cigarette. The nasty things calm her," Walter said, wiping his mouth, "excuse me."

"Was it something I said?"

"Did you have to push?" Sofia said.

"You should have stopped Nonna."

"I didn't ask if her mother was a whore. I asked about your family," Nicola said, stabbing her fork towards Maggie.

"She hasn't touched her dinner. Now she's outside bloody smoking."

Maggie's foot drove into his ankle. He grimaced.

"She's probably full after three glasses of wine."

"Oh, mother. My dinner party, ruined."

David tore apart a yorkie and drizzled gravy over it. "It isn't a party if Angelene doesn't run and hide."

Brendon rubbed the back of his neck; he wasn't supposed to care. Angelene was needy, lost and not his to worry about.

"Come on, Mags, I need help with my homework."

"Sit down, Amelia made a trifle," Sofia said.

"I don't want any bloody trifle."

"Maybe Maggie would like some," Nicola said.

"I have hours of homework and I need Maggie's help."

"You best get it done then, son. There will be plenty of pudding left if you want some later."

Brendon tugged at Maggie's chair and grinned awkwardly.

"Why'd you bloody kick me?"

They climbed the stairs. He loosened his tie and snapped it from beneath his collar.

"You were staring at Ms. Pratt again."

"I was not."

"What colour was her dress?"

Brendon pitched his tie onto a pile of Match magazines, leaned into his dresser, and fiddled with the button on his cuff. "I don't know, black."

"You were gawking at her."

"Mum is wearing black; dad's suit is black. Walter's is black with pinstripes. The only bloody people not wearing black are you and Nonna."

"You didn't meet me at the door."

"Our Lord Chancellor escorted you. He's a powerful man, a proper gentleman."

Maggie planted herself on the bed, grabbed a throw pillow, and held it against her chest. "You've been acting dodgy. You don't talk to anyone at school except Troy. The kids are making all sorts of bets."

"In case you forgot, I was a prick to Mr. Clark. I must be a model student or there goes football."

"You've barely spoken to me tonight."

Brendon lifted his gaze and stared at Maggie. He waited for the tingles to happen. Nothing. It could be Madre Innocente. She was doing an excellent job telling him he didn't deserve Margaret. It might be Padre Diavolo. He kept reminding him how great Rachel felt. Something was missing.

"I was talking to Charlie; I think I know what your problem is."

"I don't have a problem."

Maggie reached behind her back and tugged at her zipper.

"What the bloody hell are you doing?"

"Charlie told me I had to... gosh. All I want to do is make you happy."

"Do up your bloody dress. Someone could come up and ask if we want trifle."

Maggie yanked at the sleeves and tugged her dress over her hips. Brendon pushed himself away from the dresser, dashed across the room, and twisted the lock. This could be what he needed to forget about the Rachel fiasco and fall back into like.

He shimmied out of his suit jacket and joined her on the bed, kissing her below the ear. She was hip bones and collar bones, more twelve-year-old then eighteen. He had gone from voluptuous to flat.

"I asked Charlie if it hurt the first time. She said it would only hurt for a minute."

The warmth was subtle, shame and desire entwined. They were supposed to have experienced their first time together. They had talked about it, planned it. Brendon unbuttoned his shirt and dropped it to the floor. He searched her face, her top teeth dug into her lip, her eyes were intensely blue.

Maggie ran her finger over his collarbone, tilting her head. "Is that a love bite?"

Brendon kissed her softly and pressed himself against her. "Will and I got into it at the pitch. Bloody prick bruised me, it's almost healed."

"Your belt is digging into my stomach."

Brendon rolled off the bed, unlatched his belt. His trousers fell to the floor. He lay down beside her, Padre Diavolo filled his head with instructions.

"Take off your bra."

Maggie hooked her fingers in her bra strap. Her breath was shallow and rapid.

"Just relax. It's not that bad."

He crawled on top of her and propped himself on his elbows. Maggie slid her arm over her breasts and swallowed.

"How do you know?"

"Charlie."

"What are you doing talking to Charlie?"

He smothered her words with a kiss, and, unlike Rachel, who was all hands and tongue, Maggie laid still, shielding her breasts. Brendon slipped his fingers inside her panties, her thighs clenched around his hand.

"Can we just get to it?"

"Don't you want me to touch you, you know, foreplay?"

"Foreplay! I just want to get it over with."

Brendon groaned, rolled off her, and opened his nightstand. "Take off your knickers."

"I'm getting under the blankets. I don't want you to see."

"I've seen a vagina before."

Maggie peeked over the blankets, wide eyed. "When?"

"In a nuddy magazine. Will's always passing them around the dressing room."

He tossed a gold foil square on the bed and tugged at his boxers.
"Take them off under here. I don't want to see it."
"Let go of the bloody blankets. Bloody hell, it shouldn't be this much work to hump."

A voice, soft and raspy, whispered to Brendon, *be patient with her, don't force her. It will mean the world to her.*

"Fuck"

"What's the matter?"

He shook Angelene from his mind and tore open the package. "I'm going to put the condom on, okay?"

Maggie nodded and shoved her pinky into her mouth.

"Open your legs."

He squeezed between her trembling thighs and slowly moved his hips towards her. Maggie sucked in her breath and squished her eyes closed.

"It hurts."

"I haven't got the bloody thing in yet."

"Ouch, stop, I don't like it."

"It'll feel good once I start going."

She squeezed herself into the pillows and gathered the blankets. Heat fizzled and seeped from his body. She trembled as if covered in snow.

"I bloody knew it."

He tore a tissue from the box, snapped the condom off, and shoved the limp latex into it. Brendon stared at the ceiling. Sparks fluttered and flew. Angelene said everyone had the devil in them. Another lie. Maggie was an angel, moral and saintly.

"I thought I was ready."

"Cover your eyes. You wouldn't want to see a bloody knob, would you?" He jerked on his boxers, collected her dress, and whipped it. "Put your clothes on."

Maggie struggled with her bra and panties. "It hurt."

"It wouldn't have for long; Charlie told you that."

He thumped to the walk-in, grabbed a pair of jeans and a pullover. This wasn't how it was supposed to be. It should have been fiddly and clumsy. He was supposed to fall back 'in like' with her.

"Don't bloody tell me you're up for it, ever again."

"Can you stop stomping around. You're acting like Jack when he doesn't get a biscuit before dinner."

"Stop bloody crying. You know Nonna asks a million bloody questions."

He yanked on his clothes, marched over to the bed, grabbed the condom wrapper and tissue. He placed the evidence in what was a forgotten history assignment or an unfinished English paper, scrunched it and stuffed it deep into the bin.

"I better go home."

"That's the best idea you've had all night." He grabbed a pencil and tapped it against the dresser. "Stop bloody crying. Dad will want an explanation. What should I tell him? You were ready to hump, then not ready. Do you want everyone to know what we were trying to do?"

He could see everyone's reactions. His mother would be disgusted, his father disappointed. Walter would laugh and Angelene would mourn the loss of his light.

"I won't make a sound. I would hate anyone to think Mr. Wonderful is a wanker."

"No more snogging."

Maggie pushed herself off the bed, tugged at her dress, and stared at him, dumbstruck. "Are you punishing me?"

"It's bloody bollocks, getting a biggie and you saying no all the time. If we don't snog, no biggie."

"Couples snog."

"Couples have sex." The pencil snapped; he whipped the stub across the room. "Charlie does it. Fuck, even Gemma does it and she's as..."

"As what? She's a swot, a goody-goody like me?"

"No snogging. You'll get a kiss on the cheek and that's it."

"Are you going to pick me up for school?"

He shot her an 'are you for real,' glare and scrubbed his face. "I'm sticking around the pitch to work with William. If I get benched again, he'll need to be in top form."

"Get your temper under control. You wouldn't have to worry about William being in net."

"I thought you were leaving."

A sob racked Maggie's body. She fumbled with the lock and tore open the door. His brain shuffled through the night's events, Walter's never-ending tapping on Angelene's plate. The need to hold Angelene's hand but also wanting to watch her suffer, Maggie denying him. He needed to escape. The one person he could talk to was downstairs, trying to play normal. Brendon swiped his phone off the dresser and stared at the screen. The choice was not a good one. It was stupid and vengeful. He wanted something tangible, something he could feel.

"Hey, am I still your number one or have you crossed me off your list? Brilliant, I'll see you in twenty minutes. Ciao."

The sun had overtaken the clouds. Gold and soft blue stretched around the trees and moors. Brendon parked beside the Maserati, grabbed his backpack, and sauntered into the kitchen. It was warm with the scent of vanilla and cinnamon. Oatmeal simmered on the stove, coffee percolated, a bowl of mixed berries sat on the island. He grabbed a bowl and ladled creamy oats into it. Dissolving onto the stool, Brendon spooned berries into the bowl and stared at the purplish-red juice pooling over the hot oats. His mind shifted from his night with Rachel to missing Angelene. Maybe Troy was right. Angelene was a witch that had cast a spell and made him fall in love, or she was just a girl, the wrong girl. The girl he should have stayed away from.

"Are you going to eat topolino or play with it? It's my special Fiocchi d'avena, perfect for my athlete."

"Sometimes it's hard to eat after practice. Where's mammina?"

Nicola poured a cup of coffee, set it on the island, and poised on a stool. "In the bath."

Brendon poked at the berries; she was trying to get a read on him.

"What's the matter, topolino?"

"Training was tough. Working with William is frustrating. I have a whole bloody day of school to look forward to."

"Your Nonno used to get the same look on his face when Gianni would leave to go drinking with his friends, like he should stop him. He blamed himself for Gianni's accident."

"Are you saying I look guilty?"

23 GIRL WITH MANY FACES

Nicola straightened her shoulders and sipped her coffee. "Does it have anything to do with Maggie leaving in tears or you stinking of another girl's perfume last night?"

"Can I eat?"

"Go ahead, I'm not stopping you, just asking a question."

Brendon clenched his spoon and dug into the oatmeal. "How did you know you were in love with Nonno? How did you know you were ready for marriage?"

"That was a different time. You met a boy, fell in love, got married."

"It's all Maggie talks about. She's thinking of transferring to a uni in Germany."

"Why wouldn't she? You're a catch, sei bello," Nicola said, an amused smile played across her lips. "Eat up. I had to push Amelia out of the way to make you breakfast."

"You asked me to talk. Now you're going on about my looks. Why do you think I stopped shaving?"

"To drive your mother crazy," Nicola said. "Maggie is a nice girl but, she isn't the one. You have lots of time to settle down."

"I gave her a ring. I don't know what I was thinking."

"I could ask the same of your Uncle Walter."

"I take it you don't like Ms. Pratt."

Nicola set down her cup and crossed her arms over her chest. "It was hard to read her. She worries me."

Brendon had heard this before. He still had a tough time believing someone so tiny and broken could hurt anyone.

"Do I tell Maggie?"

"Tell her what, topolino?"

He swallowed a bite of oatmeal; it fell like a brick to his stomach. "That I don't want to marry her anytime soon, maybe never."

"Some promises can be broken."

"Maggie will be gutted."

"Things may change on their own. She'll be busy with her studies; you'll be busy with football. The relationship may naturally end. Space and time can make a difference."

"I have a big decision to make."

"If you feel the relationship is over, tell Maggie. Who cares if your father thinks she's perfect? You do what's right for you. The faster you tell Maggie; the easier things will get topolino. Now eat up and don't think I won't check the bin."

"Thanks for listening Nonna."

"I better get ready; I have a lunch date with the woman Walter should have married."

Brendon scraped up the remains of oatmeal and tried to swallow. Tell Maggie or not, he still hadn't decided.

***

Homey marinara and briny olives perfumed the air. The atmosphere was comfortable; the furniture was simple and rustic. Sofia clutched her glass of Chianti. She had slept terribly, plagued by the same nightmare, the sort that lingers upon waking. Every time she closed her eyes, she saw Brendon asleep, a naked woman crouched beside him, caressing him, breathing him in. The dream stayed with her while she tried to relax in the bath. It was clinging to her now.

"Should you have invited Angelene?"

Sofia shook the vision from her mind. "One night is enough. I had a horrible night's sleep; she'd drain me even more."

"Brendon was brooding into his porridge this morning. Something is up with him; I can feel it."

"He's still upset I called Liam."

"I came here to spend time with my family. That was the tensest dinner party I've ever attended."

"You said it was lovely."

"The food, gattina," Nicola said, smearing butter on bread, "I couldn't put my observation skills to use on Angelene. She kept her head down, barely spoke, and when she did, it was nothing but a peep. The only time she found her voice was when she called her mother a whore."

"She's nervous around people."

"We aren't people, we're family. I have a feeling, gattina."

Sofia understood. The feeling flickered and disappeared, erupted, and simmered. She tried to dismiss it, chalk it up to her overprotective ways. It stuck with her, sometimes debilitating and sometimes nothing more than a nauseous flutter.

"You barely know her."

Sofia pondered her comment. Neither did she.

"I know she likes her wine and topolino."

"Mother, please, I'll be in the tub all day if you don't stop."

Nicola adjusted her collar and touched the string of pearls around her neck. "She looks lovely."

"Who?"

"The woman Walter should have married."

"I hope I haven't kept you waiting. My client was crying, and I couldn't stop her. I felt bad pushing her out the door." Kate kissed Nicola's cheeks and sat.

"Years of listening to people's marital problems haven't dulled your looks."

"You can thank Charlotte Tilbury and her magic foundation."

Nicola poured Kate a glass of Chianti, her eyes sparkled. "Do you want to know my secret?"

"If it saves me from getting Botox, then yes."

"Lots of water, plenty of sleep, and great sex."

Sofia's mouth dropped open. "The table next to us heard you."

"Let them hear. Your father and I were making love until the day he passed."

Sofia pressed the napkin to her warmed cheeks. "Did you have to let the entire restaurant know?"

"I know you and your handsome husband still have an active sex life. He can't keep his hands off you."

"You never thought David was handsome. He was pasty and skinny."

"David wears a suit well. He can hold a conversation," Nicola said, passing Kate the bread basket. "I like the way he looks at you, gattina."

"Enough talk about men and sex."

"Let her speak. I like where the conversation is headed," Kate said.

"I thought you were seeing that man from Dublin. He seemed nice," Sofia said.

"He wants nothing serious. I want domestic bliss and all that stuff. I'll be forty-eight in December."

"Visit me in Milan. Leave Sofia here and we'll tour the city. Now that Walter is off the market, we can find you a nice Italian man."

"Walter had a good thing with you," Sofia said, scanning the menu. "He has a terrible roving eye."

"It didn't bother me when he'd spot an attractive woman. We're human, we look."

"There's something to be said about an older woman," Nicola said.

Sofia glanced up from the menu and raised an eyebrow. "Kate is not older than Walter. They're the same age."

"She's older than the others." Nicola winked at the waiter. "I had dinner with a buyer. He was half my age."

"That was business, not a date."

Nicola tucked a strand of hair behind her ear and gave a half shrug. "His name was Lucio; he was very handsome. I invited him back for drinks. He came." She tore her humoured gaze from Sofia and pointed at the menu. "Let's be naughty girls."

"I think you've been naughty enough."

"We'll start with the Frito miso. This is my treat. Order what you like."

Sofia studied the menu: puttanesca, gnocchi and peas, mushroom risotto. Everything looked divine and if her stomach wasn't spinning, she may have enjoyed something rich and indulgent. She couldn't get her mother's comment out of her head. She had seen Angelene's glances too.

"What are you getting, gattina?"

"The minestrone."

"You're not on one of those silly diets where you stop eating bread and pasta, are you? Men like hips, David likes hips."

"I'm feeling a little queasy, that's all."

Nicola smiled at Kate and bit into a wedge of focaccia. "She's still pouting about her dinner party."

"I'm not pouting."

"I take it, it didn't go well?"

"Angelene's mother was a puttana."

Kate choked on a mouthful of bread. "She said that at the dinner table?"

Sofia eyed the massive platter of fried seafood, placing her napkin over her lap. "Walter was so embarrassed."

Nicola picked up the tongs and placed a peppered squid ring on her plate. "I didn't need my observation skills to see how upset Walter was. You know what I see now?" She pierced a sardine with her fork and shook it on her plate. "The wrinkle between your brow, gattina is speaking volumes and you, Kate, your posture is spot-on, your smile pleasant, but you haven't taken your hand off your wrist, you're afraid to say something."

"Now isn't the time. Sofia isn't feeling well."

"You heard from Hugh, didn't you?"

"What are you two up to?" Nicola said, topping up their glasses.

"I had a PI dig up some information about Angelene."

"You talk about me, gattina."

"You saw the glances; the fidgeting."

"Looks like lunch just got a little more interesting," Nicola said.

Sofia peeled the breading off a shrimp and poked it with her fork. "Where's her mother?"

Kate reached into her bag. She pulled out a notebook and thumbed through the pages. "Dead."

Sofia shuddered. "Dead? She'd be in her early forties."

"She took her life," Kate said. "She left Paris when Angelene was thirteen with a man named Paulo Cabello. They lived together in Valencia. She was in Spain for a year before running off to Bologna with a Colonel Rossi."

"Did she stay in Bologna?" Nicola asked.

"Mr. Rossi said she left for Switzerland six months after moving in."

"Did Colonel Rossi have anything else to say about Veronique Hummel?"

"She was a hard woman to love."

"Why Switzerland?" Nicola said.

"Instead of running off with someone, she was running to someone," Kate said, skimming the page with her finger, "Roman Krieger."

Sofia dunked her spoon into the soup. She recalled conversations with Angelene, the name was familiar. "Angelene has spoken of a Roman."

"Roman Krieger is the Chief Finance officer for Credit Suisse. He wouldn't speak to Hugh."

"Did Ms. Hummel stay in Switzerland?"

"She was in Zurich for a few days, then flew back to Marseilles where she lived alone. Her landlord found her in the bathtub, her wrists... there were love letters on the floor from Mr. Krieger, an empty bottle of wine and an ashtray full of cigarette butts."

Sofia ran her fingers over her bangles. *'Angelene's wrists always covered.'*

The terrible longing Sofia had seen blazing in Angelene's eyes was more than a need for family and love. She had been alone in the world.

'It's no wonder she loves to hide and go unnoticed. She knows nothing else.'

"Ms. Hummel never went back to Paris to be with Angelene?"

"According to Colonel Rossi, she never mentioned a daughter. He didn't know who Angelene Hummel was."

Nicola reached across the table and held Sofia's hand. "How does a mother walk away from their child? It devastated me when Sofia left for Taunton."

"According to the people Hugh talked to in Paris, Ms. Hummel considered Angelene punishment from God."

Sofia gripped Nicola's fingers; sadness dripped over her. "A child is a gift, not a punishment."

Kate took a sip of water. "Elle est un diable dans beau déguisement, that's what people called Veronique Hummel."

"A devil in a beautiful disguise. Sounds like someone we know," Nicola said.

Kate pulled at her earring. "I feel like I'm invading Angelene's privacy. Do you want to hear more?"

"What about Angelene's grandparents?"

"Frieda Hummel passed from a heart attack and Bernard is in a home." "Did Hugh reach out to Mr. Hummel?"

Kate slumped into the chair and rubbed the bridge of her nose. "Bernard Hummel has the onset of dementia. The nurse at the home said he has spoken of a daughter. He said she was always running away."

"All her stories are true," Sofia said, dabbing her eyes. "Perhaps Angelene ran from Paris to get away from all the sad memories."

23 GIRL WITH MANY FACES

"She's still running," Nicola said, slicing her fork through a square of eggplant parmesan. "I see it in her eyes. She runs in all kinds of ways. She was running away throughout dinner."

"I don't blame her," Kate said, turning the page. "Emile Douchette, her landlord, took care of her. She helped clean the building, cooked for him, washed his clothes, other things."

Sofia fiddled with her engagement ring. The information swam around her mind. No mother, no father, no family history, nothing but a landlord to raise her. Run, hide, run all the way to Taunton and hide in a pretty farmhouse.

"Douchette wouldn't speak to Hugh, just told him to fuck off," Kate said, rubbing her arms. "Mr. Krieger paid the rent until Angelene was eighteen."

Sofia smoothed her blouse. "I've heard enough."

"I haven't," Nicola said, pointing her fork at Sofia's bowl, "Eat up, gattina. How did Angelene end up at the Sorbonne?"

Kate flipped the page and ran her finger over her notes. "She would visit la Cour d'Honneur and sit on the steps beside the Victor Hugo statue, reading or sketching."

"The professor, Walter, spoke about a professor who mentored her."

"Now you're interested, gattina."

"Pierre Piedmont. He taught art history, did some curating for the Louvre, painted," Kate said, scanning the page, "He did a series of paintings titled, fille avec de nombreux visages, comme j'aimais le diables."

"Girl with many faces, how I loved the devil. Do you think his paintings were about Angelene?" Nicola said.

"People assumed. He never said."

"Was he married? Victoria made that terrible comment. Angelene's cheeks were as red as my lipstick."

"Estelle Martin, a jeweller's daughter. She studied at the Sorbonne under Piedmont. He had a thing for younger women."

"Sounds like someone we know," Nicola said dryly.

"The university was tight-lipped about Piedmont. What they told Hugh was Piedmont was extremely interested in Angelene's artwork. He took her under his wing, got her a job."

"They were just friends, then?"

Kate grinned. "Hugh is exceptionally good at reading between the lines. They eventually became lovers. The Dean said Piedmont's whole demeanour changed like an addict needing a fix. He was obsessed."

'*Walter kept going back to Paris. He never chased a woman, they chased him.*'

Sofia licked her lips and rattled her bracelets. "Did Ms. Piedmont find out? Is that why the affair ended?"

"No one knows for sure. Piedmont's son got sick. They assumed that took him away from Angelene."

Sofia stared at the charm bracelet dangling around her wrist, pinching the B charm between her fingers. '*I smother you; I grip too tight. No one understands how much I love you. You put all the pieces back together.*' She understood how Piedmont could pull away. She had been guilty of ignoring David when Brendon got the sniffles.

"Did Hugh talk to the boy?"

"He didn't bother, didn't even get a name," Kate said. She closed her notebook and wrapped her hand around her wrist. "The boy is... he's in Spain studying. He left at eighteen."

"You're holding your wrist again," Nicola said, patting her mouth with the napkin. "Is there more to the story?"

"Piedmont is on a sabbatical. One student told Hugh he had gone mad for his muse. Another said he lost his most cherished possession. He couldn't cope," Kate said, releasing her hand. "Ms. Piedmont lives in Evian-les-Bain with her mother."

Sofia pinched her brow and sighed. "Angelene must have done damage for such a prominent man to take a leave."

"His muse could have been anyone. The Dean made it seem like they were tired of his philandering ways. Don't assume Sofia."

"My gut is telling me this marriage is going to blow up around Walter. You two will be picking up the pieces," Nicola said.

"They might live happily ever after," Kate said.

"My gift of observation has its drawbacks. I look for disguises, motives, and deceit," Nicola said, placing her credit card on the receipt. "What are you hiding, Kate?"

"It makes you suspicious, too."

"Thank you," Sofia said, handing Kate a cheque. "I know you didn't want to do that."

"Can we agree to leave Angelene alone?"

Sofia tightened the bow on her blouse and lifted her chin, masking her worry with forced confidence. "I promise, mother?"

Nicola reached across the table and grasped Kate and Sofia's hands. "I promise to behave."

Sofia grinned. The nightmare clung, words like muse, addiction, illness, spun around her mind. '*How I loved the devil... The devil didn't arrive on my doorstep with horns and a pitchfork. She came disguised as everything Walter ever wanted.*'

***

Angelene reread the paragraph, gritting her teeth. Tap, tap, tap, assaulted her ears. She shifted among the pillows and pressed her ear against the wall.

"Must you tap the keyboard so hard?"

"Take your book outside. Go look for your rabbit."

Angelene tucked a postcard of the Parc des Princes into her book and rubbed under her nose. "Would you like Moules frites for dinner?"

"Whatever you like."

"How long are you going to be angry with me?" Angelene said. She picked up her cigarettes, stared at Walter's tense shoulders, and tossed them back on the cushion. "Can you stop typing and look at me?"

Walter sighed gruffly and turned on the stool. "I'm looking at you."

"I'll put wine in the mussels and not my glass."

"You called your mother a whore, charged out of the dining room, stared at that damn painting all night. You could have socialized with real people, not spend the night daydreaming."

"Before we left, I practiced walking in those shoes you love. I practiced what I would say so I wouldn't sound stupid or embarrass you. As soon as I walked into the manor, I forgot everything."

Walter clicked save and switched off his laptop. "You cut yourself again. I told you not to do that."

"No one noticed. I made sure my outfit hid it." She tapped her finger against the cigarette pack. His eyes, soft blue words, cool turquoise. "The light was dim and scratched. The pact broken, my pattern fit back together so easily, it frightened me."

"What are you talking about? Light? Pacts and patterns?"

"It was overwhelming. I needed a release. I don't know what to do when my emotions tangle."

"How long have you done that?" Walter said, a frown formed around the words, "cutting yourself."

"Since I was a little girl." She hugged her knees to her chest and stretched her shirt over them. "Roman was coming for a visit. Mother and I scrubbed the floor. She always said God appreciated a clean house. I was pouring milk, and the bottle slipped. There was glass everywhere."

The memory flooded behind her eyes. *Stupid, stupid girl, you ruined everything, you're still ruining everything.* Angelene dug her fingernails into her calves. The sting stole the memory.

"It was an accident; you were a child."

"Mother screamed at me. I felt stupid, scared, angry, sad. I cleaned up the mess and ran to the street where I found a rock and scraped it over my knees, until I bled, the emotions untied, I felt a strange release, like I had been holding my breath for years, it's a habit."

Walter rose and set the kettle on the stove. "Take down your wall. Let me in."

Angelene stared out the window. The wind pushed the clouds across the sky. How could she tear down her walls when they had protected her for so long? Her walls were dangerous to scale, dark on the other side.

"You've never had to protect yourself, have you?"

Walter poured tea and shook his head. "I usually protected others. My mother after Geoffrey left. David from Richard."

"I've been constructing my wall since elementary school."

"You shouldn't keep people out," Walter said, handing her a cup. "People would like to get to know you, including me."

"I saw how Nicola looked at me. I'm not good enough for you."

Walter squeezed beside her and kissed her cheek. "Nicola thinks she works for the L'agenzia Informazioni e Sicurezza Interna, Italy's Intelligence and Security Agency."

Angelene buried herself under his arm. She had lived behind her wall for years. It would be an arduous task, taking down each brick. She had started its deconstruction, allowing Brendon in. He was dangerous, people were dangerous. Walter Pratt and his powerful black light were dangerous.

24 Trouble

Brendon tapped his fingers against the steering wheel. The secret sat like a malignant monster on his chest, mucking around his heart and lungs. He had considered telling Maggie, spill the secret, drown in the consequences. His family's motto, some secrets are best left hidden, was the better choice. Brendon grabbed his backpack and hitched it over his shoulder. He heard a deafening thump, swoosh, thump, swoosh, then silence.

"Wait up, mate." Troy dashed across the lawn, sunshine, and smiles. "Was Dawson lecturing you again? Some guys in biology said he had you cornered in the modern languages building yesterday."

Dull, grey light flowed between the Victorian buildings; the smell of rain clung to the cool breeze.

"The prick keeps sneaking up behind me. He went on and on about how much money my parents are wasting on my education. I said, I couldn't agree more."

Brendon glanced towards the ivy-covered building. Girls, mostly from Maggie's theatre class, had formed a circle around her.

"Can I ask you something, mate?"

More girls joined the circle. There was no annoying Shakespearean infused banter and theatrical one-liners. The conversation within the group looked like it had nothing to do with Hamlet.

"If it's about football, yes."

"Don't get mad at Charlie. She told me about you and Maggie. I'm hurt you mentioned nothing at practice this morning."

"There's nothing to tell."

"Wasn't it warm and cushiony like a snug glove hugging your knob?"

"I got the tip in. She begged me to stop."

"All you got was a taste, mate." Troy stopped and grabbed Brendon's arm. "What's going on? It doesn't look like they're reciting Shakespeare."

His stupid decision attacked his senses. The tiny freckle on Rachel's breast. The faded scar above her knee, her fingers clutching his back, the smell of coconut on her skin, the taste of a tropical drink on her neck.

"How could you?"

Students loitered around the Portugal laurel, playing a game of 'guess what they're fighting about'. Topics swung from the dull Margaret Thornton was a jealous cow, to the extraordinary, Brendon Cook slept with Ms. Morrison.

"I called you last night."

Maggie yanked down the sleeve of her cardigan and wiped her eyes, consoling hands held onto her shoulders. "I know why you've been acting dodgy lately."

"What did you do, mate?"

"Can we talk about this later? If I'm late for class, I'll get another strike. Dawson will call mum and no match."

"All you care about is football."

A voice flew out from the crowd. "It was Michael Collins."

Brendon scanned the mob, sparks blazed like heat sinking missiles. Michael Collins, Maggie's Hamlet, and Danny from last year's production of Grease, was rooted to his spot, his cheeks splotched, pink.

"What did you say to Maggie?"

Mr. Dawson marched across the lawn, swinging his elastic arms. "Move along, boys and girls."

A few girls from Maggie's protective circle paid attention to Dawson's warning and hurried away. Others lingered in support.

"What the fuck did you say?"

"That wasn't a swear word, was it, Mr. Cook?" Dawson said, flinging open the administration office door, "this is your four-minute warning. Hurry or I'll cram the lot of you into the room you think smells of vomit."

"I want to know what you bloody said."

"Ask him at dinner break, mate."

"I'm not going anywhere until he fucking tells me what he said to Maggie."

Maggie hiccupped and sniffled. Sparks burst into flames. Brendon's insides felt like a war zone.

A window scraped on its hinges; Dawson's pompous voice shouted from the office. "Two minutes. I suggest you get a move on. Especially you, Mr. Cook."

Students flew by, bets lacing their laughter. One pound, Rachel was the culprit. Another two, Maggie would have a nervous breakdown. Five quid Brendon would start a fight, two p, he'd take the win.

"You heard Dawson. You've got two minutes to tell me what you said."

Michael stared at his polished shoes. "I have to get to geoggers."

"You aren't leaving until you tell me." Brendon shook the tingles from his fingers. "I bloody swear if I'm late for English and get fucking pulled, you'll be reciting your lines from Musgrove Hospital."

"Stop being a wanker and leave Michael alone," Maggie said.

"Maggie's right mate."

"Talk."

Michael swallowed and shifted his backpack. "I was in Boots. I overheard Matilda tell William Rachel was hiding an enormous secret."

Brendon took a step towards Michael. Troy grabbed his arm. He jerked it free. "What else did she say?"

"Rachel bunked off school the same day you told Mr. Clark off. She said, Rachel smelled lemony fresh and had this daft grin on her face."

"We snogged. There I said it. It was the night of my party."

The words bubbled nervously from Michael's mouth. "Matilda said, Rachel crossed her number one off. Everyone knows what that means."

"Why did you tell Maggie?"

"Would you have? Maggie's brilliant."

Brendon's back pack went flying into the concrete steps, the remaining onlookers scattered.

"I should have punched Michael."

"What good would that do?" Troy said, grabbing the abused backpack. "You'd get suspended, benched for the entire season. I can't have Will between the sticks. I'd be too exhausted for my next football trial."

Maggie sniffed and rubbed her eyes. "I thought... Rachel... how could you?"

Brendon inhaled. The energy circling through his body was different, almost guilty, almost ashamed. If he had followed the code, he would have come clean, hugged all the sadness out of her and ended the drama.

"You lost your virginity to Rachel Jones?" Troy said, handing Maggie a crumpled tissue. "Did you forget about the Gentlemen's Code?"

"I wasn't thinking about the daft code."

Troy gave Maggie an awkward side hug. "I'll tell Ms. Hudson you're in the toilets. Apologize, mate, give your girl a hug."

"The entire school will know by now," Maggie said.

"Mr. Cook, I'm picking up the phone to ring your mother."

"I've got to go Mags. I can't miss another match."

"Mr. Cook, the phone is in my hand."

"I feel like I'm going to barf. Will you meet me at the park by my house?"

"I'll be there, half past four."

Brendon lumbered up the stairs and jerked the door open. Whispers and glares assaulted him. Gemma Fowler poked her head around the classroom door, staring him down, "He's coming, dirty wanker."

Brendon dropped his gaze, saluting a group of snickering boys with his middle finger. He brushed past Gemma. Rumours and insults circulated the classroom, *'it started with German lessons, footy player with a God complex, it happened under the willow tree, spoiled toff.'*

Brendon dropped onto the chair, propped his elbow, shielding his inflamed cheeks.

"Rachel Jones, mate?"

"It was once. I regret it." The lie slid off his tongue. Madre Innocente was relentless, stabbing his gut. "She's crossed me off her list, moved on to number two."

"I see the way Rachel looks at you. The slag fancies you."

Rachel was always telling him she loved him. She wrote it in his notebook and whispered 'ich Liebe dich' when they passed each other in the hall. There was no way she meant it; Rachel didn't fall in love, neither did Angelene.

"You're in a colossal mess, mate."

"It is true," Tilly said. She blew a bubble, sucking it back into her mouth. "Cheeky cow, keeping secrets."

"Turn the fuck around."

"Poor Mr. Football," Tilly said, twirling a pink strand of gum around her finger. "Was it Rachel's tits or arse? Both are lovely."

"Fuck off."

Ms. Hudson waddled into the classroom and dropped a stack of papers on the desk. "Novels open. Goethe awaits."

Brendon slid down in the chair and tapped his foot against Troy's. "How do I apologize? This wasn't just a snog."

Troy lowered his gaze. "You kept a secret. Come clean."

"Are you keeping something from Charlie? Your cheeks are as pink as Tilly's lipstick."

"Never," Troy said. "Invite Maggie round to yours. Ask Amelia to bake those biscuits Maggie loves, better yet, you bake them then give her your best, from the heart, apology."

"I better start practicing what I'm going to say."

"I hope you two are discussing Werther," Ms. Hudson said.

Brendon snapped open the novel. Humping Rachel, kissing Angelene, falling in and out of love, the list of confessions grew. He leaned across the aisle, jabbing Troy with his pen.

"Do you hate me now?"

"You're my mate. It happened; you're going to make it right. You're going to follow all the daft rules in the code and be the best boyfriend Maggie's ever had."

"She's only had one, me."

Troy hid his mouth behind the novel. "That's why you need to be sorrier than you have ever been."

'What have I done?' Brendon fanned his face with the novel. *'I'm in like with you, but I'm not sure. You belong to someone else, but I love you. I fancy you, but I'm a number on your list.'* Brendon stared at himself in the window, oblivious to the glares and whispers. He knew what he had to do.

Brendon walked along the path lined with weeds and overgrown cedars. A swift petrol scented breeze shook the groves of scraggy shrubs. Maggie swung back and forth, the rusty chains creaked, her shoes dragged in the dirt. He inhaled deeply and choked on the speech he had rehearsed. Maggie looked up from her trainers, makeup-less, blotchy, a sting, jabbed his heart.

"Jack wanted to come and practice his Choku-Zuki on you."

"Is that a punch?"

"A straight punch. Jack's brilliant at them."

Brendon dropped onto a warped wooden bench. He peeled away a layer of paint and wrapped it around his finger. Maggie squished beside him; vanilla perfume wafted in his nose.

"Why?"

He released the faded strip into the wind. It fluttered and swirled, landing in an overgrown hawthorn bush. Brendon tore at another strip of paint, watching it waver in the wind.

"It happened. Isn't that enough for you to know?"

"I deserve an explanation."

"It was the day Mr. Clark kicked me out of the class. Rachel was in the car park. We started talking and ended up at her house."

He held up the ribbon of paint. It fluttered like a tattered kite.

"That's all it took, the tart listening."

"You know how bloody flirty she is. She rubbed my shoulders and the next thing I knew; she was in her knickers."

"I bet they were lacy and barely covered her fat arse."

"I'm a prick. I got caught up in the moment."

"More like her enormous jubblies," Maggie said, pulling her hood over her windblown locks. "I guess I'm partly to blame."

Brendon released the paint chip and stared at Maggie. "How is it your fault?"

"It was supposed to be your going away present, a birthday present. I've said no so many times. We can work on things. I love you."

"Love me. I humped Rachel and when I said we snogged at my party, we did."

"I can forgive you. Look at Gemma and William. He left the party with the gum chewing tart and they're working on things."

A flood of memories surged through Brendon's head. The kiss in Burnham, holding Angelene's hand, wanting to discover Dortmund with her. It hadn't been one time with Rachel; it had been two, the second more enjoyable than the first. He had been cheating on Maggie for weeks.

"I can't do this anymore."

"Do... do," Maggie sniffed and sputtered out the words, "do what?"

"This, us."

Brendon stared at the crushed velvet sky. He missed Angelene. He missed the way she tucked her toes under his thighs and smiled in that way that said she understood. He missed how he once mattered to her. He was missing the wrong person. It should be the girl beside him.

"Do you fancy Rachel now?"

"I don't fancy Rachel. I need some space."

"Can't we talk about it?"

"We are talking about it. You're not listening."

"But we love each other. You told me the other day."

"I said it to shut you up. Are you bloody happy now? I've only been in like with you."

Maggie whimpered and rubbed her nose across her sleeve.

"I can't deal with a relationship right now. My bloody head is all mixed up," Brendon said, pushing himself off the bench. "I've got to go before I say something bad."

"That wasn't bad enough? All this time, I thought you loved me."

"Bis später Mags."

Maggie's cries carried along the wind; he pressed his hands over his ears. The truth had come out, the secret spilled, he felt empty.

Brendon shoved his keys in his pocket and hurried to the door. "Open up Angelene." He tapped his shoe into the wood and rattled the doorknob. "Open the fucking door."

"Who is it?"

"You know who it bloody is. Open the door."

"I told you we couldn't do this anymore."

Her accent was thick and raspy, barely audible.

"I need to talk to you."

"Ring Troy. Go home to your mother."

"How can you take your friendship away?" He leaned his forehead against the door. Sparks fizzled.

"I had to. I suffocate people, I smother."

"Tu me manques, Angelene."

"It's for the best. It wasn't right to ask you to help me break my stupid patterns. Walter will help."

"You never asked if I was okay with it."

The wind howled, a powerful agonizing moan, shaking the trees and blowing purple petals around him.

"You promised." He slammed his toe into the door, pain shot from his foot to his knee. "Fuck you. How many times did you come crying to me? How many times did you beg me for help?"

He slapped his palms against the door. Sadness pushed anger aside and all the places she had brought light and love, hollowed, and ached.

Brendon shuffled to the great room. Warmth from the crackling fire did nothing to chase away the cold that had settled into his bones.

"How was you day sweetheart?"

Brendon slumped into the armchair. He had left Maggie devastated, and all he could think of was Angelene.

"You look like you lost your best friend," Nicola said.

"Did you get in trouble at school again? I'm not going to get a call from Mr. Dawson, am I?"

"I finished my schoolwork, even the extra assignments."

"Why the long face topolino?"

Brendon knew it was best to come clean. Nonna had her examiner's eyes on him.

"I broke up with Maggie."

"Why? You spent five hundred pounds on that ring."

"We argue all the bloody time, that's why."

Sofia set down her wineglass, her brow furrowed. "I don't end things with your father when we argue."

"You're bloody married."

He undid his tie and balled it in his hands. Angelene had dismissed him. She didn't open the door or respond to his pleas. The ache in his heart made little sense. He should mourn the loss of Maggie, not the girl he never had.

"Are you worried my grades will slip?"

"Don't be ridiculous. Five hundred pounds, out the window. You don't think, do you?"

"I don't care about the bloody money. I'm tired of fighting with her," Brendon said, gazing at the portrait Angelene had drawn. "She's always in my head. I hear her voice, see her face. I can't fucking concentrate. She says she suffocates people. I haven't been able to breathe for weeks."

Nicola's stare was intense. "That's dramatic, even for Maggie."

"Maggie... she, uh, has shown some different sides. I don't like them."

Sofia ran her fingers along her bracelets. "Are you sure we're talking about Maggie?"

Brendon shoved his trembling fingers between his thighs. He couldn't act if his brain didn't settle. He had all the telltale signs, fidgeting fingers, beads of sweat tickling his neck, eyes shifting, Nonna would figure it out.

"Maggie's been insecure since I got back from Dortmund. I can't deal with it."

Nicola followed his gaze to the drawing on the mantle, steepling her fingers against her lips. "What's your opinion of Ms. Pratt?"

"Why would you ask him that?"

"It's just a question."

"I don't know."

Brendon cursed under his breath. Stupid, Nonna would never accept that.

"She admires you," Nicola said.
"What are you bloody talking about, admires me? She's in love with Walter."
"I don't think this is appropriate, mother."
"I want to know if Brendon sees what I do."
"You made it perfectly clear what you think of Angelene at lunch. Kate should be Walter's wife."
Nicola dismissed Sofia and stared at Brendon. "I see a girl who never fit. I see a girl who enters you like the air we breathe, filling you, lingering like that dreadful perfume she wears. Your turn topolino."
Brendon met Nicola's gaze and begged Padre Diavolo to stand by his side, help him with the performance.
"All she's known is a watered-down version of happiness. This is her chance to be happy. She's trying to fit into Walter's world and all the expectations he throws at her." Brendon ripped open the collar of his shirt, sparks flickered. "I'm hungry. Is dinner ready?"
"See what you've done," Sofia said. "Do you want to eat in here, sweetheart?"
"You're breaking the rules, mammina?"
"Just for tonight. I'll be back."
Nicola waited until Sofia had disappeared before she spoke. "Your mother is worried."
"I know."
"I see a few sides to Angelene, a girl with many faces."
"She annoys me. She could knit a bloody sweater the way her fingers are always twitching."
"I'm reading your face, topolino. I don't like what I see."

***

The doorbell gonged; Maggie's heart knocked against her ribcage. *'Brendon, please be Brendon.'*
"Can you get the door, please? I have laundry to put away," Rosie said.
"Jack can."
Rosie grumbled and stepped over a mound of textbooks and notes. "Why are you doing this to yourself?"
Jack's burbly laughter rose from the foyer. "Come see the Batcave I built, Charlie."
Maggie's heart sank.
"Margaret Grace."
"What."
Rosie set the laundry basket down, tucking a strand of hair into her ponytail. "Why are you staring at his picture?"
"I love him."
"After what he's done? I told you two years ago not to get involved with him, his face plastered all over Taunton. He's a dog with two dicks."
Maggie whimpered and shoved her thumbnail in her mouth. "I'm the reason he did what he did."
Rosie shoved the pictures aside, dropped on the bed, wiggling the tension in her jaw.

"Are you bleeding mad? You respect yourself, which is more than I can say for Miranda Jones's daughter. That girl needs a bollocking and something done with her hair. It's as wild as she is."

Maggie pressed her sleeve against her eyes and sniffed. "I bet you and dad will celebrate once I've fallen asleep. I should have just closed my eyes and let him do it."

"Be like me, desperate for attention? You're better than that," Rosie said. "I'm glad you broke up."

Maggie moaned and blew her nose in a tattered tissue. "I knew it. Gosh mum, I'm gutted."

"The relationship wouldn't have lasted, a footy player with a stadium of adoring fans. A VIP at every club."

Maggie snuffled. "You don't know that. Brendon's parents raised him to be a gentleman."

Rosie picked up a photo of Brendon, smirked, and flicked it back on the bed. "He's some gentleman. Football players marry models, actors, not girls from Taunton."

"Some footy players marry girls like me."

"I've watched Footballer's Wives."

"That show isn't real."

"You're all splotchy and have a big spot on your chin." Charlotte sauntered into the room and tossed a box of tissues on the bed. "Wipe your nose, Magpie."

"Help me out Charlotte."

"How are you, muffin?"

Maggie blew her nose and whipped the overused tissue onto a pile the size of Mount Fuji. She ripped another from the box and wiped her bloodshot eyes. "I can't believe Brendon cheated."

"See if you can't get her out of this mood," Rosie said, slamming the laundry basket against her hip. "You'd think she was dating Tom Hardy."

Maggie scaled the tower of textbooks, slammed the door, and flopped on the bed. "Troy has been taking the mick out of Brendon for years, always teasing him about being a virgin."

"Don't blame him," Charlotte said, flicking a Swarovski heart charm, "babes is not happy with Brendon."

"Is the tart Brendon's girlfriend now?"

"He's humping her. Rachel Jones does not have boyfriends."

Maggie groaned and fell back onto her bed. "Don't even say her name, stupid slapper."

"You've got to stop crying," Charlotte said, tossing her hair over her shoulder. "Let's plot your revenge instead."

"What if Troy cheated? What if he broke up with you?"

"I'd be gutted and not just gutted, but proper gutted. Babes wouldn't."

"Don't be too sure. You said Brendon was a nice bloke."

"I told you not to worry about Ms. Pratt. I still can't believe she called babes her sunshine."

Maggie blotted her nose and folded her arms over her chest. "We're talking about me right now, not that cow."

"I learned about dissociative identity disorder; I swear there are several people inside Ms. Pratt. We met Elea. The name means strange." Charlotte picked up a tube of glittery pink lip gloss, smeared it on her lips, and inspected herself in the mirror. "Ms. Pratt got starry eyed when she said babes was her sunshine, like a giggly preteen."

"Are you finished?"

Maggie had felt a distance between her and Brendon for weeks. She had a list of reasons in her journal. He was randy; football was more important. He was concentrating on not losing strikes. The list grew over two pages and at the bottom was Ms. Pratt.

"Look Magpie, Brendon is a nice bloke. He's just randy."

"Are you on his side?"

Suki meowed and strolled into the room. Charlotte picked up the cat and plopped onto the bed. "Doing something daft doesn't make you bad. Brendon is genuinely a nice boy. It must have been Rachel's massive jubblies. Babes says more than a handful is too much and mine are simply perfect. He can hold an entire boob in his hand. It's just brilliant."

Maggie dangled her sweater cord at Suki. The cat pounced onto her lap, pawing at the pink string.

"I'm gutted and all you keep talking about is Troy. I'll never get Brendon back."

"You never know. I bet the tart has moved on to number two." Charlotte shook her wrist; a heart charm caught the light and glittered. "I gave Babes a proper ear bashing. He knew about Brendon snogging the tart."

Maggie stroked Suki's fur. "Charlotte Elodie. You were pretending to be mad, so Troy would buy you that charm you wanted."

"Cheeky cow. I never told babes to buy me the charm. He did it because, well, I'm not sure why, guilt by association, I guess."

Maggie fished a tissue from within the blankets and rubbed it under her nose. "I want Brendon back. Can't you make Troy talk to him?"

"Give him some time. Brendon will figure out my bestest bestie is the bee's knees and come running back."

"What if I drink some fizzy wine and just do it."

"You drank all those alcopops at Brendon's party and look how that turned out. You don't want to barf all over him, not very romantic. Just be your brilliant self."

Maggie sniffed and ran her fingers through Suki's fur. "I don't feel brilliant."

"Put some makeup on. Do your hair, dress up your school kit. Go on a date with Michael."

Maggie picked up a picture of Brendon and bit back tears. "I wish you never introduced us, and he had stayed that boy I stared at. I wouldn't have to dress up to impress him or cry over him. He couldn't break any promises, no rejected hugs and I wouldn't be sitting here feeling like a big, boring, nothing."

"You're not boring. You're my sweet little muffin and if Brendon can't see that, then make him see it. Show the wanker you don't care."

"I'll never have the courage to act like I don't care. He looked so dishy and smelled like absolute heaven."

Charlotte collected the frames, leaned across the bed, and laid them on the vanity. "You're the best actor at Taunton College."

"Matilda and Isla Vandenberg were chatting in theatre studies; the tart is in love. Tilly said her mate is breaking all their tart rules."

Charlotte handed Maggie a tissue. "Remember when that French exchange student was chatting up babes? I dressed up cute; half the football team was going on about me being a toddy. It drove babes bonkers."

"Brendon's not the jealous type. I spent all that time with Michael rehearsing Grease. He never said a thing."

"If you show up at school looking posh and sophisticated, Michael and his drama cronies will follow you all over the place. Brendon will wish he never shagged the tart."

Maggie shoved her pinky in her mouth, glancing at the cover of a fashion magazine. She didn't find herself unattractive; she was perpetually pink-cheeked, her eyes were expressive even when she wasn't on stage. She didn't find herself attractive either. Boys never really looked at her and when they did, it was as if they were staring at their sister. The only boy who looked at her like she was pretty had cheated on her.

"It's a daft plan. I'm not a fashionista like you."

"Babes is a prat when I'm all dressed up. He can't even string a sentence together," Charlotte said, jumping from the bed. "Let's look in your closet. No wearing your mac, either."

"What if it's raining?"

"Get wet. Your blouse will stick to your baps, it'll make all the boys go crazy."

"I don't have any baps to drive anyone crazy."

Charlotte kicked the textbooks out of the way and flung open the door. "Get your makeup bag out."

"You can't be friends with Brendon and me," Maggie said, tossing a bulging bag onto the vanity. "He's the enemy unless he falls back in like with me."

Charlotte held up Maggie's school blazer and threw it on the pouf. "I'm going to be Switzerland. It's a pretty country. I might go there for my honeymoon."

"I'm trying to feel better and you're talking about a honeymoon in Switzerland."

"I don't like what Brendon did, but he's babe's bestie. If I stay neutral, no one will get angry or hurt."

Maggie leafed through the magazine. The nude look wouldn't transform her into a beauty, she'd look no different. She flipped the page, smudged liner, glittered lids. "Can you make me look like this?"

"Easy peasy. I'll need black eyeliner and an eyeshadow brush to smudge."

Maggie placed the magazine on the vanity and stared at Brendon's picture. "This is daft. The last time I wore black eyeliner was when I played Sandy and had to wear those uncomfortable tart trousers."

"You'll look brilliant."

"Do you think Brendon knows how much he hurt me?"

Charlotte held up a navy cardigan and tossed it on a growing pile of navy, grey and pink. "I'm sure he does. Boys don't admit stuff like that."

"It hurts, Charlie."

"I know, muffin. That's why we're doing this. To give you confidence," Charlotte said, scrunching her nose at a pink pullover, "you really have some boring clothes."

Maggie stuck out her tongue and ran her finger over Brendon's photo. "I never liked the stubble. It made him look older and scruffy. I'll miss it scratching my cheek."

"One look at you and he'll be scratching more than your cheek."

Maggie plucked Suki from her lap and placed her among the stuffed animals. She scooted off the bed and slumped onto the pouf.

"Are you going to teach me how to roll the waistband of my kilt?"

"There's a science to it. It must be short enough for the boys to notice but long enough, so Dawson doesn't make you sit in the room that smells like barf. I had to sit in there once and when the secretary went for lunch, babes came to say hello. We were going to hump on the desk, like an FU to Dawson, poor little crumpet couldn't get a biggie, the smell was so bad," Charlotte said, dropping an armful of clothes on the bed. "Did you just roll your eyes at me?"

Maggie propped her elbows on her thighs and rested her chin on her hands. "You can't go a second without talking about Troy."

"I love him, even when he does daft things."

"I'm going to be the third wheel if this doesn't work."

Charlotte popped open an eyeshadow pallet and lifted Maggie's chin. "Brendon won't be able to refuse you. He'll take one look and be a big, dishy puddle at your feet."

Maggie forced a smile; she'd be a six out of ten at best. She closed her eyes as Charlotte swiped shimmery eyeshadow across her lid. '*I should have worried about the tart, not Ms. Pratt. It was stupid of me to believe Brendon fancied a married woman.*'

"Sit still. I'm doing the liner."

'*Angelene came to Taunton a four, creeped up to a six like me and now, she's transformed into a nine. She's finding her wings.*'

"She's stealing feathers."

"Is that a line from one of those weird plays you like?"

"It's a play about a girl who lost her wings. She steals feathers so she can fly again."

"Sounds daft, Magpie."

"She plucks their feathers while they sleep. They can't fly once she's been round."

Maggie bit into her lip. '*They can't fly.*'

***

Angelene twirled a feather in her fingers. The doorknocker had been tapping all night. She checked before going to bed. No one was at the door. Squeak and tap followed her while she brushed her teeth and continued to rattle into the night. Three quick taps and then silence, tap, tap, tap. She had called Walter, explained to him that someone was knocking on the door. She kept him on the line while she looked. There was nothing but a frenzy of wisteria petals dancing in the wind. Walter said the walls made noises on windy nights; she was to walk up to the manor if she didn't feel safe.

Angelene placed the feather on the nightstand and crawled under the blankets. Tap, tap, tap. She clamped her eyes shut. Tap, tap, tap.

My muse, I've been knocking. I've started a series of paintings called the girl with many faces.
Do I know this girl?
You know her very well: angst, terror, distrust, wistful, wonder, melancholy.
Do you love this girl?
I'm enraptured by her.
Love drives you mad.

That is my fear, little bird.

Angelene rolled over and stared at the amber glow. The room fell silent. She exhaled through trembling lips. Tap, tap, tap. Angelene gripped the blankets, her gaze darted from the doorway to Brendon's window.

"If I run to you, would you help me? Would you chase this terrible knocking away?"

'I can't be his friend. I'll smother him.'

Tap, tap, tap. Angelene drew back the blankets, grabbed a wrap from the footboard and wound it around her shivering shoulders. She tiptoed down the hall, bracing herself against the banister. The windows rattled; a faint smell of lavender clung to the draught. She sunk to the top step. A rhythmic cadence filled the foyer. The tapping was as poetic and dreamy as Saint-Saens's 'The Swan.' Angelene leaned her head against the baluster, lulled by the melancholic knocking.

Let me in Angelene. You've been avoiding me.
I told you to stay away.
We're supposed to be friends. Please open the door.
Do you promise to sit in Roman's chair? No talk of castles and lavender fields.
Let me in, little bird.

"I'm carrying your memory and it's very heavy. My boy with liquid blue eyes." Silence swept over the house. "I can't be your friend. I can't let it happen again."

Did you have a nightmare, little bird?
I had a memory Roman, they're scarier than my nightmares.

25 Deviation

'He's the dick of all dickiest dicks.'
The whisper rolled off Brendon's back as the next one hit.
'The king slag and his queen.'
'He's a dick faced prick wanker.'
"I like that one."
Brendon swiped his notebook into his backpack and smirked. The sparks were constant now. He woke with them, went to practice with them, enjoyed meals with them. Breathing supplied temporary relief. Once Angelene popped into his head, they would flare up and he'd be at their mercy again.
"Mr. Cook, your assignment."
Madame Lafavre glided gracefully across the classroom, fluttering a paper at him.
"You can throw it out."
Ruby Lafavre flapped the paper in his face. The bright red 'zero' flashed like a neon sign.
"No offense, I'm bloody disgusted by anything French."
"You have offended me. My husband is from Toulouse. I performed with the Paris Opera Ballet. It's a country of great culture, food, and people."
Brendon chuckled, folded the paper in half, and stuffed it in his pocket. "I know someone from Paris. She crawled right out of the gutter."
"Need I remind you; I was the only teacher that would have you. Start applying yourself and lose that attitude."
"Sure thing Ms. Lafavre."
"That is Madame Lafavre. The girls may find that brooding attractive. I, however, find it repulsive. Bonne journée."
Brendon stepped into the crowded hallway and threw up his middle finger.
"Hey mate, where were you this morning? I couldn't find a quote. Ms. Hudson made me stand in front of the class and recite, he who opens a school door closes a prison. It was from this Hugo guy. Do you think the old bat is insinuating I'll end up in prison?"
"Don't mention Hugo again."

"You're touchy today." Troy checked his hair in a classroom door and smoothed his bangs. "Why were you late?"

Brendon peered through the mob of students. He spied Charlotte, and a Maggie he had never seen before. Top three buttons undone, thighs exposed, chest full of necklaces.

"I got distracted."

"What was it this time? Dortmund highlights, a write up in BILD or the colours of the sky? You're distracted a lot lately."

"Rachel got into a row with her mum and needed a cuddle."

Troy wore a look of repugnance. "You're a dirty bugger and I mean that in more ways than one."

"English or humping?"

"I told you to stop until Maggie gets over the break-up. Look at her, all dressed up and you haven't noticed."

What had attracted Brendon to Maggie was her smart, saccharine sweet, springtime pretty. This was the Maggie that stepped onto the stage, trying to convince the audience she was a vamped-up Sandy in Grease.

"Hiya babes," Charlotte said, slinging her arm through Troy's. "Brendon."

"Hello Charlotte. You're looking lovely today."

"Just because I had dinner at yours doesn't mean I'm not mad at you. Those little donuts are scrummy."

Maggie ran her fingers over the multitude of chains. "Do you like it?"

"No, I don't. You look like a tart with that stuff on your face."

"What did you call her?" Charlotte said.

"I said, she looks like a tart. I didn't say she is one. Bloody hell, I would have been sticking it to her a long time ago."

Maggie let loose the necklaces and stuck her fingernail in her mouth. Charlotte tugged at her hand and glared. "Aren't you into that type now?"

"Can you make your girlfriend stop please."

"I'm not getting involved. Today's my day to be Switzerland."

"It took me an hour to do Magpie's makeup. Can't you see she's gutted, miserable wanker."

"Can you bloody shut it? I need to eat and prepare for the match."

"I won't shut it," Charlotte said, brushing lint from Troy's shoulder. "All muffin wanted was for you to notice her."

"I'm right here," Maggie said.

Sparks vibrated Brendon's body. He tried to breathe. Fire had captured his lungs.

"You'd rather hump that slag than work on things with magpie?"

"That's all it is, humping. I'm not planning to take Rachel home to meet my mum."

Maggie bowed her head, her shoulders trembled. "Can you both stop?"

"Magpie deserves better than you."

"You're right, she does. I'm a fucking horrible person." "You're not," Charlotte said, lacing her fingers through Troy's, "other than babes, you're the nicest boy I know. Someone or something turned you into a wanker."

A sob rose from Maggie's chest, bursting from her mouth. The reaction came unexpectedly, catching Brendon off guard.

"Can you stop bloody crying."

Sparks simmered and seethed. Students slowed, loitered in doorways. A spectacle was about to unfold.

"I wanted to look brilliant for you."

Brendon reached into his blazer pocket and tossed a packet of tissues at her. "Wipe your fucking nose."

Instead of holding her, Brendon held his breath and clenched his fists.

"Unfuckingbelievable. Someone just bet 50p I'll put my fist through the wall. Two strikes, Mags, that's all I got."

"I had to get up the courage to wear this makeup and dress like this."

"You shouldn't have bothered."

Brendon had seen Maggie cry, not like this. Her entire body shook. Mascara ran like rivers of black over her mottled cheeks. All he could hear was the sound of her sobs, the whispering of bets and Angelene telling him to find God. He pressed his fists against his ears and shut his eyes.

"Will you fucking stop!"

"What's wrong with you?"

"I'm pissed off."

"You aren't the same Brendon I fell in love with. You've changed."

"I'm sure if you talk to Dawson, he'll tell you I'm the same angry dolt I was last year."

"Ever since she... I love you."

Brendon whipped his blazer and backpack onto the hardwood floor. "I don't want you to be in love with me. I'm an arsehole, a prick. Do you know what I did?"

Maggie rubbed her sleeve over her face, smudging black around her eyes. "You were under the willow tree with Rachel."

"And you still love me?"

"You aren't a prick or an arse, you're a nice bloke."

"Did you think if you showed up at school like this, I'd want to get back together?"

"Charlie said..."

"Stop listening to bloody Charlie."

"Is it her? Is everyone right about her being some devilish freak?"

"Who the fuck are you talking about?"

A whimper rolled off Maggie's lips. "You can't see it. You're so stupid."

"I'm not fucking stupid. I told you I need a fucking break; you don't bloody listen."

Michael Collins pushed his way through the crowd. "Maggie, are you okay?"

"Please go away. Brendon has the sparks. The dolt will do something stupid."

"Is that like the lurgy?" Michael said, tucking a bundle of Hamlet flyers under his arm.

Brendon glared. "It's like a punch in the mouth."

"Let's go for a walk?" Michael said, hooking her bags over his arm, "we can grab some lunch and sit under the poplar trees."

"I need to talk to Brendon."

"Just fucking go. I'm hungry and tired of listening to you cry. Fuck."

The heavy click of heels echoed down the hall. Mr. Dawson, his arms swinging like floppy noodles, charged at him. Brendon stared at the ceiling and grumbled a long, satisfying string of curse words. His shoulder buckled under Dawson's grip, sparks stormed and raged.

"Michael, escort Margaret to the toilets so she can wash her face. Mr. Cook, to my office." Dawson's bony fingers gripped Brendon's elbow, escorting him out the door like a prisoner. A group of students in togas grinned and snickered. Brendon flung his arm behind his back and shot up his finger. Sparks zoomed and zapped, sweat gathered in his armpits. His mind spun through the morning's events. Rachel straddled over his lap, Maggie in her clown costume, Angelene's voice hammering away in his head. The day was supposed to be easy. He'd control the sparks, keep his head clear for the match. By the look on Dawson's face, he meant business.

"Hold my calls," Dawson said, swinging open the door. A wave of mouldy, dust scented air clogged Brendon's nose. The secretary nodded curtly, tsk-tsking. He ignored her scolding look, jerked his arm free and dropped into an unwelcoming pleather chair. Brendon inhaled; the breath dragged from his toes to his lungs on a wave of fire.

Do you fancy me Angelene?
You're my best friend, my only friend.

A goldfinch flew from within the branches of a walnut tree, perched itself on the windowsill and cocked its head, *'you have yet to meet all her devils. This world is her hell. You are merely a pawn in it. Use your light to protect yourself.'*

"In one morning, you have used every curse word known to humankind, dawdled to French, which I learned you loathe. You missed English. To top it all off, you're failing French."

Mr. Dawson's voice drew Brendon back into the stuffy office, had the bird spoke to him?

"You've made it perfectly clear that your studies aren't as important as football."

"I'm pissed off I had to come back here."

"Whose fault, is it?"

"Mine."

"All you needed to do was complete your work and listen to your tutor. You chose not to, it landed you right back in Taunton. Now you're in the same sinking boat. Your Latin and history marks have dropped. The only class you're passing is English. You know the deal your parents and I have, don't you?"

"I fail, no football."

Dawson folded his hands, dropping them on the desk. "I'm opposed to the idea; you called the last one a prick and the German bloke an f'ing Erbsenzähler."

"He called me an arsch mit ohren, mouthy little prick, always nit-picking my assignments. He was lucky all I did was call him a name and didn't shove my cleat in his face."

"That boy had every right to call you an ass with ears. You were wasting his time," Dawson said, plucking a pen from a mug. "I would make it count this time."

"Not another bloody tutor?"

"I feel sorry for the poor soul that will have to do it," Dawson said, scratching words on a notepad. "Give this to your mother. How is she? I saw her at the butcher shop last week, looking lovely."

Brendon inhaled, envisioning a great wave of freezing water extinguishing the sparks, they lingered.

"I'm going to tell you a story."

"I'm hungry. Can you save it for later?"

"My mother forced me to take violin lessons."

"I take it you didn't like the violin."

"Hated it. I wanted to be the next Keith Richards. I did it because it made my mum happy. If you were my son, I would have left you in Germany, save the headaches."

"I guess I'm down a strike now?"

"I don't want you back here. Not today, tomorrow, or the next. Maybe wait until spring."

"Yes, sir."

"One last thing, stay away from Rachel Jones. She'll get you into a whole mess of trouble."

Brendon pulled into the pub car park, ribbons of gold and velvety purple painted the sky. Revelers gathered around the door, puffed on cigarettes, and sang a slurred version of Molly Malone. The sparks had followed him to the match and ignited into a blaze. He took it out a Tiverton attacker with a nitrogen bomb fist, received a red card and benched for unsportsmanlike behaviour. Something else had followed him to the pitch, Angelene and her devils. She tried to disguise herself in a flat cap. His hoodie gave her away. She had crawled into his head and nested, like a parasite wrecking havoc on his brain.

"What took you so long, mate? It's your round?"

"I had to drive around and clear my head. The sparks are bad."

Troy tore into a pack of Walker's crisps, shaking some into his mouth. "Breathing isn't helping?"

"Everything moved so fast."

"You're spending time with Will, shagging that tart," Troy said, tossing crisps into his mouth. "Charlie's right, you've changed."

"Dawson said, I changed, Maggie."

Troy scrunched the bag and tossed it in the bin. "What can I do to help?"

"That's just it. I don't bloody know. Everything feels heavy."

He had crossed the line with Angelene, stepped over the boundary between friend and lover, fell in head first. It was a strange, lonely place, the space between his boundary and her wall.

"Get a pint into you. You'll feel better," Troy said.

They walked into the pub. Brendon squeezed up to the bar and knocked his wallet against the scarred wood.

"What can I get you?"

"Three pints of lager."

Brendon's gaze swept over the crowd; a flash of irritation flicked the sparks into a frenzy.

"How long has she been here?"

"Ms. Pratt? Two hours. The woman can drink."

He edged himself between two men with thick beards and chests, their coveralls stinking of petrol.

"How many glasses of wine have you had?"

"I don't know, four, ten. My friend Boris has bought me a vodka."

Her accent was thick and hoarse. She stared at him with scorn in her eyes and a grin that said she was living for the moment.

"Healthy things, remember. You won't find the answer to what's troubling you in that bottle."

"It has to be at the bottom."

Mugs clattered against the bar. Brendon nodded a thank you and tossed thirty pounds on the bar.

"Are you drowning your sorrows in that mug of beer?"

"Call a taxi and go home."

"Who are you, her father? She will stay and drink with us."

Brendon glared at the heavily bearded man. "Mind your business."

"Go to your friends," Angelene said, shoving her glass towards a bottle of Moskovskaya. "Pour me another Boris. It smells like my husband, peppery and fresh. Would you like a shot Monsieur keeper?"

"I'll take you home."

"Fuck off and leave me alone."

Brendon gripped the mugs, sparks circulated, he cursed himself for caring.

"About time mate. What took you so long?"

"I was talking to Ms. Pratt."

He stared into the golden liquid. He was no better than her, drowning his sorrows.

"Ms. Pratt? I didn't see her." Troy craned his neck, raising his eyebrows. "Is she pissed?"

William snickered. "She's a minger."

Tilly slid into the booth, flinging her purse on the table. "I didn't recognize her. Is Mr. Pratt here? There's no way he'd let her leave the house like that."

"Where's Rachel?"

"Grabbing drinks," Tilly said.

Brendon gulped back the beer. Part of him wanted to take Angelene home, stuff her full of coffee, and put her to bed. The other half, the part Padre Diavolo ruled, said, fuck it. His pulse quickened, the blood drain from his face. Angelene swayed close to Rachel, her lips curled in a snarl. The black shadows he had seen hovering around her at the pitch had followed her to the pub. He kept his gaze on the exchange. Sparks glided through his gut. He slid across the vinyl bench, stopping himself from charging across the pub. Angelene had said her piece and settled onto the stool.

"My glass is half full," Tilly said, stabbing her fingernail into a lime wedge, "did the floor get a taste of my g&t?"

"I bumped into the man that looks like bigfoot. Take mine."

"You, okay?"

"Sure," Rachel said.

"You're shaking." He wound his arm around her, ignoring the 'what are you doing mate' stare from Troy. Rachel leaned into his chest; her lips tickled his ear. "She asked if I was fucking you."

Brendon bit the inside of his mouth and glared. Angelene slid off the stool, balanced on the bearded giant, and stumbled around the tables.

"I'll be back."

"Where are you going, mate? Please don't leave me." Brendon ducked into the hallway. The exit sign cast an eerie green glow over the scratched hardwood. He snagged Angelene by the wrist.

"Don't fucking grab me," Angelene said, bracing herself against the peeling wallpaper. "That girl is a putain."

"What do you care? You're honouring your wedding vows."

Angelene adjusted her flat cap. Tendrils of hair fell from beneath the brim. She looked tinier, paler, a staggering waif with 'stay the fuck away from me' blazing in her eyes.

"That girl is no good for you." "Those men you've been drinking with are any better? We aren't friends anymore. It shouldn't matter."

"You're fucking that girl, using her."

"Big deal. I love fucking her."

She stumbled and bumped into a payphone. "What happened to my sweet boy?"

"Your sweet boy is sick of you playing with his head. You said we couldn't be friends. You want nothing to do with me."Red heat flicked up his neck and onto his cheeks. He balled his hands and jammed them in his hoodie pocket. The woman swaying before him was not that scared little bird he had found under the ivy. She was ten feet tall and full of poison.

"You show up at the match, in my fucking hoodie. Did you not give a shit how I might feel?"

"I have extremely low moments where I crave your light. It's dim. I could only grab a handful."

"Leave me and my friends alone and stay away from Troy. Don't go stealing his light, too."

"Fuck off." Angelene slammed her fists against his chest, her eyes chaotic green. "Go to your slut. Brule en l'enfer, burn in hell."

"We'll burn together. Go home Ms. Pratt." He clamped his hands around her fists and shoved her backwards. She caught the dangling phone, it slipped from her hand, she crumbled to the floor.

"Your words blaze like fire. You're dark, beautiful like Lucifer. It's a trick to get me to need you again."

Brendon chuckled and held out his hand. "I could say the same about you. Now get up before someone sees you."

She slapped his hand away, gripped the wainscotting, and staggered to her feet.

"One night, a butterfly landed on the sill and distracted me. I burnt Douchette's dinner." Angelene clawed at her wrist. "Douchette grabbed my arm, he shoved me, I fell into the corner of the kitchen table. The next morning, I woke in his bed, my eye bruised and bloodied."

"I'm sorry those things happened to you. Go home, paint the bloody butterfly." She had done it again, twisted his anger and made him feel for her. "Stay away from Rachel."

"She stole your light. She introduced her devil to you."

Brendon raked his fingers through his hair. Empathy faded away. "The only thing she stole was my virginity. I was more than willing to hand it to her. I'm going to call you a taxi."

"All my life, caught in the middle, struggling, barely breathing, drowning. Every day I try to figure out where to go, which path to take, which road will lead me to yellow. I'm easily confused… always end up on the path of regret. I feel I'm heading there again."

Angelene pushed past him and disappeared into the pub. Brendon took a step, chase after her, hold her until she was sunny yellow. There would be no holding her, her fight-or-flight mode was in overdrive. Both ruled her.

"You feeling iffy? You were gone for a while," Rachel said.

"I'm fine."

He wasn't fine. He was furious and suffocating.

"We're heading to my house. Mum's out," William said.

"No, thanks," Troy said, guzzling the beer. "You coming, mate?"

Angelene bubbled and brewed inside him.

"You're not leaving, are you?" Rachel said.

"I'm knackered."

William snorted into his beer, licking the froth on his lips. "I'm thinking you two are poofters. Charlie really is a Charlie."

Tilly chortled. "Everyone knows some things are fake."

"You want me to come?" Rachel said.

Regret hung like a noose around Brendon's neck. "I'll text you."

"A delicate shade of pink would look good on you, Mr. Football," William said.

Brendon shot up his finger and pushed his way through the crowd. He glanced around the car park; she was gone.

"Talk to me, mate. One minute you look like you could punch something, then you look like you're about to cry, then you look like I do when I screw up at a football trial."

"I got into it with Ms. Pratt."

"She isn't soused mate, she's steamboats."

"I wanted to call her a taxi. She wouldn't have it. I don't know where she went.""Walter's going to be pissed off when he hears about this."

"What if she ends up in the gutter somewhere?"

"She looked like she climbed out of one. Stay away from her, mate."

"She isn't good at taking care of herself."

"She's good at one thing," Troy said, unlocking the Fiesta, "surviving. Go home. Go to bed. You look like you haven't slept in days."

Brendon slid behind the wheel. Run to her, ignore her. He was liable to confess his love or his hate, wring her neck or kiss her.

Brendon followed the brass lanterns, lighting up the drive at the McGregor's. Flood lights, hidden among the laurel hedges, cast a yellow glow across the strange collection of rectangles and squares. Brendon stepped out of the car; darkened clouds wrapped around the moon; its faint glow passed through them, washing everything in muted pewter. The door burst open; Rachel's voice blew into the night.

"You came."

A strong smell of boiled cabbage lingered in the draughty entry.

"They're in the sitting room," Rachel said, giving him a shove, "go on. I'll grab you a drink."

"No more alcohol."

"You look like you're about to tear someone's head off. I'll be back."

Brendon followed the floral runner to a sitting room crammed with a mixture of electronics and furniture.

"If it isn't Herr Wunderbar," William said.

Brendon sunk into an overstuffed corduroy couch. Furniture shoved together, overcrowded bookshelves, television jammed into an armoire, stuff stuffed everywhere.

"Is Rach getting you something to drink?"

Brendon nodded. He couldn't stop thinking about Angelene. Had she made it home or was she wandering the streets? He forced himself to shove her into the recesses of his mind and concentrate on keeping the sparks at bay. William's smirk and incessant pawing at Tilly was feeding his irritation.

"One cider for knuddlebär."

"You've been playing like shit, and you still make the paper," William said.

Tilly held up the sports section and waved it in the air. "Cook's brilliant season. Your mummy must be so proud."

"Fuck off."

Brendon guzzled the cider and shoved the glass into Rachel's hand. William's smug face, the 'I try too hard' appearance, his whistly breathing was getting under his skin.

"Can you get me another?"

"Drinking your sorrows away?" William said, sliding his hands between Tilly's thighs, "poor wee Brendon, do you need your dummy?"

"Will you stop? You'll chase knuddlebär away."

Tilly chomped and smacked her gum. "Or he'll punch you in the face."

"What's got your frilly knickers in a twist?" William said.

"You're bloody annoying. I don't know why I came."

"To have the pleasure of my company. It must be a bore hanging around Spence. He's as much a saint as Margaret."

"Don't talk about Maggie."

"Leave Brendon alone," Rachel said, handing him a glass. Cider tingled on Brendon's tongue. He tossed back the cold brew in one gulp.

"What was up with Pratt's wife?" William said.

"She was soused."

Brendon shrugged Rachel's fingers from his neck. What had pushed her over the edge? What had made her search for yellow in a bottle of cheap vodka?

'Why do you bloody care?'

"She was a gobby cow to Rach," Tilly added.

"Not a way for Walter Pratt's wife to act. Wait until mum hears."

Brendon started the countdown to calm. Angelene had made a fool of herself. Walter would find out. Concern tried to conquer anger. It shrivelled and hid.

"She'll have it spread around Taunton by the bloody morning."

William gripped Tilly's knee and leaned forward. "What's that supposed to mean?"

"You know bloody well your mum has something to say about everyone in Taunton. The bloody town knew about Walt and Angelene's do before the invitations went out." "What about your mum? She's got her nose stuck in everyone's business, too."

"Will the two of you quit it? Rach and I came for a nice evening." "Tilly, take him to his room." Rachel said.

"I think that's a good idea before I get Mr. Wonderful's posh and privileged blood all over the new hardwood."

Brendon shook the last few dribbles of cider into his mouth and dropped the glass in Rachel's lap. "When have you got into a fight?"

"Bugger off, Cook."

Brendon sagged into the couch. Padre Diavolo insisted he put his fist in McGregor's overbite. It was getting hard to ignore.

"Can you get me another?"

"You'll have to stay on the settee if you keep it up," Rachel said.

"The smell in here is making my stomach turn. I thought I smelled cabbage, it's brussel sprouts. I hate those nasty things."

"Give me a kiss and I'll get you another."

The irritation extended to Rachel and her pursed lips. He pecked her mouth and ran his hand over his lips.

"I'll be right back."

He stared at her bottom; the pleasure switch turned on. It was different, not sweet, and excited, he was going to get laid but, angry, like he despised her. An argument erupted in his head. It was intense, scolding, and provocative. Madre Innocente wanted him to find Angelene, take her home, tuck her in. Padre Diavolo cackled and snarled. He needed to stay and give the tart what she wanted. Brendon sunk into the fluffy pillows, anger clogged his heart and throat, Angelene was gone. She took her friendship, ran away and why? She couldn't tell him, another secret. Heat surged through his body as quickly as his pulse raced. Angelene and her devils had played with his heart.

"One cider for my gorgey footy player."

He reached for the glass, guzzled it, shrugging at the sparks weighing down on his shoulders.

"You're tense, knuddlebär."

"I'm annoyed, pissed off."

Rachel grabbed his glass and set it on the floor. She lowered her head; Brendon sucked in his breath and clutched the cushion. Her fingers and mouth moved over his thighs and in places he didn't think girls put their hands and tongue. Brendon leaned into the sofa; his fingers knotted in her red waves. Her mouth was warm and pretty.

"Take your shirt off."

She unbuttoned her blouse and dropped it to the floor. Brendon grabbed the collar of his hoodie and jerked it over his head. The sofa swayed.

You're so dark. Where is my sweet boy?

"Stand up so I can take your jeans off."

"Look at you, knuddlebär, demanding. I like it."

He tugged at the button; she had switched her belly button charm to a glittery green shamrock. Brendon peeled away her jeans. He pressed his lips against her stomach. The scent of baby powder filled his nose.

"Lay down."

She sprawled along the cushions, willing, waiting, a sinner like him.

"There's a condom in my purse."

Brendon tore open the package and tossed the wrapper on the nest of 'I'm trying to seem so sophisticated' books. There was a tiny star-shaped freckle on Rachel's hip bone. How many boys had seen it? Had they noticed she had a matching freckle on her thigh?

"Want to kiss for a bit?"

"Wrap your legs around my waist."

Her thighs clamped around him, and he sunk into her. The sofa screeched back and forth on the hardwood. The room swayed and bent.

"Stop."

"I'm almost there."

Rachel pushed on his shoulders and bit into her lip. "You're pounding my bleeding fanny."

"Can you shut up?"

His fingers curled around the frayed fabric, his breath rushed, the room spun around him.

"What the hell was that?"

"Sex, fucking."

"You call that sex?"

"What would you call it? Making love? Do you see any tissues anywhere?"

Rachel reached under a side table, knocked over a stack of magazines, and flung the box at him.

"I don't know who I was having sex with. I thought..."

"That you're my girlfriend now?"

Brendon staggered to his feet, dropping the ball of tissues on the coffee table. He reached for his clothes; the rug wavered under him. He waited for the noose to tighten, or Madre Innocente to prod him with her staff. He felt nothing but hate for the girl cradling her clothes against her chest.

"I really fancied you. You weren't just a number on my list."

"It's just sex."

"Where is that boy that sat in the hall and took silly photos?"

"I was another conquest, something to brag about," Brendon said, stumbling into his clothes. "Guys are with you because you don't fall in love."

Rachel stretched her arms into her shirt. "Is it because of Ms. Pratt?"

"What does she have to do with this?"

"I saw the way you were looking at her, like you cared."

"I don't give a shit about her."

He downed the last of Rachel's cider and moved on to Tilly's Red Bull and vodka.

"I thought you were different." Rachel said in a voice Brendon didn't recognize.

"You thought bloody wrong."

Round and round, the room spun. He didn't expect her chin to tremble or her cheeks to pale. She wore her sorrow like she did her flirty smile, out front for him to see.

"Put your clothes on and don't cry. I've had enough of people crying today."

"Aren't you full of yourself. I wouldn't shed a tear over you," Rachel said, kicking his shin, "you're a lousy keeper and a terrible lay, du verdammter arschficker. You damn ass fucker."

Brendon grinned.

Brendon didn't know how he got home. He remembered leaving Rachel on the sofa, starting the engine, but had no idea how he made it from William's to the other side of Taunton. He gripped the doorknob, leaning his forehead against the dewy door. He named the day, 'dulce periculum, danger had been sweet.' Brendon stepped into the foyer, Sofia and Nicola's voices carried into the entry. The conversation sounded light and nostalgic.

Brendon hobbled to the great room, willed himself to stand straight and his stomach to stop spinning.

"Sweetheart, it's almost eleven. Where have you been?"

Brendon covered his mouth; a Red Bull and cider burp rose from the depths of his stomach.

"Will's."

He rocked into the door frame and blinked. The women in the Klimt painting were swimming around the circles and squares.

"Are you drunk?"

His fingers slipped from the doorway casing. He teetered and bounced off the wall.

"You stink of cider and that awful floral perfume," Sofia said.

"I had a couple of drinks. It's no bloody deal."

"You could have been pulled over or in an accident."

"I didn't."

"You could have," Sofia said, touching his chin, "I don't know where your head is at lately. Where's my baby boy?"

"I'm not a bloody baby."

His mind buzzed. He had treated Rachel the way every other boy had, 'use her and lose her.' He shoved Angelene. Everyone was right, he was changing.

"Don't speak to your mother that way," Nicola said.

"I could be in Dortmund. I could have played in the forest and climbed trees or swam in the fucking pool by myself."

Sofia ran her fingers over her bracelets. "You know why I made those rules. I had to protect you."

"Protect me? Do you know what I was doing tonight, mammina?"

Sofia pulled David's cardigan tighter around her chest, staring at him with cool, dark eyes.

"I was with a slapper from your illustrious Taunton College. I fucked her right there on Ms. McGregor's sofa."

"Get to your room."

"Are you proud of me now, mammina? I'm failing my classes. I got a red card at the match. Want to protect your baby now?"

"Get out of my sight."

"Let's get you into bed, topolino."

"Are you going to tuck me in? She still tries to do that."

"Move your feet if you can and go. Sofia, make me some tea."

Nicola tugged at his hoodie. The marble floor shifted under his feet; alcohol tossed in his stomach. Brendon reached the top of the stairs, stared down the length of the hall.

"Why is my room so far away?"

"Just keep moving. The smell is making my stomach churn. All those years dealing with Gianni, I should be used to it."

The runner became a magic carpet, transporting him to his bathroom, depositing him in front of the pedestal sink. A flood of alcohol spilled into the white bowl.

"You can go away now."

Nicola ignored his plea and turned down the blankets. He stuck his head out of the bathroom, clumsily brushing his teeth. "Are you sick? You only drink tea when you feel ill."

"You could say that. I hope you were safe with that girl."

"I used a joy bag."

"I doubt there was any joy in it," Nicola said, patting the mattress, "into bed."

Rachel's pained face flashed through his mind. He slid onto his stomach. "I'm in trouble, aren't I?"

"Yes, topolino."

"She broke my heart."

"I'm sure you and Maggie can work things out."

His eyelids were as heavy as his heart. "It hurts."

"Get some sleep."

"We were going to walk in Westfalenpark. She said she would take a train into Dortmund."

"I'm sure Maggie will. Close your eyes."

Brendon cradled his pillows under his head, lulled by the steady beat of his heart.

"Can you turn my lamp on, please?"

He listened to the click of the switch, felt her fingers in his hair. He had been an asshole. Even a girl like Rachel Jones deserved better. His mind wandered and led him to Angelene. A painful ache buried itself in his chest. She had become nothing, a shadow in the night, a wavering promise.

***

Walter fumbled for his cell phone. It had rung three times, waking him. He drew back the blankets, scratched his head, his mind haunted with visions of Angelene. He couldn't shake the feeling something was wrong.

"Work on your mind?"

"Brendon," David said.

Walter opened the cupboard, grabbed a box of PG Tips, and dropped two bags into a pot. He filled the kettle, set it on the burner, and clicked on the gas.

"Trouble in school again?"

"He's failing his classes," David said, tossing his pen on the desk. "We let him play football. It's obvious he can't do both."

Walter had never seen a child with so much determination and skill, Brendon Cook was football. *'Brag about your kid,'* he used to say to David, *'he's going to make it to the pros.'* Uncle Walt did all the bragging. He told David to be proud. It took a different kind of smart to play football. Walter was still trying to convince him.

"It shouldn't be a choice. He followed the damn code; he conquered his goal."

The kettle hissed, Walter clicked off the burner and poured water into the pot. He dug in the cupboard for a box of digestives and shook some on a plate.

"Nicola had the audacity to pick up the phone and listen. I'm an idiot."

Walter poured tea, hooked his thumbs through the handles and balanced the plate in his other.

"You are. The boy has a gift."

"Sofia rambles when she's upset."

"She had to tell you he's failing," Walter said, grabbing a biscuit. "Brendon has worked his way through the youth system. He's done with semi-pro. It's the Bundesliga, England's national team."

"A-levels aren't that difficult." "Brendon is not..."

"Don't," David said, sipping his tea. "I'm trying to get it right this time."

"Don't you think getting it right means sending Brendon back to Dortmund?"

"He promised to finish the year. I'll hold him to it. Besides, Sofia won't let him go."

Walter dunked the cookie into his tea and took a bite. He never agreed with David, forcing Brendon to go on to years twelve and thirteen.

"We need a plan. We can't have Brendon yanked from the squad." "He's your son now?"

"Football is going to be his career; Uncle Walt saw to that."

David's lips pressed tight. "He needs a French tutor."

"Doesn't he know Italian? It should be easy to pick up French."

"The curse words. He never paid attention to Sofia or Nicola unless it pertained to football or swearing."

Walter set the mug down, amusement glinted in his eyes. "What about Ang? She's around, doing absolutely nothing. This could be good for her."

"I'll ask Sofia."

"Why would you waste money on a tutor? You're already throwing money away, paying that ridiculous tuition. Tell Sofia it's Ang or no one. Better yet, let me tell her. She never says no to me."

"Is that so?"

"I have a knack with women."

David picked up a cookie and tapped it against his lip. "Brendon may pay attention if it's someone he knows. I doubt it but, its worth a try."

"If he can learn German from Miranda Jones's daughter. He can certainly learn French from little bird."

"I hope that's what he's doing with Miranda's daughter," David said. He washed down the bite with a sip of tea. "James McGregor mentioned Brendon has been parking under the willow tree. I thought the school was cutting it down after the headmaster caught you and Pru."

Walter chuckled. "Why would they cut that tree down? Years of memories, gone."

"Call Sofia in the morning, see what she says," David said, rubbing his temples. "I never asked what you were doing awake. My apologies."

"My phone woke me."

"Was it Nicola enlisting you in the war against Fuhrer David Cook."

"It was Ang. I rang her back, she didn't answer."

"Maybe she fell back asleep."

"I talked to her this morning, asked if she would go to the auction with Sofia. She rambled on about God and seven shadows clinging to her. It was a peculiar conversation."

"Did you ask her or tell her she had to go?"

"Told, I guess." Walter snapped a cookie in half and pointed the broken piece at David. "There was a tone to her voice. She seemed disappointed or hurt, disgusted. I'm worried about her."

"She might be having a day. Sofia can start the day happy and be miserable by noon."

"I felt like I was talking to someone else. One minute a monster, the next, an angel, then a devil."

"How do you know she wasn't tackling that list of chores you left her? I'd be angry too."

Walter scratched his hair. Wasn't a wife supposed to clean the house and take care of things while the husband earned money? Normal women dreamed of becoming a wife and a mother. Angelene Hummel was not normal.

"I'm positive she was tipsy."

"Talk to her. Just like I'll talk to Brendon about school again."

"I'll sound like a father scolding her."

"You'll sound like a husband. Remember the code and be patient with her."

"I should give her a bell, see if she answers this time."

"It's late. You can charm her after you charm Sofia."

Walter placed the dishes in the sink and shut off the kitchen light. "Shall we meet for lunch tomorrow? I checked my diary. I'll be free after 1:00."

"We can devise a plan to get Brendon back on track and Angelene comfortable. We'll give it a month and re-evaluate."

Walter grinned; a lot could happen in a month.

***

Angelene tossed a crumpled ten-pound note on Malcolm's lap and fumbled with the door handle.

"Easy now, just push."

"I'm piss yellow tonight, mon ami."

"Pissed drunk, more like it."

Angelene stumbled from the seat and leaned into the car. "Are you in your dressing gown?"

"You got me out of bed. I stopped the late-night calls. The Ms. likes me home by eight."

"I'm sorry for dragging you into my mess."

"You sounded like you needed a ride home."

"Can you take me to Paris? I was going to take a train to Germany."

Malcolm stuffed the money in the cup holder. "You want help to the door?"

"Go home to your wife. I'm sorry for getting you out of bed."

She slammed the door shut; the ground tilted. Angelene grabbed hold of the wisteria, weaving to the front door. She fought with the key; the door blew open and banged against the wall. She fell to her knees. Angelene dragged herself to a wobbly stance and hobbled to the kitchen. She sagged onto a stool, cradled a bottle of wine in her hands, and snarled at a paint tray. Walter had accused her of being tipsy. She had thrown her wine in retaliation. The splat was faint under the thin coat of paint. The truth hurt. She failed Walter, just like she had her sweet boy. Brendon had been spiky black. He had looked at her like she was beautiful despite screaming piss yellow words at him. Angelene stared at the crimson stain, her head loud, bungled with thoughts. The stain spread like bloodied wings. She rose, flopped to the floor, studied every line and feathery splat. Angelene turned, pressed her back against the blemish, and grinned.

"I've found my wings."

She brought the bottle to her lips, guzzled, and wiped a dribble from her chin. The quiet was deafening. Anger yelled at her, sadness wept swollen tears, regret obsessed over patterns and sugar-sweet boys, shame berated her with words like drunk, light-stealer, smotherer. The bottle flew from her hand into the backsplash. Green shrapnel sprayed across the counter and floor. She twisted handfuls of hair around her hands and pulled. A scream tore through her throat, grungy and guttural. The emotions twirled and knotted, uncoiled, then slapped her brain. She unwound her hair, stumbled through the glass, and fell onto the stool. Little bursts of breath puffed through her lips.

I love you petite oiseau.

Do you like messes? Find a girl at school. A girl who smiles and laughs, says pretty things and is not full of scars. You have constructed a me in your head that is a deluded fantasy. My hair is a mess. My clothes are a mess, the stupid thoughts racing through my head, a mess.
Love your mess like I do. There is beauty in chaos. There is beauty in you.
"You were a stupid boy."
She swiped her arm across the island. Orange peels, hardened cheese and bread fell amongst the glass. She wiped spit from her chin, grabbed the ashtray and hurled it. Powdery grey soot sprinkled in the air.
"My sweet boy with his beautiful light, fucking the Salome of Somerset. You created a mess, God. By giving men a place to stick those nasty things."
Angelene stood. The stool clattered and bounced off the floor. She shuffled her way through the glass and ash. The noise in her head raged. The house remained silent. She picked up a shard of glass and jabbed the point into her fingertip. Angelene looped her fingers through the strings running across the hole in her jeans, tugged until they stretched and ripped. She poked the glass into her thigh. The noise continued. She dug a little deeper. The scar next to the puckering skin sang to her, calming the wicked pace of her heart.
Did you get a new book, Roman?
I bought it when I was in Berlin.
It looks too old to be new.
You make me laugh, little bird. It was a used bookstore. You won't find books more loved than those at a used bookstore.
What's it about? There aren't many words, just pictures.
It's a book about symbols.
That one looks like a tree stretching its branches to heaven.
That's the Rune symbol, Algiz. It was for protection.
Can we draw an Algiz and place it on my bedroom door? When you aren't here, it will protect me.
She scratched a line, another, one more, her mind went still. She ran a finger over the jagged algiz carved into her thigh. "Now you're always with me, Roman."

26 Two Peas in a Pod

Sofia tried to rationalize Brendon's behaviour. She blamed the Richard gene, Gianni's reckless gene, too much pressure, her smothering ways, David's demands. None of it made sense. The boy who staggered home boasting about sex with the town slapper was not her boy.

"Hang up the phone Sofia, the auction starts in an hour. I want that Paolo De Poli ring."

Sofia placed the phone on the charger and yanked on her leather jacket. "I was talking to David."

"You shouldn't be bothering him. He told you he had meetings all week."

"I want him to come home."

"He's much too busy to be commuting."

"I need him."

Nicola powdered her nose, closed the compact, and stared at Sofia incredulously. "Since when do you need a man?"

"Now, mother and he isn't any man. He's my husband."

Sofia opened the door and marched to the car. "Do you know why I went for a walk this morning?"

Nicola slid into the passenger seat and buckled the seatbelt. "To clear your head before picking up Angelene."

Sofia started the car and backed out of the carport. "I didn't want to look at Brendon."

An amused smirk brightened Nicola's face. "I recall a sixteen-year-old sneaking her father's chianti and hiding in the lemon grove with an English boy."

"Did I curse at you? Pretend to be ill? Run around like some slut?"

"You were a good girl."

"That boy who cursed at me and talked about private things, is not Brendon."
She passed through the gates and turned onto the road.

"Good thing David wasn't home to see that performance."

"Shall I call Father Sabelli? Ask him to perform an exorcism."

"Mother please. I'm worried about Brendon."

Sofia pulled up to the farmhouse. Wisteria drooped, tattered, and torn.

"Why are we bringing Angelene?"

"Walter is interested in a 17th century sideboard. He wants to turn the back room into a dining room."

Angelene stepped precariously down the walkway in stacked heels. Her movements were slow, jittery, and calculated. There was a small smile on her face. At least Sofia thought it was a smile. She could never be too sure.

"You'll be having dinner at the Pratt's. She'll entertain you with more stories about her mother."

"Be kind. David expects me to be gracious, and that goes for you, too."

"When you were young, I told you to own the room. You do that. People don't mess with you." Nicola studied Angelene, wrists full of bangles, black on black, twitching fingers. "Angelene should do the same thing. Look at her, gattina, she's striking. Her face alone is a weapon."

"That's what scares me. She doesn't know the power she has."

"It's the Marilyn Monroe syndrome," Nicola said.

"I thought Hedy Lamarr was the most beautiful woman in Hollywood."

"She was. Ms. Lamarr was also brilliant, an intelligent woman threatens men. Marilyn had a vulnerability, an innocence that made women hate her and men want to fuck her."

"What a thing to say. Brendon gets his sharp tongue from you, not Richard."

The breeze blew a silky curl, Sofia smoothed her hair and smiled. "Good morning. We were just discussing Marilyn Monroe."

Angelene pushed on her forehead and squinted, sliding across the rear seat. "My mother hated Monroe. She was too breathy; her vulnerability made her weak. Monsieur Krieger said she was a brilliant actor; she made the entire world believe she was dumb. Mother hated that."

Nicola smiled smugly. Sofia arched an eyebrow and gave her a glassy stare. She pulled on to the road. Birds chirped and darted over the moors. Spence farm was bustling. The world outside the Maserati was alive and breathing. Sofia glanced in the rear-view mirror; everything was thriving except Angelene.

"I've never been to an auction before," Angelene said.

"Let Sofia take the lead. She's a pro, always gets what she wants, right, gattina?"

"Kitten."

"You know Italian?"

"Only a few words. Mother's lover Marco called her gattina. I never understood why. She was more of a jaguar," Angelene said, clicking her fingernails, "when jaguars strike, they aim for the head, one shot and dead. Veronique was an expert in tearing the heads off men."

"Your mother sounds like an interesting woman."

Sofia opened the window, releasing the heady scent of patchouli and bleach. There was something in Angelene's stare, like she hunted and devoured her own prey.

"Mother preferred olive-skinned men. Italy, Spain, southern France. Roman and Gustav were the exceptions."

"There's nothing like an Italian man," Nicola said. "Sofia's always liked British men. Who was that actor you found attractive?"

"Jeremy Irons."

"A little drab for me. What about you, Angelene? Are you attracted to olive skinned men?"

Angelene leaned into the corner of the seat, picking at her nail polish. "I notice scents, body parts or colours."

"I appreciate a nice bottom. Some of those football players give me a thrill."

"Mother, please, let Angelene talk. I'm curious what she means."

"A friend smelled like sugar and lemons. I was always afraid he'd melt in the rain. I like Walter's hands. They're rough, not in a way that scratches my skin, more rugged like God sculpted them from rock. Another friend has incredible brown light. It radiates through his skin, stealing my breath."

"This person, the one with brown light, is he anyone we know?"

Sofia slowed the car, Angelene swallowed and swallowed like the words were clogging her throat.

"He's headed to the Second Circle of Dante's Hell where the souls of the lustful live. He might meet the Florentine lovers. Her husband murdered them. They were having an affair."

Sofia gripped the stick shift, trembling. "He doesn't sound like a good person."

"Oh, no, he is. He's lost his way."

"Good lord, this conversation has turned awfully dark," Nicola said. "What do you think of Taunton?"

"I thought it was quiet, it's loud even in the dead of night. There's always someone talking, creatures stirring, gossip travelling across the moors. Everyone knows me and yet, I don't know them."

"That would be Victoria. She never knows when to shut up."

"You need to rid yourself of her, gattina. She had the nerve to tell Daniel, the butcher, I had a drink with an AC Milan player. All I wanted was veal chops. I got an ear full of gossip."

"Victoria McGregor is a dangerous woman," Angelene said.

The light turned red, Sofia pressed on the brakes and glanced over her shoulder. "How so? She's just a jealous gossip."

"It gives her power, the wrong power."

"You have a point," Nicola added.

"I called you yesterday. Mum and I had tea by the pool. I thought you would have liked to join us."

"You mean Walter wanted you to ask. I was in town."

"You should have called. We could have gone for afternoon tea at the Castle Hotel."

"I wasn't in the mood for tea yesterday."

"What did you do?" Nicola said.

"I visited my favourite store to see if the book I ordered arrived. It hadn't, so I stopped by the pitch then the pub. I got drunk. The news of me enjoying a round of vodka with two Russians has already reached Walter."

Cake and coffee rolled around Sofia's stomach. She didn't care that Angelene was roaming the streets of Taunton, drunk. She had gone to the pitch.

"Why would you go to the pitch?"

"Why not? I love football."

Nicola touched Sofia's hand and twisted in the seat. "Did you date much before you met Walter?"

"Would anyone like tea or coffee? I can stop at a café."

"Your mother's question is fine, Sofia. I understand she's curious," Angelene said, holding up a pack of cigarettes. "May I?"

"Go ahead, just put the window down."

"My first date was with Walter."

Nicola chuckled. "First date? You never went out for dinner with a man?"

"They weren't interested in taking me for a meal or a walk along the Seine."

"It sounds like you've visited Dante's Second Circle."

"Mother. I'm so sorry Angelene."

"Don't apologize. She speaks the truth. Let me out, please."

"What a thing to say. Apologize, please."

"I'm feeling ill. Stop the car and let me out."

"I apologize. I should never have assumed your past relationships were..."

"Affairs. I've made poor decisions and I'm paying horribly for them. Please."

Sofia flicked the signal and pulled to the side of the road. "I can drive you home."

Angelene jiggled the door handle and hobbled to her feet. "I'll call Malcolm. Go to your auction. If Walter doesn't get his sideboard, I'll never hear the end of it."

Sofia stared at Nicola. "I can't leave her here."

"She's shooing you away."

"David is going to be so upset."

"And Walter will be furious. She's on her cell, lighting up cigarette number two."

"It doesn't feel right."

"None of that conversation did. All that nonsense about sugar, Hell, and brown light. The girl needs to go home to bed. She's hungover and bristly. Leave her."

Sofia didn't feel right, leaving Angelene. Something told her Angelene would have scratched and clawed her way out.

"Do you think the person with incredible brown light is Brendon?"

"Don't be silly, gattina. It's nonsense, everything she said, nonsense."

Sofia drove into the car park, the feeling returned. The darkness in her mother's eyes spoke volumes. She had never been good at reading faces, but Sofia knew Nicola had met her most dangerous adversary.

***

Brendon held his stomach; it was spinning faster than a waltzer at a fairground. An ache sat over his eyes as if screwed to his skull.

"Hey! Wanker!"

Conversations stopped, students milling about the lawn slowed their pace. Matilda flew from the modern languages building, her hands clamped tight. The ache moved from his forehead, stabbed behind his eyes, and stretched into his neck.

"I'm talking to you, Mr. Football."

Her fists pummelled his back. He stumbled from the force. "Bloody hell, fucking nutter."

"You humped her, insulted her, and tossed your spunk filled tissues at her. You're a dick."

Brendon held onto her fists and shoved them to her sides. "What guy hasn't banged her and left?"

"Hey mate, what's going on?"

"You were a good guy. You treated her with respect."

26 TWO PEAS IN A POD

"I guess I'm not so nice after all."
"Fucking apologize to her."
Brendon laughed. "Fuck that."
Tilly stood on her tiptoes, jabbed her finger in his chin, her kilt fluttered in the breeze. Brendon flew past annoyed and frustrated, teetering on the hostile stage. He grabbed her finger, the impulse to snap it, feel her finger crack, hear the pop, surged through him. Troy gripped his shoulder. He dropped Tilly's hand.
"Rachel's headed for a ciggie behind the dining hall. Go apologize."
"Get out of my way."
"Go fucking find her."
The administration office door banged against the bricks. Mr. Dawson charged across the lawn, arms swinging, his comb-over flapped in rhythm with his steps.
"Matilda Morimoto to my office. Everyone else to the dining hall."
Students dispatched in random directions. They had placed only a few bets.
"If I lose a strike over this."
Tilly shook out a piece of gum and chomped furiously. "I don't care about your bleeding strikes. I care about my friend. She's gutted."
"That's enough," Dawson said, sweeping his hair into place. "Can you not get through the day without making a scene?"
Brendon clenched and unclenched his tingling hands. "I was minding my business; she came after me."
"It's the truth, Mr. Dawson. Tilly flew right out of the modern languages building and hammered him."
"Thank you, Mr. Spence. Find your crumpet and have lunch. I hear the korma is delicious."
"I'm Charlie's little crumpet. Charlie is just Charlie."
"Whatever. Please leave the three of us," Dawson said.
"You weren't at Will's last night, were you? I told you to go home."
"Leave Mr. Spence," Dawson said, "To my office Matilda. You need to cool off."
"Brendon swore too."
"I don't have the patience for Mr. Cook right now. Get, and pull down your kilt."
Brendon breathed, four counts in, eight out. "Want me to wait in the room that smells like barf?"
"I'll expect you before your history class."
Brendon trudged across the lawn; the sparks were present but subtle. He kept his head down, ignored the stares and whispers. He needed to escape, a quick drive around Taunton to clear his head. Brendon reached into his pocket for his cell, typed in a text apologizing to Troy and finished it with, 'I need to run away.' He stared at the message and chuckled. He sounded like Angelene. She ran, he was running. She had been a hurtful, drunk, so had he. '*Two peas in a bloody pod.*'
French Weir Park was a small community space alongside the River Tone. It was a quaint neighbourhood park with places to play and pleasant paths meandering along the river. Brendon stepped out of the car; his nose filled with the scent of freshly mowed grass. Quiet was what he needed. He would avoid the children's play area and slip deep amongst the trees to hide away. Half an hour to clear his head, then he could face Dawson with no sparks.
Children ran along the river's edge outside the Centre for Outdoor Activity. Laughter bubbled through the trees. Brendon glanced into the windows of the community hub. Children sat cross-legged, listening to their teacher prattle on

about ecosystems, their eyes full of wonder and awe. The last time Brendon had felt that kind of admiration, was walking down the black and yellow tunnel at Signal Iduna Park. He continued to follow the sludgy trail, leaves swished, birds chirped. He walked around a bend and groaned softly. Angelene sat on a bench, not with the impatience of someone waiting for the bus but, with eyes savouring every leaf, every blade of grass, every wavering branch. The wind had tousled her hair from her ponytail. Her outfit suggested she was to be somewhere. The serenity on her face reminded Brendon of the French bisque doll his mother displayed under glass in the drawing room. Angelene had the same haunted look, dark-lined eyes, painted lashes, and bright pink cheeks. Brendon dug into his pocket for his car keys. Korma and poppadum sounded delicious. *'Go back to school, ignore her.'*

Brendon collapsed on the bench. Every inch of his skull pulsed with pain; he was beyond tired.

"We keep running into each other."

"I told Malcolm to bring me somewhere quiet. It's no longer quiet."

"Where are you supposed to be?"

"Here," Angelene hissed.

"You got dressed in posh clothes and heels to sit in the park?"

Angelene shook out a cigarette, flicked the lighter and inhaled. "I was supposed to be at an auction with your mother."

"Walter's going to be pissed off."

Smoke curled out of her mouth. "I don't care."

He ran his thumb over a smudge of pressed powder. Angelene tilted her cheek. Smoke blew around the words. "What are you doing?"

"You had some of that powder stuff on your cheek. Bloody hell, you're a miserable cow."

"My head is throbbing. I upset your mother and I almost honked, as you call it, in the rear seat of her beautiful car. Nicola thinks I'm a slut."

"My head feels like it's going to explode. I upset my entire household and I did honk, twice."

Angelene flicked the cigarette. Ash rolled along the path, blew up in the air in a dizzy, glowing spiral.

"Why aren't you in school?"

"I'm running away, like you."

Angelene slid a brown paper bag from beneath her purse and cradled it against her chest.

"Did you buy another book?"

"Die Haschen Schüle, Bunny School. Roman used to tell me about the little rabbits, Hans and Grete. I loved the rhymes, the way he would sing the story to me."

Brendon stretched out his legs and leaned into the wooden slats. His stomach gurgled. A trace of a smile lifted her cheeks.

"Have you eaten? You're an odd shade of green this morning. What colour is it?"

"Barf."

"For a boy in training, you don't take good care of yourself."

"And you do? Have you eaten?"

"I had to clean my mess, get ready for your mother. The house isn't up to Walter's standards. I'm a terrible housekeeper."

"You're a terrible drunk."

A brief pang stung his heart. The statement could apply to him, too.

"Why don't we go for breakfast?"

"Breakfast is over."

"There's nothing better than greasy eggs and streaky bacon when you're hung over."

"That's the stupidest thing I've ever heard."

"It's the truth. Fatty foods make you feel happy, coat your stomach."

"Go to school and leave me alone." Brendon held out his hand. She wore a pout, her eyes twinkled.

"It's bloody brekky, not a fucking date."

"I hate you."

He helped her to her feet and smiled. "No, you don't."

Brendon couldn't put a finger on what he was feeling. It had been easy lately, labelling the sparks, frustrated, pissed off, irritated. He couldn't decide if he was happy, they had found each other or angry she was her wintry self. He smoothed his tie, flicked the end, and smoothed it again. The urge to hold her hand was intense.

"How's my light today?"

"Like your words, blue mixed with grey."

"Bloody hell, really?"

"I'm afraid so," Angelene said, plucking a browning leaf from a branch. "Do you want to hear about the I Love You Wall?"

"Nope."

She twirled the leaf between her fingers and whispered. "Le Mur des Je T'aime in Square Jehan-Rictus. There are over three hundred messages written in different languages, all about love. One day we'll visit."

She had done it again, sunk into his brain, crawled under his skin, hugged his heart so tight it hurt.

"I'll fly from Dortmund, take a train, hold your hand, sound good?"

"Don't be like that," Angelene said, dropping the leaf. "We could visit as friends. Once I'm comfortable with normal and being a wife."

Brendon cursed and took her hand.

"What are you doing?"

"It's my good deed for the day. I don't want you falling on your arse."

"Your mother said a sturdier heel would be easier to walk in. She was wrong."

Her hand was warm in his and although she protested, she gripped it like she was hanging onto a life preserver. He needed the connection. He needed to know he wasn't alone. Brendon unlocked the car, yanked the door open for her, dashing to the other side. He climbed behind the wheel, shoved the keys in the ignition. Bluesy guitars seeped from the speakers. Angelene fiddled with the dial. A campy, orchestral piece filled the car.

"Danse Macabre. Saint-Saens wrote it."

"Dance macabre. Bloody hell, a little morbid, don't you think?"

Her fingers drummed against her thigh; her foot tapped along with the beat.

"Roman said it's like a poem. The violins are the devil, the oboe, a crow, listen," Angelene said, turning up the volume, "the xylophone sounds like rattling bones."

The sound was sharp and hollow. Brendon could picture skeletons dancing in a graveyard. A poem played out in his mind. All the things he wanted to say, confessions to make, feelings to divulge. He wanted to go back to the night she hid in the ivy. He wanted a do-over.

"Roman would share his favourite pieces with me. Fur Elise, Edelweiss, Moonlight Sonata," Angelene said, collecting her purse. "Shall we? Your stomach is as loud as the tuba."

Brendon chuckled. "You're bringing your book?"

"I want it with me."

The diner transported customers back to a time of floats and soda fountains. An elderly couple ate side by side, bent over their meals. A group of women chatted over a plate of hash browns and bacon. There were no familiar faces, they were safe. Brendon slid onto a turquoise bench, the tension in his neck dissolved. No one was paying attention to the boy in his school kit and the girl dressed in black. The server approached, set down two mugs as if she recognized a hungover face and poured coffee. She took their orders and placed a bowl of creamers and milk between bottles of ketchup and brown sauce.

"Your light has brightened a little," Angelene said, ripping the tab off a creamer. She tore away two more, tipping all three into her mug. "You're still sad or angry, I'm not sure which. If I were to paint you, you'd be grey, washed in brown, dotted with black."

"I'm not feeling great."

"Tell me."

Brendon gazed into her eyes. Was she angry, sad, or concerned?

"I drank my troubles away. Rachel's friends are bloody mad at me. The whole drama class, including Ms. Baxter, are still giving me the evils for cheating on Maggie."

The server slid two plates of bacon, eggs, beans, fried tomato, and toast in front of them. Brendon's stomach flipped and churned. He grabbed the bottle of brown sauce and shook a blob on his plate.

"Why are Salome's friends mad at you?"

"I thought I was like every other boy, in it for a hump. She really liked me."

Angelene piled bacon on toast, adding a splat of ketchup. "I told you not to use her."

"I didn't think I was. She's always on the pull."

"You made her feel ugly. Of course, her friends would want to tear you to shreds."

Brendon smeared the egg through the brown sauce and smirked. "You weren't kind to her. You said some shitty things."

"Did I? I remember Boris saying she looked like the girls on Vladimirsky Prospekt in St. Petersburg."

Brendon tilted his head and opened his mouth to speak. Nothing came out.

"A prostitute. He said she looked pretty but used."

"I thought I could hump her and not have to worry about her falling in love with me."

"It's hard not to."

Brendon searched her face; she was a blank canvas. Was she talking in general or speaking from her heart? A do-over, they needed to reset and start again.

"I hope you're being safe."

"Why does everyone keep saying that?"

"Because you're special. You have incredible light."

"I don't feel special. I keep fucking up."

26 TWO PEAS IN A POD

"Where's my beautiful boy?"

He slurped a mouthful of coffee and shrugged. "Hiding for now."

Brendon stared out the window, grinning at his pathetic appearance. The smile dropped. He shrunk down in the seat.

"Bloody hell, it's Ms. McGregor and Ms. Batra. I'm going to the loo. Will you be, okay?"

"I'll keep our secret."

Brendon dashed into the hallway. He slammed his back against the wall, little beads of sweat gathered under his collar.

"I guess it's past elevensies," Victoria said.

Brendon glanced at his watch. "It's almost one, daft cow."

"Eshana and I are starting the 5:2 diet," Simone said.

"Is it like the South Beach or Mediterranean?"

"I eat normal for five days, then fast for two. What did you think of that wedding gown in the shop window? Can you picture our Eshana in it?"

"Who in Taunton is she going to marry?"

"Brendon Cook. He's single now."

"What is it with you and Brendon Cook? He's been molly coddled all his life."

"He's worth a damn fortune, not to mention the football contract."

"I'm sure William will cycle through a few more trollops before he settles."

Brendon crept closer to the doorway. Angelene hadn't shrunk in the seat or hid behind the menu. She was taking little bites, chewing slowly. The evidence Angelene hadn't dined alone shone in a greasy glow.

"You could have one of those lesbian weddings. I heard Maisie fancies the wicket keeper on the cricket team."

"I thought I squashed that tittle-tattle about my daughter. Let's share a plate of chips."

"Then shoes. Sofia always has the best shoes," Simone said.

"Well, I'll be damned. Look who it is."

Brendon's bacon-and-eggs breakfast roiled in his belly.

"Ms. Pratt, what a pleasant surprise," Victoria said.

"Your ass must be jealous of all the shit that comes from your mouth."

Brendon muffled his laugh.

Victoria slammed her hands on her hips, clucking in her throat. "How rude."

"What brings you into town? Vic and I were doing some dress shopping. Next are shoes."

"I bought a book," Angelene said, in a coarse tone. "Would you like to call Walter?"

"I should. He'll want to know what his wife's been up to. Two plates of food."

"What have I been up to? Was I dining with a handsome man? Did we share little whispers across the table?"

"Maybe she was hungry and had two plates of brekky," Simone said.

"Have you looked at the size of her?"

"You don't like yourself, do you?" Angelene said.

Brendon's breath hitched in his throat. He stared from Angelene to Victoria's gaping mouth.

"You're a jealous, bitter woman. You are friends with Sofia because you think it makes you look important. You're ordinary, your children are ordinary, your husband is nothing more than a paper pusher. It kills you to be ordinary."

Brendon raised his eyebrows at the fire on Angelene's face. Who was this girl?

"You amuse me. You know little about me and yet, you have the most to say."

"Are you listening to this, Simone? I'm not ordinary."

"Shoes, Victoria."

"You might fool Walter, but I know you're just a poor girl from the slums of Paris. Play dress-up all you like; you will never be one of us," Victoria said.

Angelene crossed herself and touched her necklace. "I struggle daily with my demons. Being part of your circle would only make me suffer more. I hope you find a pair of shoes you like."

Victoria gasped. She looped her arm through Simone's and dragged her out the door.

Brendon watched Victoria clomp down the pavement with Simone in tow, unglued his feet and slid across the bench.

"Bloody hell, Angelene. You should be like that all the time. Walter wouldn't stand a chance."

"I'm only like this after I've drunk myself into a stupor. Once the alcohol wears off, I return to the trembling mess, you know." Angelene grabbed her purse and the brown paper bag. "I'm going to call Malcolm and have him take me home. My head hurts. I need quiet."

"We could sit outside for a bit."

"You're late for school."

"I'm already in bloody trouble. I should have been in the headmaster's office fifteen minutes ago."

Angelene moaned, the bag crinkled in her hand. "I want out of these uncomfortable clothes and shoes. I want to sit in the window and read my book. Forget about things."

"My head is all mixed up, too. Can't we be there for each other? One more day?"

Her eyes were wintry and far away.

"I'll be the perfect gentleman."

"I don't think you know how to be a gentleman anymore. Padre Diavolo is having fun scratching out your brown."

Brendon placed thirty pounds on the table, finished his cold coffee, and followed Angelene to the door. He glanced up and down the street, pulling up the collar of his blazer. A crisp wind ruffled his hair. The sky was blue and grey, wisps of clouds had smoothed into sheets. The day had been long and tiring. He needed quiet, her quiet.

"We can sit over there."

He pointed to a park bench hidden at the end of a cobblestone path. They waited for cars to pass, then walked swiftly to the bench, collapsing in unison.

"Where are we?"

"Bath Place. This street dates to the Middle Ages. It used to be the main road to get to Taunton from Exeter."

"I wish there were peacocks and flowers like Parc Floral."

"Would you like to be home?"

"Very much."

Brendon shrugged off his blazer and wrapped it around her shoulders.

"What are you doing?"

"Being a gentleman."

Angelene glanced at him. Her grin was frigid. "Will you do something for me?"

"If you want me to hold your hand, the answer is no. I only did it earlier so you wouldn't fall."

She unfolded the crinkled seam and slid the book out like a delicate piece of art. "Will you read to me?"

"You're bloody joking, right?"

She slid across the bench, dropped the book in his lap, and wiggled under his arm.

"I'm only cuddling because the fabric is thin and I'm cold."

"I feel bloody stupid."

"You'll like the story."

He grinned at the illustration of a mother rabbit kissing a little bunny. A re-do. If he had done what he promised and paid attention to the tutor, he'd be in Dortmund. Angelene wouldn't have existed until he came home at Christmas. By then, she would have loved Walter. Leaves scuttled through the air, the wind carried the fragrance of her hair, sadness fell heavily on Brendon's shoulders. He lost the girl he never had again.

Brendon crept silently across the foyer. Something followed behind him, pressed up against him and sucked the air from his lungs. The stairs were only steps away. He could run from whatever it was, escape to his bedroom and hide away.

"Are you trying to give me a nervous breakdown?"

Brendon gripped the banister, frozen.

"I felt like I could barf all day."

"You should have sat with a bucket at your feet," Sofia said.

He knew by the flicker in her dark eyes, hands glued to her hips, a kiss and a compliment wouldn't work. He reverted to the big, brown-eyed, 'I'm still your baby' look.

"I'm sorry. I'll go to all my classes tomorrow."

"What were you doing with Angelene?"

"I wasn't with Ms. Pratt."

"Don't lie to me. Victoria rang. She saw Angelene at that diner. She saw your car."

His heartbeat echoed in his ears. He had to think fast.

"It was a girl from school."

"I know in my gut you were with her. Ever since she arrived, nothing has been the same."

"Stop being so dramatic."

He opened his arms and stepped towards her; a hug always worked. She would forget how angry she was, tell him she loved him. Sofia recoiled and flicked her bangles.

"It'll be all over the damn town. I told you to stay away."

Sparks lit, pulsed, and whirred. *'How could I have been so stupid and not hid my car.'* He couldn't get a deep enough breath. The thing, the shadow, the feeling had suffocated him.

"If you were with Angelene, I will…"

"Will what? Shut me in the house. You've been doing that since I was a kid," he said, tearing loose his tie. "I ran into Angelene. Happy now?"

"She's a married woman. What will people think?"

"That I'm a fuck-up like dad says."

Sparks circled and spiralled. He curled his hands around the straps of his backpack, angled it behind his head and whipped it towards the den. If he were on the pitch, it would have been the perfect throw-in.

"It drives you crazy that you have no control over me."

"Until you walk out that door, you'll do as I say."

"Do you know what it's like at school? Everyone is on Maggie's side or Rachel's. All I'm getting is bloody aggro."

"From what you told me last night, I don't blame Maggie or Rachel for being upset. You thought you had aggro at school, you're about to experience some aggro."

"I think you both need to calm down," Nicola said, strolling into the foyer. "Amelia put coffee on. We can sit and talk civilly."

"Stay out of this, mother."

Nicola raised her chin and smoothed Brendon's lapels. "Breathe topolino. We don't need any of Sofia's precious antiques flying around."

"It was breakfast, that's it. Ms. McGregor has embellished the story to piss mum off."

"I know, topolino, why would you be running all over Taunton with Angelene."

"Stop fussing over him," Sofia said.

Brendon closed his eyes and imagined bombs decimating the sparks. Mammina was angry disappointed. If she were just angry, she would stand tall like a soldier, flap her hands around, reprimand him in Italian. She would yell for a bit, then unfreeze and apologize for her outburst. When her shoulders slouched and sighs spewed from her mouth, he knew she was disappointed. Angry disappointed was a whole new level of emotion. She would stand in a commanding position, letting him know she ruled the house and him. Angry was easy to deal with. He had survived disappointment on its own. Angry disappointment meant he was going to war.

"Gattina, you're letting Victoria get to you. I'm sure there's an explanation."

"I'm bloody hungover. It's as simple as that."

Sofia's eyes were cold, barren black. She sagged into the banister and folded her arms over her chest. "You've been suspended."

A sharp stab pummelled Brendon's stomach. He had bunked off school to spend time with a woman who had hurled insults at him and exposed another devil, stronger and more powerful than his. Now he was paying the price.

"You're joking? Did you call Liam?"

He knew by the look in her eyes and the 'I'm trying to keep it together,' stance she had made a decision that would cripple him. The room blurred, sparks burned his belly, he was past infuriated.

"You'll sit out both matches, which isn't a punishment considering you received a red card at the last match."

"What if I do nothing but school work? Can I play then?"

"I had to leave the auction to meet Mr. Dawson. Do you have any idea what it was like listening to the shit spewing from people's mouths? Somebody bet 50p I would tear Mr. Dawson a new one. Someone else bet two pounds he would get an erection. I was embarrassed. Thank goodness Troy was there to help me."

"He is your little meatball."

"He's a good boy, a nice boy, like you used to be. Now get your rucky and sit your ass down at your father's desk."

"You've fucked everything up for the team."

"Chi cazzo credi di essere. Do you remember who you are talking to?"

Sofia strummed her bracelets. She was buckling. It was time to strike, plea, put the blame on someone else.

"Ms. Pratt looked upset. I couldn't leave her. It's in the code."

"There was nothing sad about Angelene, she was hung..." Sofia stared at Nicola, her eyes wide, "she was hungover and nasty, as nasty as you. Were you at the pub last night?"

"Unfuckingbelievable. I was at Will's. Can this day get any worse?"

"I phoned your father." "It just got worse."

Brendon barged across the foyer, snatched his backpack, and tossed it into the den.

"Am I missing training, too?"

"I'll drive you and wait."

"Are you fucking kidding?"

"I told you to stay away from Angelene. You give her a shoulder to cry on any chance you get."

"This is fucking ridiculous."

Brendon slumped onto the wingback. His heart wanted to run to Angelene, his brain wished Walter would ship her back to Paris. He was an idiot to fall for her. The front door banged open. He dropped his chin and braced himself for the calm 'I'm so disappointed in you' lecture.

"I'm sorry, dad. I had a bloody awful day." "You can't even look at me. You expect me to believe you're sorry?"

Brendon lifted his gaze; his father was angry disappointed too.

David tossed a note on the desk and shrugged off his suit jacket. "Tell me the first amount you see."

"7,690 pounds."

"Do you know what that is?"

"One terms tuition. The second amount is six terms' worth."

David grabbed the armrests of the wingback, jerking it from its home by the fireplace. He thumped it on the parquet. It banged the leg of the desk, rattling Brendon, and the picture frames.

"Dortmund wanted me when I was sixteen. I could have saved you money."

"I understand you got another red card. I hope it was just your mouth this time and not your fists. If you continue to make poor choices. Dortmund won't want you either."

"There was a write-up in BILD about me replacing the keeper if he signs with Bayern Munich."

"At the rate you're going, I'll be surprised if Liam wants you."

"For fuck's sake, you'd think I committed murder."

David pounded his fists against the desk. The frames bounced and toppled over; the cup of pens spilled across the desk.

"Stop with the language. Stop drinking, stop using girls."

Brendon had never seen this side of his father. He had a devil looming in him, too.

"It's one girl."

"I don't care if it's one or thirty. Keep your trousers on and buckle down."

"Football is the only thing that keeps me from losing my bloody mind. Now I can't play."

"Football is a privilege."

Brendon shuddered; he was no longer staring at respectable David Cook. All the years, he had heard his grandfather complain and belittle him, welled inside him. He too had scars criss-crossing through his heart and mind. Richard wasn't dead, he was staring at him.

"You'll finish your Latin and history homework tonight, then you can get your ass to bed." David yanked down his suspenders, picked up the armchair. It landed with a clunk.

"You never wanted me." Brendon was dizzy, the room clouded around him. "It didn't work out for you, did it? Mum saw to that. I'm not the only one who has trouble keeping promises."

***

Maggie glanced around the charity shop with lit eyes. There was history among the lamps, dishes, and knickknacks. She held up a curtain rod. In her mind, it was a staff. She was a priestess, ready to lead a troupe on an adventure.

"Look what I found." Michael said, stabbing the air with a sword.

"Put that down before you hurt yourself."

"There's a bunch of stuff, crowns, robes. It's from the old theatre company."

Maggie shook out a bundle of purple velvet, crinkling her nose at the plume of musty air. "Queen Gertrude would wear a gown like this."

"Not those mini dresses Charlotte wears."

"Ms. Baxter will be chuffed. Every play is like a Hollywood production," Maggie said, placing a crown on her head. "She turns into a nutter if the props and costumes aren't perfect."

Maggie plunked an armload of dusty cloaks and dresses by the register. She set the crown on top and collected the receipt.

"I'm hungry," Michael said, grabbing the shopping bags. "I feel like a slice of Battenburg. Would you like a cappuccino?"

"With a swirl of caramel, please." She pushed open the door and chomped into her bottom lip. "Brendon wasn't in history class."

"Didn't you hear? Maisie McGregor was coming out of High Street Market and saw his car."

"Lots of people drive BMWs."

"Not with the license plate BVB1. Maisie said he was with a girl."

Maggie swallowed the lump in her throat and fiddled with her ring. She wanted to be angry. She had tried since the break-up to yell, tear up his pictures, walk past him in the hall at school with her nose in the air. She couldn't get past the pain.

"Did Maisie see the girl?"

"There were all sorts of bets at dinner break."

Michael opened the door; the air became rich with the scents of coffee and caramel. Maggie's eyes stung. She twisted off the ring and tossed it. The ring travelled along the pavement and dropped into the gutter.

"Why are you crying? He's not worth it."

"Was the girl blonde? Brendon likes blondes."

"Who cares if she's blonde, brunette, Dutch, Swedish, or from Wales. Brendon Cook is a tosser."

26 TWO PEAS IN A POD

"Do you think she was French?"

"She could be from Liverpool or Cardiff."

Maggie looked at her finger. A white line circled her skin where the ring had once been. She had been so happy the day Brendon gave her the ring. Margaret Thornton, the girl who hid in the library and had only been somebody because her best friend was dating a First player, wore a ring from Taunton's hero.

"Have you ever met Walter Pratt's wife?"

"I've only lived in Taunton for three years." Michael grabbed a napkin from his pocket and passed it to Maggie. "I know of Walter Pratt. He's our Secretary of Defence."

"His wife is French and blonde."

"You think Brendon is sneaking around with Pratt's wife? He was in the Special Boat Service."

Maggie dabbed at her eyes and blew her nose. "It was stupid of me to think that."

Maggie recalled the day Charlotte had almost run over Angelene. Angelene had a look in her eyes, like someone who had a taste of something forbidden and was dying for more.

"I know what will make you feel better."

Maggie tucked the thought away. Something about Michael caught her attention, the intelligence, his confidence. She liked how his sky-blue eyes had darker flecks of blue. Give him a Shakespeare play, he could recite a soliloquy. She wouldn't have to worry about other girls flirting with him.

"Nothing will make me feel better."

"Not even Zeffirelli's Romeo and Juliet? It's playing at the Brewhouse."

"I wouldn't be much fun." "I'm willing to take the chance," Michael said, breaking off a piece of cake. "I'll pick you up tomorrow, half-past five. We'll go to that pub on James Street near the cricket club. They have brilliant burgers."

"Brendon's Nonna said a delicious meal is the best medicine when you're gutted."

"I have one rule, no talking about Brendon."

"By the prickling of my thumbs, something wicked this way comes."

"Wrong play Maggie. We're rehearsing Hamlet, not Macbeth."

"Have you ever got the feeling something awful is going to happen?"

"Before every production. I'm afraid I'll forget my lines."

Maggie stared at the empty spot on her finger. Angelene looked like the faithful wife. She looked fragile, harmless, and 'always guilty.'

***

Angelene lifted her weary body off the stool. The plate of eggs and bacon had not cured her hangover. It had given her heartburn. The best cure for a hangover, a glass of wine. She unscrewed the cap and filled her glass.

'Thank you for buying me breakfast and reading to me, but the pattern grew like a tumour, wrapping its tentacles around my heart and lungs, suffocating me.'

Angelene finished the glass, tugged at the hem of her t-shirt, and cleared her throat, summoning the strength and confidence she had when confronting Victoria McGregor. She reached for her phone, recited the speech, her finger hovered over Brendon's number. Her phone vibrated in her hand, Rosewood manor.

'Go away, My Lucifer, he who shuns the light.'
"Bonjour, je suis très occupé."
"Stay away from my grandson."

The words glowed like a fireplace poker, hot from the coals. Angelene dropped her phone. Her scars were vivid and loud. She grabbed the bottle and chugged until she gagged and gasped. Numbness tingled her limbs, she flicked the lighter and inhaled, acrid smoke coated her lungs. Her life had been a series of warnings. Stay away, keep hidden or else, protect your light, finger wags, hands on the throat, pushed to her knees to pray. This warning, while abrasive and full of demand, was different. Nicola's fierce crimson light merged with sorrowful blue. Angelene pressed the cigarette against her wrist. The stink of charcoal and sulphur filled her nose.

Hold my hand little bird, I don't like when you hurt yourself, hold my hand as tight as you can.

What will I do when you're not here, Roman?

Imagine my hand in yours. I'll be there with you, little bird.

Angelene closed her eyes and held his hand.

27 Down the Rabbit Hole

Golden light shone through the white eyelet curtains, casting a lacy pattern over the walnut tabletop. Walter watched the early risers take in the glorious morning on Rue Neuve Popincourt. Which Angelene would he get when he arrived home? Sombre Angelene, childlike Angelene or irate Angelene. The guessing game was exhausting.

"Bonjour Monsieur Pratt."

"Bonjour, where is your daughter? I have something for her."

"Yasmine is with her new friends," Lisette said.

Walter set bags of sweets on the table and smiled. "You like your new apartment."

Lisette met his gaze with untrusting eyes. "It was very generous of you. The building is clean. The landlords are wonderful. A fresh start for Yasmine and me, just like my friend."

"You and Yasmine are special to Ang. It was the least I could do after stealing her away." Walter slid a menu across the table. "Hungry? Angelene loved the granola chocolate."

"Angelene and her sweet things. It was hard for her to keep her hands off them."

"Is having a sweet tooth so terrible?"

"I'm a pastry chef. I adore sweets. Angelene had a, it doesn't matter," Lisette said. "Why did you want to see me?"

"How long did you know Angelene?" Walter said, sliding his knife through the tartine avocat.

"For years. She was kind to me and my husband," Lisette said, fiddling with a button on her sweater. "She loved Yasmine, the best Angelene can love anyone. I had to force Yasmine into her arms. She was afraid of breaking her."

"Did she have many lovers?"

The question fell from his mouth like one would ask about the weather.

"Angelene's relationships were none of my business."

"You were her friend. Friends talk. Angelene keeps quiet about her past."

"And so she should. She's had a tough life."

Walter set down his fork and knife, wiping his mouth with a napkin. "One minute she's happy, the next, she's running away, hiding in the closet, the tub, behind a bottle of wine."

"Angelene never learned to cope healthily."

"Did you know her mother?"

"Only stories. Angelene was alone when we moved into the building."

"Who was paying her rent?"

Lisette clicked her fingernails on the table and sighed. "You need to ask Angelene these questions."

"How does a child survive on their own?"

"I know the stories and never asked." Lisette's face softened. She stopped tapping her fingernails. "A gentleman from Switzerland, I think. The building was swarming with rumours."

"She doesn't sleep. She'll lay with me for an hour then the pacing starts, shuffle, shuffle, that's all I hear."

Lisette's steely slate eyes warmed. "She went for walks when she couldn't sleep. I used to tell her it wasn't safe wandering the streets late at night. She never listened."

"Did you ever meet Pierre Piedmont?"

Lisette laughed. It rose from her belly, shaking her petite frame. "Yasmine and I used to call him Le Vampire. He only visited at night. I guess when you're married, you have no choice but to sneak around."

"I ran into him before Angelene, and I left for Taunton. He was a meek, old man."

"You never saw him behind a lectern. He could command a room, like you, Mr. Pratt." She waved her fingers at the waiter, smiled politely, and pointed to Walter's cup. "A lot has happened to Monsieur Piedmont. Some he deserved and some he didn't."

"Were there other men?"

He tried his crinkly smile. It always worked on women.

"A few. Like I said, it's not for me to speak about."

"I don't impress you, do I?" Walter said, passing the server his cup, "Merci."

"I don't trust you. You sweep in to Paris in your fancy suit and flashy watch, whisk Angelene off to your pretty house with no idea who she is," Lisette said, dropping a sugar cube in her coffee, "she's damaged and no amount of money or expensive clothes will fix her."

"Angelene will adjust. She'll fall in love with the lifestyle I've given her and forget all about her past."

"Fall in love with a lifestyle or you? You don't love her, do you?"

"She intrigued me. There's something…"

"There's something about her." Lisette blew into her coffee and laughed. "Is that what you were going to say? I've heard this before."

"You find it funny?"

"Every man who walked through her door said the same thing."

Walter pressed his fork against a slice of avocado. The first time he had seen Angelene, she was sitting on the park bench reading Hugo's Les Misérables. She was wet from an early morning rain, her sandal straps broken. She was unique, unique was attractive.

"What was it that drew you to Angelene?"

"I saw a girl starving for affection. She needed family and love," Lisette said, taking a small sip. "I didn't like the choices she made, but I couldn't turn my back on her. She tried hard to love, it pained her to feel it."

"You pity her?"

"Sometimes. There is a good side to Angelene. You must scrape the ugly parts away to find it."

"Has she made a lot of bad choices?" Walter said, scooping up a forkful of goat cheese and tomatoes.

"Hopefully, I'm not looking at one," Lisette said. "Do you know why Angelene loves being Catholic?" He never understood why anyone relied on religion. Life was up to him, not a spirit in the sky.

"You can sleep with a married man, then go sit in a pretty box. God will forgive you."

"God has nothing to do with the choices she's made."

"No but, isn't it nice someone will listen and forgive."

"She doesn't talk about things. How can I help her?"

"Does she trust you?"

"She married me."

Lisette sighed and sipped her coffee. "That wasn't the question. She won't talk until she trusts you. Until then, be patient."

Patience was coming in small doses.

"My friend David told me the same thing. It's hard sometimes, patience."

"I wanted to shake her a few times. I just remind myself she needs love."

"Does she know how to love?"

"She gets extremely uncomfortable when someone shows her love. She once told me her insides wiggle, and she gets squirmy. I remember falling in love with my husband. I felt this fluttery feeling. It made me smile, not sick. She's damaged. Damaged people find it hard to love and receive love."

The only thing Walter had seen Angelene show affection to was books, feathers, and the Hugo statue. Never anything that could love her back.

"I have a question for you," Lisette said.

"I'm listening."

"Does David have a son?"

Walter's ears perked up. "He turned eighteen in August, local footy star. He'll be off to Germany in July to play for Borussia Dortmund."

"I don't follow football."

"You should. The kid will be a star."

"He's talented?"

"The kiddie league coach wanted to start him as a centre forward because of his height and how well he brought the squad into the play. Brendon looked at the coach and said, 'I'm a keeper.' He was five."

"Would you say he's gifted?"

"I would. So would the Sporting Director in Dortmund, my friend Lukas, the fans."

"Does Angelene spend time with him?"

"He can't get ten feet away from his mother without her tugging him back. She would have no reason to. Why do you ask?"

"Angelene lives her life in patterns, always tripping and falling into them. This boy sounds special. Does he have incredible light?"

"You're sounding as strange as my wife. He has talent and passion, if that's what you mean but, no reason to befriend Ang."

"Please take care of my friend."

Walter slid thirty euros under the receipt and tried his crinkly smile again. "You should see her. A new hairstyle, beautiful clothes." "Those are just things."

"I'm doing my best to see she gets everything she needs. She's my biggest project to date, exhausting, but you should see the transformation."

"Connard!"

"Some would call me an asshole. I'm taking good care of your friend."

"I'm not so sure. What makes you different from the others?"

"I wasn't married when we met. What's wrong with wanting to turn her into Cinderella? She deserves it."

"I suppose," Lisette said, gathering her purse, "is there anything else?"

"These lovers Ang had, how many are a few? There's been talk, she's a certain kind of woman."

Lisette chuckled. "Are you asking me if she's a slut? You have to enjoy sex."

"She has a problem in the bedroom."

"I'm not a counsellor. Talk to your wife."

"Should I be concerned about these patterns, magical light?"

"She's the kind of girl that sticks in your mind and you want her forever. You can beg, plead, buy her expensive things, but there is no guarantee she'll stick around. There are years of damage to fix."

"I'm up for the challenge."

"I hope you are prepared."

Walter held open the door. The sun warmed his face. "Thank you for meeting me. I appreciate the insight."

"She drinks, smokes, wallows. Show her love and if she tries to run, stop her."

Walter had learned nothing new about Angelene. She was still an enigma, a puzzle with missing pieces. *'I hope I can find them.'*

***

"Aren't you knackered after all that shopping?" Maggie said. She glanced from her purchase of pink pens and an agenda for second term to the plethora of bags in Charlotte's hands.

Charlotte melted into the chair, dropping the bags at her feet. "Trying on clothes is very exhausting."

"Watching you try on clothes is just as tiring."

"Cheeky cow. Babes has a football trial soon. How I look is important."

"I'm sure the coaching team will decide based on your outfit."

Charlotte plucked a pepperoni swimming in a pool of grease and popped it into her mouth. "Have you ever seen Victoria Beckham look unfashionable?"

"She looks like a mindless twit," Maggie said, sliding a slice onto a paper plate, "just the type of girl Brendon will marry."

"I'm not saying a thing. It's my turn to be Switzerland," Charlotte said, slurping her soda. "I feel sorry for Brendon. Everyone at school thinks he's a dolt. William cheated too, and no one is going at him."

"They expect it from William," Maggie said. "You need to feel sorry for me. I'm the one walking around full of regrets."

"I thought regrets were life lessons?"

"I've been swimming in regrets; it's driving me bonkers."

"How was your date with Michael?"

Maggie stretched a string of cheese, twirling it around her finger. "He was either nervous or excited because one minute he was talking about the play, then he started telling me about his sister, then the last movie he saw. I couldn't keep up."

"My first date with babes, he talked about Manchester United, his brothers, Lucy the chicken, and how his mum makes the best pie and chips. After the second date, he stopped acting like a dolt."

Maggie wiped the grease from her finger and rested her chin on her hand. "I'm not sure I want a second date."

"Don't write him off because he talked about silly things. He could be your soul mate."

Maggie picked up the crust and took a tiny bite. "I thought I found my soul mate."

"Do you regret going out with Michael?"

"I like him. We have lots in common. Mum was chuffed when she met him."

"I think you feel guilty admitting you had a fun time."

"Is that so Dr. Donovan-Spence?"

Charlotte folded the slice in half and flapped it at Maggie. "I've dropped the Donovan. I've been practicing writing my signature and Charlotte Donovan-Spence is much too long."

Maggie giggled into her Ribena. "People think I'm a nutter."

"You always say life is about lessons. What did you learn from your date with Michael?"

"I still love Brendon. While Michael talked about a Netflix series, all I thought about was the Bundesliga standings. I missed listening to Brendon talk about keepers and save percentages. If I could go back in time, I wouldn't have agreed to see Romeo and Juliet."

Charlotte grabbed another slice, her mouth dropped open. "Your ring. I hadn't noticed."

"That's because you're always groping Troy," Maggie said, wiggling her finger. "Regret number two."

"If you regret taking it off, put it back on."

"I can't. I was so upset about Brendon being with a girl, I threw it away. It rolled right down the pavement and into the storm drain."

"What did you learn from that?"

"Think about things before I do something daft. My finger feels empty now."

"Did you snog Michael?"

"It never crossed my mind."

Charlotte pointed to the last slice of pizza.

"Go on. I don't know where you put all this food you eat. I've gained five pounds already." Maggie said, twirling a strand of hair around her finger.

"I burn calories by snogging babes. If I kiss him for an hour, that's 180 calories," Charlotte said, placing a stray olive on the slice. "What else is bothering you?"

"Not fighting for the relationship."

"You can't fight for something the other person doesn't want."

"Brendon and I were supposed to go to Milan in July. Mum was against it. I told her to bugger off. I should have been like that with Brendon. Put my foot down and said we aren't breaking up."

"You still might get to Milan. He just needs some space to figure things out."

"Something's up with him. Even the tart is upset. Did you know Gemma won ten quid for being closest to the number of times, he parked under the willow tree and did that."

"Someone was keeping track?"

"The gum chewing tart. Tilly would find me in the toilets and announce that's number five, number six just happened."

"Why's Rachel pissed off? She should be happy. She got what she wanted."

"Bets around school are Brendon was just using her."

"That's why she's angry? Every boy she's been with was using her."

Maggie uncurled her hair from her finger and chomped into her lip. "Isn't it obvious? She fancies him."

"Now that I think about it, she hasn't moved onto number two or four or ten. She's been stuck on number one. Who knew the queen slag had a heart." Charlotte pressed a napkin to her mouth and belched.

"Gosh, not very ladylike."

"You should eat at babes. It's like a symphony at the dinner table."

The smile left Maggie's face. "I'm worried about Brendon. He was cruel the day he broke up with me. That wasn't Brendon."

"It was guilt."

"There's something inside him, Charlie, something dark, like his eyes. They're dark all the time now."

"Stop staring at him then."

Maggie hitched her purse over her arm, collected her shopping bag, looping her arm through Charlotte's. "I feel like the coulda, shoulda, woulda's has hijacked me."

"Go out with Michael again."

"He texted and asked if I wanted to go to the Odeon tonight."

"Go. Sit in the back row and snog. Babes and I do it all the time."

"You would tell me if you knew something?"

"There isn't anything to tell," Charlotte said, clicking open the car. "Brendon did a terrible thing, I'm sure he has lots of regrets too and one of those regrets may lead him right back to you."

Maggie wanted to believe the love she shared with Brendon was forever. She knew relationships took work. No one, not even Charlotte and Troy, got it right. There were difficulties, regrets. Maggie had three and a bunch of what ifs with them.

***

Wind whipped the leaves, flicked them against the window and spun them back into the sombre sky. Brendon stared at his bowl of fruit. His heart was as heavy as the clouds, and it angered him. He wasn't supposed to be sad about her.

"Can you please eat something," Sofia said.

"I'm not hungry." "Give it here," Nicola said, "you used to like when I drizzled your melon with amaretto. You thought you were being naughty." Brendon slid the bowl down the table and sagged into the chair. "I was five." "You're acting five now," David said. "Get that risotto into you."

Brendon sighed heavily, dragging his spoon through the mushroom and parmesan scented rice.

"Take a bite, sweetheart."

"This is damn ridiculous." David said, snapping open the newspaper.

"I'll make some brodo di pollo," Nicola said.

"You've done enough Nicola. The two of you have done nothing but cater to him. Eat."

Brendon jumped at David's command and shoved a spoonful into his mouth.

"What time will Troy be here, sweetheart?"

Brendon ran his fork through the rice and stabbed a mushroom. "Soon."

"You best get that into you," David said from behind the newspaper. "You have until one o'clock. I expect you to pay attention."

"Can't you call the teacher Mr. Dawson suggested?" Brendon scrunched his nose and swallowed another bite. "Troy said Miss Kent is good."

Sofia grinned. He was unsure if it was 'yes, I heard she's an excellent teacher,' or an 'I know all about that girl,' grin.

"That's Dennis and Tabitha Kent's daughter. You remember Dennis, don't you, darling?" Sofia said, tipping coffee into her cup, "he was headteacher at the community school on School Road. He came to the gala last year in that hideous brown suit."

"How could I forget? He looked like a drunk ape on the dance floor."

"I know why Troy would recommend Teagan Kent. She's all hair and boobs."

"Walter thinks this will be good for Angelene and I agree," David said.

Brendon glanced over a spoonful of risotto; his mother was clicking her bracelets; Nicola was bursting at the seams to speak.

"Buongiorno," Troy called.

Brendon washed down a bite of risotto with a swallow of water and tossed his napkin on the bowl.

"At least someone is happy," David said.

"We're happy, we're all happy," Sofia said.

"It's nice and quiet in here," Troy said, stealing a chunk of melon. "There's a wrestling match going on at mine. Callum tagged dad in. They've turned the sitting room upside down."

"What are you two planning on doing?" Sofia said.

"I want to see how many shots I'll get past this wanker."

"I read the write-up in the newspaper. It should get you some attention."

"Thanks Mr. C," Troy said, pouring coffee. He chugged and smiled. "Mum put it on the fridge, told me I was her favourite, the easiest of the four."

"You're a ray of sunshine, like someone I used to know," Sofia said.

Brendon jerked on his ball cap; Troy was Angelene's sunshine, too. Lunch sat like a lump in Brendon's belly. He tried to steal Troy's sunshine; it was hard to absorb. He walked past Sofia; she lay a hand on his chest.

"What are you doing?"

"Checking to see if you're still alive."

He shooed her hand away, snagging her glass of water. His mouth was dry and no matter how hard he tried to summon up his own sunshine, it wouldn't come.

"Put a jacket on, sweetheart. You're rather pale."

Click, click. Brendon placed his hand over Sofia's and kissed her cheek. He followed Troy to the foyer, searching for happy, joy. Annoyed and pissed off was all he got.

"You still have French tutoring?"

"There's no getting out of it."

They walked across the lawn; a gust of wind tousled the leaves. Troy pulled two stones from his pocket, dropped one, and walked precisely eight steps before dropping the other.

"That's your net, mate."

"Those stones?"

"Get over there. We'll see how rusty you are."

"I have pylons in my car."

Troy rolled the ball between his feet. "Concentrate mate. I'm coming straight down the middle."

Brendon glanced down the hill at the farmhouse. A chill ran up his spine. He reached for the ball.

"You almost missed that."

"I wasn't ready."

"You were staring off into space again, mate."

Brendon didn't know why he hurt so badly. He struggled with his lamp at bedtime, turning it off and then on. It was silly to love her again. She was brash, a drunk. She wasn't his to love.

"Does Charlie ever make you feel you've lost the plot?"

"I texted her this morning. It took forever for her to respond. I thought I forgot something special. I stewed into my brekky until she texted back," Troy said, dribbling the ball, "I'm going to put this in the left corner."

Brendon jumped to the right. "Nice try. Do you think about her all the time?"

"Sure. This one's coming right down the middle."

Brendon grinned; the ball sailed to the left. "You'll have to try harder than that."

"Are you falling in love with Rachel?"

Brendon rubbed the back of his neck, kicking the ball into the air. He hadn't thought about Rachel since the night at William's.

"Don't be daft."

"Bets around school are she pulls a Werther."

"Rachel will not commit suicide. I humped her and left, just like the rest of them."

"What is it then, mate? You give a whole new meaning to brooding," Troy said. "Pretend there's a bar over your head. I'm putting the ball there."

Brendon jumped and tipped the ball backwards over the imaginary crossbar. He couldn't really put a finger on what he was feeling. His emotions flipped, flopped, tangled, untied. At one moment, he hated her, the next he loved her and missed her.

"It's been an awful week. Between mum's coddling, dad's constant complaining, Will in net, it's a lot."

"Do you miss Maggie?"

He hadn't really thought about her either. Drunk Angelene, child Angelene, had been on his mind. Brendon stepped to the left, snagged the ball, and clutched it to his chest.

"You sure there isn't someone else? Sometimes you make the Charlie face. The kids are making lots of bets."

"What now?"

"Maisie McGregor said she saw you with a girl."

"The McGregors always have something to say."

"It is true?"

Brendon racked his brain. It couldn't be anyone at school or someone who frequented the pitch. They couldn't be available for questioning.

"You remember those girls at the match a few weeks back? They held up a sign that spelled Cook."

"The stands are usually full of girls."

"She was blonde, held up the C."

"I know better than to gawk when Charlie's at a match. She catches me, holds up her fingers, pinching the air."

"I bumped into the girl. We had coffee. I don't know why people care so much."

Troy tossed the ball into the air and bumped it with his head. "People got to talk about something."

Brendon looked at the farmhouse, sparks flared and fizzled.

"One coffee and you can't stop thinking about her. She must be something."

"The conversation was great, I thought, bloody hell, I don't know what I thought."

Fat splotches of rain fell on Brendon's face. He was hurting; he wanted to be angry.

"You alright, mate?"

Brendon forced a smile and stole the ball from between Troy's feet.

"I'll be fine. Try to get the ball away from me."

"Did you not see me yesterday? I was brilliant, mate."

Brendon wasn't sure he would be fine. Between feeling angry and hurt, he didn't know if fine existed.

Brendon waved goodbye to Troy and stepped into the foyer, drenched. He slid off his wet trainers and ran his t-shirt over his face. From within the great room, he could hear Sofia talking about how they had turned his world upside down. He quietly walked across the foyer and leaned into the wall.

"I can't remember the last time I told Brendon I loved him."

'Neither can I, dad.'

"That was my job to smother him with affection."

"When was the last time I congratulated him on a good mark?"

"He hasn't had a grade worth celebrating."

Brendon pinched his lips together. When he got a decent mark, it had never been good enough.

"He brings out the worst in me, Sofia."

"You're nothing like Richard."

"Nine years was not long enough; it wasn't enough time."

"Stop beating yourself up. Brendon deserved to be punished."

"Not the way my father would have lashed out at me."

"Everyone regrets a time when they overreacted. I'm going to put tea on. Angelene will be here any minute."

Brendon pushed away from the wall and walked towards the stairs.

"Sweetheart, you're soaking wet."

He took off his ball cap and peeled away his t-shirt. Goosebumps travelled over his arms and chest.

"You're shivering. What were you and Troy thinking?"

"It's the only fun I've had."

He ran his t-shirt over his neck and started up the stairs.

"I'll bring you a cup of tea and some brodo."

"I don't need soup. Bloody hell, I'm wet, not sick."

He walked down the hall and stripped off his clothes. Exhaustion hung over him like an iron blanket. The doorbell rang. He told himself to keep his eyes on his notebook. It was French lessons, nothing more. He didn't know where his emotions would lead him, angry, sad, annoyed. Cold sunk into his bones. The Dortmund hoodie brought no comfort. He repeated his new mantra, *'she isn't my friend, fuck the pattern'* and trudged down the stairs. He stared into the den, saw her windblown hair, fidgeting fingers, and froze.

"Sweetheart, Angelene is waiting," Sofia said, resting her hand on his forehead. "You're very pale."

"Does she have to be my tutor?"

Sofia held his cheek. He leaned into the warmth of her hand.

"We talked about this."

"Talk to dad, please."

Sofia stepped closer and whispered. "I don't like this anymore than you do. Your father and Walter think this will help build Angelene's confidence."

Brendon took hold of her hand. His chest rose and fell in quick bursts. His mantra had failed.

"I can't mammina."

"What's the matter? I can feel your heart racing."

"I don't think I can concentrate."

"It's two hours, sweetheart. Afterwards, you can crawl into bed and watch all the football you want."

The blazing fire brought no comfort to the room or Brendon. He dropped onto the chair, breathed in patchouli and lavender. The scent enchanted him, ignited the sparks. Why couldn't she be the monster he had run into at the pub?

"I'm sorry."

"For what?"

"I don't mean to make you angry."

"I'm glad we got that out of the way. Can we get to the French homework?"

He took a small sip of tea. The fear that had frozen him switched to anger.

"I adore you. You've been a good friend."

"Stop with all the bloody compliments. Just stop."

"I wish I could be your friend. I've tried before, and it fell apart in a way I can't even bring myself to talk about."

"I don't want to be your bloody friend."

"I'm a wife."

"You should have acted like one from the beginning."

She looked beautiful, smelled lovely. The kiss, the moments that stole his breath, crashed around him. He had been stupid to believe her words and even dumber to think she'd run off to Dortmund with him.

"We better start. Mum will wonder what we've been doing."

An incredible ache throbbed in his temples. They had been vulnerable with each other, shared their frustrations. He had become her shelter. She had crawled inside him and made a home.

"Bonjour ca va bien?"

Brendon raked his fingers aggressively through his hair. He couldn't focus. The expressions were on chart paper at the front of the classroom. Madame Lafavre titled it greetings; the sun had faded the red marker and yellowed the paper.

"Je vais bien."

He was okay.

"Page cinq."

Brendon flipped through the textbook and tapped his pen. The assignment was to translate it into English. It could have been Japanese; it made no sense.

"Comprenez-vous?"

She rolled the chair closer, her sweater gaped, exposing the hollow between her breasts.

"Move away." He stared at her with cold, black eyes. "Do you have any idea what you do to me?"

Angelene shrunk into the chair. Her face spoke volumes. Something told Brendon she had heard these words before.

"Do you understand?"

"Do you fucking understand?"

"Je viens de Paris, now you."

"Je viens de Taunton, I come from fucking Taunton."

"Ou se trouve la station de métro la plus proche."

Brendon propped his elbow on the desk and placed his forehead on his palm.

"Ou se means what."

"I don't bloody know." He rubbed the aching pulse and tossed the pen across the desk. "I asked you to move away. I can't bloody think when you're this close to me. Don't you own a fucking bra!"

"Don't be like this. I don't like when you're dark," Angelene said, grabbing the pen and placing it in his hand. "The sooner we finish, the sooner you're rid of me."

"Where is, ou se is where is, bloody happy now?"

"No, I'm not happy. I'm not yellow, I'm a terrible shade of blue." She pushed and plucked at her knuckles; her gaze darted nervously around the den. "Normal feels okay for now. Okay is not good enough. Please finish the sentences." The ache crept down Brendon's neck and into his bones. Every part of him hurt. He told himself not to care, she could figure out married life and normal without him.

"Walter met with Lisette. He didn't say what they spoke about, just that he needs to sort through things. He isn't coming home tonight."

"I'm not listening to you."

The phone jangled. He heard Sofia's voice and the click of her heels on the marble. Angelene jolted the chair back, adjusting the collar of her sweater.

"Fucking unbelievable."

"Angelene, Walter is on the phone. You can take it in the kitchen," Sofia said, "sweetheart, you're flushed."

Brendon guzzled back the lukewarm tea and stared at his notebook. "I'm almost done."

He gripped the pen. Even after she left the room, her scent lingered, she lingered.

Sofia waltzed around the desk and buried her nose in his hair. "If I had listened to your father, I never would have had you."

"I'm tired mammina. I should have come in when it started to rain."

She lay her head against his and wrapped her arms around his broad shoulders. "Can I finish please."

He rustled through the pages to the glossary. Sofia placed her hand over his and held him tighter.

"Has something happened? Have you got into trouble?"

An explosion of memories burst through his mind, the kiss, the dance, lying next to her in his bed.

"Only bunking off school."

"Did you think Angelene looked guilty?"

"She always looks like that."

"You think?"

"From what I heard; she hasn't made the best choices. It's hard to forgive yourself when people keep reminding you of the things you've done wrong."

A yawn slipped from his mouth. He rubbed his tired eyes. Only four sentences to go.

"How do you know so much?"

"I haven't made the best choices lately. I know what it feels like." "I want you to finish and lie down."

He smiled, more to humour his mother than anything else. Quiet invaded the den. Madre Innocente demanded him to re-evaluate the decisions he had made. The thought of each one exhausted him further. He settled on the fact that he couldn't change what he had done. He would make better choices next time and stay away from Angelene.

***

The air was rich with the scent of baked gruyere, endive, and ham. The remains of one of Roman Krieger's favourite dishes, chicon au gratin, sat on the stove. She had lied when she said normal was okay. Normal had been like stuffing her feet into the red-soled shoes, uncomfortable.

"You said the fissures would let in light. It would be so bright; the pattern would explode. Your eyes were so blue that day."

Angelene thumbed through a pile of pictures torn from National Geographic. It had been a wonderful find. She could have as many as she wanted for five pounds. It broke her heart to see the yellow framed magazines collecting dust in the corner of the charity shop. She had spent over an hour flipping through each and selecting her favourites. She had plans for the pictures, bookmark pages of Tale of Two Cities.

Opening the book, Angelene stared at the inscription written on the inside cover, '*for my little bird.*' She turned to the first dog-eared page, sliding in a picture of an elephant and its calf.

"This quote explains self-sacrifice better than any. You got it right, Mr. Dickens. It is a far, far better thing I do, than I have ever done, it is a far, far better rest that

I go to than I have ever known. I have sacrificed my friendship with Brendon. It's a fitting quote."

Angelene turned to the next marked page, read the quote, and slid in a picture. She made her way through the book. Roman Krieger's message jumped from the page, '*this is my favourite little bird, always know you will be the last dream of my soul.*' She placed a picture of lovebirds into the spine of the book. Three hard clunks banged against the door. Her heart sputtered; three more sharp strikes reverberated off the walls. Angelene dropped the book, stuffed a cigarette in her mouth and took two quick puffs. It did nothing to please her lungs and steady her heart. Precise, authoritative raps filled the air. She pushed herself off the bench, dropped the cigarette in a cup of stale coffee, and crept to the door. Her hand trembled, her mouth pulled into a twitchy grin.

"Out walking?"

"I go for a stroll after dinner. I'll admit the view around my home is more interesting than the moors. Do you have a moment?" Nicola said.

"I was reading."

"You like books, don't you? Sofia said your favourite room in the manor is the library. The collection of books is impressive."

Angelene straggled behind Nicola, dragged out a stool and fell onto it.

"Books help me escape."

"You love football."

"Is that why you came? To discuss football?"

"You like watching Brendon play, don't you?"

Angelene slid her hands between her thighs. Nicola was watching her, taking in every twitch, every tremble. She dug her fingers into the denim and pinched.

"It's late. I must clean the kitchen and put the laundry away."

"Do you consider 7:30 late?" Nicola said, thumbing through a National Geographic, "I told you to stay away from Brendon and I mean that in all ways, physically, emotionally."

Angelene dug deeper into her thighs.

"Do you feel about Brendon the same way you felt about Mr. Piedmont?"

"Pierre?"

Angelene commanded Veronique's brash outbursts to rise from her scarred brain and heart. They wouldn't surface.

"Not him, his son."

"I only met him briefly. It was at the Hugo statue, he commented on my drawing."

"Henri Piedmont was studying to be an architect. He was talented beyond his years, like Brendon."

"I was his father's mistress. Why would I have anything to do with Henri Piedmont."

"Did you like him?"

Angelene bit into her lip. "He showed me a blueprint. The lines, arches, and rectangles impressed me. Everything came together to form a beautiful cathedral."

"That was it? He created a blueprint?" Nicola said.

Angelene sunk her tooth into her lip, tearing at a loose piece of skin. "I don't understand why you're asking me these questions."

"Before you started French lessons, Brendon seemed scared. After you left, all his energy was gone," Nicola said, adjusting the collar of her white blouse, "I won't have you destroy my grandson."

Angelene stuck her tongue in the salty indent. The fight-or-flight response was in overdrive. Her gaze darted from the kitchen doorway to the stairs. She had no fight in her, only flight.

"Brendon saved me in ways you'll never know. If anything happens to him, anything at all."

"Pl... please leave."

"Are you attracted to Brendon?"

Attracted was a funny word with many meanings. Angelene ran her hands over her sweater. The flight response was pulling her towards the door.

"You don't need to answer, Ms. Pratt. It's written all over that pretty face of yours. I'll see myself out."

She jumped from the stool and ran to the back door. Angelene glanced at the glow in Brendon's window, her heart shrivelled. She dashed across the lawn towards Rosewood manor, stopped and sucked at her breath. Turning, Angelene darted towards the road. Her feet thumped against the sand and gravel; her singed lungs struggled to breathe. She gazed around the moors, around the trees. The sky was black and empty. She spun in a circle. There was nowhere to run. Angelene flopped to the damp ground, light shone on her face and for a moment she thought God was rescuing her. She shielded her eyes, trying to make out the figure behind the wheel.

"Blimey Ms. Pratt, what are you doing sitting in the middle of the road?"

Troy closed the car door and crouched beside her.

"I was running away."

"When I was six, mum wanted me to clean my room. I told her I was busy watching a Man U game. She told me to get to my room," Troy said, extending his hand. "I threatened to run away. She handed me two bin bags and said she hoped I found a nicer mummy."

Angelene hung her head. Her messes ran a little deeper than toys and clothes on the floor. She gripped Troy's hand and stood.

"I don't have any place to run to."

"You have a home down the road. It's the best place to run to," Troy said, opening the car door. "Get in, I'll drive you back."

Angelene weaved her fingers in and out. A pattern of black, grey, and red snaked around his body.

"I'll walk."

"You look tired, Ms. Pratt."

"You look guilty."

The fight-or-flight response had disappeared. She needed a cigarette, a glass of wine and her book.

"You can't look me in the eye."

"I'm not being rude. You get stuck in my head; it takes days to get you out."

"I'm like a tumour, growing and growing until I strangled the person on the inside."

"I wouldn't say you're as bad as that. You have a way of looking at me. I forget about Charlie for a while."

"You're a sweet boy."

"My mum says I was born with sugar in my blood."

"I knew a boy who was sugar."

"Brendon's been cayenne lately. Hopefully, he gets back to the old Brendon, as sweet as me."

"Can I ask you something?"

"Don't ask me if Brendon loves Maggie again. He's all mixed up right now."

"Ms. Mastrioni, what's she really like? Is she as tough as she seems?"

"Tougher," Troy said, pulling into the laneway, "that's one lady I wouldn't mess with."

"Has her life been so bad, she needs to fight all the time?"

"It's just who she is. Generations of Mariano women were tough. Brendon said the name comes from Marius, the Roman God of War, fitting last name, if you ask me."

"She said Brendon saved her."

"He's known as the miracle baby. A lot of things happened up at Rosewood manor."

"All the more reason to stay away."

"From Ms. M?"

"I'm in my head. Thank you for the drive home."

"Do you want me to walk you to the door?"

"You've done enough."

"Sorry if I didn't look at you much. I promised to ring Charlie, and I just want to think about her."

"I understand. Good night."

She slipped from the car, ran up the walkway, slamming the locks in place. Angelene shook out a cigarette, placed it in her mouth. It stuck to the tear on her lip. *Are you attracted to my grandson?* circled her head. She never knew what drew her to men. Sometimes it was the colour, sometimes a smell, sometimes it was their light. It could be Brendon's comfortable brown or the scent of his skin. She had to stay away and not because Nicola warned her. She couldn't trust herself or the pattern. It had wrapped itself around Troy with no warning. She carried a crippling burden. She couldn't handle another.

28 SHIT, TRASH

BRENDON PACED THE NET. He didn't want to be at the pitch. He wanted to go back to bed, hide away, bring peace to his busy brain. Everything had happened so fast with Angelene. He needed to rest, to recharge. He needed a re-do.

"Deadly chip shot, Spence," Liam shouted.

Brendon picked up the ball and tossed it back onto the pitch. His heart raced as fast as the clouds storming the sky. Troy slammed his foot into the ball. Brendon stumbled. The ground was soft and squishy beneath his feet. His belly cramped; he swallowed a mouthful of warm saliva. Little stars fluttered behind his eyes; he kneaded his forehead, trying to regain focus.

"The ball went right past you," Liam said.

"I'm going to barf."

"Did you eat this morning?"

Brendon followed the principle, eat well, play well. His diet was as important as the game. He ate to keep his immune system strong, to give him the endurance to play for ninety minutes, to fuel his brain and body. It became his life, balancing carbs, and protein, getting enough vitamins and healthy fats. For the first time since devoting his eating to that of a professional footballer, he couldn't stomach food. He could see the omelette; one bite was all he could manage. He had left it sitting on the island beside an untouched glass of milk.

"Spence, what did your mummy make you?"

"Porridge with blueberries. I made it for me and my brothers."

Liam turned to William. "You?"

"Eggs and Tilly."

"Stop acting the maggot, eejits," Liam said, tossing a stack of pylons towards Troy. "Everyone ate something. Go sit on the bench for a minute." Brendon rambled to the bench, guzzled water, his stomach lurched. He spat it at his feet. *'I'm in love with someone I can't have. Fucking stupid.'* Tu me manques, she was missing from him. He would have to see her every Sunday, find the strength to face her, ignore the good and bad sparks. He'd have to find the strength to build his own wall.

"Do you still have your meal plan?" Liam said.

"It's on the fridge."

Brendon ran the water bottle over his flushed cheeks, envious of the joy and passion rising from the pitch. Football was his life. He lived it, breathed it, made it his life's ambition to be one of Bundesliga's top keepers. He didn't care.

"What's going on with you?"

"Nothing."

Liam banged his palm against his forehead and pulled a face. "Is someone up the duff?"

What little breath filtering through Brendon's lungs expelled in a groan. "I didn't get anyone pregnant."

"What is it then? You're always first at the pitch. You have everything organized before I get here."

Brendon couldn't find the words to explain. How could he tell Liam Angelene slipped inside his head and whispered to him? He had been at the pitch for an hour. His emotions had flicked from love and hate to regret and remorse and for what? A woman filled with holes and cracks. A woman who had a devil or two or three, that played tricks and got drunk and slashed at herself. None of it felt right. In some weird way, it made perfect sense.

"I feel like I've run out of steam. I can't make sense of anything."

"You left your heart in Dortmund. Who needs education when you have talent?"

"Tell that to my parents," Brendon said, crinkling the bottle in his hand, "I'm a commodity. I'm worth a lot of money to Dortmund. My market value goes down or I have a shit season, then what? If I go to uni, I have something to fall back on. Daddy will be proud."

"You'll work for the Bundesliga as a goal coach or scout."

"I want these bloody feelings to go away. I can't get rid of the sparks. They're fucking constant, when I go to sleep, when I wake up, all day, buzzing through my body."

"I'm going to make a few phone calls. Find some help for you. Do some sprints."

"I'm sweating, my mouth keeps watering, not a good sign."

"The bin is right over there."

Brendon stood; blood rushed to his head. He wobbled.

"Sprints to the pylons and back, don't think I can't see you from my office."

A strong, brisk wind whipped at Brendon's back, driving him along the grass. He swayed like the trees, blinked, and found his footing.

"On my whistle."

The high-pitched signal screeched, Brendon bolted down the field. He dropped his hands to his knees, panting.

"Still feeling iffy, mate?"

He rubbed at the black spots that had overtaken his sight. He was sure it was Troy who asked the question. The trees and houses came in and out of focus. He placed a hand against his chest, searching for a heartbeat. The pitch rose and swallowed him. Everything went black.

*

The A&E doors hissed and bumped open. Sofia teetered, cursing herself for frantically shoving her feet in spike-heeled booties rather than something practical. Sweat covered her body. She couldn't focus. Tousled hair, a fade, the hairstyle footy players sported. Broad shoulders, too broad for an eighteen-year-old. She tried to recall what Brendon had been wearing. Fright consumed every nerve.

Borussia Dortmund thermal under a First t-shirt, black sleeves, blue shirt with the TFFC logo. She scanned the waiting room; the stuffy air reeked with undertones of bleach and antiseptic. A ginger haired boy sat on his mother's lap, a plastic lined bin at his feet. His cheeks were so red and inflamed, his freckles dulled. A mother rocked her crying infant, humming Danny Boy. Neither the rocking nor the melody was comforting the child. Two men in hard hats and yellow vests conversed about an episode of Peaky Blinders, the man's thumb wrapped in a wad of crimson gauze. No espresso hair, no First t-shirt, no Liam. She was positive Troy had said Musgrove hospital. The sounds of sirens and her thrashing heart had muffled his voice. Sofia collected herself and charged past the waiting patients to the nurse's station. She had to slow her mind, her heart and the electrical charges in her stomach or she would end up on the floor.

"Can I help you?" A twenty something nurse said. She concentrated on the screen; her mile long lacquered nails clacked against the keyboard.

"You can start by looking at me."

The clicking stopped. The nurse stared emotionlessly.

"May I help you?"

"I'm looking for my son, Brendon Cook."

The surge of electrical currents sparking in her stomach whirled like a hurricane. She clutched the metal moulding. *'Breathe Sofia, breathe.'*

"Taunton's star keeper."

"He doesn't belong to Taunton; he's, my son. Is he here or not?"

The sense of urgency in Sofia's voice shocked her and the people in the waiting room.

The nurse pooh-poohed her and pointed her weapon fingernail towards a set of double doors. "Through there, bay four."

"Was that so difficult?"

The nurse forced a smile that said she didn't care who the boy was or the woman standing before her. Sofia muttered 'thank you', pushed through the door, and swallowed back a mouthful of bleach scented air. She stared at the length of the overly polished floors and pressed on, counting the curtains as she went. Bleeping machines bombarded her ears, astringent disinfectants choked her. She could only count to three. She gazed around the pristine hallway. There were only three curtains. A man in blue scrubs walked past. Sofia snagged him by the arm, stopping him from his hurried pace.

"My son, bay four."

"Right there, ma'am," he said, pointing towards a fluttering green curtain, "do you need to sit for a minute?"

The mixture of disinfectants and her poorly chosen footwear, rocked her. The bright white walls tortured her with memories.

"I need to find my son. Please, bay four," Sofia said, her voice hitched, she grabbed the man's hand, "I need to get to him, please."

"Bay four is two steps away."

She walked with hesitation. Her cashmere sweater itched. She blinked back tears and held the curtain. Guilt and panic overwhelmed her, she told herself to pull back the curtain. She was afraid, more afraid than she had ever been. Sofia held her breath and inched the army green curtain along the steel bar. She followed the IV drip to Brendon's arm. There were no machines hooked up to him, no horrifying beeps. He was okay. The mint green gown made his skin look paler but, he was okay.

"What the hell happened?"

She ran her fingers through his mussed hair. He looked younger, not a man yet. How could she throw him to the wolves in Dortmund? Who would protect him?

"Would you like to sit, Ms. Cook?" Liam said. He rose from a scratched plastic chair and pushed it towards her.

"I don't want to sit; I want to know what happened."

"I'm not sleeping mammina." "I wasn't asking you. I'm asking your coach."

"I was heading to my office, Spence yelled to call 999."

"Did he faint?"

Brendon's fingers were warm in hers. It would always be one of her favourite things, holding his hand.

"As soon as he made it to midfield, down he went. He thought he was going to boke."

"Would that be vomit?" She wrapped her fingers tighter around Brendon's. He was pale, too pale.

"If he told you he was going to be ill, why the hell did you make him do sprints? Sei un idiota del cazzo."

"It's not Liam's fault. I didn't eat, I pushed myself too hard."

"You're the fucking idiot then."

"I have to get to work," Liam said, yanking on his ball cap. "You scared me."

Brendon chuckled through a groan. "Bloody poofter."

"I'll see you tomorrow. You can help McGregor."

Sofia dragged the chair to the side of the bed and crumpled onto it.

"You gave us all a fright. Mum choked on her toast. Amelia sliced her finger."

"I'm okay, mum. I should have known better."

"What am I going to do when you're in Dortmund? The grey hairs I'm going to get."

Brendon smiled a woozy grin. "You'll never know, will you."

"Mum and Amelia are making brodo di pollo."

"Nonna swears food is the cure for everything."

"You'll eat every bite. They're making focaccia, garlic parm. You love Nonna Mariani's focaccia."

Sofia touched the wrinkle on his brow. A choked cry sat in her throat. He was a healthy boy who always ate his meals. He had never been a fussy eater. Meal times had always been happy. He would bounce in his highchair, concentrate on every bite. He never dropped food or threw it on the floor. Every piece was sacred. He'd clear his plate, bouncing and smiling the entire time. There was more to his disdain for food, skipping school, and drinking. She thought he might be holding a grudge for making him come home from Dortmund and forcing him to live up to his promise. She had discussed the idea of rebelling with Nicola over coffee and cake. He had never been a child that rebelled, he'd brood, get angry, eventually accept his fate. He had always done the right thing.

"I'm going to find a doctor. See if I can't get you out of here."

Something her mother said over coffee cracked through her head, *'Keep him away from Angelene.'*

***

28 SHIT, TRASH

Maggie plodded around the tables, her arms loaded with books, tote bags batting her hip. She released the tower of books. They toppled onto the table in a series of clunks.

"You were supposed to meet me in the library. Did you forget about the fission and fusion assignment?"

Charlotte unwrapped a package of Jaffa cakes, pushing it towards Troy. "You're so quiet, babes. Have a biscuit."

"No thanks, luv."

"The chemistry assignment?"

"You love these biscuits. I nicked them from daddy's sweet cupboard."

Maggie squished her lips together and flopped onto a chair. "Excuse me for interrupting. Chemistry."

"He'll be gutted when he fancies a cuppa and has no biscuits."

"Sweet little crumpet. You said you had the wobbles in your tum," Charlotte said, rubbing his belly. "Daddy still has chocolate fingers."

"Charlie."

"What is it, muffin? Babes is gutted."

"I've been sitting here for five minutes. You were supposed to meet me in the library."

"Babes needed me. In case you forgot, Brendon was in the A&E."

Maggie plucked a cookie from the package, chomping the chocolate-covered biscuit.

"I didn't forget. I don't want to ruin my manicure. Mum will kill me if I worry about Brendon again."

"It was awful, worst day at the pitch, other than when I got the concussion," Troy said.

"Has he caught the lurgy? When Jack gets a fever, he sees trolls and strange things in his bedroom."

"Brendon went as white as our shirts, down he went, arse over tit."

"Ah babes, should we go snog? Would that make you feel better?"

Maggie rolled her eyes and stole another cookie.

"That's a smashing idea. Do you want to sit in the hayloft after school?"

"I got straw in my bum last time."

"Will you two quit it," Maggie said. "You've made me think about Brendon and now my stomach is upset."

"He was just lying there on the pitch. It seemed like forever before he opened his eyes."

Maggie stared at her newly painted fingernails, sighed, and shoved them into her mouth. "Ms. Cook must be gutted. I bet she was jingling her bracelets the whole way to Musgrove."

"I didn't even get to tell her what happened. As soon as she heard the sirens, she hung up."

"I should give him a bell."

"You should leave him alone," Troy said. "Ms. Cook is forcing him to eat magical chicken soup."

Maggie pulled her finger from her mouth, stared from her thumbnail to the cookies, and wiggled a biscuit loose. "Why is the ginger tart coming over here?"

"Shut it and be nice. I don't want any aggro."

"Eat your biscuit, Magpie. Babes will deal with her."

In all the years Maggie had known Rachel, this was the first time she had seen her approach with hesitation. There was no 'I'm going to steal your bloke' grin on her face or a shimmy in her hips.

"It's rubbish, right?" Rachel said.

Maggie dropped the cookie and screwed up her face. "What do you care?"

"Mind your business, Thornton, I'm talking to Troy."

Maggie crossed her arms over her chest and kicked at the leg of the chair. A violent urge to hit the girl Brendon had gotten naked with overwhelmed her.

"I'll let Brendon know you were asking about him."

"No, you will not."

"Stop being a twat. Brendon isn't your boyfriend anymore."

"He isn't your boyfriend either, daft cow."

A blast of aggravated air blew from Troy's lips. "I said no aggro."

"I don't know why this slag is asking you to do anything."

"Let it go, Magpie. We'll go to the library and work on chemistry."

"Stay out of this," Maggie said, surprised at the ferocity in her voice, "go away, Jones, your tart stench is making me want to barf."

"At least I'm not an airy-fairy git."

Maggie gazed around the dining hall. Students stared over their water bottles and cans of soda; the betting began.

"Are you jealous I shagged knuddlebär? He has magic fingers, brilliant tingles every time."

Maggie flew from the chair; it fell to the floor with a thud. Utensils clattered, mouths flew open, bets changed. Maggie Thornton had Rachel Jones by the hair.

"You disgusting slag!"

Rachel twirled and squirmed. "Let go of my bleeding hair."

"Babes, do something."

"I said no aggro."

"Please crumpet. Help Magpie before she gets covered in nasty tart germs and develops a rash."

Troy placed his hands on Maggie's shoulders. She shrugged him away, stomping on his foot. "Get off me, maggot."

"Have you lost the bleeding plot? That's my kicking foot."

"Magpie, let go of the tart's hair and have another Jaffa."

"I will when she promises to stay away from my Brendon."

"He's not your Brendon. I don't need Troy to give him a bell. I've had his number long before we started shagging."

Maggie tightened her grip on the mop of curls and shoved. Rachel fell onto the floor, taking cans of soda and glasses of milk with her.

"Bleeding cow."

Rachel stood, grabbed a handful of gravy-soaked chips, and whipped them. Maggie pulled a chip from her hair, flung it, and dove at Rachel, swinging blindly. Dishes clattered, a 'what's happening in my dining hall' bellowed from the kitchen. Mr. Dawson blew through the doors, stretching around the tables in long, elastic strides.

"Margaret Thornton let go of Ms. Jones."

Mr. Dawson glared from a gravy-stained Maggie to a tousled and sticky with soda, Rachel. He smoothed his thinning bangs against his furrowed forehead and tapped his foot. "You students will be the death of me."

Maggie ran her fingers through her hair, flicking gravy to the floor.

"I hope the two of you aren't fighting over Brendon Cook. That boy can stir up trouble even when he isn't here."

The silence was intense. Not a utensil scraped across a plate. Students sat frozen in their chairs, fascinated by the new Margaret Thornton.

"I'm waiting for an explanation," Dawson said, sourly, "Mr. Spence, can you fill me in?"

"Keep crumpet out of it. He's had a dreadful morning."

"Ms. Donovan, please. Will somebody tell me what's going on or you can all march down to my office and we'll sit until someone explains this mess."

Maggie glared at Rachel. "It was her."

Rachel snatched a napkin from a muddle of broken dishes and dabbed at a syrupy splotch on her chest. "I was asking how Brendon was. This nutter attacked me."

"Mr. Spence."

"Do I have to get involved?"

"Yes crumpet, you do," Dawson said.

"Maggie pushed Rachel."

Charlotte held up her fingers. He slung his arm across his chest. "Rachel was a gobby cow, too."

"Charlotte, find Mr. Mumford. He should be in the science labs emptying the bins. You two can clean up this mess."

Maggie stuck out her tongue at Rachel and nodded. "Yes, Mr. Dawson."

"Can I go for a ciggie first?"

"No, you may not. You can get a tray from the kitchen and pick up the dishes," Dawson said, pointing a stringy finger. "You too, Margaret. The rest of you get to class."

The audience of gob smacked students sat glued to their chairs, ready for round three. Things could get interesting with mops and brooms.

"Go," Dawson hollered.

Chairs screeched along the floor; students scattered. Maggie had made history. She was no longer a boring, cry baby.

Charlotte stepped over a puddle of soda and took Troy's hand. "Brendon sure has caused a lot of trouble."

"I'd say. Something tells me this isn't the end of it either." Troy pointed his finger at Maggie. "Behave."

Maggie shot out her tongue and stamped to the kitchen. She jerked two trays from a stack and slammed one into Rachel's stomach.

"Watch it Thornton."

"Is that a threat?"

"It might be."

"Button your blouse please, your jubblies are distracting me."

"Jealous I have some and Brendon has touched them?"

Maggie tossed the tray on the table. She gathered the dishes, her insides trembled. She stared at the cans, the splatter of sausage and chips. Boring Maggie Thornton had lashed out at the queen slag and, by the look on Rachel's face, she had won.

"I'm not jealous anymore."

Rachel scooped a splotch of mashed potatoes onto a plate, wiping her hand on the tablecloth.

"You were jealous."

"What do you think? You used all your disgusting tart moves and persuaded Brendon to, you know."

"Do you think I possess some sort of magic that makes boys fall into my bed?" Rachel said, collecting pieces of a broken plate. "It's called a vagina."

"Why did you choose Brendon as your number one?"

Rachel tucked a wisp of hair into her bun, tossing a can into the recycling. "Why wouldn't I? He's the dishiest boy in Taunton."

There was a soft smile on Rachel's lips. It was the look Jack gave Charlotte when she played Batman with him. It was the look permanently etched on Troy's face; Rachel was sporting the Charlie face.

"Do you know what Brendon's favourite sweets are?"

"Smarties, just the blue ones."

Maggie sniffed and bit back tears. Rachel was in love with Brendon. She wouldn't be moving on to number two.

"You could have stayed away, respected he had a girlfriend."

"You didn't really have him, did you?"

"What's that supposed to mean?"

"If he were so committed to you, it wouldn't have been that easy to get him into bed. Look at Troy, Tilly has been trying since last term and nothing has worked. He's 100% loyal."

The wheels on Mr. Mumford's cart squeaked along the parquet. Rachel was right, Brendon hadn't been hers for a while.

"If you think Brendon would ever date a girl like you, you're stupider than I thought."

"He doesn't want a girlfriend and I don't want a boyfriend. We're perfect for each other."

Maggie could have sworn she saw Rachel's chin tremble.

"You'll never get past Ms. Cook."

"I have no interest in meeting his mum. We're having a bit of fun. I'm in lust with him."

Maggie snapped open a bin bag. She tossed drenched napkins and soggy bread into it. "I feel bad for you."

"Well, don't."

"I used to think I had to try hard to fit in. It must be hard for you, having to use your body to attract attention. I have that."

"What do you have?" Rachel said, running the mop over the floor, "Please hurry, I need to get a ciggie in before class."

"I didn't have to shove my jubblies in Brendon's face to get his attention. I just had to be me."

She tied a knot in the bag and dropped it on the floor. Maggie squeezed her eyes shut, holding back the tears. It hadn't been good enough to be her either.

"I'm going to take this to the bin. I can finish sweeping when I get back if you want that cigarette."

"It'll only take a minute. Will you take the cart back?"

"I can put the books on it. I don't know what I was thinking, taking all of them out of the library."

"You're a swot, Thornton, that's why."

"You're a slag, Jones. Don't touch my stuff."

Maggie wrinkled her nose and lumbered through the dining hall. Her hair smelled like beef gravy, her blazer and kilt stained with soda and brown sauce. She bumped the door open with her hip and dragged herself to the bins. Maggie's breath hitched in her throat, her body jerked, the bag fell from her hand.

"Ms... Ms. Pratt."

"I'm sorry I frightened you."

"What are you doing here? You know this is a school, right?"

"I was in town at the market. Someone was talking about an ambulance at Taunton Park. I wanted to know if Brendon was at school?"

Maggie shrugged at the shivers rippling over her skin and edged the bag into the dumpster.

"You shouldn't be on school property. Mr. Dawson is in a terrible mood."

"I waited in the car park. No one came."

Maggie stepped closer; her nose twitched at the smell of wine on Angelene's breath.

"Have you been at the pub?"

"I looked for Brendon's car and waited. Malcolm took me to the pub. I had a few glasses of wine and found myself here, waiting."

"Why didn't you go to Rosewood?"

"I've been told to stay..." Angelene stopped and weaved into the wall. "It's true. I had a horrible feeling when I heard about the ambulance. Sometimes the queasiness is God telling me he's unhappy. This was different."

Maggie licked her lips. There was something unsettling about the way Angelene looked at her. If she could stand up to Rachel, she could handle a drunk Angelene.

"You need to go home and have a cuppa. You can give Ms. Cook a bell after you sober, uh, rest."

"What happened to Brendon? Is it his light? It's damaged, isn't it?"

"He fainted."

"Is my sunshine here? I do like how he glows."

"Do you want me to call you a taxi?"

"Will Brendon be, okay? He was black, terribly black, and the saddest blue. It was hard for him to concentrate on French lessons."

"I'm sure he'll be fine. Ms. Cook will make sure of it."

"He brought me cornflower and fish and chips."

Maggie stumbled backwards; her fingers slid along the greasy edge of the bin. "You need to get home and sleep. Give Mr. Pratt a call."

"The next time you see Walter, look at his hands. He has golden fingertips. He can transform even the ugliest things into something beautiful."

"Give me your phone. Do you have Malcolm in your contacts?"

Angelene dug in her purse. Maggie took the phone and flipped through the contacts. She paused at the B's, no Brendon, C, only Sofia and David. Maggie scrolled until she got to M and stared at the two names, Malcolm, and my boy in brown. Brendon's face popped into her head, brown hair, brown eyes.

"Can you come to Taunton College and pick up Ms. Pratt? She needs to go straight home. Yes, she is. I'll see she gets to the road."

Maggie dropped the phone in Angelene's purse and held onto her shoulders.

"Malcolm is on his way."

"I told Brendon to stay away from that girl."

"Rachel?"

"I said she would be trouble. I was right."

"Did Brendon talk to you about her?"

"I wish I had been more like you. You're a good girl, pink, always pink, even when you're angry or scared."

They made it to the end of the drive. Maggie leaned her against the Taunton College sign.

"Wait for Malcolm here, don't leave."

"I get a strange feeling when I'm around Brendon. Do you know what it might be?"

"No, I don't. I see a black cab. Go home and rest."

The cab slowed and idled at the side of the road. Maggie rubbed Angelene's arm and forced an uneasy grin. She walked across the car park, her steps quickened, she ran to the dining hall, my boy in brown. Had Ms. Pratt stolen Brendon away? The encounter was puzzling and frightening. There was no time to think about it. She was late for history.

**

Someone once told Angelene she had the power to reinvent herself. Every winter, she became barren like the trees, blooming again in spring. When she was little, she would imagine her bones becoming brittle, her scars turning crinkled brown and falling away. She would imagine a new Angelene, one with smart things to say, flawless skin and bright eyes. Winter would come and go, and she would still be the same. Walter was hopeful his golden fingertips would transform her into someone people noticed, someone important. It was hard to believe he had any power over her winter and spring. The days when she was yellow brought hope, the person she saw in the mirror with new hairstyle and fashionable clothes, was on her way. On days like today, when she was sludgy green, there was no reinventing Angelene Hummel. She was still infecting people. There was no guilt or sadness over the day's events. There wasn't any room in her head or heart. She had shown up at Taunton College, hid by the garbage bins, a suitable place for a girl full of shit and trash. She had no reason to be there and had spilled information to the girl who was still weeping for Brendon. Maggie was smart, Maggie was a thinker, Maggie loved Brendon. Angelene had bounced into the unwise decision, tripped, and stumbled into stupid. She pinched her cross and prayed Maggie had been frightened and shrugged off the wine-coated words.

29 Lilith

Brendon pulled into the car park; the only available spot was under the famous willow tree. He backed the car in and stared at the collection of Victorian buildings. The words 'not the same kid' and 'worried' bounced around his head. He had heard that a lot lately. He was sliding into October with no strikes and had to trust he could keep his promise. School, football, and nothing else. Angelene could concentrate on becoming the best wife Taunton had ever seen, and he would sail through the year with decent grades. Brendon sighed at his optimism.

The air was warm; the wind shushing through the trees was cool. He kept his head down, strolled across the lawn, ignoring the whispers. Brendon walked into Evans Hall; students dispersed like dandelion seeds. Ms. Hudson leaned onto the yardstick, wearing a serious look as if ready to lead her students on an adventure.

"Welcome back Mr. Cook. I hope you read Tale of Two Cities."

"No, you're late?"

"Sit down and open your book."

Brendon rambled down the aisle. He'd have to hitch a ride in an ambulance more often if it meant a peaceful start to his day. He squeezed into the desk, squirmed, and stretched his legs into the aisle. A poorly acted yawn sliced through the silence. He followed the length of Tilly's arm. A stick of gum dropped from her fingers to his desk. Brendon unwrapped it and folded it in his mouth.

"How are you feeling, mate? Like a nutter?" Troy said, reaching between the desks for a piece of gum.

Students glanced over their novels; Brendon's cheeks warmed. "Keep your bloody voice down."

"Mr. Spence, I know you missed your friend; however, I need you to concentrate on the assignment. Your paper on Werther was, how can I put this?"

"You don't have to put it anyway. The book was daft, ending your life over a girl."

Laughter rippled through the classroom; Ms. Hudson slapped the yardstick against the desk.

"Thank you for your input, Mr. Spence. Perhaps you'll like Tale of Two Cities better."

"I heard a bloke dies in this book, too."

Brendon rubbed his brow, digesting the simple task. 'What is the importance of the title?' 'What are some symbols?' He recalled something about a wine bottle, Defarge's wine shop. The revolution was intoxicating. So was Angelene. Wine gave the people of Paris power, wine gave Angelene a voice. The footsteps Lucie hears, fate. Angelene had been his fate, Paris to Taunton, his story of two cities. The words flowed from his head to the paper. A shadow darkened his desk.

"That fall on the pitch must have knocked some sense into you. What else do you see?" Ms. Hudson said.

"Knitting fingers. She's always knitting her fingers. She knits the names of people who will be guillotined."

Angelene could have knit a blanket that stretched along the River Tone the way her fingers weaved. She was making her own list of the people she wanted to send to her guillotine.

"What else?"

"The guillotine symbolizes the institutionalization of the revolution; violence becomes the norm. Killing people becomes automatic and emotionless. Human life is cheap, I was cheap, she's a cheap version of herself."

"I'm not sure about that Mr. Cook but, brilliant work. You may pass my class yet."

Troy clamped his hand over his mouth and stifled a laugh. "What's wrong with you, mate? You're a keeper, not a swot."

"Troy, can you tell the class the importance of the broken wine cask?"

"No, I can't. I haven't read that far."

"I suggest you read past page one then."

Brendon thumbed through the pages. He scanned over the sentences and words. It had been the best of times. Now he was wallowing in the worst.

"Pst, Mr. Football."

Brendon looked up from the novel, meeting Tilly's gaze.

"I wanted to apologize for being a cow."

"I deserved it. I was a prick to Rachel."

Tilly flicked her ebony hair over her shoulder, angling the book at her mouth. "When Rach and I heard you were arse over tit, we were going to fake we had food poisoning and stop by your house. You never know if William is telling the truth."

"I fainted; it was no big deal."

"Rachel has bruises all over."

Brendon kicked at the toe of Troy's trainer and hid his mouth behind his hand. "What's she going on about?"

"Things got crazy in the dining hall."

"Thornton was off her bleeding trolley."

"Bloody hell, was it that bad?"

"All Rach wanted was to ask how you were. Thornton went bonkers."

"Like when she sticks out her tongue. I swear that's where Jack learned it."

"Like a proper punch-up," Troy said, shoving his notes in his backpack, "Food flying, hair pulling. Maggie could wrestle my brothers."

"Because of me?"

"Because of you, mate."

"Rach smelled awful by the end of the day, fizzy drinks, milk, gravy. See you Mr. Football."

"Sounds like I missed an exciting dinner break."

"Maggie didn't shed a tear. I've never seen her that angry."

They swished through the grass. Brendon stepped into a sliver of sunlight. He needed some warmth to take away the chill prickling his skin.

"Don't you have science now?"

"I have a meeting with my tutor. According to Dawson, I need academic support and career guidance. I told the bean pole I'm hoping to play pro footy. He said, get your head out of the clouds. Daft bugger."

Brendon chuckled. "I'll see you at dinner break."

"You, okay? I need you at 150% today."

"I'm fine. All the class participation has tired me out. I'll be match ready." Brendon waved; the smile dropped. Maggie stood by the stairs of the modern languages building, book bags strung over her shoulders.

"Hey Mags, or should I call you Lennox Lewis."

"Are you feeling better?"

"I forgot to eat, low blood sugar or dehydration. Bloody hell, people faint all the time. Tilly fainted in biology when we had to dissect frogs."

"People care about you."

"Someone bet five quid I won't last the day, another bet ten, Dawson would expel me by the end of the week. People really care."

Maggie nibbled her bottom lip and stared at her feet. "Did you have lots of visitors? I was going to drive out. Mum wouldn't let me take the car."

"Just Kate. She came to see Mum. She has a way of calming her."

"What about Ms. Pratt? Did she go round to yours?"

"Why would she come to visit?"

"She's Walter's wife, family, right?"

"I better get to class before I'm late. I doubt talking to Margaret Thornton will work with Madame Lafavre."

"Ms. Pratt was here." Maggie dumped her bags on the ground and released a breath. "I was taking the rubbish to the bins. There she was. She came from the pub, she was drunk."

Maggie's tone sounded ominous; the prickling moved up his spine and over his scalp.

"I didn't recognize her."

"You sound like a nutter."

"I knew it was her. I mean, it was like she was someone else."

"Why are you telling me this?"

Maggie nibbled on a decimated fingernail, drawing in a breath as she bit into skin.

"It was weird. Come here and for what, to see if you were okay? She could have called your mum. I had to call Malcolm to pick her up." "Malcolm?"

"The taxi driver, bushy white moustache, cheeks you want to pinch."

"Oh, right, Malcolm. She trusts him."

"She frightened me. Like that time, we sat under the tree at Vivary Park. That spider dropped from the branch onto my nose. That kind of fright. When you jump out of your skin and all the hairs stand up."

Brendon dragged off his blazer, untucked his shirt, tugging at the knot in his tie, sparks engulfed his body.

"Are you going to faint again? Do you want me to text Troy?"

"I'm angry."

"At me? This isn't rubbish Brendon, I swear."

"I believe you. What else did she want?"

"She asked about her sunshine."

Brendon undid the top button, closed his eyes, mumbling an obscenity. Maggie hadn't met Angelene, she had met one of her devils.

"I know she was talking about Troy. Ms. Spence calls him her sweet sunshine. Charlie used to sing. You are my sunshine and whenever Madame Lafavre sees him, she says, c'est mon rayon de soleil."

"She probably didn't know what she was saying if she was pissed."

"Ms. Pratt said she got a strange feeling when you're around. She asked what it might be," Maggie said, lacing her arms through the multitude of straps. "She said you bought her fish and chips."

Brendon slammed down on the curse words. That information was confidential. Leave it to the drunk devil to spew secrets around.

"William and Matilda said you bought someone fish and chips."

"It was a dream of hers to eat the shit. It meant nothing."

"It must have if she's getting a weird feeling in her belly. I get that feeling. It's called butterflies."

"Don't be daft. It was the alcohol talking."

"Ms. Pratt is like the prettiest package under the Christmas tree. When you open it, it's nothing but a lousy pair of socks. You need to stay away from her. She isn't right."

Brendon jerked open the door. Stay away. He had promised himself to stay clear of Ms. Pratt and try as he might, she still found him. Brendon rambled down the hall, searching for enough breath to squelch the sparks. He wanted to run to her, shake her, yell at her for being stupid, remind her about healthy things. He had to stop caring.

"Monsieur Cook."

Brendon froze in the doorway, glancing at his untucked shirt. "You want me to see Mr. Dawson?"

"Mon petit chou, sit. Are you feeling ill again?"

"I'm late?"

"Take a seat near my desk, just in case I have to ring 999."

"Aren't you going to give me a uniform infraction?" "Non, I'm happy you're here and feeling better. Ready class." She stood on tiptoes and twirled to the blackboard. "And one, bonjour."

An unimpressed chant bounced between the walls. Madame Lafavre clicked in her throat, rose on her toes, and raised her arm in first position. "Try again, with more enthusiasm. This is French. Bonjour."

She stretched into second position. A spirited 'bonjour' reverberated around the classroom.

"Comme vas-tu?" She was in third position.

Brendon repeated the phrase, how was he? Fuming. Angelene was back in his head. She didn't deserve a space in his thoughts or the ache in his chest. Brendon laid his forehead in his hand. The devil was a liar, a tempter, a blonde, green-eyed winter girl.

"Madame Lafavre, how do you tell someone you hate them in French?"

"Je te deteste. You shouldn't be telling anyone you hate them."

"She needs to know this."

"Do you want to get some air?"

"I shouldn't have interrupted. Go on with the lesson."

Brendon flicked his pen between his fingers. A surge of memories haunted his mind. He had to say goodbye, je te deteste, have a nice life, then it would be final.

"Madame Lafavre, I'm sorry. Can I step out for a minute?"

"I'll excuse you for today."

He grabbed his backpack. The sparks fizzled. He was numb from the dizzying spin of emotions. Brendon burst through the door, hurried down the steps, stumbling into Rachel.

"Hiya, knuddlebär."

"I was just leaving."

"Tilly texted me. She said you looked like you were going to faint. I told my teacher I had to go to the toilets."

"I'm all over the place trying to, bloody hell, Rachel, why are you even talking to me?"

"I want to apologize."

"For what? I practically raped you."

Rachel tilted her head and grinned. "Rape means you forced me to hump or threatened me. I learned all about it when mum and I took a self-defence class. You were a dick."

"I don't want a girlfriend." "I didn't think I wanted a boyfriend until I started spending time with you."

He rooted around in his backpack and pulled out a container of berries. Amelia would be heartbroken if he didn't eat the fruit she had packed. His mother would worry there was another trip to the A&E in her future. He'd force himself to eat despite his churning stomach.

"Something is missing from you, knuddlebär."

Brendon looked at the girl with wild red hair. The flirty twinkle was gone from her eyes. Something was missing from her, too.

"Do you want to sit in my car and have some berries with me?"

She laced her fingers through his and led him to the car park.

"I was so worried about you, bleeding Thornton; Troy didn't get to answer before she started pulling my hair."

"I didn't think Maggie had it in her."

"She shocked everyone. There were fifty quid on her crying. No one won the money."

Brendon tossed his backpack in the rear seat and slid behind the steering wheel. He popped open the container and tossed the lid on the dashboard.

"Can you teach me some German? It'll take my mind off things."

"Kann ich eine Beere haben."

He repeated the sentence and tossed a blueberry in his mouth. "What did I bloody say?"

"Can I have a berry?"

Brendon held out the container. She speared a strawberry with her fingernail. He grinned at the bumblebee yellow and black nail polish, on her pinkies, the tiniest BVB.

"You a Dortmund supporter now?"

"My favourite person is going to be playing for them." She popped the berry into her mouth and touched his jaw. "Kanne ich einen Kuss haben?"

"I remember that phrase."

He slid the container across the dashboard and brushed his lips over hers. Her mouth tasted sweet, not like a minty ashtray.

"One more, please."

Brendon leaned across the console and kissed her softly. His fingers dove under her kilt, her thighs were toasty. He welcomed the stir in his belly and the tingle in his groin. Padre Diavolo edged him on, *use her, give her what she wants.* The whispers were intense. He couldn't bring himself to reach further up her kilt.

"I have a condom."

"Can we talk?"

"You parked under the willow tree; you can't park here without doing something. Would you like a bj, a wank?"

"That sounds bloody fantastic but, I..."

An image of Angelene skulking around the school drunk flickered through his head. His heart split, sparks lit, squeezed, and singed.

"Will you hold my hand?"

She took hold of his hand. Comfort came, it was weak and shaky.

"One minute I'm filled with sparks and ready to explode. The next, I'm sad and ready to explode, but in a different way."

"When did you start feeling this way?"

Nothing stuck in Brendon's mind. Sometimes he hated Angelene and sometimes he wished he could have stretched the moments so they would last longer.

"Maybe I came home from Dortmund this way."

"I was glad when I heard you were coming back to Taunton. I was sad too; you only got a taste of your dream."

Brendon held their clasped hands to his lips and kissed her wrist. "I hated my dad. I didn't speak to him for days. All he could say was a promise is a promise."

"I was happy to see you at Taunton Park in your kit. You've always given me butterflies, knuddlebär, proper butterflies."

Angelene had a feeling, a feeling she couldn't describe. Brendon fell into her chest; her perfumed breasts were warm; her heartbeat, soothing.

"Would you fly to Dortmund to watch me play?"

"That's a daft question. I would fly, take a train, swim. Imagine me, Rachel Jones, the tart of Taunton sitting among those 80,000 fans, cheering for her... her friend."

Brendon kissed her collarbone and neck. He caught sight of a magazine shoved among the Double Lollies and unopened cigarette packs. The fuchsia headline asked, 'Is it love or lust?'

"Did you take that quiz?"

"Why would I take some daft test, knuddlebär?" She pulled down the visor and fluffed her hair in the mirror. "Those quizzes are silly."

Brendon held her flushed cheek and grinned. "You took the test. Are you in love with me?"

Rachel kissed his palm and dug in her bag for lip gloss. "I'm in lust."

"Lust is good." His cell phone pinged, he read the message. Troy was looking for him. "I better get to the dining hall. Troy's ordered me lunch and if I don't eat it, he'll send his brothers after me. The little dicks put me in a headlock the last time I was there."

"Nicht die Schönheit bestimmt, wen wir lieben, sondern die Liebe, wen wir schon finden."

"Impressive."

"It's not beauty which determines whom we love, but love determines whom we find beautiful. See you around, knuddlebär."

Brendon watched her walk away, all the warmth he felt puddled at his feet. The sparks were back. There had been no warning, no buildup. Angelene had come to the school, spilled secrets and talked about a feeling. He'd like to ask Angelene if it was love or lust, manipulation or one of her devils strangling him again.

***

Victor Hugo wrote, 'you would have imagined her at one moment a maniac, at another a queen.' Today, Angelene was neither.

"Didn't this room used to be Richard's den of debauchery?" Victoria said.

The room was stately and classic, framed bone white walls, each rectangular section papered with a navy and cream botanical print. The bergère chairs had been reupholstered in smoky blue damask. Vases of red roses adorned every corner, every shelf, and the credenza, which held the afternoon's selections of antipasti and drinks. It was another room, Angelene didn't fit.

"The drawing room was a place for ladies to withdraw. Richard forbid Elizabeth to enter."

"The women Richard paraded through here were not ladies," Sofia said, rearranging the stack of plates. "It was the second room I redecorated."

"I hear Brendon got suspended," Victoria announced.

"The rumour is true."

Guilt took shame's hand and dived into Angelene's heart, pushed, and stretched the muscle. Brendon should have been at school, not rescuing her, hating her, loving her, reading to her. Her boy in brown, her friend, the boy who gave her strange feelings.

"Is William perfect?" Nicola said.

The snort that blew from Victoria's nose caught Angelene by surprise. For a moment, she became the swine; she saw her as.

"William is rude, insolent, cheeky."

Sofia helped herself to a flute of prosecco, perching on the edge of the chair. "Brendon's been under a lot of pressure lately. We're working on his temper."

"He needs a night out with Eshana. She'll see he gets over what's troubling him," Simone said.

"Don't you mean you," Nicola said, dryly.

"I would invite him in for a drink, if that's what you're asking."

"I wasn't."

"How are you Angelene? You haven't said more than hello," Sofia said.

Angelene gripped the stem of the glass, raised her chin slowly, urging confidence to come. It was raw and quivering like her insides. She wanted to be brave. She wanted to defend Brendon. All the words she had practiced, how wonderful life was with the charming Walter Pratt, vanished.

"Is that a Vivienne Westwood?" Sofia asked.

Angelene recalled the conversation she had with Walter. He had bragged about the designer, thought the cut was exquisite and had been thrilled to buy the Gatsby inspired dress. To her, it was nothing more than another attempt at dress up.

"It's someone I'm supposed to know. To me, it's beautiful fabric and a lovely colour."

"It's a Westwood. I peeked at the tag," Victoria said. She pushed the crumbs stuck to her vibrant pink lipstick into her mouth and licked her lips. "Would you call the colour peacock blue?"

"I was thinking teal," Simone interjected.

"You're correct, Lilith," Angelene said into her drink.

Simone's mouth gaped open; her hand flapped to her chest. "How many Aperol spritz have you had? My name is Simone."

Victoria pointed her nose towards the ceiling and shoved an olive in her mouth. "Lilith was in the Bible. She was Adam's first wife."

Angelene threw the rules out the window and gulped back her third, fifth, eighth cocktail, she had lost count. Her Lilith wanted to play.

"There is no evidence of Lilith in the Bible. She's part of Jewish mythology. She slept with Satan and produced a horde of little hellions."

Sofia touched Angelene's arm. "How's Walter? David said he's been busy." "I frustrated Walter," Angelene said, dangling the glass from her fingers. "I've had these strange feelings and wanted to paint them. The feeling is blood red and deep pink. Walter didn't understand."

"No one does," Victoria said.

"What colour is your gown for the gala? I'm dying to know," Simone said.

Sofia glanced at Angelene; her lips pressed into a tight, red slash. "It's a surprise. I decided not to wear black."

Angelene's Lilith shrunk away; she was ruining another party.

"I can't imagine the gala without you in black," Simone said.

"Are you coming Nicola?" Victoria said, plucking a grape from Simone's plate, "it's been a few years since you've attended."

"I'll be home in Milan."

"It's the only exciting thing that happens around here," Simone said, flipping her hair over her shoulder. "Eshana and I went to Bond Street for our gowns. Brendon can take Eshana."

Angelene's chest burned. She shot Simone a furious stare. What was this feeling lighting her lungs on fire? She dug her fingernails into her hand. The feeling was as curious as the other. This one she would paint murky green with splatters of black.

"Are we back to that again?" Sofia said, jerking her cuffs. "Brendon doesn't enjoy those types of things. He'd have to shave and do his hair."

"Why don't you ever want William as a suitor for Eshana?" Victoria said, stuffing her mouth with a slice of salami. "I'd do anything to get him away from Matilda Morimoto. I walked in on the two of them, having a romp in the loo. There was my son's bare bum, plain as day."

Simone slapped her knees and shook with mirth. "Keep your hair on. They're all getting a leg up. Eshana gets it more than I do."

"Don't you dare say, not my Brendon," Victoria said, wagging a finger. "I know what he's been up to."

The feeling crowded Angelene's insides. She stared at the bottom of her empty glass, stood, and wobbled to the credenza, pouring prosecco. Angelene opened her mouth, the words sat on her tongue. She took a small sip and ran the flute over her flushed cheeks. Her mind stuttered, started, stopped, then surged.

"It's nobody's business what topolino is doing."

"I would make it my business. It's Miranda Jones's daughter. She's been through half the football club," Victoria said.

29 LILITH

"I'm sure that includes William," Nicola said.

Victoria sniffed and bit into a polenta square. "If I was Miranda, I'd be shipping her off to the Henrietta Barnett School,"

"She'd probably switch to girls then," Simone said.

"She'd be perfect for Maisie," Sofia said.

The noise in Angelene's head exploded. Fight or flight charged through panic. Angelene guzzled the Prosecco and pressed on her temples to push the voices out. She scanned the display of food, plucked a toothpick from a crystal bowl; flight was the only way to ease the cacophony.

"Excuse me."

Angelene set down the glass and left. Humming floated down the hall and staircase, Angelene was sure it was Moonlight Sonata. The conversation had switched to reminiscing about vacations, Victoria's croaky voice and Simone's gushing over flirtations, added to the symphony of noise clattering about her head. Angelene instructed her feet to move, teetered in the five-inch heels and stepped cautiously towards the kitchen. The ivy-covered doorway was the perfect hiding spot.

"Fuck."

The word was an arrow. Angelene grasped the wood trim, drew in a breath. Her spine grew straight and rigid.

"Fuck."

Heels clicked across the marble, Angelene told herself to let go. She was intruding on mother and son. Her fingers dug deep into the wood; she couldn't move.

"Lower your voice. Do you want to give Victoria more to gossip about?"

"She'd gossip about the colour of my bloody socks."

"What's got you in this mood?"

"I tipped the ball into a Yate player's foot. He scored." "This asinine mood is over a goal?"

"Do you want me to say hello to your friends?"

"Pick up your things and eat. If I hear that word come out of your mouth one more time, you won't be leaving the house for the next eleven months."

Angelene jabbed the toothpick into her thigh. It was the jolt needed to get her legs to move. She slipped into the kitchen. The scent of rosemary and thyme slammed into her nose. Angelene clutched her cigarettes and leaned into the wall. She cursed the chatter in her head, her saboteur, Lilith, Veronique, another devil. Smoke embraced her lungs. The chatter softened to a low buzz. She puffed steadily, watching Brendon slam around the kitchen.

"I can smell your fucking cigarette, Ms. Pratt."

Angelene burrowed into the ivy, puffed quickly, dropped the cigarette, and squashed it. She raised her dress, jabbing the toothpick into her thigh. The voices hummed; her heart thundered. Angelene lit another cigarette. The stool fell to the floor with a thud; she jumped.

"Hiding again?"

"I can't be around those women. There's enough going on in my head. Victoria only adds to it."

Brendon picked up the squashed butt, flicking it into the grass. "Run and hide. You're good at that."

"Walter told me I had to come. I want to scream va te faire foutre at Walter and those women."

"Go ahead, tell them to go fuck themselves."

She took a long drag and sneered. "They would expect me to do that."

"You want to tell me why you were at my school, pissed, are you stupid?"

The word pierced her. She inhaled roughly and stomped on the cigarette. Stupid, strange, ignorant. The words mingled with the chatter of emotions.

"I was shopping. Someone said an ambulance was at Taunton Park. I lost my breath and saw little stars; I knew something happened to you."

"Stupid and psychic."

"Stop calling me stupid." Angelene poked at her thigh, the ground beneath her tilted. Ivy crept around her, strangling her. "You don't know how much power that word has."

Brendon drew his tie from beneath his collar and wrapped it around his hand. "Good night Ms. Pratt." He turned, Angelene banged her fist against his back and tugged him to a stop. "Don't leave me."

"Fuck you. You show up at my school and say all sorts of shit to Maggie. Do you know how smart she is?"

"Maggie is pure and pink like a little lamb. You left her for a slut."

"You're an expert on relationships? You've been someone's mistress. That boy with the blue eyes, did you tell him you'd hold his hand and discover France?"

"Shut up."

"The truth hurts, doesn't it, Ms. Pratt."

"Solamen miseris socios habuisse doloris."

Brendon tore open the door. "I'm not impressed."

"It's from Christopher Marlowe's, Dr. Faustus. It is a comfort to the wretched to have companions in misery."

"I'll add it to my list of things we have in common. Go back to mum's do."

Angelene pressed her cheek against his back, beads of sweat snaked down her spine, emotions clamoured for her attention, her heart raged, the pain was intense.

"I love you."

Her voice was barely a whisper, it pained her to speak.

"How long did you practice saying that?" Brendon said, unclasping her hands. "The words mean nothing. It's more bullshit."

"Your light is out."

"I'm hungry, bloody exhausted. My mistake made us lose the match. That's why my light is out."   "It was me. I stole it."

"Don't flatter yourself."

She followed him into the kitchen. He jerked the stool from the floor and slammed it against the tiles.

"I would have flown home and taken a train into Dortmund. I would have held your hand in Westfalenpark."

"Va te faire foutre Ms. Pratt."

"Do you know what the feeling is? I have two strange feelings and I..."

"Get the fuck away from me. Let me eat my dinner in peace."

"I wish I could make you understand how dangerous the pattern is, how hard I'm trying to be a wife."

"Please don't make me care about you again. I don't want to feel sorry for you or want to hug you or hold your hand. The longer you stand there, the harder it is for me. Go away."

Angelene lay her hand against the wall, dragging herself from the kitchen. The foyer seemed as wide as the ocean. Amelia's humming had moved from upstairs to the great room. The tempo was upbeat and lively. The conversation had switched back to guessing the colour of Sofia's gown. Angelene pressed on her ears. The noise and clutter were alarmingly loud and alive.

I have a book for you to read.
What is it, Pierre? The book on the surrealist was wonderful.
Dr. Faustus by Christopher Marlowe. Faustus made a pact with the devil.
Why should I read a book like that?
You've made a similar deal, haven't you?

"Angelene, are you joining us?"

She pushed herself away from the door, her gaze darted nervously around the foyer. "I smoked two cigarettes in a row. I'm dizzy."

"Come sit. A cup of coffee will make you feel better."

"My head's hurting; I want to go home."

"Did you smoke outside the kitchen? You could have gone out front."

"I needed to get far away from Victoria and Simone."

"I don't blame you," Sofia said, running her fingers over her silver bangles, "did you see Brendon? Was he brooding into his chicken?"

"I didn't speak to him."

"Not even a hello?"

"I might have whispered hello," Angelene said, sticking her palm with the toothpick. "Is he okay? I heard an ambulance was at the pitch."

"He fainted. Brendon's always rushing about. He was like that as a child. Do you know how many times I had to chase him through the house to get him ready for bed? When the house is quiet, I can still hear his laughter."

The love Sofia had for Brendon radiated from her eyes. Her words were sparkling white light. Angelene clutched the doorknob, it was intense and frightening.

"I must go."

"Shall I get Amelia to drive you?"

"The walk will do me good."

A grin fluttered across her lips, the ache and chatter convulsed and jerked about her brain.

Angelene dropped her shoes to the floor, wandered into the kitchen, and snatched a bottle of Johnny Walker off the island. She walked up the stairs, the bottle at her side, emotions swirling, head pounding. Everywhere she looked, a mess. The hall bathroom was in shambles. Little piles of things cluttered the hall. She hadn't made the bed or gathered the damp towels from the floor. Angelene set the bottle on the closet floor, peeling off the dress. She sagged onto a mound of clothes, twirled the cap, and took a long drink. The magic elixir had to work; Walter swore half a glass would put a smile on one's face. Angelene reached behind a stack of opened shoe boxes and grabbed Brendon's hoodie. She draped it over her shoulders, tugged at the hood, and placed her nose in the fabric. She ran the bottle over the scar on her wrist, took a sip, for the failed attempt, to quiet the voices and another to stop her from searching for something to cut herself. The sting of alcohol didn't help with the throbbing chatter. It didn't quiet Victoria and Simone's remarks or the word 'stupid.' She gulped the whiskey for all the years of hurt scratched, poked, and torn into her skin.

Do you know what you are, Angelene? You're worse than the girls that sit in the front row of my lectures and flirt for a good grade. The devil is in the details. You are exceptionally good at getting the details right.

It was you who chose me. You asked me to go with you to that showing. The art was based on Goetia, black magic. You pursued me, professor.
Do you understand how you pull men in?
I told you to walk away. I warned you.
You said you've never been in love. You said you didn't believe in the word. That is your black magic.

A burning prickle surged through her veins.

"Brendon is strong, oui? Are you listening, God? Sofia's love for him takes my breath away. That is Sofia's crazy, the overwhelming love, the fear of losing him, having him ripped from her breast. I'm doing the right thing by walking away."

Happy birthday, little bird.
It is not a happy birthday.
You're twelve, my favourite number.
Gustav said I was old enough now. I hate the feeling I get when he is here. It's prickly and makes my head buzz. Is that why you love me?
No little bird, it's your light. You must protect it. See your light as a mighty sword and when Mr. Jenssen comes near you, you strike, understand? You must be strong. Use your light.

An incredible ache surged through her swollen veins. "I'm sorry I couldn't protect you, little bird. Forgive me."

Angelene twisted her hair and pulled. The scream released, tore through her like a shard of glass. She held a hand to her heaving breast. Angelene fished around a shoe box. Her finger moved across a razor blade; the slice was quick. Her veins shrank with every bubble of blood rising from the cut. The vortex of mind crushing emotions slowed, blurred, and hushed. Angelene gazed across the moors; his lamp was on.

30 SMUDGE

THE MOON WAS FULL, hidden behind layers of ashy grey. Its glow illuminated the clouds, touched the trees, and moors with silver light. Brendon followed Troy to the Fiesta and climbed into the passenger seat.

I love you.

"Get the fuck out of my head."

Angelene and her devils were back. He had met three. The lost child that made him feel sorry for her, the drunk banshee and the most powerful, the mother of all devils, flung desperate words at him like 'don't leave' and 'I love you.'

"Still upset about the match, mate?"

Brendon shook Angelene's voice from his head. "Goal one, from a sidekick. Goal two, through my legs, goal three, from a free kick. I played bloody awful."

"Were you brooding into your spaghetti? Is that why your dad's pissed off?"

"He's angry disappointed. I ruined mum's tea, I picked at my dinner and got a yellow card today. If he weren't stuck on the promise, he would have shipped me off to Germany."

"Your mum wouldn't allow that. She was happy your dad brought you home."

Brendon counted the cars lined up along the ditch: twenty. "Bloody hell, no one showed up at my place until almost ten."

"Will told people it started at eight. He thinks it makes him look popular," Troy said.

Brendon stepped out of the car. The wind was crisp, scented with damp earth and rotting leaves. He rubbed the chill in his arms. A maelstrom of thoughts, none of them positive, swirled around his head. He pulled a stem of fox sedge from the ditch, pushing the reddish-brown flowers along the scraggily stock.

"It's getting cold, mate. Makes for better playing," Troy said, zipping up his hoodie. "You, okay? You're looking like you might faint again."

"I'm knackered."

He focused on his breathing. The lingering sparks whirred inside his ribcage, churned the forced down spaghetti.

"How did French lessons go? I meant to ask but, every time I mention her..."

Troy's voice trailed off. He stared at his feet.

"What were you going to say?"

"Nothing mate. It must be hard to concentrate, that's all."

"She needs to invest in a bloody bra. She bends over the desk and there they are," Brendon said, kicking a stone. "I'm tolerating it and her."

"Doesn't she realize how randy we are? It's just an invitation to gawk."

"She acts like it's totally normal to walk around like that."

Brendon stopped at the end of the drive; trees shushed like whispering spirits.

"You think people will be pissed off about the match?"

"They'll be on the pull or getting bladdered. No one will care." "Where's Charlie?"

"Her grandparents are visiting. She'll be here soon."

"Is she bringing Maggie?"

"She's on a date with Michael. Bleeding Shakespeare in the Park."

Troy opened the door, a whoosh of stifling air hit Brendon's face. It was a balmy mix of cabbage, perfume, and cologne.

"Bloody hell, a lot of people are here."

They squeezed into the sitting room; crisps crunched under Brendon's feet. Most of the football team had arrived. A mixture of Taunton College students and teens from the community school had congregated in the room.

Troy shoved a can of lager in Brendon's hand, patting his shoulder. "The room is small, mate."

"All right?" William said, smiling smugly. "I'm surprised you showed up after today's performance."

Troy shot his fist into William's arm. "You play any better?"

William laughed and disappeared into the crowd. Brendon cracked open the beer and drank as if he hadn't seen water in a week.

"Knuddlebär."

Rachel stood on a corduroy ottoman, in black jeans that were more holes than fabric, and a black Adidas t-shirt that exposed her midriff. She was the only person in the room that made Brendon comfortable.

"Pass me another, would you?"

Troy dug into a mop bucket filled with beer and cider and tossed the can at Brendon.

"Babes."

It was as if happiness was growing inside Troy, lighting his smile and eyes. Brendon would give anything to feel what Troy was feeling.

"Hiya, luv, you look brilliant."

Charlotte curtsied and kissed his cheek. "You're so sweet."

"Hiya Brendon, you look miserable."

He chugged back the ale, scrunched the can and grabbed another.

"It was a tough match. I'm tired."

"I'll give you a hug. Babes says my hugs are the best medicine."

"Should you be fraternizing with the enemy?"

"I don't like that you hurt muffin, but crumpet doesn't like all the fighting and arguing." She squeezed tightly, displacing the sparks.

"Watch the ale mate, you'll be chundering all over Ms. McGregor's new hardwood."

Brendon finished the beer, exchanging it for another. "I feel like everyone is staring at me."

"No one's staring, mate."

The air was tight and hot. Chug, thump, chug, thump, pulsed out through the speakers, vibrating Brendon's chest. The walls shrank in and out with the rhythm. He chugged the beer, scrunched the can and grabbed a bottle, draining it. Sparks lit, his body was on fire, hollowing him out. 'I love you' thumped in time with the music.

"I need some air."

Brendon edged through the crowd. The floor vibrated and tilted. He reached for the mantle to steady himself.

"Knuddlebär."

Brendon glanced down at his side; Rachel smiled a 'let's run away together,' smile.

"Sorry about the match."

"I played bloody awful."

Rachel tugged at his arm and said, "I hate to say it, but Farnborough played brilliantly. I'm going for a ciggie. I keep trying to quit, then something happens. My nerves get rattled."

Brendon yanked a bottle from a galvanized pail and shoved it in his pocket. "Why are you upset?"

A black lantern lit the uneven square of concrete in a dingy glow.

"My mother."

Brendon dragged a dusty plastic chair along the cement, plunking onto it. "Did she breakup with someone again?"

Rachel dropped onto his lap, tapping a cigarette on the package. "The opposite. She's on the phone every night with her friend, Christian."

"Shouldn't that make you happy?"

"She had sworn off men. We were supposed to be doing mother daughter stuff. She's back to ignoring me."

Brendon rubbed the goosebumps on her arm. He pulled the bottle from his pocket and shoved it in a pot, tugging off his hoodie. Brendon draped it over her back, wrapping the sleeves around her like a blanket.

"You're a proper gentleman, knuddlebär."

"Depends on who you ask."

"Let me know if you want it back."

"I'm sweating."

"You feeling iffy? Your cheeks are bright pink."

"It's hard to breathe."

He understood what Angelene meant when she cried, she couldn't breathe. It was getting increasingly difficult to find a decent breath.

"What can I do?"

"Just keep doing what you're doing. No lectures, no fussing, no filling my head with rubbish."

He laid his cheek on her shoulder, savouring the warmth of her body. The patio door creaked open and whacked against the brick wall. William and the Yate keeper huddled around a skeletal cedar tree. They lit up a joint the size of a cigarette. The skunky smoke clung to the moist air.

"If it isn't Taunton's hero. You single-handedly fucked up the match today."

"Some hero, bleeding bollocks keeper."

Brendon finished what he thought was number five, tossed it in the clay pot, and grabbed the next. "Fuck off Will."

"Do you think the Germans will want you now, mate."

"I'm not your mate."

Sweat dotted Brendon's forehead, Padre Diavolo raised his baton, the orchestra of sparks began.

Rachel flicked the cigarette and shot up her middle finger. "Why are you such an arsehole?"

"You'll be taking some boilies with you to Dortmund."

William laughed; pungent, earthy smoke hovered above his head. Brendon helped Rachel into his hoodie and patted her behind. The sparks were blazing. It was a good time to listen to his father's advice and walk away.

"Didn't you hump that slag?"

Brendon stared at the boy. His sweat suit hung off his lanky body, one punch and he would be flat on his back.

"Are you going to let him speak to Rachel like that?"

"We could take turns. You're into that? A slapper like you?"

Sparks pulsed through Brendon's veins. He swallowed back the frustration, clamping his fingers around Rachel's waist. Madre Innocente and Padre Diavolo bickered, *'breathe, and walk away, slam your fist in Will's mouth.'* If things got out of hand, he could call for backup. Brendon doubt any of his friends would help fight for Rachel's honour. Brendon jerked open the door and fought with the sparks instead. He spotted a bottle of wine, grabbed it, and pushed through the crowd with Rachel in tow.

"You feel better now, mate?"

Brendon shrugged; fresh air was not the answer to his problem.

"Bloody Will, shooting his fucking mouth off."

"Just ignore him, mate. He knows you're pissed about the match. He's trying to push your buttons."

Voices muffled; the music dulled. Brendon was chin deep in a sweltering ocean of smiling faces and chugging music. Brendon tugged Rachel's hand, pushing a path through the crowd.

"Hey, Mr. Football? We'll join you in ten. Take a turn with Rach."

Brendon ducked into the kitchen, surrounded by orange-brown cupboards, wood panelling and retinol scorching wallpaper. He unscrewed the cap, swallowed the vinegary liquid, spying an iron staircase spiralling up to a hole in the ceiling. He took another swig and climbed the oddly placed staircase. The room was clammy and smelled damp. The floorboards were dusty, a light bulb and pull string dangled from the ceiling. A brass daybed leaned against the wall. Brendon washed the taste of mildew from his mouth and pulled the string. Dusty light barely brightened the room.

"Sorry to drag you away from the party."

"I'd rather be alone with you."

Brendon gulped a mouthful and set the bottle on the warped hardwood. He ran his hand under her hair and kissed her neck.

"You sure, knuddlebär?"

Brendon undid his belt buckle. The floor vibrated in time with the music. He swayed, grabbed the wine bottle, and chugged. Rachel shimmied out of her jeans and scooted to the edge of the mattress. He staggered closer. She ran a hand over him, he could feel her breath on his belly.

"I'm not sure what's happening. I'm usually ready to explode when you touch me."

"Maybe this will help."

His jeans fell around his feet, a damp chill enveloped him.

"I don't know what's happening."

"Lie down. We'll snog for a bit; you can touch me."

His fingers skated over the curve of her belly and slipped into her satin panties. He concentrated on the movements, the feel of her mouth and the little murmurs escaping her lips. He didn't know how long they had been kissing; the room was closing in; his mouth was dry.

"Do you think it's the booze? The bloody bed is floating."

"It might be. Try to relax."

Kiss me goodbye my sweet boy, find your light and kiss me goodbye.

Brendon propped himself up on his elbows and hung his head. "I can't get this shit out of my head."

"Is it me?"

"Are you bloody kidding? You're brilliant."

He hadn't felt a thing. No stirs in his belly, no tingles lighting his groin on fire. He felt nothing but a mix of tangled emotions. Brendon teetered to his feet; he struggled into his jeans; the floor boards buckled.

"Don't tell anyone."

"I'm not a cow. Well, I can be, not about this."

The mixture of ale and wine sloshed in his belly, rose into his throat, and splashed back into his spinning stomach.

"Do you think you can make it down the stairs?"

He leaned into the wall and peered down the hole. "It doesn't look wide enough."

"You got up here, knuddlebär. Do you want me to find Troy?"

"He's my height. If I fall down the stairs, he'll have a better chance of catching me. I don't want to hurt you."

"Just stay where you are," Rachel said, clutching the flourished banister, "who puts a bleeding staircase in the kitchen."

"Rachel."

"Will I run away with you? Yes, knuddlebär."

He grinned and rested his cheek against the wall. "I'm glad I'm still number one."

"You'll always be number one. Du bust mein Ein und Alles, you are my everything."

She disappeared down the stairs, loneliness gripped Brendon. The light swayed and flickered. The wall was damp and spongy. He could try to make it down the hole in the floor. All it would take was determination and a firm grip. He could face William, give him the finger, take Rachel's hand, and run away. Dortmund was a lovely place.

"There you are, mate, you pissed?"

Brendon hiccupped and swallowed back a mouthful of ale and wine. He took an unsteady step and fell back into the drywall.

"Rachel is brilliant."

Troy climbed through the hole and took Brendon's arm. "Whatever, mate."

"You're a good friend."

"Bleeding heck, mate, you smell like plonk."

"She does this thing... I can't get her out of my head."

"I don't need to know what Rachel does. You shouldn't even be with her," Troy said. "Hurry. Will's trying to pull every girl down there, including Charlie."

Brendon unglued his fingers and took a wobbly step.

"I'll go first, mate. If you fall, I've got you."

Brendon's legs trembled. He steadied himself, clamped his fingers around the banister and took a step. The staircase looked like a cage surrounding him. Music and chatter became louder, clearer. He found himself immersed in the middle of a mob, stifled by the heat.

"Told you he was a poofter?"

William snickered and wiggled his fingers.

"Just ignore him," Troy said and glanced at his watch. "How about I take you home? I'll tuck you in and read you a Paddington story."

"Where are you two going? A shag in the garden."

William dissolved into a fit of laughter. Brendon bit the inside of his mouth, Padre Diavolo lit the fuses, the sparks exploded.

"I would fuck off if I were you."

William stepped in front of him and smirked. "What are you going to do?"

"I need to get you home, mate before your mum starts texting."

"Do you need your nappy changed?"

I would fly home and take a train. I would hold your hand... tu me manques mon amour... I love you.

Brendon clenched his fists. Flashes of Burnham, waking with her, holding her, struck his mind like lightning bolts. Faces blurred and smudged; the walls shrunk around him. Go to school, get a clean sheet, impress Dortmund, get good grades, Taunton's hero. Laughter mingled with the constant chug of music. Brendon gripped his cross and stared at the ceiling.

"Brendon, you alright?"

"What do you think of your footy hero now, not so dishy, is he?"

"He's lost the bleeding plot."

Words came at him like daggers.

Do you know what this strange feeling is?

A pop and a snap silenced the crowd. Brendon stared at his torn knuckles.

William rubbed his jaw and wobbled. "What the... you're a shit keeper, a failure, fucking loser."

Brendon's fist connected with his overbite; Padre Diavolo howled in delight. The music stopped, the crowd shrunk into the walls, climbed onto sofas and tables to get away from the flying fists. William's head bounced off the floor. Brendon was oblivious to the gasps, blood, and grunts. The tangle of emotions stretched in all directions, pulling, tugging. Do the right thing, say the right thing, follow the rules, be a good boy. William grabbed Brendon's wrist, crack, crunch.

Someone wrenched Brendon off William, shoving him amongst the dazed crowd.

"There's blood all over mum's new hardwood."

Colour seeped back into the room; shocked whispers filled the silence. Brendon gazed from William's bloodied mouth to the splatter of crimson; his chest rose and fell in rapid breaths.

"Knuddlebär, your hand."

"I better get you to the A&E, mate. That looks bad."

William stuck his tongue through a gap in his front teeth. "You knocked my tooth out."

Brendon rubbed his torn fingers across his jeans. "What do you think of me now? Still Taunton's hero?"

"Shut it mate."
Troy grabbed Brendon's t-shirt and shoved him. "Move."
"You're her ray of sunshine, did you know that? Look at Troy, ladies, his smile is fucking dishy."
"Your hoodie."
"Keep it."
"I'm worried about you, knuddlebär."
He kissed her hard on the mouth, shooting up his middle finger at the gawking mob.
"She's in lust with me. What do you think of that?"
"Let's go Casanova."
Brendon stumbled down the drive. He and Angelene had another thing in common. They were both drunks.
"Look at my fucking hand."
"You really did it this time, mate."
"Sorry, I was a prick. I think it's great you're happy all the time. I could learn a thing or two from you."
"I don't know who that was back there."
"Padre Diavolo."
"Tell him to bugger off next time. You're in serious shit, mate."
"Do you think the McGregor's will press charges?"
"I hope not."
Find your light mon ami.
All Brendon had found was an unsympathetic doctor and a cast on his left hand.
"The mansion looks spooky, mate."
"It's full of ghosts." Brendon wiggled his fingers, pain shot from his wrist to his thumb.
"I'd be more afraid of your parents than ghosts."
Brendon studied the bruising wounds on his knuckles. He didn't remember connecting with William's mouth. He remembered little but a few snickering taunts and the room turning black. Brendon pressed his finger into a tooth shaped cut and sucked in his breath. "Bloody hell, I'm fucked."
"No kidding. Give me your house key."
Brendon instructed his legs to move, dug into his pocket and passed Troy the key.
"Here's the plan, mate. Be quiet."
"That's it?"
"You're going to be the quietest you've ever been. I'll get you up to your room and it's off to Bedfordshire, got it?"
"Did you know seven devils live down the hill?"
"Ghosts, devils, shut it, mate."
"They're in all of us, even you, Mr. Sunshine." "Is that so?"
"Yours is that farm. Would you make a deal with the devil to play for Man U?"
"No way, be quiet."
Brendon held his stomach and burped. His knees connected with the fountain and out spilled the ale and wine.
"Couldn't you have done it by the hedges. I could have covered it with dirt."
Brendon dragged his t-shirt over his mouth and weaved towards the front door. He ping-ponged between the cedars, his finger aimed at the doorbell.

"Bleeding heck." Troy jammed the key in the door and put a finger to his mouth. "Quiet."

Brendon stumbled over the threshold with a hiccup and burp.

"Mammina, I'm home."

Troy slapped a hand over Brendon's mouth. "I said quiet."

Brendon peeled Troy's hand away. "Mammina, your baby is home."

The hallway flooded with light, David flew down the hall, fighting the tie on his robe.

"What's the matter?" Sofia said, her silk dressing gown fluttered behind her like giant red wings.

"Hey mammina, dad."

"Do you know what time it is?" David said.

"You stink like booze," Sofia said, recoiling, "were you ill?"

"Look. It's broken."

"Did this happen at Victoria's?"

"It might have happened in the sitting room," Brendon said, weaving into the umbrella stand. "It might have been in the room above the kitchen. No, I was up there with Rachel."

"Can you help me get him upstairs?" David said.

"Do you think William will find his tooth?"

Find your light mon amour...tu me manques

"Fuck you."

"I certainly hope that wasn't meant for Troy or me?"

"No sir."

"Did you hit William?"

"He wouldn't shut his fucking mouth."

"You're going to be off the pitch for eight weeks, mate."

"I'll wrap it."

"It'll be up to the refs. Most of them can't stand you. That one ref, the rozzer, thinks both keepers should get a fair chance in net."

"You really messed up," David said, kicking the door open with his foot. "I thought I told you to walk away."

"I'm going to bloody barf."

"Take him to the toilet."

"I have to be at the stall in three hours, Mr. C."

"Then push him in."

"Sorry mate."

Brendon stumbled into the bathroom, leaned over the sink, spilling expectations and regret into the bowl.

"Do you know what memories this brings up for your mother and Nicola?"

"I'm not Uncle Gianni. I'm not drunk every day."

"Damn close. What else can I expect Victoria to blab around Taunton?"

"I tried to shag Rachel; my bloody knob wouldn't work. Ms. McGregor can announce that all over town."

David tightened the tie on his robe and glared. "It's taking every ounce of me not to slap that smug look off your face."

"Why don't you do it. It might make you feel better." "This used to be my mother's room. She would sit by the window and knit."

"She died in here too." "I used to sit at her feet and read to her. She loved Wuthering Heights." David moved to the window, standing in the spot where

Brendon remembered a rocking chair to be. "She was a wild wicked slip of a girl, she burned too bright for the world. Mum loved that line. She wished she were more like that."

Brendon yanked his t-shirt over his head and tossed it in the laundry basket. He knew a wild, wicked girl.

"Sorry I'm pissed."

David turned from the window, defeat in his eyes. "Richard used to hit mum when he was drunk. Have I told you that? She would crumble to the floor. When I went to her, he would kick me out of the way. I can still hear her crying." "It's getting really hard living with the ghosts."

"There are a lot of memories in this house."

"Don't you think it's time to let them go?"

"Go to sleep."

"You can't run from them. I've tried, they follow you around."

"I expect you to clean your bathroom when you wake."

David walked away, shutting off the light. Darkness embraced Brendon. He reached from under the blankets and switched on his lamp.

The morning sun shone through the fanlight, illuminating the stairs. Brendon clutched the banister, his legs wobbled, head throbbed, his mouth tasted like toothpaste and stale ale. He released his grip and walked to the kitchen, readying himself for his mother's wrath.

"It's half-past twelve," Sofia said, wrinkling her nose. "Why didn't you shower?"

Brendon held up his cast. "I haven't figured this out yet."

"Put a damn bag over it."

"Fatti una doccia, perché puzzi de fogna."

"He doesn't smell like a sewer mother; he smells like a brewery."

"How are you feeling, topolino?"

"I got up twice to barf. My head feels like it's going to crack open, my hand is throbbing. I'm bloody great."

"What's going on in that head of yours?"

"Nothing," Nicola said.

The doorbell was loud and brassy, Brendon managed a sip of coffee, an 'I'll answer it' hollered from the foyer. The conversation between his father and Angelene floated into the kitchen, sparks flickered.

"I'll put together lunch for you, topolino. You need to sop up all that alcohol."

He dumped the remains of coffee and tossed his mug in the sink.

"I put your things by the pool. Take Angelene a cup."

"Can I skip French lessons?"

"Brendon David, off you get."

Brendon took the mug from Nicola and left the kitchen.

"Angelene is waiting," David said.

"Sorry I got pissed. Sorry I didn't walk away."

"Your friend Rachel, if that's what she is, stayed after the party and cleaned up the blood. Victoria wants a new floor and a tooth for William."

"I'll pay for the fucking floor and his bloody tooth."

"Watch your mouth," David said, jabbing his finger in Brendon's chest, "Victoria will broadcast this all over Taunton."

"Worried about your reputation, dad?"

"You're not worried about yours? *'She's nobody. She means nothing to me.'* He repeated the words, stepping into the glass room. The air was humid, thick with the scent of patchouli, *'she's nobody, she means nothing, fuck. She looks bloody lovely. Just another one of her devils.'* This devil wore a façade of a pretty smile and caring eyes. She was worse than the mother of all devils. This one played innocent. She had no idea how enchanting she was. He slid the mug towards her, slumped into the chair, and thumped the cast on the table.

"What happened to your hand?"

The yearning to hold her hand and talk like they used to collided with hate. They ruined their friendship; she was damaged, and he wasn't strong enough to rebuild it.

"David's words are sharp red. What did you do?"

"I got in a fight."

"Will you be allowed to play?"

Brendon picked up the pen. The wounds cracked and stretched.

"The doctor said I needed to rest it for a few weeks, then it depends on the ref. Some let you play; some are afraid you'll injure someone. Considering what's floating around Taunton, they'll see it as a weapon."

"Your light is out."

Angelene touched a cut on his knuckle; he flicked her finger away. "Yup, my bloody light is out."

"If I weren't the devil myself, I would give me up to the devil this very minute. It's from Faust by Goethe. I would trade my life to get your light back."

"You'd take a train to Dortmund, hold my hand, more rubbish."

Angelene bit into her chapped lip. "The devil is powerful in you. You must fight him."

"The devil's probably laughing at me right now."

He wrote half a sentence, not sure if it was correct. He didn't care if it was.

"And sometimes he cries with you."

The adrenaline Brendon woke with unwound like a spool of thread. He sagged into the chair. "Why do I feel so bad?"

"This is what I do. I hurt people. Get the lesson done."

The words stretched and blended. An ache throbbed behind his eyes. His emotions were spinning as fast as his stomach. Love, hate, he needed her; he wanted her to go away.

Nicola marched into the room, tray in hand. "How is the student doing?"

"He's not well," Angelene said.

"He's hungover. Nothing a little food can't help," Nicola said, staring at the notebook. "What have you two been doing? There's half a sentence written."

"I can't concentrate Nonna."

Beads of sweat prickled Brendon's forehead. He wiped his t-shirt over his face and hung his head. Nicola was making observations, taking mental notes.

"Can you talk to dad?"

"Have him angry with me, too? Eat some taralli. They always helped your Uncle Gianni."

"I don't want to fucking eat."

"Don't fucking eat. Angelene can," Nicola said, walking towards the door, "Don't push me."

Brendon wasn't sure if Nicola's threat was meant for him or Angelene.

"That's correct." Angelene said, touching his shoulder.

"Don't fucking touch me."

"One day, I'll tell you why it must be this way. For now, please find your light."

"Fuck off about my bloody light. Everything is bloody bollocks right now. School, football, you."

Sparks ignited, zipped up the cord, and exploded.

"Go the fuck away."

"I'm married."

"To a man you don't love, who expects you to behave a certain way and dress a certain way. You're a fucking project, not a wife."

"David will be upset if we don't finish the lesson."

"Say you don't feel well. Say you have a painting you need to finish. You're good at making excuses."

Everything hurt, his lungs, his head, his wrist, his heart.

"I promised David your mark would improve."

"I can't deal with this," Brendon said, rising abruptly. "I can't fucking deal with you."

Brendon picked up the chair. It soared across the pool deck, crashed into the table and charcuterie. Cheese, taralli, flew into the air, olives bounced and rolled under the lounges.

"What the hell is going on?" Sofia said, "what have you done?"

Brendon's heart beat beyond any rhythm he had ever felt before. It was happening again. Padre Diavolo, the maestro of destruction, was searing his insides with a whirlwind of sparks.

"Go to your room and cool off," David said.

"Breathing used to control the sparks. Everything keeps turning black and I lose it."

"It's my fault. I pushed him too hard," Angelene said, weaving her hands. "He was frustrated and needed a break. I told him no."

"The peppers will stain the tiles."

"Sofia, put the damn tray down. The only stain in this house is our son."

The child inside Brendon raged. "I was never good enough for you. Every father sitting in the stands looks at me with pride in their eyes, like I'm their fucking kid. Yet, you don't give a shit. All you care about is my grades. Disappointing, isn't it?"

"Brendon, your father..."

"Let him say what he needs," David said calmly. "Go on son, how else have I smashed your dreams?"

Brendon stared from Angelene's knitting fingers to his mother's worried brow, back to David. An allegro of angry sparks attacked every nerve.

"I smashed your dreams, dad."

Madre Innocente whispered, *'it's time to leave.'* He had to go before his fist landed in his father's face or he lashed out at Angelene and broke the silence of their relationship. Brendon stormed from the room, bounding up the stairs. He swiped his phone off his dresser, slammed his finger on dial and landed on his bed with a thud.

"Hiya, knuddlebär."

"Where are you?"

"On the bus. I just finished volunteering. I snuck Mr. Tomlinson extra brown sauce for his sausages. He slipped me five quid and a pack of Smarties."

The sound of her voice dampened the sparks. She rambled on about blue Smarties and brown sauce. Occasionally, she would pause and say, 'Oh, knuddlebär, I was so worried.'

"She burned too bright for the world."

"Are you still pissed?"

"It was something my dad said, a quote from Wuthering Heights."

"I bet your dad's angry."

"Ashamed of me, angry disappointed, which is worse."

"Do you want me to come over? There's a Bayern match on. I need to return your hoodie."

"I told you to keep it."

"You remember saying that? You were pretty bladdered."

"Parts of stuff like my knob not working."

"We could try again. I can give you a wank while the match is on."

"Did you say that on the bus?"

The sound of Rachel's laughter pushed the sparks aside. Brendon smiled.

"A lady just put her hands over her daughter's ears."

A shadow stretched across Brendon's floor; his heart slowed to an aching pace. "I gotta go."

"Give me your phone," David said.

"Why?"

"Just give me the damn thing."

Brendon tossed it at the footboard. "You're taking my phone away. What am I ten?"

"You're certainly acting like a child."

"I need my phone to look up stuff for history. How do you expect me to pass the assignment if I can't do any research?"

"My laptop is in the den. Research all you want."

"I'm bloody sorry dad, I screwed up."

"Clean up the mess you made, then finish your homework. You can scrub your toilet as well; all I can smell is damn vomit."

"The pressure is getting to me; don't you bloody understand?"

"When you're finished cleaning your bathroom, shower the stink off you, then apologize to your mother and grandmother."

Brendon swallowed the sparks. Hate burned in his father's eyes.

"I used to make you smile, dad. You used to grin at me in my too-big Dortmund jersey, carrying Paddington around. Did that bother you too, that I liked Paddington over Winnie the Pooh?"

"You've barely been to school since I dragged you home. People are doing your homework for you. You flirt with the career advisor to get out of class. You watch football highlights when you should be doing your schoolwork."

"You never answered the question."

"Do as you're told."

Brendon scratched out his hair and glanced out the window at the farmhouse. Angelene sat on the stoop. The sky was colourless. Rain hit the glass in splats, smudging her out of his sight.

***

Sofia tightened David's cardigan around her and wandered into the great room. She adjusted a Molins-Balleste lamp, moved a burr elm bowl to the centre of the table, and repositioned a framed photo of David. She took stock of all the things she had collected over the years. Each one, a treasure with a story to tell. She had found old love letters in the Edwardian writing slope. Hikers had found the Lenzkirch clock buried under a beech tree in the Black Forest. There wasn't one style she preferred. Her taste was eclectic and driven by her mood. If she were bubbling with love, she would lean towards jewellery once given as gifts or vases to house bouquets of roses. Worry made her spend frivolously and passion brought home bulky furniture. All the stuff she treasured was nothing but things. The two most important things were at odds with one another. One sat staring blankly at the television. The other was scowling over a laptop. Sofia rubbed the chill from her arms, joining David on the sofa.

"Are you watching the television? You love this crime drama."

"I almost slapped him."   "You've never risen a hand to him. You said you'd never be like your father."

"I was standing in the middle of Brendon's bedroom; I saw mum sitting in her rocking chair. She never finished that jumper," David said, weaving his fingers through hers. "I heard her cry. I heard my father belittling her. When I looked at Brendon, all I saw was Richard."

"I know you're angry, but slap him? David, that isn't you."

Sofia never knew David to be a strike with your fist kind of man. He used words, he lectured calmly, and asked questions, 'what could you do differently next time,' and 'what have you learned?' When they fought, it was a passionate exchange of words. She would react, every word emphasized by the flap of her hands, and he would remain unruffled by her raised voice. The argument would end with laughter, David would comment on her flair for the dramatics, and she would praise him for not dropping a single f-bomb. The apology, if needed, came in the form of lovemaking. Despite heated words, it always came back to love.

"I don't understand Brendon's behaviour," David said, clicking off the television. "He's moaned about school since reception. I'd ask him about his day, he'd toss his school blazer on the floor and run off to kick the ball in the garden. I thought we were working on his temper."

"He told mum he was exhausted."

"I imagine he is with all the stuff he tries to fit into a day."

"He's upset you before. You never wanted to hit him."

"Maybe I'm exhausted too."

Sofia cuddled next to him. The scent of black tea, Italian citrus and honeyed neroli enveloped her. She nestled closer until there was no space between them.

"We made a deal; he signs the contract and finishes A-levels."

"Don't you think that was your dream?"

David's sigh ruffled her hair. "I was protecting you. The day Lukas and the sporting director showed up at the pitch, you felt faint."

"Have we done this all wrong? We promised each other we would make it right."

"If you would have waited to get pregnant."

"You've never forgiven me for that. I needed a child. I needed Brendon."

"I'm sorry. That was a terrible thing to say." He kissed her hair and rested his chin on her head. "Walt and I had lunch with James McGregor. Brendon has been working his way through the girls at Taunton College."

"There was a time Brendon didn't like girls."

"I remember Brendon picking you a bouquet of bellflower. You told him; one day, he'd be picking flowers for the girl he loved. He scrunched his nose and ran off to play football with Troy."

Sofia's eyes prickled with tears. "Remember when he came home from school and told us Sarah Grant kissed Troy with boogers in her nose and gave him a cold. He swore he'd never kiss a girl."

"There was that one kiss, the little girl in the yellow dress. What was he, five? Her mother said Brendon was impetuous."

"He's always been a good boy."

"I love him; you believe that right?"

"I do. It'll be over with now, whatever is bothering him. He can't play football for a while; he knows we're angry disappointed as he calls it. I think he's learned his lesson."

"Walter mentioned Angelene has been moodier than usual. Perhaps there's something in the air."

'Or someone.' Sofia rubbed David's arm and pecked his cheek. "I'm going to find mother and start dinner."

"She's avoiding me."

"She's been on the phone with her friend Alessandro."

"What's on the menu tonight? Another five courses?"

"Four, we're skipping antipasti."

"I'm spoiled."

"You are David Cook. A beautiful home, an adoring wife, a mother-in-law who respects and admires you and a son, who…"

"Who loves me?"

"Things will get better, darling. I know they will. They must."

***

Rain pattered against the window. The rhythm was as soothing as a concerto, exactly what Angelene needed to sweep the memories of her afternoon away. She had seen those types of outbursts before: her mother, Douchette, Gustav. She had made a habit of sticking her fingers in her ears or screaming on the inside to shield herself. She had no time to react to Brendon, no build-up, no warning. He blew up like a keg of gunpowder. It frightened her.

Angelene added a stroke of brown paint to a mountain range. A girl in a yellow dress held onto a man's hand. Winter blew behind them. They had chased the blustery winds and snow away.

"That's a change from the usual." Walter said. He walked into the room, carrying a clinking box.

Angelene picked up a fine tipped brush and dabbed navy paint along the hem of the man's trousers.

"Who are the people?"

"Roman and me."

Walter set the box on a muddle of empty canvases and thumbed through a pile of illustrations. "One of your mother's lovers?"

"He was my hopeful poppa," Angelene said, blowing her bangs from her eyes. "What do you want?"

"Can you tell me about these?"

She plunked the paintbrush in a jar, peeking into the box. It was full of empty wine bottles, across the top, her new friend, Johnny Walker.

"Why do I keep finding these around the house? Under the sink, in the shed, the recycling bin, the pantry," Walter said, releasing an impatient breath, "do you know how much a bottle of this cost?"

She looked at the navy and blue label and slowly shook her head.

"Don't you see how frustrating this is? You were tipsy at Sofia's do. It'll be all over parliament. Everyone on Via Fetonte will know when Nic gets home."

Angelene swung the box off the table, tubes of paint fell at her feet. "Gossipers, all of them."

"People are concerned."

She walked from the room; the box clacked in her arms. "Victoria and Simone only care about themselves and you, you still love Kate. You wish you had the balls to marry her. You'd have to be equals and that scares you."

Angelene waltzed into the kitchen and set the box beside the garbage bin. She turned on her iPad and tapped her fingers against the countertop.

"Are you lonely? Do you want me to commute?"

"I'm making saucisson neuchâtelois."

"Why are you changing the subject?"

"I don't want you commuting and I'm not lonely. All I want is to make one of Roman's favourite dishes."

She zigzagged around the kitchen, collected a knife, bowl and vegetables piled by the sink. Angelene dropped everything on the island. The cabbage and potatoes rolled into the fruit bowl. She paraded to the stove for a pan.

"Will you sit for a moment? You're making me uncomfortable."

"It's what I do." She set the pan on the stove, rambled to the island, and plopped on the stool. "Mother drank, so do I."

She picked up the peeler. Carrot skins flew across the cutting board and draped over the fruit bowl. She glanced at Walter's face; his eyes weren't icy blue. He was more annoyed than angry.

"Mama loved Chambord. When she was bored with raspberries and vanilla, she would switch to Calvados. It tasted like apples."

"Your mother enjoyed the taste of men too. Spain, Denmark, Switzerland," Walter said, brushing a carrot peel from his hand, "have I forgotten any countries?"

"Do you think I have a lover? Is that what you are insinuating?"

The feeling tingled in her belly. Attached to it were brown eyes and a devilish grin.

"It's been a while since we've made love."

"You don't love me, so we're not making love. We're having sex."

"We aren't having that either." Walter raised his eyebrows, mesmerized by the ribbon of potato skin. She had peeled the entire potato in one long strip. "Are you telling me the reason you drink is genetic?"

"I get very blue sometimes, smudged blue. It helps."

"Maybe you need to talk to someone."

Angelene hacked the potato into misshapen cubes and swiped them into a bowl. "Like whom?"

"A therapist. You keep all that stuff locked up inside you."
She whacked the knife through the cabbage. "I don't need a psychiatrist."
"You don't like sex. You drink, poke at your skin. Talk to me."
The words talk to me, trust me, invaded her brain and she was in the BMW, driving to Burnham. She had shared things with Brendon, opened old wounds, spilled the blood of her past over him. She wouldn't burden another.
"Did you hear me? Talk to me, your husband."
Angelene shook the memory from her head. There was no going back. Brendon was not the same boy; she had smothered him.
"I was daydreaming."
"Daydreaming can be addictive, little bird. Getting lost in your thoughts isn't healthy."
"I'm not avoiding anything. You judge me, tu es un imbecile."
"I'm not an imbecile. I'm your husband. I'm supposed to do things to help and support you."
"Stop pestering."
"Shall we move to Chelsea? We could find a place close to Stamford Bridge. You could watch all the football you wanted."
Angelene brushed the strands of cabbage into the bowl. "I like it here."
"What about sex?"
Angelene blew out an exasperated sigh, grabbed the bowl and rambled to the stove. "Are we back to that again?"
"I want you to enjoy it. Not lie there with your eyes squeezed shut."
"We'll do it tonight if it will end this ridiculous conversation."
She drizzled olive oil in the pan, went to the fridge and pulled out a package of sausage.
"People like to have sex. I like to have sex."
"It's not my favourite thing to do."
Angelene placed the sausage in the pan. Brendon liked sex. She placed her fingers on her belly. Warmth tingled and grew. It was a strange feeling; one she had felt the night she had slept beside him. She had studied his back, committed every muscle, the curve of his spine to mind. His body reminded her of Edme Bouchardon's Sleeping Faun. She had visited the Louvre for weeks, mesmerized by the sculpture. She found herself in the same entranced state when she had stared at Brendon's back. It was embracing her again.
"What about foreplay? It might help you relax."
"If it involves kissing, then I want nothing to do with it."
"You're the only person I know who has an aversion to kissing." Walter rose, walked to her, and nuzzled her neck. "After dinner, we'll crawl into bed. I'll kiss you and you'll see how wonderful foreplay is."
"I have a headache."
"This is why you need to talk to someone. I'm lonely, little bird."
"You're not lonely, you are horn-nee."
"Don't you ever get that way? None of those PSG boys didn't turn you on?"
"What is turned on?"
"Get excited, feel desirous, a tingle in your vagina."
The feeling struck Angelene. She dumped the vegetables into the pan. Was she feeling lust for Brendon?
"I don't want to talk about this anymore. It's making me feel ill."
"Didn't Piedmont please you?"

"I'm done with this conversation. I'm getting uncomfortable and you don't want me to drink. If my emotions get tangled, I won't know what to do."

"Someone must have kissed you and you enjoyed it."

"I need a cigarette."

"Go sit in the window, little bird. I'll see our dinner doesn't burn."

Angelene snatched her cigarettes and nestled on the window bench.

"I'm not sure if I enjoyed it because I didn't want it to happen. He asked if he could kiss me, and I told him no. All I remember is his mouth tasted like sugar."

"You must have liked it if it tasted sweet."

She barely remembered the kiss in Burnham. Brendon's mouth tasted of wine and all she felt was the pattern strangling her. No tingles, no warmth, just free falling into another wrong decision.

"Can we change the subject, please? Half the pack will be gone."

"I heard Brendon broke his wrist. He won't be able to play for a while."

"He wasn't himself today. It was hard to look at him."

"Why's that? Most women find the brooding attractive."

"I saw myself in him."

"What do the two of you have in common?"

Angelene smashed out the cigarette. "Do you remember what Douchette said the day I was leaving?"

"He said you had the devil in you."

"I saw him in Brendon."

Walter laughed and grabbed plates. "Should I warn Sofia?"

"I saw his eyes; they were very black."

"The only thing Brendon is good at is football. I'm sure he's angry with himself."

"Brendon threw furniture around. There were olives floating in the pool. I've seen angry, but not like this and David."

Walter set down the plates and embraced her. "What is it, little bird? You look frightened."

"David had the coldest look in his eyes, like he hated him, like my mother looked at me."

"David wasn't ready to be a father. He wanted Sofia to wait."

Angelene held her cross, it poked into her palm. "It's my fault."

Walter gave her a little squeeze and patted the stool. "Sit before you fall over."

"I'm trying to confess."

"Confess what? Were you too hard on him? Did he not like the French lesson?"

'Help me, God my saviour, for the glory of Your name, deliver me and forgive me from my sins...'

31 SEVEN DEVILS AND A BOY

By age four, Brendon had the skills to be a great goalkeeper. At seven, he was coaching his friends on what it took to be a keeper. After years of camp experience, he was mentoring hopeful goalkeepers. Since stepping foot on the pitch and telling his coach he was a keeper, he had heard the whisperings. He had what it took to make it to the pros: concentration, positioning, leadership, confidence. Brendon was lacking all four.

"McGregor, stop punching the ball. You look like you're afraid of it," Liam said. "Brendon, what should he have done? It was a high ball?"

"Caught it."

"Why?"

"There was no one around."

"When should Will punch it out? It's going to be a long eight weeks if you don't help him."

"If you're under heavy pressure and there's a crowd around you. Stretch, reach for the ball, fuck, just read the plays."

"What happens if you try to catch the ball with a bunch of players around you?" Liam pressed.

"If the ball falls from your hands... just be in the bloody game."

If Nicola hadn't forced him out of bed, Brendon would have stayed hidden under the blankets. Amelia's vitamin packed, flu blocking smoothie had done nothing to energize him.

"I'm going home."

"Get your arse inside."

The sparks were constant, sometimes dull, and achy, sometimes they came at him in a whirlwind. They were always there.

"Do you need a bleeding pram? Move."

"If I had one, I'd put you in it, mate."

Brendon followed his teammates into the dressing room and unzipped his jacket. Not only were the sparks constant, sweating, then shivering was happening too. He rubbed his t-shirt over his belly, collecting a thin layer of sweat. "I think I'm coming down with something?" "Probably a cold," Troy said, biting into a fig bar. "How much trouble did you get in? I gave you a ring, you didn't answer."

"Dad took my phone away."

"Bollocks."

"He isn't talking to me either," Brendon said, tossing his jacket into his cubby. "Not even a goodbye."

Half the team had settled onto the mats, surrounded by various sized medicine balls. The others ran on the treadmills. The steady beeps and pounding of feet sounded like bombs dropping in Brendon's ears. A steady flicker of sparks lit and fizzled.

"I'd rather Mum yell, then give me the silent treatment. She didn't speak to me for a week the last time I got bladdered. It was extremely uncomfortable."

"I have silently disappointed dad for years."

"It's that temper," Troy said, tying his laces. "You were doing good at controlling it. I'm worried about you." "Don't be. I'm feeling sorry for myself, that's all."

When he got in a spat with Maggie, he would go for a drive, run it off, breathe through the anger and sort it out. Hurt mingled with anger, which danced with disappointment and tangled with regret. A long run on the treadmill would sweat out the emotions and shake the fairy tale titled, 'A Mess Named Angelene.'

"Why'd you let me get so pissed?"

"You're not blaming me for your stupid mistake."

He set the treadmill to four miles and froze.

"You okay, mate?"

He didn't know how to answer. He wasn't sure if it was Angelene the person, the silly promises that spilled from her mouth or her vacant 'I love you.' It could be a stew of school, poor decisions, screw-ups, or nothing.

"I don't know."

"You promised me if you were getting to the point of blowing up, you would let me know."

"Promises are broken all the time."

"I don't know what's got into you, but you better figure it out before everything blows up around you."

Brendon kept up the pace, his heart thumped, sweat ran down his back. Angelene had warned him. Terrible things happen to people who love her. Not everything she said was a lie.

Brendon slid off his trainers and zipped his First jacket to his chin. His legs felt heavy as he lugged himself up the stairs. He glanced from his room to the room no one talked about and followed the sound of hushed voices.

"Sofia, you're worrying for nothing."

"The last time I sat in this room, Brendon was four. He hugged me all day; said he was squeezing the sad out of me. I lied to keep him out of the forest. I said the witch from Hansel and Gretel lived in there."

"Parents say all sorts of things to protect their children. Out of this room, David doesn't want you in here."

"I needed comfort; crazy, isn't it?"

"This room brings no comfort. Come, I have a flight to catch."

The mattress creaked. Brendon walked down the hall, cursing the ache in his legs. The enormous bed, adorned with pearl inlay and brass ormolu details, called to him. He stripped out of his clothes and crawled under the blankets.

"You're going to be late for school."

"I feel like shit."

31 SEVEN DEVILS AND A BOY

"Where is the 'I did twenty extra box jumps'," Sofia said, laying a hand on his forehead. "You feel cool."

"I'm going to barf."

"All you have in your belly is that dreadful smoothie."

"I want to sleep."

"What's got into you, little man? Your omelette is sitting on the island," Amelia said, passing Sofia a stack of clothes.

"He feels ill."

Brendon grimaced; it was Amelia's turn to do the forehead swipe.

"Some girls at Sally's school have been out with the flu," Amelia said, tugging the blanket around him. "It could be the ale you drank. It takes our Tim a few days to recover when he's drank too much."

"It isn't the alcohol, it's me."

Sofia clicked through her silver bangles. "Call Dr. Weiss. See if he'll do me a favour and stop by?"

"I don't need a bloody doctor. I need to sleep. Will you both go away."

"David wants him at school," Amelia said, twisting her apron ties around her hand. "He'll be upset Sofia. He's already angry."

"What's going on in here?" Nicola said.

"I want to bloody sleep and these two are bickering over me going to school." He dragged the blankets over his head and rolled to his belly.

"There are coffee and scones on the table," Amelia said.

"Sofia Francesca, go eat. You're a damn hypocrite nagging topolino when you haven't eaten breakfast, either."

"How can I eat when my baby..."

"I'm not a bloody baby," Brendon interrupted. "Go eat a scone."

"You heard topolino. Off you get."

Brendon cradled the pillow under his head. This was the norm when he got sick. Sofia would click through her bracelets and glue herself to his side until he was back to his smiling self. The kitchen would smell of simmering brodo di pollo. Amelia would ensure there was bread for toasting, bowls of magical soup, pots of tea and lots of cheerful humming. The constant fussing had always irritated Brendon. Today it was worse.

Brendon yawned and gazed around his bedroom. He had slept the day away. He dragged the sheets around him, reaching for a hoodie tangled amongst them. His head was full of visions of Angelene and the words, 'I love you.'

"You awake? Dr. Weiss is here."

How could he share with Edward Weiss what was troubling him? Devils, falling in love with Walter's wife? It had to be a fever or a cold or both, exhaustion from dealing with Angelene.

"Would you like a cuppa, toast? I can heat some brodo?"

"Just tea."

Amelia spun around and splayed her hand across her breast. "Goodness, you couldn't wait downstairs?"

"I didn't mean to frighten you," Dr. Weiss said, smiling an apologetic grin. Edward Weiss was a smile. It was present in his demeanour and mannerisms, an understated happiness a person could count on. He was the safest person in Taunton.

"I should have known you would have made your way up here. Can I make you a cuppa?"

"No, thank you."

"I'll leave you two then."

Edward dragged over the clothing covered chair, smiled, and dropped his valise on the floor.

"Just dump the clothes on the floor."

"I don't think your mother would appreciate that."

"She's worried. She won't notice."

Edward grabbed an armful of clothes, piled them on top of the dresser, and settled into the chair. He smiled, studied Brendon's face, and smiled.

"I got the report from the A&E. that's some break. How did it happen?"

A flutter mingled with the sparks; Dr. Weiss knew the details. All of Taunton would have learned of his Saturday night adventure.

"I was pissed, got in a fight."

"Your temper has been getting you into trouble."

"It was William McGregor. He was chatting up every girl at the party. He called my friend a slag," Brendon said. The sheets were damp within his hands, "he called Troy and I poofters."

Edward tilted his head and leaned forward in the chair.

"Poofs, you know, a bum chum."

Edward smiled, not one of disapproval, not an angry smile, 'now I understand, but you could have used a better term,' smile.

"You and Troy are not homosexuals and even if you were, it shouldn't have bothered you."

Brendon released his grip, blaming William was an excuse.

"Have you forgotten about your breathing? You had your temper under control before you flew to Dortmund."

Moments with Angelene spun around his head. They were sharp, cutting through him. He hated her again.

"The sparks explode before my first inhale."

Edward opened his valise. He wound a stethoscope around his neck. The thermometer beeped. He stuck it in Brendon's ear, smiled, and stuck it in the other. "I'm going to listen to your heart."

"I have a fever, right? These chills are horrible."

"Normal," Edward said, dropping back onto the chair. "Your heart sounds strong. How about you tell me how you're feeling."

"My head hurts, my body aches. I feel like I'm losing my mind."

What sounded like the Death March warbled from the hall. "Your tea. I put Jacob's crackers on the plate. They always help Georgie and Sally when they feel poorly."

"You're brilliant Ame."

She nodded and scuttled from the room.

"Have you eaten today? You were in the A&E for dehydration, low blood sugar."

Brendon nibbled a cracker; it was dry and tasteless.

"I had a smoothie."

"How tall are you?"

"Six-two."

"A boy your height, training the way you do, needs calories. No wonder you're tired and nauseated."

"Nothing tastes good to me. The house smelled brilliant the whole time Nonna was here. I can't seem to stomach anything."

"How's school? Margaret? I saw Jack the other day. He showed me three new karate moves, left a bruise on my shin."

Brendon smiled weakly. "I don't miss that."

"Jack said the smelly dolt isn't visiting anymore. You and Margaret broke up."

Shivers rippled over Brendon's skin; he drew the sheets to his chin. "I don't see what any of that has to do with the constant chills and aches."

"Sometimes our bodies react to how we're feeling. School? Are those rumours true?"

"Bloody hell. I wish people would mind their own business."

Edward set the stethoscope and thermometer in his bag; the smile dropped from his face.

"I've been out to a few matches; you've had a rough go on the pitch."

"Liam pushes and pushes. I'm expected to lead the team. There are ten other players on the pitch."

"You're a natural leader. Why do you think Dortmund wants you."

"I don't have it in me."

"Stress can affect your health."

Tu me manques mon ami.

Brendon shook her voice away. "Stress?"

"It can do all sorts of things, affect your concentration, overwhelm you, make you feel tired and achy."

"What can I do? Everything was good, well, school was bollocks but, everything seemed fine. I could control the sparks. I was happy."

"Take a few days. Eat, drink. I'll stop by Friday and see how you're feeling."

"Dad will be pissed off I'm missing school."

"Your father is due for a check-up. I'll talk to him; suggest he back off a bit. You're trying. That should count."

A heavy weight crushed Brendon's chest; sparks flew in a frenzied dance. "Can someone die of a broken heart?"

"Time heals. You'll eventually feel better about your break-up with Maggie."

"No lolly, doc?"

Edward smiled and dug into his breast pocket. He tossed a Double Lolly on Brendon's lap.

The sound of the front door slamming resonated through the house. Brendon raked his fingers through his hair. His mother was rambling about the traffic and, had it not been raining, she would have been home sooner. It would have been nice, her stuck in traffic. He could have said goodbye to Weiss and pretended to be asleep.

"I'm glad you haven't left. Can I get you a scotch?" Sofia said. She stepped into the bathroom, grabbed a towel, and ran it over her hair.

"I was just leaving."

Brendon jerked on his hood and dodged Sofia's hand. "Dr. Weiss checked. I don't have a fever."

Sofia clacked her bracelets, squishing her eyebrows together. "Have you looked at him?"

"It's stress, mental exhaustion."

"Fighting, getting drunk, that nasty stuff he's been saying, is stress?"

"Dr. Weiss has diagnosed me. I feel like I'm dying, but if he says it's stress."

"Never say you're dying."

"Bloody hell, mammina, it's just a saying. I feel like shit. How's that?"

Brendon glanced from Edward's pensive face to Sofia's. She was doing everything she could to hold back the tears.

"What about sending him to Dortmund?"

"Can you write that on your prescription pad and give it to dad? He might take it seriously then."

"You're not going anywhere, not like this."

"Rest, put some food in your belly, and practice your breathing."

"Has somebody done this to him? Has somebody got into his head?" Sofia said.

'Angelene smothers people, suffocates them.'

"It's stress, Sofia, nothing more. I'll see myself out."

Brendon grinned a 'thanks for trying' grin and rolled his head across the pillow. He knew in his heart it had been half his doing, falling for a woman he couldn't have. Angelene and her devils had taken up permanent residency in his heart. Rest, clear his head, forget about her.

"I thought you were staying in London to have dinner with dad?"

"How did you know about that?"

"I heard him remind you before he left, some posh restaurant."

"He's taking Walter. You're more important right now."

Sofia stopped clicking her bracelets and snuggled beside him. "Who's playing? Not Dortmund, they don't look like bees buzzing around the pitch."

"Schalke and Dusseldorf."

"Who's better?"

"It's the start of the season. Schalke is higher in the standings."

"I went for a walk this morning. I bumped into Angelene."

Brendon gripped her fingers; he wasn't supposed to be thinking of her.

"She was looking for faery doors."

She was spilling secrets again.

"You and Paddington used to wait by the edge of the forest for the faeries."

"Uncle Walt told me about the faeries. He must have told Angelene."

"Shower and meet me downstairs."

Brendon scratched at his hair. It was dirty and itchy. If he had any energy, he would take a selfie and post it to Facebook, knock himself off the dishiest footy player list.

"Give me fifteen minutes."

He would title this chapter 'missing pieces.'

"I thought you were going to shower?"

Brendon sagged into a chair and sniffed his armpit. "I'm up. Isn't that good enough?"

"Hobnobs and my amaretti, almost as good as Nicola's." Amelia said. She set down a tray, pulled at her apron ties, and fiddled with the ends. "Sometimes Georgie gets blue. It only lasts a little while, then she's back to her old self."

He wasn't blue; he was in love with Angelene. The doorbell gonged, Amelia flapped a tie at him and scurried from the room.

"I'm going to my room."

"No, you're not. We're having tea."

"You're not disturbing us. I'm not sure what a knuddlebär is, but Brendon and Sofia are sitting by the pool."

A whisper of a smile touched Brendon's lips; it grew as Sofia's eyebrow arched.

31 SEVEN DEVILS AND A BOY

"Don't get too close, he hasn't showered," Amelia said, patting Sofia's shoulder. "Dinner is in the oven. See you in the morning."

"Mum, this is..."

"Miss Jones," Sofia said, taking inventory of the girl's red Rapunzel hair and painted-on jeans. "You're the one."

"The one and only."

"I'll go call your father and beg him to forgive me again."

Brendon glanced at his rumpled t-shirt and shorts. What did he care? He wasn't out to impress anybody.

"Do you want some tea?"

"Please. Your mum is proper posh."

"I'll tell her you said that. Milk and sugar."

"Just milk."

Brendon poured two cups, splashing milk into their cups. "That's how I drink my tea."

"Don't forget how I take my tea. It's important."

"I've heard."

"I remember the first time I saw you coming off the Taunton First bus. It was at that match in Weston. You had on a navy suit. All I thought was he's fit as fuck."

"Was that when I climbed to number one?"

"You've been number one since we started sixth form and I made the daft list," Rachel said, rummaging through her purse. "You look like you've gone to the dogs."

"Thanks."

"You still look dead gorgey, just a little rumpled." She placed a permanent marker between her teeth and bit off the lid. "Give me your hand."

Brendon thumped the cast on the table. Rachel grinned at the pictures and messages. "Does that say, little star?"

"I told mum to write it in Italian. It's embarrassing."

"You are a star," Rachel said, flipping his arm over, "dein lachein verändert meinen ganzen Tag." She added a heart and snapped on the lid.

"You better not have written anything dirty. My mum thinks..."

"I know what your mum thinks. She tried to hide it; her arched eyebrow gave it away."

"Did you write fuck off?"

"Don't be daft. It says your laughter changes my whole day."

"I haven't been laughing much lately."

"I know, knuddlebär, that's why I'm here."

"You drove all the way out here to make me laugh?"

"I would fly to the moon to hear your laugh."

Brendon hooked his pinky around hers, waited for the warmth to travel through his veins and ignite the fire, heaviness slumped his shoulders, it was gone.

"Dawson suspended me. Now we'll both be away from school."

"What did you do this time?"

"Another uniform infraction. Dawson went bonkers over my kilt. His comb over was flapping. His cheeks were a lovely shade of purple."

"Did you have to sit in the barf room?"

"Until mum came, do you know what she said?"

Brendon shook his head, stared at the line of Hobnobs, and crinkled his nose.

"She said I was a brilliant student, and he needed to stop whingeing about my uniform."

"Proof she loves you."

"I think she's falling for her friend from Berlin. A guy from the bank asked her out for drinks. She turned him down to talk on the phone. She was making this daft face the whole time."

"The Charlie face."

"Is that how Donovan stares at Troy?"

"Kind of."

"Why are you so sad, knuddlebär?"

Brendon rose and wandered to the glass wall. He gazed above the trees to the stars dangling from the inky sky. He must be feeling sad. Anger had left, guilt had shrivelled, something had hollowed his insides.

"You need to make a wish."

He wound an arm around her and drew her close, longing for warmth.

"I gave up on wishing a while ago. It got chaotic."

"I will then."

"Can you tell me?"

"It won't come true, knuddlebär."

"Have you ever had someone talk about things they want to do with you, even though they know they can't?"

"Guys say lots of stuff to me."

"Does it make you feel bad or empty?"

"Only once. I thought he might have liked me for more than my fanny."

Brendon drew her into his chest and kissed her hair. "Sorry about that."

"We're friends and if you ever want to hump, I'm your girl."

They strolled back to the table; Brendon sagged onto the chair.

"I feel hollowed out, like I know I'm pissed off, but the bloody sparks don't light."

Rachel wedged herself between his thighs and held his cheeks in her hands. "Who hurt you?"

"I'm a dolt for believing the shit."

"Does she go to our school? Who's the cow?"

"You look brilliant when you're pissed off."

He ran his hands over her bottom and laid his head against her chest, soothed by the rhythm of her heart.

"You smell, knuddlebär. It's like stinky sweet, I'd still hump you." Rachel pecked his lips, dropped to the floor, and crossed her legs. "How long will you be off? Latin is dreadfully boring without you."

"The week."

"Troy looks lost. It's weird not seeing the two of you together."

"I hear they won the match."

"Tilly wouldn't shut up about Will not letting a goal in," Rachel said. She tilted her head and smiled warmly. "He'll never be as good as you."

"You don't have to say that."

"There are good keepers and great keepers. You are one of the greats."

"I don't feel very great."

Rachel ran her black and yellow painted fingernails up his calf. "You will."

"Busted wrist, bruised knuckles."

"You still have it, knuddlebär."

"I wish I could see what you see."

"You're a little lost right now." Rachel stood, slurped back the tea, and squished his cheeks in her hands. "Get your brilliant bum back to school. I miss you." She pressed her mouth against his. Brendon tried to capture the warmth.

"Did I breathe any life into you, knuddlebär?"

He shook his head and smiled a flimsy smile. If only he could go back to September, back to the way he was before Angelene, not so lost, not so empty.

***

Taunton First was celebrating their first victory in weeks. The final score was 1-0. Troy peeled off his jersey and tossed it on the bench. The win was bittersweet.

"You rallied the team today. You did good," Liam said.

"Someone has to set up the plays."

"I've been hearing some buzz about you. That scout from Newcastle was back."

"That's brilliant."

"Get in the shower. I've got a phone call to make. A friend of mine joined the coaching team for Arsenal."

"Are you going to tell him about this ace defender you know?"

"Just keep dazzling on the pitch. I won't have to say anything."

Troy grabbed a towel, Brendon's number one jersey hung, match ready. It wasn't the same without him. They had been playing on the same team since the youth leagues. Nothing but Dortmund was supposed to separate them.

"I got my first clean sheet," William said, 'we don't need Mr. Football now. I've proved that."

Troy gripped the towel. A hush swept through the dressing room. "Would you like to repeat that?"

"Calm down and give me some credit."

"You did nothing but stand there. I was keeper and defender."

"Liam can start me now. I've proved I can play ninety minutes."

"Standing in the box does not make you first choice keeper."

"You must really love your boyfriend, defending him on and off the pitch."

Troy dropped the towel, his muscles quivered. There were no sparks like Brendon said, just a pulsing heart. It caught Troy off guard. He had earned the nickname Switzerland for good reason. He wasn't a fighter and never took part in any wars, even if it involved his best mate. Troy played the role of mediator. He made sure everyone had an opportunity to speak. Sometimes the title of Switzerland earned him bruises or taunts. It was worth it to save face with Charlotte and keep up his reputation as the nice guy.

"You guys would rather have this dolt in net."

The dressing room remained silent.

"We won, didn't we," William said.

Someone shouted from the shower. "Cook should be happy. He finally humped."

William snorted. "He did stick his dick in Rachel."

Troy jumped over the bench and snagged William by the neck. "What did you do that was so brilliant?"

"Have you lost the plot? "

Troy tightened his grip, shaking William. "What did you do other than keep the net warm?"

"I was on the pitch not whingeing into mummy's tits."

A series of snickers and laughter circulated the dressing room. Troy lifted William another inch and shoved him into the wall. "You did nothing. I communicated to the team. I yelled push up, I called keeper's ball."

"Let me go."

Troy dropped him and glared. "You're a shit keeper and you know it."

William adjusted his jersey and kicked off his cleats. "Nilsson and Barnes will see Brendon doesn't play a match for twelve weeks. Those refs think he's a showy prick."

Adrenaline raced through Troy and into his fist. William staggered backwards, crumpled over the bench and onto his backside. Hoots and hollers exploded around Troy as he stared from his hand to William's reddened cheek.

"Cook is a moody piece of shit. Taunton's hero, my ass."

Troy put his fist in William's face, the other in his stomach. Brendon was a hero. He believed in him, not just as a defender, but as a person and friend. He never had to explain his feelings or frustrations, Brendon just knew. Spence and Cook until the end.

"What the hell is going on?"

Liam burst through the door, grabbing Troy by the waistband. Troy's chest expanded in quick bursts. He was the only person allowed to talk shit about his mate. He struggled free and plowed towards William. Liam growled and hooked a finger in his shorts.

"Will you stop acting like a bunch of eejits?"

William wiped blood from his chin, flinging the gob of crimson saliva at Troy's feet.

"You're lucky you didn't knock my other tooth out."

"What the hell are you two fighting about?"

Troy drew in a quick breath, jerking his shorts from Liam's thumb. "You aren't first choice keeper."

"The team knows that," Liam said, grabbing a damp towel. "Clean up your blood McGregor, Spence in the showers."

"You're no Brendon."

William mopped up the blood and smirked. "Don't you hate being in Cook's shadow? He walks onto the pitch, the crowd roars. Who roars for you?"

"I could ask you the same question."

Liam pushed himself between Troy and William, laying a hand on their chests. "You want a wake-up call McGregor? You didn't do a damn thing out there. The defence did all the work."

William shoved Liam's hand away and threw up his middle finger. "You're a bleeding poofter."

"I'm not the one with a bloodied lip. Anyone else have something to say?" Troy said, ripping his towel from the bench. The room stayed silent. "I didn't think so."

The word defender took on a whole new meaning. He defended his mate on the pitch, off the pitch, and at school. He would defend Brendon until the end, even if there was nothing in it for him. That's what a defender did.

Troy pulled into the Tesco parking lot, still defending. He spent the drive pleading with Charlotte to understand. Charlotte didn't want a boyfriend who fought. She wanted her sweet little crumpet. He was in for a long night if her mood didn't change.

"I just pulled into Tesco luv." Troy parked the car and dug through the console for a pen. "What's mum going on about? Is she whingeing we don't eat enough veg again?"

Troy scribbled down the additions to the list, mumbled 'I love you' and returned the air kiss. He added cherry Bakewell's and Jelly Tots, if he was going to plead for forgiveness, two gifts were better than one. Hopping out of the car, Troy sauntered across the car park. He mapped out his route, checked his hair in the window and jerked a trolley free.

"Your hair looks fine."

Troy shifted from one foot to the other. "Hey Ms. Pratt."

"You looked like you stepped off the set of an old Hollywood movie. My mother would have devoured you."

"Ms. Thornton calls it a low fade with a side part."

Angelene's calm composure put Troy on edge. She looked happy, her eyes said she was holding in a scream.

"Where's your friend?"

"Charlotte? She's helping mum with dinner. I'll see you."

"Brendon. Was he not at the match?"

The doors wheezed open, Troy clenched the handle, swinging the trolley to the produce aisle. He stared from the list trembling in his hand to the row of lettuces.

"He's in bed."

Troy bagged romaine and tossed it in the cart.

"Is he not well?"

Troy swallowed. He couldn't decipher if she was concerned, scared, or both.

"Give Ms. Cook a call. She'll tell you."

"I saw her today; she said nothing. She seemed worried," Angelene said, wringing her hands. "Why are your words black? Where is your sunshine?"

Troy moved the trolley around the displays. Cucumber, no he needed celery. Patchouli followed him down the aisle, the list crumpled in his hand.

"I had to defend and be a keeper. I'm knackered."

Angelene touched his hand. His legs quivered.

"You have cuts on your knuckles. Who stole your sunshine?"

"I'd love to chat, but mum is waiting to get dinner on and if I don't get Charlie some sweets, she'll be mad all night."

"Where's your smile?"

"It's as tired as I am. See you around."

"How sick is Brendon? Is it his wrist?"

"I'm not sure. We talked briefly after the match. Dr. Weiss thinks it's stress."

"This is part of the pattern."

Troy scrunched the paper. The scream lingered in her eyes.

"I think it has more to do with school and wanting to play football."

"I thought it was for the best."

Troy dropped a box of cherry Bakewell tarts into the trolley. "Do you need me to call Mr. Pratt?"

"He wouldn't understand. I'm sorry for troubling you."

Troy smoothed his bangs. He was all about helping a friend, except he didn't consider Ms. Pratt a friend. She was a pretty woman he fantasized about. He conjured up a picture of Charlotte and pulled Angelene in for an awkward side hug. The scream had moved from her eyes to her twitching mouth. She was unravelling.

"What did you come to Tesco for? I have a few more things to get."

"I was going to make sole meuniere. I can't remember the recipe."

Troy smoothed the paper on his chest and laid it across the handle. "Grab me a box of Shreddies. I'll get the recipe off my phone."

Troy tapped open his phone, his mind spun. She had gone from Angelene's happy to silently screaming.

"Your Shreddies."

"You need sole, lemons and some things called capers."

"I remember now," Angelene said, placing the box in the cart. "Will Brendon be, okay?"

"It's my mate. He's the healthiest kid in town."

"Are you sure? I couldn't live with myself if something happened to him."

Troy watched the pink fade from her cheeks. He was afraid to look too long in fear of falling victim to her again.

"I have Jelly Tots, OJ, and some crisps left to get. You grab what you need, and I'll drive you home."

"I've run my whole life. When things get tough, when things make little sense, when I don't understand my feelings. I eventually come back, but then run again. It's a terrible pattern."

He wanted to ask her what it had to do with Brendon. He kept quiet. Talk about patterns and running had him feeling uneasy, more witchcraft.

"I'll wait by the registers for you."

"I'll say a prayer for Brendon."

"You better make it to the footy gods, so his wrist heals quicker."

He ducked into the aisle of crisps; his heart raced. She wore the Charlie face.

***

Angelene dumped wine into a mug and stepped back from the easel. She examined the painting; seven cloaked figures surrounded a boy. The creatures had red eyes, horns, all of them tearing at the boy's wings.

"You never got to tell your side of the story. Are you using Brendon as your voice?"

She gulped the wine, wiped her mouth on her sleeve, and tossed the mug on the table.

"I'll title you Seven Devils and a Boy."

Angelene flicked off the light and padded to the bedroom. She stared over the moors; her heart snapped. His lamp was on.

Pierre, is something wrong with your son? He usually comes to meet you for lunch. It's been weeks.

He speaks in riddles. He says he fell in love with winter and spring chased it away.

Angelene gripped her crucifix and paced.

32 STAIN

Walter's gaze swept over a photo of Brendon after First won the league championship and a plaque that said, "I can and I will,' he had yet to add a photo of Angelene. When he visited colleagues' offices and saw collections of family photos and wedding pictures, he reminded himself to do the same. When he would feel inclined to add a photo, something would happen. A spat, tears for no reason, finding random wine bottles, he would decide against it. London was becoming a welcome relief.

"Shouldn't you be leaving?"

Juliette Hawley, his secretary, and personal shopper, stood in the doorway smiling an 'I'm here if you still need me' grin. Named after the Shakespeare character, she was fiercely independent and tolerable to Walter's demanding ways. She found him challenging, intellectually and personally. Juliette shared his philosophy, "I can, and I will.'

"I'm in no rush to get home."

"Would you like me to get my notepad?"

Walter smiled. The girl was always working and always dressed in a way to say, 'I'm smart and good at my job.'

"Where did you get that frock?"

"Hobbes. Do you need me to find Ms. Pratt another dress?"

"It's lovely. You must have spent a paycheque on it."

"It cost 89-pounds. I don't dress to turn heads. I dress for myself," Juliette said, "if I dressed for you and the other ministers, I'd be in nothing but heels."

"You're a real go-getter, aren't you?"

"I'm here to do a job, not find a husband. I went to Pitman."

Walter glanced at the photo of Brendon. "I know someone else like you."

"Are you hanging around to ask about my dress?"

Walter clamped his hands on the armrests and rose. He paced, slow and in thought like he did before a presentation, practicing lines, preparing for the razzle-dazzle.

"Can you shut the door, please?"

"Is everything all right?"

"My wife is a loner."

The words had sat on his tongue for weeks. It felt good to say them.

"An introvert?"

"I thought that, but Ang avoids the company of others. Introverts are uninterested in people. She's fearful."

"She's shy then."

"Introverted, shy. Ang is a drunk. I'm sure you've heard. The building talks."

"I don't listen to gossip."

Walter slid his wedding band up and over his knuckle. "I took her on her first date. Can you believe that?"

"Please excuse this question, but how old is she?"

"Twenty-five. The way she pouts and stamps her feet, I feel like I've married a nipper."

"Do you think her age has anything to do with it?"

"You're twenty-four. You act more mature than her." He stopped pacing and leaned into his desk. "Bottles, Juliette, empty bottles everywhere."

"Have you talked to her family or friends?"

"She has no family and her friend, Lisette, was very hush about things," Walter said. "She's always alone, locks herself in the house, paints the most horrific things."

"If she's used to being alone, it's become part of her being. You know, I'm my own best friend."

"She says she enjoys being alone."

"Then she isn't in any pain? It shouldn't worry you."

"So why drink?"

"To cope?"

"If not from loneliness, then what? You've helped pick out her clothes. You know how much they cost."

"Things don't fill voids. Alcohol may make her feel fifty feet tall and powerful."

Walter slid his ring down his finger and sighed. "It's hard to be a good husband when your wife is a drunk."

"Maybe all she needs is for you to listen and understand."

"My friend told me I needed to be empathetic."

Juliette grinned. "David Cook. I was hoping his secretary would have retired by the time I graduated."

"How did you know I was speaking about David?"

"That was the only gossip I listened to. When you're ready to trade me in for someone dazzled by your flirting, put in a good word for me."

"You can forget about David. I'm keeping you," Walter said, flashing her a, 'I'm Walter Pratt smile.'

"Your smile may have made your other executive PAs swoon, not me. You have a bigger challenge than trying to get me to fall for that grin."

"My wife," Walter said, rolling the tension from his shoulders, "the Mount Everest of women. Dangerous and cold with an intriguing mystique."

"If anyone can conquer her, it's you."

"Do you think I'm a fool, like everyone else around here?"

"I think you're a smart man who saw something in her. Find it again, go home, hold her, kiss her, tell her you missed her."

"You don't know my wife."

"Neither do you."

Walter reached for his briefcase. It was that simple: listen and understand. David seemed to have mastered the 'happy wife, happy life' concept. If David could, it should be no problem for him.

"I hired you because you're a smart woman. You remind me of someone I know. She has the same strong, I am woman, hear me roar, attitude."

"From that twinkle in your eye, I'd say you should have married her."

"Thank you for listening."

"We can't have King Midas lose his golden touch, can we?"

Walter folded his suit jacket over his arm. "Where did you hear that?"

"See you Monday."

Walter chuckled, sliding file folders into his briefcase. A tiny shred of hope burned inside him. He hated failure. He had hoped marriage would be easy and his damaged little bird would find her wings. Walter grabbed his keys from the drawer and left his office. He ran through a list of things he would do when he got home, compliment her, force a kiss, and listen.

Walter forgot his list.

He closed the front door; the air was thick with sandalwood. He glanced into the front room, the pillows and cushions were in disarray. Two wine bottles lay amongst a muddle of charcoal pencils and paper. He set his briefcase down and walked to the kitchen, crumbles of mud and grass squished under his feet. Walter scowled at the dishes in the sink. A fallen souffle sat untouched on the stove.

"Bloody woman."

Walter thumped up the stairs, kicked a sweater down the hall, and growled at the mess in the bedroom. A jewellery box lay open on the bed. Walter closed his eyes, mumbled an obscenity, and banged his fist against the bathroom door. Candles flickered, creating a merriment of shadows on the wall. He glared at Angelene, chin deep in bubbles, a wine bottle bobbed between her legs.

"Did you not hear me?"

"I did."

"Are you drunk?"

"Je suis bourre."

"Our home is a damn pigsty."

"I'll clean it, once I'm done washing my sins away."

She grabbed the bottle. A flood of water spilled over the side of the tub and splashed at his feet.

"What is it this time?"

"Me."

He wrenched the bottle from her hand and poured it down the sink.

"I've been away all week; this is what I come home too?"

Bubbles cascaded down her body. She ripped a towel from the rack, winding it around herself.

"Tell me to fuck off. Isn't that what you want to say?"

Walter tossed a towel on the floor and mopped at the water. "What is all over the bed?"

"Don't touch it."

"You're dripping water on the floor." He strolled to the bed and picked up an article. "This is about Brendon."

Angelene collected the clippings and postcards and shoved them back into the box. "He's family, non."

"Do you have more?"

Angelene clutched the box to her chest. "Non."

"Empty the damn box."

She shook her head vehemently, like a dog shedding water from its shaggy coat. "You stay out, or I'll chop your fingers off."

"You're a devilish little bird when you drink. Shall I get a knife?"

"Keep out of my things."

Walter rubbed the veins bulging in his neck. "What are you hiding? More articles about Brendon? Things from past lovers?"

Angelene rose on her toes and jabbed her finger in his chest. "What have you done for me besides try to change me?"

Walter staggered backwards, his nostrils flared, she continued to jab.

"You embarrass me with your ridiculous bravado. Golden fingertips. You're my biggest mistake yet."

It took a second for Walter to react. He stared from his hand to Angelene's bloodied lip.

"Fuck you," she said and spat at his feet.

Walter stared at her limp body and breathed as if relief had finally come.

***

"Sono felice di vederti," Sofia said, tugging David's braces, "you must be tired."

David set his briefcase down and savoured her kiss. "I'm happy to see you, too. Your bracelets are missing."

Sofia stared at her wrists; she must have forgotten to put them on. There were more pressing matters than accessorizing an outfit.

"How's Brendon?"

They walked to the great room. Sofia shivered; the room was chilly despite the fire blazing.

"Edward stopped by. He thinks it's mental exhaustion."

David pulled the stopper from the decanter and poured half a glass. "If that's what Edward thinks, then it must be."

"You, of all people, should know about stress. Law school, years of commuting, the pressures of the political world."

"Has he left his bedroom or talked to Troy?"

"A girl from school came to visit."

"What girl? Margaret?"

"That girl, you know, the girl."

David gulped back the scotch. "Have you two eaten?"

"I was waiting for you so we could eat together."

David set his glass on the tray, threading his arms through his suspenders. "I'll go change and get him out of bed."

"Be kind."

"Why wouldn't I be?"

"You haven't been kind or patient with him."

"How can I be? The entire House of Commons knows he's a hothead."

Sofia's fingers went to her wrist. There was nothing to flick. She fiddled with her wedding band, hurrying after him.

"Set the table, Sofia."

"Mental exhaustion builds. It can lead to changes in behaviour, irritability."

Sofia clung to the words. It had to be true. Edward knew Brendon, he brought him into the world.

"Training, school, mentoring aspiring goalkeepers, flying back and forth from Dortmund. The contract with Protein Plus. I'm exhausted." She charged into Brendon's bedroom and grabbed David's arm. "What do you see?"

"I see our son lying in bed and you worried."

"Brendon's favourite Christmas was when you got him the subscription to Match. You would look through it together," Sofia said, trying to mask the desperation in her voice, "the trip the two of you took to Dortmund. You told me the best day of your life was seeing his face light up when you entered Signal Iduna Park."

A muffled groan rose from within the mound of pillows. "Stop trying so hard mum, dad doesn't like me right now."

"You're worrying your mother."

Brendon rolled to his side; the cast clunked on the nightstand.

"Go get washed up."

"I don't feel like it. Mum made me eat toast. I almost barfed."

"I don't care," David said, pulling at his tie. "You have five minutes to get out of bed and downstairs."

Every haunting memory David had shared crept from the corners of Brendon's room, gripping Sofia's heart, reading at Elizabeth's feet, bringing her tea, watching her die. David swore he'd be different with Brendon. He swore he would love him. There was no love in the room.

"Get changed, David. I'll get Brendon up."

David eyed the opened notebook and novel on the floor. "I suppose you've neglected your studies."

"Bloody hell, I can't keep my eyes open. You expect me to read?"

"Five minutes and you better be downstairs." David tossed a wrinkled pair of jeans on the bed and pointed at his watch. "You have four minutes now."

Sofia hung a hoodie over the footboard, managed a worried grin, and trudged behind David.

"He's got you wrapped around his finger. He's not sick, he's upset with himself for making poor choices."

Sofia ran her finger down a stack of sweaters, chose a navy pullover, and held the wool to her nose.

"Edward said it, not me." She handed David the sweater, a pair of khakis, and sat beside him on the bed.

"I couldn't protect you the last time. If Brendon doesn't get himself together and something happens to you. I'll hate him."

"Give Brendon the weekend. I'll call Troy. Rachel. I'll do anything to stop the bickering."

"Families fight Sofia."

"Do you know how many times Victoria has phoned about new flooring and William's tooth?" Sofia said, taking his hand. "Something is not right; I can feel it."

"Let's get through dinner."

Brendon met them at the top of the stairs, hope dinner might be argument free, settled into Sofia. David had worked hard to erase the blemish that surrounded the Cook's name. They were pillars of the community, Lord Chancellor and his elegant wife, their son, a superstar. The last thing Sofia wanted was for the blemish to return.

"Amelia made potato leek soup, focaccia." Sofia ladled soup into bowls and passed one to David and Brendon.

"What should we talk about?"

David smeared a layer of butter on a piece of bread and dunked it in his bowl. "What are you reading in English?"

"Tale of Two Cities."

"Is there a passage you like?"

"Ms. Hudson starts each class with a quote, then makes us share a favourite. I've marked a few."

"Can you share one, sweetheart? "

"A dream, all a dream, that ends in nothing, and leaves the sleeper where he lay down, but I wish you to know that you inspired it."

Sofia touched Brendon's hand; the feeling twisted in her stomach. "Why that quote?"

"I've been doing a lot of dreaming lately, nightmares mostly."

The doorbell gonged, David wiped his mouth, and dropped the napkin beside his bowl.

"Are you expecting anyone?"

"Victoria was going to stop by with a quote from the dentist. I told her no."

Sofia tipped the bread basket at Brendon, her eyes blurred.

"Please eat something. I can't take the tension between you and your father."

"I can't get it off my fingers," Walter said, scrubbing his hands on his trousers. "I hit her."

Brendon's fingers curled around his knife. Sofia laid her hand over his and pushed it loose.

"Go to the great room and finish your dinner."

Brendon made a tower of dishes and nodded towards his empty glass. "Can you grab me some milk?"

"Have you forgotten your manners too?" David said.

Sofia raised her eyebrow, shooting David a 'I've had enough' glare, jerked open the fridge and grabbed the milk jug.

"Take it and leave, please." She waited until Brendon was out of earshot before she spoke.

"I've seen you angry, but hit a woman?"

"I didn't come home to my wife," Walter said, resting his forehead in his hands. "I don't know who that woman was."

Sofia was sixteen when she met Walter. There had always been someone on his arm whenever she flew into Taunton. She had met Prudence, Jane, Abigail, and each girl had the same thing to say. He was charming, his crinkled smile was brilliant, he was a flirt but sweet. Walter had never raised a hand to a woman. He believed it was his job to protect them, not beat them down. Sofia didn't recognize the man slumped on her kitchen stool.

"Juliette and I were talking about Ang's drinking. She told me to be empathetic. The entire drive home, I said, Walter, put yourself in Ang's shoes. I came home to a mess and a drunk."

"Why didn't you walk away?" David said.

"It was like my hand had a mind of its own," Walter said. "I know I can be an overconfident arse, but I love women. I don't push them around."

"Why don't you two go for a drive?"

David clapped Walter's shoulder. "That's a good idea. The house is suffocating tonight."

Sofia watched David and Walter walk away. A prickly tingle crawled up her spine. She needed comfort; she needed her son.

"You ate."

"Dad's still angry disappointed. I thought it was best."

Sofia settled onto the sofa, curling her feet under her.

"Your reaction when Walter said he hit Angelene, sweetheart. You looked like you were ready to stab him." Brendon jerked the throw over his legs and burrowed into the sofa. "Angelene was probably a blizzard."

"What do you mean?"

"Icy, howling, bitter."

The tingling was back. It crept like prickling fingers up Sofia's back.

"Have you seen Angelene like this?"

She tried to remember Nicola's observation techniques; her mind was blank. She couldn't see anything but a sadness in his dark eyes.

"Has Angelene acted this way with you?"

"I overheard Walter telling dad, she could be cold as a winter's day," Brendon said, flipping through the channels. "You've seen her, her mood can switch like the bloody seasons. One minute she's sweet like spring. The next dismal, dreary, full of snow showers."

"I've never thought of her that way before. Rather descriptive for you."

"You can thank Ms. Hudson for that," Brendon said, dropping the remote on the floor. "Our family documentary is on, The Godfather."

Sofia grinned and placed a pillow on his leg.

"We used to cuddle like this when you were little. You were the only three-year-old that would rather watch football than the Teletubbies."

"They were weird. The sun with the baby face on it, bloody creepy."

"Do you think I should go check on Angelene?"

"I think you should stay out of it, especially if she's pissed."

Sofia couldn't decipher the look on his face, fear, guilt, 'please don't leave me.'

"She must have been really drunk for Walter to hit her."

"People do and say stupid things when they're soused," Brendon said, holding up his cast. "I'm not saying she deserved it. Walt has looked a little tense lately, like he's got a whole mess of shit bottled up."

"We've all been tense."

"Let's watch the movie. Uncle Walt will make things right. I've never seen him look so upset."

Sofia cradled the pillow under her arm. Memories hung like shadows, crept out from under the furniture, dripped from the ceilings, stretched, and spread around her. She had spent years redecorating, removing the terrible memories so they could build new ones. It was dark and lonely. Sofia snuggled deeper under the blanket; the hair on her arms stood up. Warmth scented with damp earth and chocolate digestives wrapped around her legs.

You're scared, I'm here. I'll protect you.

Sofia jerked and gasped. She stared around the great room, holding a hand to her thrashing heart.

"David, you scared me."

"Come to bed. It's my turn to cuddle with you."

"Should I wake Brendon?"

"Leave him."

Sofia draped the blanket around Brendon, gathered the dishes, and hung the milk jug from her thumb.

"How's Walter?"

David clicked off the television and frowned. "Still in shock."

"It's been nothing but chaos since Angelene arrived."

David flicked on the kitchen light, took the dishes, and set them in the dishwasher. "Life has always been a hectic around here."

"Mum left upset. Brendon's not well. Walter is an idiot and you; you're tense all the time."

"Are you suggesting Angelene is at the centre of this turmoil?"

"Life was normal before she came."

"Normal? We had to fly Brendon home twice because of his temper. Dawson gave him three strikes. He burned through them in a month."

"Maybe he's been stressed longer than we've known."

"Angelene isn't to blame. Nicola's suspicious nature gets her all worked up. Brendon is allowing his temper to control him and I'm having a tough time understanding."

Sofia poured a glass of water and clutched the glass. "Brendon talked about Angelene like he had seen this side of her before."

"Angelene hasn't turned Brendon into a miserable sod," David said. "He isn't exhausted. He's holding a grudge."

"Have you looked at him?"

"I can't. All I see is Richard."

"That's your son. Have you no sympathy?"

"He's making the choices."

Sofia dumped the water down the sink, set the glass on the counter, and looped her arm through David's.

"There's more to it."

"Life has placed another bump in the road. We'll figure it out, we always do."

"I want my normal back. I want to find grass swept under the runner in the foyer and hear him rushing in from training. I miss him. Aren't you worried about him?"

"He pouted for weeks when we brought him home last spring. He moped around when Lukas and the sporting director couldn't convince us to let him stay. The Facebook fiasco, he grumbled no one would take him seriously as a goalkeeper."

"There's more to it, I know it."

"I want to believe you; I just don't think there is."

"You haven't seen him. You haven't been here."

"You're right, I haven't been here."

Sofia held David tighter, remembering Brendon's first steps. Edward Weiss said he would run before he could walk, and he did. They had picnicked in the garden. Brendon had pulled himself to stand, gurgled a smile and walked to Sofia, arms outstretched. He was nine months old. His first word came as no surprise, footy and a long string of mum, mum, mum. First tooth, bedtime stories, bath time, had all been her. She knew Brendon Cook. That was not her son.

***

Brendon blinked sleep from his eyes. He heard his parent's voices from the foyer. They were going to the farmer's market. He rubbed at the kink in his neck. The doorbell gonged. Was it Walter coming to say he hit her again? He knew how frustrating Angelene could be when she was drunk. She must have forgotten his advice and neglected to read Walter's face. She might have been too drunk to notice.

"Troy, I'm so happy you're here. I've missed my little meatball."

The hope and joyful tone in Sofia's voice was grating. Didn't people understand that not answering his phone meant he wanted to be alone?

"You look so handsome. See if you can't wake sleepy head."

"Thanks, Ms. C, it's all about impressions. Before I get on the pitch and when I'm defending."

Brendon fought the urge to toss the blanket over his head and pretend to sleep. He didn't want to see anyone, especially Mr. Happy.

"I'll get him off the sofa. Hey Ms. C, you forgot to put your lipstick on."

Brendon stared at the ceiling; Sofia Cook didn't leave the house without her signature red lips.

"If you break into 'you are my sunshine,' I'll bloody thump you."

"You like when I sing to you."

Brendon stood, wobbled, and steadied himself. The ache in his neck had kidnapped his legs and spine.

"Blimey mate, you look like shit."

Brendon brushed past Troy and headed to the kitchen.

"I like looking like shit. I don't have to hear, you're so dishy."

He grabbed a glass from the cupboard, filled it with water, and gazed out the window. Sparrows flitted around the trees. What was Walter's little bird doing? Tending to her broken beak?

"Good luck at the match. I'll see you when I see you."

Brendon grabbed the coffeepot and held it up. Troy shook his head and snatched an apple.

"Is that any way to treat your best mate?"

"It's nice to see you. Now kindly go away."

"Haven't you missed me?"

"Nope, bloody poofter."

"I was thinking," Troy said, munching around the apple, "you should come to the match."

"Did mum put you up to this?"

"Put your suit on and get your arse on the bus. All you'll be doing is sitting on the bench." "Watching Will fuck up. Dr. Weiss said I need to relax, that will stress me out."

This could be the ultimate FU to Angelene, prove she hadn't gotten to him. Madre Innocente whispered, *'mammina will be so happy.'* Padre Diavolo cackled, *'fuck little bird.'* His heart wept.

"I'm knackered."

"Sleep on the bus." Troy shoved a banana in his pocket, fluttered his eyelashes and grinned. "Please, for your little crumpet."

"You're not my crumpet."

"Shower mate," Troy said, rummaging through the fridge. "You smell."

"You already stole fruit. What else are you going to nick?"

"I'm making you brekky." Troy placed the tray of eggs on the counter and flashed him another grin. "My speciality, an omelette."

Brendon choked back the coffee.

"What are you going to fill it with? Snot and spit."

"Sunshine and love mate, off you go."

The half-time whistle blew. Gosport was ahead by two goals. Terrible words sat on Brendon's tongue, a goal between the legs, a goal from a batted ball. He was mute, everything bottled inside him.

"Wish you didn't get into that fight?" Liam said.

"People do daft stuff when they're pissed."

'Like grow fifty feet tall and point a finger in Walter Pratt's face.'

"Wish you didn't get shitfaced?"

"I have some regrets."

"Should I switch to a 3.4.3? It doesn't look good out there."

"You're the coach."

"You used to give me insight. No one could read the match better than you."

Thoughts and emotions pressed down on Brendon's shoulders. He leaned into the fence; his suit was uncomfortably hot despite the chilly breeze. If he were any kind of leader, he would be in the dressing room encouraging the team to give it their all. It wasn't in him. For a kid who lived, breathed, and loved the beautiful game, he couldn't find the passion in himself. How could he expect it from others?

Brendon turned up his collar, sheltering himself from the crowd. His prediction for the game, another two for Gosport.

"Hey mate, you missed the team meeting. We could have used you in there. Everyone's miserable."

"It's killing me watching William."

It was a lie. He wanted to feel angry. It laid stagnant in his belly.

"There's forty-five minutes left, maybe forty-nine, with stoppage time. I need you here."

"You play just as brilliantly when I'm not."

"Send me a text so I know you got home."

Brendon walked to the car park and dialled a cab. Gray clouds rolled across the sky, rain fell, plunk, plunk, harder, stronger. Potholes filled with water; wind tore leaves from trees. God's tears were icy and violent. Nausea swirled the Spence speciality around Brendon's stomach. He should have fancied Angelene from afar and never rescued her. Rachel should have stayed off limits and not been a toy for him to play with. He should have stuck to what he knew, being a good boy and fulfilling his father's expectations. Brendon opened the gallery of photos; rain smeared the last picture taken, Burnham, the beach. Angelene's winter blew through him, stinging and freezing his insides. A black cab pulled alongside the curb. He took one last look at the photo and deleted it.

"If it isn't Taunton's hero."

Brendon stared at the man with a head full of white hair and a bushy moustache.

"Hey Malcolm."

32 STAIN

Brendon leaned his head against the window and watched the terraced homes fade away. He recalled a game he and Troy used to play. They'd make up stories about the people in the homes. The stories would change depending on who they saw and how much action was taking place. The game lost its appeal after Maggie wouldn't stop talking about a book she had read about a girl on a train. It took all the fun out of it.

"Must be hard, standing around the pitch."

"The fall of a hero, wasn't that what the papers said?"

"Don't let it get to you. The headlines need to be dramatic; no one would read it."

"I can't wait to get to Dortmund. I can go about my business without everyone sticking their bloody noses in."

"You think it'll be easier when you're playing pro footy? You make a lousy save; have a terrible season. It'll stretch across Europe."

"Between my dad wanting me to be a scholar and mammina wanting a good boy. Ms.... people expecting me to be full of bloody light. It's exhausting."

"Expectations can push you."

"I'm not smart, and I'm obviously not a good boy."

"You know who else has some lofty expectations, Ms. Pratt."

Angelene bounced into his head. He didn't place her there, didn't want her there. All it took was the mention of her name. She was good at getting stuck in his head. Had she made someone hollow before, scooped out their insides? He didn't know how to fix the empty spots. They had become part of him. She had become more of a nightmare than a dream.

"I picked her up from Tesco. She was tipsy again. Kept talking about a boy in brown and scaring her ray of sunshine. Nonsense really, I feel bad for her."

"Don't. She's a nutter and Walter's problem."

"She's lost, buried under expectations, just like you."

Rain smudged the farmhouse. Was Walter apologizing, wooing her with his crinkly smile, swept away in her beautiful?

"Here you are. This house has been the centre of gossip for centuries, gives you the wobbles."

"At least people had enough respect to leave one secret alone."

Malcolm rounded the fountain and parked beside the walkway. "That was a sad day in Taunton. Someone paid a lot of money to keep it out of the newspaper."

"I can handle the ghost of my grandfather, but that ghost got the expectations right. He reminds me all the time."

Brendon placed money in the cupholder and drew his suit jacket over his head.

"Thanks, and thanks for taking care of Ms. Pratt. She needs a friend right now."

Brendon trudged up the walkway. He missed what he never truly had. All the hope filled moments were just that, a moment. What happened to the leader his teammates saw? Where had the boy people rooted for gone? He wasn't Taunton's hero. He was a shell of himself. The headlines should read, 'the boy is broken.' Brendon stepped into the foyer covered in God's tears.

"Sweetheart, I was worried."

"I went to the match."

"Did Troy drive you home?"

"I don't want to talk about it."

"Join us for dinner. Your father would appreciate if you ate with us."

"I'm not so sure about that."

"Please come to the table. I want the bickering to end."

Brendon made his way to the dining room, his movements slow and controlled. Marinara, basil, and warmed focaccia penetrated every corner of the room. Mammina's lasagna, gooey layers of cheese, sauce simmered all day. His belly grumbled; he didn't feel hungry. He grasped the doorframe, dizzy from all the thoughts barrelling around his brain. Tiny sparks of anger, a touch of sad, a tad of guilt. Brendon draped his wet suit jacket over the chair and flopped onto it. Rules clattered around his head. Were his elbows on the table? Were his shoulders straight and squared?

"You be on your best behaviour tomorrow. Angelene has been through enough this weekend," David said.

"You feel sorry for her?" Sofia said.

"She didn't deserve a slap. Walk away if you're angry."

Brendon pushed the pasta across his plate, summoned a spark. He got nothing but soot.

"I apologize again for hitting the prick."

"Don't you think you were the prick?"

"Enough. I can't stand the arguing," Sofia said dolefully. "Can we talk about something else? Did the team win or lose?"

Brendon rubbed his brow; he had promised to be there for Angelene. Just keeping his lamp on hadn't been enough. If he could find the strength, an ounce of empathy, wrath, he would run down to the farmhouse and drive his good hand into Walter's mouth. The emotions tangled, and he slipped back into 'I don't care.' Angelene was needy. She had made peace with Walter.

"Your mother asked you a question."

"They lost."

"How was Troy? I miss seeing him around here," Sofia said.

Brendon flipped over a layer of pasta, mozzarella, creamy parmesan, ribbons of basil, just how his father liked it. This was his mother's devil, soothe with food.

"It's Troy's turn to shine now. The scout from Newcastle was at the match again."

"Were Liam and the team happy to see you?" David said.

"Liam's pissed off. Will kept sticking his tongue in the space where his tooth used to be. The team couldn't give a shit."

Brendon dropped his fork. A spark or two would come in handy. He could blow his top, get a lecture about respect, and sent to his room. Padre Diavolo was hiding.

"Liam shouldn't be angry, sweetheart. You're injured."

"He isn't injured." David said, severely.

"I know it's my fault. Do you have to keep reminding me?"

"I will until you're truly sorry for this mess you created."

"Can I be excused?"

Sofia reached for her bangles and stared at her empty wrists. "You haven't eaten anything."

Brendon poked at the layers of pasta, begging Padre Diavolo to light the orchestra of sparks.

"You should have stayed in London. All you've done is bitch at me."

Sofia gasped and held her napkin to her mouth.

"Sit up straight and eat your damn meal. Whingeing every day, you feel ill. You don't eat!" David said.

Brendon shovelled a forkful into his mouth, gagged, and swallowed. Dinner had always been a huge production. The entire house would smell of a Mastrioni masterpiece. They would eat by candlelight, the table adorned with roses. David would talk about his week in London, and Sofia would prattle on about what treasures she had discovered at an auction. He would fill them in about the matches he had played and the Bundesliga standings. Dinners had been a time to relax and be together as a family. The candles weren't lit. The roses hadn't left their home on the sideboard. His father looked at him scornfully.

"I'm taking Angelene to the auction in Bridgewater."

"Walter mentioned it. I'm glad it will be just you and Angelene, not those other two."

Brendon's leg bounced; his stomach rolled. If Sofia made peace with Angelene, she would be around all the time. Afternoon teas, walks among the roses, dinners throughout the week. He clung to each breath, one second, two, three.

"She's a friend now?"

"I'm trying. Walter's trying, Angelene is trying, we're all damn trying."

"Everything is okay, mammina."

He wanted to believe that. The look of disgust on his father's face made him want to peel it off. He wanted the hollow spots to fill so he could get angry, feel sorrow, get the amazing tingles Rachel gave him. He wanted to go back and walk away from William. A re-do.

Brendon slid his fork through the pasta and shoved it into his mouth. Between his mother's attempt at hiding her worry and his father's disappointment, he would call the night, 'the devil is at the dinner table.'

"All done."

"Every day, force you to eat, force you out of your room, force out conversation," Sofia said.

"You should talk to Angelene. Walt was telling me she knew a boy who didn't come out of his room for weeks. She might have some words of wisdom."

"What do you mean, she knew a boy," Sofia said, "is she suggesting Brendon is going to be housebound?"

Sofia reached for her wrist; her fingers trembled. Brendon pushed his chair beside her and held her hand.

"She was just trying to help, make it seem normal."

"You don't bloody listen. I feel awful, like the worst illness ever."

David tore into a piece of bread and dragged it through the sauce. "Stop being so dramatic. We should send you to Dortmund, guaranteed you'd feel better."

"We're not sending him anywhere, not now. Not when he's sick."

"This is to get back at us for bringing you home. What did you say? We ruined your life?" David said. "We kept our end of the bargain."

"So did I. It was hard balancing training and school work."

"I don't want him halfway across Europe. What if he gets worse? What if I can't get to him in time? Can't you see this is not an act?"

"He chose to miss classes. He got in a fight, and he cheated on Maggie."

"We could go back to church. He could confess, God might listen this time."

David wiped his mouth, tossing the napkin on the table. "He doesn't need a priest. He needs a swift kick in the ass."

"Your father is frustrated. It's been a tough weekend."

"He's been pissed off since the day I was born."

"That's not true. Tell him, David, we needed you."

"You needed me. Dad didn't want me, just like Richard the prick didn't want him."

A sob rose from Sofia's throat. She pushed back her chair and fled. Brendon stared at his empty plate. No sparks, no tears, nothing."

"Why must you upset your mother?"

"You think this is intentional? You think this is all an act?"

"I don't know what to think anymore."

"Aren't you curious about this kid who locked himself in his room? Isn't it strange Angelene knew a boy feeling just like me?"

"Not in the slightest," David said, placing his utensils on his plate, "don't you have highlights to watch?"

Brendon cursed Padre Diavolo for staying silent. He needed a healthy dose of the sparks to get back at his father and say something hurtful. He walked away.

***

The sun warmed the cut on Angelene's lip. She had fallen asleep with her memory alive and woke with it buzzing. The different compartments remained open, oozing past hurts. Brendon's skin smelled like warmed lemons, which smelled like Henri Piedmont, which smelled like the Limoncello she would smell on her mother's breath. The pulsing sting reminded her of Douchette's hands, Gustav Jenssen's fingers, the prickling words hurled on the school playground.

"Do you not understand?"

Brendon chewed on the pen; his leg bounced under the desk. "I understand one word."

"Which word? It may help you understand the sentence."

"Toilettes."

Her smile was slight and pained.

"Comment va-tu ?"

"I'm okay."

"In French s'il vous plait."

"Je vais bien. That's a bloody nasty cut. Why did Walt hit you?"

"Do your work."

"Tell me," Brendon said, tapping his pen against his notes, "I'm having a tough time figuring out my emotions. This may help. The emptiness is strangling me."

'It isn't emptiness, it's me. I steal light, breath, I tear wings to shreds.'

"I was drunk."

"You've been pissed before."

"I had been drinking all day. The house was a mess."

"He shouldn't have hit you."

"I was a bitch and deserved to be shut up," Angelene said, circling a word in red, "Try again."

Brendon scribbled out the word. "Still no excuse."

"I couldn't read his face. Everything was black and squiggly red. He's sorry for what he did. Quid pro quo mon ami, why did you hit that boy?"

A smile quirked Brendon's lip. "I'm not your friend and you know the story; I was pissed too."

"You've been drunk before; you haven't reacted that way."

"It was the alcohol. Padre Diavolo possessed me, both."

"Now you're hurt too."

"I'm exhausted. My mind is full, but I can't get any of the words out. I don't feel anything but hollow. At least that's consistent."

Angelene grasped his bruised fingers. She studied the drawings and signatures on his cast.

"May I?"

"I don't want any reminders of you. I want you to go away."

She plucked a permanent marker from the cup and twisted off the lid. "Trouve ta Lumiere sil te plait, find your light please."

"I'll find mine when you find yours."

"You're very black and blue."

"No bloody kidding." Brendon wrote a sentence and scribbled it out. "Are you going to stay with Walter?"

"He's apologized and I'm going to stop drinking."

"You could go back to Paris."

"To what? I have no job, no flat. There are too many memories."

"I could fly you to Dortmund, rent you an apartment."

Angelene sighed and held her cross. "This is my home with Walter."

"Never doubt you're an artist. You paint some lovely pictures." He closed his notebook and tossed the pen across the desk. "Why did you tell me you loved me?"

"It was the prosecco. I say stupid things when I've been drinking. It gets me into trouble. Au revoir."

"Not a bientôt?"

"Goodbye, my friend."

Angelene tossed the sponge in a caddy. The sink gleamed; the island was clutter free. Her hands were raw from scrubbing. She flumped on the window bench and leaned into the window; the grass glistened under the fading sunlight. The sky was empty, as empty as Brendon had looked.

She didn't mean to make men fall in love with her. She never meant to say the words to Brendon. Roman Krieger believed it was important to say I love you. She never told Roman how much she loved her hopeful poppa. She never told the boy whose world was lines and shapes.

"I'm sorry, little bird."

Walter cupped her chin and ran his thumb over the wound.

"It isn't in your hands to be rough."

"How are things at the manor?"

"Very grey."

"Are you hungry?"

"I'm the deepest, darkest blue."

"I'll make us a plate, cheese, fruit, like the picnics we used to have in Parc Floral."

She lifted herself from the window bench and moved to a stool.

"Why is it when you try to do the right thing, it ends up the same."

"We're going to try again. You'll give up the booze and I'll work on being empathetic," Walter said, placing sliced cheese on a platter. "You going to paint?"

"I'm not feeling inspired."

"Would you like to go for a walk? We could go to Spence farm. I know you like to look at the animals."

Troy's face flashed in her mind. He hadn't been the same with her. His sunshine was gone.

She plucked a grape from the stem and rolled it under her finger. "Can you take me to St. Georges? I need to confess."

"I'm the one who should be confessing."

Angelene popped the grape in her mouth and cringed as the juice squirt into the cut. "Come in with me, Father will bless you."

"Can I ask you a question without the plate flying at my head," Walter said, sliding a wedge of brie on a cracker, "why did you keep that article about Brendon?"

Angelene plucked at her skin, trying to distract her from the strange flutter in her belly.

"He's going to play professionally. I can brag I knew him."

"Do you fancy Brendon?"

Angelene stopped pinching and looked at Walter. "You're not a jealous man."

"Anastasia used to fuss over him. I have PTSD from her flirting."

"It's just a news article."

"Why hide it?"

"I put many things in that box."

"Should I be worried?"

Angelene touched her cross, prayed for normal, prayed for Brendon, prayed her devils away.

"Don't be silly."

33 Nefelibata

Sofia stepped into Brendon's room. She gathered the duvet off the floor and laid it over the footboard.

"Time to get up, sweetheart." She gripped the curtain; it clacked along the rod, revealing a sky washed in soft yellow and blue. Every day, she told herself to look past the boy crumpled under the sheets, focus on Paddington Bear and the joyful things in his room. Every day, she ignored her advice. She missed the rush, the smell of eucalyptus, listening to him curse his school kit. She missed the mornings. Monday, a kiss to send David off. Friday, waking, knowing he would soon be home and all the in between days with Brendon. She missed it.

Sofia picked up a wrinkled t-shirt and dropped it in the laundry basket. "Out of bed sleepy head. I've let you stay home for three days now." She pulled back the blankets and frowned. "Did you sleep with your hood on?"

"Don't make me go to school."

Sofia peeled back his hood and held his cheek in her hand. "I've told your father you've been at school."

"I'm bloody knackered. I can't shake it."

"I've lied. We've always been honest with each other." "Not all the time. You hid being pregnant."

"That was different." Sofia tucked the blankets around him and smoothed his hair. "He's been in a good mood. I don't want to ruin it."

Brendon plonked the pillow over his head and burrowed under the blankets. "He thinks I'm at school."

"One more day."

"I love you, mammina."

"Don't say because you think I need to hear it. I want you out of bed by noon. Amelia will put your lunch in the great room. I'm not having Edward come up here."

"You cancelled the appointment. I don't want to see him."

"He wants to see you," Sofia said, patting his leg. "We'll go for a walk later. The leaves are changing."

"Have fun at the auction, mammina."

Sofia picked up his crumpled suit and held the bundle to her nose. A hint of cologne lingered on the lapels. She tried to remember the last time he hugged her, the old way, complaining and rolling his eyes. Her heart cracked; confidence gone, competitive nature disappeared, his fight had slipped away.

Sofia walked out of his bedroom and bumped into Amelia.

"He's not going to school again?"

"I have to figure out a way to tell David."

"What can I do?"

"Make him lunch and change his sheets."

Amelia hummed under her breath, fluttering the ruffle on her apron. "I keep cycling through my weekly schedule of sheets."

"Purchase more, I don't care about the colour. A new duvet as well. He's sweating horribly every night."

"You're going to be late."

"How selfish of me, leaving Brendon," Sofia said, her eyes shifted to the locked door, "damn Walter. He should take her to the auction after what he did."

"Flowers are arriving at the farmhouse daily, Walter's trying," Amelia said. "I'm going to make those drop scones Brendon likes. One sniff and he'll come running. What's his record, fifteen?"

Sofia wound her arm around Amelia. She sagged into her as they walked down the stairs. "Eighteen, Troy ate fifteen."

"Give me Brendon's suit. I'll take it to the cleaners." Amelia pried the bundle loose and laid it on the umbrella stand.

"David has a suit that needs cleaning. My beaded gown, the one I wore to La Bohème, should be… That was an incredible night. I love David in a tuxedo."

Days of worry sat on Sofia's shoulders. She couldn't crumble, she was Sofia Cook.

"I want him well."

"Worrying will not help," Amelia said. "Think of all the treasures you may find."

"I already have a treasure."

"Brendon will be fine. I'll put an extra glug of syrup on the stack."

Sofia managed a thin smile and grabbed her purse.

'Someone make him well. I don't care if it's the damn devil. Make my boy well.'

Sofia had been quiet on the drive to Bridgwater. Guilt hitched a ride and worry furrowed her brow. She had managed 'good morning' and 'it's a beautiful day.' It would have done her good to talk, pass the time. The words would not come.

"I feel like I've stepped onto the pages of Pride and Prejudice," Angelene said.

The room was imposing, wood-panelled walls cluttered in Venetian paintings and mirrors. Braided cords tied back heavy brocade curtains; crystals dripped from chandeliers. Sofia angled down a row of Gothic Windsor chairs and melted into one. The scent of cracking oil paint and worn leather would have once caused a stir in her belly. The smells of aged things and Angelene's 'I don't belong here' expression wore on her.

"Have you got your paddle?"

Angelene nodded and fanned it over her flushed cheeks.

"Is my outfit, okay? What about my lip? Can you notice it?"

Sofia studied the layer of foundation and pressed powder. The bruise was barely noticeable; the wound was healing.

"You look lovely."

'*Like a cracked porcelain doll,*' Sofia mused. Walter's transformation was working. The bulky black turtleneck and slim trousers were the perfect ensemble. Red soled shoes, hair in a flirty ponytail, wrists full of baubles. She looked exquisite. '*Welcome to jealousy,*' Sofia thought. *She had forgotten accessories, hadn't styled her hair, 'you're not a jealous person, women envy you. You have more important things to worry about than bracelets and clothes.'*

"Walter said to dress nice. I wasn't sure what he meant."

"You look more put together than me. Those shoes, the Vuitton bag. You fit in."

A painful electrical storm clattered around Sofia's head. The people she loved and trusted kept assuring her Brendon would be fine. Edward would heal him, ease the stress, mend whatever needed mending. The constant headache and thundering panic had taken her hostage.

"He needs to get well."

"Did you say something?"

Sofia gazed around the reception room. '*I'm at an auction in Bridgwater.*' She cleared her throat and tried to smile.

"I was daydreaming, thinking about... it doesn't matter."

"Nefelibata, it's Portuguese for cloud walker. Roman told mother I lived in the clouds of my imagination. Mother would pull my hair and say it was my devil plotting."

Sofia pulled a catalogue from her bag, cloud walker, devil. She needed a distraction.

"Did you have time to look at the items up for auction?"

"There's a painting, 'The Girl with the Haunted Eyes.' They don't know who the artist is. I'm drawn to it."

Sofia flipped through the glossy pages and stopped at a photo of a girl poised on a black velvet stool in a black velvet dress. Every ounce of the girl wept. Sofia glanced from the photo to Angelene. She wore the same 'I live in a world of secret sorrow' look.

"When the auctioneer starts the bidding, raise your paddle. If someone bids against you, raise it again. The price will rise until someone wins."

"This is exciting. I'll have to be strong like you."

You must be strong, Sofia. Stand up for yourself. Don't hide behind David. You deal with Richard, and rule that house. Don't look pitiful or weak. I didn't raise you to be timid.

Sofia repeated Nicola's words like a mantra; it wasn't in her to be strong.

"This is what I'm bidding on," Sofia said, pointing to a pair of navy and gold vases. "They'll look lovely in the dining room."

"How is Brendon?"

Sofia slid the catalogue into her purse. For a moment, the thrill of winning the Royal Dalton vases concealed her worry.

"At home again. If you're speaking to Walter, please don't tell him. I haven't told David yet."

"I won't say a thing. You must protect his light."

Sofia gazed at Angelene, puzzled. She had spoke of this 'light' before as if it were magical.

"What do you mean by his light?"

A group of people dressed in grey, and navy walked onto the stage, adjusted chairs, and set a tea set on display. Sofia slumped into the chair and rubbed at the ache between her brows.

"Tell me more about Brendon's light."

"It's his spirit. The first time I saw him, the purest white light surrounded him."

"He isn't pure anymore," Sofia said, tapping the paddle against her knee. "How do you see this light?"

"In a smile, their words, their eyes, it's all around them."

"Are you talking about an aura? There was a psychic fair, a few years back. Victoria convinced us to go. The medium said my spiritual energy was black. I was holding onto negative emotions."

"Brendon has beautiful light."

The room tilted, Sofia gripped the edge of the chair, breathed through the dizzying electrical charges.

"You see this in Brendon?"

"I have seen it once before. A boy, he lost his light."

"The boy who locked himself in his room?" The words spilled from her mouth, coated in fear.

"How did you know?"

"Walter mentioned it to David."

Her mother's voice raged in her head, *keep Angelene away*, another voice whispered, *something is not right, ask about the boy.*

The air became soupy and musty. A man in a pinstriped suit took his position behind the podium and tapped the microphone. Sofia lowered her chin to hide the tears stinging her eyes.

"Welcome ladies and gentlemen, we will begin in five minutes."

"What happened to the boy?"

"I don't know."

Angelene's lips moved in prayer. Sofia could hear the whisperings of wash me from my guilt and cleanse me of sin, Psalm 50:4-5. Nicola used to make Gianni recite it after a night of drinking.

"How well did you know this boy?"

"Our first item up for bid is an 18th century Royal Albert tea set. We'll start the bid at two hundred pounds."

An arm, clad in purple silk, shot into the air, waving a paddle.

"I met him briefly. He was a beautiful boy like Brendon."

Sofia tugged at her cashmere sweater. What had her mother told her to look for? Perspiration, fidgeting? Angelene's knee was bouncing, her manicure nails tapped on the paddle.

"You think Brendon is beautiful?"

"He's such a healthy boy, watching him on the pitch. He takes my breath away."

"Are you attracted to Brendon?"

"There is a difference between being attracted to someone and finding someone attractive."

Sofia's head swam. Nothing was making sense. Walter oozed experience and confidence. Women found him handsome, men found him powerful.

"Isn't it the same?"

"Our next item is a painting; legend says it's cursed. If you stare into the girl's eyes, horrible things happen. We'll start the bid at one hundred pounds."

"Angelene, hold up the paddle."

Angelene stretched her arm. The paddle wobbled. Another shot up. Sofia placed her fingers on Angelene's elbow and forced her arm higher. The bidding war began.

"Pierre knew everything about the Impressionists. He had a brilliant mind."

"But you were involved with him. I don't understand."

"Attracted is a force that pulls you towards something. Attraction is a quality you admire." Angelene lowered her eyes. "Attracted requires feelings."

A whirlwind of thoughts spun around Sofia's head. Attraction, attracted, she never answered the question.

Sofia turned onto High Street. Autumn's magic was touching the trees in chartreuse and burnished bronze. She had walked this street with Kate for years. She knew every crack in the pavement, where the cobbles met the tarmac. Sofia was having trouble finding the entrance to the law firm. Her heart wanted to drive home. She was struggling with the definitions of attracted and attraction.

'Attract, evoke, have a sexual or romantic interest in, exert force. Attraction, the action or power of evoking interest, pleasure or a liking for someone or something.'

Sofia parked the car. Her insides quivered. Was Angelene attracted to Brendon or his light?

"I'll just be a minute."

Angelene tore her gaze from the painting. A triumphant smile brightened her face. "It's beautiful, isn't it?"

Sofia grinned and stepped out of the car. Her senses were on high alert. Every flutter of a leaf caught her eye. The smell of petrol was strong, the shushing leaves deafening. The door banged open, a woman with red, puffy eyes flew past.

"I'll be in touch," Kate said.

"Another affair?"

"Her husband got bored. Thirty years in the bog."

"David and I have been together that long."

"She can't get through a day without Prozac and the night without Lunesta."

"I could use some sleeping pills. Quiet the chaos in my head."

"Tough morning?"

"It's been a tough month. Brendon, Walter, her."

Sofia jingled her car keys, flicking through each trinket. The Italian flag once belonging to Gianni. The key ring with dangling hearts, David had left on her pillow and the Dortmund logo Brendon had given her. She touched each one, her heart aching.

"What's the matter with King Midas?"

"You haven't spoken to him?"

"I've been giving him space."

"He hit Angelene."

"He's a cocky ass, not an abuser."

"She was drunk. The house was in shambles. They fought, he reacted."

"She must have been off her face."

Sofia looped her arm through Kate's. "Keep this to yourself, David said she frightened him."

"Walter was in the Special Boat Service; you're telling me that five-foot waif scared him?"

"I've never seen Walter so rattled. The last time was... long ago."

"How's Angelene?"

"She's acting like it's completely normal. Brendon isn't any better."

"I read an article about a player from Liverpool, nineteen years old, suffered from burnout. It happens to athletes."

"He was friends with Angelene. Look at Walter."

"You think there's a link?"

"I don't know. She's touched both their lives and ..."

"You're tired. You're worried about Brendon."

"Do you think there's a difference between attracted and attraction?"

Kate gripped the door handle and smiled. "Maybe. I have an attraction to your Dolce & Gabbana sunglasses, but I wouldn't want to marry them."

"Angelene said there is. I asked if she was attracted to Brendon."

"Get in the car. You need to eat, then have a rest."

Sofia climbed into the car. She listened to Kate and Angelene exchange hellos and backed out of the car park. Walter wouldn't have hit Kate. He would not have come home to a messy house or a drunk. The problem, Kate would never be Walter's 'Fair Lady.' Sofia had gone to the play with David and Nicola. Nicola hated the play. Eliza Doolittle was a cliché; it was another Cinderella story. Would Angelene's story end the same, happily ever after?

Sofia left High Street and headed towards the roundabout; the traffic sped past her. Was she driving that slowly? She was never one for speed limits, David complained she drove too fast. Everything was moving too fast. The cars, Walter's marriage, Dortmund was approaching.

"I'll buy a pair of cleats, so I hear the click on the marble."

"Are you talking to yourself?" Kate said, snapping open a compact and dusting her nose, "you need some sleep."

"I won't redecorate Brendon's room. I'll leave it exactly how it is. A t-shirt on the floor, the towers of football magazines. I'll even turn on the television to hear those annoying commentators."

Kate closed her compact and dropped it in her purse. "July is months away."

"What do you think of the painting Angelene bought?"

"It gives me the creeps, no offense," Kate said, grabbing her purse, "the restaurant Sofia."

Sofia jerked the car into the car park. She could do this, get through lunch. Sirens whirred in her head; her heart thrashed in her ears. The visions and sounds shook her.

"I have to get to Brendon."

"He's okay." Kate climbed out of the Maserati and took Sofia's hand. "Amelia is there. Dr. Weiss will be there soon."

"I prayed for Brendon. God will look out for him."

Sofia tried to rustle up a witty remark about God's lack of sympathy, nothing would come. She opened the door; the dining room was white and grey with pops of pink and yellow. Sofia had always liked Gerbera daisies. They were happy flowers.

"I'll ask Peter to purchase some."

"What are you going on about?" Kate said.

"Gerbera daisies. They would look pretty around the pool."

Kate pulled out a chair and rubbed Sofia's shoulder. "Let's get some food into you."

Sofia sank onto the chair. She needed to be home, not eating lunch with friends.

"You're not wearing your lipstick," Angelene said. "I thought something was missing."

Sofia picked up the knife and studied her reflection. She must have forgotten.

"I admire you for being confident enough to wear it. I still haven't worked up to the colour yet. My friend, Madame Rousseau, gave me a tube; she said every French woman should own red lipstick. Mother made me throw it out."

"I had other things on my mind."

"Have you given Amelia a bell?" Kate said.

"I texted her. He's still in bed."

"He needs to find his light," Angelene said, sipping her water.

The conversation on attraction and attracted snuck back in Sofia's head. Was Angelene attracted to Brendon like the Klimt painting, or did her feelings run deeper? She still couldn't read Angelene's face.

"Brendon's presence is calming. He has a way of making me relax."

The words fell from Angelene's mouth so nonchalantly, one would think they were talking about the weather. Sofia snapped open her napkin and patted her upper lip. It had been weeks of walking on eggshells, not knowing if he would lash out or brood. There was no calm, just constant aching and worrying.

"Look at the menu, Sofia, the dover sole looks good," Kate said.

"Archangel Michael will protect him. God will see his angels keep him safe."

"From what? Who?"

Sofia's mind raced, the patchouli scented sheets; the wine scented bedroom in Burnham.

"What type of relationship have you had with Brendon?"

Kate reached across the table and took Sofia's hand. "Angelene is just being kind. Brendon has a way of making people feel comfortable, that's all."

"You met him for breakfast that day."

"I didn't plan to." Angelene broke off a piece of bread and rolled it between her fingers like plasticine.

"You just happened to be in the same place as him? You were supposed to be at the auction with mum and I."

"I bumped into Brendon in August, remember, just before he went back to Dortmund. We grabbed lunch," Kate said.

"I was upset I troubled you and Nicola. Malcolm drove me to my favourite bookstore. I stumbled into him. Neither one of us had eaten."

Sofia's mind replayed the entire day, the phone call from Mr. Dawson, Victoria's smug tone.

"He missed classes that day. He was in a terrible mood."

Kate opened the menu and laid it over Sofia's plate. "You can't nag Brendon to eat if you aren't."

Sofia studied the selections. Dorset blue souffle, pear, and walnut salad. Angelene still hadn't answered the question.

"I can't decide.""I'll make it for you," Kate said, summoning the server, "we'll both have the souffle with salad. Angelene?"

"I'm sorry Sofia. I don't mean to upset you."

"Make that three souffles," Kate said.

"I'm so frazzled. I can't think straight. Mental exhaustion..."

"Edward knows what he's talking about," Kate said.

Sofia held her breath, desperate to slow her thundering heart. "I met the girl."

"Femme fatale. I told Brendon to stay away from her."

"How do you know about her?"

"I saw her at the pub. She reminded me of my mother, flaunting and fawning over Brendon."

"You don't think someone broke his heart, do you?" Kate said.

"Somebody hurt him, something... I feel it."

Attracted, attraction, the boy locked in his room, the girl with the haunted eyes, beautiful light. The noise raged in Sofia's mind. She scolded herself for being stupid, it had to be nonsense. Sofia glanced over her wineglass. Angelene looked calm, despite the bombs she dropped. *'They're just words, Sofia, it's what's behind the words? Did I see a twinkle in her eye? Was there a hitch in her voice when she spoke of the boy locked away? Did breathless mean she loved Brendon or is she in awe of this breathtaking light?'*

***

Brendon nibbled a pancake, staring blankly at the Dortmund, Bayern match.

"It's taken you three hours to eat a drop scone," Amelia said. She ran a feather duster over the mantle and dropped it in her apron pocket. "If you'd let me make them with castor sugar, not protein powder, you might have finished by now."

"Afternoon. Peter let me in," Edward said, smiling warmly.

Amelia fluffed the throw pillows and pat the cushion. "Would you like a cuppa?"

Edward wedged himself between the pillows and set down his valise. "No, thank you."

"You can take the tray away. I'm finished."

"You better eat the soup I made for dinner. My goodness, little man."

Brendon stretched out along the sofa, dragging his hood over his head.

"Back again, doc."

Edward reached inside his valise, pulled out a file folder, and flipped it open. "How are you feeling today? Feverish, chills, sleeping?"

"I can't sleep. I get hot, then cold. All I do is think."

"Have you tried a meditation app like Liam suggested or counting sheep?"

"They pronounce crisps, sheeps in France."

"I'll remember that," Edward said, scanning the paper, "Liam and I agree it's mental exhaustion."

Brendon knew exhaustion. He had trained with the elite squad in Dortmund. Hours of rigorous practice drills, rounds of box jumps, plyometrics.

"I feel sick. Mum keeps sticking a thermometer in my ear. Ame has been humming depressing songs. All I want to do is sleep."

"How's the hand?"

"Itchy."

"Sofia said you went to a match. That must have felt good."

"I stayed until half time and came home. I felt nothing."

Edward pushed his glasses up his nose, the smile dropped. "Nothing?"

"Will played lousy. I didn't care that the team lost. The old me would have lost his temper. The words, and not nice ones, were right there, but I couldn't get them out."

"What do you mean?"

"It's like something has pulled everything out of me. I feel empty."

Brendon sat up, tugged off his hood and fanned his inflamed cheeks. He tilted his head and listened for any movement in the foyer. There was no humming, no rambling about last-minute chores or dinner prep.

"You're a man right?"

The smile came back to Edward's face.

"The last time I checked."

"You know what happens to a guy in the morning?"

"It annoys my wife."

"It isn't happening. Bloody hell, sometimes I have no control over the thing. It does whatever it wants and at the worst times. It happened once in Latin. Rachel bent over her desk and her kilt lifted."

"Are you not getting erections?"

"Not for a while. The other morning, I thought about Rachel and nothing."

"Stress will do that."

"I felt something the other day."

"Are we still talking about erections or something else?"

Brendon transported himself back to French lessons. It was right when Angelene walked into the den. The sun shined on the cut. His hand had formed into a ball, sparks disappeared as quick as they came.

"It might have been anger, frustration. It only lasted a second and went away."

Edward closed the file and took off his glasses. "It's a start."

"Can you talk to Mum? I want to stay home."

"Getting back to your routine will help."

"That's what dad said. He's beyond angry."

"You're concerned?"

"He blames mum. They've been fighting since this started."

"Arguing is healthy. Bottling things up isn't."

"Mum and dad aren't afraid to fight. Dad was always calm; mum was the yeller. It's the opposite now."

Brendon jerked at the throw and draped it around his shoulders. He shivered and sunk deeper into the sofa. "It's me. Dad hates me."

"He might be ashamed he's reacting like Richard."

"He can't stand to be around me."

"Amelia hums sad songs. Your mum thinks the worst. Some people lash out when they're scared. It could bring up past hurts for your father."

A heartfelt rendition of 'Where is Love' from Oliver spilled into the room. Brendon dropped the throw and stood.

"I heard mum telling Ame she has Couvade syndrome. Is she sick?"

Edward chuckled as they walked to the door.

"It's sympathy pains, like an expectant father feels."

"You'll be checking in on mum soon."

Brendon opened the door, his heart dropped. Mammina was home.

"I'll see Sofia. I want you to do one thing from your old routine. Can you do that?"

"Sure thing, doc."

"I'll walk out with you." Amelia said, "there's ribollita on the stove, you eat."

"Do you see what I put up with? If it's not mum fussing, it's Ame."

Edward smiled and held out a lollipop. "Do as she says."

Brendon put the lolly in his pocket and glanced at his watch. It was half past four, what would he be doing? Match day, he would be on the pitch. There would be dragons in his belly, he would be happy. He stared at the cast, rambled up the stairs, and ducked into his bedroom. He waited until she was in her bedroom, groaned, and forced himself to go to her. Old Brendon would be heartbroken to see mammina in pyjama bottoms and his father's pullover. He couldn't remember the last time he had seen her hair in a ponytail.

"Jimjams already?"

"I'm exhausted."

'Sounds familiar'

"I spoke to Edward, another week. I don't know how I'm going to tell your dad."

"Ame made Nonna's ribollita. You know what Nonna says: food and humping cures everything."

"Making love, sweetheart."

"I did my homework; tell dad that. It'll soften the blow."

They walked arm in arm to his bedroom and dropped onto the bed. The doorbell echoed through the house. Brendon's heart clunked to a stop. Would Angelene visit? She had a habit of showing up and spilling secrets.

"Are you expecting anyone?"

"I haven't looked at my phone."

Brendon reached into the rumpled sheets and tapped his phone. "It's Rachel. I'll text her to come in."

"So much for a quiet evening."

"She's not that bad."

"She has a reputation."

"You don't even know her."

"I'm coming up, knuddlebär, you better be decent."

Rachel pirouetted into the room. Her black baby doll dress floated around her hips. It covered her breasts, giving the impression she knew how to be a lady.

"Bloody hell, you look nice."

"You didn't get dolled up for him, did you? He hasn't showered."

"I went to dinner with mum and her friend, Christian."

"Another boyfriend?"

"It's her friend from Berlin. The one I told you about."

Something stirred within Brendon, a flutter, a tingle. It was weak, quietly whispering what he had thought for a month.

"Du bist sehr schon."

Rachel's smile was shy. He grinned at the blush on her cheeks.

"You never told me I was beautiful before."

"We were about to have dinner. Why don't you stay and have a glass of wine with me?"

"I'd love too, Ms. Cook. Mum said two words to me over dinner, eat and manners. I don't know why she cared; Christian is just a friend."

"I'll go dish it up. Five minutes and I want you downstairs."

Brendon reached for Rachel's arm and dragged her closer. "Why'd you agree to stay?"

"Your mum looks gutted."

He brushed her hair over her shoulder, running his thumb down her neck. "You think so?"

"She looked proper posh when I visited before. She's in pyjamas." The last time Brendon had seen his mother was in the morning. She had fussed over the hood on his head, swiped her hand over his forehead. Brendon rolled his knuckles over the heaviness in his chest. She hadn't put makeup on. Memories stretched through his mind, playing in the garden, football matches, Tesco for milk, red lips. Her light was missing, too.

"You feeling iffy? You want me to get your mum?"

"I don't know what I'm feeling, sad?"

He moved his hand to her cheek and kissed her, waiting for whatever feeling was loitering in his belly to move to his groin. It disappeared before turning into that wicked heat that made him ache for her.

"Are you worried about your mum?"

He didn't know if it was worry, guilt, or sorrow. Feelings floated around, dangled, teased, and tormented, nothing stuck.

"Maybe mum has caught the lurgy."

"I don't think so, knuddlebär."

He took her hand, his heart didn't thud, the butterflies had flown away.

"Can you act surprised when you go into the kitchen? Mum still hasn't found out about my party."

"Anything for you."

Brendon grinned and pressed his lips into her hair. It smelled like honey and apricots.

"Every room in the house is brilliant," Rachel announced. "Who has chandeliers in their kitchen?"

If Brendon could trap a feeling, it would be embarrassed. Sofia had filled the island with scrapbooks. Each one opened to a specific page, Brendon, through the years.

"Please don't show Rachel my baby pictures."

"I thought the scrapbooking phase was silly. Why would you put your memories in a book when you could display them?"

"Mum stopped taking pictures of me after dad left."

"I have a book for everything, my wedding, David and Elizabeth. Most are of you."

"Please don't cry."

He dunked his spoon in the thyme and garlic scented broth, bobbing cannellini beans up and down.

"I can reminisce without crying," Sofia said, holding up a baby blue book. "This is my favourite page."

Brendon rolled his eyes at the Paddington Bear decorations surrounding his smiling face.

"You loved Paddington? Oh, knuddlebär, how cute."

"Do you know how excited I was when Edward told me I was pregnant?"

"You've told me a million times, mammina."

"I sat in the garden and said please make him a boy with dark hair and dark eyes. Someone listened. You were perfect."

Brendon pushed a carrot around and rested his forehead on the frayed end of his cast. "I'm not so perfect now."

"Have you ever seen anything as sweet as that face," Sofia said, presenting a photo of Brendon in his highchair, his cheeks smeared with chocolate gelato, "you would bounce up and down, clean your plate. Now you barely eat a thing."

Brendon set his spoon down and held Sofia's hand. He knew it was the right thing to do.

"You had to have a sundae every night after dinner. We'd read the Tutti-Frutti Rainbow, then you had to have a bowl of chocolate gelato so you could be like Paddington in the story."

"I'll remember that, chocolate gelato," Rachel said.

"You aren't eating."

"Neither are you mammina."

"You sure you don't want some? Amelia always makes too much."

"No, thanks. Mum made me eat all five courses. The first was scallop tartare," Rachel said, scrunching her face. "It had caviar on top."

"Please eat."

"I'm trying."

He liked ribollita. It reminded him of rainy days in Milan when Nicola would whip up a batch and they would sit in front of the television watching hours of Serie A football. The reboiled soup was comfort in a bowl, there was no comfort in it today.

Rachel tugged the placemat, ladled broth, and vegetables on the spoon, and swallowed.

"Go on, knuddlebär, it's moreish. You've got that dishy body to fill."

Brendon dragged the placemat back and filled his spoon. He swallowed and repeated, more from instinct than hunger.

"You need to join us for dinner every night."

"I'd love that. I'm usually sitting in front of the telly with a bowl of cereal watching Corrie Street." Rachel wrapped her pinky around Brendon's and grinned. "You need to get back to school. I miss you."

"Soon as I feel better."

"One more week, sweetheart." Sofia dipped bread into the broth, munching the crust. "Do you plan on going into finance like your mum?"

"I'm applying to King's College in London for nursing."

"The Florence Nightingale faculty is one of the best schools in England. What type of nursing?"

"Geriatrics"

"She wants to change nappies and wipe drool."

Rachel swatted his arm. "Geriatric nurses are bleeding important, knuddlebär, even a minor issue can turn into something major."

"I'll be one of those old people."

"I'm not changing your bloody nappy." Brendon pushed the glass of wine at Sofia and snatched a piece of bread. "You drink it."

"Milk, you always drink milk with your meals. Chocolate after practice, white the rest of the time. How could I forget?"

"You finish eating, Ms. Cook, I'll get it."

"Will you stay in London or move back to Taunton?"

Rachel stared helplessly at the cupboards. Brendon grinned; she could give Maggie a run for her money.

"Cupboard beside the fridge."

"I'm not sure where I'll end up. Mum is busy doing her own thing and dad, I haven't seen him in years."

She filled a glass, set it down, and wound her arms around his neck. "I could go to Manchester or Berlin. I could take the train to Dortmund. Imagine me Rachel Jones sitting in Signal Iduna Park, watching knuddlebär light up the pitch."

She pecked his neck and flopped down on the stool. Brendon tilted the bowl and filled his spoon, glancing at Sofia. She had a dreamy look on her face, like she was lost in a precious moment.

"Mammina?"

"I like the way Rachel looks at you."

Brendon choked back the milk and squeezed Sofia's hand.

"We're going to my room."

"Go sit by the pool."

"Bloody hell, I'm not going to hump her with you in the house."

"Making love, sweetheart, one day you'll see there's a difference," Sofia said, stacking the dishes, "the pool or the great room."

"William said you had an indoor pool. I thought he was telling me a porkie."

Brendon helped her off the stool, yearning for the warmth of her fingers to heat the hollow spots.

"I thought your mum said she had too many pictures to frame. Everywhere I look, there's a photo of you."

"She doesn't want to forget a moment. If something happened to me, I'd always be around."

"You don't need pictures. I feel my gramps all the time. When I'm down, I feel a little tug on my hair. I know he's there."

"Mammina is a little obsessive. It devastated her when Uncle Gianni passed. She ran around the house looking for photos. He was drunk in the only photo she found. She was angry and not just at God for punishing him."

"God doesn't punish people."

Brendon laid his hand over the light switch. The room flooded with an aquamarine glow. "Try telling mum that."

"God would never take you away. People need you."

Brendon lounged on a chaise and patted the space between his legs. "I'm no good to the team. Mum's sad, dad hates me."

"You're important to me."

He ran his hand under her hair and caressed her neck. She was always there when he needed. Angelene had promised and ran. He leaned his forehead against hers, breathed in summer flowers and apricots.

"You wanna snog?"

"I thought you'd never ask, knuddlebär."

He parted his lips. She washed over him like a wave of summery heat. She touched him; no fire lit in his belly. He loved her body. Every inch of it, every curve, all the spots that made her sigh with pleasure. Nothing. He kissed her harder. She touched him in her fearless way that if it were any other day, he would have exploded before he had laid her down. A murmur of voices hit Brendon's ears. He couldn't stop himself. The hollow spots were still empty. He was desperate to feel something. Books and papers toppled to the tiled floor; Brendon pulled his mouth away.

"What are you doing here?"

"I... do up your trousers."

"Dawson asked Troy to bring his homework." Rachel said, tugging at his zipper, "you're interrupting."

"You can't return a text or go to school, but you can snog that tart."

"You don't understand."

He dropped his head against the cushion and stared at the ceiling. No one understood.

"I'm going to go." Rachel said, untangling herself, "you two talk this out."

He didn't want her to leave. The damn thing hadn't woken up yet.

"How about you leave Mags."

"Text me, knuddlebär. I'll be here whenever you need. I…"

"You what?" Maggie said, stacking the books. "You love him now?"

"Don't be daft, Thornton. I miss him. Bis Balt, knuddlebär."

"Ms. Cook is right down the hall, gutted, and you've got your hand down his trousers."

"He had his hand up my skirt. What's your point?"

"Can you both stop?"

"Gute Nacht," Rachel said, smothering his mouth with a kiss, "next time I visit, I'll bring a takeaway and the three of us will eat together again."

Maggie stuck out her tongue and marched herself into a chair.

"Did you beg Troy? Did you cry?"

"I'm worried about you."

"Don't be."

"You aren't at school, practice. You don't return phone calls or texts. You're a mess."

Angelene was a mess. It must have rubbed off on him, another pattern?

"You brought me my homework. Go."

"I wish Charlie never introduced us. Then I wouldn't care so much."

"We finally agree on something."

"I love you. I would have done anything for you."

"No tears?"

Maggie stood and unlatched her teeth from her lip. "You've never said sorry. You've never acknowledged you hurt me."

"Can you go? My head is pounding. I'm tired."

"I thought if I gave you time, you'd see what we had was good. You weren't a number on a list."

"Go see Michael. He'll make you feel better."

"For what it's worth, I'll always love you and one day, I'll visit Dortmund. By that time, you'll see what a brilliant girl I was. Gute Nacht, cuddle bear."

Brendon grasped at a spark. It fizzled. Reaching into his hoodie pocket, Brendon gripped his phone and knocked it against his forehead. Bloody Troy, always Switzerland.

"Hey mate, we lost 5-0"

"Why didn't you bring my homework?"

"I was going to but Maggie… she's gutted, mate."

"You know I don't want to bloody see her."

"You're seriously giving me aggro over this?"

A spark came, danced in his belly, sizzled, and died.

"You fucking promised."

"Fuck you."

Brendon stared at his phone. Had those words really come from Mr. Sunshine's mouth?

"You have no idea what my life has been like since you went MIA. I'm a defender and a keeper. Even off the pitch, I'm defending you. I nearly got myself benched for trying to shut Will's mouth. You're a dick, you don't even care."

"I'm trying to care. No one bloody understands."

"The next time someone calls you a nutter or a daft keeper, I'm going to keep my mouth shut. Shoot me a text when you can appreciate your mate."

Brendon scrubbed a hand over his face. Fuck the stupid sparks and Troy. He didn't need a friend.

"What's going on? Rachel left, upset. Maggie stormed out the door without a goodbye. Now you're yelling at Troy."

Brendon grabbed the neck of his hoodie, dragged it over his head and mopped his chest. "It's fucking hot in here."

"Why were you cursing at Troy?"

"He's a wanker."

"Troy is not a wanker. You're going to chase all your friends away with an attitude like that."

"Your little meatball is bloody perfect, always smiling. Fuck him."

"No, fuck you and your miserable attitude," Sofia said, hugging herself. "I'm going to call my mother."

"Not dad?"

"He hung up in my ear."

Brendon tapped his cast against the armrest. He had lost his mind trying to understand the girl who didn't want to be understood.

***

Walter cracked open a beer and handed it to David. "Another row with Sofia?"

David tore open a takeaway bag, sliding the containers across the island. "What's she going to do when he's in Dortmund, fly there every time he has a poorly tummy?"

Walter passed out plates, stuck spoons in the pans, and chuckled. "She hasn't purchased a flat yet?"

"She keeps hinting."

Walter swigged the beer in two gulps. "You still think it's all in Brendon's head?"

"Life exhausts you. It will not get any easier when he's out on his own."

"You could have stopped the coddling and spoiling."

"She would have done it anyway. Brendon is her life; she's made that perfectly clear."

Walter had never seen David this agitated. David's mad was calm, direct. As teenagers, David had perfected his lectures with Walter at the brunt of them. David had a gift for staying calm. Over the past week, Walter would say his friend was ready to blow.

"When I came home, no bracelets, no lipstick. What does Sofia do at six o'clock every Friday?"

Walter spooned rice on his plate and grinned. "Puts her face on. Is it Sofia or Brendon you're annoyed with?"

"I've loved Sofia since the day I spotted her on Corso di Porta Ticinese. I found a happiness in her that was so foreign to me. Can't Brendon see what he's doing to her?"

"If he isn't in a good headspace, how could he?"

"She goes into that room after I told her not to."

"Have you let go?"

"It's not the same. There's nothing wrong with Brendon."

Walter set the kettle on the stove. The element popped and hissed.

"Ang enjoyed the auction; she bought a painting." "Sofia bought a set of vases. They're still in the box."

"I'm glad Ang got out. It'll help get her out of that depressing bubble she lives in."

David spooned prawn biriani on his plate and finished the beer. "She may catch the auction bug and go all the time." Walter nestled the tea pot between aluminum pans, grabbing mugs from the cupboard. "I'd rather have a hole in my wallet than find empty wine bottles around the house."

He dropped onto the stool and dragged a piece of naan through a puddle of chili sauce. "You'll never guess what it's called."

"The spoiled prince of Rosewood manor."

"Girl with Haunted Eyes. It's cursed. People die when they stare at it."

"Sounds like something Angelene would like."

"Sometimes I wonder if she came out the trollop's womb jinxed, and it's hung on for twenty-five years."

David pierced a cauliflower, wiggling it on his plate. "The sorrow Angelene carries around is her curse."

"Juliette asked if I had been understanding." Walter said, pouring tea, "I didn't have the heart to tell her Ang was drunk, and I hit her. What's happening to us?"

"Life is happening. It can't be pretty all the time."

"No curse then?"

David shook his head and passed Walter the milk. "You're trying to fit a poor, uneducated girl into this idea you have. You need to accept her for who she is."

"Is Brendon a scholarly gentleman?"

"I'm his father. I'm supposed to teach him right from wrong, guide him."

"You've spent years trying to turn him into the perfect son. Didn't you think there would come a time when it blew up in your face?"

"What about Angelene? You've seen her temper. Aren't you afraid the next time may be worse?"

"I'm trying to have faith in her word."

Walter stared at his hands; women loved his hands. They were rugged, strong. His touch had always been gentle, made women sing. His hand never hurt a woman.

"Something cursed my fingers."

"Something or someone?"

"I wouldn't put it past, little bird. She's probably sticking pins in a voodoo doll right now."

***

You haven't been cursed; you are a curse.

A clattering of memories rattled around Angelene's brain. She had a habit of replaying moments, hoping she could make a better choice and it would play out differently.

Angelene grabbed a bottle of wine. She had kept her promise for a few days, only taking sips to coat her tongue and throat. She was the reason Brendon suffered. It was never her intention; she wasn't being malicious. She yearned to bathe in the light. The more she drank it, the more her body craved it. If she became Brendon's friend again, his light may glow. Sofia would wear her red lipstick. She thumbed the cork loose. Amber light shone from his window. She wore her curse well.

34 A PRETTY MESS

Troy burst through the dressing room doors. Nothing had been right since his argument with Brendon. His game was off, his smile gone. His mood was as chilly as the breeze fluttering Charlotte's kilt. Arguments never lasted long. They'd give each other the silent treatment for an hour, then banter playfully about the Bundesliga and Premier League. This one stuck worse than the smell of manure.

"Maybe this will put a smile on your face," Charlotte said, shoving a pink bag at him. "Have you spoken to Brendon yet?" Troy plonked behind the steering wheel and kissed her cheek. "I have no interest in speaking to that dick." He shoved a donut in his mouth, sugar dusted his tie.

"He needs you babes."

"He doesn't need me. He has a mum and a housekeeper."

The pitch faded away; it had been their pitch. Their safe place, a place of dreams.

"If anyone calls him a wanker or a shit keeper, I'm not saying a thing."

Charlotte pulled apart an iced bun, shoving a wedge in her mouth. "There's a jam filled donut in the bag, you like those."

"I don't want to talk about that dolt."

Troy flung up his finger at the Taunton College sign and parked under the willow tree. He switched off the car and leaned back in the seat. One by one, memories popped into his head. The kiddie league, jumping from hay bale to hay bale, Dortmund against Man U in the garden.

"We made a brilliant team on the pitch."

"You will again when his hand heals, and he feels better."

"It's not just our love of football. Brendon gives the best you'll get off the farm talks. He never complained when we started dating and spent all that time together. He knew I was falling in love."

"If it makes you feel better, he was nasty to Magpie, too."

Troy reached into the bag and grabbed the jam donut. He split it in two, licked at the oozing strawberry goo, and passed half to Charlotte. "I should have taken him his homework. Maggie looked at me with those I'm about to cry eyes and I couldn't say no."

"Ah, little crumpet, you're so sweet. Sweeter than these scrummy donuts."

"Promise you won't think I'm a poofter."

"I wouldn't care if you were. We'd be the best of friends."

"I miss him, and not because he understands those daft books. I miss debating English football is better than German. He makes stupid jokes. I miss seeing him kiss his cross before a match."

Charlotte crumpled the bag and tossed it on the floor. "Do all athletes do something, or is this another silly thing you and Brendon made up?"

"Lots of pro footy players do things, some pray, some wear lucky socks. Liam used to sit on the same seat on the bus when he played for the Rovers."

"What do you do, babes?"

"I pray the football director from Man U shows up and whisks me off to Old Trafford."

"That's all you do?"

"I can't tell you."

Charlotte walked her fingers up his thigh and fluttered her long lashes. "Please babes."

"I kiss your picture."

Charlotte flung her arms around his neck and smothered his cheek with kisses.

"I remember the first time I saw you at the pitch. The guys were talking about your new jubblies. All I could think about was lying in the hayloft and watching the stars with you. Will wouldn't shut up. He wanted to know if they felt like real boobs. All I thought about was holding your hand."

"That's the nicest thing a boy has ever said to me."

"I had a tough time defending that day. I had never seen hair so shiny and your smile."

"That was the Chesham match." Charlotte said, applying lip gloss, "why didn't you talk to me? I had to go to four more matches before you asked me to McDonalds."

"Brendon told me to stop being insecure and ask you. He was sick of me talking about you." Troy flicked the Man U key chain; he could hear Brendon's voice.

This is Troy. He's Taunton First's best defender. He heard you like Malteser McFlurry's. Can he buy you one?

A small grin brightened Troy's face; Brendon had always been there.

"One time I heard Brendon's mum say she loved him before she knew him. I took the piss out of him. You know what? That's how I felt about you."

"Look what you've done, babes." Charlotte said, flipping down the visor, "I spent twenty minutes perfecting my eye makeup."

"You still look beautiful, like those cute raccoons we saw at Tropiquaria Zoo."

"Let's get in the rear seat. We have fifteen minutes." Troy climbed out of the car, slid onto the seat, and laid his head on her lap. He pressed his lips against her belly and took her hand.

"Go talk to Brendon, babes."

"Just because I miss him doesn't mean I'm not pissed off at him."

"You'll be miles apart in July."

"Good."

"Your smile is the best medicine," Charlotte said, running her hand over his groin. "Can I be on top, so my hair doesn't get ruined?"

"I'd rather hold hands."

Troy laced his fingers through hers. It was the perfect time to confess about Angelene. Charlotte was lovestruck. It would hurt. He'd get a pinch, but she would get over it because she was the luckiest girl alive.

"I never saw you as a farm boy. You were just Troy Spence, my sweet little crumpet. I'm glad we shared the McFlurry. I wouldn't want to share one with anyone but you."

Troy kissed her wrist. Now wasn't the time to break her heart.

"We better get to class."

"I wish we could bunk off and run away."

"Me too but, English awaits. I have a chapter abstract to present. All I've read is it was the best of times; it was the worst of times. I agree with Mr. Dickens."

Troy crawled out of the rear seat, hitched his backpack over his shoulder, and took Charlotte's hand.

"There's Magpie. She still looks gutted."

"Does Brendon know what he's doing to people?"

"Something happened to him first, babes. It's trickling on to everyone else."

Maggie hobbled towards them, shifted her book bags, and chomped into her lip.

"Michael doesn't want to see me anymore."

"You kinda rushed into it."

"Shut it, Troy. Matilda blabbed I interrupted him and Rachel."

Charlotte scrunched her face. "They weren't humping, were they?"

"They were snogging, just as bad."

"You never should have gone. It was a bad idea."

"You didn't know Rachel would be there, babes."

"Michael accused me of still loving Brendon."

"Why don't you ask Michael on a date, make it up to him."

"I asked him to that BBQ restaurant on Bridge Place. I thought it could be our spot. He said he was busy, then told me it was over."

Troy saw the same look on Maggie's face that he had sported only minutes before. Maggie was still in love.

"Have you put Brendon's pictures away yet?"

"No, I haven't got to that point of it's over yet."

The autumn sky was pale grey. A brisk breeze carried the scent of old leaves and damp bark. Troy smoothed his bangs and lifted his lapels. "What does walking in on him and Rachel snogging tell you?"

Maggie tore at a hangnail. "He's randy."

"I've got to run, babes. I forgot I had an appointment with Ms. Morrison. She thinks I need to go to uni. I love you."

Troy smiled and kissed her hard on the mouth. "Love you too."

"You two are so sweet. I wish Brendon and I... love isn't in the cards for me.""You're eighteen. You got plenty of time to fall in love.""Out of all the girls adoring Brendon, he chose me. For two years, I competed with the other girls, Rachel, Franca, Ms. Pratt."

Troy wiggled his tie and swallowed. "What about Ms. Pratt?"

"She's shown up at the pitch, here," Maggie said, grabbing onto his arm. "She was one of those girls."

"Don't be daft."

"He said he never fancied her. You said he did. Maybe he's denying his feelings."

Troy knew all about Ms. Pratt, how she crawled inside and stole your thoughts. That's all they were, thoughts. Sure, they made him feel guilty. Only Charlotte was supposed to take space in his head. They never lasted, they never hollowed him out.

"I'm going to be late for class."

"He was always running to her rescue; I swear she had the Charlie face the day she was lurking around the garbage bins. Do you think..."

"You're overthinking as usual."

"He looked gutted, Troy, like heart broken gutted."

"He can't play football. I'd be gutted too."

"Can you visit him and see if you see it, too?"

A week ago, Troy would have rushed to the Fiesta and drove to Rosewood Manor to save his friend. He walked to English instead.

***

Brendon blinked at the golden light oozing between sheets of sombre grey. He went over his routine, go to the toilet, brush his teeth, training kit, sprint to the BMW, 4x4 until Liam arrived, rush home to mammina. It wasn't in him to get out of bed.

"Brendon David."

"What?"

"I'm going to London."

Brendon groaned sleepily. "Why do you do that? March in here and announce you're going out. Bloody hell."

"I'm practicing being tough. Your father wants me to be tough."

Brendon rubbed his eyes and stared at her nude face. She was in denim and a simple black pullover. London meant shopping on Bond Street, dinner at a posh restaurant.

"Why are you going to London?"

"I'm picking mum up."

"I thought she wasn't coming back until Christmas."

"Some of us need our mothers."

Brendon stretched and yawned. The blankets were warm. The cocoon he had built for himself was safe.

"Bloody hell, will you stop trying to make me feel bad."

"Shower, eat and get some fresh air."

It sounded rehearsed, like she had been practicing over her coffee. Brendon could picture her in the kitchen, mug in hand, savouring the notes of chocolate and dried fruit. She would have practiced with Amelia, raised her chin, 'up you get, shower, and eat.' The hitch in her voice told him she was drowning in worry. There had been no rehearsing over a mug of Lavazza.

"Are you coming home?"

"I'm staying in London."

Brendon whipped back the sweaty sheets, perched on the edge of the mattress, and blinked the dizzying orbs from his eyes. "I need you mammina."

"Your father and I have been arguing all week. I'm tired, tired of the quiet in the house, tired of you sleeping the days away."

Brendon stood and sluggishly moved past Sofia. He brushed his lips over her cheek and squeezed her shoulder. "I'm up. Get Nonna."

"I don't have it in me to be strong. I can't stop worrying about you. Eighteen years of you filling all the empty spots."

"You think I enjoy feeling this way? I'm tired of feeling tired." Brendon spit out a mouthful of toothpaste and poked his head out the door. "I'm sorry mammina. I don't mean to worry you."

"I'll see you tomorrow... you'll be fine. It's one night."

"Breathe mammina, I'll text you every hour."

"I've been holding my breath for weeks."

Brendon's heart sank, no I love you. She had forgotten to say the words. It didn't matter if she was angry, disappointed. She always said I love you. It was a promise they made to each other when he was five. Mammina would say it first and he would follow with a snuggle and a kiss. Brendon picked up his phone, tapped in the words and a heart. He would follow her instructions, shower, eat and, if he had any energy left, fresh air. If he did two of her requests, it might appease her, and he would see her red lipped smile again. Step one, shower. Brendon stripped out of his damp t-shirt and shorts, stepped under the hot water, and searched for his lost emotions. He needed guilt to kick his arse for worrying mammina. Anger to keep Angelene out of his head, happiness to enjoy football and remorse for telling Troy off. Step one, complete, his body was clean, a week of sweat washed down the drain. Step two, eat. He dried himself, hung the towel behind the door, and wandered to the walk-in. Brendon dug out his favourite jeans, a Nike t-shirt, and a Dortmund hoodie. His heart thundered, thump, thump, thump. He closed his eyes, focused on his breaths, and instructed his legs to move. A sombre melody floated into the foyer. Amelia's humming was as grey as the sky.

"Egg white omelette, porridge with berries. Where are the blood sausage and fried bread?"

"Those things aren't good for you."

"Neither are kale and protein powder," Amelia said, shoving her hands in a heart-shaped pocket. "What can I make you?"

Brendon collapsed onto the stool and held out a mug. "I'll have coffee."

Amelia opened a bag of Warburton's bread, depositing two slices in the toaster. "Your mother said the same thing."

"Mum always gets dolled up when she's going to see dad."

"Sofia doesn't need all that goop. She's beautiful without it."

She grabbed a dish of blueberries, strawberry jam and shoved them down the island.

"She used to make the effort."

"Have you looked at yourself lately?"

The toaster popped; Brendon gazed at the blueberries. Step two, eat. He had to eat for mammina.

"I'm exhausted, like when the entire match is out front of me, but ten times worse."

Amelia set down the plate and snuggled his shoulder. "It's hard for me to understand. If I'm stressed, I just go on."

"Maybe you're stronger than me."

"There's strength in you, little man. Toast and berries gone by the time I get back from switching the laundry."

Brendon smeared a layer of jam over the toast and bit into the corner. He had been an ass to Troy, the person who defended him, on and off the pitch. They had promised each other, in year one, they would be friends forever, promise broken. He couldn't give Rachel the brilliant tingle. He tore out Maggie's heart. Brendon sandwiched the toast, gobbled it in three bites, washing it down with coffee.

He was ready for step three.

"I'm leaving early today; I have to pick Georgina up from the train station. She's home from uni," Amelia said, setting a laundry basket on a stool.

"What's she studying again?"

"Forensic Science. She got to examine evidence from an actual crime scene."

"Georgie must have been over the moon, all that blood and gore."

"Tim thinks we should have called her Morticia." Amelia said, placing a stack of tea towels in the drawer. "What do you want for dinner?"

"I'll have Coco Pops. Mum wouldn't let me eat sugary cereals when I was a kid. They're in the house now."

"She wants you to eat. I'll whip up some chicken and peppers. You can roll them up in a wrap."

"I can scramble some eggs."

"I was watching videos on YouTube with Sally. She fancies a defender from Manchester City. I know what you need to stay fit, as in healthy, not fit like Sally means."

"I thought she liked De Gea, the Man U keeper?"

Amelia chuckled and placed a pepper on the counter. "She still goes on about him. There's a new one every week. Blueberries after your walk."

Brendon stepped onto the cobbles, pondering where to go. The rose maze, the forest, hesitation, and the chilly air split his breath. Amelia would be busy prepping his dinner. She had laundry to finish, beds to make. She wouldn't notice if he ducked into the forest. He put his head down and headed towards the forest's edge. Whispers of drab light filtered between the swaying leaves. Loam and pine clung to the damp air.

"Bonjour, comma ca va?"

Patchouli caught on the breeze and filled his hollow spots. He tried to shake the scent, fill the holes with anger. Nothing came.

"Qu'est-ce que tu fais ici?"

"It isn't Sunday." Brendon ducked under the warped roof and slid across the bench. "I could ask you the same thing. What are you doing here? Do you always sneak up on people?"

Angelene perched on the edge of the board, setting a wicker basket at her feet. "I'm collecting pine cones. I'm going to paint them silver and gold for Christmas."

"Keep walking. There's a whole bloody forest of them."

He turned to look at her, cursing himself. Golden strands of hair fluttered around her pale cheeks. Her mouth was glossy. She looked lovely, another devil, the trickster. She wasn't pretty. It was all in his head.

"I'm going to St. Georges today."

"Going to confession, Ms. Pratt?"

"I like the smell of frankincense. God holds my hand when I'm in His house."

Her fingers weaved and plucked; Brendon stuffed his hand in his pocket. He wouldn't hold her hand. She didn't deserve it.

"God listens."

"He's ignored you a few times."

"I pray for what I truly need and always remember to thank Him. Every time he forgives me, I'm grateful."

The floors she scrubbed, the fight to claw herself free, each painting she created written in her hands. Something tiptoed out of a hollow spot. He held her hand.

"Walter hates when I fidget."

"It makes me sad."

Brendon leaned against the tree trunk; sorrow burst through him in a blaze of shimmery blue sparks. He parted her bracelets and ran his thumb over the scar. "Where was God then?"

"He was testing my faith." "You've been beaten, forced to do things..."

Another feeling flooded the hollow spots. He had been that man. He was no better than the men who abused Angelene.

"You've suffered and you still think God is brilliant? He wasn't there when Richard the prick shook me and screamed at me. He took my Nonno away, he takes things, ruins people's lives."

"God is the only thing that has never left me."

"Where's God when Padre Diavolo is around?"

"Who are you praying to for help? God or your precious Father Satan?" Angelene clutched his hand tighter. "Pray with me now."

"I don't want to bloody pray. I want my hand to heal." A few sparks lit and floated around his body. "I want back on the pitch. I want... it doesn't fucking matter what I want."

Sparks continued to awaken. All her devils were out to play. Hurt and anger smoldered. He jerked his hand away.

"Lord, you invite all who are burdened to come to you, allow your healing hand to heal me."

The words floated around Brendon, emotions seeped from the holes and hollows. Angelene crossed herself and leaned into him. He tried to shrug her away, he couldn't move. The words were like glue. He was stuck.

"God will hear me, and He will bring you peace. Do you believe me?"

"I believe nothing you say."

"You must. Please look at me."

"It hurts too much. We always end up finding one another and every time, you look so pretty."

A whirlwind of dried sparks and ashy emotions whirred around his body. It wasn't supposed to happen like this. His hand was going to heal. The hollow spots would fill on their own and he'd be okay. She wasn't supposed to have anything to do with it.

"Please look at me."

"Fuck off."

Brendon jerked at his cuff and dabbed the tears stinging his eyes. He hated her and loved her again.

"I've wanted to cry for weeks, but the tears wouldn't come. I've wanted to bloody scream. It wouldn't come. What's the matter with me?"

"I steal light so I can fill the holes in me. I steal breath so I can breathe."

"Is this how you felt the day you wanted to die?"

Angelene gripped her cross, her eyes grew wide and brilliant green. "People need you. No one wanted me."

"I've messed everything up. I can blame Padre Diavolo all I want. It was me."

"Ignore him. Listen to your heart, listen to me. Hold your cross."

"No more bloody prayers."

The words spilled, fast and furious, like the sparks whizzing through him. He whispered 'amen,' exhausted.

"I've never been able to return the light once I've stolen it. It fades out and then they're gone."

Brendon ignored her warning. Something passed between them.

"I've been a dick."

"God will forgive you."

"How do you know that? I've chased everyone away, including Troy."

God, fate, what was it that drew him to Troy that first day of reception? He remembered feeling for the boy crying against his mother's leg. He had been excited to start school, new rucky, new football. He had asked Sofia to keep Paddington company, kissed her cheek, and dropped the ball at Troy's feet. He shared he was a keeper and handed Troy a tissue. Evelyn Spence had wiped Troy's nose and nudged him forward. He was a defender. It could be God or fate; Troy had always been a good friend.

"Troy will forgive you."

"I don't know why I'm telling you this stuff. I bloody hate you. You keep telling me to find my light. How can I when you stole it?"

"I still see it. I haven't sucked it all out of you yet."

"What colour am I?"

"Blue. Your brown is smudged."

"Go find your pine cones."

A pretty mess, pretty mouth. Life had not been kind to his green-eyed little bird. He had not been kind either. There was nothing between him and Angelene. It had all been tricks and lies, her grasping at normal and trying to break patterns. She meant nothing.

***

People bumped around Sofia; the neon yellow screens glared in her eyes. She heard whisperings of hellos and gushes of 'I've missed you.' The smell of flowers, perfume, and sweat nauseated her. It seemed like hours waiting for Nicola's arrival. A long, fatigued breath emptied from her lungs. Sofia moved through the crowd and embraced Nicola as if it had been years between visits.

"You're going to wrinkle my blouse, gattina."

"How was your flight?"

"The turbulence was terrible. I prayed the entire two hours."

They dodged around luggage and snaking queues towards the sliding doors. Sofia took Nicola's Gucci duffel bag. She looked calm despite the bumpy flight into London; she hadn't fallen apart.

"We're staying in London tonight."

"You're leaving Brendon alone. You haven't left his side for weeks."

They walked to the short stay parking; fluorescent lights competed with the fading sun. Sofia's nose filled with petrol, her mind with Brendon.

"He's texted every hour. He's ate, went for a walk, showered."

"That's an improvement. You should be happy."

"I need to see David."

"You need to see David, need to see me."

"I don't know what to do. David told me to be tough. I forgot how."

Sofia paused and gripped the steering wheel. She needed the M4. Was it Contrail Way to Inner Ring Road or the opposite?

'It's Tunnel Road, I need to stay right.'

"I let Brendon stay home. David's angry."

"Dr. Weiss recommended it, not you." Nicola said, clutching the seat belt, "do you need me to drive?"

"A4 to the Hogarth Roundabout. Knightsbridge to Piccadilly, I know this route, I've driven it a million times."

"Gattina, slow down. I survived the flight; I'd like to survive the drive to David's flat."

"I keep confusing the directions. My heart wants to go home."

"Then we'll go. What's another fight with David?"

"I've neglected David." Sofia veered into traffic; a horn blasted. She tightened her grip. "Shit, milk. I forgot to buy milk. We need two jugs in the fridge."

"Gattina, pull over and let me drive."

Nothing had been more perfect than her son. Nothing could take him away. Sofia turned onto the A4, repeating the directions in her mind. She needed the roundabout. She needed milk, her boy, and an understanding smile from her husband.

"You remember that boy that used to hug me when I was upset or make those terrible jokes to get me to smile. He's gone."

"Hogarth's Roundabout, Sofia."

She yanked the steering wheel, maneuvered the car around the front end of a Land Rover, her heart pounding along with the blasting horn.

Nicola held a hand to her heaving chest. "Brendon is still there. He's in his head, brooding like Anthony used to do."

"The other day I put the sugar in the fridge. I ran a bath and forgot I was going to have one."

"Nonna is here. There will be no more lying around or forgotten baths."

"I took Angelene to an auction. She bought a painting."

"Let me guess, demons and ghouls."

"It's of a little girl with the most disturbing eyes, so sad, like Angelene."

"Sounds like something Angelene would like."

"David told me she once knew a boy who locked himself away. I asked her about it. She avoided the question and prayed."

"Would the boy be Pierre Piedmont's son?"

Sofia's nails dug into the leather steering wheel. "She never mentioned a name."

"I did a little investigating."

Sofia turned onto Constitution Hill; relief washed over her. She could see the gates to Buckingham Palace and the Victoria Monument in the distance. She would be with David soon.

"What did you find out?"

"His name was Henri. He was obsessed with buildings, drew his first blueprint using an architect's scale at age five."

Sofia pulled in front of the building. David was waiting in his charcoal suit and suspenders. She jerked the wheel and bumped over the curb. "A prodigy."

"We'll continue this later."

Sofia nodded and stepped out of the car. She went to David, smoothed his lapels, and searched his eyes. There was a touch of 'I'm happy to see you' in them.

"How was traffic?"

'Not how's my son?' Sofia thought.

"I've been praying the entire time. First a bumpy plane ride, then this one driving."

"You're here now," David said. "The key is in my pocket."

Sofia reached into his suit jacket, kissed him, inhaled his cologne. She missed the smell. She had been missing a lot of things lately.

"I'll Park the car. You two wait inside."

She kissed him again, yearning for the warmth his lips used to bring. The kiss was quick, tense like him. They entered the lobby; Sofia had always liked the contemporary décor. Black walls, gold accents, chandeliers dripping in white beads. She collapsed on a black velvet chair; the luxurious entry felt cold.

"Tell me more about Henri Piedmont."

"There was talk Henri and Angelene were involved."

A burst of energy shot through Sofia. Her shoulders stiffened, memories stormed her mind like shooting stars, Burnham, his light, breakfast together.

"What do you mean, involved? Friends? Lovers?"

Nicola ran her finger along her pearl necklace and raised an eyebrow. "That was one answer I couldn't get."

"Why did he lock himself away?"

David walked into the lobby; his smile was brief. "Walter cleaned the loo for you."

"Is he not home?" Nicola said.

"He booked himself into the Mandarin Oriental. He needs a night to himself."

The elevator doors hissed open, David ushered them in, and pressed number eighteen.

They rode the elevator in silence. Sofia's mind spun. Henri Piedmont a prodigy. Brendon, gifted. Kate said Henri Piedmont was in Barcelona. She had worn the same look as Nicola when speaking of Henri. Had Henri's light burnt out too? The doors bumped open, Sofia rubbed her arms, jumping as the lock clicked.

"Pour *gattina* a drink, would you?"

Sofia fell onto a chair, draping her arms over the sides. "You haven't asked how Brendon is."

"How's our son?"

"I had to drag him out of bed." She dug in her pocket, tapped her phone open, and read the text. "He's working on English."

"Did you have to force him to do that, too?"

"All I've eaten since leaving Milan is a handful of Ferrero Pocket Coffee. I'm famished."

"Do you want to go out or grab a takeaway?" David handed out glasses of scotch and perched on the armrest.

"Put your lipstick on, *gattina*."

"I didn't bring it."

"Sofia Francesca, enough."

"Where is that tough girl I fell in love with? You were never afraid to stick your finger in my father's face."

"I didn't love him."

"Do you feel like curry?"

"I don't care, mother."

"A little tough love, and he'll come around," David said.

"I'm afraid of losing him. I couldn't bear it, not after everything that has happened."

"I'm going to run you a bath. You can have a nice soak. By the time you're done, dinner will be here." Nicola said, gulping the scotch, "I've decided we're having Lebanese."

"I don't want a bath. I want my son back."

"Tough love Sofia. We need to do this together," David said.

Sofia grabbed her overnight bag and trudged to the bedroom. Tough love had never worked on Gianni. It might with Brendon, it would come from a place of deep love and that would make it okay. It might set him straight, get him back on the pitch, back to her.

'Henri Piedmont was a gifted architect, touched by Angelene. Brendon, a top-notch keeper, touched by Angelene.' She unzipped her bag and shuddered. There was no proof Angelene, and Henri Piedmont had been involved. She had nothing on Brendon, other than pangs in the belly and odd coincidences.

"What in heaven's sake are you wearing?" Nicola said.

"Brendon's t-shirt and my pyjamas," David said.

"Leave me alone, both of you."

"Have you thought about sending him to Dortmund?"

"He can finish school like he promised."

Sofia flopped onto the sofa and rubbed at the pain in her forehead. "He isn't going anywhere. Not when he's like this."

"I didn't raise a quitter."

Nicola scrolled through a menu on her phone and glanced up. "It wouldn't be quitting, David. It might help."

"What good is he to Dortmund with a busted wrist? He'll do as he's told and finish school."

"Brendon will be fine. I made sure of that. I feel like mutabal and kofta."

Sofia curled her feet under her and cradled a pillow. Fine was a stupid word. It was satisfactory, not great, or fantastic. Satisfactory was not good enough.

"She stole his light."

David lifted Sofia's legs and laid them across his lap. "Close your eyes for a bit."

'Henri must have had beautiful light too.'

***

Angelene tapped a cigarette against the package. Brendon was still a mess. It had spilled onto Sofia, struck the woman down. People were shadows of themselves. It was her fault. A scream stuck in her throat; her skin stretched tight over her bones. She had done well, putting on a smile and pretending life was okay. No one noticed the pain she hid; she had become an expert at blending in. Angelene closed her eyes and pressed her palms into the sockets. Sadness, self-pity, frustration battered for a spot in her brain. She promised not to hurt herself, not to drink, not to smoke. The tornado of emotions tore through her. Angelene focused on the glow in Brendon's window, gripping her cross. The gnawing feeling slashed at her belly. Angelene flung open the drawer, rattling the clock and lamp. She pushed papers aside, sucking at her breath as something poked her thumb. Angelene moved another finger over the push pin and poked, circle, jab. She held up her hand. It looked like a pincushion. Her breath quieted; her mind slowed. Angelene ran her finger over the dots of blood, circled, and weaved. She stared at the smeared labyrinth. It reminded her of Hecate's wheel. She had read a book about Greek goddesses and learned about the ancient wheel. Her mother had accused her of witchcraft. Angelene liked the symbol, birth, life, death. Her heart clattered; she would not be responsible this time.

35 Saudade

After Gianni's death, Edward Weiss gave Sofia a book about the five stages of grief. According to Elisabeth Kubler-Ross, she would experience denial, anger, bargaining, depression, and acceptance. Sofia had been angry for years.

"Up you get topolino," Nicola said, marching across the floor. "Sofia the curtains."

Sofia dragged them along the rod and leaned into the sill. "I'll get your clothes."

Nicola yanked the sheets from Brendon's hands and shook his shoulders. "Up."

"Jesus Christ Nonna."

"Don't bring Jesus into this. I've let you lie around for a day. Enough is enough."

"Mother, let him be."

"How about you both go away."

"Sofia, turn on the shower."

Sofia laid an armful of clothes on the bed and lugged herself to the bathroom. If she could find the energy, she would try bargaining with God, make Brendon well and she would attend Christmas Mass.

"You're wasting water."

"Couldn't you have stayed in Milan?"

"You're lucky I didn't wake you with a bucket of water. Gianni hated that."

Sofia cradled a towel in her arms, wishing Brendon had the flu or measles or chicken pox. People might understand.

"Are you feeling better, sweetheart?"

"I don't know."

She was sick of hearing, 'I don't know, I'm tired.' She wanted football stats and Dortmund highlights and ti amo mammina.

"Shower topolino. Sofia, come down for lunch."

"Out of bed before she comes marching back in with the water."

She wrapped her arms around herself and trudged down the stairs. She could hear Nicola and Amelia discussing what to have for dinner, pasta, or something light. Cacio e pepe was on the menu.

"Is he in the shower?"

Sofia slumped onto the stool and nodded.

"Go put your face on. We must be a unified front."

"Later."

"We're going to battle, Sofia Francesca."

"This isn't war. It's my son."

"Do you think I met perspective buyers in an old pullover?"

"I don't want to push him."

"He's been home for weeks," Nicola said, taking the frittata out of the oven. "It's time to get him back to routine."

"I agree," Amelia said, pouring two mugs of coffee. "The mood around here is very bleak. It's worse than when Richard was alive."

Sofia cradled the mug and stared into the coffee. "He looks so sad."

"Moping around isn't helping. I want the key to that room, gattina. No more sitting in there and crying."

"It helps to clear my head. I feel things."

"Sadness," Nicola said, slicing the frittata. "Put that key on my dresser and you, Ms. Potter, start humming something upbeat. The three of us must stand together. Brendon will have no choice but to get out of this funk he's in."

"You think so, Nonna?"

"Yes, topolino, I do. Hug your mother."

Sofia took his hands and drew him closer. "You smell good."

"Any requests while I'm dusting?" Amelia said.

"Surprise us."

Sofia picked at the wedge of frittata. The comforting smells of parmesan and prosciutto wafted from the steam. She couldn't eat. Brendon had showered, his cheeks were rosy, something was missing.

"Do I need to feed both of you?"

Sofia sliced through the frittata. "I'll take a bite, if you do."

"Topolino, you need 3200 calories a day. You're withering away."

"When I'm training and playing. I'm not doing either."

Nicola passed him a glass of milk and lounged on the stool. "Sofia, we're going for a walk afterwards. Topolino, you're going to get that school work done. Your mother is beside herself and I'm tired of it."

They ate in unison, bite, drink, bite, drink until their plates were empty. Nicola grinned triumphantly.

"No football or Xbox until your assignments are done."

"Jesus, Nonna."

"Stop bringing him into this. The poor man has suffered enough." "I think I'll go for that walk now."

Sofia smiled a lousy 'I'm okay' smile and wandered from the kitchen. She pulled David's cardigan from the banister; shrugged it on. It brought no comfort. Sofia stepped onto the walkway, the fountain gurgled, a crisp breeze shushed through the trees. She tried to let go of anger, forget about bargaining and depression, just accept her fate. She had spent years doing different things to ease it, boss the football board members around, practice pasta making, yoga. For years, the anger twisted like the ivy clinging to the manor. Sofia tucked a strand of hair behind her ear, a scent she loathed, masked the roses.

"Am I disturbing you?"

She wanted to say yes and tell her to leave her alone. The concern on Angelene's face had her reaching for her hand.

"The house is so quiet. I came out here for noise, the birds, the leaves rustling, something. The quiet is killing me." "How's Brendon?"

Sofia gazed over the lawn. Every inch of the garden held a memory. Imaginary Signal Iduna Park, Brendon's first birthday, tea with Paddington, dancing with David, kisses under the stars. Life happened at Rosewood manor. She felt like she had slipped back in time and the darkness returned.

"Every time David and I made love, I hoped I'd get pregnant. I told God he had been cruel, and he owed me. I cursed Him. Do you think God is punishing me? Would he take Brendon from me because I despise Him?"

"God doesn't punish."

"Brendon was meant to be my son. He filled all the empty spots and now, they ache."

"I know you don't trust God but, I've been praying for Brendon. He'll get well, I know it."

"How can you be so sure?"

"God has told me what to do."

Sofia fumbled with her cuff, twisting the fabric around her fingers. "Are you some sort of messiah?"

Sofia turned Angelene's hand over, touching a tiny prick mark on the tip of her finger. She slid the bracelets apart and gasped at the sight of the scar. Walter hadn't been spoiling her with expensive baubles, he was hiding her past. Angelene pulled her hand away, reached for a fallen leaf, and tore it along the browning vein.

"I have moments where my thoughts are brilliant, like shooting stars. My insecurity disappears, the right words come, people listen. The problem is, they come too fast, and it overwhelms me. Emotions can be like a wicked thunderstorm. Have you ever heard nature scream, Sofia?"

"I've heard trees cry and birds' weep. I stood under a great oak and felt its tears. I'm feeling that pain now."

Sofia pulled her cardigan tighter, shielding herself from the wintry despair that blew from Angelene.

"Henri Piedmont."

"Leave him alone, Sofia. He's suffered enough. Let him build his castles."

"Did God restore his light, too?"

"He did and He will see Brendon gets better and you'll get stronger too," Angelene said, crumpling the leaf. "You frightened me the day I met you. The elegance and confidence were overwhelming. I always saw you as sophisticated black. Find it again." She touched Sofia's arm and walked away.

Sofia twisted her wedding band around her finger. Angelene was having trouble being a wife. She couldn't have that kind of power over Brendon. She pushes men away, runs, hides like Walter said she had done when he wooed her.

'That is her power,' Sofia mused. 'She runs, and men pursue. It's like a game of cat and mouse, the prize, a green-eyed little bird.' A brisk breeze scented with freshly dug earth wavered around her. Sofia shivered and yanked the cardigan tighter.

"I'm overthinking, aren't I?"

Warmth nestled into her side, she held onto her breath and closed her eyes, overthinking went hand in hand with perfectionism. Every detail, think and rethink, design, and redesign until she was satisfied. It was never enough.

"I thought I got things right. I don't know how to start over."

Sofia clung to the warmth, held it like a hand. She would have a cup of coffee, call Kate. If she had any strength left in her, make a list of how to make things right. First on her list, leave Henri Piedmont alone.

**

Brendon stared at the text. The pull happened, faded, curiosity kicked in followed by a spark of anger. His first response, 'fuck you.' He didn't owe her anything. Brendon stepped into the hallway, quiet attacked his ears. Strangled emotions screamed at him, warned him. He glanced down the hall. No light seeped from beneath the bedroom doors. His heart thundered in his ears as he made it to the kitchen. He unlocked the door, touched his cross, and asked Madre Innocente to forgive him and protect his mother. She had been a mess after her walk, mumbling about wishing to start over. She had nearly fallen asleep in her pasta. Nicola had put her to bed, which was exactly where he should be, not following the smudged clouds in a sky painted black and inky blue. Brendon wrangled his breath, stopped at the bottom of the hill, and glanced over his shoulder. A shadow wavered in his bedroom window, begging him to come back. Brendon urged himself forward. He stepped over the crumbling stone wall. Angelene had cocooned herself under a wool blanket. Candles flickered atop the window ledge, dripping waxy tears onto the stones. He leaned into the wall, gripping the jagged stones. Padre Diavolo hovered above him.

"Sit with me."

"No bloody way. Talk."

Angelene lit a cigarette off a candle and blew a mouthful of smoke towards him.

"You remember the boy I mentioned?"

"You liked his light, too."

"His name was Henri."

Brendon stared at her trembling fingers and the darkness looming in her eyes. He cursed at a momentary flicker of 'I care.'

"Henri Piedmont, Pierre's son."

"Bloody hell, father, and son. Do you like my dad too? He's a bloody powerful guy."

"I'm trying to do what I don't do well, talk." She dragged the cigarette over the bricks, blowing out a ragged breath. "These fucking patterns, they're like a kaleidoscope, starting off mixed up, then coming together to make the most beautiful picture. You twist and turn; it falls apart into an ugly mess."

"Get to the point."

"I was sitting at Hugo's feet when Henri introduced himself to me. He commented on my drawing and showed me a cathedral he had designed. I had never seen anything so beautiful."

"He was smart. I know this already."

"I never meant for things to happen. It became a pattern, meet at Hugo's feet, share our drawings. He would tell me about his favourite buildings. Henri loved Basilica of the Sacre-Coeur. It has the largest bell in France."

"Did you visit the I love you wall? Kiss under the Eiffel tower?" He crossed his arms over his chest and stared at the graffiti on his cast. "If mum wakes up and sees I'm missing, she'll lose her bloody mind. She's already lost the bloody plot."

"One day I stopped into the lecture hall and there was Henri. Pierre introduced us and I ran."

"Thanks for giving the boy with the liquid blue eyes a name. That's him, right?"

He turned to leave; shadowy fingers clamped on his shoulders. *'Bloody Padre Diavolo always getting in the way.'*

"I stayed away from Hugo for a few days, hoping Henri would forget about me. He was a pretty boy."

A sharp pang poked Brendon. Her daydreamy smile lit a spark, it burned.

"Henri had tousled waves of brown hair, eyes the colour of spilled ink. He wore black-framed glasses that would slip down his nose, his smile, full of sugar."

"Is that why you fancy Troy? You have a thing for smiles?" Brendon said, yanking on his hood, "Henri was fit. You fancied him. Gute Nacht."

Her ragged breath invaded the quiet, another spark lit. Anger, jealousy.

"Don't go. I need to talk about this. I've held on to it for so long."

"Fucking talk then. The longer I stay here, the harder it is to keep you out of my head."

"I was sitting for Pierre's class. I was uncomfortable. The sheet kept slipping and exposing my scars. Henri joined the class and while everyone drew my breasts, he drew my hands."

"He fell in love. You should have lived happily ever after. Bonne nuit Ms. Pratt."

A growl, rough and jarring, startled Brendon. Her hands dug into the rotting straw and dirt like claws.

"Please, this is killing me."

Brendon clamped down on the curse words and perched on the wall. There weren't enough sparks to get angry.

"Pierre was so angry. He told me to stay away. He said his son looked lovestruck. I tried my best to avoid Henri. He always found me. He appeared out of the blue, blue was his colour, always changing from inky blue to the colour of the sky."

Crimson stormed her cheeks, crept down her neck, another spark lit, sympathy.

"I told Henri we could be friends. I wanted to break the pattern. He said friends were better than nothing."

"Sounds bloody familiar."

The sympathy spark blew out, hate smoldered. Words like pathetic, needy, desperate danced around his head.

"We kept our friendship hidden; it stayed that way for a while."

"Did you fuck him, or did you make love? You don't know how to love, so you fucked him. His dad, who you were also fucking, found out, end of story."

Angelene gripped handfuls of hair, twisted and pulled. "I ended it. Pierre had a feeling something was going on. Lisette was angry. God had condemned me."

"You confessed; you're forgiven."

"Henri was heartbroken. He locked himself in his room."

Brendon stepped over the wall. He had to walk away. The sparks were frustrating and dizzying. Nothing stuck except the sadness looming in her eyes.

"He killed himself."

Brendon's heart clunked to a stop. The colour had drained from her cheeks, her eyes had flooded with tears.

"Pierre said he would kill me if I went near Henri. Henri took his life to save another."

"Did he get that from Tale of Two Cities?"

"Please don't," Angelene sobbed. "I thought you were stronger than Henri."

Sparks turned to ash. He was too tired and damaged to resist. Brendon dropped beside her and took her hand.

"It wasn't your fault."

"Pierre blamed me. I should have run from them both."

"That's why we couldn't be friends."

"I thought I could this time. I was married, not a lover. You were such a nice boy."

"We could have been friends. I would have accepted it."

"You're suffering because of me, just like Henri. Sofia has fallen apart."

The sky was all the shades of Henri's blue. Ashes blew from the holes in his heart.

"I can't keep going back and forth with you. Love, hate, friends, enemies."

Angelene nuzzled his neck and tightened her grip. "Your scent has changed, sweet and salty."

He tucked his arm around her. It made sense. She had something to prove to God and herself. She needed to show the world she could be friends with a man and defeat her demons.

"I've never been this confused before. All my emotions are dull, just floating around. I tried to persuade my heart to beat and my lungs to breathe."

"I was feeling strange. It frightened me. You said all those pretty things. I had to run."

"I loved you, then hated you. You were beautiful, then ugly. I wanted to save you, then I couldn't care less." Brendon laid his head against hers. "I've been confused since the day you said you couldn't breathe."

"The last thing Henri said was the triangle is the strongest part of a building. It holds its shape and has a sturdy base. He said our trusses were not balanced. We were like an arch, leaning against one another, built on a fault line."

"I want to go to the pitch, feel the dragons in my belly, get angry when I don't understand the Latin homework. I want to enjoy Nonna's spaghetti."

Angelene removed his hood and held his cheeks in her hands. The warmth from her fingertips seeped into his skin.

"Go to practice tomorrow, then meet me at your old fort."

"I can't trust you."

"I couldn't save Henri; I can make you well."

"My head is saying run as fast as you can. My heart says it's the right thing to do, for mammina, not you."

"You'll do it, go to practice?"

"I'll think about it."

***

Walter rolled the chair back, searched his brain. What drew him to Angelene Hummel? She had been the first woman to run. It could have been the thrill of the chase. He knew it wasn't love, he was struggling with like most days. He had conquered the sea, the political world, being a husband was proving to be his biggest challenge. Walter searched through his irritation. There had to be something. He smiled; she was turning into quite the chef. It amused him when she fussed around the kitchen, cursing in French when she cut her finger or burned the first attempt at a bechamel. She was finding her wings, his little bird, however forced it may be. No matter how lovely the meal, she drained him. The innocence, helplessness, all the things that made him want to be in her presence, trapped him. He didn't know how to escape. Walter Pratt never failed.

"You still up?"

"I'm supposed to be reassessing the security and defence needs. I can't wrap my brain around it."

David filled a glass with water and dissolved onto the sofa. "Who could at midnight."

"Why are you awake?"

"I had another argument with Sofia."

"Let me guess, Brendon?"

Walter stretched out his legs. He was glad he passed on being a father. He never dreamt of playing football or having tea parties in the garden. It was a role that didn't appeal to him, what did, playing uncle. He enjoyed spending time with Brendon, happy he could hand him back.

"Have you ever known Sofia to be a crier?"

"I've seen her at her lowest. She didn't cry that day."

"Look at me going on about Sofia. Talk, you look miserable."

"I need a glass of scotch. You?"

"It might help me sleep."

Walter yawned, stretched his arms, and walked to the liquor cabinet. He filled two glasses and passed one to David.

"I tell Ang to stop drinking and it's the first thing I run to."

"You can stop at one. Angelene can put back a bottle."

Walter chuckled. "She could drink any punter under the table. It's what she becomes when she drinks." "I can't imagine running to the bottle to escape. All those forgotten, wasted days."

"She cuts herself."

"I've noticed some scars."

"She says it helps when she's overwhelmed. Hell, I jog, I call you. I used to have sex. She doesn't want to do that."

David took a sip and grinned. "I can't say my sex life is any better. I crawl into bed and Sofia's wearing one of Brendon's shirts, not a clean one either."

"Ang has always been like this."

Walter reminisced about the times she pretended to be asleep, had a headache, or forced herself to do it. He hadn't tried to have sex with her when he was first wooing her. It took forever for her to stop running. Sex would have complicated things. The first time they had sex was on their wedding night. It hadn't been romantic and full of fireworks; she had laid still and scrunched her face. The rejection was eating away at him.

"You'd think by looking at her, she'd know how to have sex. She lays there like a bloody corpse."

"Have you tried holding her hand or asking about a book she likes? Conversation is amazing foreplay."

"She doesn't like to hold hands. She just finished a book about a man named Werther. He offs himself over a woman, depressing stuff."

"What's something you both like? Sofia and I love travelling. We cook together."

"Ang says sex feels like death. Has Sofia ever said that?"

"Maybe religion plays a part. Sex is a sin."

Walter had dated a Catholic before. A devout Irish woman as wild as the horses that raced over the moors of Connemara. Sex wasn't a sin, it was an adventure, ending with an exhausted 'Jesus, Mary, and Joseph.'

"If Anastasia weren't in the mood, I could kiss her neck, bury my face between her legs. I'd have her writhing in delight. Ang squeezes her eyes shut and bites into her lip. I feel like I'm forcing myself on her."

"Have you talked about it?"

"She doesn't talk about anything; just hides away like this jewellery box she has."

David looked at Walter, puzzled. "What does a jewellery box have to do with sex?"

"It's the secrets inside it. She protects it like she does herself."

"Everyone has secrets. Look at that damn house I live in; every room has a secret," David said, "we protect our secrets in fear of judgement. If she's scrunching her face in disgust, it must be one hell of a secret."

"Her whole life is probably in that box."

"She'll share when she's ready. Some secrets are worth sharing, some hurt so bad, you tuck them away."

Walter rose, went to the desk, and shut off the laptop.

"Kate called; she's worried about me. Kate doesn't worry."

"She cares about you."

"I'm struggling with marriage, Ang."

"Divorce her. Set her up in a flat in Paris like you did her friend."

"How about you buy a flat in Dortmund? Let Brendon do the thing he's damn brilliant at."

"Well played," David said flatly, "we flew him back and forth to Dortmund. He messed up. He's still messing up."

"The first time I saw Angelene, I knew she would be mine, the potential I saw. I don't quit."

David collected the glasses, walked to the kitchen, and set them in the sink. "You better start accepting her faults then."

"Brendon is a genius on the pitch, not school."

"Don't drink anymore and don't let Angelene get into your head. You've been hard to live with lately."

Walter grabbed the bottle; a long sigh blew from his mouth. Angelene was good at crawling inside him. She stuck. Walter set the bottle in the cabinet and pressed the door closed. Their pieces hadn't fit together yet. He'd find a way to assemble them. He was, after all, Walter Pratt.

***

Angelene thought the confession would bring her peace, like the wound on her thigh, it bled.

"I can make this right. Henri was sensitive. Brendon needs his light."

She dabbed at the blood, tossed the tissue in the toilet, and crawled into bed.

"I ran from you, hid myself away. You did matter to me, 'out of the blue' Henri. I was afraid to show you my insides, afraid you would do the running. That is my confession to you."

36 Walls & Boundaries

BRENDON WOKE WITH ONE intention: build a wall. One of stone, raw, durable with no gates or doors, a towering wall, bigger than the one Angelene lived behind. He guzzled a mouthful of water, swished, spit it at his feet, unsure why he ventured to the pitch. He owed her nothing.

"I didn't think I'd see your face around here for a while," Liam said.

"I hear Will could use some pointers."

"Sprints?" "I don't think I can. It took all my energy to walk from my car."

"How about four team, it's a simple warm-up drill."

Brendon stared down the pitch, raised his hand to wave at Troy and dropped it. There was no sunshine on Mr. Sunshine's face.

"I'm gonna go. It feels weird being here."

"Call the colour, catch the ball. Throw it back to someone with the same-coloured bib, quick throws," Liam said enthusiastically. "I'll blow the whistle at the two-minute mark. You can rest."

Brendon twisted his cap around; he would keep up his end of the bargain, his deal with the devil.

"What's next?" Troy said, running from midfield.

"Four team. Hand out the bibs. Glad you're back, Cook."

"Can I talk to you?"

Troy grabbed a net bag, scattering bibs across the pitch. "I have nothing to say to you."

"Bloody hell, I'm sorry."

"Four team. Everyone grab a bib."

"I apologize for being a dick. I'm messed up."

Troy dragged a blue bib over his head, passing a ball between his feet. "Get in net."

Brendon jerked off his hoodie and tossed it towards the bench. How could he concentrate on the drill with a brain jammed into protection mode and his best friend pissed off?

"I'm scared. I'm afraid it will fall apart again."

Troy bopped the ball from knee to knee, his voice icy and hard. "Everything you want is on the other side of fear."

"Where did you bloody hear that?"

"I read it somewhere. You're a keeper. You told me that on the first day of reception, prove it."

The team scattered around the pitch. Brendon walked to the net, if he made rules and boundaries, he wouldn't be another casualty. The whistle pulled Brendon from his thoughts. What was he supposed to do? He searched the pitch, yellow bibs, blue, red, call a colour.

"Blue."

Rule one, friends, no acquaintances. Rule two, small talk, meaningless conversation that couldn't lead to heartfelt discussions. Rule three, no dinners, rule four, no attending his matches. A flash of black and white soared towards him. He sorted through the chaos in his head, *'hold out your hands and catch the bloody ball.'* He reached and clutched the ball to his chest. Boundaries. He was his own person; his needs were more important than hers. He imagined a bright yellow line around his fortress. He would be there for her, just in a different way.

"Yellow."

He focused on the pitch, dropping to his knees to catch the ball.

"Yellow."

The ball sailed towards him. He snagged it and tossed it.

"Blue."

A tiny, competitive spark lit. The yellow line of protection glowed. Rule five, she needed his permission to climb over the wall. The ball flew back and forth across the pitch, his reflexes on fire, every save, made. She wanted him to find his light, he'd find it, with or without Troy.

Brendon wasn't confident in the construction of his wall. Henri Piedmont, the architect, couldn't build anything strong enough to keep her out. Brendon stared at the text; he'd meet her. He'd be respectful, follow the code. One last meeting to set up the rules. A nasty taste filled his mouth. He swallowed the acrid lump, ducking as Sofia flew across the foyer, arms outstretched.

"Where have you been? I was worried sick."

"Training."

"You're supposed to be resting."

"I worked on my core, some squats, nothing hard."

"What if you collapsed again, and I had to go back to the A&E."

"Stop, gattina, we should be celebrating." A grumble erupted from Brendon's belly. He clutched his stomach.

"I'm hungry."

"See Sofia, I told you I would make topolino better."

Brendon followed Nicola to the kitchen. Coffee was brewing, eggs, onion, and a tin of San Marzano tomatoes were on the counter. Brendon planted himself on a stool, coaxing calm to come out of hiding. This wasn't just a kitchen. It was the place Amelia baked scones and fret over healthy meals. His mother planned her parties here, filling notebooks with drawings of labelled platters and tea sandwiches. It was the spot he and Troy celebrated a win, whipping up pizza and enjoying playful banter on German and English football. Normal dinners happened in la cucina. He could slouch, put his elbows on the counter and forget about napkins on the lap. It was the first place he had spoken to Angelene. Brendon pressed on his jittery belly; calm was still hiding.

"What are you making, Nonna?"

"Uova all 'inferno.'"

"What's that?"

"Eggs in purgatory," Sofia said. "Mum made it for dad when he needed a little pep in his step."

"And your brother when he was hungover."

"Sounds like the brekky for me. I've been in hell for weeks."

"It's a good way to start the day, topolino. It'll warm your belly."

I need all the help I can get,' Brendon thought. Madre Innocente gave him a quick jab; *'go to school, swim, anything to make the pieces fit without including her.'* Padre Diavolo snickered; *'she can save you.'*

"I've missed you," Sofia said, setting down a glass of milk. "I've seen more of you in the last little while, and I've missed you."

"Training is a start. Nonna's eggs in hell will kill whatever is ailing me."

Nicola held out a knife, frowning. "Chop the onions, gattina. Let the poor boy breathe."

Brendon rubbed the back of his neck. Angelene didn't love him, couldn't love him. She ran from love, which might be all the protection he needed. He held his cross and set out his intention, *'she doesn't love, so I'm safe. She's married, so I'm safer.'*

"Why did we stop going to church? I get you're angry with God. He might have eventually helped."

Sofia ran the knife through the onion in slow, precise chops. "I was waiting for God to explain Himself to me."

Nicola kissed Sofia's temple, gathering the onions, and dropped them in the pan.

"You were impatient, gattina."

"He never gave me an answer. Just takes without thinking about the people left behind."

"Aren't you pissed off, Nonna? God took Uncle Gianni?"

"Booze took Gianni from me," Nicola said, stirring the onions. "I go to confession once a month."

"I thought you only went at Christmas and Easter mass."

"It's important to ask for God's forgiveness," Nicola said, dumping tomatoes in the pan. "It would do you good, gattina, apologize to God, do a little praying."

"He never listened before. Why would he now?"

"What do you need to confess, Nonna?"

"Not going to confession is a sin," Nicola said.

"I hated going to confession. I told Father Murphy I broke that vase and hid the broken bits in the bin. You were so mad; I swore God told you what I had done."

Sofia grinned softly. "It wasn't God, Amelia cut her finger. I never found another Fukagawa jardiniere."

"You're restored to grace when you confess," Nicola said, grabbing the egg tray. "Why are you so interested in religion all the sudden?"

"Lots of people believe God helps. He might help me."

Nicola poured the tomatoes into three baking dishes, cracking two eggs in each. "You don't need a church. God is always around; he'll hear your prayers."

"You're putting a lot of faith in someone who tests you," Sofia said, sliding the dishes into the oven. "I'll slice the ciabatta."

"I still want to know why you're going to confession every month."

Nicola's eyes twinkled. "I've had some fun."

"I don't want to know what you and Alessandro have been up to."

"Sometimes I get busy and forget to say good morning to Anthony." Nicola set her coffee cup down and crossed herself. "I curse Gianni for loving the drink more than his wife and daughter. Sometimes it's as simple as taking the biggest slice of cake and leaving little for everyone else."

"Ms. McGregor would have to confess every bloody day."

Sofia smiled, refilling his milk. "There's an extra pinch of pepper flakes. You may need this."

"A little fire to get the devil out."

Brendon grabbed a slice of ciabatta. He had never given much thought to the devil. He was just a guy who pissed God off. Angelene had seen the devil in him, she had coaxed him out to play. All it got him was a broken heart and wrist. Brendon had seen Angelene's demons, they were cruel and untrusting.

"Do you think people have the devil in them?"

"We're all sinners, topolino."

The egg timer buzzed, Sofia opened the oven door, wrapped a tea towel around the dish and set it in front of him. His stomach lurched and growled at the sputtering tomato sauce.

"Sounds like you have the devil screaming in you. He's hungry," Nicola said.

"It's a lot easier to blame the devil for your mistakes than take accountability. Lucifer's been everyone's scapegoat for years."

"You feel sorry for Lucifer, mammina?"

"It's hard to believe someone as loving as God can be so cruel."

Nicola perched on a stool, dipping her spoon in the sauce. "I know someone else, just as powerful and beautiful."

Sofia shook her head, dunking bread into the poached egg. "Has someone told you the devil is in you?"

"Nonna just did."

He plunged the bread into the peppery sauce, took a bite, it tingled on his tongue. The devil, bad choices. It had been more fun to give in to Padre Diavolo's temptations.

"It's harder to be good, making sure I'm saying the right thing, looking for that affirmation, the pat on the head."

"Your choices haven't been the greatest. It doesn't mean you're bad. You're a good person, sweetheart."

Brendon spooned up the last bite, grimacing as his stomach cramped. Forgive me Father was no use to him now. He had sinned too many times and was on his way to commit another.

"I'm going for a walk."

"You're still in your training shorts. It's chilly out," Sofia said.

"I won't be long. If I don't move around, I'll barf."

"Go on topolino. We'll do up the dishes and map out our trip."

"Where are you off to?"

"Antique shopping. The Valentino dress didn't put a smile on gattina's face. I'll try something else she loves."

Sofia smoothed out his hoodie, plucking a blade of grass stuck to the pocket. "The sauce put colour in your cheeks."

"Sofia Francesca, it's a damn walk."

"Stay out of the forest."

"Bloody hell, mammina, I'll text you from every corner of the property."

"Cheeky," Sofia said, touching the stubble on his chin.

"I thought you didn't like it."

"It's become part of you, and I love every inch of you. I'd rather see stubble on your face than not see you at all."

Brendon gathered courage and began his trek. He squeezed past gnarled branches, ratty brambles, and dripping ash keys. A shimmer of gold fluttered in the breeze. The tightness in his chest choked him. Friends, acquaintances, could he go back to the start? He wanted a re-do; it might be too late. The boundary was weak, his walls ready to collapse. Brendon stepped over a tangle of moss-covered roots and plunked beside her.

"Did you go to the pitch?"

"I did. I ate brekky too."

"How do you feel?"

"Like I could barf."

Angelene pressed a hand to her mouth, laughing softly. Her nose was pink from the cold, eyes bright green. Something crept out of a hollow spot. He pushed it back inside.

"If we're going to be friends, we need to establish some rules." He placed the stones that had fallen from his wall back into place and strengthened his boundary. "I went to training. The drive to do ten more crunches wasn't there. I want that feeling back and if you fuck with my head again."

"No kissing me, not on my forehead or cheek. No sharing a meal. Those are the rules."

"I have a few to add, no calling me mon amour. Don't tell me you love me, which I know was rubbish, but don't bloody say it. Don't comment on my looks or my light."

"The world would be empty without you. I'll follow your rules."

"Shake on it."

He held out his hand. Angelene stared into his eyes, a little tug pulled at his heart. He needed stronger boundaries, barbed wire to snag her before she crawled back inside.

"You must go to school."

"I can try."

"And football, go to your matches."

"When I saw Will this morning, he stuck his tongue through the hole where his tooth used to be. Troy isn't talking to me."

Angelene blew into her hands, rubbing them together. "I want you to feel alive again."

"You think getting angry and being your friend will get rid of this miserable feeling?"

"I could not be the friend Henri needed. We never set rules."

"I've built a bloody wall. You can wave to me from the other side of my moat."

"Roman said my wall was as big as the Great Wall of China. We're both safe."

Brendon dusted his shorts; his wall crumbled. When Troy introduced him to Maggie, there was no lightning bolt of love. The tingles he got from Rachel came from her hands and lips. At this moment, the breeze fluttering her hair, Brendon got a glimpse of her truth. He rebuilt the wall and electrified the boundary.

"Would you have come to Dortmund?"

"What does it matter? We've established the rules."

"I need to know."

"Fall in love with Maggie, Rachel. Give your heart to one of them."

He walked away, pleased he had survived the meeting. He had fortified his wall and was prepared to do what it took to keep her from crawling over it. All morning there had been small sparks, little flutters, bits of emotions. Brendon opened the kitchen door and grinned; he was feeling things.

"Feel better?" Sofia said.

"I'm going to force myself to do things."

"That must have been some walk."

"Nonna and dad are right. I need to get back to my routine."

"You shouldn't push yourself." Pretty green eyes and shimmery hair danced around his mind. He pushed the thought away and added another layer of stones.

"How else am I going to get better?"

"A walk around the house has given you the strength to get out of bed?" "My coaches called me a prodigy. That motivated me and gave me the determination to be the best bloody keeper Taunton had ever seen. I knew my strengths then and mastered them. I've got to do that now."

"I want you well, sweetheart."

"Then let me try this. I promise if I feel iffy, I'll call you."

"Mum prayed, she made me hold her hand."

Brendon grinned at the annoyed look on Sofia's face.

"God might watch out for me."

"I was only humouring her."

"Can I invite Rachel over? She's good at Latin. I could use her help." "Shouldn't she be in school?"

Brendon hesitated. He wanted her to like Rachel in case he took Angelene's advice and fell in love.

"She got suspended."

"Call Margaret for help," Sofia said reproachfully.

"Maggie will think we're getting back together. Rachel is safer."

It was the first time Sofia had laughed in weeks.

"Are you looking for help in Latin or something else?"

"Latin, I swear."

He gave Sofia a quick kiss and bound up the stairs. Rachel could coax more feelings out. She would see he was whole again. It was worth a try.

Brendon had slept an hour before the text arrived, letting him know she was on her way. He yawned and scratched at his rumpled shirt, dragging himself from his bed. The house was alive. The scent of ladyfingers was as wonderful as Amelia's rendition of 'What's New Pussycat.' Things were looking brighter. Brendon stood in the den's doorway; one thing hadn't changed. Mammina still looked doubtful a miracle had happened.

"What are you looking at?"

Sofia turned from the window and smiled wistfully. "When I first came here, all you could see was grass. You see nothing but roses now."

"I'm sure Richard appreciated that."

"I was bringing love to Rosewood manor. I was determined to get rid of the sad memories."

Brendon set down his text and notes, resting on the edge of the desk. "Richard never went to your wedding, did he?"

"He had better things to do." She chuckled, picking up a wedding photo. "He was afraid of mum. He called her the queen of casa del grande."

There had always been something about the den he didn't like. It wasn't uncomfortable or unpleasant. There was a certain charm about the wood-panelled walls and leather furniture. It had never felt cozy. Richard lingered.

"What really happened to Richard? No one talks about it." "I had to carry you up to bed that night. You fell asleep in the car, exhausted from your match, five years old and playing like a teenager. You slept through the noise."

Brendon grinned at the only memory he had. "I was still in my kit at breakfast."

"Richard went for a walk. The transformation in the great room annoyed him. There was a knock on the door and not a pleasant, I've come for a visit, knock but a demanding thump."

Brendon moved along the desk and fell onto the chair.

"Ame and I stared at the door. When we finally got up the nerve to open it, a beast of a man with a scraggily blonde beard and barrel chest demanded to see Richard. I told him Richard was somewhere in the garden and he walked away, yelling Richard Cook, come out from hiding."

"Bloody hell, mammina, you must have been scared."

"Beyond. Ame and I ran in here. We heard a crack and thump, another pop, then silence. Ame ran to the door and locked it. We heard tires screech, and I called 999."

"Who was the man?"

"The husband of Richard's lover. He got as far as Spence's farm when the police caught him."

"Dad said Richard's miserable spirit and poor choices took him away. It did."

"Excuse me, would you like me to put tea on?" Amelia said.

"Mum was just telling me about how Richard died."

Amelia lifted her apron, hiding her smile. "Tim and I had drinks to celebrate."

Sofia wound David's cardigan tighter around her. "Tea and coffee. Mum has been itching for the tiramisu."

The doorbell gonged, Amelia flapped her apron ties at them and scurried to the door.

"Guten tag Ms. Potter."

Rachel waltzed into the room, jeans full of holes, wearing his hoodie. "Hiya Ms. Cook. I like your hair up."

"You don't think she looks like a frump?" Nicola said.

"Are you daft? She may be in jeans and a jumper, she's still beautiful."

Brendon stifled his laugh.

"I'm not daft, I'm Brendon's grandmother Nicola, you are?"

"Where are my manners?" Rachel said, flinging out her hand. "I'm Rachel Jones. You don't look like a grandma."

"I might like this one, topolino."

"That's brill. I usually frighten mums and nans away."

"You can't help your curves, just don't try so hard," Nicola said.

"The coffee is on; tea is brewing, the tiramisu is done," Amelia said.

"My stomach hurts. I'll have tea."

"Perhaps Rachel would like some. Those curves are a sign of a good appetite."

"Must you be so bold, mother."

"I mean no disrespect. Walter Pratt is the only man I know that likes skin and bones."

"Mum tells me I have a fat bum all the time. I'm used to it."

Brendon jerked the ruler from the cup holder and lifted the hoodie. "It isn't fat. I like it." "Brendon," Sofia said, frowning, "Would you like some tiramisu?"

"I've never had it before. I hear it's moreish."

"Never had... you don't know what you're missing. Amelia dish her up a plate with a cup of coffee. Rachel can dig into that instead of my grandson."

"Oh, mio dio, mother."

Brendon chuckled at Sofia's flushed cheeks. "You sure are observant, Nonna."

"Rachel likes you. Is that better, Sofia?"

"Would you prefer tea, Rachel?" Sofia said, shooting a 'behave yourself' look.

"I always drink coffee with mine," Nicola said.

Rachel dove into the wingback chair and looped her arm through his.

"Coffee it is."

"Sofia was saying you're going into nursing." Brendon sunk into the warmth of her body. Like osmosis, it creeped into his pores and heated his insides.

"She wants to treat old people."   "Somebody must look after them. My mother-in-law lived with us," Nicola said.

"I went to a senior care home with Maggie to meet her great gran. The whole place smelled like piss."

"I'm happy you're getting your cheek back, sweetheart." Rachel snuggled closer, resting her chin on his shoulder. "My gran has dementia. She wears the same ugly dress everyday waiting for gramps to come home for dinner. Gramps has been dead for years."

"Geriatrics means more to you then," Sofia said.

"I volunteer at a senior care home. I could sit and talk to them for hours."

"You wouldn't want to talk to my grandfather, Richard. He told me footballers were a bunch of prima donnas. He said I'd fit right in because I was a spoiled, whingey brat. I was four."

"Has he passed? I don't want to work at the home he's in."

"The prick is gone. He got what he deserved."

"That he did," Nicola said, tugging Sofia's arm. "We've hung around long enough, gattina."

"How do you get into those jeans? You must be terribly uncomfortable."

"Now who's being bold?" Nicola said. "Like the rest of us, one leg at a time."

Brendon flipped open his textbook, papers spread across the desk. He relaxed into the chair, twirling Rachel's hair around his finger.

"I like your Nonna."

"I like her too."

"I wouldn't want to mess with her."

"She ran the textile mill, let mum move away, laid my Uncle Gianni to rest then Nonno. She's been through a lot and never shed a tear."

"She doesn't seem the type to cry."

"Strong women don't cry; they go into battle."

Rachel ran her fingers along his neck and kissed his jaw. "How are you, knuddlebär? You look better, smell better too."

"Food's tasting good. Training was okay."

"I heard you and Troy are fighting."

"I was a prick. I let him down."

"Do you need a kiss?"

"Your tiramisu could arrive any minute."

"Just a small one. Then homework."

He brushed his lips over hers. His heart slowed; every muscle relaxed. He kissed her and kissed her, savouring the taste of cherries on her lips. To hell with his mother and the tiramisu. Angelene wanted him to fall in love. This could be the moment where time stood still, and lightning bolts happened. Brendon fumbled under the folds of fabric, touching her breast. It was warm and glorious, covered in satin and lace. Something was stirring, something was coming alive.

"I have your tea and dessert."

Brendon jerked his hand away, staring at his lap. The thing was awake. He leaned forward, placed his elbows on the desk, concealing the evidence.

"Tiramisu and coffee. Tea for you, sweetheart," Sofia said, eyeing the empty notebook. "How's the studying going?"

"Extremum vitae spiritum edere, mammina."

Rachel licked the spoon, her eyes sparkled. "Impressive, knuddlebär.""Give up the ghost mammina."

**

Of all the churches in Taunton, Angelene preferred St. Georges. She loved when the sun was setting, and its rays shone through the Gothic style windows. The intricately carved arches and chancel took her back to the Gothic churches Henri loved. Angelene pressed her back against the wood. It was a habit, sitting still and silent. She could hear her mother whispering, *'god is watching,'* feel the jab in her ribs. She clutched her rosary, touching each bead. God had to hear her. She was in his house. She had confessed about Henri's death and haphazardly mended the wound. All the years she punished herself and wallowed in shame sat differently in her heart. Angelene twisted the rosary around her hand, *'Help me strengthen my walls. Help him find his light again.'* She gazed around the white arches and wooden pews for a sign God had listened. It was selfish of her to think it would come so quickly. She closed her eyes, muttered a prayer, reminding herself God loved her and continued to love her with every tumble into an unwise decision.

Angelene kissed the pewter St. Jude. A grin twitched her lips. It was a suitable saint for her, desperate cases, she had been one all her life. She tucked the rosary into her purse and thanked God for listening.

"Sorry I took so long. I lose myself in church."

"No worries. I was talking to my wife. She needs me to pick up some bits and bobs from Tesco. Three things turned into ten," Malcolm said. "You headed to Taunton Park?"

"I will only go with my husband from now on. Can you take me to the bakery on Station Road?"

"Anything for my favourite passenger."

"Me? Most people loathe me after a while."

"I like your stories. You have an interesting perspective on things," Malcolm said, slowing the car at a stop sign. "You probably think that telephone pole is beautiful."

Angelene followed the length of the pole with her finger, tracing along the wires. "All the words exchanged through the wires. All the goodbyes, I love you, I miss you, the connections made. It's beautiful."

Malcolm signalled and rounded the roundabout. "Only you would see that."

He pulled alongside the curb; his moustache fluttered. "I have another pickup. You want me to come back after?"

"I'm going to explore for a bit. I'll call you."

She pressed money into his hand and smiled. She had made the right decision, even if God hadn't answered yet. Brendon would be back to his old self. Sofia would be the glamourous woman who intimidated her. She was making the effort at normal, buying Walter's favourite, raspberry roly-poly. God knew her intentions were good. Angelene strolled into the shop, gazing at the pastries. The first time Walter had brought her to the bakery, the simplicity had amazed her. Chelsea buns, Bakewell tarts, where were the macarons, profiteroles and milles feuilles? Walter called her a pudding snob. She didn't know what he meant. Pudding came in pots, petite pots au chocolat, crème brûlée.

"May I have two jam roly-poly please?"

She studied the display. Squares of pink and yellow Battenburg caught her eye. The checkerboard slices were cheery. It suited her mood.

"Two slices of Battenburg, please."

Angelene smiled politely, took her change, and made her way to the door. She spotted an Asian market two doors down. Roman loved Pak Boong Fai Dang. He had it every time he was in Thailand. She had researched the recipe, memorizing the ingredients: morning glory, Thai chili, soybean paste, oyster sauce. Today was a day to celebrate. She needed to share her joy with her hopeful poppa. Angelene kept her head down, reciting the list, listening for God, and bumped into a man's chest. She drew the pastry box into her chest and glanced up. The shock of nearly knocking someone over disappeared.

"Blimey, Ms. Pratt, you need to watch where you're going."

"You aren't sunny yellow. You're muddy yellow."

"I was just grabbing some Chelsea buns for Charlie."

Pierre had taught her a technique to examine artwork, a simple formula developed by Erwin Panofsky. The first was to look. Was it rough, shiny, carefully made, haphazardly thrown together? Step two, see, apply meaning to it or symbols, Panofsky called it 'iconography.' Last, she was to put everything together and think about the painting's meaning. Like everything in her life, it became a pattern when visiting the Louvre. Troy Spence was sunshiny yellow, lean, and athletically built. He was a product of love, cultivated in the rich soil. His yellow was constant and flowed through his veins even on days when it was dark.

"What brings you into town?"

"God and jam roly-poly."

"You have a nice night."

Angelene stared at her feet. If she wasn't running, people were running from her.

"Have I made you uncomfortable?"

"You know the opening line from Tale of Two Cities."

"It's one of Dickens's best. It was the best of times; it was the worst of times."

"It's the bleeding worst. Brendon and I aren't talking. Maggie thinks... I can't, bleeding heck, Ms. Pratt, you look at me with those eyes and I'm a dolt," Troy said, jingling his car keys. "How are you getting home?"

"I'm going to the Asian market to buy ingredients for Pak Boong Fai Dang. I'll call Malcolm."

"Pak what? Sounds funny."

Angelene held a hand to her mouth, grinning. "It's a Thai dish."

"I'll grab the Chelsea buns and go with you." "You're relaxing a little. Your yellow is brightening." "I'm invoking protection from the Great Mother. Amelia's daughter, Georgina, is into white magic. She invoked the Great Mother last summer at a BBQ at the Cook's. It was to protect Brendon and I on our travels to Dortmund and Manchester."

He moved past her. She caught a whiff of his scent. Tonka beans, almonds, cinnamon. It reminded her of a sunset. The scent stayed with her. She studied his lean body and square jaw. Something stirred in her belly. She touched her cross, confused by the sensation. He had moved her like Eugene Delacroix's Dante and Virgil in Hell.

You are a painting, nothing more.'

"Everything good? You have goosebumps."

"Kama muta, throbbing, molten yellow. The feeling is in motion, coursing through my veins."

"That's not like the Kama Sutra, is it? Charlie's parents have the book. We found it in Ms. Donovan's yoga room. Charlie and I tried the Lotus. She was sitting cross-legged. Sorry, Ms. Pratt."

"It is nothing like the Kama Sutra. It's a feeling, like when Man U is behind and pulls out the win or you hear a song, and it reminds you of something or someone."

They made their way towards an open set of doors. Spicy, unfamiliar smells floated around them. Troy threw his hand over his nose, coughing. "What's that smell?"

Angelene laughed at the aversion on his face. "It's durian fruit."

"Bleeding awful."

"I'll get the morning glory. You find me soybean paste and oyster sauce."

"I've never heard of this stuff. Where is the treacle and malt vinegar?"

"What's treacle? I've never heard of that."

"It's syrup, sweet and sticky."

"I've learned something new, too."

Angelene gazed over the rows of cardboard boxes, stuffing morning glory in a bag. She added lemongrass, galangal, and kaffir lime leaves to her basket. Tom Yum Goong would be on the menu tomorrow. Roman loved the spicy shrimp soup. He had said it warmed him from his head to his toes. There were prawns in the freezer. She would see if it had the same effect on Walter.

"Do you need anything else?"

"That's everything."

"I'm going to pull the car up. I couldn't put my finger on the smell when we first walked in. Rotten onions and our socks after a match." Angelene grinned. It was the eighth smile of the day, a record for her. She set her basket on the counter, gazing at the cluttered displays. Her heart expanded. Smile nine appeared, White Rabbit candy, Panda biscuits. The memory was vivid.

Where did you fly to this time, Roman?

I was in Hong Kong. There are lots of tall buildings. The signs were brighter than the sun.

Was it busy?

Busy in a good way, little bird, like it had its own heartbeat.

I was so happy when mother said you were coming. She's been terribly grumpy. Monsieur Douchette bought her a bottle of Chambord. She must have missed you too.

I bought her a kimono. She can wrap herself in that the next time she misses me. These are for you. There's strawberry cream in the cookies and this.
It's a little cat.
That is a Maneki-Neko. He'll bring you good luck.
When God doesn't hear me, I'll have my lucky cat.

Angelene placed the biscuits and candy on the counter. She paid the clerk, rushing from the shop. There were too many memories waiting to steal her joy.

A dance beat thumped from within the Fiesta. Angelene touched her cross. She was doing nothing wrong. Troy was a painting, nothing more.

"You didn't buy any of that stinky fruit, did you?"

"Once you get past the smell, it's delicious. The insides are sweet and custardy."

"I'll stick to apples and bananas."

The poppy hip-hop music thrummed in Angelene's ears. Sometimes she would hear similar sounds coming from behind the doors of her apartment building. Roman had introduced her to classical music, her mother, Edith Piaf. Veronique would play the records while she waited for a lover to arrive. One of the few times Angelene heard her mother laugh was when she danced barefoot in the kitchen with Roman to Piaf's 'La Vie en Rose.' Angelene listened to the whoosh of the high hat, clapping hands, and synthesizer. It was as extravagant as Mozart's Sonata No.17; she tapped her fingers against the pastry box.

"What do you call this music?"

"It's Nicki Minaj. Have you never heard of her?"

"This song is as yellow as you. It makes me happy."

"Turn Me On, was playing the first time Charlie and I, sorry, you don't need to know that."

They passed an apple orchard, children ran among the trees, sticks in hand, laughing and smiling so brightly, it pained her.

Once upon a time, there was a girl who lived in a rabbit den of concrete and glass. Outside her window, puddles became oceans. Birds were airplanes, taking her to all the places she yearned to see. A boy lived across the street in a giant, concrete beast. She was queen of the concrete castle, and he was king of the gargantuan steel fortress. His name, Francois, and she, Angelene.

Angelene splayed her hand against the window, inhaled, filling her lungs with the children's joy.

"What was Brendon like as a child?"

"He never sat still, always got in trouble for moving about."

"Was he bored?"

"He was goalkeeping in his head," Troy said, turning onto Taunton Road. "The teachers used to change his lessons, so he'd pay attention. If you made ten saves and then another five, how many saves did you make? He'd sit then."

"Was he happy?"

"All the time, unless his game was off, or Mr. Cook gave him a lecture on his grades. Mum says he broods. The girls find it dishy."

"He hasn't been happy lately."

"I'm not sure what's up with him. Everyone has a theory. Some say a broken heart, some say a guilty conscious, Maggie thinks... it doesn't matter. He's not the same. He's a dick."

"I've asked God to watch over him." Melancholy was invading her yellow. Brendon would not heal if Troy weren't by his side. "Can you forgive him? He needs your yellow."

"I'm tired of defending him, on and off the pitch."

Angelene undid her seatbelt and rested her arms on the dashboard. "The cows are wonderful."

"They're a pain in my arse."

"You could put bells around their necks. Imagine how pretty that would sound."Angelene grinned. She was proud of herself for conquering sad before it stole her happiness.

"May I say hello to the cows?"

"Now?"

"You're uncomfortable again. I'm sorry."

Troy turned onto the lane leading to the barn. A wrestling match was taking place in the garden. He waved to Callum and Brian and parked beside the wooden fence.

"I've got my protection spell around me."

Angelene laughed, climbing out of the car. "You don't need protection from me."

"You don't know what's been going on in my head," Troy said, climbing the fence. "That's Blossom. She was a runt. Mum said she blossomed, we named her that."

"May I?"

She reached through the gap and ran her hand over the cow's snout.

"Your parents are magicians." "I feel like the flies that get in our house and buzz around my window, stuck with no way out."

"I got out of Paris." "No sporting director or scout is going to drive down Taunton Road looking for me."

She stroked the cow, marvelling at how the skin felt rough then soft depending on the direction of her hand.

"Don't you see the beauty surrounding you? The earth, the animals."

"I smell shit."

"You mustn't give up on your dreams. You radiate vibrant yellow light."

"Maybe my yellow, as you call it, can attract the coaches at Man U."

Angelene nuzzled the cow's neck. She understood Troy's struggle.

"I gave up on my dreams. Don't lose your light."

"Bleeding heck, my protection spell isn't working. You've got into my head again."

"All your hard work will pay off. It's building character, which will take you far."

She jumped from the fence and plucked a stem of red campion. "May I?"

"It grows all over. I doubt mum will miss it."

"I'm going to press it in a book. When I see you on television in your red and gold kit, I'll have this flower as a reminder of the boy and his chickens." She ran her fingers over his bangs and pecked his cheek. "Always stay bright yellow."

Troy swallowed and stared at his feet. "I'll take you home now.""Can you ask your father to put bells on the cows? I could hear them every morning."

"Sure thing," Troy said, touching his cheek. "The spot you kissed tingles. You are a witch."

The words floated in her ears. "My mother said I was wicked. She said once someone caught my attention, I claimed them.""I meant nothing bad," Troy said, opening the car door. "Did you do this to Brendon? Did you put a spell on him too? Not that I care."

"I don't have that kind of power. You'd have to think you were someone special to have that kind of effect on people." She slid onto the seat, blew the cows a kiss and set the box on her lap. "People feared the witches. They should have been frightened of the people who accused them of witchcraft."

"Sorry, it was a daft thing to say."

They backed out of the lane. Angelene turned in the seat, tilting her head. "Are your brothers fighting?"

"They think they're professional wrestlers."

"It looks like fun."

"Not when you get put in a headlock."

Troy turned onto the farmhouse drive; the stones glistened like little stars in the fading lavender light. It was charming, less haunted, like a house out of a fairy tale.

"Give me your palm."

"Is this more magic?"

Angelene took his hand and flipped it over, moving her finger along the lines and crosses. "Your heart line is long and curved; passion and desire drive you. Your lifeline is short."

"Does that mean I'm going to die young? My uncle died at 38."

"It means you're controlled by others."

"The farm."

"Don't lose hope. There's a break in it. You'll have a change in your lifestyle."

"You believe that?"

"The question is, do you believe?" she said, winding her fingers through his. "You bring such joy to people."

"I take it back," Troy said, smiling. "You aren't a witch. You see things differently and I like that. Enjoy your Pak whatever."

Angelene touched his cheek. She was up to smile twelve. "Please forgive Brendon. He needs you."

"I'll think about it."

"I want to hear the clanging of bells. Bonne nuit."

Angelene floated to the door, embraced in yellow. She had spent time with a boy and hadn't stolen his light. She slid the box onto the island and carried the ingredients to the counter. Her task, enjoy a bowl of Pak Boong and read. A muffled chirp came from within her purse. Walter insisted the notification suited his little bird. Angelene rummaged through her bag, clicking on the message. Her yellow mood slopped at her feet, red flooded in. Walter had bought her a gown for the gala, an Alexander McQueen masterpiece. Angelene cursed. She had made it perfectly clear; she did not want to attend the event. Walter had not listened.

Angelene tossed the cell into the fruit bowl, grabbed her Benson & Hedges, and poured wine into a mug. She flipped through the pages of the Hunchback; an illustration of the Pont Alexandre III floated to her lap. Henri had kissed her on the bridge. He said he would never forget the kiss; she swore it would never happen again. Angelene scrunched the cigarette package. Red remained. She took Henri's friendship away with no thought of how it might break him. How could she be Brendon's friend? Angelene gulped the wine and refilled the mug. She would be Brendon's friend from a distance, wave from the laneway, casual conversation at dinner parties. She would paint him like she had Troy. He would be nothing more than that, a painting.

37 Rub till it's Numb

Troy hung his blazer and deposited his keys on the half-moon table. Grunts and laughter bounced off the thin walls. He walked to the sitting room. Brian stood on the sofa, ready to pounce. Troy scooped Callum onto his back, swinging him in a dizzying helicopter. He tossed Callum on the sofa, ducking as Brian came in for the clothesline.

"We're in trouble now. Frilly Knickers Donovan is here," Callum said. He dove from the sofa, the cushions flopped to the floor. "That girl was here again. She was cuddling Blossom this time."

Charlotte cocked her head to the side in a distractingly charming, inquisitive way.

"What girl?"

"I got you two Chelsea buns. You want a cuppa?" Guilt rattled him. He flung his arm across his chest, slipping past her. "I put them in my room so my brothers wouldn't eat them."

"Troy Alexander, who was here?"

"They'll be no rumpy-pumpy now." Brian hollered.

Troy shot up his middle finger and marched down the hall. He slammed open the door, kicking a pathway through the clothes on the floor. Charlotte pushed aside a stack of magazines and sunk onto the mussed bed.

"Is that why you didn't answer my text? You were busy with some girl?"

"I answered it."

Charlotte flipped open the lid, pierced a current and stuck it in her mouth. "Three hours later."

Troy flung his shirt into the basket; he had never purposely hidden anything from Charlotte. He'd take the pinch, compliment, and kiss her until she forgave him. Troy stripped out of his trousers, dove onto the bed, puckering his lips for a kiss.

"No humping. I'm gutted you had some girl over."

"Are you having that PSM or PMS thing again?"

"Where were you when I text?"

"Buying you Chelsea buns. Pretty thoughtful of me."

He didn't know how Brendon could have hidden his secret from Maggie for so long. He was drowning in guilt.

"It was Ms. Pratt." The words flew on a ragged exhale.

"What were you doing with her?" Charlotte said, licking sugar glaze off her fingers.

"We went to the Asian market. She was making Pak something. I offered her a drive home."

"Why stop here?"

"She begged to see the cows." Troy pushed off the bed and ripped his shirt and trousers from a hanger. "I've never seen anyone so excited over bleeding cows. She looked happy, like proper happy instead of how she usually looks." "Do you fancy her now?"

He wrestled into his clothes, threading his tie around his collar. "Don't be daft. I was being nice."

"Are you going to drive Tilly home now? Double date with Brendon and the tart."

"She made me see things differently."

Charlotte dropped the bun in the box and closed the lid. "Who is she, Mother Teresa?"

"She talked about the farm like it was a living, breathing thing. She made me realize how hard mum and dad work. I'm lucky."

"Are you giving up on being a pro footy player now?"

"I'm going to get off the farm. She saw it in my palm." He latched his belt and tore his backpack off the floor. "She gave me hope. She said chores and hard work are building character."

"Brian said again. Was Ms. Pratt here before?" Her voice was flat, her expression let him know her entire world was falling apart. "Why don't you go have Pak something with Ms. Pratt."

"Do you have to do this before a match? You're messing with my game," Troy said, chasing her down the hall.

"I knew when I met you, you were the only boy for me. We just fit."

"We still do." Troy reached for her wrist, she slipped out the door. "She's just a friend." "She's a married woman. She shouldn't be friends with you or Brendon. It isn't right."

"I don't mean friend friends. She's Walt's wife. I have to be nice." "Do you have any idea what someone like Ms. Pratt can do?"

Troy knew what she used to do, made him think many inappropriate things. He had fallen asleep feeling grateful for life on the farm.

"Ms. Pratt stares at you like she's stealing your soul."

A little shudder crawled down his spine. Had she got in Brendon's head too?

"You never told me she visited before. You kept it from me," Charlotte said, plunking behind the steering wheel.

"I was going to tell you the day we parked under the willow tree, but we said all those brilliant things. I didn't want to hurt you."

Charlotte turned onto the road; her cheeks grew chalk-white, tiny beads of sweat dotted her upper lip. "Ms. Pratt is manipulative. She wants to control people because she's never had a voice. She's been powerless all her life."

"You should go to uni to be a psychologist. You've got it all figured out."

"I used to think Maggie was daft for thinking Ms. Pratt was an evil spider, spinning her beautiful web. I believe her now."

37 RUB TILL IT'S NUMB

Troy dug in his pocket for a tissue and patted the sweat from her lip.

"Has something happened between you and Ms. Pratt?"

"It was a while back, the day Maggie and I bunked off school. We were leaving your house; I nearly ran her over. She called you her sunshine, told me to not steal your light. It was the way she said it, like a threat."

"Why didn't you tell me about that?"

"By the time the match was over, I convinced myself it meant nothing."

"We're equal then. You hid something from me."

Charlotte pulled into the pitch car park and parked beside the fence. "Have a good match."

"My kiss for good luck."

"Goodbye, Troy Alexander."

"You're not staying?"

"I'm going back to yours to crochet with your mum. I have a new stitch to learn."

"You want someone to take pictures?"

"I have enough," Charlotte said. She reached across his lap and opened the door. "Au revoir Monsieur Spence. Bonne chance."

Troy reached over the seat for his backpack, his heart stopped and thumped heavily against his ribcage. "Why are you speaking French?"

"You must like French things now."

Had his theory been right? Was it another trick to get him to fall for her again? Troy shook the thought from his head. She was a different Ms. Pratt. She made him believe life on the farm was okay and not his devil, as Brendon had once said. He wouldn't worry about it; he had a match to play.

***

Brendon stared at his graffitied cast. He should have ended the chapter titled 'Ms. McGregor's New Floor' with a fuck you, instead of his fists. The fans wouldn't look so sombre. He should have edited the chapter, 'Welcome to Taunton, Little Bird.' He would have grabbed drinks, ignored the girl hiding in the ivy. It was a good try, erasing, forgetting, rationalizing. The lack of excitement on his team mates faces reminded him there was no rewriting.

"Whoa, slow down." Brendon grabbed Troy's arm. He halted to a stop.

"I've got a match to play. Bugger off."

"You look like you've lost your best friend."

"I have," Troy said. "I also got into an argument with Charlie. She's going back to mine. Mum started teaching her to crochet a while ago. She mastered the single stitch."

"Does she need me to take pictures?"

"I asked. She said she had enough."

They walked towards the dressing room; Brendon squeezed his shoulder. "Buy her another charm. She'll forgive you."

Troy shoved past him and tore open the door. "You know how your parents get angry disappointed. She's angry sad."

"You want to talk about it?"

Brendon scanned the bleachers. Fans gripped cups of coffee and First flags, hope on their faces that today would be the day First dug themselves out of the losing streak. Of all the people in the stands, one person stood out. She tried to blend in, wearing a brown flat cap and brown sweater. He had added barbed wire barricades and land mines for extra protection. She shouldn't be able to get in. She had somehow slipped past his barricade.

"It was Ms. Pratt. I bumped into her. She talked about durian fruit and a Thai dish and the cows' wearing bells. Nicki Minaj was playing. She came alive, like she became part of the music. She was beautiful, like I was noticing her for the first time."

"Did you want to snog her again?"

"For a second or two. She started talking about how brilliant the farm is. I was watching her mouth move; I felt the urge."

"She takes you to a place you shouldn't go."

"I'm thinking you snogged Ms. Pratt."

"Don't get wrapped up in Angelene, not unless you have a fifty-foot wall around you."

"I don't even know why I'm talking to you. I've got a match to play."

Which devil had attacked Troy? Had one of her devils attached to every boy whose light she admired?

Brendon gripped the steering wheel, added more stones to his wall, and turned on to the tire-worn path. Angelene stood amongst the brambles. Which devil was waiting for him, liar, selfish?

When a woman is talking to you, listen to what she says with her eyes.

The words fell freely in his mind. Angelene had thrown the Hugo quote at him like she did all the others. He would take Hugo's advice and find the hidden meaning in her eyes. Brendon parked the car, set his landmines to destruct and replaced the barbed wire with razor wire.

"Why?"

"My disguise didn't work?"

He studied the tilt of her pouty lips and wide eyes. He couldn't decipher which devil had come.

"No matches remember, your rules." "Your light is dazzling today. I thought I was dreaming."

He bounced between '*I love you*,' *I hate you, you're a mess, you're lovely.*' The words zipped around his brain. The landmines deactivated; the razor wire coiled into a tight bundle. Brendon shrank into the seat; she had done it again.

"I'm pissed off at you."

"I drew this for you," Angelene said.

"The branch is going to break. What if the bird gets hurt?"

"Be as a bird perched on a frail branch that she feels beneath her, still she sings away all the same, knowing she has wings. That's one of Roman's favourite Hugo quotes. The branch hasn't broken yet. Use your wings."

"Why don't you find Roman? You can show him your wings."

"I'm not sure Roman would like the new Angelene."

"You could fly home, take a train into Zurich, hold his hand and walk in Parkanlage Zuerihorn."

"That was unkind." Brendon flicked the BVB key chain. It felt good to give her a little stab.

37 RUB TILL IT'S NUMB

"I'm bloody pissed off. You show up at the match and now you're acting like everything is normal."

"Have I ever told you about the Bridegroom's Oak?"

"I'm supposed to be telling you to fuck off for breaking the rules, not listening to your bloody stories."

"Roman told me about the oak tree. It's in Eutin, Germany. People searching for a spouse put a letter in the tree and hope to find a partner."

"That's the stupidest thing I've ever heard."

"People want to be loved."

"Except you."

"Walter bought me a new dress for the gala. I don't want to go."

Brendon's fingers bit into the steering wheel. She was avoiding things, talking in riddles, hiding behind her carefully constructed wall.

"You don't have to; you can say no."

"Walter's eyes are cold. I don't know why we're going; he's been distant."

"Mum wants to give up her tickets." "I do hope Sofia is going. I can't be on my own." "Nonna convinced her. She said it was just what mum and dad need to stir up some romance."

Angelene rubbed at her charcoal-stained fingertips and shrunk into the seat. "I've recited everything I need to say. I filled a champagne flute with water, practiced holding it, took tiny, ladylike sips."

Brendon's wall shook. Which devil was playing with him, liar, desperate? He wasn't supposed to be feeling anything but annoyed and angry. The shifting from love to hate was strangling him. His fingers itched to hold her hand. Brendon slid his hand between his thighs and lit his boundary on fire. She'd burn if she stepped any closer to his wall.

"No more breaking the rules."

"I promise. Can you take me to St. Georges church?"

"You need to pray?"

"I need to be forgiven." Brendon started the car and slowly backed onto the road. He had to get rid of her before his wall crumbled and he fell back in love.

"Did you have fun with Troy?"

"Are you jealous?"

"I don't like you. How can I be jealous?"

"Your words are green."

"How about we stop talking?"

Angelene plucked her cigarettes from her pocket, shook one into her hand, and placed it in her mouth. It bobbed up and down as she spoke. "Troy is going somewhere, far from the farm and Taunton."

"Did you read his palm, or did God whisper it to you?"

"Troy's angry with you. You're going to need him. Make amends."

Brendon kept his eyes on the road. He was a mixture of blue and green. Strength drooped, he struggled to hang onto hate.

"No more matches."

"I promise."

He slowed the car at a stop sign. Her eyes were grey green. It was hard to see if she was telling the truth or playing with him.

"No more promises, either."

"Can I borrow your wings for the gala?"

"Borrow someone else's, mine are being mended."

"Walter is upset with me."

"He'll put on his tuxedo; you'll be in that posh dress. Walter will forget whatever is eating him up."

"How could he forget when it's me?"

"St. Georges church, Ms. Pratt. God awaits."

"I guess this is see you soon."

"I'd rather say goodbye, if that's all right with you."

***

'If we confess our sins, he is faithful and just and will forgive us our sins and purify us from all unrighteousness.' John 1:9.

Angelene didn't know how long she had been whispering John 1:9. The mysterious feeling bounced between exhilaration, euphoria, anxiety, and panic. It showed hints of itself around Troy when she dove into his yellow. It burned when she was with Brendon. Angelene held her cross. What was the feeling and why did it spread from her belly to her thighs? She had felt this feeling before and dismissed it. Memories of the evening were vivid. The sky had been midnight blue, dusted with stars. She had thought his blueprints were prettier than a Degas or Klimt. His skin smelled of citron broyé. He had begged for a kiss. She remembered protesting but allowing it. Angelene squeezed her eyes shut, dug her cross into her palm. The memory would not come together. He had been his blue, sugary sweet, inky blue. He had wrapped her in his calm, it might have been his arms. The memories were foggy puzzle pieces bouncing around her head. She couldn't recall if she enjoyed falling into Henri's blue.

Crossing herself, Angelene stood and wobbled. The chips of memories weighed heavily. She stepped into the confessional. The voice on the other side was monotone and gentle.

"Forgive me Father, for I have sinned. It has been two days since my last confession. I accuse myself of the following sins. I'm feeling something and it frightens me. When I think of him, I shouldn't be feeling warmth, not there."

She drew in a rattled breath and clutched her cross. "I'm a drunk like my mother. It's easier to drown the screams in a bottle. I'm sorry for these sins and all the sins of my life."

Angelene scratched at the scar on her wrist. It had been goodbye this time.

"Do not act on this feeling. Pray to release it from your mind."

"People say I have the devil in me. Would the Vatican perform an exorcism?"

"Stay true to God, trust Him, He will guide you."

Angelene breathed in her penance, her sins pardoned. The feeling lingered. She crossed herself, scrambled from the booth, and dropped to her knees. She began the Hail Mary's rocking and repeating, '*I will ignore the feeling. I will respect Brendon's boundaries.*' Angelene stood and ambled to the door. The air was cool. Night had settled in, wrapping itself around the rectory. She made a quick call to Malcolm and sagged against a tree; the feeling was gone.

'*I thought if I were brown today, I would blend in and go unnoticed. I'm wearing brown. I envisioned myself surrounded by brown. Yet, you spotted me.*' Angelene made her way to the road, shook out a cigarette, gazing at the spirals of smoke. '*I never liked the colour brown, not until I met you.*'

37 RUB TILL IT'S NUMB

She took two long drags, scraped the butt along the cement and shoved the filter in the package. Today should have been a brown day. It turned out to be a kaleidoscope of colours that never came together. Malcolm honked and pulled alongside the curb.

"It was a beautiful autumn day. I hope you got to enjoy it," Malcolm said.

"I would describe the day as lovely, hopeful, blissful, frightening. I prefer spring."

"I don't like winter. The world looks bare and the snow showers."

"We need winter. Things must die to be reborn. That's why I love spring. What winter steals, spring returns. People do it too."

Malcolm's cheeks ballooned into a smile. "You're telling me people are like seasons?"

"People change, parts of them die and new parts appear. My hopeful poppa said I was winter. He always tried to chase it out of me."

"What am I?"

Angelene tilted her head and held a finger to her lips. Summer was like a warm blanket.

"You're summer, shining as bright as the sun. You're green, sometimes orange, sometimes yellow."

"How did you know green was my favourite colour?"

"I didn't. I just know I was lucky to find you."

"I hope Mr. Pratt knows how special you are."

"Odd, you mean."

"It's an interesting way to look at people, as a colour or a season."

Angelene leaned into the seat, fiddling with her engagement ring. "What colour am I?"

"Blue. You're smiling but, your eyes are sad."

"I'm a little anxious. The gala is tomorrow."

"I drove two ladies to the salon today. They were giggling like a couple of schoolgirls." "It's stressful. I must act. I'm no Catherine Deneuve."

"Just be you. Let the rest of them act."

Angelene laughed softly. Being her was more difficult than acting.

"Do you think it's a sin to think about someone's light?"

"It depends if you're admiring it or... I'm too old and happy to be thinking about another woman's light. If that's what you mean."

"I get this feeling sometimes." Angelene glanced at the farmhouse and swallowed nervously. "What colour am I now?"

"Black."

Angelene tucked a folded bill in his hand, forcing a twitchy grin. "Black makes sense. I'm unsure of Walter's mood and I'm petrified to attend the gala."

"You'll be fine. Can I give you a piece of advice?"

Angelene opened the car door and nodded.

"Stay away from other people's light. You have enough of your own."

Malcolm tooted the horn, Angelene waved and rambled up the walkway. The house was fragranced with lemongrass and galangal. Walter was singing a duet with Mick Jagger. She tiptoed to the kitchen; he was reheating the tom yum boong. His light was static and electrified, not soft like Brendon's. She shook Brendon from her mind. She was supposed to be thinking about her husband so she could fall in love. Her mother had said love made her crazy. The feeling she felt could be love, and that's why it troubled her. She might have been insanely in love with Henri, a mad woman scratching at his light. She might love Brendon, which was why she had trouble breathing when he was around. It could be her devils tempting her.

"You liked the tom yum boong."

"It's quite tasty," Walter said, carrying his bowl to the island. "Where have you been? You've been gone all afternoon."

Angelene slid onto the window bench. Walter hadn't looked at her yet. He had come home from London, sat at his laptop, and worked into the night. They had passed by one another at breakfast with no good morning. He was present, but far away.

"I went into town to hunt for books at the charity shop and ended up at St. Georges."

"You've been going to confession a lot lately."

"I've been unpacking my baggage."

His eyes never left the bowl. Angelene pushed at the trembles in her belly. Walter's static energy was attacking her. She had to switch from black to yellow. She wouldn't survive the gala if she were black. Paint, take herself away, Troy Spence and his chickens would be her inspiration. His yellow was infectious.

"Do you know how long it's been since we've had sex or had an actual conversation?"

Angelene tucked herself in the corner, hugging her knees. She could try to find a smidgeon of love for Walter, go mad for her husband. Her nails sunk into her calves; the air was as prickly as Walter's tone.

"Shall we have sex, little bird?"

"I'd rather have a conversation."

"Sex is a conversation. You're talking with your bodies. You're using your lips and hands to tell someone you love them."

"I'm trying. I told God I would try."

"Shouldn't you be telling me?"

Angelene shuddered, the hairs on her arms stood up. His eyes were the coldest blue.

"I wouldn't know if I was in love. I don't understand it, and it frightens me."

"Everyone has their own idea of what love is. For some, it's that head over heels rubbish you see in movies. For others, it takes time and grows. Love is simple, little bird. You run from it."

"I promised God. I'll try to love you."

"Don't you think having sex might make those feelings grow?" She rocked gently, her mind spinning. She had daydreamed sex led to love. The night Henri laid his body against hers was the start of something, love, madness. She stared at Walter; confidence oozed from every charismatic pore. He didn't make love; he had sex; fucked.

"Sex leads to many things. I don't like it." "My exes never complained."

"They wouldn't. Not with your golden fingertips."

Walter tipped back the bowl, swallowed, and smirked. "Why don't you allow my golden fingertips to caress you? I feel like I'm forcing you."

"I have known none other way."

The memories floated in shards; she might have enjoyed it with Henri. It might have been all those things she had dreamt. Angelene unclenched her fingers, gripping the ends of her hair. Her emotions were on overdrive, Walter's black was prickling her skin.

"I can be gentle. It's been weeks."

"Not now."

"Not now. Not in the morning, not at bedtime, never," Walter said. He rose, carrying his bowl to the sink.

"Please don't be angry with me. I'll paint a scene as scandalous as Bosch's Garden of Earthy Delights."

"You'll head back to confession," Walter said, rinsing his bowl. "Does God not approve? Has the church made you feel guilty for thinking lusty thoughts? We'd all be damned to Hell."

Angelene wrapped her hair around her hands and tugged. "That thing shoved inside me, the grunting and sweating, stuff spat all over me. Men think they are as wonderful as Jesus when they fuck a woman." Walter placed the bowl in the dishwasher and leaned against the counter. "God created us with those things. One fits within the other. If He didn't want us to have sex, He should have made us differently. What about touching yourself?"

Angelene released her hair, fumbling for a cigarette. She scrubbed, she removed scents and stains. There was no pleasure.

"God is watching. He would not approve." "Do you think God sits and waits for someone to touch themselves so he can punish them? Paralyze their fingers, strike them down?"

Angelene lit the cigarette, holding the smoke in her mouth. Her lungs and heart quivered; the conversation dug into her.

"What pleasure can come from a spot that has been rubbed until it is numb?"

Walter groaned, gripping the back of his neck. "Is it because you'd be concentrating on how good it feels rather than praying and finding pleasure in Him?"

She took another drag and stubbed it out on an ashy plate.

"You don't want to be a trollop like your mother, is that it?"

Angelene lay her head against the window, fixing her gaze on the trees. After a lover left, Veronique would lie on her bed for days, wine bottles would clutter the nightstand, the ashtray stuffed with ashes. She would fall hard for a lover, submerge herself in their flesh and devotion, then hide away after they left. When they returned, she would lash out and accuse of them of abandoning her. When they proclaimed their love, she ran. Angelene shook out a cigarette and flicked it between her fingers, love made her mother a stranger, distant, insane.

"My mother loved her men more than me."

"I'm tired of this conversation, little bird."

"Then please leave me alone."

She dropped the cigarette and slid from her perch, her skin tight and itchy. The day was no longer lovely brown; it was muddy.

"I'll be down here, staring at the telly. Join me if you want to cuddle or hold my hand."

Angelene hung her head and conjured Roman Krieger's hand in hers. She bit the inside of her mouth until she tasted the saltiness on her tongue, trudging to her bedroom. Angelene lay on the bed and stared at the glow, it burnt her eyes and heart.

I'm going to take you to cloud nine petite oiseau.

She blinked away tears, clutching the pillow against her chest. Henri's cloud nine was a rooftop garden. He had held her hand while they climbed a secret staircase and took a magical lift to paradise. They had shared ganache chocolat and drank champagne. The sky was the colour of his eyes. She had felt something. It frightened her.

'Maybe I loved you. In my odd, bungling way. Non, it couldn't have been. Mother said I was not worthy of love. She said love burns and makes you crazy.'

Angelene folded the pillow over her head. It was as smothering and hot as her thoughts. Pierre called his love for her an addiction, an extraordinary high that made him delirious and crave her. She had seen Veronique's craziness, obsessing for days, waiting for a lover, always wanting, and needing, more than they could give. Angelene unfolded the pillow, her breath escaped in quick puffs. After all the madness, love leaves.

38 Forelsket

When Brendon woke, he had three things on his mind. Why had Angelene broken the promise? How could he build stronger walls and why hadn't he reached the dreaded explosion?

"What are you working on?"

Brendon tossed the novel on the desk, stretching his legs. "An essay."

David glanced from the few scribbles written on the paper to the blank laptop screen.

"It doesn't look like you're working on anything."

"Don't start."

"What's the essay about?"

"The themes in Tale of Two Cities."

David studied the paper. "Class struggle and family. That's the best you can do?"

Brendon tapped his fingers against the armrest. Sparks were simmering.

"I only need to write about one."

"Pick it and tell me about it."

"Where's mum?"

"In the tub. She didn't sleep well." David perched on the edge of the desk, picked up the novel and flipped through it. "She expects you to complete your assignments, too."

"Who says I'm going back to school?"

"You mentioned feeling up to it. Are you going to break another promise?"

Curse words slammed against his teeth. He wheeled himself into the desk and stared holes into his notebook. He could write pages on broken promises.

"I pick family. Happy now?"

"What about family?"

"It's an appropriate thing to write about considering ours is bollocks."

"Whose fault is that?"

"Every bloody shitty thing that happens is my fault."

David set down the book and walked to the window. "Lately, yes." "Just admit it. You've been pissed off since the day I was born." Brendon rubbed his aching forehead. "It's hard to love something you never wanted."

"I love you unconditionally."

Brendon gripped the pen and tapped it against the desk. "Your love comes with all sorts of conditions. You're forced to love me."

David turned from the window. "You must let go of this nonsense."

"It's been written on your face since the day I picked up a football instead of a chess piece."

"I won't argue with you about this."

"Why? Because you know I'm right. I didn't like Winnie the Pooh or learning the piano and it pissed you off. I signed with Dortmund and there went your dreams of having your son follow in your footsteps. Bloody hell dad, I'm not..."

"Don't you dare."

Hate danced in the sparks. Brendon opened the book and breathed through the blaze. "Can I get to the essay? I don't want to be stuck in the den all day. The ghosts are especially bothersome today."

"Family is the perfect topic for you. You can think about how damn lucky you are."

Brendon rubbed his brow, the words jumped from the page, *'she was the golden thread that united him to a past beyond his misery, and to a present beyond his misery: and the sound of her voice, the light of her face, the touch of her hand, had a strong beneficial influence with him almost always.'* Lucie Manette, the golden thread, she supported others. How had Dickens described her, *'a pretty figure, a quantity of golden hair,' religious, sometimes regarded as a child.'* Brendon chewed on the pen, his fingers hitting the keyboard. Lucie weaves the golden thread, knitting all the characters together. Lucie's love has the power to transform those around her. Brendon stared at the words on the screen: him, Troy, knitting fingers, Walter, thirteen knots in her golden noose.

***

Sofia walked into the salon. The music was bright and cheery, matching the afternoon sky. She loved getting pampered. Harrison & Co was its own community where people came to meet, share a glass of champagne, and feel good. It had been hard to leave the manor. Brendon's transformation, sullen to happy, had been quiet, not instantaneous, but it was happening. The constant knot in her belly told her she didn't trust it.

"Hello Ms. Cook," Rosie said. "Off to the gala tonight?"

"It's the last place I want to be."

"It's been a while since you've been here."

Sofia slid off her coat and handed it to Rosie. "A manicure was the last thing on my mind."

"Margaret said Brendon hasn't been well."

"He hasn't. He isn't himself."

"All that pressure," Rosie said, placing Sofia's coat on a hanger. "Always the bleeding hero. Unless it was with our Maggie."

"Taunton made him a hero. Excuse me."

Sofia walked to the manicure station, collapsing onto a velvet chair. She lay her hands on the table, staring at the rows of nail polish.

"Rosie Thornton had to get a dig in." "She's a mother protecting her daughter. Sound familiar?" Kate said.

Sofia frowned, pointing to a bottle of crimson polish.

"What do you think? It's sangria, which reminds me, we need to book our trip to Andalucía."

Sofia watched the manicurist file and shape her nails, mesmerized by the movement and scratching sound. "Book it. I don't care."

"We've talked about Spain for months. Smile, would you."

"David and Brendon have been at each other. Mother is whipping up pasta and pizza dough, which means she's upset." Sofia blinked at the tingle of tears. "There's a huge black cloud over my home."

"Brendon's been at training. He went to the match. Those are all good signs."
""He isn't the same boy. There are pieces missing."

"It's bound to take time."

"It used to drive me crazy when he would rush into the house, cursing about being late. I miss that."

"You'll have that again. I'll have to listen about the grass in the foyer or how he left the house with his shirt untucked."

Sofia grinned wistfully. It was funny how the littlest things meant the world to her. Grass-stained knees, tousled hair, stubble on the chin, football boots dropped at the front door.

"What were David and Brendon arguing about?"

"An essay. Everything Brendon does seems to aggravate David."

Kate handed the manicurist five pounds and spun in the chair. "Maybe David's feeling neglected?" Sofia slid her hands under the heat lamp. She hadn't thought about David. She always made a point of welcoming him home, taking his briefcase, or tugging playfully on his suspenders. The routine had changed. She couldn't remember the last time she greeted him or kissed him goodnight.

"Dance with David. Pay him some attention. He needs your love, too." How could she be romantic when they had been at odds? Romance was the last thing on her mind.

"Brendon asked about God and the devil. He wanted to know why we stopped going to church. We talked about religion over eggs in purgatory."

Kate reached into her purse and handed the stylist a picture torn from a magazine. "People travel to find themselves, drink, look to religion when things get messy."

"God isn't my friend and hasn't been for years," Sofia said, tipping the nail tech. "I don't understand Brendon's interest in Catholicism all the sudden."

Sofia grabbed her purse and followed Kate to the waiting area.

"Georgina practices Wicca. Angelene goes to church. People search for things to help when life gets stressful."

Angelene was the most devote Catholic Sofia knew. Had she told Brendon he had the devil in him? Had she got to Henri Piedmont too? Words floated around Sofia's head and tumbled from her mouth.

"Why didn't you tell me Angelene had been involved with Henri Piedmont?"

"Hugh mentioned nothing about a relationship. Are you wearing your hair up or down?"

"Down, David likes it down."

Sofia glanced at Kate. She wasn't perspiring, fidgeting. She was calm Kate.

"You should hire my mother to do your PI work. She found out many things."

"Rumours. The way people talk, Simone would be sleeping with Brendon."

"The boy locked himself away, just like Brendon. Henri Piedmont is a gifted architect. Brendon a phenom."

Kate reached over and squeezed her hand. "Mr. Piedmont might have been an awful father. He certainly wasn't a good husband."

Rosie Thornton waved at Sofia from the row of chairs. She managed a grin, took Kate's hand, dazed from all the thoughts swimming around her head. She sank onto the chair, staring at her reflection in the mirror. It would take more than a new hairstyle to hide the worry.

"I apologize for my comment. If Maggie is still chewing at her fingernails, you must be out of sorts."

"You're a mother. You know what it feels like when your child gets sick."

"You'd never know Jack was sick. He could have a fever of 105 and still be bouncing all over the house."

"Brendon did a horrible thing. David and I raised him to be a gentleman."

"It's for the best they broke up. They're both headed in different directions." Rosie tied a smock around Sofia, pulling her hair from the neckline. "What are we doing today?"

Who could she be? Certainly not Sofia Cook. That woman had vanished. Claudia Cardinale, Sofia Loren?

"Make me a sixties starlet, big hair, sexy, so my husband looks at me like he used to."

"David's crazy about you," Kate said. The chair hissed as she dropped onto it.

"Flirty, that's what I'm going for."

Nicola told Sofia to be flirty, to dance close to David, to flutter her lashes. It wasn't in her.

"You don't think it's strange the similarities between Brendon and Piedmont's son?"

"There are boys all over France who are talented in something. I will not assume Angelene was involved with all of them."

"That nutter showed up at Taunton College. Scared the hell out of Maggie."

Sofia fanned the smock in front of her face. "Was she lost?"

Rosie rolled a section of hair and clipped it. "It was the day Brendon fainted. Maggie was taking out the rubbish, her and that Jones trollop got into it. Ms. Pratt was lurking around the bins."

"She doesn't know her way around Taunton. She took a wrong turn," Kate said.

"There was nothing wrong about it. She was asking about Brendon."

Fear clung to Sofia; Angelene touched Henri Piedmont. Her son with his incredible light, touched by her too.

"Angelene should have stopped by if she was concerned."

Rosie folded over a clump of hair, teased it, and carefully laid a section over it. "Maggie said she was tipsy."

Kate leaned across the chair, snagging Sofia's hand. "There's your explanation."

"Can you ask Hugh to find Henri Piedmont?"

"No, I won't. We're going to let this go."

"I shouldn't have brought it up," Rosie said, spraying Sofia's hair. "I'm sure Ms. Pratt was concerned, that's all."

"My hair looks lovely, thank you."

She laid twenty pounds on the counter, clutching her purse handles. Why show up at the school? Why get drunk, appease her guilt?

Sofia shrugged on her coat, passing Kate hers. "What are you doing now?"

"Soaking in the tub and shaving my legs."

"You haven't shaved your legs?"

"Why would I? It's just me and the telly," Kate said, opening the door. "Stop worrying about Brendon, celebrate he's coming around."

Sofia held a hand to her chest. Angelene would have no reason to go to the school unless her fears were true.

"I'm dizzy."

"Take a few breaths. You've been holding it for weeks."

"Why would Angelene show up at the school?"

"Stop, Sofia," Kate said, pulling her against her shoulder. "She might have thought you'd be too worried for company."

"I can't stop thinking Angelene had something to do with Brendon's illness."

"You're not thinking rationally. Go home, cuddle with David."

"There are too many similarities."

"Angelene would grasp onto to anything to fit in and feel normal."

"That's what scares me."

Sofia climbed into the Maserati. Was it coincidence Henri Piedmont and Brendon were similar, eighteen, gifted in their passions? Had it been random the day Angelene met Henri? Was Brendon supposed to drive Angelene to Burnham? Who was Henri Piedmont, dark-haired like Brendon? Was his smile sweet and dimpled? Did he carry around a pad of paper and pencil like Brendon had a football? An image of a boy tangled in a web, struggling to breathe, bombarded her mind. She parked the car and took a shallow breath, searching for the confident Sofia everyone expected. There was nothing in her. How could she pretend she was part of a happily married couple?

'This shouldn't be happening. We power through storms, not hide from them.' Sofia mused.

She marched down the walkway, gripped the doorknob, and shuddered. *'The empty vessel makes the loudest sound.'* She never understood the Shakespeare quote. It made perfect sense now. Angelene was empty, a hollow shell. Her silence screamed the loudest.

"I'm losing my fucking mind," Sofia muttered, dropping her purse and coat on the umbrella stand. "Go for an hour, complain of a headache, and leave."

Sofia leaned into the arched doorway, lightheaded.

"Hey mammina, your hair looks nice."

"Where's your father?"

"He's pissed off my essay was bollocks. I'm rewriting it."

Sofia trudged to the desk and perched on the corner. "I love you."

"I know."

"Do you know how much? How deep it is?"

"To the moon and back."

"Saying it is one thing. Do you feel it?"

Brendon pushed the chair back and took her hand. "You're the best mammina in the world, a little clingy. I couldn't ask for a better mum."

"You feel it, though? Please, it's important I know this."

"When you pass me the broom and tell me to sweep up the grass, when you text me to get home safe, when you come into my room at night and kiss my hair."

"You're supposed to be asleep when I do that."

"All those things show you love me."

Sofia pressed her lips against his cheek, savouring the scent of his skin. Her heart swelled; eyes blurred. There were too many similarities with Henri Piedmont.

"Has Angelene ever mentioned a boy to you? On the drive to Burnham or when you had breakfast?"

Brendon turned to the laptop. "No, why?"

"I'm curious about the boy who locked himself in his room. She spoke about it at the auction and seemed so sad." "We talked about football. She likes PSG, bloody daft."

"Just football?" "We've talked about our expectations."

"I guess you have that in common." Sofia rubbed his back and stood. "She showed up at Taunton College. Rosie mentioned it."

"Maggie told me."

"What did Maggie think? She's a smart girl."

"She thought it was weird. Ms. Pratt was also tipsy; she could have been looking for Tesco."

Sofia glanced at him; his ears turned red when he lied. His cheeks were rosy, his demeanour hadn't changed.

"You better get ready, mammina. The limo will be here soon," Brendon said, tapping on the keyboard. "Can you put your face on, please?"

"You only started showering again and you're telling me to put makeup on."

"Ms. McGregor has spread all sorts of rubbish around town about you."

She blew him a kiss and wandered across the foyer. David's cologne hung in the air. From deep within the house came the tinkling of piano keys.

"You're playing Braham's Lullaby."

"Op.49, Cradle Song, we never finished learning this piece."

"Didn't you try to teach Brendon?"

"The farthest we got was Twinkle, Twinkle Little Star, and that was a task."

Sofia bit down on her tongue. She fought the urge to slam the cover on David's fingers. "Can't you say anything nice? Why is it always about a failed exam or he couldn't sit still? Mother put me in piano lessons. I danced instead of learning the damn thing."

"I promised no bickering. This is supposed to be a night of romance."

Sofia settled onto the bench, hugging herself. The ballroom was cold. It could be her. She hadn't felt warm in weeks.

"How's my hair? I know you like Cardinale and Loren."

"I like you and you look beautiful. Your turn."

"You look handsome. You always look good to me."

"Even when I'm an ass to our son?"

"You've barely spoken to him today."

"You've been damn ignorant," Nicola exclaimed, parading into the ballroom. "You picked at him like Richard did with you."

"It's all I seem to do lately," David said, kissing Sofia's shoulder. She brushed him off and stood.

"Help me with my gown, mum?"

"I've finished my essay," Brendon announced.

Sofia reached for her bangles, her shoulders drooped, no bracelets, no red lips, tension all around her and a head full of unanswered questions.

"What did you write about, sweetheart?"

"Family." Brendon said, handing the paper to David.

David scanned the first page and flipped to the next, muttering under his breath. "You think Lucie is the thread that links family together?"

"She plays a role in all the characters' lives."

Like someone we know,' Sofia thought.

"You want help with the pizza, Nonna?"

"You can slice the mozz, topolino," Nicola said. "You two stop bickering. I'll be up in a minute, gattina."

Sofia fell into David's chest; the chill had settled deep into her bones. "Just love your son. I shouldn't have to keep shoving him into your arms."

She pulled away; exhaustion clung to every step. Laughter spilled from the kitchen. Once upon a time, it would have warmed her to hear the joy of grandmother and grandson. She couldn't muster any. Sofia walked into her bedroom, flicked on the light, and stared at the Valentino gown. The deep crimson velvet clung to her curves and exposed just enough leg to be sexy yet sophisticated. Sofia slowly undid the buttons on her denim shirt and dropped it to the floor.

"You'll need a strapless bra, gattina."

Sofia pointed at the drawers in the closet and collapsed onto the bed.

"I read your lips when we were in the ballroom."

"Lucie was the thread that links everyone together. That's all I said."

"Like the pretty golden one we know," Nicola said, tossing a bra onto the bed.

"That golden thread is wrapped around Walter's neck. It's choking the life out of him."

"Do you think it's wrapped around my family?"

Nicola took the gown off the hanger and draped it over the bed. "Let's get you into the dress."

Sofia teetered, steadied herself, and slid out of her jeans. "I don't want to go."

"You need this. David needs this. The tension in the house is as thick as fog."

"I'm glad you're here."

"Me too. Someone needs to cut that damn thread."

"I'll change into my lingerie, then you can zip me up."

"Hurry, gattina. I left Brendon in charge of the toppings. He likes to put hot peppers on it." Sofia slipped into the lingerie, shimmying the gown over her hips.

"It feels loose."

"I wouldn't be surprised with all that worrying you've been doing."

"How do I look?"

"Stunning. Put your makeup on," Nicola said, swatting her hip. "You rule Taunton."

Nicola winked and smiled a 'chin up' smile. Sofia strolled to the vanity and sunk onto the bench. The smell of damp earth, chocolate digestives and honeysuckle materialized from the corners of the room. Her hair fluttered; the scent spiralled around her.

"I know you're here. I can feel you." Goosebumps rippled over her skin. "I thought I got it right this time." Warmth spread over her fingers and onto her palm, "You think I should go too? You always sided with her."

Sofia opened the drawer and pulled out her makeup bag. It was a simple routine for date night and events, an upsweep of black liner, red lips. Sofia placed the back in the bag and slid her feet into her stilettos. She latched the buckles and dragged herself to the hall, curling her fingers around the banister.

"Bloody hell, mammina, you look brilliant."

David held out a wrap and laid it around her shoulders. "I always thought you were too good for me. You're proving that tonight."

"I'm glad I look the part."

A horn honked, signalling the limo's arrival. Sofia stared at Brendon. There was no golden thread around his neck.

Clouds, heavy with the promise of rain, swept along the dark blue sky. The driver nodded a hello and opened the door. Sofia slid across the seat next to Kate, touching the ruffle on her gown. "Teal is a lovely colour on you."

"People will be surprised. You're not in black."

"I'm glad I chose this colour; my entire world seems black."

Walter refilled his glass with scotch and poured one for David. "When a person speaks, my wife sees the words in colour. Mine are red and not in a passionate way."

Sofia shot him a 'now's not the time' look, reaching for David's hand.

"She's an artist. They often see things uniquely," Kate said.

Sofia glanced at Angelene. Her dress had a black velvet bodice and a full skirt of black tulle. She reminded Sofia of an incredibly sad, ready to give the performance of a lifetime ballerina.

"Your dress is lovely."

Angelene opened her mouth. Walter smirked and interjected. "Little bird doesn't like it."

"You should have come to the salon with Sofia and I, not that you needed to," Kate said, shooting Walter a questioning look. "That updo is brilliant."

Angelene's smile came and went. "I found a picture of Bardot with her hair up. I thought it might please Walter. All it did was remind me of how much my mother hated her." Angelene pushed down the layers of tulle and stared out the window. "She told me I was like Bardot, flaunting and using my parts to lure men. I don't like my parts. Why would I use them to attract men?"

"No one wants to hear your stories, little bird."

"There are two ways of seeing: with the body and with the soul. The body's sight can sometimes forget, but the soul remembers forever," David said.

"The Count of Monte Cristo," Angelene said.

"I spent an entire summer memorizing every page of Dumas's book, plotting my revenge on my father," David said.

"I was going to go hunting for pheasants and accidentally miss."

Sofia tightened her grip on David's hand and turned to Angelene. "What have you done all day? Did you hang the painting of the girl?"

Walter snorted and shot back the scotch. "Avoiding me and painting. A boy and his chickens, she called it. There was a hell of a lot of yellow in it. It's my wife's favourite colour."

Sofia leaned across the seat and took the glass from Walter's hand. "You need to breathe. This is supposed to be a nice evening."

"I could say the same to you, Sofie. You've been holding your breath since we left the manor."

Sofia grabbed David's arm, Troy Spence. "Wh... why chickens?"

"What else is there to paint, cows, trees?" Kate said.

"Malcolm drove me home from church. I saw the chickens. Klimt's Garden Path with Chickens is one of my favourites. I wanted to paint like Klimt."

"You know Malcolm, been driving a taxi for years. He understands her," Walter said.

David finished his scotch, reached across Sofia, and placed the glass in the cup holder. "That's good. You've found someone you can trust."

"What's his colour, little bird? Golden yellow like the sun? Certainly not fiery red like me."

"Can you be quiet, Walter. I've been hating the quiet for weeks and now I need it." Sofia said, rubbing the wrinkle on her brow.

A line of limos and Bentleys snaked around the drive. Attendants in white gloves opened doors, waving guests onto the ivy-covered porch. The estate sat on one hundred acres of parkland, surrounded by walnut groves and orchards. Sofia studied the architectural masterpiece; would Henri Piedmont have found it beautiful?

"This is an important event, little bird. The media will be here. I suggest you follow Sofia and Kate's lead. Shoulders straight, chin up."

"You sound like my mother," Angelene spat. "Are you going to pinch me if I slouch?"

Sofia sighed heavily. "Just be yourself. No one expects you to be anything but Ms. Pratt."

Sofia slid across the seat, held onto the attendant's hand, and climbed out of the car. A man dressed in tails opened the door. The entry was a spectacle of Taunton's elite. It would be tomorrow's gossip, who looked the loveliest, who tried too hard, who was wearing a knock-off. Victoria stood in the middle of the crowd, smiling a contrived smile, her hand rhythmically shooting out to snatch hors d'oeuvres. Simone and Eshana wore matching pink gowns and tiny rhinestone tiaras. The production had started, lines rehearsed, and everyone was in their costumes. Sofia knew how the evening would unfold. Conversation would revolve around local news and gossip. It would turn to talk of the Prime Minister. Political banter would lead to polite arguments. Once the champagne kicked in, politics would switch to who was getting soused or flirting. Sadness embraced Sofia, she felt like she didn't belong. Her place was at home with Brendon, not at an enchanted soiree forcing out conversation and smiles.

"I need to go to the bathroom," Angelene said.

Walter grumbled under his breath.

"Merda," Sofia said. "I'll take her. Find our table."

Sofia took off her wrap and handed it to David. They walked down a hall; Sofia lifted her skirt and bumped open the door with her hip. The mansion's opulent décor spilled into the bathroom, turning a mundane loo into a lavish experience.

"Magnifique. There are sofas in here."

"Let me help you with your skirt or you'll be peeing all over the marble floor."

"How do you do it? Walk into an event like this and hold your head up?"

"It's taking every ounce of me to be that confident woman people expect me to be."

"My insecurity has led me to the wrong people and the wrong places."

Sofia followed the map of veins travelling through Angelene's pale skin. Had Henri Piedmont run his fingers from east to west?

"The boy who locked himself away, was it Pierre Piedmont's son?"

Sofia sighed, long and heavy. She had said it, got the question out of her head.

"Yes," Angelene said, pumping soap on her hands.

"Were you friends?"

Sofia gripped the back of the sofa, waiting for an answer. She told Brendon to stay away. Nicola had warned her to keep him away from Angelene.

"Did you like Henri? Did he have a light too?"

"Please don't make me talk about this."

Sofia held open the door, her heart aching. She had seen the same look in Nicola's and Kate's eyes when they spoke of the boy. *'Everything is fine, Brendon is fine, my marriage is fine.'*

Sofia headed to the ballroom; Rachmaninov's Piano Concerto No.2 floated in the air. The décor was classic, a vase of ivory roses sat in the centre of each table. Waiters balancing silver trays of champagne moved around the tables. Sofia pictured herself among the guests, admiring the months of planning, the thought-out menu and décor. She flopped onto a chair, staring across the table at Walter. "How many have you had?"

"Five, and you're done, right?" Kate said.

Walter finished the drink and set the glass on the table. "It's five courses, little bird. I hope you're hungry." A waiter paused at the table. Walter plucked a flute of champagne off the tray, clinking his glass against Kate's.

Sofia wrapped her fingers around David's. The tension was as thick as the cloud that hung over Rosewood manor.

"I feel out of place, not hungry," Angelene said.

"Of course, you do. Act, everyone here is," Walter said.

Kate took the empty champagne flute from Walter's hand and handed it to the waiter. "There's an art gallery a few doors down from my office. You should take your paintings there. They highlight local artists."

"What would they title the exhibition? Monsters and demons? Chickens?" Walter said.

"Have you not seen a painting by Goya or Dali's Face of War?" Kate said.

"I have and I don't like them."

"You're an expert now?" Angelene peeped.

Sofia rubbed her brow. "Look Kate, Nathan Fischer is here. He's single."

"Just because you were fucking Piedmont, doesn't make you an expert either."

A waiter strolled over to the table; Sofia smiled politely as he set a plate of salad in front of her. She knocked her knee against David's and nodded towards Walter.

"Come with me Walt. I'm sure they have a pot of coffee brewing. We'll grab you a cup and get some air."

"Did I offend you, little bird? You made love to Piedmont. No wait, you don't do that either," Walter said, loosening his bow tie. "Eat your damn salad."

"Let's go," David demanded.

Sofia patted her napkin on her warmed cheeks. "What a terrible thing to say. I'm sorry Angelene."

"Don't apologize. I've made Walter angry."

Kate picked up Angelene's plate and scraped half the salad on hers. "He's being an ass.""I struggle with happiness; how can I shower him with it if I don't feel happy?"

'It's your golden thread choking him.'

Victoria walked towards them, fluttering the bronze ruffles on her skirt.

"Did you do the seating arrangements? I'd like to talk to whoever stuck Simone and I in the corner."

"Hello to you too," Sofia said, rolling a walnut under her fork. "I had nothing to do with it. Just the menu and the décor."

"It's going to cost two-thousand pounds for William's tooth."

"Send me the bill."

"It looks like your husband has had a few too many glasses of bubbly. I would watch him if I were you. He gets flirty when he drinks."

Angelene set down her fork and patted her mouth. "He's had a long week."

"James said he's been miserable, growling around the office. Poor Juliette, run off her feet catering to him," Victoria said, plucking a walnut from Sofia's plate. "He bit the head off one of the MPs. The poor man couldn't finish his comment."

"People have bad days. Don't read into anything," Kate said.

"Shouldn't you be getting back to your table? The second course is about to arrive," David said, running a hand under Sofia's hair.

Victoria smiled insolently and laid her hand on her breast. "You look very dapper tonight, Lord Chancellor."

Sofia rubbed her forehead, glancing at the corner of the room. "Your husband is waving you over."

"Tata," Victoria said. "Save me a dance David."

"Where's Walter?" Kate said, hiding her smile behind a spoonful of soup.

David sunk into a chair and poked at his salad. "At the bar."

Angelene bowed her head, picking at her nail polish. "I'm to blame for his mood. I've been ignoring him."

"He needs to sober up," David said.

Kate set down her spoon and pat her mouth. "I'll get him. Start your soup."

Sofia frowned; this was Walter's time to shine. There was no confident smile, no gathering of people around him. Brendon had worn the same angry look before he unravelled. Sofia dabbed at the perspiration dotting her forehead, Angelene, the thread.

A sleepy rendition of Moonlight Sonata swept through the room. Sofia gazed dreamily at David; the song took her back to their wedding. She ran her hand over his. She needed to feel something other than annoyance and anger.

"Would you like to dance?"

"I need an escape from the table."

Sofia pushed back her chair, took David's hand, leading him to the dance floor. She rested her cheek against his, tuning out the stares and whispers. She needed to reconnect.

"I made Walter promise no more. I don't think he's going to listen."

"It's the golden thread."

David moved his cheek, puzzled.

"It's something mum, and I talked about. I'm worried about Walter."

"Walter will figure this out," David said, drawing her closer. "I've missed you."

"I can't stand the bickering. I prefer when we fight and get it over with. This is lingering,"

"Will you wear one of your silk nightgowns to bed?"

"If you promise to be kind to Brendon."

Sofia glanced across the dance floor. Angelene sat with her head bowed. Walter scowled into his soup. She wasn't sure if the thread had wound itself around her family. It had strangled the life out of Walter.

***

Angelene gathered the tulle. A sense of vertigo rocked her. Her heart beat sluggishly, despite the uncontrollable shivers trickling up and down her spine. Little scratches and ticks crept from the attic and clawed behind the walls.

"I'm having a nightcap."

"You punish me when I'm drunk and look at you, you can barely stand."

Whimpers and whispers slipped from behind doors and darkened corners. The ghosts were alive.

Walter tossed his tuxedo jacket in the front room and barged past her. "I'd like to forget the evening,"

"No more yelling at me when I'm drunk."

"Do you see any broken dishes? Have I hidden bottles?"

"You were cruel tonight. I wore the dress. I sat up straight and ate my dinner."

"Shall I ring the Taunton Times?"

Angelene opened her mouth, waiting for harsh words to spring from her tongue. She was mute. Collecting the tulle, Angelene rustled to the stairs. She teetered on each step, cursing herself for not taking off her shoes. Flicking on the bedroom light, Angelene peered into the murky night. A thick blanket of fog crawled over the moors, climbed the hill, and veiled Rosewood manor in an eerie shroud.

"Do you know how much I paid for that dress?"

"I didn't ask for an expensive gown. You need to make an impression. That's all it is with you, impressions, and look at me."

"You confuse me, little bird. You want to work on the marriage, but you want nothing to do with me."

"You're frightening me."

"How did you think I felt when you screamed in my face?" Walter said, clinking the ice around his glass. Angelene tore her eyes from Walter's frigid gaze to the manor. Brendon's lamp glowed. Walter ran the glass down her neck and over her shoulder. She shuddered.

"Casse-toi." Her words were weak.

Walter pressed his lips against her neck. His breath was hot, steeped in scotch. "I should tell you to fuck off."

His hand tightened around her stomach; screams simmered in her throat.

"Please let me go."

Walter set down his glass, his fingers sunk into her hips. "You're denying me again."

"I won't have sex with you when you are like this."

"Consider it fucking. Would that make you more comfortable?"

He jammed his groin into her back. She tugged at his fingers, stumbling into the bedframe. Walter collected layers of tulle, ran his hand over her bottom. Years of memories stretched through her mind. The smells of sweating skin and stinking breath. The sound of grunts, her voice muffled by a hand on her mouth. An ache scratched behind her ribcage, tearing, and ripping to get out. She squeezed her eyes closed, clutched the duvet.

"Heavenly Father full of grace…"

"Pretending to be asleep, afraid God will judge you."

Angelene dug her nails into the mattress and dragged herself across the bed. She fell headfirst onto the floor.

"You're a damn tease. Do you know what you do to me?"

Angelene pushed herself off the floor and charged past Walter. He snagged her by the wrist. "Where do you think you're going?"

Angelene wrenched her arm free and hurried towards the door. Walter tore at the tulle, ripping it from the seam. A deep growl followed her down the stairs. She spotted her phone by the fruit bowl, hobbled to the kitchen, and snatched it. Her fingers trembled as she fought with the locks. She hurried to the shed and hid among the brambles.

"Little bird, get back here."

She tucked herself deeper in the scraggy hawthorn, scrolled through her contacts and listened to the rings.

"Please help me. Please, he's very drunk."

The door slammed, his car tore from the driveway, barrelling down the road in a spray of dust and gravel. She ran, her heels dug into the damp earth, faster and faster, clutching handfuls of grass as she climbed the hill. She urged her lungs to breathe, her heart to stop the frenzied rhythm thrashing in her chest and stepped on the muddy path. The forest sounded like an eerie symphony, branches clacked, trees moaned. She glanced over her shoulder; the heel of her stiletto rolled over a rock. She spiralled to her knees. Pain seared through her wrists, dirt and pine needles rose between her fingers. She clawed at the bark, scraping her knuckles along a burl, and stood. Angelene tore her skirt from a branch and ran. She was to go through the carport. He would wait at the servant's door.

"Be bloody quiet." "Where are David and Sofia?"

"In their bedroom."

Angelene followed him through the kitchen, clutching handfuls of tulle.

"You're dropping leaves."

"I didn't know what to do."

"We'll talk in my bedroom. Get close to the banister to avoid the creaks." She squished herself against the railing, her limbs shook, her heart was ready to explode. Angelene tiptoed to Brendon's room and collapsed on the bed in a plume of black tulle. Walter's voice raged in her mind. She could feel his fingers sinking into her skin. All the years, her face shoved into a mattress, all the years of silence, blurred her eyes with tears.

"What happened? Did you fall?"

Brendon dropped the crinkled leaves on the dresser and walked to the bathroom.

"Walter insists I wear these stupid shoes. If he wanted a leg-ghee woman, he should have stayed with the Russian."

Brendon moved layers of tulle and sat beside her. He ran a washcloth over her hands. She drew in a tiny breath; the soap stung her torn knuckles.

"He's very drunk."

"Did Walter rip your dress?" Brendon said, lifting her chin. "Bloody hell, did he try to force... fuck."

"I've been denying him for so long. I deserve it."

"Don't be daft."

"I was so scared. It took me back to all those horrible memories I've tried so hard to forget."

Tears spilled over her cheeks. She sniffed at the snot dribbling over her lip. Brendon reached over the mountain of tulle and tore a tissue from the box, blotting her nose.

"Look at you, washing my hands and wiping my nose, just like Roman used to do when I was little."

"I'd only do it for you."

She curved her body to fit his, breathing in the warm, citrusy scent. "Bad things keep happening. I'm so frightened of my past, the future, what tomorrow will bring."

"You're safe now."

Angelene snuggled deeper into his chest, tears fell, staining his shirt darker blue. "I've broken the rules again."

Her chin trembled. She wasn't sure if her heart was swelling or breaking. She stared into his eyes and saw safety blooming in the brown. Angelene pressed her mouth against his, breathing in the life that flowed from him. He was the oxygen for her empty lungs. She was safe.

"I didn't think I could hurt anymore. I'm so damaged. What more could happen?"

She sniffed back a dribble of snot, lacing her fingers through his.

"Bad things happen to all of us," Brendon said, running his t-shirt over her nose.

"I feel safe with you. Henri made me feel this way, too."

She laid her cheek against him, the feeling that sunk into her flesh and warmed her bones, enveloped her. She closed her eyes, lulled by the sound of his heartbeat.

"I'm tired. Tired of running. I'm tired of the buzzing in my head. Tired of fighting."

Brendon kissed her head and rubbed her back. She held him tighter.

"I know what will make you feel better."

She wrestled with the tulle and snuggled into the pillows.

Brendon pulled a book from the shelf, tucked Paddington under his arm, and snuggled beside her.

"Are you going to read me a story?"

"A Bear Called Paddington. Mr. and Ms. Brown took care of Paddington. I'll take care of you."

A little pain poked her heart, her tattered and plucked wings fluttered. She flew.

Morning light shone across the hardwood, illuminating the torn dress. Angelene plucked leaves from the netting and scrunched them in her hand. She had broken the rules, climbed over Brendon's wall, found solace in his arms. His light had rejuvenated her. She found peace. Parts of her glowed yellow, other parts were black.

Angelene dabbed patchouli on her wrists, heat rose in ripples from her toes to her cheeks. She cranked open the window, crisp apple scented air washed over her face. *'I should have been more like mother and taken lovers.'* She would have had the pleasure of the charismatic Walter Pratt, sugary sweet Henri, brooding then smiling Brendon, the sunshine of Troy Spence. She could have had a lover for all her devils to play with.

'Being like mother would come with a price. I'd have to please them all, learn their bodies, spread myself so thin so each felt special.'

A sharp, piercing pain shot through her heart; God was angry.

"You've made quite the effort for French lessons."

Angelene twisted around, her eyes fraught with fear. Walter blocked the doorway. She had nowhere to run.

"It's lip balm and perfume," she said, timidly. "No different from any other day. Where did you go last night?"

"I had to leave before I did something I would regret. You?"

Angelene stared at the tears in her knuckles, the abrasions on her palms. She hid her hands between her thighs. "I smoked in the garden."

Walter strolled towards her; the drawer pull shoved into her back.

"Are you scared of me now?"

"Y... yes."

"It was the scotch."

"Isn't that an excuse?"

She stood, dug deep inside herself for the woman she becomes when she drinks. Her brain was too foggy to grow fifty feet tall.

"You never said where you went."

Walter hung his tuxedo jacket over the footboard, undoing the buttons on his rumpled shirt. "I went to Kate's."

"Did you..."

"Don't be stupid. We talked, she made me coffee."

Angelene turned and stared at Rosewood manor. "She is your safe place, oui?"

"She makes me see things, like my fear of failure, my arrogance."

She grabbed a wrap from the bed and wound it around her. "I have to go."

"We'll go for a drive when you get back, grab a takeaway, see where the day takes us," Walter said, cupping her cheek. "I'm sorry."

Angelene hurried past him, flew down the stairs, and stuffed her feet into her shoes. Her mind buzzed and zapped. She had kissed Brendon. It wasn't a proper kiss. She didn't open her mouth or touch his tongue, just placed her lips on his and inhaled his breath. A kiss for preservation. It may have turned his strong brown, white, cold, and empty. He may be angry with her for doing the thing she had scolded him for.

The laneway to Rosewood manor seemed longer. Her lungs were struggling, her body numb and clumsy. Angelene sunk onto the edge of the fountain and stared into the cloudless sky. The feeling was back and intense.

"Forelsket, am I falling in love? I'm asking out of curiosity, God, nothing else."

Love made you crazy.

Angelene pressed on the ache in her chest. Had she blown Brendon's wall to bits and left him empty white? Sighing, Angelene gave herself a quick pinch to numb the buzzing.

'Please make him brown, not angry red or spiky black.' The door opened; she grabbed her cross. "You're brown."

Brendon plucked at his t-shirt. "My shirt is blue."

Angelene sucked in her breath, inundated with a burst of emotion. It tingled and flashed, painting her insides yellow, electric blue, and pink. She floated into the foyer. Addio Fiorito Asil played softly from the great room. Angelene grinned. Madame Butterfly was one of Roman's most loved operas.

"Where are David and Sofia?"

"In bed. Mum came down in her nightgown, grabbed two cups of coffee, and went back to her room. Nonna's reading."

Angelene nestled into the wingback chair. The fire crackled and popped, warming her chilled skin. Brendon plunked beside her. She touched the ends of his hair, still damp from the shower, and breathed in eucalyptus. Her belly quivered. She moved her hand.

"How was Walter this morning?"

"He's very rumpled."

Brendon reached for her hand and ran a finger over a scratch on her knuckle. Her breath caught in her throat. The slightest touch made a colour burst in her belly.

"I'm sorry for breaking the rules."

"You're not much of a rule follower."

She closed her eyes to the warmth. Her heart was full. Yellow invaded the black spots.

"I shouldn't have kissed you."

"I wouldn't call that a kiss," Brendon said, flipping open his notebook. "You made me feel something. I don't like it."

"When I think of you, my belly flops. It scares me."

"Do you think you're feeling love?"

"I know what anger feels like, shame, guilt. I feel those colours all the time but love, I wouldn't know."

Brendon laid his hand on her cheek and pressed his mouth against hers. "How do you feel now?"

"I told you what happened to Henri. He said those words, he kissed me, he left me." "Answer the question. Stop running for once."

"I promised to be a good wife."

"Walter hurt you last night."

"Don't make me sin again."

"It's not a sin if you're in love."

"I don't understand these feelings. I'm so scared. I don't know what to do."

Brendon held her cheeks in his hands and kissed her forehead. "We're here for each other. Nothing bad can happen if we look after one another."

"We made rules. You built a wall. God will disown me."

"I love you."

"Don't say that."

Her mind whirled. Love makes you crazy. It drives people to do horrible things.

"Love Maggie. You'll disappear if I steal your light. I can't do that to Sofia. I can't steal her son."

"I'll give you my light."

"You don't know what you are saying."

"This strange feeling you keep talking about sounds like love to me. Don't be afraid of something that feels good. I'm going to kiss you and you're going to kiss me back. Rules gone; wall demolished. You're not stealing my light if I'm giving it to you."

Angelene's heart thundered, the electrical circuits in her brain crackled and sparked. "A kiss is the trick of the devil, making you fall under love's spell. Love makes you crazy. Mother said so."

His mouth pressed against hers. Regret dripped in angry sparks from the sizzling electrical circuits.

"We better start the lesson," she said, touching her cross. "Page cent vingt cinq."

She leaned into his arm, resting her cheek against it. She reflected on the list of poor decisions and bad luck that had come into her life. This couldn't be one of them. She was safe with Brendon.

"Isn't this cozy."

Angelene jerked away. Nicola's glare was intense.

"Hey Nonna," Brendon said, holding up his notebook. "Five sentences complete."

"I made you a sandwich, topolino. It's in the kitchen."

"I'll just finish this, then grab it. I'm on a bloody roll."

Angelene licked her lips, pushing at the skin on her torn knuckles.

"I made one for you too, Ms. Pratt. I even put crisps on the side."

"You shouldn't have. Je ne mérite pas votre gentillesse."

"Topolino, your lunch. Go."

Angelene's gaze followed Brendon. She wanted to run after him, tuck herself inside him. It was a mistake, diving into his light. She should dive into her husband.

"You're right, you don't deserve my kindness," Nicola said.

"I was correcting his work."

"If you were any closer, you would have been on his lap."

Angelene pinched her knuckles. The fire was pleasant. The smell of cedar and lingering eucalyptus was divine. Nicola was prickly red.

"Cat got your tongue, Ms. Pratt?"

"I didn't mean to sit so close."

"I told you to stay away," Nicola said coldly. "I know things. You will not destroy my family."

Another feeling, dark and jittery, crept through Angelene. It could be her body responding to another wrong decision or God telling her the good that could come from sharing his light.

Everyone is damaged little bird.

My scars Roman, I've stitched my heart back together so many times. The pieces aren't right; they don't fit.

The best remedy for a broken heart is love, little bird.

39 TORN

THE BEECH TREES SURROUNDING Taunton College blazed red in the afternoon sun. The aspen glowed like burnished gold. Everywhere Brendon looked, glorious shades of emerald, topaz, and copper. There was no solace in autumn's beauty. The jitters were back. Angelene had kissed him. It was obvious she didn't want to. Her lips never softened; he hadn't felt her heart racing. It was the right thing to do, like when she said I love you.

"I can do this," he mumbled. "You can make everyone happy. Angelene wants you at school." The pep talk did nothing to steady his nerves.

"Training was fun. I love three on three, twenty seconds to get the ball past me. Makes you think fast."

Troy's voice lacked sunshine. If Brendon were to put a colour to his words, they would be weepy blue and dismal grey.

"I can't get out of my car."

Troy stopped, waved to the group of boys. No smile, no yellow light. "You've got your feet on the ground. That's a start."

"Don't take the piss. Every nerve is on fire and not in a good way."

'Breathe Brendon, grab your rucky, and bloody breathe. I'll visit Angelene after school and see if the kiss meant anything. I'll offer her my light again.'

"Remember when we used to pretend, we were playing in the Euros or the World Cup."

"That was a long time ago."

They strolled across the lawn; the traffic of students was heavier than usual. News of his return had spread. People had to see if the gossip was true. Jittery shivers marched through Brendon's limbs; the whispers were incessant.

"How many times must I say sorry? I was a dick, a prick."

"As many as it takes. You're different. You're not you."

"Charlie, still mad at you?"

"Do you know what it's like to love someone so much, all you want to do is kiss them, so they know how you feel? Charlie would rather crochet."

Tension bounced between Brendon's shoulders. He bent his head from side to side, sighed through the ache. He knew.

"Have you missed me?"

"I'm pissed off at you. See you around." Troy fixed his bangs in the window and vanished into a mob of students.

Guilt had once been a good thing. He'd get a brief pang in the belly letting him know he had done wrong. Guilt had him swinging from the gallows. Brendon edged down the aisle. He placed his backpack on the floor and stretched his legs. Two classes, then he could go to Angelene. He wiped his sweating palms on his trousers. His heart beat out a 'crazy in love' rhythm. It could be one of her patterns, break through people's walls to see if she could. He couldn't go back to that place, where the world was dull and colourless. She could be anyone of her devils when he arrived.

Brendon turned to Maggie. Her expression was inquisitive and pretty. The love of history burned bright in her eyes and rosy cheeks.

"Are we still studying the Black Plague?"

"It fascinates Mr. Clark. We started the unit on the Industrial Revolution. He was ridiculously excited about the Spinning Jenny. Then we were back in 1348. It's been very confusing."

Mr. Clark lumbered into the classroom, took his usual spot in front of his desk, and cleared his throat. "I have a wonderful lesson planned. You're going to map out the Black Death."

"Bloody hell, is he going to spring a biggie?"

Maggie giggled, swatting his arm.

"Do you have something to share, Mr. Cook?"

"No sir."

"I expect your full attention after being absent for so long." Mr. Clark picked up a pointer, swishing it through the air like a magic wand. "Things to consider. The rate at which the plague spread. How rapidly it progressed and the mortality rate. You may work in pairs, have fun."

Brendon flipped open his text. He raised his eyebrows at a painting of a couple laying in bed, covered in pustules. "What a bloody awful topic."

"You should have seen him the day we discussed the symptoms," Maggie said. "We might as well work together."

"We usually do."

"I always did the work."

Brendon chuckled, digging in his backpack for a pen. "You'd get whingey if I didn't get the facts right. You'd take right over." "You're a wanker. You'd have the football highlights on, you'd want to snog."

"Rats spread the bubonic plague. Fleas carried the plague across trade routes into Europe. Write that in your notes."

Maggie smiled, tapping her pen against her lip. "This is nice, us talking." Brendon shifted in the chair, sorting through the mess in his head. Lie and make her happy, be honest, and break her heart again.

"It has been nice." "Charlie is still upset with Troy. I've never heard her call him Troy Alexander as much as she has lately. The four of us…"

"Troy's pissed off at me. I've been trying to make amends. He's being stubborn."

His cell phone vibrated. He kept his eyes on Mr. Clark, tapping his phone. A photo filled the screen, freckled breasts, fingers shaped in a heart. Brendon expanded the photo, grinning at a heart-shaped freckle on her collarbone.

"What a thing to send."

"I didn't ask her to send it."   "She's still coming between us."

"There is no us."

She wound her arm around the desk, shielding her notes. "Do your own assignment." "Unfuckingbelievable."

"Did you swear Mr. Cook?"

"Sorry, sir, this unit is too much. All the suffering."

A ripple of laughter spread through the classroom. Brendon crossed his fingers there would be no trip to Dawson's office.

"Shall I tell you about my relatives? Poor sods died from the plague."

Brendon groaned softly. Between Maggie's gnawing and Mr. Clark's family history, it would be the longest thirty minutes of his life.

The day had dragged. Brendon had learned every symptom associated with the plague and how Mr. Clark's relatives succumbed to it. Latin had been easy once he convinced Rachel to put his blazer on. The heart-shaped freckle was too distracting. He had one thing left to do; it was making his insides tremble.

"Guten tag, knuddlebär." Rachel snaked her arm around him and squished her breasts against his arm. "I was in the toilets and overheard Thornton. You two have been talking. You aren't going to leave me for her, are you?"

"I'm not leaving anybody," Brendon said. Her embrace was tight, suffocating. "Can you let me go? You're waking my knob up."

"Is that so terrible, knuddlebär?"

"In front of Evans Hall, yes."

"Come round to mine. I have Smarties. I'll pick out the blue ones."Brendon unwound her arm. "Another time."

"I thought you'd be happy to see me. You stared out the window most of Latin, barely said two words."

"First Maggie, now you. Bloody hell, I feel like I've gone from one prison to the next."

Brendon trudged towards the car park. Madre Innocente was relentless, stabbing and tearing at his heart. A quote from F. Scott. Fitzgerald slashed through his brain. His first day back at Taunton College, Ms. Hudson greeted him with a quote from The Great Gatsby, 'The loneliest moment in someone's life is when they are watching their whole world fall apart, and all they can do is stare blankly.' Rachel's world was falling apart and all he could do was drive towards Angelene.

Brendon turned onto the farmhouse laneway and parked the BMW under the willow branches. It had been a while since he felt the flutters and although it made him nauseous; he was revelling in the feeling.

"Quick, get inside."

Brendon pulled himself from her grip and tossed the keys onto the table. "Bloody hell, what's got into you?" He wiggled his tie loose, tossed his blazer on the floor, collapsing on the sofa.

"Will anyone see your car?"

"Come sit, bloody hell."

Angelene's lips trembled around the words. "Sofia, Nicola, what about Aim-Mee?"

"No one can see my car. I made sure of that."

She pinched her cross and sunk onto the sofa behind a wall of throw pillows. Brendon stared at her bare feet; she had painted her toes canary yellow. He had never noticed a girl's feet before. It had been about breasts or bottoms. She had the tiniest feet and delicate little toes. Brendon shoved his hand under his thigh. The yearning to touch them blazed in his fingertips.

"Where does Sofia think you are?"
"At the pitch."
"Will she come looking for you?"
"She's bloody happy I went to school," he said, undoing his tie. "I've seen you nervous before, not like this. If you're regretting kissing me, let me know. I left Rachel on the lawn of Taunton College. I feel like a wanker. She's gutted."
"That look Nicola gave me yesterday scared me."
"Everyone feels that way until they get to know her." "She thinks I'm going to hurt you. I could see it in her eyes."
"She gets extra suspicious when mum's a mess. Throw me into the mix, she would think Troy was out to get me." The throw pillows dropped to the floor. She bounced into his arms, knocking the breath from his lungs. "Tu me manques."

Brendon lifted her chin and stared into her eyes. They were clear, vivid green, no haze, no clouds. He touched his lips to hers, his heart clunked, hard and fast.

"Open your mouth a little. You look like you've eaten something dodgy."
"I don't know how to kiss."
"I'll teach you. Open your mouth and relax your lips."

Brendon could feel her heartbeat, taste apple on her mouth. He removed her splayed hands from his chest and wound each one around his waist. Brendon grinned at the tiny pecks she pressed into his upper lip, then the bottom.

"What's so funny?"
"Let me kiss you. Follow my lead."

She clutched at his shirt, mimicking the movement of his lips and tongue.

"Do you want me to kiss you again?"

She nodded; he lowered his lips on hers. He slipped his hand under her shirt, his fingers danced over her skin. She quivered with every touch. Brendon lifted her arms and took off her shirt. Her breath grew ragged.

"You shouldn't be here. It isn't right."   "How are you feeling right now?"
"Like I'm waiting for the blade to fall and my head to drop into the basket."
"Do you know how hard this is?"
"Please don't make me do this. I'm married. I promised God."
"I won't force you to do anything. We'll just kiss."
"That's scaring me too. I'm getting that feeling again."
"That feeling is love."
"Is that why I feel like I'm going to lose my mind?"
"Absolutely."
"I want to touch you. Is that horrible of me?"

Brendon took off his shirt. Like a sculptor creating a work of art, Angelene's fingers drifted over his shoulder blades, followed the length of his spine, traced around his lower back. Her fingers floated to his neck, over his abdomen, circling his belly button. He laid her on the sofa and tugged at her zipper, dragging her jeans over her hips. Brendon ran his finger over an irritated wound on her hipbone and kissed it.

"God will be so upset with me. He will cause a great flood again, leaving me nothing to build an ark. He'd watch me drown."
"I can leave. We can promise to never kiss again and rebuild our walls."
"I don't know what to do, close my eyes and dream myself some place else."

He lay his body over hers, drew her legs around his waist. Warmth surrounded him, they melted together. He kissed her neck and collarbone. The murmurs falling from her lips were shaky and sweet. He brought her breast to his mouth.

Her skin tasted like spiced honey. It was at that moment Brendon learned the difference between humping and making love. Heat moved through his body. Her breath hit his neck, their bodies sticky with sweat. Brendon rolled to his side, squished into the sofa.

"You're so beautiful."

"I'm yellow. Sunburst yellow."

"What colour am I?"

"You're the most magnificent shade of purple, luxurious, magical purple."

He kissed her temple. She placed her fingers against her mouth and grinned, tilting her cheek towards him. "Here please."

Brendon brushed his lips over her flushed cheek.

"And here," she said, burying her nose into the pillows, exposing her neck. "Here too."

He followed her fingers, kissing her collarbone and the space between her breasts.

"Make love to me again."

***

Walter knew marriage wouldn't be easy, and he'd have to tend to his project every day. He never expected marriage to drive him this close to madness.

"I've finished typing your paper," Juliette said.

Walter glanced from the spot where he was going to add a picture of Angelene and forced a smile.

"Did it make any sense?"

"I corrected a few errors. No one will know you've had your head in the clouds."

"You've noticed?"

"Must be all that fun you had at the gala. Angelene love the dress?"

"The answer is no, to both questions."

"Knock, knock."

Walter rubbed his brow and groaned. He had been ignoring David, leaving the apartment early, anything to avoid conversation.

"Hello Mr. Cook," Juliette said.

"This one still grumbling?"

"I've got a few smiles; I'll leave you two so I can prep for your meeting tomorrow."

Walter propped his elbows on the desk, dropping his forehead on his steepled fingers.

"What brings you to the Defence department, Lord Chancellor?"

"I thought we could go for an early dinner."

"You heard Juliette; we have a meeting to prep for."

"You've been avoiding me. Don't you think you should talk about Saturday?"

"What's to say? I got drunk."

"I worked through lunch. It's my treat."

Walter tore his suit jacket from the back of the chair and stomped across the office.

"I'm leaving. See you first thing. I'll bring coffee."

Juliette glanced up from the keyboard, wiggling her fingers at him.

"Beatrice is retiring in a year," David said, pressing the elevator button.

"Don't think of stealing Juliette."

Walter leaned into the mirrored wall and flicked at his wedding band. "How can one girl be so normal and another a total mess?"

"I take it you're talking about Angelene."

"Angelene is a constant mess. It spirals around her like a damn tornado."

The doors slid open, Walter waved to a group of women, their eyes followed them into the street.

David chuckled. "Your admirers didn't make you smile. You must be upset."

"Upset, frustrated, angry. Need I go on?"

David held up his hand, hailing a cab. "At whom? Yourself or Angelene? Whitehall Court, please. The Royal Horseguards Hotel."

They dropped onto the rear seat. Walter scowled, jerking at his cuffs. "You and Sofia looked cozy."

"She didn't come to bed in Brendon's t-shirt."

The cab parked alongside the curb, Walter handed the driver fifteen pounds, trying to control the agitation in his voice. "How's Brendon?"

"He went to school today," David said, holding open the door. "It only took two days and me prying the truth from Nicola."

Walter held up two fingers at the maître' d, following him to a banquette covered in crimson damask.

"What can I get you to drink?"

"Tea, please, Walt?"

"The same."

Walter skimmed over the menu, feeling uncharacteristically at a loss for words. David pinched his lips together, nodding a thank you to the waiter. He tipped tea into their cups and studied Walter's face.

"Stop worrying, Davy boy, I'm fine. I'll get the club."

"Make that two. We'll start with the mezze platter," David said, passing the menus to the waiter. "Let's talk about Saturday night. Not the usual scene you make. People usually run to you, not from you."

"She frustrates me. Why can't she be damn normal?"

"Is anyone truly normal?" David said, spooning sugar in his tea. "Aren't we all just doing our best?"

Walter fiddled with his cuff link. *'Normal, conforming to a standard, usual, typical, or expected.'* Angelene was none of those things.

"I talked to her about sex, like you said."

"I take it that's what started things."

"She's damaged. It's as simple as that."

Walter stared into his tea. Memories of what should have been a glorious evening burned in his brain. There should have been no arguing over a dress or drowning in alcohol. He shouldn't have forced himself on her. He shouldn't have ended up on Kate's sofa, moaning into a cup of coffee.

"Everyone is damaged," David said diplomatically. "Look at the hurt I've lived through. Life throws curveballs. You accept them, work through it, end the chapter."

"You and Sofia haven't closed a chapter."

"I'm not ready to end that chapter. There are things I still need to say."

"Richard called you stupid and look at how far you've come. He paraded women around. You worship Sofia and value your marriage. Angelene hasn't moved on from any of it."

Walter eyed the platter of olives, hummus, baba ghanoush and pita. The smells of lemon, oregano, and garlic took him back to a trip he took with Anastasia to Greece. They had spent the first days in the room, snacking on mezze and each other.

"Have you heard about disassociation?"

Walter dipped a pita triangle in hummus and shook his head. "Educate me."

"I was around ten when mum started sitting by the window and knitting. All day, she sat and knit. I called my grandmother. She sent the doctor around," David said, scooping up a blob of baba ghanoush. "I heard him tell Richard mum had dissociated herself or detached from the abuse."

"He told Richard he was abusive?"

"We never saw Dr. Palmer again. Anyway, I researched it and the doctor was right. Mum had completely pulled away from her life."

"You think Angelene has done this?"

"It's a way to survive."

Walter pulled at his collar and swallowed. Angelene had struggled and run. "I feel even worse now."

"You've seen Angelene's scars. Think of the ones you don't see. I don't think she had time to heal before the next happened."

"She doesn't want to heal. Clings to the hurt like that blanket you dragged all over the garden."

"Drove Richard crazy. It was a sign of weakness."

The waiter set down their sandwiches. Walter stared at the basket of chips. Angelene had been a hard woman to conquer. She fought every step of the way, was still fighting.

"Ang said her wings never grew. Funny, all she does is fly away."

"Angelene may not think she deserves a better life, so she sabotages or runs."

"She certainly did Saturday night."

"What did you do?"

"I was in the mood. She dismissed me. I got a little aggressive."

"You thought she'd want to make love after the way you treated her?"

Walter took a bite, pondering his actions; he had been a hypocrite too. "If I wasn't soused, I would have done what I usually do, curse and walk away."

David topped up their cups and frowned deeply.

"Stop looking at me like that. Kate already gave me a lecture."

"I think I know the answer... when did you see Kate?"

Walter wiped crumbs from his fingers and rubbed his brow. He didn't know how he ended up at Kate's. He didn't remember driving down Taunton Road, past Tesco, or knocking on her door. He had somehow steered his Aston Martin to a destination he hadn't planned to visit.

"You didn't try it on Kate, did you? Sofia will kill you."

"Of course not," Walter said, harshly. "She made coffee, called me an arse and went to bed." "I hope you learned your lesson."

"Wives are supposed to make love to their husbands."

"Is that written somewhere, a law I'm unaware of?"

Walter sipped his tea. He hated to admit it, even to his best friend. He was suffocating. Unravelling was one thing; he could wind himself back in. Suffocation led to death.

"Every time she rejects me, I get more pissed off."

"You mean your ego gets bruised."

"I won't cheat. I won't be like my father."

"You're randy. You always have been. Poor Pru was stuck in the barn every day after school."

Walter stabbed his fork into a chip, dunking it in ketchup. Even as a teenager, girls didn't deny him.

"Think about what I said. Be gentle with Angelene. Take her flowers, buy her a book, look at her paintings without judgement. She'll relax and be comfortable."

Walter smirked; he wasn't sure he had it in him to make the effort.

"How many times can someone try?"

David finished his sandwich, wiping his fingers on his napkin. "You only knew her a few months. Patience."

Walter had run out.

***

Sofia held a photo of Brendon against her breast. It had been greedy of her, longing for the old Brendon. She should be grateful for the improvements, instead of yearning for what he once was. Who was she to demand her son get well? Fear lingered in her heart.

"What are you doing, gattina?"

"Thinking."

"You have that look on your face like you're about to cry. You should be over the moon; Brendon is back at school. You and David are getting along."

"I'm afraid I'll wake up and find Brendon back in bed.""Now you know how I felt, all those years watching Gianni drink. He'd get sober for a week; I'd be able to breathe, then back to the bottle."

"What if he's never that sweet boy again, and he goes off to Germany numb?"

"Lukas will let you know. They want my topolino. They'll let nothing happen to their investment."Sofia set the photo on the coffee table. She followed Nicola into the kitchen, passing by shrines of Brendon. Her heart swelled and shrank with each arrangement of photos.

"How do I get over it?"

"You never get over it. You learn to live with it," Nicola said, passing her a bowl of mushrooms. "Place them on skewers."

Sofia took the bowl, picked up a skewer, and pierced a mushroom. "All I ever wanted was a happy, healthy child."

"We fill our minds with all sorts of hopes and dreams for our children. It isn't our right to mould them into our dreams. They must live their own lives," Nicola said. "You won't always have that boy who clung to your side.""Are you going home soon?" Sofia said, passing Nicola the plate of skewered mushroom and shrimp.

Nicola placed the skewers in the pan. It crackled and sizzled. "I have to keep my eye on a few things."

"The Pratt's?" "I saw something during French lessons. It's made me curious."

Sofia dumped orange slices in a pitcher and stirred the sangria. Questions bounced around her head, something intimate, something frightening?

"Girls fall hard for Brendon. Maggie, Rachel, Franca," Nicola said, cubing potatoes. "I'm concerned someone else may have fallen for topolino."

"You're not talking about Angelene, are you?" Sofia said, opening a can of tomatoes. "One minute I trust her, then I don't."

"Put the knife down and come sit."

Sofia set the knife on the cutting board; she fiddled with her engagement ring; more questions filled her rattled brain.

"Henri Piedmont is dead."

"From an illness? An accident like Gianni?"

"He committed suicide."

"Oh, God, Kate said…" Shock flashed across Sofia's eyes. "Kate said he was in Barcelona."

"Don't be upset with Kate. She was protecting you."

"You think Angelene…" Sofia's eyes stung with tears. "Henri locked himself in his room. He was a prodigy."

"I believe Angelene was involved with Henri, as involved as she can be." "Angelene said they were just friends."

"And you believe that? Did you look in her eyes? Were her fingers twitching?"

"I couldn't focus. I can't focus on anything except Brendon."

"Angelene is one of those starry-eyed girls," Nicola said. Her eyes were damp and vivid brown.

Sofia's feet slipped from the rungs; it had been years since she saw her mother scared.

"Burnham, the sheets… Brendon likes Rachel. He denies it. I've seen the way he looks at her."

"That's the look of a horny teenager. I saw a different look."

"From… from Brendon?" Sofia stared at her white knuckles. Brendon was a nice boy; rule nine of the Gentlemen's Code, comfort a woman. Brendon might fancy Angelene. He liked women who didn't doll themselves up, natural beauties, *'women like Angelene. She might fancy him. There has always been a line of women trying to get a piece of him.'*

After a long silence, Sofia cleared her throat. Her eyes drifted to the arched doorway. "I think I heard the door."

"Don't mention Henri Piedmont. Brendon doesn't need to know."

"How am I supposed to act in front of him? My thoughts are racing." "Shove it to the back of your mind, gattina, be observant."

How could she act like she wasn't shocked and scared? Had Angelene fallen for Henri Piedmont? Did she hollow him out too?

"You're just in time, sweetheart."

Brendon jerked his tie loose and tossed it on the counter. "For what?"

"Dinner in Spain, topolino," Nicola said, sniffing him.

"It smells bloody brilliant."

Sofia studied Brendon's face. There was a healthy glow on his cheeks, eyes, dreamy.

"Did you work up an appetite at school or the pitch?" Nicola said, pouring glasses of sangria.

"The pitch. I was helping the keeper from Chesham United. Liam's considering him for my spot next season."

"It must have been quite the practice. You're flushed," Nicola said.

Sofia gazed at Brendon. He looked like he always did after being at the pitch, alive, happy.

"You're in your school kit. Did you play in it?"

Brendon dropped his fork and pushed his plate away. "Bloody hell, what's with all the questions? I wasn't going to drive home to change and drive back into town."

Sofia took a sip of sangria, moistening her dry throat. "How was school?"

"Bloody boring." "Something exciting must have happened. Were your friends happy to see you?"

She would keep the subject to school, deter Nicola from asking questions. His eyes were darkening.

"The teachers backed off, which was nice. Rachel couldn't stop hugging me."

"I like Rachel."

Brendon stabbed his fork in a tomato. "Mum doesn't."

"I never said I didn't like her. It's hard to get past what she did to you."

"She didn't do anything to me. I was more than willing."

"She knew you had a girlfriend."

"The girl has balls, gattina," Nicola said, tossing a chunk of bread on Brendon's plate. "She knows what she wants and goes for it. She's feisty, doesn't wallow like someone we know."

Sofia shot Nicola a 'please mother' glare, peeling the shell from a shrimp. "You've met Rachel once and you know this about her?"

"She's got sass. She'd keep you on your toes, topolino."

"I'm not interested in a girlfriend right now. I'd still be with Maggie if I were," Brendon said, swiping the crust through a blob of sauce.

Sofia found solace in his empty plate, jutting out her cheek as he stood.

"Bloody hell, mum."

"Make her happy, topolino. She smiled once today, a genuine smile, not that fake one she's been giving us."

Brendon kissed Sofia's cheek and set his plate in the dishwasher. "I'm going to shower, then call Troy. Try apologizing again."

"How's my little meatball?"

"Charlie's mad at him."

"About what?" Nicola said.

"A girl."

"A girl from school, sweetheart?"

"She's in his, uh, biology class."

"Is she blonde, topolino?"

Brendon grabbed his tie, rolling it around his hand. "Does it matter? Charlie is pissed off, and he's gutted."

'The boy with his chickens. The painting Walter talked about, bright sunny yellow. Troy.' Sofia pushed her plate away. *'I'm losing my mind, strangled by the golden thread.'*

"Go smell his shirt."

"Why would I do that?"

"Quick gattina, before he gets out of the shower."

Sofia sighed heavily and marched from the kitchen, sunny yellow, the architect, her son. Sofia walked into Brendon's bedroom, eucalyptus and citrus scented steam wafted from under the closed door. Her gaze drifted over the dresser to crumpled leaves on a stack of magazines to the heap of clothes lying by the laundry basket. She picked up a shirt and held the collar to her nose. Sofia scoffed at Nicola's suspicion. She was being ridiculous, rooting through Brendon's clothes on a silly hunch. The shower stopped; she heard the snap of a towel. Dropping the shirt onto the pile, Sofia hastily made her way to the hall. A little tug pulled her pinky.

'You're angry with me for sneaking into Brendon's room.' Sofia stared at the locked bedroom door, rubbing her goose pimpled arms. *'Give me a sign Brendon is telling the truth.'*

Sofia held her breath, waiting for her hair to flutter, a familiar smell, a light to flicker. Nothing came.

***

Angelene tapped her cigarettes on the armrest. Every corner had eyes on her, every creak a scolding voice. How quickly she had turned on the rules and her promise.

'Perhaps if I scrub myself clean, God will forgive me.'

A knock, loud and hard, drowned out her thoughts. Angelene crawled across the sofa and tiptoed to the door. The knocking grew louder, heavier. Angelene's hand shook as she opened the door.

"Bonsoir Ms. Pratt."

"Nicola."

Angelene peered around the laneway. The night sky was clear, glittering silver and dark blue. She opened the door wider, stepping back from Nicola's intense stare.

"Shall we sit?"

"I put coffee on. We can sit in the kitchen."

"Am I making you nervous?"

Angelene weaved her fingers in and out. Nicola's stare was severe, suspicious. Her perfect posture and commanding, accusatory tone, did more than make her nervous, it clogged her senses.

"People make me uneasy."

"Were you nervous when you first met Walter?"

"I ran from him."

Nicola chuckled. "Most women run to him. Things must be tense between the two of you. I hear he was drunk at the gala."

Angelene fled the foyer, squeezing into the corner of the window bench. She fumbled through the ashtray, lighting a bent cigarette. "He was drunk, I have been too. Walter and I are equal now."

"Are you saying Walter had retribution on his mind?" Angelene blew out a long trail of smoke. "I'm not saying anything."

"Does Brendon make you feel uneasy?"

Where was Veronique's 'I'm the queen of this house' attitude when she needed it? Angelene stared at an opened bottle of wine. Bravery and inner Veronique were underneath the cork.

"I don't feel anything."

"Nothing?"

Angelene rubbed out the cigarette, stood, willing her legs to stop shaking. She raised her chin and walked to the counter. "Would you like a cup? Walter says I make it too strong."

"I must have imagined you and Brendon snuggling in the den."

Coffee splashed on the counter, Angelene ran a cloth over the spill, cursing her trembling hands. "I like Brendon. Is that what you want to hear?"

"What did I tell you?"

Angelene gripped the mug, searching her buzzing brain for the words.

"To stay away."

"I saw the way you leaned into Brendon, your fingers gliding over his. You don't need to tell me how you feel about him. Your flushed cheeks and twitching fingers tell me everything. Guilt and shame."

"There's a difference."

"I know the difference. Both dwell inside you. You've done something bad, and you feel you are a bad person. Am I right?"

Angelene scratched at a freckle of black paint, bracing herself against the counter. "I have done bad things and I believe I'm a bad person. I have since I was a little girl."

"Is that why you tried to commit suicide?"

"I didn't know what to do. I had no reason to live."

"Were you having some sort of existential crisis?"

Angelene gripped her wrist, digging her fingernails into her flesh. "I don't want to talk about it."

Nicola relaxed onto a stool. She picked up a pile of drawings, flipping through. "Just like Henri Piedmont. You don't like to talk about him either."

The skin puckered around Angelene's nails.

"Did you think you could waltz into Taunton without me knowing who would interact with my family? I don't listen to gossip, I get facts."

Angelene unclenched her fingers, stumbled to the window bench, and flicked through the ashtray. A package of cigarettes flew in her direction. She snagged it from the air.

"There's a keeper in you. Did Brendon teach you that?"

Angelene shoved a cigarette in her mouth, inhaled and blew smoke towards Nicola. "I will not discuss Henri with you."

"You were involved with Henri Piedmont. You admire my grandson. I'd say you have a thing for teenage boys." Angelene took another long drag and smashed the cigarette in the ashtray. Was Brendon's scent on her skin? Was his light shimmering around her?

"Can you look at me, Ms. Pratt?"

Angelene stirred up the winter, freezing her insides and held Nicola's gaze. "I was not involved with Henri."

"I know what I saw in the den. I've seen it before, at his match, over meals. You can't take your damn eyes off him. I will not let you destroy Brendon like you did Henri Piedmont."

"Please leave."

"Stay the hell away from Brendon. You need to focus on your husband."

A deafening bang rattled the walls. Angelene ripped at her hair, releasing a scream from her lungs. She flipped the ashtray to the floor, stepped through ash, leaving a trail of footprints across the foyer and up the stairs. She dashed down the hall and climbed onto the bed, gazing at the lamplight glowing in Brendon's window. Tingles spread like melting butter over her thighs. "Go away, whatever you are."

She pushed until the feeling subsided. Shame tormented her. She was supposed to stay behind her wall and he behind his. Brendon had been dangerous from the start. The two of them were dangerous together.

40 Hikikomori

It had been a curious morning. After training and before he started his porridge, mammina had sniffed his neck and clothes. Brendon couldn't make sense of his mother's odd behaviour or the dream, which wasn't a dream. He had made love to Angelene. He expected guilt or regret to wrap around his heart when he walked past the photo of Walter and his father sipping caffe on the Piazza del Duomo. The feelings slumbered.

Brendon climbed out of the car, sprinted across the street, and grinned. She hadn't changed her mind. He pushed open the door. Dust motes shimmered like comet tails, pungent incense tickled his nose and coated his mouth. He snuck up behind her and placed his lips behind her ear.

"It smells funny in here."

She didn't look annoyed, a little guilty, which was nothing new. An overwhelming urge to kiss her glossy pink lips took him hostage. He tucked the yearning away; this wasn't the place for PDAs.

"It's the dragon's breath incense," Angelene said.

"There are dragons in here."

"Don't be silly."

Brendon held on to all the things he wanted to say, *'leave Walter, run away with me, I love you.'*

"Are you okay mon amour? May I call you that?" Her lips moved around the words. A flutter rippled through him. She sounded as beautiful as she looked.

"I prefer that over friend."

Angelene touched his cheeks, running her pinkies over his lips. "Your eyes are dark."

"Rachel wanted to talk. I ignored her. She hasn't moved me from number one yet."

"You're my number one."

The ferocity in her eyes and voice took Brendon by surprise. Since when was she possessive? She ran, she didn't hold tight. Did she forget she was married or not care about her vows?

"I'm yours if you want me to be. If you want this, us?"

Her hand cupped his cheek. He melted into her touch. "This is the start of madness."

A jangle of clicks and clacks interrupted the pan flute music.

"I have your book."

"Was it hard to find?"

"Not as hard as the others."

Brendon peered over Angelene's shoulder. A witch stood by a cauldron; two children cowered by its edge. He never liked Hansel and Gretel. The thought of an old woman living in the woods cooking children scared him. Sofia had said an old crone lived in the forest behind Rosewood manor. As he grew older, he learned there was no witch in the woods. The only monster was the one she was holding on to.

Brendon strolled between the displays of crystals and incense burners while Angelene explained to the clerk the importance of fairy tales. He stopped at an ornate bookshelf and read the various titles, 'White Magic,' 'The Kitchen Witch,' 'Celebrating Samhain.' Who knew someone could craft a spell out of household items.

"I'm hungry."

"I'll grab us something from the cafe. You wait in my car. I parked under those ash trees."

He held the door open and walked by her side, keeping a respectable distance. He ran through a list of excuses in case someone drove by: she was lost; she didn't have enough money for a taxi. All lame, but it was something until he could concoct a more elaborate tale.

"Malcolm told me they have the best Ham and cheese and lemon meringue pie and milkshakes."

"Bloody hell, I'll see you in a minute, quick, before someone sees you."

"More hiding, the same old pattern."

"It has to be this way until you come to Dortmund."

Brendon delighted in the thought of her in the bleachers at Signal Iduna Park. She'd forget all about Paris St. Germain. She'd don the black and yellow proudly. He placed their order, checked his watch. Twenty-five minutes was long enough to enjoy lunch in the park. Brendon handed the clerk thirty pounds and grabbed the bag. He glanced up and down the street, sprinting to his car.

"Your lunch and these." He passed Angelene a bouquet of slightly wilted yellow flowers. "I picked them this morning. They're creeping all over the school grounds. The caretaker says they're a nuisance."

"Like me."

"Not like you. You like yellow. I want you to be yellow all the time."

Angelene kissed his cheek and stuck her nose in the bouquet. "That was very sweet."

He turned into Ash Meadows car park and parked. Brendon dropped his keys in his blazer pocket and ran around the car to get the door. He grabbed the bag and took her hand; it was cold and trembling.

"I need quiet," Angelene said, somberly. "I dreamt we were making love. God was crying and the queen, with her crown of thorns, kept shouting off with her head. Her words burned my skin like holy water. I woke sweating and out of breath."

"You feel bad about what we did."

"I've asked God to understand."

"Not forgive?"

"Understand."

Brendon led her towards a park bench hidden amongst a grove of trees. A group of women walked by, pushing prams. Brendon hung his head and tugged her towards the bench. The hornbeam branches dipped low, surrounding them in a green shelter.

"You liked Hansel and Gretel? That book scared me."

Angelene slurped her milkshake and dug into the bag. She unwrapped her sandwich and took a small bite.

"Mother used to read it to me when she was angry. I told her God did not make witches, she called me a witch for seeing words as colours. Roman fixed the story so it wouldn't frighten me." "Did he change the words? My teacher had to make up a whole new story after Troy's mum complained. The witch baked biscuits, and they had tea in the garden."

"Roman told me witches didn't exist. He hiked the Black Forest and if witches existed, they would live there. I told him witches existed. I lived with one, mama."

Brendon laughed and took a bite. "I bet he kept that to himself."

"It was our secret," Angelene said, setting her sandwich in her lap. "I have something for you. Hold out your hand."

Brendon gobbled his sandwich and tossed the wrapper into the bag. He opened his hand; she placed a shiny, black stone in his palm.

"It's obsidian, for protection."

Brendon rolled the stone around his hand. "What do I need protection from?"

"Me."

"More like Rachel and Maggie. They both stare at me during class. They'll hold up their notebook and peer over the top. It's funny."

"Those girls adore you. It's hard not to."

"Are you saying you adore me?"

"Tu es ma Chérie pour l'éternité."

Brendon slipped the crystal into his pocket. "I don't know what you said. It sounded bloody pretty."

Angelene sipped her milkshake and tucked her feet under her. "Roman used to say that to me. You are my darling for all eternity. I was, for about six years."

Brendon pressed his lips against her forehead, his stomach dropped. Music in the Park happened every autumn. This was Victoria McGregor's chance to outdo his mother. Brendon pinned his back against the bench and shrank behind the ash keys dangling from the branches. He peered through a gap in the leaves. Victoria's ample bottom was out of sight.

"What's that over there?"

Brendon held his breath and hoped she wasn't pointing at Victoria McGregor.

"That's the fountain. It's bloody old."

"Can you show me?"

Brendon wiped his palm on his thigh and scanned the park for Victoria's navy trench.

"I should get back to school."

"Please, a quick look."

Brendon surveyed every corner of the park, over the flower beds, around the trees. The women had parked their prams, laid out a blanket and chatted while their babies played. A couple tossed bread to the woodpigeons. There was no woman wearing a navy trench.

"Finish your sandwich. I'll take you to the fountain and then home."

Angelene swallowed it in three bites and washed it down with the milkshake.

"I'll save my pie for later," she said, holding his cheeks in her hands. "I'm going to kiss you."

She kissed his top, then bottom lip. It was salty, and chocolaty. Brendon tossed the bag into the bin and took her hand. They walked across the grass and stepped onto a concrete pad. A group of joggers ran past, Brendon dropped his chin. He gazed nervously around the park, still no Victoria. The joggers in their matching pink and black outfits faded out of sight. Love was making him crazy.

"It's beautiful."

"They built it for Queen Victoria." He glanced at his watch: 1:00. He could tell Mr. Clark he barfed, was tired, overwhelmed. "Hasn't Walter brought you to the park?"

"He's promised."

Brendon searched the park for Victoria. The women chatted and fed their babies. The couple and the woodpigeons had left. He wound his arms around her waist and drew her close.

"You don't need a stone for protection. You fit perfectly in my arms."

She snuggled closer. All the crazy emotions zapped through him.

"I feel calm when I'm with you. It's a tricky thing for someone to do, quiet the noise."

"You're making me feel lots of things."

"Irritated? Flustered?"

"I love you."

"Please don't. No, I love you."

"I like you a lot. How's that?"

"Even that scares me." She took his hand and tugged him along the path. "Is that a bandstand?"

Brendon gazed nervously around the park, searching for Victoria. She'd have to talk to everyone, people at the coffee shop, playing mini golf, groundskeepers, and not just about Music in the Park. She'd have to squash the rumours about Maisie fancying the cricket keeper, complain about the blood imbedded in her new hardwood, William's missing tooth, him.

"I'll show you the sensory garden. There's a mosaic water feature and sculptures. It's quiet."

He led her down a path. Squirrels skittered across the grass, birds chirped, and flew between the ash trees. Brendon pointed to a park bench, ornamental grasses whispered and rustled in the rosemary and lavender scented breeze.

"God is unhappy with me. I can feel it."

Brendon glanced down the path. Ducks, wood pigeons, no Victoria. He could finally breathe.

"Are you worried I'll go crazy like Henri?"

"Don't talk about Henri. I drove him there. He loved me, and I ran. Love made him crazy."

"I was in the same place as Henri. I have to trust you won't run from me and drive me right back to my bloody room."

Angelene brushed her hand over the yellowing strands of pheasant's tail grass. "Beautiful hands, a beautiful mouth that says pretty things, beautiful eyes that see past my scars."

"I'm just a list of things. Bloody great."

"Whenever I feel my heart getting full, I get scared. Love, after all the madness, leaves."

"Henri didn't leave you. He would have loved you and built you a bloody castle. You would have lived happily ever after."

"Happily ever after is terrifying. Who lives happily ever after, Cinderella, Sleeping Beauty?"

"You don't think you deserve love. You do."

"I'm afraid to feel love. I'm afraid it's only a dream. God will judge me, and I'll go to Hell. I'm afraid of the vows I took."

"You're afraid to feel love, but you're feeling something, fear. Fear is bloodier scarier than love. It makes your heart race, your muscles tighten, you can't breathe."

Angelene smoothed his lapel, leaning her cheek against his shoulder. "Love does all those things, too."

Madre Innocente and Padre Diavolo bickered. It had been a while since the two of them had a fight, stay, run.

"We better end whatever this is. I can't bloody deal with the hurt again."

"I don't want you to leave. You're mine."

"You don't want me to leave or stay. You can't love me, you're married. Bloody hell."

"I'm frustrating."

"Since the first day we met, I chose you. Even though I knew it was wrong, I kept choosing you and I will, until the day I die. God wants you to feel love."

"It's a dangerous game we play. Worse than Russian roulette."

"I'll take my chance. I'm extremely competitive. You've seen me on the pitch."

"I must go to confession."

"I'll drop you off."

"God is not happy."

"Dad tried to read me Winnie the Pooh when I was little. I never liked the bear; Paddington was more my style. His adventures were better."

A slight smile brightened Angelene's face.

"There's a quote mum and dad love. Piglet asks Pooh how you spell love and Pooh says, you don't, you feel it. If you're too afraid to tell me you love me, look at me like you did a minute ago and I'll know I'm more than a list."

"Russian Roulette."

"I love," he cursed at the wrinkle in her brow. "I like you a lot. I'll take your madness and play the game."

"I don't like this."

"I don't like sneaking around either, but until we decide what to do, we have no choice."

"Hikikomori. It's a Japanese word, pulling inward or confined. We're confined to walls, hidden, locked away."

"We better go. I have this weird feeling we're being watched."

"That is love. I told you, it makes you crazy."

They dashed to the car. If there was such a thing as walking on cloud nine, he was doing it. Madre Innocente led her army of guilt through his brain and body. He had kissed her, touched her in places only a husband should. Brendon gripped the wheel of what was once Walter's car. It was Walter who told Lukas about the Bundesliga's next superstar. Walter, who made him feel okay when he deviated from the code. Walter's wife he was in love with. Cloud nine blew up.

***

Maggie had spent most of the day thinking she and Brendon would reconcile. He was kind of himself, kind of smiling, kind of brooding, sometimes moving between both in a of matter minutes. Hope had ballooned in her chest when he texted asking her what the connections were between the Black Plague and the changes adopted by the ruling class. It fizzled when he didn't respond to her goodnight. There was something in his brooding, more than football stats. She had a feeling what it might be and thought herself silly for thinking it. Maggie heaved her book bags over her shoulders. It would be a long bus ride home hauling half the library.

"Thornton."

Maggie bit into her lip and hobbled faster towards the bus stop. She was in no mood to talk to the girl behind the desperate sounding voice.

"Do you need help with your bags?" Rachel called.

Maggie spun and teetered under the weight of her books. "If you're here to gloat, you can bugger off. I've had the worst day."

"Did Brendon piss you off?"

"I was tutoring. The boy's breath smelled like onions."

"Can you stop for a minute? I'd like to talk to you."

Maggie dropped her bags with a hefty sigh, books spilled at her feet. "Your knuddlebär is at a match. You should know that."

Rachel gathered her hair and twisted it atop her head. She laid her tie over her cleavage and scratched at a pimple on her chin.

"What do you want?" Maggie shoved up her cuff and stared at her watch. "I'm going to miss the bus."

"You were with Brendon for a long time, right?"

"Until you crawled all over him."

"I'm sorry about that."

"Please. You loved hurting me. It made you feel good when people placed bets on whether you'd be his girlfriend. You aren't sorry."

Maggie released a quick burst of breath and grinned. The vent felt fantastic.

"I didn't lure him into my bed." Rachel lit a cigarette and blew a mouthful of smoke towards the sky. "It felt good to be with him. He introduced me to his mum, Ms. Mastrioni. I felt like somebody, not the tart of Taunton."

Maggie had seen the 'crushed on the inside' look before. She had worn it for weeks.

"Brendon has a way of making you want to be with him."

"You looked like you were getting along the other day." Rachel took a long drag and stubbed the cigarette on the sole of her shoe. "Gemma bet 50p you and Brendon would be back together by the end of term."

Maggie grabbed a book and shoved it amongst the others. "She might as well kiss her money goodbye. We ended up fighting when you sent him the picture of your jubblies."

"You saw that?"

"You should have seen the stupid look on his face."

"Sorry, I don't know why I do those daft things."

"I don't know why, either. You don't need to push your jubblies up or wear all that makeup. Boys will still look at you."

"And they don't look at you? I've been jealous of you."

Maggie dropped her head back and cackled. "Of me? Boring Margaret Thornton."

"I was thinking about what you said and you're right. You didn't have to try to get Brendon's attention. He loved you, for you."

Maggie crossed her arms and kicked at a stone in the grass. "He was in like with me."

"For a while I thought he liked me, too. Brendon respects you. I'm just a set of tits." Rachel sniffed and blinked. Maggie reached into her blazer pocket and handed Rachel a package of tissues.

"He obviously respects you too. He invited you to his house. You met Ms. Cook, which means something."

Rachel dabbed her eyes. The tissue looked like an ink blot. "Don't be telling people I cried. If I hear anything, we'll have another row in the dining hall."

"I have no desire to mop the floors again."

Rachel blew her nose and scrunched the tissue. "He's changed. It's like he wants nothing to do with me. I pulled up the football highlights in Latin and he stared out the window."

"He hasn't been the Brendon I've known for a while. I think there's someone else."

Rachel tilted her head, puzzled.

"He's been distant and irritable. I thought it was because I wouldn't, you know, do that with him."

"It wasn't me. He'd smile that brilliant smile when I'd flirt, but that was it. He'd talk about some daft code he had to follow. It was just German lessons, I swear."

"I have a feeling I know who it is."

Rachel wiped her nose and stared at her scuffed high tops. "Anyone I know?"

Maggie looped the straps over her arms. "It's my insecurity making me think I've figured it out. I have this feeling. I've had it for a while."

"I shouldn't have fallen for him." Rachel said, heaving a book bag over her shoulder.

"It's hard not to," Maggie said. "I accept your apology. It doesn't mean I like you."

"I don't like me much either."

They hobbled beside one another; book bags banging between them. "I may end up in Dortmund, surprise him."

"Brendon cheated; you'd still visit him?"

"Wouldn't you?"

"Probably."

Maggie looked at a defeated and heartbroken Rachel, her insides turned to mush. If her theory were correct, there would be more devastation than just Rachel Jones.

***

Bubbles crackled and popped against Angelene's skin; a bottle of wine bobbed between her legs. Brendon had been there, placed himself inside her. She had allowed it. There were moments when she found herself free from the guilt and enjoyed his skin against hers. Shame would embrace her, she suffocated. He was addictive, like her cigarettes and wine, just as bad.

"I know I should stay away," Angelene said, taking a swig. "I know it's wrong, but I can't lose him like Henri."

She finished the wine and plucked the bottle from within the bubbles. Angelene patted herself dry, dropped the towel and wine bottle and walked to the bed. She crawled under the blankets; they were cool against her warmed skin. Angelene rolled to her side and grinned at the glow in his window. A little fire burned in her belly. She placed her fingers on the heat, staring at the amber glow.

"Please forgive me God for running from normal and jumping into a pattern I know I shouldn't. Lisette said I may regret marrying Walter; I may meet a man who is my soul mate and be stuck. Am I stuck, God?"

Her cell phone chirped; she jerked her hand away.

"Bonjour Walter... I had a confusing day. I danced with joy, then stumbled into an old pattern. I learned to play Russian roulette... I'm being silly, what am I doing now? Laying in bed thinking of you."

41 Enfant Épouvantable

Brendon had convinced himself Victoria McGregor was around every corner. He could have sworn he saw her lingering around the dressing room, in the bleachers, lurking around the car park. His paranoiac thoughts had taken him on a roller coaster ride with his two new friends, panic and paranoia. He called this chapter 'Parisian roulette.' The sound of crunching gravel pierced Brendon's ears. His gaze darted manically around the car park. He let out a huge breath. He had to give Rachel credit; she was persistent.

"I heard Thomas Wagner moved to number one." Rachel laid her arm across the window and rested her chin. "He isn't you, knuddlebär."

"What do you want?"

"I'm in love with you."

"That's bloody brilliant, but I have to go."

Rachel climbed out of the car and smiled a smile wild with temptation. Padre Diavolo whispered, *take her into the rear seat of the BMW, watch her face when she reaches the brilliant tingle.* He flicked Padre Diavolo away. There was only one girl he wanted to quiver and moan. She was waiting for him.

"I'm mad at you for breaking my heart. However, I'm all about second chances." She tucked her hands in his hoodie pouch, rose on her tiptoes, and grazed his chin with her glossy lips. "Walk with me, knuddlebär."

Brendon ran his sleeve over the sticky smear. It had been a while since he saw Rachel's smile. Angelene scolded herself for being a light stealer. He had stolen Rachel's. He had bypassed her in the halls, ignored her flirty texts. One last walk to say goodbye.

"To the end of the street and don't grab my bum."

"Oh, knuddlebär, I'll make you love me yet," Rachel said, clapping her hand in his.

"Do we have to hold hands?" "Look at me, Rachel Jones, holding a pro footy player's hand." "I could be number two keeper, even three. Dortmund may keep me on the U19 squad."

"I've read BILD. Rumours are the keeper is going to sign with Bayern Munich. The writer mentioned you as the replacement. I put little stars around your name."

"That paper is in German. You could read it?"

"Most of it. Christian is visiting again. He helped me with some words."

Dusk settled over the pitch. Orange, gold, and pink wrapped around the houses and radiated through the trees. Brendon surveyed the street, panic and paranoia skipped along beside him. There was comfort in Rachel's fingers, a familiarity like home. Guilt tagged along.

"Is your mum dating him?"

"I'm not sure. She was going on about how he works at a robotics company. He's a bit of a swot, a little older than her. It might be what she needs, someone stable."

"Maybe he'll be your stepdad."

"Mum told me over brekky, she'd move to Berlin to be with him. She said she'd want me to come. I'd be four hours away by train.""You might not fancy me anymore. You could meet Mr. Right in uni."They got to the end of the street. Brendon spun her around, hurt tapped him on the shoulder. Rachel was smiling, the sparkle had disappeared from her eyes.

"I doubt it, knuddlebär. You've stolen my heart. Keep running to whoever you're running to. You'll see who was best."

Brendon's stomach clenched; he kept his eyes on the pavement. "Who says there's someone else?"

"Margaret Thornton, that's who."

"When were you talking to Maggie?"

"I apologized to her."

Brendon gently nudged Rachel. "You're bloody lying."

"I have a heart," Rachel said, shoving him back. "You should know, you broke it."

Brendon clutched Rachel's hand. Maggie was smart. She had a way of figuring things out. When they had worked on maths together, he'd stare at the problem, juggling quadratic functions around his brain. Maggie would dissect the assignment like a puzzle and carefully put it back together. If anyone could figure out who he had been spending time with, it was Maggie. Panic and paranoia giggled with delight. Parisian roulette was getting riskier.

"Do people at school think there's someone else, like Will?"

"William's busy trying to juggle Gemma and Tilly."

"I'm not seeing anyone," Brendon said. He dug his toe in the gravel and kicked at the stones. *'Maggie doesn't know anything. Ms. McGregor didn't see me. She was busy trying to outdo mammina.'*

"I'm trying to hate you, knuddlebär. I told myself you're a secret poofter, the way you and Troy go on.""You think I'm a poofter?"

"I think you're brilliant. I hope this girl is worth it," Rachel said, wiggling his pocket. "One kiss, for old time's sake?"

"I'm a poofter. I don't kiss girls."Rachel puckered her lips, reaching for his neck. Their foreheads touched; Brendon pecked her lips.

"I never thought you were a slag."

"That's why it hurts so much." Rachel pressed her lips against his cheek and tapped his bottom. "I'm going to beat Thornton to Dortmund and sweep you off your feet. That gobby cow told me she might visit you. Bis später, knuddlebär."

Brendon dropped behind the steering wheel and touched his cheek. What was he doing? Rachel was available. There was still a giant wall between him and Angelene, one with huge, rock like hands. He was Rachel's knuddlebär and the love of Maggie's life. There would be no sneaking around. He wouldn't have to worry about Victoria McGregor.

Brendon turned onto the farmhouse lane, parked under the willow tree, and pushed regret from his mind. He closed the car door and spied a clump of purple flowers growing around the tree's roots. He plucked a handful, walked to the door. The house was quiet. There was a basket of feathers beside her wellies, a collection of broken eggshells, and a trail of faded wisteria petals leading to the kitchen.

"You promised."

Brendon looked at the half-drunk bottle of wine and ran his hand through his hair. Which devil was greeting him?

"I'm here now."

"Where were you?"

"At the pitch."

She curled her fingers around the wineglass. With one quick flick, it flew from her hand. Brendon ducked; glittery fragments fell at his feet.

"What the fuck are you doing?" Brendon kicked the glass into a pile and tossed the flowers on the island. "I should throw the flowers at you."

He slammed onto a stool and rested his head in his hand. Rachel's forced smile and downcast eyes haunted him. Maggie, the girl who put puzzles together with little thought and did crosswords with a pen, bounced between images of Rachel. The girl, with fire in her eyes, hissed at him.

"That's devil's bit, seems appropriate, doesn't it?"

"Which one of your devils am I dining with tonight? Wrath, envy, drunk?"

"You ruined everything."   "It's cold, not ruined."

She gripped the ashtray, ash and butts scattered across the cushion and floor.

"Don't bloody throw that."

"What took you so long?" Angelene dropped the ashtray and gripped the cushion. "Tell me."

"Rachel showed up."   "Fucking Salome."

Brendon pushed the plate away, sparks lit, heat prickled his neck and cheeks. "Her name is Rachel. She's a friend."

"Rachel is not your friend. You have done to her what you do to me." Brendon rose, ripped the bottle of wine off the island, and shoved it between her legs. "Finish it." She gripped his arm. He stooped under the force. Her grasp was as fierce as her eyes.

"Don't leave me."

"I'm going to say something bloody awful if I don't leave."

She jumped from the window bench, gripped his hoodie, and jerked him to a stop. "Don't go."

Brendon tugged himself free. "You were bloody right about love. It turns you into a fucking nutter."

Angelene reached for a plate, tossing it like a frisbee. It painted the counter beige and white.

"Stop bloody throwing things."

"Why does everyone leave me?"

"Because you're fucking crazy."

Angelene wilted against the island and scrubbed at her face. "Please. I don't want to be alone."

"You're not alone. You have Walter." Just like he had Rachel, the girl with a different kind of fire. Brendon leaned into the doorway and knocked his forehead against the wood trim. His heart was telling him one thing. Panic scrambled his thoughts. Paranoia screamed at him to run.

"Do you like Rachel? Do you wish you never ended things with Maggie?"

"Bloody hell, Angelene, I ended things with Maggie and Rachel because of you."

"You're going to leave me like Roman and Henri, like Francois."

"You're screaming at me; I don't feel like dodging plates. Who is Francois? Another boy you loved?"

He met her gaze; the darkness had left her eyes. Brendon sighed, left the safety of the doorway, and drew her into his arms. Her scars had opened. Years of hurt spilt at his feet.

"Francois was my best friend in elementary school. I lost him too. Are you going to leave?"

"Stop bloody pouting and go sit in the front room."

Angelene scooted off the stool, grabbed the bouquet, and shuffled away. Her shoulders drooped like the flowers at her side. Brendon stepped over the proof, love made her crazy, grabbed a plate from the cupboard, divided the food and heated each one in the microwave. He filled two glasses with milk, defeated and tired.

"I don't deserve these," Angelene said, sniffing the flowers.

"No, you don't."

He set a plate on her lap, taking the flowers from her hand. Brendon flopped to the floor and crossed his legs. Sparks flickered and fizzled. They were tired too. She sat still and picked at her meal, her cheeks flushed from wine and rage, eyes as grey as a winter's day. She was a mishmash of disgraced red, icy white, and winter blue. He would title the night, 'little bird found her voice.'

"I don't want to lose you."

Her voice dripped with desperation and melancholy, oozed into his ears like a nerve agent, strangling his heart and lungs.

"You're married, in case you forgot," Brendon said, stabbing his fork into a roasted carrot. "Get some bloody chicken into you."

"I should have kept running from Walter all the way to Switzerland," she said, poking at the chicken. "After mama chased Roman away, I used to see a magpie out my window. I thought it was Roman checking in on me. Magpies are smart birds; Roman was the smartest person I've ever known."

Brendon gulped the milk. The flush had crept down her throat, washing her chest in red.

"My year one teacher taught us a rhyme about magpies. One for sorrow, two for mirth, three for a funeral, four for birth. I would kick the ball around the garden reciting it. Mum thought it was a bloody awful poem to teach children," Brendon said, wiping a dribble of butter from his lips. "I never understood why mammina hated the poem. Until I overheard her telling Amelia they stand for loneliness and death. According to mum, a magpie sat outside the kitchen window for years. After I was born, it was gone."

"I begged my wings to grow so I could join magpie Roman and fly away."

She sniffed and ran her t-shirt under her nose. "Goodbyes were never pleasant for me. They were always final."

Brendon pushed himself off the floor and sat beside her. He scooped up some mashed potatoes and stabbed at a piece of chicken, nudging the fork at her lips. "Open up."

Angelene took the bite, chewing slowly. "Do you know what hurt the most after Roman left?"

Brendon pushed the fork into her hand and kissed her temple. He'd re-title the night 'when little bird cries.'

"I kept losing him. Every day, his scent would fade from the apartment. I hate goodbyes. I hate when people leave."

"I won't leave you. We'll figure out a plan to get you to Dortmund."

Angelene nibbled a bean, staring wistfully at the fire. "It's only a matter of time before the pattern breaks apart. It always ends the same, moments of yellow then black."

"We can make our own pattern, something just for us. Yellow, pink, and brown."

"Why pink?"

"It's how bloody fast my heart beats when I look at you. The colour of your lips. My insides glow when we hold hands. It's how you make me feel."

"I'll stumble again. I'm terrible on my feet."

"I'll catch you."

Angelene set her plate on the coffee table and curled into the corner of the sofa. She drew a hand over her mouth, yawning.

"Do you want me to leave so you can sleep?"

"Please don't say leave."

"I'm going to migrate to my house and migrate back here tomorrow. Better?"

"Will you stay until I fall asleep?"

"I'll even tell you a story."

He lifted her onto his back and held her hands. The weight of the evening was heavier than her.

"Your light is prettier now. It was staticky a while ago."

"I was angry. I told you healthy things. It pisses me off when you don't try."

Brendon crouched. She climbed off his back, tearing the blankets away.

"It's a habit. I'm sorry."

"Quit apologizing. You bloody apologize for everything. Sometimes it isn't your fault," Brendon said, running his fingers down the length of her arms. "Raise your arms. You've got snot on your shirt."

"There's a yellow shirt in the second drawer."

He dropped the t-shirt in the laundry basket, opened the drawer and lifted a stack of shirts. Brendon studied the faded picture of a building made up of colourful boxes and the words Musée du quai Branly, Jean Nouvel.

"Are you hiding this from Walter?"

"It was Henri's. He loved Nouvel. We went to the museum. He told me all about the concealed light sources and shifting ceiling heights."

"And you got pissed off at me about Rachel."

"Henri can't interfere in our relationship. Rachel can."

"Go brush your teeth."

Angelene wiggled into the t-shirt and padded to the bathroom. Brendon walked to the bed and jammed his toe into something hard. He sunk onto the mattress, rubbing his foot.

"Bloody hell, what do you have under the bed?"

"My jewellery box," she said, gurgling the words.

"Why don't you keep it on the dresser?"

"Special parts of my life are in there. It must stay hidden."

He stared at Walter's pillow; guilt coiled around his neck. The faint scent of peppery cologne lingered on the sheets. Memories of making love to Angelene stormed his brain.

"You want to go downstairs and watch telly?"

"After a tantrum, I feel like I haven't slept for weeks."

"Why don't you show me what's in the box? I'll make us a cuppa; we can watch the highlights."

"Everything in there has a pattern attached to it. Every postcard, every drawing has goodbye."

Brendon pictured himself on his own bed, bunched the pillows, and opened the box.

"Show me something and tell me about the wonderful parts. The sad memories will go away if you remember the happy bits."

"I've tried. Sad is stronger than happy."

"When my Nonno died, all I could remember was him lying in the coffin. I couldn't shut my eyes without that image in my head. Then I remembered all the things I loved, like watching AC Milan or his laugh. He had the greatest laugh; his belly would shake, and his entire face would light up."

"It's been a pattern, looking, remembering." Angelene pulled out a postcard, Switzerland embossed on the cardstock. "This was the last postcard from Roman."

"What makes you happy? Look at the picture, something Roman told you."

"Roman grew up on a dairy farm in the Canton Graubünden. He told me about la désalpe, where the cows come down from the mountains in winter. There was a festival, the alpine descent. Roman would parade the cows through the streets wearing bells and flowers."

"Instead of thinking how your nutter of a mother chased him away. Think about how his stories made you feel."

Angelene kissed the postcard and tucked it back in the box.

"Is that?"

Brendon flipped through the drawings and postcards. The mystery of the missing Dortmund jersey solved.

"I missed your scent horribly that day. I'm sorry."

"Keep it. You can wear it when you watch me play in Dortmund. Everyone will know you're my girl."

Angelene gazed at him. There was a look in her eyes, like she was committing every inch of him to memory.

"Am I your girl?"

"Snot, tears, tantrums. I choose you." Angelene pressed her lips against his arm and held up a drawing of a castle. "Henri drew this for me. He was going to build me the prettiest castle."

"He's building it for you right now. Beautiful towers, battlements to protect you and a footbridge lined with every yellow flower on the planet. He's on the other side of that door, ready to take your hand. There's a problem, though."

Brendon lifted some postcards and pulled out a drawing of a gothic mansion. "A brilliant knight heard about Lady Angelene and challenges Henri to a duel."

"If you defeat Henri, he'll be sad. I couldn't hurt him again."

"We could share you for a bit, but you'd have to choose. Prince Henri, the architect, or Sir Brendon of Dortmund." Angelene flipped under news clippings and photos, grinning at a tag dangling from a yellow ribbon. "This is from Henri's favourite patisserie. He had a terrible sweet tooth. Sugar ran through his veins."

Brendon dug through the box, holding up postcards from Kyoto, Hong Kong, and Nuremburg.

"He'd be the perfect boyfriend for Maggie."

"I always told him to find someone sweet. He said he preferred my spice."

Brendon set the postcards on the lid and unfolded a newspaper article. He read the headline, 'Taunton First will be first with Cook back in net.' He placed the article on the postcards and pulled out another, 'Brendon Cook, Taunton's hero.'

"When I first met you, all I could see was this incredible light. I could feel it when you shook my hand. There was something about the way you looked at me, like you knew how to tear down my wall."

"I wasn't the only one. Henri and Roman knew how to scale that bloody wall of yours. That's what you need to think about when you look at these things, how precious you were to Henri and Roman."

Angelene closed the lid and cradled the jewellery box in her arm. "I'm tired."

Brendon placed the box on the floor. He, too, was tired, wrapped in the heaviness that came with comforting little bird.

"Will you tell me a story?"

"There once was a boy named Brendon who lived in a beautiful manor surrounded by a bloody enormous forest. Every day, he would look out his window and stare at the trees. He wanted to play in the woods. Queen Sofia said it was too dangerous. A horrible witch named Veronique lived in the woods."

Angelene giggled sleepily, tucking her knees into her chest.

"One day Brendon decided he would disobey his mother. He was tired of all the rules she and King David made. He snuck into the woods and at first, he was frightened, but then he remembered he was brave and had his brilliant light to protect him. Brendon walked deeper into the forest and found a wall made of gold and platinum bricks."

"Were there flowers?"

"Yellow flowers along the edge and between the bricks."

"Did Veronique live behind the wall?"

"She had her evil monkeys, Douchette and Jenssen, build it. Veronique was jealous of her daughter. She had the wall built to shut her away."

"Did Brendon climb the wall?"

"He climbed the ivy. I forgot to mention the ivy. When he reached the top, he almost fell to the ground. He had never seen a girl so beautiful. She wanted to run; she is exceptionally good at running when she's scared."

"Did she?"

"Brendon said please don't run, tell me your name, and she said, little bird. Brendon said, 'why do you look so sad?' Little bird said, 'I've lost my wings.'

Brendon reached over the wall and said, 'I will share my light with you, and we'll fly'."

Angelene closed her eyes and clutched his hoodie. Which devil had he met? This one was full of fight, too scared to do anything but scream and stamp her feet. Enfant Épouvantable was the perfect name for the devil snuggled next to him. Brendon eased himself off the bed and covered her with the duvet. He was no longer on cloud nine; he was floating on cloud thirteen. A frigid breeze fluttered the curtains, Brendon shivered. Thirteen steps to the gallows, thirteen knots in a hangman's noose. Judas was the thirteenth dinner guest. He was Uncle Walt's Judas. Cloud thirteen suited him. He would take a chance on Enfant Épouvantable. He would take the thirteen steps.

***

Walter liked London at night. He described it as vibrant and suffocated when the fog was thick. He had moments throughout the day when he described himself the same way.

"Good night Mr. Pratt. See you tomorrow."

"Thank you for staying late. I couldn't wrap my head around that budget report."

"I was happy to help," Juliette said, pointing her purse towards Horseguards Avenue. "You have company."

Walter grumbled, curling his lip, Victoria McGregor stood at the bottom of the stairs, tapping her foot.

"Good luck," Juliette said with a smile.

Walter gripped his briefcase, dodge back into the building, or walk right past her. It wouldn't be the first time someone ignored Victoria.

"Shouldn't you be in Taunton making dinner for your children?"

"William is eating McDonalds with Matilda and Maisie is studying maths with the keeper from the cricket team."

"Maths or her?"

Victoria pinched her plump lips together, scowling. "The rumours are true then. You are working late."

"You should know. You started them."

"It's in my nature. I was born a gossip."

"Nobody has gossiping in their DNA. You're insecure."

"People are saying you've changed. You always were a pompous ass, never rude."

Walter's eyes narrowed. Why had she come? Victoria never had anything important to say.

"It's late and I'm tired. If you'll excuse me."

"Taunton has been full of gossip lately. Brendon Cook beat our William, ruined my new hardwood."

"The whole damn town knows Brendon has a temper; that's nothing new."

"There's trouble in the Cook's marriage. They looked cozy at the gala. They were the biggest actors in the room."

Walter set down his briefcase, flexing his fingers. "There's nothing wrong with David and Sofia's marriage. Do you not have anything better to do than gossip?"

41 ENFANT ÉPOUVANTABLE

Victoria jerked the ties on her trench and pointed her chin to the sky. "People come to me for news."

"You've been a busy body since primary. Hand-me-down school kits, you lived in a crumbling terraced home. You're a jealous woman, always have been."

"How's your wife?"

Walter grabbed his briefcase and brushed past Victoria. "You should know."

He had asked himself the same question over tea and biscuits. Angelene had been happy to hear from him. Her tone had been unusually pleasant, the conversation had been light and easy, too easy, as if she had practiced what to say.

"I saw Angelene coming out of the Asian market on Priory Bridge Road with Troy Spence."

"Good night, Victoria."

"Troy wouldn't shop there. Evelyn and Harrison are bangers and mash people, not pad Thai."

"Evelyn makes a brilliant curry."

"Troy looked smitten. I've never seen your wife happier."

Walter stopped and turned. "It's your currency."

"Excuse me?"

"Gossip. It gets you the better seat at the table, a one up. It gets you noticed," Walter said, smirking. "Not by everyone."

"What's that supposed to mean?"

"David. You've fancied him since secondary school. He never paid attention to you. It's eaten away at you since then."

"You're the jealous one. Women have always fawned over your charismatic smile. Not me."

"Don't flatter yourself," Walter said, shifting his briefcase to the other hand. "Why are you here?"

"Is there someplace we can talk?"

"Call Juliette in the morning and have her pencil you in."

"Shouldn't you be heading home to Taunton?"

"What are you implying?"

"I have currency."

Walter rubbed his neck, blowing out an irritated breath. Victoria was in a prickly mood, and he didn't do prickly. The feeling swarmed his brain. Something told him to hear her out.

"There's a pub around the corner."

They walked in silence, Walter two steps in front, mulling over Angelene's good mood, Victoria's unexpected visit, and the feeling that had sunk to his gut. He opened the door, a spirited jig, spilled onto the street. They entered a room which could have been an extension of his lounge: familiar, cozy. There was an odd mixture of jumble sale trinkets lined up along shelves and hanging from the walls. Walter marched past the gleaming wood bar to a table hidden in the corner, signalling the server.

"Affligen blonde, Victoria."

"Wine, white, something Australian," Victoria said, tugging at her coat sleeves. "You like blondes, don't you?"

"Not particularly. I've dated mostly brunettes."

Victoria touched her peroxided locks. "James has always fancied blondes. Sienna Miller, Rose Huntington. You'll remember from primary, I'm brunette."

"Did you wait outside the Ministry of Defence to remind me you were once a brunette?"

He dropped twenty pounds on the waitress's tray and leaned over his beer. "Do you think I want to be here? You aren't my favourite person."

"The feeling is mutual."

"You didn't have a fun time at the gala." "You're making assumptions. I had a brilliant time."

"You were drunk."

"So were half the guests there. Get to your point. I have work to do and you're wasting my time."

Victoria jerked her blazer over the bulge sprouting from her waistband and stared down her nose. "I was at Vivary. I plan Music in the Park every year."

Walter snort into his beer. "Not very well. You got that awful Beatles tribute band to play. Half the crowd left before they finished their first set."

"I saw your wife there."

"Impossible. That was last October. I hadn't met Angelene yet."

Victoria's lips disappeared into a magenta slash. "Not then, the other day."

Walter chugged the beer and slid the glass across the table. "Good night, safe travels."

"Hear me out."

"I've been promising to take Ang to Vivary. I haven't had time. Spread that around Taunton."

Victoria took a small sip, clicking her nails on the table. "She wasn't alone."

"You look worse than the people you spread rumours about."

"I would want to know if James was up to something."

"How do you know Ang was up to something? Did you see someone with her?"

Walter grinned at Victoria's attempt to furrow her Botoxed brow.

"There were four legs, dark hair. The ash branches were hiding his face. They were wearing grey trousers."

Walter shook his head, holding up his empty glass. "You let the whole town know Simone was out for dinner with a man. It was her cousin from Bolton. You smeared mine and Kate's names around Taunton when we went for coffee, said I was already stepping out on my marriage."

"You and Angelene didn't look happy at the gala."

"My marriage is not your concern."

"You'll thank me when the truth comes out. Grey trousers." Victoria said, snootily.

"Ms. Holloway would never have known about Pru and I snogging in the cupboard had you not opened your mouth."

Victoria finished her wine, snapped open her purse and root around the contents. She pulled out a tube of lipstick and smeared it on her lips. "This is not gossip. I know what I saw."

"Have you ever thought about writing a novel?" Walter said, pointing to his front tooth.

Victoria snapped open a compact, opened her lips and scrubbed at a lipstick mark.

"I have. A book about Taunton's scandals. I could start with Richard Cook and Geoffrey Pratt. It would be a best seller."

"The first chapter could be about a snooty little girl who intruded on everyone's lives because hers was so incredibly boring."

Victoria jammed her arms in her coat and yanked it over her shoulders. "Don't say I didn't warn you."

"We'll celebrate with Moet when the details come out. Have a safe trip home."

"Somebody was with your wife."

"Maybe it was Troy Spence." Walter took out his cell phone and scrolled through the menu of a pizza place. "Didn't you say he looked smitten? I can see the headlines now; farm boy has an affair with politician's wife. Put that in your book."

"Why you pompous…"

"Now, now Victoria, you're getting prickly again. I don't do prickly."

Victoria moved along the bench and whipped her purse over her arm. "You put me in this mood."

"God help William if he has Dr. Morimoto's daughter on all fours or Maisie's diddling in the girl's shorts. Look at your own family before you judge someone else's."

"Mark my words, Walter Pratt. Your wife is up to something."

Walter gulped back the beer, set the mug on the table, and rubbed his brow. What had ruffled Victoria's feathers? Angelene's gown? Sofia's accolades for a successful event? Whatever it was, Walter would not entertain the nonsense. He was tired and had bigger concerns than grey trousers. His wife's terrible acting.

***

Morning came at Angelene in a blaze of golden yellow and fiery orange. Her devil, wrath, woke with her and try as she might to tuck it away, wrath lingered in ribbons of scratchy, vengeful red.

"What brings you to Taunton College?"

"I need to speak to someone." "Do you need a ciggie? You're looking really agitated."

"Am I red today?"

Malcolm smiled and chuckled. "I'd say. I can feel the heat coming off you."

Angelene spotted twins getting out of a Mini. She pushed open the door and grinned, an icy, plastic smile.

"I'll only be a minute. Can you wait?"

"I'm not going to leave you. Not like this."

"When I'm done, I'll be saffron. I'll treat you to a café au lait."

Angelene scrambled from the car, blew into her cupped hands, and sniffed. The breakfast of cigarettes and wine clung to her breath.

"Excuse me."

The boys turned. Their grins were lop-sided and curious. Angelene straightened her pullover and shoulders. Wrath was giving her confidence.

"I'm looking for a girl, Rachel. She has red hair."

One boy looked at the other, shrugging. "If it's Rachel Jones you're looking for, she'll be in the building by Evans House."

Angelene tilted her head and crept closer to the boys. "What do you mean house?"

"Some students live here. There are six houses, students belong to one."

The shorter boy fiddled with his cuff and glanced at his watch. "If you want to talk to Rachel, I'd hurry. Classes are about to start."

"Non, this must be a secret. No one must know I'm here."

A group of students walked past. She dragged her hood over her head and lowered her voice. "Here's twenty pounds. Find her and tell her to come here?"

The taller of the two snickered and elbowed his brother. "Did she try to pull your man?"

"Please, I have little time."

The boys held out their hands, Angelene placed crumpled bills in each. She paced, practicing her lines. She had to be direct and firm, no hesitating. News travelled fast around schools. The entire playground at Maxime Henriet Public school had known of every lover that visited her mother before she did. Angelene glanced up from the tracks she had made in the gravel, shielding her eyes. Rachel approached, veiled in shimmery white joie de vivre. Wrath stepped aside for a new devil, envy. Rachel was whole, not shabbily stitched together. Angelene glared at the girl who had kissed Brendon, was the first to touch his skin and dive into his light. Envy and jealousy hung by wrath's side; Brendon belonged to her now.

"What are you doing here, Ms. Pratt?"

"You can't speak of this. Brendon must not know."

"It depends on what you're about to tell me," Rachel said, tugging at her kilt. "Can you make it quick? I snuck out for a ciggie the other day. The headmaster's been lurking around the laurel bushes waiting to catch me." Angelene pawed at her burning cheeks. "Stay away from Brendon."

Rachel stepped back, fumbling with the buttons on her blouse. "He's my friend."

Smoke smoldered inside Angelene. "Stay away from him. You stole his innocence."

"Are you a nutter? We had sex. He liked it."

"Leave him alone."

She could feel herself shrivelling. The wine, her inner Veronique, wrath, were tired and moving on.

"Brendon's light is weak. You'll ruin it. You'll ruin everything." Angelene sucked at her breath, her cheeks burned, her eyes stung. She ran her sleeve over her nose and tripped backwards, grasping the hawthorn branches. "Brendon was using you. You made yourself available, and he used you. Stay away from him."

Rachel flattened her tie, licking her lips. "When you use something, you throw it away. Brendon hasn't thrown me away yet."

With each passing second, Angelene could feel herself growing frail. She demanded wrath to come back. She couldn't lose Brendon, not another. Her emotions twisted, jealousy, envy, shame, and anger entwined and knotted. She pushed at her knuckles, praying the tugs would ease the constriction.

"God has given you a purpose, that disgusting thing between your legs. You're nothing but a vessel for Brendon to fill. Leave him to heal or every time you turn around, I'll be there."

Wrath scurried away; shame strangled her. She was exhausted.

Rachel held out a trembling hand. "Are you okay?"

"Don't tell Brendon I was here."

"I got it Ms. Pratt. I won't tell him."

"You mean nothing to him."

Angelene reached into her pocket and placed a cigarette in her mouth. Rachel's white shimmer had faded to foggy blue.

"Everything good?" Malcolm said.

Angelene slumped into the seat, dropping her chin. "What colour am I?"

"Gloomy grey."

"She needed to know."

"We can skip that coffee. You need to go home."

"Take me St. Georges please. I need to confess."

42 Mutterseelenallein

THE HALLS AT SCHOOL had been quiet that morning. A feeling like everyone knew a secret, and he wasn't in on it, gnawed at Brendon's gut. The person who may know why the world was upside down sat under a beech tree.

"I saw you at the bus stop. I honked, you ignored me."

Rachel kept her eyes on her notebook and tugged her cardigan over her breasts. "Can you go away? You smell brilliant and look even better."

Brendon glanced at her notebook; 'forget knuddlebär' filled half the page. Under that, a list of names. She wasn't studying, she was making a list.

"Why are you sitting by yourself?"

"It's too noisy in the dining hall. I'm trying to concentrate." She pointed to her textbook and stumbled through her words. "On natural selection and evolution." "Troy's in your class. You're studying Mendel and his peas."

Brendon dropped beside her, crossing his legs. She scooted along the grass and set her purse between them.

"Have I done something wrong?"

"You used me," Rachel said, spinning her hair into a bun.

Brendon plucked at a blade of grass, tearing it along the seam. "I thought you were okay with humping. You're my girl."

"I was a vessel for you to dump your spunk in."

Brendon tossed the strips of grass onto the lawn and stared at his feet. Where was the flirty girl who gave his tie a wank and stared at him like he was a delicious piece of cake?

"You're my friend."

"Right, a friend," Rachel said, folding her arms over her chest. "Go away, please. You're making it difficult to study."

"You're not bloody studying."

Brendon reached for her hand. She jerked it away and scanned the school grounds.

"I don't understand what I've done."

"Has Ms. Hudson started the unit on poetry and Tennyson? It's better to have loved and lost than never loved at all?"

"We're still on Tale of Two Cities. Why?"

"Tennyson is daft. Loss hurts, love hurts, and sitting here with you hurts, so go away." She searched the lawns and wrapped her arms around herself. Brendon followed her wild-eyed gaze. Had she made friends with panic and paranoia, too?

"I'll remember that when I write the essay." Brendon laid his hand on her thigh; she flinched and flicked his fingers. "Has Maggie said something to upset you?"

"No." Rachel sniffed and rubbed her finger under her nose. "If I tell you everything is fine, will you go away?"

Brendon unzipped his backpack and fished for a pack of tissues. He leaned towards her. She squirmed and ripped the tissue from his hand.

"Bloody hell, Rachel, you're not fine."

"Mutterseelenallein. I'm alone, all alone. Now, go away."

"I know you. That's not it."

"You don't know me; you know my tits and fanny." Her voice was tiny, panicky, and intense.

"You want to be a nurse. You're good at those paper things."

"Origami. Fick dich arschloch."

Brendon recalled a late-night conversation. He fumbled through things she loved and disliked. "You love Lord of the Rings. You volunteer with old people, you can't eat spotted dick because of the name."

"Do you know my favourite quote from the movie?"

"You never told me."

"Gandalf says to make the best of the time we're given. I plan to do that."

The breeze picked up, tossing leaves into his lap. It was as chilly as Rachel and did nothing to cool his heated cheeks. None of this made sense. Her breasts covered, the constant surveying of the school grounds, hair tied in a bun.

"Have you started a new list?"

"I'm starting with five. I like that number. Mum wears Chanel #5. Fabian Schar's number is five."

"I thought you were a Dortmund fan. Are you going to cheer for Troy if he joins the Newcastle defence squad with Schar?"

"I'm avoiding anything to do with Germany. Which is proving to be quite difficult," Rachel said, dabbing her nose. "Mum's swooning over Christian. There's German beer in the fridge. She made sauerbraten and spaetzle for dinner. She bought a Union Berlin jumper because Christian adores them."

Brendon pointed at number three. "Eleanor Baker. You like girls?"

"Why not? It's the trendy thing to do. Maisie McGregor said snogging a girl is brilliant."

"Finn Anand?"

"His father is from Kalimpong. I always wanted to visit West Bengal."

"Hunter Jacobson, the Hendon midfielder?"

"He posed for Nike. He's pretty in that Beckham kind of way."

"Too bad he doesn't play like Beckham." Brendon peered over her hand. "There's no number one."

"I have a number one. He's hung up on someone else and I really hope it isn't… dreckige hure."

Brendon lifted her chin; her eyelashes were shiny with tears. "I've been practicing German. I kept all the notes you made me."

Rachel jerked her chin away. "I used to hate Mondays; it was a start to another long week of school. You started back to school on a Monday. I saw you come into Latin. My heart beat so bleeding hard. I looked forward to Mondays because I got five days to spend with you."

"I didn't know you felt this way."

"You're bleeding stupid, knuddlebär."

"We're friends. You were okay with that."

Rachel's gaze darted across the lawn. "You've been using me. You made me think you liked me, that I meant something." She sniffed and ran the crumpled tissue under her nose. "You broke my heart three times."

"I was honest with you. I told you I didn't want a girlfriend."

"I keep telling myself to move on and forget about you. You always look so bleeding dishy."

"I do like you."

"You like my jubblies and arse," Rachel said, sniffling between the words. "I like you and not because you're minted or that daft contract. You talked to me, really talked to me. You were the first boy who told me I was beautiful."

Brendon ran a thumb over her cheek. She slapped his hand away and ran her tie over her eyes.

"You're my girl."

"Stop saying that. I'm not, someone else is."

"Can't we be friends?"

"No, we can't. You've broken my heart four times now."

Rachel dug in her purse and clutched a pile of ripped paper. "I did this for you." Scraps of paper scattered across his lap, the famous list, destroyed. "I was your sometimes girl. When you wanted to shag, a friend. Sometime isn't now."

Brendon scratched at his hair and stood. A lump bobbed in his throat. What was he doing? Throwing away a sure thing for someone taken?

Everything around him moved at a slower pace. The trees swayed gently; students looked like zombies trudging to classes. His cell phone beeped; Brendon stared at the message. 'Ich bin in dich verbliebt. '

He tapped his cell against his lip and turned. Rachel was gone. Nothing made sense, Rachel's edginess, the silence that had swept over the school. Brendon spotted Troy coming out of the dining hall. He sprinted across the lawn. Somebody had to make sense.

"Do you know that last word? Verbliebt?"

"I took Spanish. See ya."

"Will you stop for a minute, fuck."

Troy stopped; his jaw clenched. "I'm late for class."

"How's Charlie?"

"All she's said to me today was, see you for dinner. She doesn't even sit beside me anymore."

"It's been a strange day. My classes were quiet. Maggie is pissed off at me for making Rachel cry, since when has she cared about her?"

"Why's Rachel upset?"

"It isn't all over school? No one was placing bloody bets?"

"Like you said, the school's been quiet. It's like something blew in and stole everyone's voices."

"Rachel thinks I used her."

"You did."

"I broke her heart. I didn't think love mattered to her."

"Take it from me, it matters." Troy hung his head and walked away.

Drizzle fell from the clouds, darkening the sky. The type of love he felt for Angelene hurt. It was the kind that stings and breaks people. His mother would mourn the loss of her son, his father would disown him for ignoring the code. He'd lose Walter. This love would knock all the people he loved on their asses.

***

The day had been strange for Sofia. She had always been the one to balance the household finances, how much came in, where the money went. Receipts and credit card statements were meticulously organized. She had sorted through a handful of receipts tossed on David's desk for new linens, wallpaper she had no intent of putting up, and seven Borussia Dortmund mugs, one for each day of the week. She faintly recalled buying the items. Throughout the day, she had sniffed through Brendon's laundry basket. The strangest feeling, when Brendon walked out the door, an emptiness grew inside her, like goodbye forever. When he had arrived home and she could finally breathe, the strangeness of the day lingered. He looked like he had experienced odd and strange things, too.

"I'm glad you stayed for coffee and cake."

"I was happy you asked," Amelia said, pinching crumbs under her fork. "Tim's at the pub, Sally's with friends. Besides, I enjoy eating off these posh plates."

"You'll have to visit me in Milan," Nicola said, winking. "We'll shop on Via Dante, drink espresso." "What would our Tim do?"

"Survive, like all men do," Nicola said, gliding her spoon through a slice of zuccotto. "You need to get out of that routine of yours."

"Life is easier when you have a solid routine. Most people get bored doing the same thing day in and day out. Not me, keeps me sane." Sofia sipped her coffee and grinned. "That's why Richard hired you. He always knew where you were."

When Sofia first moved to Rosewood manor, she learned Amelia Potter was routine. Not just breakfast at eight, lunch at noon, and tea at three. Each day had its list of chores, Monday, dusting, Tuesday, laundry. She had a schedule for changing the linens and opening windows. She never deviated from her routine. Amelia was okay with her predictability; people could count on her.

"I was Collywobble manors' saving grace."

Sofia set down her cup, curled into the sofa and tugged a blanket around her shoulders. "I forgot you called the house that." "Got the shivers the first time I stepped in the foyer. I ignored it and mapped out the house so I could plan my schedule and build a routine. I was determined to bring sunshine into this home."

Nicola finished her cake and set the plate down. "The look on Richard's face every time you hummed around the house, priceless."

Amelia's cheeks lifted; she rubbed her hands together like she was hatching an evil plan. "I didn't care what Richard thought; this house was my stage, made me feel cheeky to annoy him. I enjoy taking care of people and houses, especially this one."

"We were lucky you took the job. Richard must have interviewed ten, twenty women."

"The house made people nervous," Nicola said. "Richard made people nervous."

"He was everything the town said he was, rude, haughty. I remember driving up the laneway, practicing what I would say," Amelia said, twisting her apron ties around her hand. "I pictured a fat, scowling man, expecting me to bend the knee. Richard was in full dress, ready to impress. I would have found him attractive if he weren't so miserable."

"Thirty years and not once have you deviated from your routine."

Nicola tucked a leg under her thigh and tapped her lip. "Something else hasn't changed. You fiddle with your apron ties when you're nervous."

Amelia loosened the straps and pinched her lips. "I also overreact and overthink."

Sofia shot up; the pillows dropped to the floor. She knew Amelia had been part of her strange day. The constant fluttering around the house, avoiding conversation. She hadn't sat still, not even for their usual tea and biscuit break.

"Where's Brendon?" Amelia said.

"In his bedroom, watching football and attempting his homework."

"If you have something to say about topolino, just say it. I'm going to call the house Collywobble manor again. Everyone has been acting so damn weird."Amelia wiggled in the chair and flapped her apron tie. "I ran into Victoria McGregor at Tesco"

"What was in her trolley?" Nicola said, her lips quirked into a smile. "Jaffa cakes, Cadbury mini rolls?"

Amelia stifled a laugh, clearing her throat. "She saw Angelene at Vivary Park."

"Wow, that's some news," Nicola said.

"Victoria said someone was with her. He was wearing grey trousers."

Sofia licked her lips. She had smelled Brendon's collars, lapels, t-shirts and got nothing but citrus or tuberose.

"Did she say it was Brendon?"

"I feel awful for saying these things. I love Brendon. The joy he brought me after eighteen months of sadness. I can still see him standing on the stool in the kitchen, helping me make shortbread, his little hands covered in flour."

"Amelia, please, this is no time to reminisce."

Sofia wound David's cardigan tighter around her chest. *'Breathe, just breathe,'* she commanded herself. This wasn't her. She never paid attention to gossip. She could no longer discern what was real and what was Victoria McGregor's tittle-tattle. Sofia rubbed her brow; the colliding thoughts were making her head hurt.

"I'm sorry Sofia. I've worried you again."

"Did she say it was topolino?"

"She didn't, just insinuated. It could have been anybody, really." Amelia tied and untied the apron straps. "I don't know why I listened to her. Forgive me Sofia."

Sofia propped her elbow on the armrest and leaned her cheek against her hand. "I told him to stay away."

The strange day just got stranger. It made sense, and it didn't.

***

Walter laid his hands on his desk and rolled his chair back. He was tired, hungry, and try as he might, he couldn't get the conversation with Victoria out of his head. He had spent the night mulling over the accusation, analyzing, cursing himself for wasting time on gossip. Victoria had to be wrong.

"I'm sorry for making you work late again. Can I bring you back a takeaway?"

"No, thank you, Mr. Pratt. I'm almost finished."

"No cravings today? You don't need me to grab you a kebob or roti?"

Juliette glanced up from the keyboard and grinned. "Aren't I supposed to be getting you dinner?"

"You're not my errand girl. You're holding me together."

"I appreciate the offer, but I'm on a roll here," Juliette said, turning back to her computer. "I was burping garlic and cumin after the last takeaway. Not very ladylike when you're on a date."

Walter pulled on his coat and grabbed his briefcase. "I appreciate the long hours you've put in. I can't seem to wrap my head around things."

"I'm going to finish the report, then get your diary organized. You're flying back to Scotland."

"What's on the docket this time?"

Juliette stopped typing and ran her finger over the dates. "A tour of the Hydro Group, Wings for Warriors, and Lossiemouth."

Walter sighed heavily. "All that in a day?"

"I get exhausted looking at your diary. You should go home; you look like you haven't slept."

"I don't feel right leaving you here."

"I have about fifteen minutes left, then I'm meeting someone."

"That MP I saw you chatting up in the courtyard the other day?"

Juliette's fingers tapped against the keyboard; her cheeks flushed. "I wasn't chatting anyone up. We were discussing Brexit."

Walter ticked things off his mental checklist: confident, gracious, smart. He scratched his hair and sighed; he'd give Angelene street smart. Her experience made her wise in the construction of gigantic walls.

"Thank you again," Walter said, sighing for the third time. He was becoming an expert at the sigh. "I appreciate everything you do."

"Get some dinner, go for a walk, clear that brilliant mind of yours. Oh, and say hello to my future boss."

Walter managed a thin smile and walked to the elevators. He pushed the button; the doors hissed open; he stepped inside. 'She's a lady' played softly from the speaker. He sang along, style, grace, a winner. Angelene was none of those things either. A ping and whir signalled he had hit the first floor. Walter waved to the security guards and pushed open the door. His brow furrowed, then softened. Kate stood at the bottom of the stairs of the monolithic building, fidgeting with her pendant. She was worried. Kate Miller was not a worrier.

"Come to stare at the architecture, the sculptures, Earth and Water?"

Kate adjusted her purse strap and looped her arm through his. "Burberry. I need a new suit for court."

"You're lying barrister. You're wearing the same look as Sofia. It isn't very becoming on either of you."

"I miss your smile," Kate said. "You're one of the toughest men I know. You look defeated."

"Try hungry."

"I was hoping we could grab a bite to eat."

"There's a pub on Craigs Court."

Walter watched people stroll past, on their way to somewhere or some place. If he could be anywhere, he would travel back to Paris. He would have been the one that ran, not little bird.

"Should I ring David?"

"I'd rather we were alone."

"Are you chatting me up?"

Kate grinned and nuzzled his arm. "Get over yourself."

Walter's mental checklist surfaced again: witty, intelligent, independent, inflexible.

"Victoria McGregor paid me a visit."

"Oh, god, I'm sorry."

Walter pointed his briefcase at a black lacquered door. A ceramic butler held a placard boasting the perfect gastropub experience.

"Was she gossiping again? The whole town knows Hans Larson was in the coat cupboard with Marcus Bower's wife."

Walter led Kate to a booth, away from the crowded bar. He slid across the bench and leaned his briefcase against the wall.

"She saw Angelene at Vivary Park." He picked up the menu, studying the selections. "They make a delicious burger here, serve a dish called poutine."

Kate tugged off her coat and laid it over her purse. "Poutine? Sounds interesting."

"One owner is from Montreal. It's quite popular in Canada, chips smothered in cheese and gravy. Damn good."

"I don't care about chips and gravy; I care about you and Victoria's latest tale." A young girl, her hair tied in a Vikingesque braid, approached the table. She flipped open a notepad and grinned. "Hiya, Mr. Pratt."

"Hello Kiersten. This is my friend Kate; I'll have my usual."

Kate perused the drink menu, cucumber and gin, rosewater and vodka.

"Gin and tonic, please."

"Can you bring us an order of poutine? Kate's never had it."

Kiersten scratched down the drink order, sliding the notepad in her apron. "It's moreish, you'll love it."

Kate unrolled the napkin, setting the utensils on the paper place mat. She laid the napkin over her lap, her eyes pensive. "Victoria."

"She thinks Ang was at Vivary with someone."

"Who?"

Walter shrugged and blew out an exhausted sigh. "Grey trousers, dark hair."

"Do you believe her?"

Kiersten set their drinks before them along with a steaming bowl of chips smothered in beer scented gravy.

"I don't know, no, maybe."

Kate forked a gooey pile of chips, globs of cheese oozed onto her plate. "You're a smart man. You know the stuff coming out of Victoria's mouth is half-truths."

"I took a tip from David's playbook and started calling Ang before bed. She told me she was thinking of me. Little bird does not think about me."

"Maybe she's falling in love."

"She used to tell me about her day, fill my ear with all sorts of nonsense. She tells me she's tired and needs to sleep. Ang does not sleep."

Kate squeezed the lime into her drink and stirred. "She's moody, a little bit sideways from the norm."

"I gave her a ring one afternoon; she was out of breath and giggly. Have you ever heard her giggle?"

"Victoria has made you suspicious."

"We haven't had sex in weeks. Women love having sex with me."

"I wouldn't know, would I?" Kate said, smearing a chip through a blob of gravy.

Walter washed down a mouthful with a gulp of beer. "You were the only one I couldn't get into bed." "I was a different challenge."

Walter met her gaze and ran his fingertips over hers. "You're one of my closest friends, if I lost you…"

"I'm not going anywhere. Someone needs to hold you accountable."

They dug through the bowl, dragging chips through the gravy, quietly eating. Walter stared at the last chip, then Kate and pushed it towards her.

"Do you think Angelene is seeing someone?"

"I toss the thought around, then I get pissed off at myself for letting Victoria place doubts in my head. Grey trousers."

"I own several pairs of grey trousers. How does Victoria know it was a man?"

Walter leaned over his beer and clasped his hands. "Victoria saw Ang and Troy Spence coming out of an Asian market. Taunton College's school kit, grey trousers."

"This is ridiculous. Troy is a boy."

Walter washed the sour taste from his mouth and sagged into the booth. "I'm being stupid. I'm Walter Pratt."

"You are and you're a great man." Kate clinked the ice around in her glass and sipped. "I had Victoria pegged from the moment I met her. There isn't a redeeming quality about her, always picking apart other people. Angelene is the perfect target. Look at the transformation. She's stunning."

"She's ugly inside."

Kate finished her drink and held up the glass as Kiersten whizzed past. "I'm worried about you; you know I hate to worry."

"Don't be. I'll just keep trying."

"You show up at my home drunk. You're worn out, miserable."

"Is there anything else you'd like to add to the list?"

She squeezed lime into the drink and stirred. "You're the most incredible man I've ever met."

"Tell my wife that."

"Angelene will never see you as I do."

"Thanks for the vote of confidence."

"The qualities I admire probably scare the hell out of her."

Walter spun the mug around, stopping it mid-spin. "Why did she marry me?'

Kate scraped her fork through a blob of cheese and licked the stringy glob. "You'll have to ask her that."

"I'm afraid of the answer."

"Angelene has a history with older men. She wouldn't be running around Taunton with a teenager."

Walter caught the hesitation in her voice. "Are you hiding something from me? Was there someone else in Paris I don't know about? A boy, like Troy Spence?"

"How would I know?" Kate said, setting down her fork. "All I know is what Sofia told me."

"Maybe Angelene is looking for a father figure? No wonder she won't have sex with me. God isn't judging her. I'm like a daddy."

Kate unfolded the menu, scanning it. "You're a powerful man. She's never had power. That's attractive."

"Do you think there's another man? Be honest, you see this stuff all the time."

"If she can't love one man, how could she love two?"

Walter held up his mug and wiggled it at Kiersten. "She's damaged."

"Some of the most beautiful things are full of scars and broken parts. She might be worth it."

"I have my doubts. Just like I do about the mysterious person in the park," Walter said listlessly. "Perhaps it was a woman, and Ang doesn't have the heart to tell me she fancies girls."

Kate gave him a dismissive blink. "It could have been a wave of the branch, the sun in Victoria's eyes. She has so much Botox in her face, it's eaten away at her brain. I'm surprised she isn't accusing you. You're more likely to step out of the marriage than Angelene."

Walter smiled at Kiersten and cradled the mug. "I do struggle with monogamy. I could pick out ten women right now I'm attracted to and wonder what it might be like to be with them. My willie wants one thing, my heart and head tell me to be a gentleman. I don't know how David does it."

"David knows the grass isn't greener. He does an excellent job tending his own garden."

"It helps when your wife wants tending."

"That night you called Angelene. She might have been thinking about you. Absence makes the heart grow fonder."

Walter grumbled. "Out of sight, out of mind."

"I can't picture Angelene having an affair. She was never the pursuer, men pursued her. She's timid, socially awkward."

"Someone chased after her then, paid attention to all the odd things that come out of her mouth."

Kate dunked the lime with the swizzle stick and tilted her head. "What have you done to make things right?"

Walter twirled a coaster under his finger and raised his shoulders. "Nothing."

"Hire me. Divorce her, problem solved."

"Have you ever known me to give up?"

"Then you need to pick up the pieces and love her. Stop being so stubborn. She will not come running to you. She's proved that."

"I adore you. I should have put more effort into keeping you."

"You couldn't handle a woman like me," Kate said, pointing to a picture of a Wagyu beef burger. "You said the burgers are good?"

Walter gave her hands a gentle squeeze and waved Kiersten over. "Two of the Wagyu burgers, bacon, cheddar, onions."

"Good choice, Mr. Pratt. It's nice to see you smile. It's been a while."

"I see I'm not the only one who missed your smile."

"Kiersten's a good girl. Best server in London."

"Is she one of the ten?"

Walter snort with a flimsy chuckle. "Even she's too young for me."

The smile dropped from Kate's lips. "Your project, the reassembling of Angelene, may be too big of a DIY, even for you, King Midas."

Walter stared into his beer. He believed it and doubted it. He was hopeful about the marriage and saw its demise. The suspicion and discontent had to stem from somewhere, Angelene, Victoria. There was a hardness growing in him, the fear that in another few weeks, it would spread like a tumour.

***

Angelene kneeled in the booth. She shifted from knee to knee, studied the priest's profile through the latticed window and made the sign of the cross.

"Bless me, father, for I have sinned. It has been a day since my last confession. I have a feeling, it's strong and takes my breath away. My friend says it is love."

"Do you think it is love?"

Angelene clasped her hands tighter. "I feel myself going mad with delight, fear, joy, and shame. If that's love, then I'm not sure I like it."

"Love is not a sin."

"I'm married."

She rocked on her knees; the ornate box closed around her. "I have given in to jealousy. It controlled me. I became vengeful."

"What compelled you to do this?"

"That feeling, love."

"Love is kind and beautiful."

She unclasped her hands and braced herself against the walls. "My mother said love makes you crazy and if that is what I'm feeling, then it has."

"Did you speak badly to someone?"

"I thought more horrible things than I said. She has what belongs to me." "No person belongs to anyone. Is she involved with your husband?"

Great swirls of emotion rocked her, her knees buckled, she dropped to her bottom. "It's the other way around. This girl will ruin everything."

"Say goodbye to this man, you're married, you took vows." His voice swept through the screen, shackling her.

"My husband is a powerful man." She dug her cross into her palm and rose to her knees. "I thought his power, this incredible black light, would seep into my bones and I too, would be powerful."

Angelene squeezed her eyes shut, her nose tingled. She didn't get the feeling when she was with Walter. She had hoped it would grow and fill her empty spots, repair the cracks, and give her light. It had yet to come.

"This man sees past my scars, wipes my nose, tells me stories to help me sleep. He's always there, even when I don't deserve him to be."

"I can't tell you what to do or who to choose. I can only remind you of the vows you took."

"I'm good at getting into messes. It's as natural as breathing."

"You can get out of this one. You know how."

Angelene bowed her head and gripped her cross, her mind a mess. She was too tired to clean it.

43 Once upon a time..

Dr. Weiss's waiting room was a busy, cheerful place. An enormous bay window housed plants. Sunlight bathed the room, illuminating the black and white photos of steamer trains. Children sat on the floral area rug, books, and toys at their feet. The once ostentatious Victorian townhome was as bright and smiley as Dr. Weiss.

"Brendon."

He followed the nurse up a bleach scented flight of stairs, his mind wandering. Angelene had rambled when he phoned. She spoke of her friend the rabbit and wanting to slip down the rabbit hole. The desperation she tried to hide made him miss her more.

"My son misses seeing you on the pitch. He's looked up to you since you were the mentor at the football camp. He's going to make brilliant dives like you."

"I hope to be back on the pitch soon."

Brendon removed his blazer and flopped onto a chair. The tiny room held the sharp odours of disinfectant and hand sanitizer. There were jars of cotton swabs and tongue depressors arranged from largest to smallest on the Formica countertop. Photos of trees in full bloom, a colourful cross-stitched sign exclaiming, a smile was the best medicine, hung on the milky blue walls.

"I'm going to take your blood pressure."

Brendon rolled up his sleeve and presented his arm. "Why did you want to become a nurse?"

"When someone is sick, they're at their lowest. It makes me feel good to give people the reassurance they'll be okay."

Madre Innocente whispered a name in his ear, an ache crawled into his chest. Rachel had been there. She had shared her light when he needed it. All he had done was break her heart.

"My friend is going to uni for nursing, geriatrics."

The cuff blew up around his arm in steady puffs. "She must be a special girl," she said, unwrapping the cuff. "It takes a certain nurse to work in Geriatrics. Can you step on the scale, please?"

Brendon stepped on the ancient silver contraption. Rachel was special. She was fireworks, orchids, and gone.

"What do I weigh? My coach says I'm down a few pounds."

The nurse looked from his chart to the scale and scribbled down a number. "You're down a bit. Dr. Weiss will be with you shortly."

Brendon smoothed out his tie and leaned back in the chair. Everything he loved about Angelene was the opposite of what sent his hormones into a frenzy when he thought about Rachel. Angelene was the flower shy to bloom. Rachel blazed like the scarlet pimpernels that ignited the roadside in fiery red. Maggie was sweet as a daisy. Angelene wasn't his flower to pick. She had promised to be faithful to Walter, forsaking all others until death do they part. Brendon slumped forward, burying his face in his hands. Her boy in beautiful brown light had diverted her attention. Brendon rubbed his face and sat up as the door opened. She should have said, 'till a better choice comes along.'

"Morning Brendon." Dr. Weiss plunked onto a stool; smiled and wheeled himself closer. "It's nice to see you out and about."

"I haven't enjoyed going back to school." He shivered as Weiss placed the stethoscope against his chest. "I'm happy to be at the pitch. Liam thinks I'll make a brilliant coach when I retire."

Edward wheeled the stool into the stainless-steel drawers and smiled.

"How have you been feeling lately?"

"It's hard getting up in the morning."

"Not sleeping?"

That was an understatement. He cuddled with guilt, lust, and reckless nightly. Dreams of his happily ever after were more of a nightmare.

"I have a lot on my mind."   "Like what?"

"When I'll be in net. I lost all my strikes at school, other things."

"Are you worried about leaving for Dortmund?"

"I can't wait to leave. I need to get away from mum. She's been worse since I got sick. She tells me she misses me. I haven't left the bloody house."

Edward chuckled and folded the paper over. "Sofia gives a whole new meaning to empty nest."

"Don't tell her I said that."

"It's our secret." When Edward Weiss said it was 'our secret,' Brendon knew it was as good as a pact written in blood. Weiss was the go-to when he didn't understand the ache in his testicles. Troy said his knob was frustrated and needed to release all the built-up spunk. Weiss told him it was natural. Mammina never learned about that conversation.

"Can I talk to you about something?"

Edward set the clipboard on the counter, clasping his hands. "This sounds serious."

"I've been seeing this girl. I was late showing up at her place. She went bloody crazy. She kept screaming at me, you're going to leave me. It was bloody awful."

"Those are some heavy words to throw around. What do you know about this girl?"

"I know she's had a hard life."

Edward took off his glasses, wiping them on the hem of his lab coat. "I thought you were concentrating on football and getting well."

"I love her."

A hundred tabs opened in Brendon's brain, each with a title, what he loved about A, why he should stay with A, why you don't get involved with a married woman, how to punch Uncle Walt in the gut without using a fist. He had promised to stay focused on football and while the need to get back on the pitch was intense, Angelene had taken up residence in his head and heart.

"She's married."

It sounded worse when he said it. The smile disappeared from Edward's face. Brendon reached into his shirt and held onto his cross. For the first time in a long while, Brendon prayed. This secret was bigger than aching testicles.

"How long has this been going on?"

"We were friends at first. Things got more serious."

"Are you sexually active?"

Brendon bowed his head, hiding the flush rolling over his cheeks.

"Are you using protection?" Edward's voice was formal. The smiley tone had vanished. He was all business.

"We were in the front room snogging and next thing I knew. Bloody hell, Dr. Weiss, things happen."

Brendon ran his sleeve over his face, reckless happened.

Edward spun around, yanked open a drawer, and tossed a handful of condoms. "What do you know about her sexual history?"

"I know a bit."

"You're being very irresponsible. This woman sounds like an awful lot of trouble, too much for an eighteen-year-old to deal with."

"I love her."

"She's having an affair. What does that say about her? Have you given any thought about her husband?"

He had moments of guilt, moments of anger and frustration. It was never enough to end it.

"He doesn't love her."

"Do you want my advice?"

"Not really."

"Run like you've never run before and start using condoms. Pregnancy isn't the only thing you need to worry about."

What did he know about her? She was blonde, her body was thin. He knew the pout, the scowl, the hissing, and sweetness. He knew her paintings, the books she loved.

"Are we done?"

Edward put on his glasses, reached for a pad, and ticked a series of boxes. "See Kalisha, give her this."

Brendon took the paper, a plastic cup, examining the letters and words. Sweat gathered in his armpits. "What is this? Antigen, antibody?"

"Bloodwork. Any discharges or rashes?"

Brendon's vision blurred. He reached for the examining table and steadied himself.

"Where?"

"Where do you think?"

"There isn't anything wrong with my, uh, it."

He hadn't thought about STDs or pregnancy. Parisian roulette took on a whole new meaning.

"Take a seat if you're feeling lightheaded," Edward said sternly. "I'll give you a bell."

"You won't ring mum, will you? She'll tell dad. He's so bloody smart, he'll figure it out and lecture me on breaking the gentlemen's code."

"What we talk about is our business." Edward placed a hand on Brendon's shoulder and lowered his voice. "You have opportunities millions dream of. Don't destroy it over a girl, a girl you shouldn't be involved with. Run, before it ends in disaster."

Brendon stuffed the paper into his pocket. The only place he would run to was Dortmund, and he'd be holding her hand. Brendon walked down the mint green hallway. The mixture of disinfectants nauseated him. He handed the nurse the crinkled paper and dropped onto a plastic chair.

"I'll need your arm."

Brendon fumbled with his buttons and shrugged his arm out. Cold whirred from the vents, blowing over him. The needle poked into his skin. He shivered and bit into his lip.

"Do you do these types of tests often?"

"More than I'd like," the nurse said. "I thought the kids attending Taunton College were smart."

"Apparently not."

Brendon held up the strip of condoms. The nurse rolled her eyes and pointed to the cup. "The toilets are around the corner. Aren't you that footballer everyone talks about?"

"Nope, just a stupid kid."

The farmhouse looked lonely despite a backdrop of a cerulean sky. Dr. Weiss was right, he should be running away, not walking towards her. Brendon ambled up the walkway, the scent of yellowing wisteria surrounded him. He grasped the doorknob and let himself in. His head hurt, his eyes burned, his mouth was dry. They were in love and if he had to, he'd steal her from Walter. People would have to understand. Love had made him crazy.

"Bonjour, mon amour."

Brendon collapsed on the sofa. He grinned sleepily and glanced at the drawings covering her lap.

"You've been busy."

He picked up an illustration. Winged devils dug their gnarled fingernails into the shoulders of a boy. Was it her devils clawing at him? Angelene shuffled the illustrations into a pile and lay them on the coffee table.

"I went to confession today."

"Is that why it felt like you didn't want to talk to me?"

"This is hard for me."

He was too tired to look in her eyes, too exhausted to ask her, who are you, do I really know you? Do you know we're having an affair?

"Hungry?"

"Why do you always change the subject?"

"I made flammkuchen."

Brendon undid his tie, rolled it, and shoved it into his pocket.

"What's that?"

Angelene covered her lips with her fingers and smiled.

"It's like pizza. I'll put it in the oven for you."

Her excitement over flammkuchen warmed him. She wasn't yellow, more ochre like the painted cliffs he saw on a trip to Australia, deep yellow, porous, and jagged. Brendon stretched, yawned, and thumbed through the drawings. A little girl stared out the window at a bird, soaring across an indigo sky, a crying girl clutching yards of yellow ribbons, a woman holding a girl's head under water,

43 ONCE UPON A TIME..

her mouth wide, screaming the words 'scrub, you must scrub.' A tiny pain shot through his heart; her paintings were her voice. Brendon set the drawings on the table and drooped into the pillows. Run, stay, steal her away.

"For you." She stood before him; arm outstretched, smiling a smile that said she was proud of herself.

"It looks good, smells good, too."

"I burnt the first one. A swallow distracted me; they'll be leaving for Africa soon." She set the tray on the table and nestled into the cushions. "Male swallows visit the nest of other swallows to find a mate."

"I'm a swallow swooping into Walter's nest."

He broke off a piece and took a bite. Only minutes ago, he was okay with stealing her away.

"Your light is flickering; your words are dismal blue." "I had an appointment with Dr. Weiss. He made me talk about stuff. Rachel's ignoring me. In fact, she isn't talking to anybody. I won't learn German." "Do you need to know German? Is it that important?"

Brendon pulled a piece of bacon from within the crème fraiche and nibbled it. "The coach and sporting director in Dortmund think it's important." "We'll learn together then." She helped herself to a piece, twisting a string of gruyere around her finger. "I'm half German. I should know the language. We have each other."

"Do we really? I'm a swallow sneaking into another man's nest." Brendon wiped his fingers on a kitchen towel and stared at his palm. "I've broken a lot of hearts to be with you, and I can't really be with you."

"I don't like when you're blue."

"We've got to figure this out. I can't keep sneaking around. Bloody hell, this plaster is itchy."

He reached up his sleeve, tore the bandage, and tossed it in the ashtray.

"Are you sick?"

"Dr. Weiss made me get blood work done."

"For what?"

"STDs."

"Has your doctor scared you?"

"Rachel and I always used condoms. I don't know how many partners you've had."

Angelene pushed herself into the corner of the couch. Reckless had been fun. Dodging bullets was exhilarating. It was an innocent question. Brendon regretted it. Her eyes were grey and damp.

"You make it seem like I wanted to sleep with those men. You want a number, six."

Brendon yanked down his cuff, leaned across the sofa, and wiped her eyes.

"Only two matters. I may have wanted Henri. I don't remember, we had been drinking, and I was scared. You're the other." "Walter is your husband. Sex with your husband matters."

"We've had sex three times." She twisted his shirt around her hands and licked her lips. "Walter thinks he's some sort of messiah. He gasped when he saw my scars. Pierre had to pop a little blue pill. He always wore a condom. He said I had a devil's snatch. I remember every time. Gustav covered my mouth. Douchette grunted like a pig. Pierre was more disgusted than I was. Six men, four don't count." "I didn't mean to make you cry. Dr. Weiss put all this stuff in my head. I got scared." "I'll get tested."

Brendon laid out along the sofa; his feet dangled off the armrest. Angelene pressed herself against him. He kissed her forehead and ran his thumb over her cheek. The fire crackled, forked flames danced frantically around the logs. He would spin the revolver one more time and pray the chamber was empty.

"Are you sure you're coming to Dortmund?""Roman passed through Dortmund once. He said the stadium was like a church, full of worshippers."

"You'll be one of those worshippers."

She slipped her fingers inside his shirt. Brendon quivered. Winter clung to her fingertips.

"It's a beautiful thought, sitting among the congregation, a sea of black and yellow."

"What else will we do?"

"We'll visit the Bridegroom's Oak, put letters inside, wait and see if anyone responds."

Brendon grinned sleepily, lulled by her touch.

"We'll follow Hansel and Gretel's trail of breadcrumbs and protect each other from witch Veronique."

"She really gets around."

"In more ways than one." Angelene's lips tickled his as she spoke. "We'll eat pretzels outside Kölner Dom. Henri loved that cathedral. Oh, and Neuschwanstein Castle, we must see it."

Brendon cradled her cheek. The story in her eyes differed from the childlike wonder in her voice. He couldn't tell if it was shame, sadness, guilt or all three mingled in the grey and green.

"Roman loved Rothenburg ob der Tauber. He said it was like stepping into a fairy tale. Lake Constance, to Flower Island, visit the Schmetterling Haus and Schloss Mainau."

Hope was a powerful feeling. His mother had hoped Dortmund would forget about the wonder kid from Taunton. His father hoped for a chess playing scholar. Angelene dangled hope in front of him and it hurt. He didn't see any hope in her eyes.

"Dortmund won't be so lonely if you're with me."

"You won't be lonely. 80,000 fans will adore you and, the girls. They'll wait outside Signal Iduna Park waiting for a glimpse of you."

"I don't want any girl but you."

Brendon tightened his arm around her. She wound a leg over his thighs.

"Quiet, exhausting, Angelene?"

"I like that your quiet, it keeps me guessing what's going on in your head. I like how your body fits perfectly against mine, how you pause and think before you speak. You nibble your lip when you're thinking."

"You've noticed all that?"

"I notice a lot about you. You have a heart-shaped bum."

Angelene giggled and dropped her head against his chest. Brendon rested his chin on her head. It sounded wonderful touring Germany together.

"What are you going to do about Walter?"

The giggle faded; she kept her face buried. "I told you. I'll fly into Paris and take a train."

"It's not that simple. You can't run away, you're married."

"I've already run from Walter."

"We have to come up with a plan."

"How will I get money? Walter gives me money for groceries, not much more."
"I'll buy the bloody tickets before I leave."
"Will I escape in the night? Wait until he's in London and have him come home to an empty house."

Brendon searched her face; her eyes were wild and frantic.

"You'll get Malcolm to drive you to Heathrow and fly straight to Germany. Fuck the train."

"Your light is flickering."

"I'm getting frustrated. You could be bloody honest and say you're leaving. You could ask for a fucking divorce."

She pulled her hand from his shirt, rolled off the couch, and walked to the window.

"It will destroy Walter. He doesn't like to fail."

"Staying with him will destroy you."

His cell phone buzzed. Brendon grabbed it from his pocket and stared at the screen. Mammina.

"You need to go. Sofia will be worried."

"She's getting better."

"She looks like someone has ripped her heart out."

Brendon followed the curve of her spine to her shoulder blades that jutted out from beneath her thin t-shirt. He pushed himself up, dizzy, dangling from hopes' noose.

"Please come to Dortmund. All I want is to wake up with you and have a cup of coffee."

"With schneeballen?"

"What the bloody hell is that?"

"Snowballs. Roman loved them. We can get some when we visit Rothenburg."

"We can eat all the snowballs you like."

"Henri said it was a fitting pastry for a girl as cold as winter."

Brendon swallowed her in his arms and kissed her. "I'll call you before I go to sleep."

"Will you tell me a story?"

"I'll tell you about this boy who goes to Dortmund and waits, every bloody day, at the train station for his girl to come."

"Even the darkest night will end, and the sun will rise."

"Let me guess, Victor Hugo."

"Oui, Les Misérables."

"Remember how strong we are in happiness and how weak he is in misery."

"Tale of Two Cities," Angelene said.

"It's an appropriate quote, don't you think?"

"It fits us."

Brendon stole one last kiss and jingled his car keys. "You asked me once what my favourite colour is. It's blue."

Brendon could feel his insides sink. The pain in his chest came back. Something in her eyes told him all the wonderful words weren't true. Trust was as heavy as hope.

"Topolino."

Brendon tucked his thoughts away, dried his weeping insides and pasted on a smile.

"Hey Nonna. I expected to see mum, she's been texting."

"You were supposed to text after your appointment. She's worried sick. I made her get in the bath. You're flushed."

Detective Mastrioni was on the case of the missing boy. He hadn't thought of an excuse. The story needed to be good and believable.

"Come to the kitchen. I'll reheat your lunch."

The last thing on Brendon's mind was food. He had barely touched the flammkuchen.

"I have to get ready for the match."

Nicola persisted. "Humour an old lady."

"You're not old Nonna. Rachel told you so."

"What happened to Rachel?"

He followed Nicola into the kitchen, slumped onto a stool and ran through the things he needed to do to outsmart detective Mastrioni. Keep his feet still, blink, watch his breathing.

"I saw Rachel yesterday. She's fine."

He didn't know what happened to Rachel. She had gone from hot to cold overnight.

Nicola set down a plate of tagliatelle and poured milk. "Maggie, Rachel. How many girls do you have on the go?" She placed the glass beside his plate, leaned into the counter, and twisted her pearl necklace around her fingers. "It isn't nice to lead girls on, topolino."

"I'm not leading anyone on. They all know I want nothing serious right now."

Nicola's glittering eyes transfixed him. He wasn't playing Parisian roulette anymore. She held the gun.

"I bumped into Rachel."

"When?"

"I was at the butcher shop on Riverside Place. Rachel was coming out of La Belle Boudoir, cigarette in one hand and lingerie in the other." Nicola unwound her necklace from her fingers and crossed her arms over her chest. "She was on her way to the corner shop to pick up milk and Smarties. She told me you like the blue ones."

Brendon shifted on the stool, downed his milk in two gulps.

"Most mothers wouldn't want a girl like that around their son. I liked her." She grabbed his glass, rinsed it, filled it with water and slid it across the island. "You used her."

Brendon undid a button, releasing the heat that was gathering under his shirt. She knew something.

"You're sweating."

"Bloody hell, Nonna, I feel like I'm on trial."

"I expected Gianni to run all over Milan, a different woman in his bed, not you."

"Did she tell you I used her?"

"She was breaking at the seams to tell me something. There was something she wanted me to hear."

Brendon ate another bite and forced it down with water. "I will not discuss Rachel with you. She's just a friend."

"Alessandro is my friend; I'm not sleeping with him. I feel for Rachel."

"Well, don't. She's a tart. She was probably buying lingerie for her number two."

"Brendon David Anthony." Nicola's eyes flashed as bright as the obsidian in his pocket. "Rachel is stuck on you, you hurt her."

Brendon pushed his plate away. He picked up the glass and ran it over his heated cheeks. "Rachel has never fallen for anybody. I didn't think she would fancy me like that."

Nicola straightened her collar, her sharp eyes fixed on his. "What is it about that girl?"

"Bloody hell, Nonna, I do like Rachel. I'm all mixed up right now."

"Not Rachel. Ms. Pratt."

Brendon gripped the napkin; his palms were sweaty, his leg wanted to bounce. He developed the nervous habit at school to help soothe him when class got stressful. He had to sit still and keep eye contact, no matter how fierce her look.

"What does Ms. Pratt have to do with this?"

"You've been with her. You stink of her perfume and that awful incense she burns."

"We're friends, just like you and Alessandro."

"That girl does not know how to be friends with men."

Beads of sweat trickled down his spine. He had to make it seem innocent, a lonely girl and a boy willing to be her friend.

"She doesn't know anybody. I check in on her like dad and Walter asked."

"Her ex-lover was a married man. She was involved with his son, too."

Anger welled inside him, sparks zipped and whirred.

"Uncle Walt's ex belonged to the IRA. Richard had ties to the Russian mafia. You imagine all sorts of stuff."

Nicola took his plate and scraped it into the compost bin. "Should you be calling Walter, uncle?"

"We're friends, that's it."

"She had another lover; he was married too. The man went crazy, lost everything. Pierre Piedmont's son ended his life. Do you see a pattern here?"

Brendon chugged his water and ran his arm over his mouth. He did, he created a new one, pink, yellow and brown.

"You should consider becoming a PI."

"Who is Angelene married to?"

"Walter."

"How has Walter treated you?"

"Like a son."

It stung to say the words. All the years Brendon felt shunned by his father, Walter was there. Daddy number two.

"That man loves you. He held you before your father did. He boasted around town a footy star had been born."

The ugly shadow of guilt left Brendon's body and hovered over him, held him down, tied the thirteen knots.

"Are you involved with Angelene? If you are, topolino, end it."

"I'm not involved with Ms. Pratt."

Nicola walked across the kitchen, perched on a stool, and took his hands. "Everyone touched by Angelene has died, run, or lost their minds. Look at your Uncle Walter. He isn't the same man. If something happens to you, I'll kill her." Nicola leaned across the island and tightened her grip. "You saved this family. Stay away from Angelene."

'Hold her gaze,' Padre Diavolo whispered. *'She knows too much.'*

"I'll stay away."

"I won't tell you again," Nicola said sharply. "The girl is dangerous."

Brendon tugged his hands free and chuckled. "Dangerous? She doesn't come out of her shell long enough to do any damage."

"I'm not talking physically. Angelene is needy, unpredictable. She's the type of girl who gets stuck in your head. She makes you feel you need her forever. Angelene Hummel does not give forever."

"I'm just her friend."

It hurt to call her that. Why did she have to be a secret? Why did Walter have to find her first?

"Angelene is damaged. Walter doesn't have enough magic in his golden fingertips to put her back together."

Brendon stood and kissed her cheek. "Just friends."

Bullet dodged and if he had to keep dodging them until he made it to Dortmund, he would. Brendon walked across the foyer and hauled his backpack over his shoulder. His body was heavy, weighed down by Angelene's plans to discover Germany and his Nonna's suspicion. Brendon stopped at the landing; light flooded the hallway.

"Why are you in here?"

Sofia glanced up from the Winnie the pooh clutched in her arms. "Something is different about you."

"I'm tired. My head hurts."

"That's not it."

"If you weren't sitting in this bloody room, you wouldn't be thinking these daft things."

"Maybe it's selfish of me to expect you to be the boy you used to be."

Brendon slumped under the weight of his backpack. He was different. He had fallen in love with the devil. Every time he came up for air, Angelene drowned him with words coated in honey. He loved the woman that was destroying him. Her destruction made him feel alive. He had changed. He was in love.

"My head's a little jumbled. I usually feel that way after school."

Sofia laid the bear on the pillow and touched its bead nose. "It isn't fair. God keeps taking from me. What have I done that was so bad He has to take the things I love?"

"God hasn't taken me. The pressure is back. I'm trying to keep my head above water, so I don't end up back in bed."

Brendon dropped his backpack. Shadows flickered in every corner; the scent of damp earth overwhelmed him.

"I miss that boy who rushed around the house, the boy who told me everything. You're hiding things from me. Things are happening, but I can't make sense of it," Sofia said. "I don't want to say goodbye. I don't want you to go to Dortmund."

Brendon stepped deeper into the room. He glanced nervously from the bookcases to the collection of glittering rocks and specimens of wood. Goose pimples prickled his skin.

"It's never goodbye, mammina. It'll be see you at international breaks and Christmas." "I won't be able to hold my breath that long."

A chilly draught wound around Brendon's legs. He shuddered. "Can we get out of this room? I shouldn't be in here. The ghost wants me out."

43 ONCE UPON A TIME..

"I ate a pretzel when mum and I were in Somerton. I don't know how people eat them. It's all dough and salt, no cream or sugar. You're like that now, just dough, twisted into something I don't recognize."

Brendon reached for her hand, helping her off the bed. He grabbed the key from within the duvet and led her from the room.

"When I think about you running through the house leaving a trail of grass, I get angry it won't happen anymore. That trail always led me to you."

"I'll bring home grass from Signal Iduna Park and sprinkle it across the foyer. That pitch is one of the best in the Bundesliga."

"I wandered through the house for years, wondering where he went. He couldn't have just vanished, he had to be somewhere. I'm doing it again, searching for you, listening for the tap of your cleats. You're not my boy, you've changed. I don't care how selfish it is of me. I want him back."

Brendon kissed her cheek and gave her his best dimpled grin. "I'm fine."

"I must call your father. He's changed too."

Brendon kicked his backpack towards his room. He would dodge as many bullets as he had to.

***

Streams of sunlight pierced the clouds, warming the grass. Maggie blew her bangs from her eyes and dropped the 'supposed to be a scarf' onto her lap. She watched Charlotte's fingers hook and loop a chain of stitches like she had been born with needles for fingers. It had taken Maggie a week to complete a tangled row.

"Have you seen Rachel today?"

"The slag had the nerve to add Troy to her list."

Maggie unwrapped a Starbar and broke it in half. Caramel oozed from under a layer of chocolate. She twirled the sugary strands around the bar and passed it to Charlotte.

"They're making plenty of bets. Someone said she was pregnant. Gemma heard she caught one of those nasty tart infections. William mentioned someone gave Jude and Jaden twenty pounds to find her."

Charlotte chomped the candy bar in two bites. "Ask the twins."

"They won't talk, said they were sworn to secrecy." Charlotte set down her needles and cracked open a can of Fanta. "Remember, at the end of last term, that girl showed up and threatened to hang her by her hair if she didn't stay away from her boyfriend."

Charlotte passed Maggie the can. She took a sip and passed it back. "I almost put two pounds on Brendon being the culprit. He's good at breaking hearts."

Charlotte pushed the can into the grass and rubbed under her nose. "You didn't sniff or bite your lip when you mentioned his name."

"I get a little itch in my nose. Heartbreaker or not, Brendon is the dishiest boy in Taunton, or would that be your little crumpet?"

"Troy Alexander is a wanker. I'm glad he has a match this afternoon. I'm sick of him asking for a kiss."

"He hasn't been your little crumpet for a while."

"He's Troy Alexander." Charlotte picked up her needles and yarn. Click, clack filled the air. "He kept things from me."

Dizziness attacked Maggie; she had seen fingers move like that.

"You're not being nice, going round for supper and sitting with Callum, who really is a younger version of Troy."

Maggie couldn't take her eyes off Charlotte's hands. It was no longer the speed keeping her mesmerized. It was the weaving, in and out.

"We agreed to always tell each other everything."

Maggie stuck her thumbnail in her mouth. Brendon had kept things. "Can't you just pinch his nipples and get over it?"

Charlotte glanced up from the ribbon of stitches. Her hands moved rhythmically as she spoke.

"Troy has lovely nipples. They're small and pert. I couldn't pinch them; it would give me the tingles."

"I feel bad for Rachel and Troy."

"You're such a sweet little muffin. Troy Alexander must realize he can't keep secrets." Maggie shoved the wrapper into her purse and frowned. "It's not like Troy kissed Ms. Pratt. He didn't cheat like Brendon."

"I know he thought about it. He made that daft Charlie face whenever he spoke about her. That's cheating."

Maggie stared at Charlotte's fingers. Dinner at Rosewood manor, the wedding party, Angelene's fingers had weaved in and out. Rachel had constantly looked over her shoulder, hurrying from class to class like someone was chasing her. Maggie gasped and tore at her fingernail.

"Ms. Pratt."

"I don't want to talk about her anymore. Every time you mention her name, I think about Troy, and I don't want to."

"What did Rachel look like in psych?"

"She had her hair in a bun and not a stitch of makeup. She looked pretty without all that gunk on her face."

"Not her appearance, her. Did she seem scared or nervous?"

Charlotte finished a row and stared at Maggie. "She looked like a girl who had her heart broken. Poor wee tart."

"Maybe someone did show up and threaten her." A muffled ping came from within Charlotte's purse. She plucked her phone from the mess of makeup and hair products, staring at the screen. "Troy Alexander loves me, poor sod." She tossed her phone on the grass and chugged the Fanta. "It wouldn't surprise me, the way she's been moving through her list."

"I overheard Tilly bad-mouthing Rachel; she broke the number one tart rule, love them and leave them, Rachel stopped at Brendon."

Maggie's mind cycled through the excuses Brendon had told her, the missed phone calls, the distance he had put between them. If Ms. Pratt fancied Brendon, Rachel was a threat. The strange day at the garbage bins. There had been a terrible fear in Angelene's eyes, like she was desperately clinging to someone.

"I'll be right back."

"Where are you going? If Troy texts again, I'll need you."

Maggie dug in her pocket and clutched five pounds.

"I have a bet to place."

***

43 ONCE UPON A TIME..

Smoke swirled around Angelene's head; ash dripped onto her bare feet. She was part secretive turquoise, her other parts sad black. God was not happy. He had been giving her the silent treatment for days. She tried to break the pattern, boy finds her, boy forbidden, vow to stay away, break the promise. Henri had started that pattern. Angelene ran a hand over the tiny pulses aching in her thighs, sugary sweet, out of the blue Henri. Anguish burned in her chest; her love had strangled him; his goodbye was forever. Life in Germany sounded wonderful. Coffee together, a kiss before he left for training, adventures through Bavaria and North-Rhine Westphalia. Normal things, dinners together, going to the market, making love. Angelene stared at the ceiling. Who was she fooling? She didn't do normal; it didn't come naturally to her; Walter was miserable. She had pissed on her vows. Maybe Walter was in love, and she was his crazy. Angelene lifted her camisole and traced along a faint pink scar.

"This one was for you, Douchette."

She pinched the pink wrinkle of skin. Her throat and nose itched with tears. "This was for you, Gustav." Angelene pulled at her skin and gazed at a scar running alongside a blue vein. "This was for Roman. That was the hardest goodbye."

Angelene ran the camisole over her nose. Her entire life was written in the map of criss-crossing lines. One for Paolo, one for Veronique, two for shame, three for Walter. One for all the frightening emotions Brendon made her feel. Angelene gripped the cushion. A scream ripped through her throat. She uncurled her fingers, her chest starving for air. She breathed through the bits of stuck scream. Turquoise seeped from her body, replaced by smudged yellow, red, and grey. It smeared across her skin and stained her insides. The story Brendon told her dripped from her memory, covering her with sludgy sadness.

Once upon a time, there was a boy who waited at the train station every day for his girl to arrive. The boy had moved from his home in England and could still hear his mother crying. Bring back my boy, please don't take my boy.

Angelene pulled her cardigan tighter around herself and nestled onto the window bench. She lay her cheek against the glass; the sun had dipped behind the trees; painting the bark gold. Her whole life had been once upon a time.

Once upon a time, there was a little girl who lost her mother. She had no fairy godmother to protect her. The big, bad wolf, Douchette, had plans for the girl. He would look after her. He was crazy in love.

Angelene splayed her fingers across the glass. She could see the cows plodding across the field. *Once upon a time there was a man who smelled of brandy tobacco, and edelweiss. The man loved little bird and wanted to be her father. The evil queen Veronique was jealous of his attention to little bird and chased him away.*

Patterns and, once upon a time, summed up her life. There had been no glass slipper, no kiss to wake up the sleeping princess, just walls of thorns, poison apples and evil queens. Angelene brought her knees to her chest. Her limbs prickled and numbed. She shrank as far into the corner as she could.

Have faith, little bird. The reason a bird can fly, they have faith in their wings. Yours will come, little bird.

Angelene dug beneath a stack of books, gripped her cell phone, and tapped in the number.

"Lisette."

"It seems like forever. How are you?"

"I'm feeling numb. Can you fly to Taunton?"

Lisette's sigh blew like a winter wind. "What kind of trouble have you gotten into?"   "I haven't heard from God in a while."

"The last time I heard you say that, was before you married Walter."

"I'm questioning things Lisette. My faith, my life, my marriage."

"You should have listened when I told you to wait for the man who was supposed to love you. Remember, he wouldn't be married or cruel or ask you to become something you're not."

"I wouldn't need wine, cigarettes, or sharp things. I would have my Prince Charming."

"You had your prince, the boy who drew you castles."

Muddled colours smeared and smudged her insides.

"Are you there, Angelene?"

"Yes, and no. My brain won't shut off Lisette. I've prayed for silence."

"Ask Walter to fly you home, get away from whatever mess you've created."

Angelene stared at her palm and traced her heart line. "Do you believe in love?"

"Love is powerful. All your scars would heal if you let love in."

"Love makes you crazy. Henri proved that. Mother was delirious with every man."

"Corinthians 13:13 says three things will last forever: faith, hope, and love. Tell me the truth. Are you in love with another man?"

Angelene clutched her cross. "I'm not sure what this feeling is. It's sweet, pink, comforting brown and wrong."

The door creaked. She heard shoes drop to the floor and the rattle of keys on the table.

"Angelene, you'll never guess what happened."

"Is that your Prince Charming? Angelene, are you there?"

"I must go."

"I'm going to call you tomorrow; this conversation is not done."

Angelene stared at Brendon. His cheeks were pink, knees grass stained, his smile dimpled and bright. His light burned her.

"The ref let me play. William buggered his shoulder at the end of the first half. Liam told the ref he had to put me in. Troy was bloody brilliant; the fans were cheering. We won, 2-0."

"You're still in your kit?"

"I was so excited. I had to tell you." Brendon walked to the sink, grabbed a glass, filled it with water and gulped. "I played bloody great. The dragons are back."

'And I'll slay them.'

Angelene slid off the window bench, took his hand and tugged him towards the stairs. "We're having a bath."

"Do I smell bad?" Brendon said, sniffing his jersey. "I have that after a match smell. Most girls find it bloody brilliant."

"I need the water. I'm messed up today."

"I haven't had a bath in years. I used to run away from mum, up and down the halls, completely naked. She had a habit of interrupting mine and Paddington's football matches."

"I need this. I need you."

Angelene led him down the hall. Brendon stood at the threshold and shook his head.

"No way, that's Walt's room. I felt bloody awful the last time."

"It is a bathtub; it's made for two."

She let go of his hand, continued into the bathroom, and spun on the taps.

Angelene lifted his jersey and pressed her lips against his chest. "Your skin tastes salty."

She demanded her lungs to breathe and her thoughts to clear. Her lungs ignored her; the whirlwind of thoughts slowed. She dropped her clothes to the floor, sunk into the water, and gazed at his back muscles. The tingle prickled her thighs. She filled a cup with water and poured it over his head. Rivers of water snaked down his back. She squirted shampoo into her palm and moved her fingers through his hair. The colour changed from melted chocolate to espresso.

"Can we bathe together in Dortmund?"

"Every night."

Angelene rinsed his hair and laid her cheek against his back, trying to synchronize her breathing with his. Her lungs struggled; her eyes stung.

"Once upon a time, there was a girl who fell in love with a boy. God forsake her. Lucifer wept for her." Water lapped against the sides of the tub. Angelene leaned back and drew Brendon between her legs. "The girl had a magic mirror and everyday she would say to the mirror, mirror, mirror on the wall who deserves love most of all. The mirror replied, you do, little bird."

"Are you cold? You're shivering."

"Can we lie together? I need you to warm me."

"In Walter's bed?"

Angelene stood and tore a towel from the vanity. She ran it over her body and patted Brendon dry.

"It's just a mattress and sheets. His scent isn't there. I need your light."

Angelene draped the towel over the toilet and walked to the bed. She laid on the mattress, a gasp slipped from her mouth, she clung to his neck, ran her fingers through his hair. Fairy tales, faith, love, sprang from all corners of her mind, twisting, weaving, smudging the colours until they were empty black. His kisses lulled her aching parts. She flew, soaring through golden yellow and blue. Her wings carried her through clouds, away from her scars and sad memories. Angelene held him tighter and buried her nose in his neck. Her eyes darted to the door, she spiralled from the sky.

"Brendon, the fairy tale is over."

44 Thirteen Knots

"Angelene, what's the matter?"

Brendon rolled over, clutching the blankets around his waist.

"All be damned, Victoria was right."

"Uncle Walt, bloody hell, I can explain."

The smile dissolved from Walter's face. "You tripped and fell into bed with my wife. I'll leave you to dress."

Brendon gripped his chest. Shots fired.

"What are we going to do?"

"Go home before he gets angry."

"He's livid. You can see it in his eyes."

Brendon crawled from beneath the blankets, a sick feeling stirred his insides. He fumbled into his kit. Angelene wore a look like she had expected this to happen. Brendon kissed her forehead, the noose tightened, he dangled from the gallows.

"I love you."

Angelene rolled to her side and curled into a ball. The urge to throw her over his shoulder, blankets, and all, tingled in his limbs. There was no getting out of this. Guilt and shame would follow them to Dortmund.

"People will understand. We went about it the wrong way, but it's love. It makes you do crazy things."

"Please go."

The noose tightened; he couldn't clear the sour taste from his throat.

Walter's voice, calm and colourless, drifted up the stairs. His heart clunked slowly; his legs wobbled. He could only hope Walter, the winner, would be too embarrassed to admit his wife was a cheat. Brendon glanced towards the kitchen. '*Go to Walter, beg, admit he's in love, run.*' He needed his brain to slow down. He had to get a grip on what happened so he could crawl out of the mess with only minor damage. Brendon chuckled; damage done.

"How could you?"

Brendon stumbled backwards. His backpack and school uniform fell from his hand. He touched the sting on his cheek, staring wide eyed at Sofia. Play dumb, act innocent? Lie and say it was Rachel or Maggie.

"Walter loved you like a son."

Brendon wiggled his jaw. His parents didn't believe in spanking. They would take his football away, no highlights, a firm talking to. His mum had a decent right hook.

"What's your father going to say?"

"I can explain." Sofia glanced up from her reddened palm. He wasn't sure if she was going to burst into tears or smack him again.

"You have changed. You aren't my boy."

"Are you going to cut off your arm? You said you would do that if you hit me."

His mind switched from the sting on his cheek to Angelene. Walter was calm angry. There was no knowing what he might do. He was surprised, he had walked out of the house unscathed. *'I pulled the trigger. I destroyed Walter. Walter will get over the hurt. He doesn't love her. There will be another woman to take her place, someone confident, less complicated.'*

Brendon sagged into the umbrella stand, dizzy. Questions swirled around his head. What if she stayed with Walter and tried to make it work for the fourth time? He'd fight for her; would she fight for him? Did she really love him? Would she come to Dortmund?

"Don't you see what you've done?"

"I love her."

"She isn't yours to love."

"Walter doesn't bloody love her."

"And that gives you the right? How long have you been involved with Angelene?"

Brendon pondered the question, emotionally or physically, as friends or lovers? "Since the day I met her."

"You were a good boy until she came along. Have you had fun acting out?"

"I should have fought to stay in Dortmund. I should have left when I was sixteen. Dortmund wanted me. Dad bloody didn't."

"That's not true. It was me who couldn't let you go."

"You should have. None of this would have happened."

Sofia stared at him with piercing eyes. "Don't you dare blame me for this."

"This is fucked."

"Make me understand and please don't say love. There are reasons Walter hasn't grown to love her."

Sparks flickered and tingled. Walter would never love her; she'd never be the woman he expected her to be. She'd always be awkward and frustrating. There wasn't an ounce of a socialite or elegance in Angelene Hummel.

"You can't help who you fall in love with."

"No, you can't but, if they are already spoken for, you move on."

"I tried to be her friend. I couldn't."

"I told you to stay away. Angelene is dangerous, she gets her, feel sorry for me claws into you and you can't get her out of your head. She drives people mad. Look at Walter," Sofia shivered. "You'll end up like Henri Piedmont... You should have known better. I can't say the same for Angelene. I'm not sure she knows what it takes to have a healthy relationship of any kind."

Out of the corner of his eye, Brendon watched his father drive around the fountain and into the carport. He heard the slam of the car door and heavy footsteps. The door opened and banged against the wall; air rushed out of him under his father's grip.

"What the bloody hell are you doing?"

"You're going to pack. I've booked you a flight on Sunday." David said, dragging him up the stairs.

Brendon struggled free, ducking as David flung a suitcase from the closet. Clothes flew in every direction.

Sofia scooped up an armful of shirts, charging past David. "I told you no."

"Walter may want to work on his marriage. He won't be able to with him around."

"You're not sending my son away."

"Can you both bloody stop. I can't stand the two of you fighting."

David tore the garment bags from the rack and tossed them into the room. "You should have thought about that before you fucked my friend's wife."

Sofia dropped the clothes, her chest heaved, she fled the room. The sound of Sofia crying reached inside Brendon and tore at his heart.

"You could have had your pick of women and you chose Angelene," David said, kicking his way through the mess of clothes. "This will be all over town if it isn't already. Your mother and I will have to live with this every day."

"Are you worried about your reputation?"

"I couldn't give a damn what people think of me. It's you I'm concerned about."

Brendon smirked; childhood hurts rode on the fiery sparks. "You don't give a shit about me. The only time you do is when I fuck up."

"You have no remorse or guilt?"

"Remorse, no. Guilt, yes." Brendon grabbed a hoodie from within the mess of clothes and tugged it on. "Walter doesn't give a shit about her. He's hit her, changed her, forced himself on her. Did your friend tell you that?"

David unzipped the suitcase and shoved clothes inside. "Do you remember the Gentlemen's code?"

"How could I forget? You've been slamming it down my bloody throat for years."

"Any girl," David said, releasing an armful of clothes onto an ever-growing mountain. "All I asked was you finish school, be a decent man. You cheated on Maggie, you've used Rachel Jones and now you love another man's wife. You've broken every rule in the code."

Sparks exploded and seared, rupturing Brendon's insides.

"I never wanted to play chess or the bloody piano. You've tried to replace him with me. It didn't work out for you, did it? I'm a goalkeeper, not a fucking academic. I'm not bloody Ethan."

***

Sofia swallowed a mouthful of brandy. Brendon ended the relationship with Maggie, tossed Rachel aside, the perfumed sheets. She cursed herself for being a fool. Sofia drank another mouthful and gazed at the photos on the mantle. Her heart swelled, filled her chest, and cut off her breath. She never wanted a girl, not that she would have loved a daughter any less. She needed a boy. A strong, beautiful boy with dark hair and dark eyes. She had gotten her wish; she didn't think it would turn out like this.

"I wish I could have slowed time and kept Brendon as a boy a little longer."

"I said the same thing, gattina, when you accepted David's proposal and told me you were going to be the queen of Rosewood manor."

"Angelene touched him, like she did Henri Piedmont. She got to him."

Nicola moved across the sofa and touched Sofia's hand. "How exciting it must have been, sex with Taunton's hero."

Sofia shut her eyes and gulped the brandy. She gripped the edge of the sofa to stay upright. There were no answers to the questions clashing about in her head.

"Angelene doesn't have sex with Walter. Why did she choose my son? He's my life. He's the reason I could live," Sofia said, her voice trembling. "Oh, God, mum, Henri Piedmont loved her and took his life. What if Brendon... Oh, God."

The glass slipped from her fingers; she fell into Nicola's arms.

"It won't happen to topolino."

"Do you think Angelene caused his illness? She couldn't save Henri Piedmont. She used Brendon to make amends with God."

"Always pointing the finger at Angelene. That little bastard is as much to blame."

Sofia pulled away from Nicola. She stared at the disgust and rage darkening David's face. She never knew David to be an angry man. He was the kind of man who called her lovely, who showed her off to Taunton as his partner. She would marry him again and again. Not this man. She didn't know the man standing before her.

"I spoke to Lukas. Dortmund wants him so bad; they can damn well have him."

"I'm not happy with topolino either. Don't send him away. Don't do this to Sofia." David walked to the liquor cabinet and poured a scotch. "He's going."

"Don't take my son," Sofia said, desperate tears spilled down her cheeks. "Please, I'll see he finishes school. He'll never leave the house, no football."

"I don't want him in my home," David said firmly. "Have you considered Walter?"

Nicola picked up the glass and set it on the table. "Angelene seduces men and makes them fall in love with her. Awful things happen. Look at Walter, the Piedmont's, your son."

David tossed back the scotch and chuckled. "Do you know how ridiculous you sound? Angelene is not a seducer. Hell, she doesn't even touch her own husband. You're both trying to justify Brendon sticking his damn penis in my best friend's wife."

Nicola raised her chin and pressed her shoulders into the sofa. "I confronted Angelene. For a woman who doesn't know how to love, she was certainly feeling something for Brendon."

Sofia dug into her pocket and pulled out a wrinkled tissue. She dabbed her eyes, twisting the tissue in her hand. "Ever since Angelene has come into our lives, it's been nothing but turmoil, running after her, protecting her, sheltering her."

David slammed the glass down and laced his arms through his suspenders. "You're acting like Brendon is the victim."

Rage burned Sofia's insides; her world was crumbling around her. She had spent years creating the perfect home and the perfect family. It was falling apart.

"Have you not seen the way Angelene is? She was all over you in Burnham." "I've seen a meek little girl," David said, his voice flat.

Sofia stood and paced. She couldn't lose her son, not yet. She wasn't ready to let him go. There was a party planned for July. Then she would fly with him to

Germany, see him off with a hug, tour Dortmund to know he'd be safe. She had an itinerary set, visit the stadium, drink a beer at the Züm Alter Markt. Sofia grabbed a photo of Brendon. Rage puddled at her feet.

"Angelene is to blame. All those pathetic stories. Brendon would have listened. He would have been kind. Isn't that part of the code?"

"I asked Brendon to check in on her, not sleep with her."

Sofia cradled the photo against her throbbing heart. "You never wanted him. That's why it's so easy for you to send him away."

"I wanted you to wait. There's a difference," David said. He collected the glasses and sighed. "If you'll both excuse me, I'm going to call Walter and apologize again."

"Brendon did a terrible thing. I feel awful for Walter, I do. I can't let Brendon go; David can't send him away."

"If anyone is leaving Taunton, it's Angelene."

"I was thinking about the day Brendon was born. It was humid. The roses were in full bloom, as if they were waiting for his arrival. I was so in love, someone had listened to me and got it right. I tried to get it right. The night I brought him home, I was so afraid to let him go. Do you know what I said to him?"

"Tell me again, gattina,"

"Hello little star. I've been waiting for you."

***

Walter loved the view from the kitchen window. Each season brought a new picture to look at. Radiant green, until autumn swept in and decorated the foliage in a rich tapestry of colour. Shades of grey and dismal blue, rain, and snow showers. As he stared at the reflection in the window, the view turned sour. Angelene looked younger, tinier, in his Royal Navy hoodie and baggy sweatpants. Walter grinned at the dishevelled mess piled atop her head. He used to find the tangly bun endearing. It fit the moment.

"Half of parliament told me to stay away."

Angelene shook out a cigarette, lit it. Smoke circled her head like a dingy halo. "You should have listened."

Walter inventoried his project. He had always excelled at projects in school. Volcanoes were boring and overdone. No one cared about the strength of magnets. Walter built ships and mapped out their course across whichever ocean he chose. The coordinates were exact, the destinations impeccably plotted. This project had proven difficult. He should have hidden her away until every detail was complete. The transformation had come too quick. He had rushed it, forgetting to mend her broken heart and stitched lungs. He had focused too much on the outside, leaving the most important pieces for another man to pick up.

"Why me? What made you stop running?"

"I have a pattern: run, succumb, endure, run. I don't think of the risks or consequences, not even God, until it's too late." The cigarette bobbed as she spoke, ashy snowflakes fell at her bare feet. "They fall in love. I run, taking their light and breath with me. You weren't in love with me."

Walter drooped onto the window bench. He picked up Tale of Two Cities and thumbed through the pages. "I was a project for you too."

Angelene slid down the wall and drew her knees to her chest. "I wanted to see if I could do normal things. See if I fit instead of standing on the other side of a glass wall with my nose pushed against it."

"Were you attracted to me?"

Angelene inhaled until the cigarette turned to ash. "You have powerful hands, strong shoulders. You have control over your life."

Walter dug his fingers into his hand. All her stitched and restitched pieces had split at the seams. He hated her for disrespecting him. The vulnerability slumping her shoulders made her beautiful.

"I could handle a punter from the pub. I might not care that you cheated."

"I don't know what to say."

Walter pounded his fist against the wall. "Brendon was a virgin. Was that the attraction? He was a conquest."

Angelene plucked at her knuckles, her voice brittle, accent thick. "It was Rachel Jones, not me."

"How long have you been sleeping with him?"

Angelene peeled herself from the wall, walked to the island, dropping the cigarette butt in the ashtray. "It doesn't matter, I'll end it."

Walter's cheeks burned with fiery heat. He rose and hammered his fists on the island. "How long have you been fucking him?"

"Not long."

Walter rubbed his clenched jaw, her trembling and pathetically squeaky voice fed into his anger.

"When? Where?"

Angelene shuddered and backed into the wall. "The house on the sea."

Walter laughed through his rage. "You fucked him in Burnham. That's why you were so miserable? The guilt was too much. God wouldn't forgive you?"

"We, he kissed me. We snuck into town and got drunk."

"Brendon was miserable. You were washing yourself in God's tears. For a man good at puzzles, how did I not see it?"

Angelene paced and scraped her wrist. "I've done a horrible thing again. God has been ignoring me for weeks. He's sure to abandon me now."

"Again? Who, Troy Spence? Victoria said she saw you with him." Walter clapped his hands, laughing. "The painting, a boy and his chickens. Were you fucking him too?"

"It was Pierre's son."

"Do you prefer boys? Is that it?"

"I told Brendon it was a mistake."

Walter grabbed a tea towel. He twisted, squeezed, picturing her slender neck.

"I never wanted to get married. Who wants to spend their life splitting up chores, watching the relationship turn dull and routine? I chose you, little bird. I gave marital bliss a shot with you."

Angelene unleashed her hand and fumbled for a cigarette. "You should have walked right past me."

"This is my fault? Choosing you?"

Walter wrung the tea towel into a tight coil. He glared at her shaking fingers, guilt-ridden face. How quickly someone could turn ugly. Her vulnerability was no longer lovely. She was a shamed mess.

44 THIRTEEN KNOTS

"What is it about Brendon? The dimples, his body, those damn Italian suits?" Walter wrenched the tea towel. "The football contract? Do you get wet when you think about him in his kit?"

Angelene leaned into the wall and dragged on the cigarette. Her silence infuriated him further. Walter flung the tea towel. The muscle above his lip quivered. He tried to get a grasp on the turmoil burning his gut. *'I could snap you like a twig, little bird. Who would miss Angelene Hummel?'*

"I asked you a damn question. What is it about Brendon?"

"He's kind, understanding. He never saw my scars like you did."

"What a saint. He's a damn prince charming, swooping into my home and fucking my wife."

Walter stomped from the kitchen and swiped his keys from the table.

"Don't leave me."

"If I don't leave, I'll... I don't want to be the bad guy."

"I said vows," Angelene pleaded. "I promised myself to you. God heard me."

"You've pissed all over those vows."

"Please, I beg you, don't leave me."

"Get your coat, little bird. I'll drop you off while I drive around."

Angelene smashed out the cigarette. "I don't understand."

"Confession, Mademoiselle Hummel. If you ever needed your God, it's now."

Dawn seeped into the kitchen, painting Walter's cheek pale gold. He rubbed his bleary eyes and walked to the coffeemaker. Walter spooned coffee into the basket, filled the reservoir with water. It hissed and gurgled. A knock filled the silence. He smoothed his wrinkled shirt and walked to the door.

"Davy boy, you'll be stuck in traffic if you don't hit the road."

"I wasn't sure you'd be awake."

"I've slept an hour, maybe."

"I'm disgusted. You need to know that."

"Brendon's young, full of promise, dishy, that's what Juliette said. It was the first time I saw her blush."

"It doesn't excuse what he's done."

Walter strolled into the kitchen, poured coffee into mugs, and set them on the island.

"It's the damn code. We never should have written it."

David sipped his coffee. "Why's that?"

"It's no wonder Brendon fooled around with Ang. It's hard to follow those rules all the time."

"Open the door, help with chores, give a firm handshake, don't covet your best friend's girl. Doesn't sound hard to me."

"He's a randy teenager, if she was offering," Walter said soberly. "It makes sense, Ang avoiding sex. It wasn't her fear of God, it was me. She didn't like me."

"Are we okay?"

Walter chuckled, rose, and topped up his mug. "You're my best friend. I won't let my wife's actions come between us."

"What are you going to do?" David asked, holding out his mug.

Walter poured coffee and set the pot on the island. "Hang around here, think."

"That's just like you. Stick around and face it while I run."

"You're not running. You're afraid of what you might say to Brendon."

"I don't like him right now. I haven't for a while," David said. "He's to stay home. I can't trust he won't show up and cause trouble. If Sofia knows best, she'll keep him locked up."

Walter gulped his coffee, tipping more into his mug. "How is Sofia?"

"Devastated, embarrassed, worried."

"Worried about what? I would never hold this against either of you."

"I'm sending Brendon to Dortmund."

"Banish the boy from the kingdom. Don't punish Sofia."

David set down his mug and pinched the bridge of his nose. "Do I ever use the word fuck?"

Walter snorted and filled his mug. "It's part of the code. People respect a man who can speak without using words like fuck and bollocks."

"If the word isn't flying out of my mouth, it's bouncing around my head. On the drive here, I said it three times, fuck the code, fuck Sofia, fuck Brendon." David smoothed his tie and took a sip. "Brendon must go. I must learn to like him again."

Walter pawed at his chest and dumped the coffee in the sink. "Brendon's a good kid. Ang has a way of drawing people in."

He sunk onto a stool, words escaping him. He had failed. Golden fingertips, not this time.

Walter spun his wedding band around his finger and glanced at the doorway. He wasn't staring at a seducer. He met the eyes of a scared little girl.

"I'm sorry David."

"David doesn't need apologies. He needs peace before driving to London. Fly away, little bird."

Angelene shuffled to the island and took hold of David's arm. "I tried to stop it. It's one of my patterns."

Walter growled, propped his elbow, and rested his chin in his hand. "Grab a coffee and go away."

"Do you believe in fairy tales?"

David scratched at his stubbled chin. "I believe in the lessons fairy tales teach us. Triumph over evil, courage, asking for help — those types of things."

Walter groaned and rubbed his brow. "Here's a fairy tale for you. Once upon a time, a man visited the prettiest park in Paris and saw the most intriguing little bird. He was duped, the end."

Angelene lit a cigarette, took a drag, and blew smoke at the ceiling. "I used to stand in front of the mirror and wish all my scars away. I would pretend I was a beautiful, confident woman. My prince charming would come. We'd live happily ever after."

"Look around you. Here's your castle. You've transformed into a beautiful woman. Walter is your prince, not my son."

Walter glanced at Angelene; she looked fragile; her stitches pulled apart. '*Try again, walk away.*' Walter groaned and scrubbed his cheeks. "Please go away, little bird."

"Are you in love with Brendon?" David said.

Walter massaged his temples. He needed to hear this. His decision to stay or go might be easier if he knew the truth. If she loved Brendon, he could walk away, let her live her fairy tale with the boy wonder. If she didn't, he'd take a step back, be patient, get counselling, try again.

"I want to be in love with him." Smoke trickled from her mouth. "The same way I wanted to fall in love with Walter and Henri. I think I'm in love with the idea of being normal. I'm terrible at picking partners. Then again, I never do the picking. They pick me."

Walter waved the smoke from his face and watched her walk away. "I don't think she answered the question. You see how frustrating she can be?"

"You didn't see it in her eyes?"

"What? Guilt? Sorrow? Regret?"

David stood and glanced at his watch. "She loves Brendon or the fairy tale that comes with him."

Walter snapped a banana from the bunch and peeled back the skin. He opened his mouth, turned up his nose, and laid it on the counter.

"Do you think you can forgive her?"

"Forgiveness is a complicated thing. She betrayed me with someone I love."

Walter followed David to the door, sandalwood lingered in the air. He would miss that smell. It was the first thing that greeted him when he came home from London.

"Did you have a hunch, or did you believe Victoria?"

"I forgot my notes on the P-8A Poseidon patrol planes. I thought the drive home would help clear my head. All I got was more clutter."

"Whatever you decide, Brendon will be out of your way."

"You're going to tear Sofia's world apart."

"This goodbye isn't forever."

"Sofia may follow him to Germany."

"My fairy tale won't have a happy ending. I'll call you later."

Walter opened the door, soft, golden sunlight slipped between his fingers; a chorus of birdsong filled the crisp air. "Fairy tales are silly, Davy boy; all they do is give people hope. Look what hope got me."

The luminous sunlight took him back to Parc Floral. He had saved the damsel, marriage, and normal was her reward. Walter grinned. Angelene Hummel was a fairy tale.

**

Troy read the text and read it again. The dining hall buzzed with energy. Students munched on cottage pie or tikka masala. Rumours floated from table to table. This had been the best news about Brendon Cook.

"Guten tag."

Troy dropped his phone and pushed a chair towards Rachel.

"You sure Charlotte won't mind?"

"Charlotte heard about Brendon and thinks I shagged Ms. Pratt; she's ignoring me. Sit, keep me company."

Rachel flopped onto the chair and shoved a tendril of hair into her ponytail. "Charlotte's still in it."

Troy grinned a 'thanks for giving me hope,' grin and pushed his fork through a mound of salad. "She's still calling me Troy Alexander. That's not a good sign."

"When Charlotte stops getting mad at you, you know the relationship is over. She drives out to the farm, holds back her tears, calls you Troy Alexander. That proves she still wants you."

Troy picked through the salad and pierced a cucumber. "I can't believe Brendon was so stupid."

"You can't help who you fall in love with. Look at me, I fell for him. Brendon Cook is so far out of my league."

"You're better than Ms. Pratt."

"William bet two pounds he slept with Eshana's mum."

"Will's a dolt." Troy rolled the cucumber back and forth, wincing. "Ms. Pratt gets stuck in your head."

The colour drained from Rachel's cheeks; her eyes misted with tears. He set down his fork and took her hand.

"Can I tell you something? I've been holding it in for a while, eaten my weight in chocolate." Rachel jutted out her chin and pointed. "Look, I've got spots from all the sweets."

"If it makes you feel better."

"Ms. Pratt came here."

"All those bets placed about a nutter showing up at school were true."

The shocking truth slammed into Troy. The strange silence made sense. His friends, the kids in biology, had looked like they had a million things to say. The silence had been loaded with the crazy truth.

"She told me to stay away from Brendon. She said my life's purpose was to be a tart."

Brendon had said Angelene was a nutter. All he had seen was a sunny girl who tapped her feet to music she had never heard and loved the cattle. Troy blinked his eyes, stunned. It made sense, Brendon's devotion to Angelene, his downward spiral, the dreamy expression. He had gotten sucked up in it, too. The day at the farm, she had moved him, made him believe life would be different for him. She had been gentle, not crazy, and possessive.

"I can't believe she would have the balls to show up here and say those things."

"After she left, I thought she and Brendon had to be involved. Maggie said Brendon got distant with her, he was the same with me. I didn't want to believe Brendon could be that dumb."

"Maggie has been saying things for weeks about Brendon and Angelene."

"I can understand why she told me to stay away."

Troy rubbed his forehead; Maggie had whinged about Brendon fancying Angelene. She said she had a feeling something wasn't right. He and Charlotte had laughed, called her daft. Margaret Thornton had been right all along.

"You feel sorry for her?"

"I hated her that day. By the time I took my seat in biology, I felt sorry for her. If she's had to fight all her life for the things she loved, why wouldn't she fight for Brendon?" Rachel said, pointing her chin at his tray. Troy pushed it towards her. She picked up the fork and bit into the cucumber. "I get why Brendon fell for her. You want to protect someone that sad. You want to fill their miserable life with rainbows and sunshine."

"I went to grab Charlie some Chelsea buns, and I bumped into her. Ms. Pratt was happy, the happiest I've ever seen her. I wanted to be with her. I wanted to listen to all the weird stuff she says. If she's comfortable with you, she's just her, and that's what draws you in." Troy leaned back in the chair, fiddling with the end of his tie. "Who knew when Walter brought her to Taunton, everyone's lives would be shaken up?"

"I feel for Brendon too."

"He broke your heart four times."

"No one's supposed to know that."

"Will's been spreading it around the dressing room. He and Tilly think you're a bore now."

Rachel reached into her pocket and shook a tube of Smarties onto the tray. "Tilly tells me every bleeding day. Don't eat the blue ones."

"I'll leave them alone."

"I'd love to go round to Brendon's and give knuddlebär a big hug."

"I wouldn't. Mr. Cook is proper mad, not lecture mad but sending Brendon to Dortmund mad. I'm pissed off at him but, what am I going to do without my mate?" Troy said, tossing a smartie in his mouth.

Rachel rolled a Smartie under her finger and grinned. "Never say goodbye because goodbye means going away and going away means forever."

"That's ace. Did you just make that up?"

"It's from Peter Pan." Rachel reached for the napkin and ran it under her nose. "I haven't said goodbye to knuddlebär and if Mr. Cook sends Brendon away, it's see you soon. It won't hurt so bad because you know there'll be a next time."

Troy knew he had been wrong about Rachel. He had spoke bad about her, called Brendon a dolt for liking her. She was just a girl who, like Angelene, was desperate for love.

"You're different and not because you covered your jubblies. You're quieter. Everything about you is quiet."

Rachel tossed a Smartie into his mouth and sighed. "My mum's friend suddenly became her boyfriend. She's been flying to Berlin on the weekends. I'm trying to forget Brendon. I used to have my nan to talk to. She has dementia."

Troy scooted to the edge of the chair and held her hands. "I thought missing Charlie was bad."

"It happened so fast, mum's new boyfriend, Brendon ignoring me, Ms. Pratt. I didn't have time to process one thing before the next happened." Rachel pulled a sheet of paper from her bag, folded it into an envelope and dropped the blue Smarties in the pocket. "I'll do what I always do, accept the in-love Miranda Jones, quiet Rachel and go on."

"I like the new Rachel. Just don't be moving me up to number one. I'm in enough trouble."

"Charlotte will come around. She's never had to compete with anyone. That's why it hurt so bad."

"How do I get Charlie to believe I love her? I only thought about Ms. Pratt for a day. Well, more, but I didn't love her. I love Charlie."

"Just keep being you. You're dishy when you smile. Your bum is brilliant."

A warm flush crept over Troy's cheeks. He held up his middle finger at a group of snickering boys and smoothed his bangs. "You still love Brendon?"

"He'll be my number one forever. Someday, knuddlebär will see I was the girl he loved."

Troy glanced at his watch and tossed the remaining Smarties in his mouth. "Should I forgive him?"

"He's going to need a friend. Even if he is a wanker." Rachel wound her purse strap over her shoulder, dropping the Smartie filled envelope in the pocket. "Go see Charlotte. She's crocheting in the library."

"Charlie hates the library."

"It's the best place to go when you're sad. No one can see you cry. See you tomorrow. I'll save you a seat in biology."

Troy tapped open his phone and pulled up the text. He read it and read it again. *I've been involved with Angelene. Dad wants to send me to Dortmund.*

He was shocked when he first read the text. Now, he was sad. This was wrong in all sorts of ways, wrong woman, wrong kind of love. Troy slid the tray in his hand, a single blue Smartie dropped at his feet. *'The right person has been standing in front of you the whole time.'*

***

Angelene perched on the toilet seat and pushed at her pruned fingers. The air was moist, scented with lavender and patchouli.

"God, please tell me if this is love."

The bathroom was silent, no tug at her heart or swirl in her belly.

Sinner, whore, always stealing from people what is missing from you.

Angelene clamped her hands over her ears and shook her head furiously. The voices knocked about; each word struck her forehead viciously. The walls pulsed and screamed, *sinner, whore, let Brendon go*. Her scars vibrated. She was a sinner; she was a victim of love.

"God, I'm begging you. Do not abandon me. I'll give you until the morning and if I don't hear from you, I'll pull out my hair and scratch at my skin. Please don't leave me."

45 Lebensmüde

Brendon kicked the pillows to the floor and drew in his legs. He would title this chapter, 'how to break the Gentlemen's Code and other things'. Sofia asked him not to speak about the brother he never knew. It felt good to say his name. Old wounds bled; it was his fault.

"He better bloody jump."

Sofia plucked the pillows from the floor, tossed them onto the chair, and flopped next to him. "Who? The goalkeeper or the one in front of the net?"

"The keeper. He needs to jump and tip it over the bar."

The goalkeeper ran into the mob of players, jumped, and tipped the ball over the crossbar.

"You knew what the goalkeeper was going to do."

"I may not know bloody history or French but, I know football."

"We need to talk, sweetheart."

"Is dad coming home? I overheard you telling Nonna he's staying in London."

"I don't know. Our conversations have been very brief."

"I texted him again, apologizing for mentioning his name."

Sofia looked away; tears welled in her eyes. "His name is Ethan Luca."

"Isn't it time you talked about him? The place has been haunted by his ghost for years. He wants you to let go."

"It hurts too much. I would have to face his death again," Sofia said, drawing David's cardigan to her cheek. "We only had nine years with Ethan."

"Nine years with the son dad wanted."

His phone buzzed. He reached into his pocket and clenched it. It was bad enough facing mammina's sorrow. The constant texts of disappointment were irritating. He buried it under a stack of football magazines, out of sight, out of mind.

"Angelene and I have something else in common. No one wanted us."

Brendon recoiled; Sofia's eyes were piercing black. "You filled the emptiness. I needed you. I loved you more."

"Not dad. Ethan was just like him, smart, respectful."

"You came too soon for your father. Time hadn't healed him yet."

Brendon stared at his palm and traced along his life line. "When Ethan died, he took the father out of dad."

Sofia scooted across the sofa and raised his chin. "Your father's an excellent role model. He taught you to drive and shave, why he wasted his time doing that."

Brendon pulled his chin away and flicked off the television. "Dad rejected me before I was born. It's hard to build a relationship with someone you didn't want."

"The entire ride to the hospital. I had your father on the phone. I kept repeating, this is not goodbye, this is not goodbye and your dad..." Sofia paused, her voice wobbled. "He kept saying, tell Ethan to hang on until I get there. Ethan passed before he said goodbye."

A low hum rose from beneath the football magazines. Brendon tucked his toe under the corner and shoved them aside. He glanced from Sofia to his phone. His heart thundered.

"What are the two values your father cherishes?"

"Respect and monogamy."

"You did a horrible thing. It's going to take time for him to forgive you."

"Have you forgiven me?"

"No. I understand why you fell for Angelene. It was all the things we heard from Walter. She's a perfect balance of enticing and inaccessible, the forbidden fruit. Take a bite and you find out she's rotten to the core."

'She's just a girl'

A girl that flew into Taunton ripped out his heart and shoved it back inside. Her game of catch me if you can, was never ending.

"It was easy for you to fall out of love with Maggie and Rachel. You must realize loving Angelene is wrong."

"I was in like with Maggie. I never loved Rachel."

Sofia struggled with a grin. "You loved Rachel; Angelene was blocking your view. It might have been intentional if she saw it too."

His phone buzzed. Brendon fumbled under the magazines and hid the screen from Sofia. A cold sweat prickled his neck. "I'm going for a walk."

"You can't love Angelene. She's Walter's, you respect that."

Brendon glanced at his phone, clenching it. He checked the number again and shoved it into his pocket.

"I won't leave the property."

Brendon left Sofia, his mind jumbled and twisted. Forget about Angelene, stop loving her, pretend she never existed.

"Where are you off to?"

Brendon slipped on his trainers and gripped the doorknob. "For a walk. Ethan's floating around, following me from room to room, pissed off I hurt mammina and dad. I need to breathe."

"Don't forget what your father said." Nicola's voice was sharp. "I'm making his favourite; he might come home."

Brendon opened the door, welcoming the mild air and smoky grey skies. "I'll be on a plane Sunday. Dad can come home then."

The anger dissolved from Nicola's face. "Go for your walk before I slap that lovestruck look off your face."

Brendon snuffed out the sparks and stepped into the dull afternoon. Butterflies broke free in his belly, ferocious, stinging, whipping their wings, stirring up the sandwich he had eaten for lunch. Madre Innocente hissed at him, *'do as you're told,*' Padre Diavolo howled, '*spin the revolver one last time.*' Brendon trudged on; Angelene had been right when she said love drove people crazy. His thoughts had a mind of their own. They raced through his brain at a hundred miles per second. Paranoia grew inside him, like a living thing, attaching to his heart and lungs. Brendon moved along the path; five minutes was all he needed, a quick look, one last 'see you soon', one more moment to stretch from Taunton to Dortmund.

"Are you okay?"

"I'm pink, black, grey, timid, sad, and indecisive. The colours never change, just shift."

Brendon kissed her forehead and ran his thumb over her chapped lips. "What colour am I?"

"Blue. Sad, depressed blue."

Brendon held her hand and leaned his back against the tree. "I'm starting to detest the colour. How's Walter?"

"He hasn't left the kitchen, just sits at his laptop. I feel if I walk the wrong way or say the wrong thing, he'll explode."

"But you rang me? Dangerous move, Mademoiselle Hummel."

Angelene's gaze darted around the forest. Her grip tightened. "Take me to Dortmund."

Brendon searched her eyes. Desperation, help me, frantic love.

"How will you get past Walter?"

"He's been drinking a lot. I haven't had a drop; he can't go a few hours without it." Angelene picked at a blob of yellow paint and bit into her lip. "Malcolm can take me to the airport. I'll wait for you there."

"Do you mean it?"

"I was painting, an abstract, yellow triangles, splashes of pink, dribbles of orange, splatters of green. You've been my normal the whole time."

Brendon drew her into his arms, rested his chin on her head, and slipped his fingers into a hole in her sweater. "This sweater is falling apart."

"It was Roman's. He left it in mama's closet. I stole it."

"You like to do that, don't you?"

"The wool used to smell like Roman's tobacco. It brought me comfort."

"I'm going to find us the perfect place. Somewhere close to Westfalenpark."

"Nicola visited last night. She told Walter she'd kill me if I went near you. He said, not if he killed me first. It might be dangerous for me to come."

It was a simple decision: find a place, board the plane, happily ever after.

"Leave a note. Say you returned to Paris, don't say where you're going."

"I'll still be married. God isn't speaking to me; I need Him to guide me."

"There are plenty of churches in Dortmund. I'm sure God will be at one of them. Do you want to come or not?" He extinguished the sparks. She was trembling, getting angry would make her run. "You trust me, don't you?"

"I'm trying. It's a beautiful thought, you, as my normal."

Brendon tapped his foot against a root. She was faltering, dancing between what was right and wrong, what frightened her and gave her joy.

"If Sunday is too soon. I'll get to Dortmund and send you money. Walter won't be working from home for long."

"April would be better. We can visit Bonn and see the cherry blossoms."

"April, May, bloody hell, next it will be July. It'll be like the story I told you. I'll be waiting at the train station for you."

"I learned a German word," she said. Her voice was as hollow as the wind. "Lebensmüde, life tired. I'm so exhausted."

Brendon raised her chin and kissed her like it was the last kiss they would share. He gazed into her eyes. The look, the silence, said everything. There was no trace of love. Something inside him broke. She dissolved out of his arms.

"I thought your mother had you locked up?"

Walter reached within the dilapidated walls and yanked Angelene's sweater. Brendon stumbled over the twisted roots, missing her hand as she fell into a fern.

"I can't lie down without you running off to him?"

Brendon swallowed and gazed nervously from Angelene's crumpled body to Walter.

"It was me. I gave her a bell."

Walter banged his fists against the decaying wood. The board rattled and fell at Brendon's feet.

"Why can't you let her go? She's my wife."

Angelene scrambled to her feet and tugged at Walter's jacket. "I rang Brendon. I asked him to meet me. C'est fini."

Fini, the end.

"You don't kiss someone like that if you're ending it."

Brendon stepped around Walter and reached for Angelene. Walter's hand wrapped around his throat; Brendon cried out. No sound came.

"Nicola, your father, your damn mother, told you to stay away."

Brendon struggled and gasped, pinned to a splintered plank. "You never treated her like a wife. She was your bloody DIY."

Brendon's head bounced off the board, black flooded his sight. Walter's fist smashed into his stomach; a sharp pain seared his gut. He buckled and grimaced. "Who asked Lukas to watch you play?" Walter said, driving his fist. A crack filled the air, Brendon's lungs burned.

"Walter, please, hit me, beat me."

"Isn't that sweet, wanting to save your prince."

"Fuck off," Brendon croaked. "You're pissed off because I won."

Brendon hammered his cast into Walter's head, wiggled himself free, plunging his good hand into Walter's stomach.

"You're driving my car. I was there when your father wasn't," Walter said, bulldozing into Brendon. Brendon slid across the damp foliage, grunting as his back hit a tree trunk.

"So-fee-ah, please come."

"Mum!"

"So-fee-ah."

A muffled crash and bang mingled with the rustling of leaves. Brendon bat and tugged at Walter's fingers.

"Mammina."

"Brendon, not my boy. Please, not my boy."

Brendon grabbed Walter's collar. He dragged him into an oak tree, peering around twisted branches. Sofia stood at the mouth of the path, her cheeks ashen, her bare feet rooted in the ground.

"Mum, hurry!"

"I can't breathe, sweetheart. Everywhere I look, I see him."

"I'm at my old fort." Brendon's fingers sunk into a mossy burl. He gasped and choked with every punch to the gut. "Mum, please."

Brendon grappled with Walter, knocking him into a board. Heavy, rock-like hands closed around his neck.

"Don't be scared, mammina. Ethan's with you. He'll hold your hand."

"You couldn't keep your damn hands off her. Million-dollar hands, I'll break the other."

Brendon hung limp from Walter's grasp.

"Walter, stop," Sofia said, slipping on the rocks. Her toe caught under a root, she fell to the ground, her sweater tangled in the brambles.

"Let fucking go." Brendon rammed his cast against Walter's arm. "Mum's fallen on the roots where Ethan died."

"Brendon, I'm scared. Ethan, you're here. I'm sorry I wasn't there."

Walter clutched his throat, Brendon choked, the words sputtered from his mouth. "If there ever comes a day when we can't be together, finish it, mammina. Tell Ethan." Brendon coughed and gasped. "He wants to hear the words. He needs to hear them."

"Keep me in your heart. I'll stay there forever. You and Winnie the Pooh, best friends."

"It wasn't your fault, mammina. I need you now."

Sofia wiped her tears, smearing dirt across her cheek. "Walter! Please don't take my son from me." She found her footing, ran, and propelled herself into Walter's back. "Not my son, not again."

Walter unleashed his hand. Brendon touched his throat, gasping for air. Sofia grabbed his cheeks and ran her hand over his hair and jaw. She pried his lips open, examining his bloodied gums.

"Mum stop."

"You didn't do a good job keeping him in the house."

Brendon wiped his mouth on his sleeve and placed a hand on Sofia's shoulder. "Can we go home?"

"Not until she hears what I have to say."

Sofia locked eyes with Angelene. "You took my boy from me."

"Take Brendon home before I throw my fist in his face again."

Brendon tucked Sofia under his arm and nudged her towards the path. "I'm dizzy. My chest hurts."

"Do you know how many sympathy cards I received after Ethan passed? All those kind words, none of it erased the hurt. Nineteen years, blaming myself, David blaming himself for not protecting him. You've stolen Brendon from me. His death has been a whole different kind."

She pressed her shoulder into Brendon, raised her chin, blazing with indignation. "You took my son."

"Go home, little bird," Walter said.

Angelene walked away. Brendon's heart cracked; icy splinters stabbed his gut. The cord that tied him to her pulled and snapped. She was gone.

"How could you? He's just a boy."

Walter snort and smiled. "He isn't a boy. He's certainly proved that."

"I deserved it mammina."

"You could have killed him. Instead of the blood being on that damn oak tree, David swore he'd have Peter cut down. It would be on your hands."

Brendon rubbed Sofia's back and forced her to take a step. "I need to rinse my mouth."

"Pack up her shit and drop her off at St. Georges. Let God deal with her."

Walter ran his shirt over his bloodied knuckles. "You don't blame Brendon at all, do you?"

"Angelene is damaged. Damaged people will do anything to make it hurt less. They'll use other people's happiness or light to mend their wounds. I blame your wife."

"Maybe this is her penance, staying married to me," Walter said. He stepped forward and jabbed his finger in Brendon's chest. "Stay the fuck away."

"You're a lousy fucking husband."

Brendon stumbled as Sofia jerked his hood, tugging him down the path.

"She needs to go. She's infected you, drove David away, turned Walter into a horrible beast."

"It wasn't all her mammina. I'm to blame too." Brendon pulled leaves from her sweater, tossing them on the path. "You didn't put shoes on."

"I heard your voice; my entire world blew up. Ethan never called for me. He tripped on the root and bled to death while I was sipping tea and planning his birthday party."

Brendon pushed open the door, dropped onto a stool, and inspected the tears on his knuckles.

"How could you be so stupid?" Sofia cuffed him across the back of the head and wet a tea towel. "Do you know how much I paid for your teeth?"

Brendon ran his tongue along his gums. The taste was metallic and salty. "There's nothing wrong with my teeth. I have them all."

He stared at the puddle of coffee and the broken mug, wincing. Angelene was alone with Walter. He was furious.

"You couldn't stay away," Sofia said, dabbing the cloth under his nose. "Why the hell would you meet with her?"

"I promised I would always be there for her."

"Isn't that damn romantic." Sofia folded the tea towel and blotted the blood. "I'd like your father to come home. This will keep him away forever and you'll be on a plane. Walter will make sure of it."

"Am I allowed to play in the forest now?"

"Watch your mouth, topolino," Nicola said. She walked to the coffeemaker and flipped the switch. "I told you to stay away."

Sofia tossed the towel into the sink. "How am I going to convince your father to let you stay?"

Nicola spooned coffee into the filter. "You're not. See what you've done, you and that puttana."

Brendon shoved his torn-up hand into his pocket and hung his head. "Dad will come home when I'm in Dortmund."

Nicola bent over and mopped the coffee. "If you would have stayed away. There may have been a chance you could stay. You've broken your mother's heart again."

"I'm good at breaking hearts."

"Things will not be the same. You'll be in Dortmund; I'll hate David for sending you away." Sofia said, picking at the dirt under her fingernail.

"David Cook isn't David Cook without Sofia by his side. Things will be okay, mammina."

"I couldn't wait to be a mother. Remember mum, I'd play for hours under the fig trees with my dolls."

Nicola stood and threw the towel on the counter. "I do, gattina. You were a wonderful mother to your dolls, and you are now. Ethan's death was not your fault. That boy was always climbing trees and digging under rocks. He was reckless in a different way."

Sofia slumped onto a stool and buried her face in her hands. "I failed both my boys."

Brendon climbed off the stool and held his chest through a painful, laboured breath. "You're a brilliant mum. You've put up with me." He pulled a burr from her sweater and kissed her cheek.

"I smothered you because I was afraid of losing you. I wanted you to always need me so you wouldn't leave."

"I couldn't stop Gianni from driving drunk anymore than you could stop Ethan from exploring the forest."

Brendon raked his fingers through his hair. The notion that love made people crazy was alive in la cucina. His mother looked a mess. Nonna, enraged. He was ready to bolt to save Angelene and risk having his head blown off.

"You don't deserve my love right now. I should pack your bags and kick your ass out the door."

"I'm going to run you a bath," Nicola said. "Le tue azioni hanno portato vergogna alla famiglia."

"I am a bloody disgrace to the family."

"If only Kate and I made that stop in Paris."

Brendon poured Sofia coffee and handed her the steaming cup. He turned on the tap and ran his hand under the stream of water. "Are you talking about the time you went to Avignon Provence?"

"We stayed at the L'Atelier Du Renard Argenté, a bed-and-breakfast near Mornas and took a cooking class. Kate sliced her finger instead of the aubergine. She was flirting with the chef, trying to forget Walter was getting married. We were going to surprise Walter, get a peek at this mysterious woman. I could have talked him out of marrying her."

Brendon flicked the bloodied water away and rinsed the sink. He ripped a sheet of kitchen towel from the roll and wrapped it around the abrasions. "You wouldn't have stopped him."

"I'd like to tie a rock around her waist and throw her in the River Tone," Sofia said.

The doorbell chimed; Brendon's heart rattled. "I hope that isn't Walt coming back for round two."

"I'm going to have my bath. If it's your Uncle Walter, duck."

Sofia patted his shoulder and slowly walked from the kitchen. The doorbell rang again. He heard Nicola's disappointed tone and a sweet, apologetic 'sorry for bothering.' Brendon gathered the broken cup in the blood-stained tea towel and shook the bits into the bin. He dried his hands and left the kitchen. Maggie stood by the umbrella stand, staring at him with a loving expression. He felt like a fool. She still loved him, despite what he'd done. She was the beauty who didn't know she was beautiful, who dazzled him with the history of Great Britain, the girl he destroyed.

"You want to sit in the great room? Ame will be racing through the door soon. She had to run to Tesco for chili flakes. Nonna's in the mood for penne all'arrabbiata. She eats it when she's pissed off."

Maggie dropped her purse next to her shoes and trailed behind him.

"Have you come to gloat?"

"I came to see how you are, by the looks of things, not well."

Brendon glanced at his blood-stained hoodie and flopped onto the sofa. "I did something stupid."

He picked up a magazine and flipped through the pages. It was hard to look at her. Guilt had resurfaced. It was like he cheated again.

"More stupid than getting involved with Ms. Pratt? The kids are placing all kinds of bets, horrible ones too."

"You want to hear it from me? You want to know if all the stuff you accused me of is true."

"Don't you think I deserve the truth?"

Brendon tossed the magazine onto the coffee table. He had fallen for Maggie in spring. Since then, she had been his springtime girl, smelling sweet like apple blossoms and delicate like the snowdrops. He had stomped on her, destroyed her. It was time for her to blossom.

"I was involved with Angelene."

Brendon braced himself for the downpour of tears, the quivering lip. She sat still and plucked her thumb from her mouth.

"Did it start on Burnham? Is that why you didn't want me to come?"

Brendon poked at a tear in his knuckle. Honesty, get that part of the code right.

"It started the first night I met her. I thought she was the most beautiful girl I'd ever seen."

"Were you and her? Gosh, Brendon, I thought Rachel was..." Her voice trailed off. He waited for the sniffing. Her face remained springtime pretty.

"I kept running to her instead of you for emotional support. I've been cheating from the start."

"All those times you said you were moving furniture or helping your mum."

"It was innocent at first. We were just friends. I fell in love."

"By talking to her?"

"It was more than that. She said she would come to Dortmund."

Maggie unclasped her hands and batted his shoulder with a pillow. "I told you that, wanker. So did Rachel. Didn't you think it was wrong? It's your Uncle Walter's wife."

"I tried to switch the feeling off. Bloody hell, Angelene and I weren't talking at one point."

"Is that why you got sick because of Ms. Pratt?"

"Have you ever had someone say things to you and it turns out to be shit?"

Maggie held up her hand and pointed to her ring finger. "He gave me a ring."

"I don't know what to say to make you feel better."

"You can keep being honest with me. Did you fancy Rachel? Is that why you cheated and no daft excuses like you were angry with the world."

"You can't cry. I can't take much more."

"Who says I'm going to cry? I feel sorry for you. You had two brilliant girls, and you chose someone you can't have."

Brendon rubbed at the pain in his chest. He wasn't sure if it was from a cracked rib or the sadness dwelling in Maggie's eyes.

"I fancied Rachel and not just her jubblies. I looked forward to German lessons and Latin because I wanted to be near her."

"You fancied Rachel, loved Ms. Pratt. What did you feel about me?"

"I thought I was in like with you, but sometimes when I can't sleep, I want to hear your laugh, that little snort you do. I want to hear you call me a wanker. When I'm near you, I crave a biscuit."

Maggie threw her arms around his neck. Brendon buried his nose in her hair, closing his eyes to the scent of vanilla. An ache welled in his heart, expanding like a balloon.

"I'm sorry for being a prick to Jack, for cheating on you, for making you think I wasn't in it."

"You're still the dishiest boy in England."

"I'm a fucking idiot. I know I shouldn't love her. Bloody hell, I've told myself a million times, it isn't right."

"I wish it were me. Rachel wishes it were her," Maggie said, twirling the string on his hoodie. "Does Ms. Pratt love you?"

"I don't know. Sometimes I see it in her eyes. She flips through emotions like Charlie does outfits."

"What about your parents and Walter?"

"It's a bloody mess. Mum and dad are fighting. Walter would have killed me had Angelene not screamed for mum."

Maggie let loose the string and touched his wounded knuckle. "Walter did this?"

"And this," Brendon said, pointing to his swollen lip. "He might have broken a rib."

"You deserve it."

"I know I do. He was bloody calm the day he found us. All the hurt and anger must have caught up to him."

"He found you?" Maggie dragged his arm around her shoulder and snuggled against him.

Brendon would never forget the look on Walter's face, like he knew what he was coming home to. "We were in his bed. I would have preferred he beat me then."

"You were... I would have been gutted if I walked in on you and Rachel." "Good thing you stayed clear of the willow tree at school."

"I didn't want to believe the bets. Every morning?"

"Rachel likes to hump."

"She likes you. She thought sex would make you fall for her."

"Why all this sympathy for Rachel?"

"I know how badly she's hurting. I felt it too." She unwound his arm and pecked his cheek. "I better go. Charlie's coming over."

"Her and Troy still not speaking?"

Maggie smoothed out her blazer, reached for his hands, and tugged him off the couch. "You can thank Ms. Pratt for that. She's like an itch mite, burrowing under your skin, laying her eggs, so she'll always be a part of you."

Brendon grinned, leave it to Maggie to be descriptive and dramatic. "You sure you can't stay? I won't make you watch football or play Xbox."

"If I stay, I'll remember how much I love you, then I'll surely cry. It's been weeks since I shed a tear."

It had been a good two years. It wasn't time to mourn the relationship. He'd celebrate the joy she had brought him, once upon a time.

Maggie slid into her Mary janes and smiled. "It's okay if I wasn't the best chapter in your story. I hope when you get to Dortmund, you'll read it and smile."

Brendon kissed her forehead and dragged her into his arms. "Can I lift your kilt for old time's sake?"

Maggie giggled and pushed his arms away. "We might run into each other someday. I won't be so insecure; you'll be a pro footy player, still as dishy as ever. See you soon, wanker."

Brendon closed the door, clutched tightly to 'see you soon' and her springtime. He had loved Maggie.

"How was Maggie?"

Brendon blew out a heavy sigh. "Adorable."

"You should have realized that months ago," Sofia said, handing him a clean hoodie. "Change please."

Brendon dragged his hoodie over his head, tossed it towards the stairs, and shimmied into the clean one. "Where are we going?"

"To the A&E. You need your ribs x-rayed."

"You hate the hospital."

"I hate the forest. You forced me to face it," Sofia said, shrugging on her coat. "It's about time you face some things."

"What's that?"

"How wrong you were. How many people you've hurt?"

Brendon opened the door and stared into a sky of melted pewter.

Once upon a time, there was a boy who was in love with a girl who blossomed like spring under his touch and blew like a fierce blizzard. One day, she blew with such ferocity the whole town disappeared under a blanket of the coldest snow. Some suffocated, some clawed their way through, and some hung onto hope they would survive.

***

Maggie plucked Suki from the stone wall, snuggling its neck; proud she had walked away from Brendon without shedding a tear. She had expected a boastful Brendon, testosterone bubbling over, arrogantly strutting about, bragging of his conquest. She had found a broken boy instead.

"Why are you waiting outside?" Charlotte said.

"Mum doesn't know I went to Brendon's, so keep your mouth shut."

Charlotte grabbed a bulging paper sack, closed the car door, joining Maggie on the walkway.

"Rosie still doesn't want you to visit?"

"Ms. McGregor was in the salon boasting about how she tried to warn Walter. She claims she knew it was Brendon all along, gobby cow. Mum hates Brendon even more now."

The door swung open, Jack grinned, biscuit in one hand, Batman in the other. "Have you told Troy I'm your boyfriend?"

"I have, and he's gutted."

Jack bounced on his toes and poked at the bag. "What did you bring?"

"Stop bothering Charlie. She's here to visit me."

"I went apple picking with Ms. Spence and made my first pie," Charlotte said, peeking into the front room. "Hiya, Ms. Thornton. I brought you some apples."

Rosie turned down the corner of a magazine and smiled. "Maybe you can teach our Margaret to bake."

"That's boring, Charlie. Mum makes me eat an apple a day to keep Dr. Weiss away. I had to see him last week."

Charlotte ruffled his hair and reached into her purse. She pulled out a crocheted rectangle and unfolded it. Jack's eyes brightened.

"It's a Batman mask."

"The ears were bollocks. I had to get Ms. Spence to help. Try it on. It should fit."

Jack tugged the hat over his head. Bits of sandy blonde poked through the stitches.

"What do you say?" Rosie said.

"Thanks. I'm never taking it off."

"He probably won't," Maggie said, grasping Charlotte's hand. "He'll be thirty and still wearing it."

"How was Brendon? Gutted? Dirty bugger."

"Ssh."

Maggie twirled Charlotte into her room, scanned the hall, and closed her door. "Black and blue."

Charlotte sunk onto the pouf and dropped her bag to the floor. "Are you speaking in colours like that cow? Ms. Pratt said Troy was yellow."

Maggie flopped onto her bed and scrunched a pillow under her chest. "Literally black and blue. He and Walter got into a fight."

Charlotte flicked her hair over her shoulder and raised her chin. "Poor Mr. Football, cheating again. I bet Troy shagged her."

"Don't be daft. Troy may have looked. He might even have fancied her, but do that, no way."

"Was it hard seeing Brendon?"

"Despite the puffed lip, he's as dishy as ever," Maggie said, eyeing the empty spots on her vanity. "He was a nice bloke until Ms. Pratt came along."

"Do you think it was Ms. Pratt's fault and not Rachel?"

Maggie rolled over and squished her back into a mound of pillows and stuffed animals. "Rachel was no different than me. She went about it the wrong way."

"I don't think Troy humped her. Ms. Pratt looked differently at him than she did Brendon."

Maggie petted the ears of a stuffed pig and tilted her head. "What do you mean?"

"She looked at Troy like she wanted to dive into his smile and soak in the happiness." Charlotte closed her eyes and took a quick breath. "She looked at Brendon like he was everything she yearned for but couldn't have."

"When did you see that?"

Charlotte hung her head and flicked at her plum nail polish. "That day in the pool."

Maggie flung the pig at Charlotte; she took aim with a stuffed cat. "You cheeky cow. You told me I was imagining things."

"You were gutted. I couldn't. All those glances you noticed; I saw them too."

Maggie cuddled the stuffed cat. She could feel Brendon's presence beside her, smell the citrusy scent of his skin. Something inside her broke. That sad feeling only Brendon Cook could give her ached.

"Why couldn't Ms. Pratt stay that? A Ms. I don't particularly like older men, Walter Pratt has a charm about him."

"I thought you fancied our Lord Chancellor?"

Maggie dropped her forehead on the stuffy and giggled. "You swore you'd never mention that. We were discussing the German invasion of Poland. It's a crucial event in history. Mr. Cook had so many interesting things to say."

"Did you get a tingle?"

"Charlotte Elodie," Maggie said, shoving the cat within a mound of stuffed animals. "Ms. Pratt has caused a lot of trouble."

Charlotte glanced at herself in the mirror, angling her head from side to side. "I spent an extra fifteen minutes on my hair and makeup. Troy didn't even notice."

Maggie flopped to the edge of the bed, opened the vanity drawer, dug in her stash of sweets, and tossed a Double Decker at Charlotte. "Chocolate will make you feel better."

"The last sweet my little... Troy gave me, was one of these."

Maggie grabbed a bag of Drumstick Squashies and tore it open. "Are you ever going to forgive him? It's extremely uncomfortable at school."

"Troy was coming out of the shower when Ms. Spence and I got back from apple picking. I told myself, Charlotte Donovan, don't go staring at that gorgey body or dishy face, go straight to the kitchen. You know what that dolt did?"

Maggie hid her smile behind the bag.

"He kissed my cheek and walked to his room. He didn't even get a biggie. You can usually see it; the towel pops up."

"Can you please forgive him?"

"Have you forgiven Brendon?"

"I was happy Brendon was hurting as much as he hurt me. Then I thought, if I keep hanging onto the hurt, he'll still be hurting me. I forgive him," Maggie said, biting into the candy. "I'm worth more than Brendon can give right now. I'll be okay without him."

Charlotte gobbled the chocolate bar and tossed the wrapper in the bin. "I'm not ready to let go. Troy needs to hurt as much as me."

Maggie gobbled the sweets and tossed the bag on the vanity. "I'm done with boys for a while, especially footy players."

"I thought you fancied the keeper from Swindon."

"Not after I found out he's done it with Matilda."

"You're completely over Brendon?"

"For now."

Thumps rattled the thin walls; Jack flew into the bedroom and dropped a block structure into Charlotte's lap. "For you."

Maggie giggled at Jack's Charlie face. "What is it?"

"A key to the Batcave."

Charlotte held up the odd cluster of bricks and smacked her lips against his cheek.

"Yuck. You can still give me the lurgy, even if you're my girlfriend."

"Take a sweet and go," Maggie said.

Jack peered into the collection of candy and grabbed a handful. "You promised to play with me."

"I will when Charlie leaves."

Jack flapped his cape and thumped from the room.

"You're playing with your brother now?"

"I only got annoyed because Brendon did. Hey, I just thought of something." "You do like the Swindon keeper."

"If you and Troy break up, you can wait for my brother. We'll be sisters-in-law."

Charlotte placed the block key in her purse. The smile dropped from her lips. "Don't you miss Brendon? I miss Troy horribly."

"I miss how he used to sneak a peek at my knickers, helping him with his homework. I miss mum pulling out the milk jug and cursing because he drank it all."

"Did you throw out your wedding scrapbook?"

"I chewed every nail before I put it in the bin."

"I still have mine," Charlotte said, shoving onto the bed. She leaned her head on Maggie's shoulder and twiddled the ears of a stuffed hedgehog. "I keep it beside my bed and add things to it. My wedding colours were going to be lilac, Kelly green, teal and white before Troy fancied the French tart."

"You might still have your boho wedding and I might show up in Dortmund."

"I don't need Troy, you know."

"Oh, I know, Miss. Independent."

"I want him, and that makes the difference. Pass me my phone."

Maggie reached for Charlotte's purse and dragged it to the side of the bed. She dug around the massive bag, snatched the phone, handing it to Charlotte. A photo gallery entitled 'Little Crumpet' filled the screen.

"Troy waited four months before trying to hump me."

"Gosh, randy Troy," Maggie said, tapping on a photo. "He looks dishy in this photo."

Charlotte shooed her hand away and dropped the phone in her lap. "He was the first boy who didn't want to feel my new tits."

"It's hard to imagine yourself with someone new. I miss Brendon, but he doesn't want me. He doesn't want Rachel. Troy wants you."

"He hurt me. He kept secrets."

"I saw how you looked at his pictures. It's time to let go."

"Of my little crumpet?"

"Of the hurt. Forgive him."

"You're the smartest girl I know. I should listen to you."

"Falling in love is easy. Letting go, that's the hard part. It took a while for me to realize I had to. Your heart will give you the right answer. Mine said, not now."

***

Angelene was scared and not the fear of spiders or heights scared but deep down in her marrow, scared. She had spent the rest of the day a blend of timid pink and cowardly yellow.

"I won't be able to go back to London with that bastard around," Walter said. He pushed the SIM card from her phone, snarled, and bolted from the kitchen. Angelene wrestled with her breath and left the security of the window bench.

"David will surely send Brendon away."

Walter stopped halfway down the hall and glared. "It'll be all over the Taunton Times, the battle at Rosewood manor, the fall of Walter Pratt." Angelene climbed the stairs two at a time. She scrambled down the hall and froze, staring at the contents of the jewellery box.

"Did he give this to you?" Walter said, shaking the Dortmund jersey. "Answer me."

Angelene dug her fingers into the door frame. "I took it."

Walter chuckled and whipped the jersey. "You stole it? Unbelievable."

She uncurled her fingers and hurried towards the bed. Walter snagged her wrist. She gasped. There was no gold in his fingertips, only wrath and rage.

"Sit," Walter barked, shoving her to the bed. "Articles about Brendon, his jersey. You really did fancy him."

"You have no right going through my things."

"No right? This is my home. I told you no secrets."

He fished in a pile of postcards and held up a photograph. Angelene wiped at the beads of sweat prickling her upper lip. Henri, sugar smile and liquid blue eyes. Lemon macarons, his scent, like crushed lemon peel, his death, ripped through her brain like grenades.

"Who is this? Another boy you loved?"

"Henri, it's Henri."

Walter flicked the photo onto the bed and unfolded a news article. "What is it about these young boys? Shall I drive you to Spence farm?"

"It just happens," Angelene said, digging her fingernails into her forearm. "The boy chooses me. I want their light. They fall in love. I run, snuffing them out."

"You didn't run from Brendon, you keep running to him," Walter said, crinkling the article. "All I asked was you wear a few posh frocks, mingle with the other wives."

"I don't want that. I never wanted that."

"But you want this," Walter said. He whipped the article and scrunched another.

"I was ending it. That is why I asked him to meet me."

"It certainly didn't look like you were ending it. You never kissed me like that. Hell, we don't kiss at all."

Angelene gazed at the glow in Brendon's window. Her heart twisted. "I felt something. It frightened me."

"You're finally being honest with me."

"Once upon a time, there was a girl who pushed people away and closed herself off from love. She saw love leave, turn people into monsters. She couldn't love, love means goodbye."

"I'm not a fool. I saw the two of you kissing, fucking, doing the things we don't do."

"I want to stay married. Brendon's light is too bright. He'll soon see, he'll hate me."

Walter threw up his hands and grumbled deep in his throat. "You decide what you want."

Angelene gathered the postcards and drawings and cradled them in her lap.

I made you a picture today.

How pretty. It's springtime, little bird. You've drawn baby birds and cherry blossoms.

Will you put it in your office?

I'm going to frame it and put it in my house for all my friends to see.

Roman, I love... Don't be afraid to say those words, little bird.

Angelene stared at the glow. "I don't want to chase my springtime away. Please God help me."

You'll find your springtime, little bird. When you do, run to it as fast as you can.

Angelene placed the postcards and drawings back in the box and shut the lid. She spotted Walter's phone buried beneath a tie. Angelene jumped from the bed and rushed to the doorway. Walter was at his laptop. The rata-tap-taps were as fierce as a machine gun. Angelene swiped open the phone. She hit send, then removed it, fear and frantic captured her. Money. She needed money for a taxi, a plane ticket, a hotel. Angelene scurried to the closet and lifted a stack of ties. Her eyes widened at the rolls of bills. She stretched her neck and stared into the hallway, tap, tap, tap. Angelene bit into her lip, snatching a bundle. She squished the roll in her pocket, shoved aside Walter's suits and dragged out the duffel bag. She placed the jewellery box inside and hurried to the dresser. Angelene flung stacks of clothes into the bag and wrestled with the next drawer. She zigzagged back and forth, tossed jeans and sweaters onto the accumulating pile. Brendon's hoodie, her books.

"My paintings."

She stopped to catch her breath. There was no time to collect them. Dortmund would be springtime. Her paintings would be new, happy, normal.

'I need a plan. I don't like to plan, but I must.'

Angelene flopped onto the clothes and hugged her knees. Henri told her every building starts with a solid plan. Every angle, shape, and line formed an incredible structure. Angelene composed her blueprint.

'I'll hide my bag until Walter falls asleep. Steal his cell phone, walk as far as I can and call Malcolm. Scotch, I'll offer him scotch with dinner, ramble on about fairy tales, and Victor Hugo. Bore him to drink.

"What are you doing?"

Her heart leapt and raged. "I'm leaving... leaving you."

"Where are you going to go?"

"I don't know, but I can't be here with you."

She climbed off the duffel bag and steadied herself against the footboard. Disappointment flooded her; the blueprint vanished.

"I'll walk into town, call Malcolm. He'll take me somewhere."

Walter spied his phone. He reached for it and slid it into his pocket.

"Please let me go."

Angelene stared from the door to Walter. If she ran quick, ducked around him, she could escape and run to Troy, beg him to take her into town.

"Did you steal my money?" Walter said, spying the mussed tie box. "You aren't going anywhere. I'll decide if you stay or go."

"You don't love me."

"You don't love me. We're a perfect match."

"Go see Kate, talk to her. You'll see she's better suited. It's written across your love line."

Walter picked up a pile of clothes and shoved them in the drawer. "You have no job, no money. People will never forgive you for cheating on me."

"How can you still want me?"

"I don't like to fail," Walter said, his face softened. "Put your clothes away, little bird, then come downstairs. Skysports is replaying the Dortmund match. You can envision your lover in net."

Angelene watched him leave, her eyes blurred.

"I can't stay in Taunton without you. Who will save me when life gets complicated? Who will hold my hand? I was barely living after Henri disappeared from my life."

Don't you think you build these walls to see who will tear them down? Find your springtime, little bird.

"If I'm in Germany, I could take the train to Zurich. I could find you Roman. My Opa and Oma are in Berlin. I could have a family."

Angelene withdrew the money from her pocket and tucked it beneath the clothes. Blood pounded in her ears; the floor tilted under her tingling feet. She laid a hand against her pounding heart; she couldn't stay with Walter. Things would never be the same. She had damaged his ego. Sofia and David would look at her with hate in their eyes.

"I need to think, clear the doubt from my mind."

Angelene padded to the bathroom, turning on the taps. She poured bubble bath under the flow of water and closed her eyes to the warmed scent of patchouli. Angelene sunk into the tub and scooped a handful of bubbles.

What does love feel like, Roman?
Like the sun has warmed your insides. You glow, little bird.
Mother says love makes her crazy. She's horrible until you arrive.
Love can make you do silly things. It can make you angry and sad, but it can also make you incredibly happy.
I don't like to feel angry or sad, especially when they're mixed. I don't want to fall in love and be like mama.
Allow yourself to fall in love, little bird. It will help you find your wings.

"I should have run after you, Roman." Bubbles flew into the air as she spoke. "I should have screamed, I love you. You might have come back. You were fairy tales and adventure, Edelweiss and chocolate shaped like the alps. I love you."

Angelene fumbled in the wire rack and grasped the bottle of shampoo. She unscrewed the cap and sniffed. The scent carried her to Henri. She could see him sitting at Hugo's feet, sketch pad in hand. The memories reached her heart and grasped it.

Do you like your castle? There are fields of lavender surrounding it, and a garden full of buttercups, daffodils, edelweiss, and cornflower.
It's prettier than Versailles.
My blue and your yellow will make the loveliest shade of green. See how lucky we are.
I am a hard person to love, out of the blue, Henri.
It's been easy for me to love you, petite oiseau.

Angelene moaned softly, sending bubbles into the air.

"I love you, Henri. Please hear me, I love you. Your persistence made me red and spiky black. You also made me yellow. Your fingertips smelled of graphite pencils and lavender petals. You were shapes and dreams, stars, and sugar, with eyes the colour of spilled ink."

Her breath snagged in her lungs. She clutched the edge of the tub and plunged under the water. A scream burbled, she rose, gasped for air. Angelene wiped the bubbles from her face. Goosebumps prickled her skin. She closed her eyes and imagined herself beneath Brendon, wrapped in his arms, his scent, his light.

It is late, mon amour; you should be sleeping.
I can't. I was thinking about you, waking up with you, drinking coffee together. It's going to be bloody brilliant coming home to you.
Shall I tell you a story? Once upon a time, King David banished his son from the kingdom. He brought shame to his family. The boy waited at the train station every day for his girl to arrive.

Does she come?
She comes, mon amour.
"I love you and your beautiful, comforting brown. You are light and magic. The prince of the pitch, lemons, and kisses. You are a glorious sunrise, the stars I see glowing, even on the darkest night. I love you."

Tears stung her eyes; an ache hollowed her chest. Love screamed in her head. She dug her fingernails into her thighs. Desperation, shame, and regret tumbled and thumped. The words spewed from her mouth in sludgy black.

"I ran from Henri and Brendon in different ways than Walter. His black was powerful and intense. I had moments of love with King Midas. I loved and hated his hands. You were a crinkled smile, strong, overwhelming love. You saw my worth. I love you, Walter Pratt."

Are you coming, little bird?
Where are we going, Roman?
To find your springtime. Hold my hand, ready, little bird?
"Yes, Roman, I am ready."

46 Blue

Sirens shrieked. Brendon fumbled within the blankets for the remote and clicked off the television. He snuggled under the blankets and closed his eyes. Sirens wailed. Brendon rolled over and stared at the television screen. He leapt from the bed and rushed to the window. Flashes of blue flickered between the willow branches. Brendon grabbed a wrinkled pair of shorts, jerked them on, and ran from the room. He flew down the stairs, jamming his feet into his trainers. Brendon swung open the door. The sky was intense blue, his eyes swelled with tears. Panic grew, blue light burned his eyes.

"Sweetheart, stay away from Walter's." Sofia wound a wrap around her shoulders and reached for his arm. He ran. The world blurred around him and not in the way it had when he had first laid eyes on Angelene. Panicked tears smudged the trees and road. Brendon thumped to a stop and tugged at Nicola's sweater.

"Go home, topolino."

"You threatened to kill her if she went near me. Nonna..."

Nicola gripped his shoulders and shook him. "You don't need to see this. Go home. I won't tell you again."

"You killed her. You threatened her, you said hurtful things."

Brendon shrugged himself free of her grip and ran. Walter stood among the yellowing wisteria, his t-shirt, stained crimson. Two paramedics rolled a stretcher out the opened door. Brendon wobbled and raked his fingers through his hair. His eyes darted from Walter's shirt to the sheet covering her body.

"What have you fucking done?"

Walter was still as a statue, expressionless, with icy blue eyes.

"Go home."

"You hit her again. You hurt her."

Brendon stepped towards the stretcher. Walter reached and snagged him by his t-shirt. He coughed and gagged. Thirteen coils in the noose, thirteen steps to the gallows, thirteen things that defile a person, adultery, murder, covetousness. Judas, the thirteenth guest at the last supper. Brendon swung his arm behind him and pounded his cast against Walter's hip. Thirteen steps to her.

"Stop."

"Out of the way, son."

Brendon gripped the cold metal frame and dug his feet into the ground. "Please stop."

He stared at the sheet and the red stains. The world was silent. He bent over the stretcher and laid his head on her chest. "You can have my light; you can fucking have it."

He clutched the sheet, his chest tightening. This couldn't be the end of his story.

"You need to let go, son."

"Fuck off." Brendon dug under the sheet. Her skin was cold and clammy. "Goodbye means forever. This is not forever. I will not say goodbye." He pressed his lips against the sheet and closed his eyes. "This is not goodbye."

"Sweetheart, hold my hand."

He dropped to the ground; held his face in his hands and conjured her sometimes smile. He remembered how she slept in a little ball and painted her toes lemon yellow. He was her first kiss, first dance.

"You wanted her dead. Nonna wanted her dead. Walter hated her."

Sparks singed his heart and tore through his lungs.

"He did this." Brendon freed himself from Sofia's arms and charged at Walter. "He's hit her."

A police car pulled into the driveway; Brendon shoved Walter. "Officers, he did this. He's hit her before. He's fucking killed her. My Nonna threatened her. Please... somebody..."

"Sweetheart, we need to go."

"I don't want to leave her. I promised I would be there for her. This can't be goodbye."

"Say until we meet again."

The doors to the ambulance closed, sparks exploded and fell like powdery ash, numbing his insides. Brendon gazed into the sky; the sun painted the moors yellow. Somewhere within the trees, a bird chirped. He'd call this chapter, 'you found your wings.'

47 Commuovere

London was alive and bustling. Stars twinkled as bright as the Christmas lights decorating the nostalgic buildings on Story Gate. Walter squeezed up to the bar, ordered a lager, and turned towards a chorus of giggles. Kate Miller was in the middle of the group. She caught sight of him. Her smile was slight and tired. Walter ordered her a gin and tonic and waved her over.

"What brings you to London?"

"My niece's hen night. I'm not sure I'm up for a pub crawl."

Walter grabbed their drinks. They shoved their way through a group of people wearing laminated name tags and slid into a booth. "You kept up with me in Dublin."

"I feel like I've aged twenty years. I'm tired and not long days in court tired."

"I'm sure your niece's excitement will rub off and you'll be ready to party until dawn."

Kate glanced at the gaggle of girls in glitter and stilettos. "Sofia made me come. She said it would be fun to get away, act twenty-five. Twenty-five doesn't exist in me. I've been living on black coffee and adrenaline for weeks."

Walter nursed his pint; he was the blame for Kate's lack luster smile. He caused her to do the thing she hated the most: worry.

"You don't look a day over thirty."

"Still charming," Kate said, swirling the ice around her glass. "What brings you out on a Friday night? You haven't been a Friday night at the pub kind of guy for years."

Walter cradled the mug. The answer was simple: escape.

"You haven't returned my phone calls either."

"I've been busy."

Kate tossed the swizzle stick on the table. "Too busy to call a friend."

"I haven't been in the mood for I told you so. I get enough at work. Damn James McGregor is as much a gossip as his wife."

"No one cares in Taunton anymore."

Walter managed a thin smile. "I'm still the hot topic around Taunton. Politicians' wife found dead."

"You looked good in that news article about the allocation of resources. It was a dull read but, you'd never know you were hurting."

"That was Juliette. She made me fix my hair, change my tie. She's been lovely."

Kate raised an eyebrow and gave him a glassy stare. "You haven't learned your lesson."

"Not lovely in that way. She's saved my arse on more than one occasion." Walter said, taking a hearty sip.

"Where is our Lord Chancellor?"

"David has become a boring workaholic."

"David hasn't been home in over a month."

"That's how he deals, submerges himself in judicial policy."

"He needs to go home to Sofia."

Walter had given little thought to home. The day he found Angelene limp in the tub, he lifted her body from the chilly water, held her against his chest and tried to breathe life back into her, horrified at the gashes on her wrists. After the ambulance had taken her body away and the police had left, he had wandered around the house. Lavender and patchouli had followed him from room to room. He had escaped into the night, switching from anger to grief, grateful to have known her and sorry for the pain he had caused. The road took him to London. He hadn't looked back.

"How's Sofia?"

"The same. Worried, angry, sad. She's never been good at forgive and forget."

"David said she stayed with Nicola for a bit. Shopping at Versace and Valentino, didn't make her happy?"

"You, of all people, should know things don't fill voids. Amelia rambles around the house. Brendon isn't doing well."

Walter fanned his reddening face with the cardboard coaster. "Good."

"He's hurting too."

"He should be, and not because Angelene took her life."

"He's seeing a psychiatrist."

Walter set down his mug and massaged his brow. What bothered him the most wasn't the humiliation or failure, it was the betrayal, the snap of his heart by the one person he loved the most.

"Angelene had a jewellery box filled with newspaper clippings and other mementos. From the moment she arrived in Taunton, every article about Brendon. A jersey, a hoodie."

"Did you burn it?"

"I thought about it," Walter said, gesturing to a server. "I left it by the potted cedar at the manor. Brendon loved her. It seemed fitting he should have it."

Kate studied Walter's face; her brow creased. "You look like you're going through the motions of normal. You smell good, you're dressed to impress, you're going to work. Underneath this fantastic façade, you're not okay."

"I'm fine," Walter said dryly. "Shouldn't you be off to another pub?"

Kate scanned the crowd; her niece and entourage were enjoying a round of vodka shots with a group of men intrigued by the bride to be.

"It doesn't look like I'll be leaving anytime soon. Talk to me."

Walter handed the server thirty pounds, clinked his glass against Kate's and took a sip.

"I hired cleaners to rid the loo of the blood. I've bought some new clothes. Sofia was right, Armani makes a nice suit. No wonder all the ladies swoon over Brendon."

Kate squeezed the lime, dropping it in her glass. "You know I don't like to worry."

"Don't. I'm fine."

"I'm worried for Sofia, David, Brendon, you," Kate said, pointing to the wrinkle between her brows. "I'm going to need Botox. You know how I feel about that."

"I took her ashes to Parc Floral; she loved those damn peacocks. I had Lisette and Yasmine join me. Yasmine still wears the pendant Ang gave her. Damn thing cost me a fortune."

"Angelene spoke of the girl. She loved her."

Walter grinned. If there was anyone Angelene Hummel could have loved, it was Yasmine.

"I kept the drawing Yasmine did. Put it in my room." Walter leaned over his beer. His breathing was slow and pensive. "Lisette blamed me. She said I killed Ang the day we met."

"What a horrible thing to say."

"Lisette was right. I took everything that made Angelene who she was and destroyed it. I started the process of her death."

Kate reached for Walter's hand. "Did she ever come around?"

"Once Yasmine took my hand and led me to Ang's favourite bench."

"What about Hugh? Was he helpful?"

Walter took a small sip and ran his thumb over Kate's palm. "I should have asked for Hugh's help sooner. Krieger could have helped her."

"What was he like?"

"I can see why Angelene loved him. The man has class."

"Was he upset when you told him?"

"It surprised him she lived to twenty-five. He still has the pictures Ang drew hanging in his office and sitting room. His biggest regret, not taking Angelene with him. She was the prettiest little girl Krieger had ever seen. He adored her. He fancied Veronique, but it was Angelene that kept him there."

"Is he married?"

"He married a German woman. They have homes in Zurich and Ingolstadt. He bought the home in upper Bavaria because Angelene loved the painted ceiling in St. Maria de Victoria Kirche. It made him feel closer to little bird."

"Roman Krieger could have been Angelene's escape."

After meeting Krieger, Walter imagined what life could have been like for Angelene. Private school in Zurich, studying at the ZHdK, University of the Arts. She would have been confident yellow, blossoming under Roman Krieger's love.

"It could have been the fairy tale Ang wanted. My life would be different. David and Sofia would be together. Brendon would be that carefree kid he used to be."

"You can't blame yourself. You didn't know she would take her life."

"I could have spent more time with her. I might have seen the red flags. It would have been me running, not her."

"No one blames you."

Walter chuckled, curling his fingers around Kate's. "I'm sure everyone except you and David blames me. I lie in bed at night, replaying all the things I could have done right. Guilt sleeps with me, that, and regret."

"You can't live with regrets. You tried, she tried. It's time to heal."

Walter glanced across the pub. A girl in a pink glittered sash stretched her arm above the crowd and waved furiously. "You're being summoned."

Kate squeezed his hand, clinked the ice around, and finished her drink.

"I'm staying in London for the weekend. Would you like to meet for lunch tomorrow?"

Walter grinned at the posse of girls shooting back vibrant blue cocktails.

"You think you'll be in shape for lunch? You might be getting in at that time."

Hoots, whoops, and resounding cheers lit up the pub. Kate tugged her purse strap over her arm. "I have two pubs left in me, then I'm calling it a night. What do you say? Lunch with an old friend."

Walter glanced at Kate. McCartney wool coat, dark wash jeans, Louboutin booties, Tiffany earrings. She was stunning, put together, unlike any woman he had seen.

"I'd love that."

"I'm staying at the Savoy."

"Impressive. We'll drive to Kent. There's a charming restaurant on the Folkestone Harbour."

She leaned across the table and pressed her lips against his cheek. "You have lipstick on your cheek."

Walter laughed and touched the mark. "It might bring me some attention. The women may think I'm still fit."

"You're still fit, just a little broken."

Kate slid out of the booth, grabbed her coat, and placed a hand on his shoulder. "Forgive Sofia and Brendon. They're hurting too."

"There's an Italian word, commuovere, to stir, to touch, to move. Angelene did all those things. She moved us all to tears, both good and bad."

"Everyone has lost something, everyone is suffering. Let it go."

The afternoon sun lit up the apartment in streams of golden light. Walter dropped his keys on the island, his ears filled with rap, rap, rap. Walter approached stealthily, afraid to disturb his friend. When he had left, David was at his laptop, furiously tapping, phone under his ear, the conversation neither heated nor friendly. He hadn't moved from the desk or his work.

"Were you talking to Sofia earlier?"

David glanced at the handwritten report and back to the keyboard, rap, rap, rap.

"She's coming to London. She wants to have drinks."

Walter slid onto the sofa, giddy, feeling something he hadn't for a while, alive. Lunch had been like it always was with Kate, easy, like he opened a forgotten book and remembered how much he enjoyed it.

"You don't look excited for someone who hasn't seen the love of their life in over a month. Put on one of those posh suits and your silk braces. I never understood what Sofia finds so attractive about braces."

"We're going to a pub," David said. He stared at a yellow notepad, mumbled something under his breath and pressed save. "There's no need for a posh suit. How was lunch?"

"It was nice. The conversation was delightful. She's witty, keeps me on my toes."

"Will there be another?"

"We're talking about you and Sofia." Walter said, stretching along the sofa.

"She chose sides. It wasn't mine."

"She's going to look fantastic."

"When doesn't she? Even when Brendon was going through his heartache and she wore my jumper, she looked beautiful."

"You don't believe it was exhaustion anymore?"

"The relationship started from the moment Angelene arrived in Taunton. She knew it was wrong, tried to end it. Once she gets stuck in your head, she's hard to forget."

"Nicola and Sofia thought someone hurt him. Nicola hinted it was Ang. I laughed it off."

"They said the same to me. I should have listened. I might have been able to stop it from going further."

Walter plucked a blanket from the back of the sofa and laid it over his legs. "Have you spoken to Brendon? I hear he isn't doing well."

"He has Edward Weiss, Sofia, Amelia."

"He needs his father."

David pushed the chair back and stared at Walter incredulously. "Have you forgotten what he's done?"

"If you would have asked me yesterday, I would have told you I hated him. Kate said it was time to forgive. She said I'd be able to move forward if I let go of the anger and hurt."

"It's not that easy."

Walter curled a pillow under his arm and relaxed into the cushions. "Ang gave Brendon parts of her she wasn't comfortable sharing with me. He loved her, I didn't."

David opened the drawer and reached for a frame. "I've been hanging onto the hurt for nineteen years."

Walter stared at the boy with dark hair and David's hazel eyes, nodding heavily. "Ethan was a good boy. Curious, too smart for his own good, like you."

David set the photo beside Sofia's picture, touching the boy's smile. "After Ethan died, I divided my life into two parts, before and after. I've been stuck in the before. After came too soon."

"The after hasn't been too bad."

"When I would come home from work, Ethan would run to the door and hug my legs." David pressed his fingers into the corners of his eyes, catching the tears. "He'd hug them so tight I'd almost fall over. Death took the father out of me; I've lost two sons."

Walter tossed back the blanket and walked to the kitchen. He shook the kettle, set it on the burner, and grabbed mugs from the cupboard.

"I forgive Brendon. I understood why Ang ran off to confession so often. It's a heavy burden to carry."

"I never wanted Brendon. I didn't want to live in that damn house or replace Ethan."

The kettle whistled, Walter took it off the stove, dropped tea bags into the mugs and poured water. "Sofia needed him. If you let go of all the hurt, you might realize you needed him too."

"After Ethan died, I found a home in Knightsbridge. It was a converted church, seven bedrooms, vaulted ceilings, original stone pillars. Brendon could have gone to Westminster school."

Walter flipped the tea bags into the sink and grabbed the mugs. "Ethan would have gone to a prestigious school. He would have gone to Oxford and become a barrister or a doctor. The little nipper was always researching and discovering things in the forest. Brendon is a goalkeeper and a damn good one."

"Brendon is nothing like me."

Walter lounged on the sofa and shoved his feet under the blanket. "No two children are alike. Look at Prudence. She was wild and free. Her sister, a bookworm. You see Richard and Gianni in Brendon. That's what you don't like. Accept Brendon for who he is." He blew into his tea and took a sip. "If I had accepted Angelene as the bohemian artist she was, I might not have found her in the tub with her wrists slashed."

"Brendon loved Sofia more. They would greet me at the door, he would cling to her leg like I was some stranger."

"She was a desperate mother, fearful of losing another child. She's lost Brendon too."

"He's reckless, disrespectful."

"The kid cares deeply. He loves things other people don't see worth loving, like Ang and Rachel Jones. He may not be a scholar, but underneath that stupid behaviour, is a good kid."

"He slept with your wife."

"Get your hands off his throat. Stop carrying the burden around. You'll learn to like him again."

David finished his tea and cradled the mug in his hand.

"Meet Sofia tomorrow, give her a kiss, tell her you love her. It's time to heal."

A chill covered Walter's body. He tucked the blanket tighter around himself. It was a scary thought, admitting defeat, forgive and heal. It was another project to conquer. He'd do it. He was Walter Pratt.

***

A damp breeze seeped through Troy's jacket. He blew into his hands and gazed at the empty net. The first half of the season had ended. First had fallen to fifth. Matches were quiet without Brendon bellowing out the plays. Troy missed his friend.

"Troy Spence."

Troy shoved his hands in his pocket. It had been a while since he heard her voice. It was sticky sweet like candy, taking him back to sun soaked afternoons and irresistible kisses.

"You didn't answer my text," Charlotte said. She collapsed onto the seat beside him and dropped her purse at her feet. "I texted to see if you wanted anything from McDonalds. I'll share my Malteser McFlurry."

"How did you know where I was?"

"I rang your house. Your mum said you've been hanging around the pitch lately."

Troy shifted in the chair; it hadn't been in him to talk to anyone. He fumbled through the days, thinking of all the ways he could have shared his yellow with Angelene. He had dreamt he had baptized her in a pool of sunny yellow water and healed her scars. When he found a random feather or nuzzled Blossom's snout, he thought about her. He thought about how Angelene's death had obliterated Brendon. He thought about losing Charlotte.

"I didn't mean to ignore you. My mind is full."

"I deserve it." She ate a spoonful of ice cream and squished herself closer. "I was a cow, trying to hurt you."

"I come here to think. Some of my best memories are on the pitch. Brendon and I..."

He stopped himself. An ache throbbed in his chest. He missed the back-and-forth banter about which football league was better. He missed the secret pep talks before a match, the sprinting competition, laughs over pizza.

"I miss the old Brendon. I visited Ms. Cook. She said Brendon wanders around, brooding."

"It's going to take some time. Regardless of the yuck factor, you know, her being married, Brendon lost her and not in the break-up way, she's gone."

Troy tucked his arm around her and buried his nose in her hair. He breathed in orange blossoms and mimosa. That 'I miss you' feeling gripped his heart.

"I'm on loan to Newcastle. The Premier league like to do this, give us little guys match experience. The scout, Paul, says this is my shot."

"That's brilliant, but what does that mean?" Charlotte licked the back of the spoon and turned to him. "You'll have to move to Newcastle. You'll be gone."

Troy touched his forehead to hers and slipped his hand under her hair. "Mum is gutted. Brian and Callum have more chores to do. They're annoyed. Dad's been bragging."

"I won't see you."

Troy kissed her forehead and eased into the seat. "This could be my chance."

"Newcastle is on the River Tyne."

"It's about a five-hour drive from here."

"Is there anything brilliant about Newcastle? Manchester has the Trafford Centre. There are over two hundred shops."

"You don't know?"

Charlotte shrugged and stirred the ice cream.

"It has St. James Park where I'll be playing. What more do you need?"

"Shopping, posh restaurants."

"There's the Millennium Bridge. The Victoria Tunnel."

Charlotte fed him a spoonful and sighed. "I'm going to need more than a tunnel."

"Are you going to visit me? I thought you'd be happy to see me go."

"I've been thinking a lot since Ms. Pratt died. How empty everyone must feel. I don't want to feel that way."

Troy took the cup and placed it on the ground. He wrapped his hand around hers and grinned at the Manchester United inspired fingernails. "I missed you, even when you were right there crocheting with mum." He kissed her cheek and tapped his thumb on hers. "You're going to have to change your nail polish. Newcastle's home kit is black and white."

"That's boring babes."

Troy grinned. It wasn't his favourite pet name, but it was a start.

"Do you still love me? Bets around school are you and Declan Burke fancy each other."

Charlotte tossed her hair over her shoulder and laughed. "Don't be listening to those daft bets. He asked me to the pub, I told him no. No boy stands a chance. They don't compare to my sweet little crumpet."

Troy touched Charlotte's cheek. The distance between them had been the loneliest time of his life. Brendon would be empty for a while.

"Cyan, fuchsia, lapis, and gold."

"Are those the colours our apartment is going to be, if you come to Newcastle that is."

"Those are our wedding colours, for now. I change my mind every few months. Can you picture it babes, boho inspired, lots of flowers, greenery, antique crystal?"

"Didn't you say Ms. Pratt dressed like that?"

"Before Mr. Pratt changed her. I put myself in those brilliant Louboutin shoes she wore. It helped me understand. She wanted to feel that sunshine that makes you Troy Spence. That's all she wanted, was to be happy."

Troy squeezed the tears from his eyes. "Please say you'll visit me. I don't want to feel like my mate."

"I'll drive up every weekend and Easter holiday."

Troy rubbed his hand over his eyes and wiped it on his jeans. "Brendon was my biggest fan, other than you. Spence and Cook until the end. Every time I look at the pitch, my heart breaks."

"Then call him, babes."

"I thought memories were supposed to warm you up."

"We can't have my little crumpet sad. I have a brilliant idea."

Troy grabbed her purse and yanked it over his arm. "Another McFlurry. That one melted."

"We shared one on our first date. See, not all memories are sad."

He grabbed her hand and led her down the stairs. That first love feeling filled him.

"We can get the works, burgers, chips. Maybe eat it in my room."

"Oh, babes, it'll be like a picnic. Afterwards, we'll get starkers."

"It might be a long afternoon. When I said I missed you, I meant all of you." Troy tossed the soupy cup of ice cream into the bin. "I can't smell you on my pillow anymore."

"I better stay the night then," Charlotte said, snuggling into his arm. "Newcastle on Tyne, sounds like a fairy tale."

"You're okay with the tunnel, then?"

"I'm going to make a list of all the restaurants we'll eat at." She jumped into his arms and smothered his cheeks with kisses. "Every girl at school will be jealous. You're going to be on the telly. My little crumpet, a pro footy player."

"The coach will have to put me on the pitch first. I may sit on the bench."

"Ms. Pratt said you'd make it." She unwound her legs and jumped to the ground. "She saw people as colours and yours was the brightest. Brendon's is a little muddied. He'll be okay."

Troy unlocked the car. A flock of bramblings flitted around the beech trees, chirping playfully. Maybe Angelene was among them, wings strong and full. A quote from Tale of Two Cities burst into his head. It was the first novel he had finished for school; he wasn't sure if he enjoyed it or tolerated it, but the words resonated with him.

For you, and anyone dear to you, I would do anything. I would embrace any sacrifice for you and for those dear to you. And when you see your own bright beauty springing up anew at your feet, think now and then that there is a man who would give his life, to keep a life you love beside you.

Angelene had committed the ultimate sacrifice.

***

Brendon stood at the window. Tiny snowflakes fell from a white and smoky blue sky. The world looked cold, gleaming under the pale sunlight. When he first arrived in Dortmund, he ached for the familiarity of Rosewood manor, the smell of cedar, Amelia's humming. This was home now. Routine had helped take his mind off Angelene. Wake up, practice, eat, practice, come home, eat, sleep. Before he fell asleep, he would switch on his lamp, so she knew she still had a safe place to go.

Brendon grabbed his backpack and suitcase, glancing around the apartment. He had put the cornflower drawing in a little frame, placing it beside a collage of Henri's castles. It was the least he could do. Henri had loved her too. He framed the postcards and hung them above the kitchen table. Every morning when he sipped his coffee, he looked at one place Angelene wanted to visit and imagined her there. The jewellery box had a home on his coffee table and nights when his heart ached, he opened the lid, closed his eyes, and danced with her.

Locking the door, Brendon walked down the stairs and waved to Lukas. Lukas had been his saviour when he arrived on Dortmund's doorstep. Lukas, the sporting director, and coaching team believed in him when he didn't.

"Don't forget to finish your homework from Dr. Candler. Ten reasons playing for the U19 squad as first choice keeper is great." Lukas looked up and down the street and pulled onto the road. "Then start the next. Why going home will help you heal."

"I'll try. The last one got heavy, five reasons she killed herself."

"From what Walter told me, she was brave to live as long as she had."

"I don't think she wanted to die. She wanted to stop the pain."

Lukas flicked the blinker, looked in the side mirror and moved over lanes. "No one wants to die. The pain gets heavy. You, of all people, should know that."

"If Angelene was alive, she would say I was cold, painful blue."

"Angelene sounds like an interesting woman. I was scouting this kid at the Paris Saint-Germain academy and ran into Walter. He said she was a delicate flower ready to bloom. He saw something in her."

Brendon flexed his fingers; the wrist splint was tight and itchy. "Everyone did but her."

"It's a four-hour drive to Schleswig-Holstein."

"I promised Angelene. I won't let her down."

It seemed silly. Put a letter in a tree addressed to a dead girl. Dr. Candler suggested it would be therapy, face her death, say a last goodbye. Brendon wasn't sure. He faced her death every day and at the oddest times, brushing his teeth, showering after a gruelling training session, going wee. Facing it was one thing, saying goodbye was the tough part.

"This will cheer you up. The keeper from the senior squad signed with Bayern. You'll be starting keeper next season."

Brendon gazed out the window. He had yet to discover the city. He tried to walk around Westfalenpark. He never got further than a few feet down the path before he missed her and had to leave.

"I thought you'd be jumping out of your seat with the news."

"It's bloody brilliant. It's, well, she was supposed to be here."

"Walt is one of my closest friends. I'm not sure how I would have felt had she come with you."

Brendon laid his cheek against the glass and watched the buildings pass by.

"Thanks for not holding it against me."

"I said to Walt, du bist Ein volltrottel, you're an idiot marrying some girl you hardly know. I'm sure he has regrets."

"I have regrets."

Lukas swerved around a car. Brendon grabbed the grip handle. Lukas was pushing 130 mph. "What do you regret? If you ask me, the relationship should be a regret."

"I should have stayed her friend. Things might have worked out differently."

"It's hard to stay friends when feelings are involved."

"I would have tried. She may still be alive. Walt wouldn't hate me; my parents would like each other."

"You can sit and wonder all you want. It will not bring her back. Use this time to clear your head and enjoy your family."

Family. He didn't know what that meant anymore. Dortmund had become his family. He wanted to be the family Angelene never had. His own family, blown apart, mum, not mum, dad had run.

"There's another rumour floating around Signal Iduna Park."

"Cook's a knicker snatching hot head."

"Keep your wife away."

"I have no intention of sleeping with anyone's wife. Bloody hell, I didn't chat Angelene up, it just happened."

"Nothing just happens. You had a choice," Lukas said. He turned onto a forest road and nodded towards an oak tree. "Here we are."

Brendon stared at a fenced walkway and ladder. The famous tree looked no different from any of the others surrounding it.

"Why that tree?"

"Legend says the daughter of a Dodauer forester fell in love with a chocolate maker. They had to keep the relationship secret. They'd put love letters in the tree, married under it. People heard the love story and hoped for their own."

Brendon chuckled. "The tree was the first dating app."

"I guess it was."

"Dr. Candler said it'll take two years to get over the grief."

"You can't put a time limit on grief. You need it, it's a form of love, keeps you connected to the person. Go put your letter in the tree, I'm sure she's waiting to hear from you."

Brendon stepped into the brisk air. Snowflakes melted on his eyelashes and nose. He walked to the wooden walkway and gazed from the tree to the wavering canopy of leaves. Brendon gripped the rungs of the ladder, clearing the sting from his throat. This wasn't goodbye, it was until we meet again. He would see her on cloud nine in the prettiest yellow dress with the most incredible wings. Brendon pressed his lips against the envelope.

'I still choose you. I loved you even though I wasn't supposed to, and you loved me the best you could. We'll always have forever, cornflowers and coffee in the morning. Tu me manques, little bird.'

Brendon stood beside the luggage carousel, the orange light flashed, the conveyor belt chugged to life. Bags circled past him, his had the BVB logo. The signature suitcase said he was one of the mighty. Lukas's words, grief was love, danced around his head. All the love he still had to give sat in the corners of his eyes, bittered the lump in his throat and hollowed his chest. He missed the connection, how they always seemed to stumble into one another. Dr. Candler said the memory of the blood-soaked sheet and her wintry hands would eventually disappear. His mind would fill with happy moments, yellow moments, her fingers slick with oil, salty from first time fish and chips, teaching her to kiss, stumbling drunk along the beach. It was time to close the chapter he called, 'La Douleur Exquise, Exquisite Pain.'

Brendon grabbed his suitcase and stepped through the sliding doors. He scanned the crowd, around welcome home signs and bouquets of flowers. The feeling of home and, 'yes, you fucked Walter's wife, but you're still my son,' swarmed him. Brendon dodged around people headed to their gates and into outstretched arms.

"Ich vermisse dich, I miss you."

"Look at you, you look just awful. Do German girls like the scruffy look?"

Brendon kissed her cheek. She looked like mammina, red lipstick, wrists full of bangles. Sadness lingered in her dark eyes; she was trying her best to act the part.

"It's been a long day. You look brilliant."

Sofia smoothed her black pencil skirt. There was a hint of optimism in her thin smile. "I'm meeting your father tomorrow. I'm practicing."

The doors slid open, a blustery wind soaked in God's tears and scented with jet fuel, whipped around him.

"I wanted to tell you about the last match. I made this save. It was one on one, bloody brilliant."

"You can tell me about it later. I need your dad to come home. Mum is flying in tomorrow. It would be nice to have my family together."

"What if I need you?"

"I've been there for you, sweetheart. Your father needs me now."

Brendon studied Sofia's face; it was her time to heal.

"How am I going to get home?"

"I ordered you a taxi. I think you'll like the driver. He needs a friend too."

Malcolm leaned against the cab, twiddling the end of his moustache.

"Did he find out from gossip, or did Walt have the decency to tell him?"

"Walter met him for coffee. It devastated the poor man."

Brendon shifted from foot to foot and flicked the strings on his hoodie.

"Did Walt mention what I did, we did, about her and me?"

"He told Malcolm she took her life and gave him a drawing." She rummaged around her purse for her keys and touched his cheek. "How do I look? I want a reaction."

"Bloody brilliant. It's nice to see you out of dad's jumper."

"It's been painful with you and your father gone. I have nothing but photographs to prove we were once a family."

"We'll be a family again."

"I hope so, sweetheart. See you soon."

She walked away. A little tug pulled at his heart. Confident but not confident, mum.

"This is a first for me, having a pro footy player in my taxi."

"I play for the U19 squad."

Malcolm smiled, took his luggage, and set it in the rear seat. "I've read the papers. Taunton's hero will replace the first team keeper."

"I'm no bloody hero."

"Angelene said you'd be a star. She saw that light in you."

Brendon watched a plane split through the clouds and dropped onto the seat; *she took my light with her.*

"Are you happy to be home?"

"It feels weird. Like when I flew into Dortmund. You don't know what to expect or how people will react. There's a lot of talk floating around Taunton."

"I don't pay attention to gossip. I just take people where they want to go and mind my business."

Brendon laid his head against the headrest. Kate had sworn the gossip had settled; his mother told him otherwise. She had become a defender of the Cook name, her son, her family. She had gone as far as having Troy round for pizza to give her the scoop on what makes a great defender. According to Troy, there were five attributes of a central defender: positioning, communication, strength, technical ability, and composure. She told Brendon, on a nightly phone call, she had been practicing each. She placed herself close to Victoria McGregor to bat away any garbage spewing from her mouth. Her opinions were forceful yet polite. She was slowly finding her strength to hold back the tears when faced with whispers, your son is a dirty prick, or your marriage is falling apart.

"I drive past Angelene's favourite book store now and then. It used to make me sad. It makes me happy now, knowing she loved that place." Malcolm switched on the radio. Gorecki's Symphony #3 resonated through the car. "I've experienced every emotion, sad, angry. I've accepted her death."

Brendon rolled his head towards Malcolm. Angelene had said Malcolm was twinkly green, he was dull, and murky.

"Already? Dr. Candler told me it would take time. I've cycled through anger, denial, I'm stuck on depression."

"Sometimes it takes people a little longer. I talk to my wife about Angelene and when I see certain things, like telephone poles and little birds, I remember how special she was."

Brendon relaxed into the seat; his heart filled with memories: rabbits, Victor Hugo.

"Angelene had an interesting way of seeing the world. I remember picking her up from the charity shop on North Street. She had rescued a stack of National Geographic, her words. That's what I loved about her," Malcolm said, flicking on the indicator. "What are some things you liked about her?"

"I don't want to talk about her anymore." Brendon pushed back his cuff. Two and a half hours had flown by. "Taunton still looks the same."

"It helps to talk."

Brendon had heard this for weeks, from Dr. Candler, his coach, his teammates. He'd talk about how heavy his heart was, then switch to goalkeeping.

Malcolm slowed at a stop sign and patted his arm. "Three things."

"I liked the sound of her voice, how she pronounced certain words, like phoot-ball. I liked her love of books. She had a quote for any situation." Brendon ran his finger under his nose and sniffed back the sting. "I liked her paintings, even the sad ones."

"Mr. Pratt gave me a drawing. Angelene titled it, je ne peux pas vivre sans toi. I can't live without you."

"What was in the drawing? She was obsessed with creepy things in cloaks."

"A brown rabbit, a little yellow bird, and a mouse with topolino written on his shirt. They were having tea."

"I feel like I'm stuck holding all her pieces. I never got the chance to put her back together."

"Each day, take one of those pieces, say what it is, and put the intention out there. God will listen and make her whole."

"You sure? God didn't help her. She asked. He ignored her."

"That's anger talking. If God's offended by someone's actions, He won't listen."

An ache scratched and clawed at his gut. They had spit on her vows, stained Walter's sheets. He wore a black spot of shame just as Hester Prynne wore her scarlet A.

"Bloody hell, Mr. Thornton still hasn't figured out how to hang Christmas lights."

The same wreath with faded candy canes and silver presents hung on the door. Strings of multi-coloured lights dipped and dangled precariously from the eavestrough. Suki laid on the brick fence; her paws crossed, the faithful watch cat.

"I drove Margaret home after drama practice with Charlotte Donovan. They were giggling something fierce, made me chuckle."

"Is Maggie in love? She giggles when she fancies someone."

"There was one rumour I listened to. I'll let Troy Spence tell you that."

The row of terraced homes faded, moors cloaked in dark green and brown rose on either side of the car. Spence's farm sprawled across the land. Brendon smiled. Charlotte's car was in the driveway.

"You can't give me a hint. Troy and I aren't really talking."

"His news to tell."

They whizzed past the farmhouse; Brendon cranked his neck to get a look. He was positive Malcolm had sped the car up. The house looked lonelier, overgrown hawthorn and cedar clogged the flower beds and front door.

"I appreciate you driving me home."

"Your mother paid me well, gave me a Christmas bonus."

"What colour would you say my mum was?"

"A mixture of black, blue, and purple, like a bruise taking too long to heal."

"I would add a little green for hope."

"Tragedy makes you realize how important family is. You find that joy, find your light."

"Thanks for being Angelene's friend."

"The friendship may have been brief, but it was worth every second."

Brendon stepped out of the taxi and grabbed his luggage. Amelia's car was in the carport. He didn't get to say, see you soon. He didn't know how she was feeling or if she forgave him. Brendon trudged up the walkway and opened the door, welcomed by a spirited rendition of 'My Favourite Things.' He glanced around the foyer. The Christmas tree that had a home by the staircase was missing. There was no garland wrapped around the banister or familiar smells of cinnamon and shortbread perfuming the air. Brendon walked up the stairs. The door to the room that had been forever locked was open. He shoved his backpack and suitcase towards his room and stepped cautiously. Mammina had redecorated.

"Bloody hell. I hope she didn't..."

Brendon rushed down the hall. His room was exactly how he left it. The struggle, the desperate goodbye, and pleas of 'don't send my boy away,' lingered. Brendon scraped his fingers through his hair and followed the melody. He stopped at the table outside the great room doorway and touched the photo of the brother he had never met.

"My goodness, look at you," Amelia said, scurrying from the kitchen. "You look like a proper footy player." She reached and held her plump hands against his cheeks. "I've missed having you around here. The house is quiet."

Brendon wound his arm around her. They walked to the kitchen.

"I'm baking pork pies for David. I'm hoping he comes... I made your dinner and turned down your bed. You must be tired."

Brendon stood in the doorway. The cedar boughs that decorated the cupboards and pantry door were missing. There was no wreath hanging on the window or mulled cider bubbling on the stove. The mistletoe Sofia hung, so she could steal a kiss from David or him or anyone she could torture, was missing too.

"Pappardelle ai funghi. Nicola's recipe," Amelia said, handing him a plate. "Milk?"

"Please. What the bloody hell is going on? I'm home for Christmas. The place looks worse than the day I left."

Amelia stirred the pork filling, walked to the fridge, grabbed the milk, and poured him a glass. "I'm making spongata di Natale. Sofia and David like to have that cake with tea."

"A bloody cake will not bring Christmas into the house."

"Your mother isn't in the Christmas spirit."

"I'm not either. Maybe if the trees were up, the twinkle lights, we'd feel like celebrating."

"I asked Sofia if she wanted me to drag everything out. You know it takes a month to decorate this place. She didn't want to." Amelia said, spooning filling into pie shells.

"How is she and don't say fine?"

"Sad. Wanders around here, sits in your room, Ethan's room. She's worn a hole in David's jumper."

Brendon guzzled the milk and set down his glass. "I thought she would have come home with me."

"David needs her."

"I need mum."

Amelia popped the tray in the oven, grabbed the pan off the stove and rinsed it. "She pushed David out the door. He needs her love now."

"Bloody hell, I made a mess of things."

"You sure did. You and that girl."

"I don't want a bloody lecture. I live with the fucking guilt every day."

Brendon twirled the pappardelle around his fork. She wasn't some girl. She was part of his story, the chapters he read and reread.

"I wish Walter never brought her to Taunton."

"I wish she never killed herself. People keep telling me I'll be okay. I don't want to be okay. If I'm okay, it means I've forgotten her. I promised I'd always be there."

Amelia wiped her hands on her apron and perched on a stool. "Haven't you met someone?"

"I haven't gotten over Angelene. I go to Westfalenpark and sometimes I see her sitting on the park bench with her books and drawings. When I can't sleep, I hear her."

"I'm sorry you're hurting."

"I watched Angelene lose bits of herself every time Walter tried to change her. I picked up the pieces and let her be her."

"You were a good friend. You should have stayed that way," Amelia said, weaving the apron ties between her fingers. Brendon watched the tie loop over her thumb and under her finger. Who would hold Angelene's hand when it trembled?

"Can you take the pies out in twenty minutes?"

"You're leaving?"

"I was doing Sofia a favour. I hate seeing her sad."

"I don't want to be alone. It's bloody creepy in here."

Amelia folded the apron and tucked it into the drawer. "Think how Sofia feels. All those memories stirred up, only me to help with the loneliness."

Brendon massaged the ache bouncing around his forehead. "You don't like me very much, do you?"

"I love you. I don't like what you did. Twenty minutes."

Brendon grabbed his plate and headed to the great room; the room was as bleak as the rest of the house. He set down his plate and pulled his cell from his pocket, setting the alarm for twenty minutes. Tossing the phone on the sofa, he walked to the armoire and pushed the door open. He grabbed the remote, glanced at the mantle, and stumbled, bumping into the armrest. He stared into the eyes of a girl in a black velvet dress. She looked eerily familiar. Brendon found his footing, scrambled onto the sofa, clutching a pillow against his thundering heart. A voice whispering *'tu me manques'* crept from the shadowed corners. She was always with him, in his heart, in his head and now in the great room. Brendon grabbed his cell and punched in a number.

"Can you come over and quick?"

Brendon stared at the girl and shivered. The resemblance was frightening. How could he let go when she was all around him?

"Mr. Football, where are you?"

"In the great room." Brendon turned his back to the painting and grinned.

"Did you sprint?"

"I drove," Troy said. He flung his arms around him and squeezed. "I missed you, mate."

"Bloody hell, let me go."

"Dismal in here."

"It's like I never left. My school kit is still on the chair, piles of football magazines everywhere. The clothes dad threw on the floor are still in a pile."

"Walter caught you kissing Angelene and next thing, you're on a plane. Why were you so stupid, mate?"

"I think my heart knew it would be our last kiss."

Troy slid over the armrest and smoothed his bangs. "It's funny how we just know these things. I went to leave the pitch. Something told me to stick around. Charlie showed up. We talked."

"Is that the good news I heard about?"

"I'm on loan with Newcastle. No more A-levels for me."

Brendon picked up his plate and swirled the pasta around his fork. "That's bloody brilliant. Is Charlie going with you?"

"Her dad wants her to finish school. She's already looking at homes, two million pounds, mate. How are the German girls? Do their jubblies look ace in those dirndl dresses?"

"Do you think they walk around in those? Bloody hell, they look like normal girls."

Troy gazed at the painting on the mantle, blinked, and shook his head. "You've been looking?"

"I went to a café last weekend. This girl said she recognized me from a match and offered to buy my coffee. I looked, but that was it. I bought our coffee."

"How are you? I've been meaning to call."

"It still hurts. Don't bloody lecture me about loving Angelene. I already got an earful from Amelia."

"I wasn't planning on it."

"I have good days and bad days. More good than bad, thanks to Dr. Candler and the coaching team."

Troy tossed a pillow in the air, stared at the painting, and recoiled. "That bleeding painting is spooky. It looks just like..."

"You can say her name. It looks like Angelene." Brendon twirled pasta around his fork and slurped. "I thought I might call Maggie."

"Leave her alone. She hasn't cried for a month. You look at her with those brown eyes and that dimply smile and Charlie's life will be miserable. I won't be around to make her feel better."

"How's Rachel?"

Brendon had moments when he thought about texting her and apologize for hurting her. He couldn't bring himself to do it.

"She comes to school and goes home. Tilly doesn't speak to her anymore, says she's as boring as Maggie."

Brendon, the heartbreaker. He lived everyday numb, desperately trying to stitch up his heart. Rachel was doing the same. More damage done.

"Should I give her a ring?"

"And break her heart for the sixth time?"

"How do you know how many times I broke her heart?"

"We talked. I felt bad for her. She loved you, mate, like proper loved."

"The day Angelene... when I ran to the farmhouse... I held her hand to warm it, it stayed cold."

Troy dropped the pillow, flopped onto the sofa, and touched Brendon's shoulder. "I don't know what I would do if I lost Charlie. The entire time we were fighting was the loneliest time of my life."

"I was walking in Westfalenpark, an ambulance drove by sirens blaring. I bloody lost it. My heart bounced up to my throat."

"The night it happened; I was wrestling with my brothers. The cows were mooing, the chickens wouldn't settle. Dad grabbed his gun, thinking something was in the barn. By the time he got to the back door, it was quiet. I went numb, mate, like I knew something bad happened."

Pain swept through Brendon. He remembered laying in bed, staring at the text, she would meet him in Germany. He had fallen asleep clutching hope, only to wake around midnight with tingly wrists, hearing her whisper tu n'es plus là ou tu étais, mais tu es partout là où je suis, you're not where you used to be, but you're everywhere I am. He had fallen back asleep pondering the Hugo quote. She said one day he would understand. When he woke to sirens, he knew she was everywhere around him and gone.

"I feel guilty for missing her. Guilty for loving her. Guilty for hurting everyone. How can you grieve when the guilt strangles you?"

"You did a terrible thing, mate; guilt will last as long as the grief. One day, you'll wake up, think of Angelene, smile instead of feeling sad."

"Sorry for bothering you. I hope you and Charlie weren't busy."

"She's baking ginger biscuits and shortbread with mum. I was going to watch her. She gets flour on her cheeks. It's brilliant."

"Do you think she'd come over? I might put the Christmas tree up, surprise mum."

"Ours has been up for weeks. Brian and Callum knocked it down a few times. It's Christmas at Spence farm."

"The house feels bloody empty."

"I'll text Charlie. We'll bring some cheer to the old manor."

"There was one change."

Troy glanced up from his phone, pausing mid-text.

"The door to his bedroom is open."

"His room? Ethan?"

"Mum redecorated it. The walls are yellow, the bed is new. She painted the side tables and fireplace white. There's a chandelier that looks like tree branches. She put Winnie the Pooh and Ethan's picture on the mantle. The throw pillows are yellow with little birds on them. It would be the perfect room for..."

"Angelene would have loved it," Troy said. "It was probably therapeutic for your mum."

"I made them face his death. I made her go into the forest." Brendon slurped up the last string of pasta and set the plate on the floor. "I said some bloody awful things to dad."

"No offence to your folks, but it was time. It wasn't right to hide the sadness, lock the door and make daft rules to protect you. I used to believe a witch lived in the forest. Do you know how many nights my mum had to sleep with me?"

"You always were a crybaby."

Troy shot up his finger and grinned. "All I'm saying is, you've got to face the hurt. That's how I know you'll be fine."

"How so, Dr. Spence?"

"You know you're sad. You're telling people you're sad. You're facing it. Eventually, it won't hurt so bad."

Brendon reached for his phone and swiped it open. His finger hovered over Rachel's name. "Maybe I'll text Rachel."

"No, you won't. Don't use her to numb the sadness. Have a wank."

"Bloody hell, I haven't thought about sex for a while. I feel bad for hurting her. I'd like to apologize."

"There will be plenty of time to say sorry. Let everyone heal first, especially you. You'll get one look at that red hair and her arse; you'll head up to your bed for a hump."

"She has a nice bum. Is it still round, like a juicy apple?"

"She wears trousers and a jumper long enough to cover it."

"She really is boring."

"She's hurting, like you," Troy said, swiping his finger across his phone. "Charlie will be here in ten. She wants to give you a hug."

A flush warmed Brendon's cheeks. He hung his head. "How can I face her?"

"Like you always do, with that dishy smile."

"I've got to face the ghost. My shrink wants me to go to the farmhouse."

"We'll do it together after we put up the Christmas tree." Troy looked at his phone and smiled. "Charlie is bringing biscuits. Be nice."

"I'll tell her they're the best biscuits I've ever eaten."

"She made curry last week. It tasted delicious."

"She'll make the perfect wife."

"I think so. I can't imagine my life without her."

What is love, mon amour?

It stirs you, reaches inside you and touches your soul; it moves you to tears.

Then this is love, my beautiful boy in brown.

Tinsel sprouted from boxes; glittered balls rolled around Brendon's feet. He stepped back, sipped his coffee, and admired the lopsided stockings.

"Are you looking after her? She's got seven devils with her. Enfant Épouvantable is a bloody brat. I'd watch out for that one."

A lump rose in his throat and snagged his breath. He squeezed away the tears and plugged in the twinkle lights. The room tilted and blurred; patchouli wafted in the draught. They had danced in this room, held hands, shared secrets, and scars. She was everywhere and nowhere.

Brendon dragged his sleeve over his eyes and stepped into the garden. The air was crisp and brittle. Brendon had spent many nights wondering why she killed herself, consumed with the possibilities, what her reasons were, why she changed her mind about coming to Dortmund. Dr. Candler had given him many reasons, depression, trauma, substance abuse, they all seemed to fit, yet didn't. If she could have seen what he saw, the brilliant gold light that shined behind her scars, she may have chosen differently. She may be still alive.

"Sweetheart, what are you doing out here?"

Brendon walked back into the house; he met his father's gaze and looked away.

"I put the tree up. Troy and Charlie helped."

"It looks lovely."

"Walter texted; Nicola's flight is delayed. He'll ring us when he gets to Kate's," David said.

"I'm glad Walter is spending Christmas with Kate. No one should be alone," Sofia said.

She kissed Brendon's cheek and left the great room.

Brendon slid over the arm of the sofa, clutched a pillow, and wound the tassels around his finger. The quiet had been hard before. It was killing him now. He couldn't read his father's face, disappointment, forced to play happy family.

"Walter said you played well your last match."

Silence broken.

"I've had a decent start."

"I should have been there for you."

"I have the team, my coach, mum, Dr. Candler."

"When you were growing up. I wasn't there when I should have been."

"If you think that would have changed what happened, it wouldn't have."

"I was something to everyone," David said, perching on the armrest, "a good barrister, a good MP, a good husband. I was a lousy father."

"I'm sorry I'm not like Ethan."

"I was too stubborn to accept I lost Ethan. I was angry at your mum for getting pregnant and not giving me time. Can you forgive me for forcing you to be someone you're not?"

"You were just being a dad."

"I needed to be a father. Ethan was Ethan and you're my athlete."

"I never meant for it to go as far as it did. We tried to be friends. I really loved her. Why did she kill herself?"

"Angelene is happier in death than she was living. Someday you'll understand that."

"I wish Walter never married her." "If Walter didn't bring Angelene into our lives, I never would have realized how badly I've treated you; how much I love your mum, my family."

"It hurts, bloody bad."

David laced his arm around Brendon and squeezed his shoulder. "Angelene gave you wonderful memories, terrible memories, sad ones. All those experiences will help you grow. This will give you strength. You remember that."

It sounded like respectable David Cook advice, accepting it meant he had to say goodbye.

"Are you going to divorce mum?"

"Not in a million years. She was meant to be my wife."

"We have a lot of healing to do."

"I blamed you and Angelene for tearing my family apart. It brought us closer together," David said. "More coffee? Your mum has a day of shopping planned. I better get some caffeine into me."

"Thanks for not hating me."

"I love you. James McGregor can't say his son plays for the Bundesliga."

Brendon dragged the blanket over his legs. Patchouli wafted around him. He closed his eyes to the prettiest sound.

C'était toujours toi, it was always you, mon amour

Epilogue

Brendon glanced at his watch; ten minutes had passed since he last checked. He straightened his tie, brought the bouquet of roses to his nose, inhaling the sweet fragrance. Afternoon heat rose from the pavement and stretched around the platform. Brendon's heart inflated and deflated in a crazy rhythm; he could see the train approaching. He wiped his hand on his trousers, switched the bouquet to the other and repeated. The soupy air and his racing heart made it hard to breathe.

The train puffed and screeched to a stop. The door hissed open. Brendon grinned. She didn't look like a schoolgirl anymore. She wore a sundress, sandals. Her hair was deeper in colour. The sun had kissed her cheeks. Brendon's smile grew. She was beautiful.

"Bloody hell, you look brilliant."

"What would you do if I kissed you right now?"

"I'd kiss you back."

"Knuddlebär."

Brendon buried his nose in her neck. She smelled like a bergamot sunrise and blooming jasmine.

"I don't want to let you go."

"I'm here all week, knuddlebär. You can hug me all you want."

"Mum said red, I picked yellow. I hope that's okay," Brendon said, shoving the bouquet in her face.

"You're the first boy to buy me flowers. They're beautiful."

Brendon picked up her bag. They strolled into the station. A burst of chilled air cooled his cheeks. It was hard not to stare. She was a stripped-down version of herself. He felt thirteen again, not knowing what to say or how to act. He welcomed the bumbling. It was nice to feel alive and normal. It was time to try love again.

"How was Berlin?"

"Mum's in love. For the first time in her life, someone loves her."

"Is she moving to Berlin?"

They moved through the station. Brendon pushed open the door. The sun was setting in streams of gold and orange. His car shone inky liquid blue.

"She gave her two weeks at the bank. Christian is going to take care of her."

"You'll be visiting Berlin more often?"

"Have you missed me, knuddlebär?"

"I didn't think I did until I saw you. I mean, I did but, bloody hell, I can't think straight."

"Mum wants me to transfer to the Hochschule Osnabruck nursing program in Lingen."

"Where's that?"

"Two hours from Dortmund."

Brendon chuckled. "You already know the travel time?"

"Can you imagine me, Rachel Jones, travelling by train to see her footy player?"

Brendon unlocked the car and placed her bag in the rear seat. He could.

"Nice car, knuddlebär. You miss your BMW?"

"It was never really my car. This Audi A7 sport is all mine."

"It's brilliant like you."

"I don't know about that."

"Don't be so modest." Rachel slid onto the seat, closed the door, and buckled the seatbelt. "You've been ace on the pitch. I told the girls at uni we snogged."

Brendon glanced down the road and pulled onto the street. "You did?"

"They didn't believe me at first. I had to show them the pictures on my phone."

"You still have the pictures we took?"

"You're still my number one and not because you're a pro keeper. I never stopped thinking about you."

"Even after I treated you so bloody bad?"

"It wasn't my time yet."

"I'm sorry for hurting you. I was going to text when I came home for Christmas, both times. Troy told me to leave you alone."

"Mr. Newcastle. That contract they offered him made the front page of the Taunton Times."

"I'm flying home next summer. You can come with me, if you're in Lingen, that is."

"Your mummy missing you?"

Brendon laughed, turned onto a drive, and pressed the code for the underground parking. "I finally got mum down to one call a week. Troy and Charlotte are getting married. I'm the best man. I should have a date."

"Charlotte would die if she saw me with you. Maggie will be her maid of honour. I'll absobloodylutley go with you."

He parked the car and turned to face her. "I still have the text you sent me. The last one where you told me to fuck off."

"I see your German hasn't gotten any better."

"Are you going to tell me what it said?"

He swiped open his phone and scrolled through the texts until he found it. His heart cracked; he had broken her heart the fourth time that day.

"It says you're a wanker and smell like dog poo."

"You could have told me that. What if I asked one of my teammates to translate it for me?"

"Oh, knuddlebär, it says I'm in love with you."

"I wouldn't blame you for hating me after everything I've done."

EPILOGUE

"I tried to hate you. I must have called you an arschloch a hundred times, a wanker, a prick, then I'd cry and call myself a dumme Kuh, stupid cow. I could never hate you."

"You want to see my bedroom? I've got a king-sized bed and no mammina telling me to keep girls out."

Rachel climbed out of the car and sniffed the bouquet. "Can we talk?"

Brendon grabbed her bag, puzzled. Who was this girl?

"You were the last boy I've been with. I don't want to be a fanny."

"I didn't mean to upset you. You look so bloody beautiful."

"I know what you thought. That girl is no longer me. I want to mean something to someone, to you."

"You mean something. You always have. I was too stupid to realize it."

"Don't think this is easy for me," Rachel said, tugging at his tie. "You look fit, like grown-up delicious fit. The first thing I thought when I stepped off the train was how fast I could get into your trousers."

"We'll talk then."

Brendon jingled through the key ring and shoved the key into the lock. "I grabbed some wine. Mum told me to make an antipasti board. It's a Vesper board, a snack between the main meal as Lukas's wife calls it. I'll take you out for a late dinner."

"I'd rather stay in tonight."

"Whatever you want," Brendon said, waving her in. "What do you think?"

Rachel glanced around the living room. "It's brilliant. Christian said Westfalendamm is an excellent area. Westfalenpark is close by."

"It's about ten minutes from here, the zoo, Rombergpark. We can take the subway into the city centre."

"I was expecting black, white, and modern, Borussia Dortmund posters. It's pretty, white, yellow, and grey. No offence."

Brendon tossed his keys on a table and tugged off his suit jacket. "When I first moved here, it was white, bloody white everywhere. Mum took me shopping when her and dad visited in May. I thought yellow would be nice."

"Because you play for Dortmund?"

Brendon took the bouquet from her and plunked it in a pitcher. He walked to the kitchen, filled the jug with water and set it on the counter. "Angelene's favourite colour was yellow."

He rooted in the drawer for a corkscrew, pulled the cork and poured two glasses. His nerves jangled. There were reminders of Angelene all around the room. Yellow throw pillows, paintings of little yellow birds. He handed Rachel a glass and settled onto the sofa. He promised his dad he'd follow the Gentlemen's code. Rachel deserved honesty. She deserved to know Angelene still lived with him.

"Did she draw those?" Rachel took a sip and nodded towards the collage of castles.

"His name was Henri Piedmont. He was going to build Angelene a castle."

"He loved her, like you did."

"Bloody hell, Rachel, you just got here and I'm talking about Angelene."

"Do you miss her?"

Brendon set down the glass and took her hand. "Sometimes when I can't sleep, I feel her beside me. If I'm having a tough time on the pitch, I hear her telling me to find my light. It doesn't hurt as much. I miss her."

"She wasn't a nice person. I saw a horrible side of her."

"Those are her devils," Brendon said, running his thumb along hers. Her nail polish was purple, the colour of the last kit he wore. "She felt threatened by you. She had every right to be."

"I don't understand. You chose her. You loved her."

"I think she knew you were truly the one."

"You've been single. I checked all your social media accounts. You sure have lots of followers, Hannah, Adelaide, Tatiana, to name a few."

Lemon yellow, castles, and postcards. All his reminders stared back at him. Angelene would want him to be happy, even Enfant Épouvantable.

"Does it bother you I have all these memories of her?"

"You loved her. It's my turn now."

Brendon kissed her wrist, picked up his glass, and took a sip. "I was happy when you text me. I'm bloody happy you're here."

Rachel pushed up his sleeve and traced her finger over a tattoo. "I bear the dungeon within me. Within me is winter, bleeding depressing, knuddlebär."

"Angelene loved Victor Hugo. She was winter. Nothing could melt her icicles, not even me. She called me her spring."

"Which season would I be?"

Femme fatale, Salome. "Summer, hot and sultry."

"Don't be a wanker. I don't want to be that girl. Well, for my gorgey footy player. If we're together."

"I've wanted to text you for a long time. I wasn't sure you'd want to hear from me."

"It took a while for me to get over the hurt. When I saw you on the telly, I nearly choked on my tea. That text sat in my drafts for weeks."

"You haven't dated anyone? No dishy doctors?"

"I wanted to find me and love me. Angelene said I was a vessel for boys to dump their spunk in. It made me feel awful, but it was true. If I'm going to be a tart, I want to be one boys' tart."

"You want to be my tart?"

Rachel threw her arms around his neck. He closed his eyes and held her.

"I missed you, knuddlebär. I've only ever wanted you."

"You got me. You hungry?"

"Starved."

"I cut everything up and rolled the bloody meat like mammina said. She told me how to arrange the plate, wash my sheets. Amelia told me to clean the loo for a lady. I didn't know there were different ways to clean the loo." He opened the fridge and set a stack of containers on the counter. "Dad told me to open the door for you, sleep on the sofa. Bloody exhausting, the three of them."

"How are your parents?" Rachel said. She popped open a container and dumped cubes of Butterkäse on the platter.

"In love. They can't keep their bloody hands off each other. I gave them a tour of the training centre and dressing room. They were giggling like bloody teenagers. It was embarrassing." He plunked a disk of brie in the middle of the platter. "I'm happy they found their way back. When he gets home, Ame said, they go to their room for some romance."

"That's cute, knuddlebär. I hope I have a love like that."

Brendon stabbed a fork into a pile of rolled Krakauer and shoved it amongst the cheese. "I had a brother."

EPILOGUE

"My mum said sad things happened at Rosewood manor."

Brendon held up plates. Rachel grinned. "Your mum told you to eat off plates?"

"She was going to send linen napkins. A lady is supposed to eat off a plate with a napkin on her lap."

"I'm good with a kitchen towel and my fingers," Rachel said, grabbing the wine. "Can we sit on the balcony?"

Brendon took the platter and nodded towards the sliding door. A little tingle fluttered. She still had a great wiggle.

"What's your brother's name?"

Brendon hooked his foot around a rattan table and dragged it between the two chairs. "Ethan. He died before I was born."

"Was he sick?" Rachel said, she set down their glasses, filling them with wine, "nobody has ever mentioned anything."

"It was the only time Ms. McGregor had any respect. He was playing in the forest. Dad said he liked to hunt for treasures, bloody swot."

Rachel fired a cube of cheese at him. "Don't be a wanker."

"He tripped over the roots of an oak tree and hit his head. Mum called him in for lunch and when he didn't come, she found him. He died on the way to the hospital."

"No wonder your mum is so protective of you."

Brendon sliced into the brie and placed the wedge on a piece of Vollkornbrot. "Ethan was smart, like my dad smart. He could name every bloody mushroom and flower in the forest."

"Did he look like you?"

"He was a miniature David Cook. There are pictures of him around the house now. I'll show you the next time we visit."

"You're going to take me home to your mum?"

"I'll even introduce you as my girlfriend. Don't expect to sleep in my room. Mum has a strict, not until you're married policy."

"How awful, losing a child."

"Neither one of them forgave themselves for Ethan's death."

"Death can make you feel many things, especially when it happens suddenly and there's no time for goodbye."

Brendon leaned into the cushion. A crescent moon had risen, slicing through the darkened sky. He had been that person, angry at God for turning his back on Angelene. Angry at Angelene for leaving him. Scars were forming over his wounded heart. The hollow spots, filled by 80,000 adoring fans and the girl sitting next to him.

"It's still hard to say goodbye."

"Then don't. Never say goodbye because goodbye means going away and going away means forgetting."

"You make that up?"

Rachel tossed a cube of cheese in her mouth and smiled. "Troy said the same thing. It's from Peter Pan. My nan used to say that to me. She even called me Tinkerbell."

"Can I call you that?"

Rachel tore a piece of bread in two and shook her head. "No, you can not."

"You call me knuddlebär," Brendon said, plucking a grape from the stem. "Just don't when I introduce you to the guys. They took the bloody piss out of me when mum brought Paddington into the dressing room."

"She did that? How awful."

"I used to pretend the garden was Signal Iduna Park. Paddington was my defender. She thought he'd like to see the stadium. The bloody team teased me for weeks."

"You're going to introduce me to your teammates?"

"You said you'd always be my girl."

Rachel jumped from the chair and planted herself on his lap. Brendon ran his fingers through her hair and kissed her.

"You don't taste like minty cigarettes anymore."

"I haven't had a ciggie in over a year. You're getting a whole new Rachel."

"I liked the old one," Brendon said, pressing his fingers into the small of her back. "This Rachel is brilliant."

"You don't have to sleep on the sofa."

"My dad told me to be respectful but, if you don't mind."

Rachel pecked his mouth, climbed off his lap, and nestled onto the chair. "I don't. How's the queen of Milan?"

"Nonna visited last April, brought her friends Leonara and Sabra. I've never met a randier bunch of women."

"I hope I'm as spunky as Nicola when I'm that age."

"She asked the sporting director out for a drink, in front of the entire squad. First it was bloody Paddington, then my Nonna chatting everyone up."

"What about Mr. Pratt? Has he forgiven you?"

Brendon finished his wine and set the glass down. "Forgiven me, yes. Have I seen him, no. He sold the farmhouse to Troy's parents. They tore it down and bought more cattle. Do you know what they did?"

Rachel shook her head and bit into a strawberry.

"They put bloody bells on the cows. It's all mum hears, mooing and jingling."

"Is Walter dating? Mum hasn't seen him around Taunton."

"Mum's friend, Kate. They bought a house in Chelsea."

"Do you know who I saw, knuddlebär?"

"Tilly?"

"I haven't talked to that gobby cow in a over year. When I needed a friend, she wasn't there. Troy was."

"Bloody William McGregor."

"He hasn't been back to Taunton since he left for Brunel. Didn't even say goodbye to Tilly, just ditched her."

"No Oxford?"

"He made up some dumb excuse that Brunel was more his style. I ran into Maggie."

"I texted her when I was back home playing for England, Cook and Spence together again. Her number wasn't in service."

"She was at Vivary with her brother. It was eighty degrees out and the kid had on a crocheted Batman hat."

"Did you talk to her? How is she?"

"She was with her boyfriend, some guy she met at uni. His name is Grayson. She's happy."

"I'm glad. That's all I wanted for her."

"Do you miss her too?"

"I had some brilliant times with Maggie, but those chapters are closed."

"I'm tired knuddlebär."

EPILOGUE

"You get ready for bed. I'll put the food away."

Brendon grabbed the platter and slid the door open. He walked to the kitchen and smiled as Rachel hummed her way to his bedroom. Brendon fumbled around the drawer for plastic wrap, ripped a sheet, and spread it over the platter. He corked the wine and shoved the plate in the fridge. The words going away mean forgetting wavered in his heart. He wouldn't forget Angelene, and her sometimes smile. He had to let her fly free. He had to let her go.

"I'm coming in. You better be decent."

"Mum made me bring pyjamas. She told me to be a lady."

Brendon dragged his tie from his collar and tossed it on the dresser. "I sleep in my boxers. I may have a pair of pyjama bottoms somewhere."

"As long as you don't sleep naked. I saw a picture of you on Insta. You were on a beach in Capri. Your body is even dishier now. I may turn into the old Rachel."

"That wouldn't be so bad," Brendon said. "What do you want to do while you're here? I've been so busy with football; I haven't really discovered the city. Hey, that's my hoodie?"

Rachel held the pillow up to her face and peeked over the edge. "It goes everywhere with me. I'm like a kid with a blanket. Do you think I'm a dolt?"

"I think it's sweet," Brendon said and slid out of his trousers. He yanked off his socks and strolled to the bathroom. "Do you want to go to Westfalenpark?"

"Christian said it was a must. Shop on Westenhellweg, try lippischer pickert."

Brendon brushed his teeth and dived under the blankets. There were little stars on her pyjamas.

"I have something for you." Rachel crawled to the end of the bed and rummaged under her clothes. "Ready?"

Brendon grinned at the folded paper star. "Let me guess, blue Smarties."

"I picked out every last one."

"Mum put all the cranes and boxes you made me on the shelf where Paddington used to sit and a star on dad's desk. She said it reminded her of you. She liked the way you looked at me."

"You don't look happy. That star was especially hard to make. It took a lot of cutting and folding. I was going to make it out of black and yellow paper. I know your favourite colour is blue."

"I'm learning to like the colour again. I love it."

"I'll send you one every month, so you don't forget me."

"I won't forget you." Brendon pulled her beside him and nuzzled her hair. "Did you ever think you'd end up here?"

"That night when we sat by the pool and I wished on the star, I wished we'd end up together."

She reached across him and grabbed the lamp chain.

"Don't turn it off."

"Are you afraid of the dark? I'll protect you."

"I promised Angelene I would keep it on."

"Every time you think of her, you're leaving your light on. The drawings, all the yellow things, being a brilliant keeper. You've kept the light burning."

"Will you put your arm around me so I can sleep?"

Rachel snuggled into his side and tucked her arm around his waist.

"She came into your life to give you the love you needed. The light will always be on and your light, knuddlebär, will be brighter because of her."

Brendon closed his eyes. The curtains fluttered; patchouli wafted in the air.

"One of her favourite quotes from Tale of Two Cities was, I wish you to know you were the last dream of my soul."

"You were, knuddlebär."

Brendon reached out from beneath the blankets, whispered I love you, little bird and turned off the light.

Acknowledgments

THIS BOOK WOULDN'T BE possible without the love and support of the following people.
Mammina, for the hours you listened, revision after revision. Daddy, for ensuring pitchers of your magical brew, was always overflowing. Sweet pea, for helping me step into the mind of an eighteen-year-old boy. I need to give a shout out to the Bundesliga. I watched hours and hours of football to research the beautiful game. I'm with Brendon. It is excellent football! Lastly, to my brother Jay. I know you are looking down at me and smiling. Tu me manques, Bubba.

Manufactured by Amazon.ca
Bolton, ON